CATHERINE GASKIN

The Ambassador's Women

FONTANA/Collins

First published in Great Britain by William Collins Sons & Co. Ltd 1985
A Continental edition first published by Fontana Paperbacks 1986
This edition first issued in Fontana Paperbacks 1986

Made and printed in Great Britain by
William Collins Sons & Co. Ltd, Glasgow

The Ambassador's Women

CATHERINE GASKIN was born in Ireland, grew up in Australia and, after spending eight years in England, married an American and lived for ten years in New York. She and her husband then moved to St Thomas in the Virgin Islands where they lived for two years, before moving to the Wicklow Hills in Ireland. They now live on the Isle of Man.

Catherine Gaskin's first novel, *This Other Eden* (now *The Lynmara Legacy*) was published when she was seventeen. Her many bestsellers include *Sara Dane* which was made into a TV mini-series, *Family Affairs* and *Promises*. Her sales in Fontana alone total well over 6,000,000 copies in paperback.

Available in Fontana by the same author

All Else is Folly
Blake's Reach
Corporation Wife
Daughter of the House
Edge of Glass
A Falcon for a Queen
The File on Devlin
Fiona
I Know My Love
The Property of a Gentleman
Sara Dane
The Tilsit Inheritance
The Lynmara Legacy
The Summer of the Spanish Woman
Family Affairs
Promises

To Winsome and Ian Grey
With love and thanks for so many years of friendship.

PROLOGUE

The Ambassador was dying. The words seemed to beat and mark every step of the way up to the house from the town, as they had done for weeks now. Livy could not deny the fact, or get around it. Her steps dragged, as if she were trying to draw out time – time for him.

She had known this house all her life, had been part of it, and yet had tried, at times, deliberately to distance herself from it, because she feared to be possessed by it, by the house and the family. She had been born down there, in the small town whose manor house, or castle – once its fortress – this was. She had lived in both places: the house on the height from where the whole sweep of the bay could be seen, and out beyond to the Atlantic; down there in the town where the houses huddled together in the narrow, ancient streets, sheltered from the Atlantic by the hill which brooded over its harbour, a harbour town now too well known, too much photographed to make it entirely comfortable to live in during the tourist season. She had been part of the family of this great house, and yet apart from it. An outsider and an insider. They had given her many things. Generous, careless, lavishing on her love and friendship and encouragement, when they had had nothing more to give. They had also lavished money when it had come. They had loved, quarrelled sometimes, made up, and never succeeded in hating. The Ambassador had been a major part of the complex relationship, but now his part in it was ending. He would die soon. The Ambassador's wife had told her yesterday that she must telephone the families to say that it was time to come. They would come, bringing with them the trappings of their various worlds, the riches, the power, the influence. They would bring their bright cleverness, their glamour. They would come bearing also the scars of their various lives, their pain and hurt.

7

Livy looked down at the flowers she carried, the simple, bright bunch of chrysanthemums and dahlias. The house was always filled with masses of sophisticated flowers and plants from the hothouses. These were from her own garden, probably from stock planted by her mother, appearing in their cheerful, carefree fashion year after year. Her mother had had a great sense for growing things, as she had for everything in nature. These flowers, she knew, would go in the Ambassador's room. He would know them. Even through his weakness and the haze of drugs, he would ask where Livy's flowers were. She sighed, and started once again on the steep upward climb, wondering how many more days were left when she could bring flowers to the Ambassador.

The drive was smooth, free of weeds and ruts, bounded on both sides by huge rhododendrons and the trees which had managed to defy the Atlantic gales. Livy could remember when the drive had not been paved, when the house had leaking roofs and some broken windows; when the wind blew straight off the sea, some rooms had been miserably cold. All that had changed. The house still presented its almost quaintly muddled façade; the Tower, which had been its fortress beginning, was as old, some people said, as the legends that were attached to this place. In Tudor times a more comfortable house had been begun and it was added as need and money decreed, until it became a pleasant hotch-potch of styles. Here, one of England's great naval heroes of the seventeenth century had been born. They said down in the town – a story passed on through the generations – that he had been miserably seasick each time he had gone out with the local fishermen. But he had won two famous victories, this frail and sickly man, and the grateful nation had given him a title and a handsome sum of money. He had squandered most of it by adding yet more to the house. The family had had other famous sons. One, a retiring mathematician whose theory, expounded early this century and largely ignored then, but which now bore his name, was used as the basic principle for guided-weapon systems. Another of the family had been a reforming prime minister.

This house had always been a magnet for the family, even though at times there had been no direct heir, and a nephew or a cousin had inherited the title and the house, and whatever lands and assets had gone with it. There had been marriages for love, and there had been marriages for money, as in most great families. Sometimes both had combined. She thought now that once again a sweeping change would come, and her steps slowed even more.

She reached, at last, the plateau on which the house and the Tower stood. Here Livy turned to look down on the town, as from the town she had looked up towards the house. That was her secure world down there, small, snug, sheltered. The family lived here on the heights, and had invited and forced her to endure the buffetings of the winds which blew in their world, their world of power and poverty, of riches and risk. Without them she would most likely have spent her life down there, as cosily domestic as the chrysanthemums and the dahlias, her vision bounded by the snug harbour. They had compelled her to look further, to the wider horizon. Sometimes she had almost wished they had never done it.

She turned back to the house and looked towards the windows of the room where the Ambassador lay. At this odd hour of the early afternoon, someone was closing the curtains. For an instant she frowned in puzzlement. Then she knew. The flowers slipped from her suddenly nerveless hand. Then she realized there was no point in haste. The Ambassador was dead.

Chapter 1

Livy couldn't remember just how old she had been when she had started climbing the hill from the town to the house with her mother. Down in the town it was always called 'the House' or 'the Castle'. Its name was Tresillian, so called after the fortified tower, which brooded over the headland, almost derelict now, and unsafe, her mother said. Here, below the Tower, the sea and a river had cut a vicious slice into the coast line. More than a mile away, often not visible through the mist, was the opposite headland, called St Buryan, desolate, uninhabited, part of the Tresillian estate still, and dotted with the chimney stacks of the pumping houses of the abandoned tin mines, which had once given Tresillian and most of Cornwall its wealth. In between were the infamous Tresillian Rocks. At low tide they were revealed in all their frightening beauty, jagged fingers of rock pointing skywards, set in a deceptively calm and serene stretch of white sands. When the tide turned this inlet sucked in the sea with breathtaking speed; the Atlantic rushed in to take back what it had, a few hours ago, reluctantly given up. It hissed and swirled around the Rocks; some were submerged, and only the tips of others showed. Because of the fierce pull of the tidal race, it was the graveyard of many ships. Sometimes after a great storm, when the currents had been particularly strong, the bones of some hulls would show above the sands. Then another tide would come and they were reburied, and the inlet would wear its deceptively peaceful air again. Livy both loved and feared the Rocks.

Tresillian also had its stable block, and a great walled area, built to shelter its garden and orchard from the fierce gales. This wall was beginning to crumble, and on some of the outbuildings the roofs had collapsed. The rain poured into the empty frames of the greenhouses. But for all its delapidation, and the menace of the Rocks, Livy liked the Castle. It was very different from the small rooms of the little house on a narrow, steep street in the town where they lived. She was happy exploring the vast rooms here, taking off the dust sheets that draped some of the massive pieces of furniture, scrambling on the four-poster beds which dominated some of the grander bedrooms while her mother dusted or polished the floor. Best of all she liked it when her mother cleaned in the library. It was the grandest room in the house, rising the height of two storeys, with an intricately-wrought-iron gallery at the second floor level, giving access to the thousands of books stored there. Many were old, and not to be touched, not even to be dusted. Her father had occasionally come up here, and sighed over the treasures he saw, but he had never borrowed any volume, even though no one would have known. He noted the ominous water stains on the ceiling, and sighed for the fate of these precious books.

Livy's imagination took flight at Tresillian. Once she had pulled off a heavy bedcover, rich with faded embroidery, draped it around herself, let it trail behind her, and descended the magnificent carved staircase into the hall, pretending, with great seriousness, that she was the princess doomed to wait long years for the return of her lover, whose ship would evade the clutch of the Rocks, and come safely to harbour in St Just. She was the princess doomed to a fatal love. She enacted the stories told to her by her father. He didn't read them from a book, he just told them to her. For everyone knew that Cornwall was the kingdom of Arthur and his faithless wife, Guinevere, and her lover, Lancelot. This was the kingdom from which King Mark had sent Tristan to bring the king's bride, Iseult, from Ireland, to be betrayed by them both. People in Somerset and Wales might dispute that, but all the Cornish knew that this was Arthur's and Mark's kingdom. She loved all his stories, the stories of the battles against the English, while the Tower withstood both the battles and the Atlantic gales. She didn't like it so well when she and her mother had to go up to the Castle in the teeth of the wind. It always met them as they emerged from the shelter of the town and started to climb. The rhododendrons and the oaks crashed and swayed, the gulls flew inland, and her mother held her hand to help her on the upward climb. These were the days when Livy stayed close to her mother within Tresillian, and didn't go exploring.

They were quite alone in the Castle. The young man, who had fairly recently inherited the title, Tresillian and its lands from a father who had not himself lived there for years, rarely came to the place, and then it seemed with some reluctance. The townspeople guessed that since he could do nothing about its decay, he preferred not to see it. He lived on the small income the tenant farms brought in and roamed the world restlessly, occasionally writing pieces for newspapers and magazines about his travels. Mostly he loved to climb mountains. He took every penny he could from Tresillian to join mountaineering expeditions, and he must have greatly regretted the lost wealth of the tin mines. Livy didn't mind if the heir, Lord Camborne, never came to the Castle. This way she could continue to think of it as her own. She could be its Princess as long as everyone else stayed away. Five days a week her mother went up to the Castle, systematically cleaned and aired each room on a schedule she had devised, and when all the many rooms were done, she started at the beginning again.

On entering Tresillian in the mornings her mother would start the fire in the big, old, iron stove which dominated one end of the flag-stoned kitchen. At first it gave warm water for her to clean with; by ten o'clock it was hot enough to boil water for their tea; at noon one of its several ovens heated their pasties for lunch. Livy ate the pasties greedily and with huge enjoyment; everyone said her mother made the best pasties in St Just, potatoes, a little meat, wrapped in the lightest pastry. Her mother was clever at many things; her movements were neat and deft and quick. She was one of the old Cornish, of the family of Tregenna, and she had inherited the red hair that had reappeared in the family for many generations. Some said there was an Irish streak in the Tregennas. She was deeply Cornish, of a sea-going family, but she had married an Englishman, a stranger, and no one in St Just could understand that. Why throw away her gifts, her winning graces, her beauty, on a man so much older, lungs gassed in the Great War, a man who had stumbled, almost, into St Just, carrying a bulldog puppy and a shabby suitcase which was filled mostly with books. He had been persuaded to come there by the hospitality of artist friends. Their letters told of the mild winters and the cottages which were to be bought cheaply. He had sampled the place, liked it and bought one of the cottages, a small one, with a walled garden which gave him space and privacy, a place to sit in the sun and write his poetry. He enjoyed wine with his friends, and beer in the pubs. Others like him had drifted there, painters, writers. They came mostly in summer, renting or buying cottages, setting up their easels to paint St Just's stunning bay, or to walk the rugged coastline, and talk of poetry and literature, to compare and criticize one another's work. These things were foreign to the townspeople, who were mostly fisherfolk, but tolerated because the strangers brought money in the summer to see them through the winter.

It was a shock, a surprise, a disappointment to some, when Iseult Tregenna had married the poet, Oliver Miles. She just barely knew that she was called after a queen of legend, but she was sprung from fisherfolk, and the man she married was a gentleman, educated, with a degree from Oxford, a writer of poetry which was printed in books, but which sold few copies. A shabby, tall gaunt man with dark eyes whose expression was sometimes pained, as if he remembered too much, and a gentle smile. The townspeople didn't know that he was a well-reviewed poet, but a printed poet he was, and for that they had to respect him, as if he had some power in their ancient, largely unwritten culture. But he had only a meagre disability pension, and a tiny income inherited from his parents who had both died in the pandemic of the Spanish influenza which had swept through the world at the end of the war. He had sold his parents' house, and on the proceeds and the little income, he had managed to go to Oxford. When he had come down he had eked out a living as a copy-editor and proof-reader for a London publisher, and striven to write his poems. He had striven against the terrible wastage of his lungs. Finally he could take the London soot and fog no longer, and he had come, as a desperate measure, to St Just, to breathe its clean air, to take its mild winter sun. As if it were a gesture to declare that he would live a life of a normal span, the last thing he did before leaving London was to buy the bulldog puppy whom he called, not very originally, Bully. The puppy went everywhere with him, and in a year had grown to a massive size. It had a brindle coat and a dark muzzle, on which the skin fell in mournful-looking folds. Bully loved his master devotedly, and for his sake, he loved his master's friends. The women of the town said the poet spent more on feeding the dog than he spent on feeding himself. Oliver Miles first saw Iseult Tregenna when she stopped to feed half the pasty she was eating to Bully as he sat like a sentinel by the open door of his cottage. Bully rose, licked his lips and wagged his thick short tail at her. Oliver Miles rose from the table where he was correcting the proofs of another writer, and went to speak to her. A few months later they were married.

If Iseult Tregenna had decided to marry outside her folk, then the townspeople of St Just thought she might have made a much better marriage. She might have married one of the farmers who lived inland, might have been mistress of a prosperous house, had horses, even a motor car. Instead she had loved, and married, this sick, penniless poet. She mixed with his friends when they came in the summer, and shared the lonelier winters with him. She was shy in the company of his friends, and said little. But she cooked them marvellous food, things that came from the sea, and the farms around, and from her own little garden, which for her seemed to yield up things her neighbours couldn't grow. She read her husband's poetry over and over, only half understanding it. It was mostly about war, and it was sad. That side of it appealed to the deeply Celtic streak in her. She sensed its rhythms, its sweet melancholy, as she sensed the rhythms of the sea. She was awed by these slim printed volumes of verse, and realized, vaguely, that in the world far away, in London and even beyond, there were people who admired her husband, who thought him a true and wonderful poet. They were few enough, though, and the royalties were small. But it seemed a miraculous thing to Iseult that he was actually paid money for writing. He earned far more from the manuscripts he copy-edited, and the proofs he corrected; but even putting it all together, it was very little.

Oliver called her Isa, and he loved her. When their only child was born in 1931, three years after they had married, she was named Olivia Iseult, and was called Livy, because when she first began to speak she couldn't pronounce her name. To Oliver Miles the child was a miracle he had never expected to happen. He was deeply protective of his two women, and he worried about their future.

He worried aloud to his friends, Thea Sedgemore and Herbert Gardiner. Thea was a noted but controversial sculptress, still known by her maiden name; Herbert Gardiner was a no less respected painter. They were considered mildly scandalous as they had not bothered to marry until years after their two children had been born. They lived in a house not far from Oliver's cottage, and had separate studios. Thea's opened on to a large, steep, walled garden where some of her largest pieces stood, surrounded by the sub-tropical trees and plants that flourished in that climate. It was a town sight to see one of those massive pieces of stone being hauled along the narrow, steep streets and manhandled through her garden gate. It needed great strength and delicacy of touch to do this. It was even more a thing of wonder to see the great crates, which had to be specially built by one of the town's carpenters, taking away a finished work. They marvelled that she was paid to create such strange objects, which they could understand no better than her husband's impressionistic paintings. It was the urging of these two, Thea and Herbert, which had first brought Oliver Miles to St Just.

'What shall I do for them, my lovely women?' he asked of Thea and Herbert. 'I'm hardly able to deal with the few manuscripts they send me for copy-editing. I grind my teeth to make myself correct the proofs. I'm no good for work, except to write my bits of verse. And that comes so slowly.

16

Isa has to go out to work to help with the money. It shames me.'

'Isa is happy,' Herbert said. 'She loves you.'

'Can that be enough?'

'For Isa it is.' It was true. Isa had grace and beauty, and rough, red hands. She revered the man she had married. She didn't care at all that she had to work to supplement their income. It was natural for her to do so. She did it cheerfully. She was more than content: she was happy.

'May you be as beautiful as your mother,' Oliver said to his daughter, who didn't then understand what he was saying. 'May you be as wise. And with luck, you may be happy.'

They were happy, Isa kept telling him, but her voice was stilled by fear at the times when his lungs grew worse. There never would be a cure for those tortured lungs, and it didn't help that Oliver Miles was a heavy smoker. It was a habit that all the men who had served in the trenches in Flanders had seemed to acquire, and he could not give up. That winter Oliver grew worse.

He spent most of it by the fire. On sunny days he went into the garden where Isa wrapped him in blankets, and he watched while Livy played close to him. She sat on a whitewashed rock near him, and listened to the stories he spun for her. She talked back to him, riding along in imagination with the things he said; she had developed a precocious vocabulary, and she spoke with his accent. She had begun to accompany him when he was strong enough to make his walks to Thea and Herbert's studios. She was silent as she watched them work, because her father was silent. She learned that their work was important, and must not be disturbed. 'Your work is important too,' she insisted. 'Mother says so.'

He ruffled her bright copper hair lovingly. 'Your mother thinks everything I do is important, pet. Your mother is a wonderful woman.'

Livy had, at five years old, been enrolled at the dame school, a little place run by two maiden ladies with genteel manners and voices, who charged a small fee, and to whom the children of the fishing community were never sent. It pleased Oliver to learn that Livy was placed in a higher class than her age warranted. Oliver had already taught her to read quite well, and had begun her on simple arithmetic. But part of him was loath to hand her over to strangers for what he considered one of the most important things in life, learning. But he sent her for the sake of the companionship she would have at school, companionship different from that of her Tregenna cousins.

The time came when Oliver seemed disinclined, or unable, even on fine days, to walk to his friends' studios. He drew his chair nearer the fire, and rarely took up the pad and pen to try to write. He didn't know that the Gardiners had filled the coal hole for Isa, so there were fires in each of the rooms, upstairs as well. As his energy drained away, his despair and worry grew. Isa had to bring a bed down to the front room of the cottage because the effort to climb the stairs was now too much for him. He confided to Herbert, who brought him bottles of whisky and the cigarettes they both knew he shouldn't smoke. 'I wish I could stay with them, Herbert. Isa will be a bit lost without me. And Livy. I wish I could do more for Livy. She must keep on at the dame school, but in a few years she'll have outgrown that, and need something better.' He was ashamed that he didn't want his daughter to attend the school in the town. He wanted better for her. The child was lovely, and quick and intelligent, he thought. She should, some day, experience the world beyond St Just. 'I planned to teach her myself, and when she was old enough, well, somewhere like Paris for a while.' He shook his head impatiently. 'Just dreams. There won't be enough money for that.'

As he talked with Herbert, his hand absently stroked the dark head of the kitten, called Tubby, which purred on his lap.

'Thea and I will see to things, Oliver,' Herbert said. 'But don't worry about them. You'll be here to see to things yourself.'

Oliver took what comfort he could from the thought. But Thea and Herbert were middle-aged. Their two children were grown up and had left home. A young child would be a nuisance and an intrusion in their lives. But he was grateful they were there. Livy would have their guidance, and their presence would ensure that she was not totally absorbed back into Isa's family. He wrote to his publisher, Venables, a patient, kind man who had encouraged and guided him since the first poems had been written at the end of the war. 'Of course we'll do anything we can, old man,' the answer came at once. 'But you're going to be around to look after her yourself.' Oliver knew he would not be around. He longed for the winter to be over. If he could just last through the spring or perhaps one more summer. Another summer to be with Isa and Livy. He kept hoping.

The early Cornish daffodils had already been picked and shipped to the London market when Oliver died. It was a blustery, rainy day. Isa had not gone to the Castle. She had called the doctor, because Oliver had not been able to raise his head even to drink. But she knew there was nothing the doctor could do. 'I'm so sorry Mrs Miles. But he lived longer than I expected. He lived because of you . . . and the child.'

The Times published a long obituary, and telegrams and letters came from people Isa had never heard of. Thea and Herbert took over answering the letters. Oliver's publisher came all the way from London to attend the funeral. A lot of the townsfolk walked in the funeral procession to the Anglican church at the top of the hill. They had liked the poet, even though he had been an Englishman, and a stranger.

After the funeral Isa went back to her work at the Castle. The little money she earned was more important than ever. She could not accept the help already offered by the Gardiners; she would never accept help unless she needed it desperately for Livy. On Oliver's death his life insurance policy had been paid up. It was a small sum, but the most Isa had ever had at any one time. She was told that the tiny income he had from some shares left by his parents would continue. She would manage. She was glad of her work up at the Castle to distract her from her grief. She wished it were more demanding, and that it tired her enough to give her sleep at night. She felt the desolation of a great loss, and, when she knew Livy was asleep, she gave way to tears. She felt the responsibility of Oliver Miles's child more than she would have felt the responsibility of a child of some other man, some man of her own kind. She knew his pride in Livy, sensed his hopes. All she could do now was try to help her bear the pain of her father's death. Livy attended the dame school dutifully and without fuss, because she knew that was what her father had wanted, but at other times she sat listlessly in the little garden, Bully and Tubby for company, on the white-washed rock by the garden seat where Oliver had talked with her through so many hours. How was Isa to teach her? What did she know except how to cook and sew and grow things? The loss of her husband seemed doubled because of what the child had lost.

In the spring had come the news that the young heir to Tresillian, Lord Camborne, had been killed in a climbing accident in New Zealand. For a while Isa was frozen with worry. It was 1937, and there were six women in the town for every job that might possibly be offered. She had to think of Livy. She could not go away from the town to seek work elsewhere. People in the town tried to remember something of the cousin who had inherited, since Lord Camborne had not married, and had no direct heir. No one could even recollect that the new Lord Camborne had ever been to Tresillian.

It was welcome news when Isa learned from the Camborne solicitors that the heir and his family would come to Tresillian to spend some time during the summer. Two other women, both her cousins, were engaged to come daily to help clean at Tresillian while the family was there. Some attempt was made to clear a part of the wilderness of the big walled garden and to plant a vegetable garden to supply the Castle's table. But money was limited, the solicitor who had come to make the arrangements warned. He engaged the services of two young men to dig the garden, and of one old man to tend it when it was planted. That was all he was authorized to do. He arranged for some of the broken window panes to be replaced; about the places where the roof leaked he could do nothing. He could authorize nothing until he personally had spoken to the new Lord Camborne. Even then he had little hope that money would be forthcoming for anything like the work Tresillian needed. The income from the estate was little enough, and the late Lord Camborne had been willing to spend none of it on his inheritance. It had been the same with his father. From what he knew of the heir, the solicitor had little hope that the situation would be any different.

So late in May Isa packed some clothes, her husband's books of poetry, and the books Livy cared for most. She closed the little cottage in the town, and took her cat and her dog and her child, and went to live in the Castle.

Chapter 2

Both women were always to remember the precise details of how they met. It was late afternoon in November 1930. Dusk was gathering over St James's Park; it had rained earlier, and chill droplets seemed still to hang in the air. Mist shrouded the outline of Buckingham Palace; the lights had come on in The Mall. Dena Penrose lingered, her hand on the rail of the bridge over the lake, to watch the ducks begin to seek their roosts for the night. Light and graceful, they floated off. She wished she could float too. She sighed; she was more tired than she had realized. She would have to walk to the end of Birdcage Walk to get a taxi. She shivered a little; it had grown colder as the dusk closed in. She turned to go.

'Snap!' a woman's voice said quite close to her. She hadn't noticed the woman. A low laugh followed the one word. For a moment they stared at each other. Then Dena laughed too.

'I suppose we do look funny,' she said. The woman's body, wrapped in a fur coat, revealed just as much as her own cloth coat her swollen shape. They were both well advanced in pregnancy. 'I suppose,' she added, 'that you've been doing what the doctor says, and getting your exercise? Isn't it all a bore? The waiting, I mean.'

'When?' the other woman asked.

'Next month.'

'For me, too.' In just those few words she had spoken she declared her American birth. She was tall, and she wore a neat little fur cap over her dark blonde hair. She was not strictly beautiful, but even in the growing darkness Dena could see the good bones of her face, the sharp, patrician line of her chin, the deep-set eyes, whose colour she couldn't then tell.

22

'I'm afraid,' Dena continued, 'I've overdone the exercise a little. I'll have to find a taxi to get home. It's just along Knightsbridge, but it's too far to walk.' They became conscious that the gentle flow of the afternoon strollers had become a purposeful stream of people walking towards Victoria. The offices were closing; the homeward rush had begun.

'A cab at this time can be difficult,' the woman said. She hesitated just a little, looking very closely and carefully at Dena. 'Why don't you let the rush hour go? Come and have a cup of tea with me. I live close by – just across The Mall.'

Something gently persuasive, almost wistful, in the woman's tone touched Dena, or was it that she was really tired, and the thought of a cup of tea became almost irresistible. And the woman herself, attractive, friendly. Her voice was warm.

'That's kind,' Dena said. 'I'd love that. There's no one at home . . . just now.'

'Settled, then.' The woman moved closer and took Dena's elbow, steering her gently across the bridge. She was some inches taller than Dena, and her manner was protective. Dena thought they must be close in age, and yet the stranger acted as if she, Dena, was a mere child, someone in need of help. 'My name's Ginny Clayton.' They were walking now at a fairly brisk pace towards The Mall. Dena fancied that everything this woman did would be brisk and decisive from the way, as they came to The Mall itself, that she held up her hand and the traffic slowed and halted. Dena would never have dared to do that. 'Might as well take advantage of the mother-to-be bit. After all, there are two of us. Who'd dare run us down? Can't you see the headlines? Two expectant mothers die under the wheels of the First Lord of the Admiralty's car. And practically in view of Queen Mary's sitting-room!'

Dena started to giggle. They reached the Green Park side of The Mall safely, and the traffic rolled again. This Ginny Clayton, Dena thought, was accustomed to getting her way, not imperiously, but just as if it were a natural thing. 'I'm Geraldine Penrose. Dena, they call me. I can tell you're

American, of course. An Englishwoman would never have spoken to me, much less asked me to tea.'

'People miss so much by not speaking. You looked somehow frail, and cold. And rather tired standing there watching the ducks. And yes, I agree. Being pregnant gets to be a bore, especially towards the end. This your first?'

'Yes. And yours?'

'I have a little boy of three.'

They did not take the usual route past St James's Palace, but went farther, to Queen's Walk, the broad pathway through Green Park that led directly to Piccadilly, passing Lancaster House. The traffic roared along Piccadilly; the Ritz was outlined against the lights up there. Here there was just the dim light cast by the old-fashioned, gas lanterns which still illuminated this part of the city. The autumn leaves had been swept into huge piles against the beech hedge. They were not going as far as Piccadilly. Ginny Clayton steered her towards an opening in the iron railing on their right. They moved along the narrow brick-paved walk called Milkmaid's Passage which separated the gardens of two tall, graceful houses which stared across the park to Buckingham Palace. They came out into an open space behind St James's Palace and turned to the left. Ginny Clayton took a key from her handbag, and unlocked a wrought-iron gate at the side of one of the houses. Dena knew it. Seymour House. One of the grandest houses in this grand area of London. In her debutante year she had been to a ball here. When they reached the top of the steps Ginny Clayton rang the bell of the front door. She was not the sort to let herself into her own house.

With great promptness the door was opened. A butler, not a footman, greeted them. 'Mrs Clayton, good evening, madam. I'm very pleased to see you. I was getting a trifle worried. It's dark, and you've been out quite a time in the park. I was just about to send Alfred to see if he could find you.'

'Kind of you, Griffin.' Ginny Clayton was slipping out of her coat, shaking her hair, which she wore rather long, from the confines of the snug fur cap. 'But I'm not a invalid, you know.'

24

'Of course not, madam, but what would Mr Clayton have said . . .' He took her coat and hat, and turned to help the unexpected guest off with hers. They had emerged fully into the light of the great staircase hall, the graceful curving staircase, the Adam fireplaces, the moulded ceiling just as Dena remembered it. The butler hesitated just momentarily. 'Why, it's Lady Geraldine, isn't it?'

Ginny Clayton had given her the man's name, and now Dena vaguely remembered his face, pink, well nourished, but mostly a discreet mask. But at which of the houses she had known as a debutante, or even before that, had he worked? She couldn't remember. Now that bland pink face smiled. 'It was at Blenheim, m'lady. And how is Mr Penrose?'

Dena smiled back. 'You don't forget anything, do you, Griffin? He's very well, as far as I know. Still in Cairo. Second Secretary.' The butler's formal demeanour returned. 'May I bring you something, Mrs Clayton?'

'I promised . . . er . . . Lady Geraldine some tea. In the library, Griffin, please.'

'Very good, madam.'

The curtains had been closed against the dusk, and the fire was cheerful. Dena went to it gratefully. 'I used to come here sometimes when I was a little girl. And I remember a ball the year I came out. That isn't so long ago, but it seems a lifetime.' She turned back to her hostess. 'Are you renting? Is it rude of me to ask?'

'No, not rude at all. I wish more of the British were so forthcoming. And no, we're not renting. It was for sale or rent. When we bought, Griffin was available too, so we kept him on. After all, he knows where everything is.'

'It's a lovely house,' Dena said. 'You must be intending to stay for some time.' She smiled. 'I hope so. Not everyone brings in strangers from the cold. I hope I shall know you.'

'Why else would you be here? Yes, we'll be staying, on and off.'

Griffin brought tea, with the usual accompaniment of small sandwiches and cakes. Ginny Clayton poured from a magnificent old silver service. They drank and ate almost in silence, but it was a companionable silence. 'I do get so hungry,' Dena said apologetically, as she finished the last sandwich. 'I suppose it's part of being pregnant.' She looked gratefully at the mistress of this house, seated on the other side of the fireplace. 'This has been so nice . . . so terribly kind of you. I'd have been making tea all by myself in the kitchen and no delicious little cakes, either.'

Griffin came to take the tea things away. 'I must be going,' Dena said. 'There should be plenty of taxis now . . .' But she didn't immediately rise to her feet.

'Don't hurry. If there's no one at home . . .' She knew now that Dena's husband, Harry, would not return from Cairo until close to the time the baby was expected. 'I'm alone too. My husband's in Zurich. There's nothing much to do at this stage of a pregnancy . . . except wait. As you said, rather boring. I don't know many people in London. Tell me . . .'

The conversation she was leading into stopped when a middle-aged woman knocked at the door and entered before Ginny could reply. 'Good evening, Mrs Clayton. I'm sorry to disturb you. Master Alex has come to say good-night. Griffin told me you had a guest, so I assumed you wouldn't be coming to the nursery just yet.'

A very dark haired boy, almost black haired, came running to Ginny. Her outstretched arms greeted him. 'Momma . . . why didn't you come upstairs? We waited.'

'Darling, we have a guest.'

The child turned and stared at Dena as if he resented her intrusion. 'You must shake hands, Alex. Lady Geraldine, this is my son, Alex McClintock.'

Dena's instinct was to hug the child, but she knew such a gesture would be unwelcome to him at this moment, since he wanted his mother to himself. He was beautiful. There was no other way to describe him. His eyes were a much darker shade of grey than his mother's but they were as deeply set under dark, straight brows. His head was beautifully set on straight, broad shoulders. He was tall for his age, and graceful in his movements. Had his mother said he was only three years old? Rather reluctantly he left his mother's arms and advanced towards Dena, holding out his hand as if his manners had been well drilled into him. He showed no trace of shyness. Dena accepted his hand gravely. 'I'm delighted to meet you, Alex. Your mother very kindly brought me in to tea. It was so cold in the park. That's why she didn't come up to you straight away. She was taking care of me.'

His resentment seemed to melt. He looked at her with new interest. 'Were you lost?'

'Not exactly. A little bit tired.' She looked across at Ginny Clayton. 'A little bit lonely, too.' On looking back it seemed to Dena that a friendship that was to be forever began by their staring first at the ducks passing under the bridge, and by the look they exchanged over the dark head of this beautiful child.

'You won't be lonely with my momma.'

He left with his nurse, after kissing his mother. Dena pondered his name. McClintock. And Ginny's name was Clayton. The two names were known even to the still rather unworldly Dena. There was a story to tell. Dena suddenly realized that she already knew a small part of it.

'Won't you stay and have a drink . . .?'

No one was expecting Dena in the small flat in Knightsbridge. She smiled, and accepted. 'I feel such . . . such a sponger.'

'Don't! I invited you. I've . . . I've been a bit lonely, too.'

They had drinks, and Griffin seemed delighted when Ginny told him that Lady Geraldine would be staying to dinner. By the time Dena was driven home in Ginny Clayton's Rolls-Royce, they knew a good deal about each other.

That night each woman lay restlessly in bed, twisting her heavy, burdened body in an effort to find a comfortable position, dozing fitfully, waking, recalling the conversation by the fire with the other woman, the talk, the revelations. They were almost the same age: Dena twenty-two, Ginny twenty-four. Their growing up had been in the same years. Their experiences had differed widely, but the framework had been the same. They had known privilege, if not always wealth. They lived again their own brief lives in thinking of the other's.

Chapter 3

Ginny's had been a graceful and relatively carefree growing-up. Washington, the capital, was close at hand, and often visited, but the family was pre-eminently Virginian. Her mother's maiden name was Lee, and they had been closely related to the South's great hero of the War between the States, as they still called it, Robert E. Lee. Her father's family could claim kinship with another hero of that war, 'Stonewall' Jackson.

Each family had suffered personal and financial loss during the war. In the case of Ginny's mother, it had meant near-ruin. Ginny's grandparents had only their pride and their memories to give their children. They had encouraged the courtship of their daughter, Rosemary, by the young congressman, Thomas Jackson. The Jacksons had managed to keep their graceful, spacious house, Pointerstown. In the poverty to which most of the South had been reduced, they were comparatively affluent. They weren't downright poor. So Rosemary Lee had gratefully married Thomas Jackson, and settled down at Pointerstown to raise a family of Southern gentlefolk. Three children were born: Lucy, Robert, and a third child they called Virginia.

Things moved in rather a different direction from than Rosemary Jackson had envisaged. True, they had their life at Pointerstown, and she cherished it; they had their black servants, their horses, and, increasingly, an amount of modest luxury. But Thomas did not settle down to the life of the Virginia country squire and landowner as Rosemary had expected. She had thought that his being a congressman would be a passing phase, a sort of hobby that he would tire of as soon as he had had his spell in the intense, bustling life of the capital, and had shown those Yankee congressmen, with whom he was forced to mix, just how things were conducted in the South. Instead, Thomas showed considerable political skill and ambition.

To Rosemary's dismay he renovated a house in Georgetown, which had been among the family holdings, a modest enough house, tall, narrow, sitting cheek-by-jowl with its neighbours. There he moved his family when Congress was in session.

As the years passed, he gained seniority in some important congressional committees. When he was approached to run for junior senator for Virginia, he thought it was high time to make the try. But Thomas did not ask Rosemary's opinion of this step. All he asked was that she remain the charming hostess she had become, that she take care of him in and out of bed, that she bring up his children as he thought they ought to be brought up. He rarely bothered about what opinions women might hold. They had their place, as wives and mothers. He honoured it. He hoped his daughters would grow up like their mother. They would certainly grow up as daughters of a United States senator. He had come in as junior senator with a large majority. He began to accumulate power, and for Thomas Jackson power was more pleasurable than money. In due course the senior senator retired, and as Thomas Jackson was returned to the Senate for this third six-year term, he knew he was a force in the land. Thomas Jackson had been active in politics long enough to know that a purely Southern view on the world could be a limiting thing, especially for this new generation. So when his children each came to the age when he judged they should see and know a wider world, he sent them to schools in the North. Rosemary thought this an unnecessarily harsh action on the part of a father who had always shown affection and consideration for his family. 'Why there's our own university right here in Virginia,' she had protested. 'And for the girls, all they need to know is how to behave as ladies.'

'They need to know far more than that. It isn't enough these days, Rosemary, for them to be able to say their family name is Lee. The South's got to put the past behind it. They can be proud of their birth and this history, but they have to know it isn't the only thing that matters in this country.'

So Lucy, and then Ginny, had gone to Miss Cole's School for Ladies in Connecticut, and when he had finished his prep school, Robert had gone to Princeton. And then to Harvard Law School. Lucy's lack of intellect disappointed her father, but she was a very pretty girl. He had somewhat modified his views that he wished his daughters to be just like their mother. In time she married much as he had expected her to. She married a young captain highly regarded in the Department of Defence. Robert had gained a place on the Harvard Law Review. The Senator had already ear-marked the law firm in Washington with whom he would start when he graduated. It was one of the best. Only Ginny's future remained to be settled.

There was nothing about Ginny which disappointed the Senator. She was not as conventionally pretty as her sister, but she was more striking, taller, with lovely graceful movements. She was the sort of girl people noticed favourably. There was nothing of the Southern belle in her demeanour. She didn't simper or flirt. She had a strongly defined chin, a high forehead, and light grey eyes. As he watched her grow, he thought of his lovely thoroughbred fillies in the paddocks of Pointerstown. He saw their flowing manes in the proud toss of her dark blonde hair. There was an as yet unguessed potential for this his last, secretly, his most loved child.

She finished at Miss Cole's at the top of her class, and astounded Rosemary and delighted the Senator by declaring that she had applied to and been accepted by Radcliffe. Rosemary wept and raged at the decision. No woman of her family had ever been to university. And no one of them would ever have considered that bastion of blue-stocking Northern Yankee women as a place to be considered, even if they had aspired to this fad for higher education.

'No one will ever marry her,' she had wailed to the Senator. 'Now Lucy – she's done so well . . .'

'Just watch what Ginny will do,' was all the Senator had said.

'I don't want to watch my daughter become a . . . a . . .' Rosemary didn't know what sort of woman she tried to describe. Rosemary shared the Senator's ambition for their son; she knew he could have a brilliant future in law in Washington. Never had she thought one of her daughters might aspire to something other than husband and children. 'Why couldn't she be more like Lucy?'

'Thank heaven she isn't,' the Senator replied.

So Ginny went to Radcliffe and thrived in its air of intellectual challenge. She didn't even seem to mind the terrible Northern winters. When she returned home for Christmas her mother was relieved to see that she didn't actually despise her family. Having a brother at Harvard made her familiar with the ways of young men, and she seemed to enjoy the Washington parties. Rosemary's anxieties lessened, but she said as little as possible to her friends about Ginny's future ambitions. 'Oh, she'll settle down one day, just like Lucy.'

Ginny came back to Pointerstown for the long summer vacations, and seemed perfectly content with its quiet routine. She brought a pile of books with her, and began to use her father's library. And every day she rode. She rode as naturally as she danced. The house sounded to the jazz records she played, and at weekends there was a stream of young men who came to dance with her. But every morning she was up at sunrise to ride for an hour or two before the heat of the day. Sometimes she went to the Georgetown house, and even accompanied her mother on shopping trips and to elegant teas with her mother's friends. She dated friends of her brother, Robbie, and young men who worked in the Senate office building. Less pleasing to her mother was the fact that she haunted galleries and the Smithsonian, and, before Congress broke for the summer recess, she attended sessions of both the House of Representatives and the Senate. Whenever she was home from Radcliffe, she was in the Senate each time her father made an important speech. Father and daughter grew closer. For her twentieth birthday he gave her her own morocco-bound edition of the *Encyclopaedia Britannica*. She thanked him gravely, and said she would be happy to take it to her new home.

'I have to continue my education somehow.'

'You're . . . you're not leaving Radcliffe?' The mention of a new home greatly disturbed the Senator.

'No, Daddy. I'm going to marry Alex McClintock.'

The Senator slumped back heavily in his chair. 'McClintock!' He took a long, deep breath. They were seated across the breakfast table at Pointerstown. Already, around them were the sounds of the preparations for this evening's birthday party. Rosemary's voice was heard directing where the last of the decorations were to be hung. Men were stringing paper lanterns along the wide porch. The Senator stared at his favourite child, dismayed. Filled with fear.

'McClintock!' he said again.

The McClintock name was known throughout Washington and Virginia, and very much further. There were McClintock buildings in the capital, in Pittsburg, on Wall Street and in Chicago. There were offices in other great cities of the world. There were factories. The Senator couldn't even begin to remember where the factories were scattered, or the diversity of the products they made. The present McClintock was a man, they said, ahead of his time. The first McClintock Washington and Virginia had known was a man thoroughly hated. His son, who now owned and ran this financial and industrial empire was scarcely more liked. His grandson was an unknown quantity to the Senator. And this was the man his beloved Ginny proposed to marry.

James Alexander McClintock had arrived on the Washington scene at the end of the Civil War. He had come from New York with the reputation of a war profiteer, worse, a war racketeer. McClintock had troubled to deny nothing. It was as if what the Southerners thought of him was a matter of indifference. He had come to Washington, not as a common carpetbagger, but a man well known and, in financial circles, respected. The McClintock Bank had funded and helped raise a great deal of the Union Army's loans. There was the McClintock steel works in Pittsburg, and European connections of which less was generally known. James McClintock had come to pay his respects to the new President, Andrew Johnson, after the assassination of Lincoln. He had lingered a little in Washington, looked around Virginia, and for almost no money, because the war had ruined its owner, he had bought Prescott Hill, one of the South's finest *ante-*

bellum mansions. It stood, shaded by its great oaks, on its green and gentle hill, like a Grecian temple.

If McClintock had tried to integrate into the life of Virginia, perhaps eventually he would have been accepted, or if not he perhaps his son. James McClintock's Yankee wife had died giving birth to his only child, a boy, in 1877. But the years went on, and the McClintocks, father and son, spent little time at Prescott Hill. A great house, inevitably called the McClintock Mansion, was built on Massachusetts Avenue in the capital.

Nothing changed when James Alexander died at an unexpectedly early age. His son, Andrew Alexander McClintock, continued in his father's ways. It was said he had even a better head for business than his father, and he had much smoother manners. But he continued to ignore his Virginia neighbours. He married a Russian princess about the turn of the century. When their son was born two years later, the papers said the Czarina was godmother, by proxy, to the child. The McClintocks occupied the mansion on Massachusetts Avenue and a great house in New York. The princess's jewels were reported to be almost beyond belief. It was some of these jewels, as many as she could get into her possession, which she used to fund herself and her lover when she ran away with a Russian cousin, Count Bolivsky, when her son was three years old. McClintock was unforgiving. He refused a divorce. He refused her her child. She was believed to have died in near poverty on the French Riviera in 1920. She never saw her son again.

McClintock remained a secretive, elusive man. His wife's desertion had embittered him, and her name was forbidden to be mentioned. His son grew up without any personal knowledge of his mother. His father had discreet mistresses, but he never married. Prescott Hill remained mostly unvisited by its master. It was never shuttered. A staff of servants remained always in residence, and McClintock would usually arrive without warning and expect the great house to be in readiness for him.

The stock market boom of the twenties only made Andrew McClintock richer, while others still struggled, very slowly, from the genteel poverty the long-ago Civil War had thrust upon them. Long before the United States entered the European war in 1917, McClintock factories were turning out arms and materiel for the Allies, and, it was rumoured, through neutral sources, for the Germans. But the Allies and eventually the United States needed the McClintock arms. It might be said that the whole world despised the men who made munitions, but they were needed. In the midst of all his other concerns, it seemed that there was no place in McClintock's life to care what people thought of him, most certainly not his snobbish, poor Virginian neighbours.

Now Senator Jackson's beloved daughter, Ginny, sat across the table and told the Senator, on the morning of her twentieth birthday, that she was going to marry the son of Andrew McClintock.

He went around the table and sat down beside her. Very calmly she poured a fresh cup of coffee and placed it before him. He ignored it.

'Why?' he said.

'For the usual reason. I love him.'

'And he – this Alex McClintock?' He almost stumbled over the name. He had heard it only rarely. Alex McClintock played as little part in the life of his neighbours as his father. No one knew when he had ever visited the mansion. Someone said he had once gone out hunting with the local pack.

'He loves me. Why else would he have asked me to marry him?'

'We . . . we don't even know him.'

'*I* know him, Daddy. I was the one who invited him to the hunt. That story's true. But we didn't ride together. Barely spoke. I thought it was a joke . . . you've all been so stuffy about him.'

'But how do you know him?'

'For the last three summers I've gone out riding with him whenever he's been at Prescott Hill. We met one morning, quite accidentally. He's a splendid rider. I was still in school, almost, but he treated me like a grown-up lady.'

'And since?' The Senator didn't attempt to hide the innuendo.

'He has continued to treat me like a lady. In every respect. And he wants to marry me. I want you to announce it at the party tonight. We're going to be married in about a month's time. He starts working for his father this fall. He wants to be married by then.'

'Impossible. I'll never agree to it. You know this man's reputation.'

'I know his father's reputation. Do you know a single thing against Alex McClintock?'

'I know nothing in his favour, either.'

'Then why judge? If you refuse, I'll marry him anyway. Even if I have to run away with him.'

His eyes deepened with a painful suspicion. 'Ginny, you're not . . . not in trouble, are you?'

She spoke frankly, in the manner of one who has learned something at Radcliffe: 'If you mean, am I pregnant . . .? I'm not. I'll marry Alex, and soon, because he's the only man I'll ever love in my life.'

'Ginny! You're too young to say that!'

'What am I supposed to say? I'll think about it? I'll wait? I'll think and I'll wait until I'm thirty, and I've lost Alex? If I'm not sure of this, then I'll never be sure of anything in my life. We'll announce the engagement tonight, and I'll take the same chance on marriage as everyone else takes. It will either succeed or it will fail. That I'm even willing to consider failure tells you how much I've thought about it. All this past year at Radcliffe. I hoped he was going to ask me. I was ready to say yes. I love him, Daddy. His father and I have met, and there's no opposition.'

The Senator's face reddened. 'I should think not!'

'Daddy, let's stop arguing, and tell Mother. Let her get her hysterics over. Alex will be here at nine-thirty to see you.'

'Good of him,' the Senator said bitterly. 'I suppose he'll ask for your hand like any gentleman. After he's already got you to agree.'

'I practically had to ask him. I thought he'd never notice I'd grown up. But I have, and I intend to do what I want. It's the only thing, don't you understand, Daddy? There's

35

nothing else for me. No one else. If you refuse this, and force me to do it on my own, I'll never speak to you, never see you again.'

The Senator, studying her expression sadly, knew she meant it. Her face was stern with determination, and at the same time radiant in a way he had never seen it before. Just talking about the man could transform her. He loathed the thought of marriage to a McClintock, and yet he had to respect the judgement of this, not only his most beloved child, but also the most intelligent, the most sensitive. He looked at the simple cotton dress she wore to receive her future husband; he considered her innocent account of a courtship which had seemed to take account of her innocence. She looked at him with such frank and open honesty that he could not doubt one word she said.

The effect of the news on Ginny's mother was predictable. It did Rosemary credit, the Senator thought, that never once did she seem to consider what wealth her daughter was marrying. Or was it that her narrow pride saw only one aspect of this unknown man? McClintock. That was all they knew to be wrong with him. His father's name was McClintock.

The argument raged between them for the hour before Alex appeared at Pointerstown. When he was announced by their butler, they knew at once why it had happened.

Alex was almost impossibly handsome. Black hair, perfectly regular features, dark straight brows, dark grey eyes. He had not the clean but rather bland good looks of the boys Ginny knew as neighbours. If it had not been for his accent and what Rosemary could only think of as courtly Southern manners, he might have stepped straight out of a tale of Old Russia. Had her daughter fallen in love with the prince from *Swan Lake*? But then, Alexander McClintock, sprung from rude Scottish forebears, the grandson of the robber baron, was, indeed, a Russian prince. Rosemary, who had been standing, full of matronly dignity and indignation, abruptly sat down. What could she do or say, faced with a man like this?

The announcement was made at the party that night.

Virginia society got its first good look at Alex McClintock, and was impressed by what it saw. But his father did not attend. He had urgent business in New York. The marriage was announced for one month later, and many Virginian matrons asked the same question as the Senator. Why the almost unseemly haste? What time was there for the preparation of a grand wedding? Where was the trousseau that such a marriage would demand? Why there was barely time to think of a wedding gift. Where would they go on their honeymoon, Ginny was asked? They hadn't thought. They might just take off in a car and stay wherever their fancy took them. Those who had visions of a long European honeymoon were disappointed. It all sounded very patched together, dullness where there should have been dazzle.

The wedding at Pointerstown was not disappointing. The Senator virtually emptied his pockets to provide that, and a trousseau at which neither Andrew McClintock nor anyone else could sneer. He sent Ginny to New York to shop. And people did discover that there was time to find suitable wedding gifts, and because of the McClintock connection, they spent rather more money than they normally did when the children of other friends were married. Invitations to the wedding were eagerly sought, but no invitation was more eagerly looked for than the one to the ball to be given on the wedding night at Prescott Hill. At last those closed, indifferent doors were being opened to Virginian society. The President and First Lady would attend, and all but one of the nine Supreme Court Justices. The wedding, which had been beautiful, was eclipsed by the ball. Prescott Hill did not disappoint. It was as magnificent, and as unlived in, as everyone had supposed, despite the festive air given by the lighting and the flowers. Keen connoisseurs of rare books envied McClintock his library. The pictures were of excellent quality, mostly horse and hunting pictures, suitable to this country, Stubbs, Landseer, Jacques Laurent Agasse. The really great paintings were said to be in the Massachusetts Avenue house, and in New York. The women tried to price the carpets, the curtains, the chandeliers, the silver; tried, by discreet means, to count the number of marble bathrooms.

Andrew McClintock was reckoned to have had the laugh of the evening when he found a distinguished Washington hostess in his bedroom. 'Good evening, madam. May I be of service to you?'

Everyone had to wait until the President departed, which he did considerably early. The dancing went on. No one noticed when Andrew McClintock slipped away. And then it was found that the bride and groom were also gone. The guests were left to dance and drink champagne, and they realized that although they had seen Prescott Hill, they were unlikely to grow very familiar with it. It suddenly began to seem that Ginny had gone over completely to the McClintock side. The Senator and Rosemary were left to take the good-byes of the departing guests. All through the next day the servants and those hired as extra help cleared up, removed the marquee, replaced any plants which had been damaged, removed and replaced worn turf. By evening, Prescott Hill was immaculate, and its usual silence had descended on it. Then Ginny and Alex came back from one of the group of guest houses sited among the plantation of magnificent cedar trees which James Alexander had ordered to be planted about half a mile from the main house when he first bought Prescott Hill.

They spent an idyllic two weeks riding Prescott Hill's many acres, reading the books in the library, making love whenever it pleased them. The servants and stablehands remained discreet; if they came on the lovers in any of the groves of trees that dotted the estate, they moved quietly away. They told no one where the young McClintocks were. Telephone calls to the house were answered politely and dismissively by the butler. All the servants knew that if it leaked out that Ginny and Alex were at Prescott Hill, they all would be instantly dismissed by Andrew McClintock. Each bedroom and its adjoining bathroom in the mansion was made up, supplied with fresh sheets and towels. There was some gossip in the servants' quarters that just about every bed had been used and tried. 'Quite the little princess, ain't she?' one of the maids remarked. 'Looking for the mattress without the pea under it.' She was sternly rebuked by the butler. They were ordered to do their jobs silently, and stay out of sight. Only the butler brought breakfast to whatever room Ginny and Alex had decided to use the night before; only he served their other meals, and withdrew until a bell summoned him back. Once the swimming-pool, fashioned after a Greek temple, with columns of real marble, had been cleaned in the early morning, all the staff were forbidden to approach it during the day, and most particularly at night. But the sound of laughter and splashing carried on the still night air. It was a warm Virginian September night when a young stable lad crept quietly through the shrubbery and along the tall stone wall which surrounded the pool. He never spoke of what he saw. He had come as a voyeur and to snigger; he left in a state of awe. He had never imagined a naked woman could be as beautiful as Virginia McClintock.

And Ginny had never known she could be so happy.

After two weeks it was time to move to the Massachusetts Avenue house. They would live there as Alex began his life in the Washington office of McClintock's; he would work, for the first year, mainly in the legal department. His father would continue to run the Wall Street office, and make his frequent visits to Washington.

Ginny turned to look back wistfully at Prescott Hill as they left. Could any time ever again be so wonderful? 'We'll come back every chance we get,' Alex promised.

The McClintock mansion oppressed Ginny. It had all the elaborate furnishings, the grandeur of the last years of the opulent nineteenth century, a ballroom, a marble fountain in its hall, and a conservatory. Here the pictures were indeed magnificent, as was everything else. The staff were silent and punctilious. Everything was what any woman might have dreamed of.

To Ginny the house was coldly formal, and neither she nor Alex had much desire to become known as party-givers. Alex had inherited much of his father's temperament in this respect, and for the time being Ginny wanted only to be with him. She had yet to find her feet as a married woman, much less the woman who had married the McClintock fortune. The worst part of living in that house, she found, was that

Andrew McClintock still regarded it as his home. He wasn't there very often, but his arrival was always as unheralded as it had ever been. Every day Ginny saw that fresh linen and flowers were placed in the suite he always used. Every evening a place was laid for him at the long table in the panelled dining-room. Ginny found it nerve-racking to be constantly prepared for a demanding guest who so rarely appeared. When he was present, she experienced at once the constraint he placed on Alex and herself. She began to think nostalgically of the rather shabby house in Georgetown which the Senator and her mother occupied.

But Alex made it worthwhile. She wondered how it would be possible to love him more. It was an on-going honeymoon; there were flowers and small gifts sent to her, as if she didn't already have the ability to command whatever she wanted. She cherished the books that arrived, always by special messenger, because they signalled the fact that Alex had taken part of his lunch hour to select them. She knew instinctively that they had not been ordered by telephone by his secretary. He gave her modest gifts of jewellery. They pleased her more than the lavish ones she knew he could afford. He often brought work home from the office in the evenings, and they sat companionably in the library, she reading while he worked. And they were sitting in such a way late one evening when Andrew McClintock arrived. He entered the room unannounced.

Alex got to his feet. 'Father, I do think you could have had someone telephone Ginny that you were coming. It's hardly fair to her –'

His father cut him short. 'Ginny has servants to look after my needs. I don't much care for hotels. I've told Taylor what I want to eat. He'll bring it here on a tray.' He strolled over to the desk where Alex was working, and without permission, glanced at the papers. 'Glad to see you keep busy.' He turned to Ginny, his sharp eyes reading the title of the book she was reading. Hazlitt's essays. 'Still at Radcliffe, I see. You'd be better reading some American stuff . . .'

'I think you might leave Ginny's choice of reading to her,' Alex said.

His father laughed. 'Touchy young bridegroom. I rather sense Ginny can speak up for herself. Well, it's good to see you two young people like each other's company. Too damn much partying goes on in Washington to my mind. Though . . .' He looked at Ginny again. 'Being the daughter of a politician you must know how much politicking goes on at parties. You'll have to start giving some dinner parties. This house hasn't had a hostess since . . . well, for a long time. I don't have to tell you, a Senator's daughter, how much a wife, the right wife, can help a man. Though, God knows, anyone invited to the McClintock house would beat a trail here, even if the hostess were a barefoot kid out of the hills.'

Ginny knew that his acceptance of this marriage, to which she had brought no money, had been conditioned by the fact of her father's political power, and her mother's breeding and reputation as a hostess. She knew very well the job Andrew McClintock expected her to do.

'I think all newly-weds are given a grace period, Mr McClintock.' She felt goaded by his reference to a bare-footed kid. 'After all, you expect great things of Alex. You don't want people deferring to him just because he's your son. And as for me . . . well, I think I'll need a little time before I launch out. I'm going to have a baby.'

The two men seemed, for an instant, frozen. 'Ginny!' There was profound hurt in Alex's tone. 'You didn't tell me! I should have been the first —'

'I only knew for sure today. I was waiting until you were finished with your work, when you were having your night-cap.' Her look pleaded for Alex's forgiveness. He went to her and kissed her fully on the mouth.

'Thank you, my darling. Let it be a girl. I'm greedy. I want another Ginny.'

'It had damn well better be a boy,' Andrew McClintock said. But he went to Ginny and kissed her on the cheek. Never before, not even at their wedding, had he done that. A handshake was the most intimate contact they had achieved. 'Well done, girl. Let there be lots of them. Boys and girls. It was always a damn shame Alex never had any brothers. Too much on one man's shoulders.' He moved to the bell cord and pulled it. I'll cancel that order for claret. This calls for champagne.'

When his light meal was over, the bottle of Veuve Clicquot drunk, and Taylor had cleared away, Andrew McClintock went to a wall safe that Ginny had not known existed. It was behind a row of false books that in this room which held thousands of books she had never noticed. Typically, Andrew McClintock had no need to consult a notebook to remember the combination. He thrust aside some papers, and took out a large, flat jewel case. 'Took it out of the bank in anticipation of some happy news of this kind. Here you are, my dear. When the baby's born, we'll hold a christening party, hell, no, we'll have a ball, so you can dress up. Of course, they really need resetting. A little old-fashioned now, I'd say.'

He held towards her the box in which lay, on black velvet, an emerald and diamond necklace, with long matching drop earrings and an emerald and diamond bracelet. Ginny had never seen any jewels so dazzling in her life. She heard her own gasp. She realized she was looking at some of the jewellery which the Russian princess had been unable to take with her. She backed away from it. It was something no girl who was still under twenty-one should ever wear. It was something for a duchess, for a queen. 'I couldn't . . .'

'Don't be foolish, girl. You're a McClintock now. Besides, you've got the neck for it.' It was the first compliment he'd ever paid her.

Alex put his arms around her. Neither of them looked again at the contents of the velvet-lined box, although Ginny was sure that for him, also, it was the first sight of them. 'I love you,' he said. Ginny thought of the simple, delicate little pieces of jewellery he had given her. His love had been shown in them in a way that these great green stones never could convey. She would wear the McClintock emeralds because it was expected of her, but she would cherish and love the pieces Alex had given her.

'I love you, too.'

They had managed to exclude Andrew McClintock and his emeralds. They knew from the way he testily bade them goodnight, that he hadn't liked it. He was not used to being shut out. When the library door closed behind him, Alex put his arms about her once again. 'In future we won't save up things to tell each other. Or he'll take them away from us.' He looked about him. 'This damn house! We should never have agreed to come here. When the baby's born, I'll tell him we have to have a place of our own. We're getting out from under him. In another year I'll come into the trust fund. He won't be able to stop us.'

He had never before revealed his feelings about his father. 'I hope it is a girl. Serve him damn well right!'

The months of her pregnancy pressed heavily on Ginny. Or perhaps it was, she thought, the McClintock house. Andrew McClintock appeared there more frequently, and he enquired about her health in sometimes embarrassing detail. She wasn't sure that he hadn't tried to get even more information from her doctor. 'Well, you come from good, healthy stock. Good breeding stock. Your sister Lucy's having another, I hear.'

They took to going to Prescott Hill every weekend to escape the Washington house, and with the hope of escaping Andrew McClintock. Often he followed them there. He was obliged, for the sake of humouring his pregnant daughter-in-law, his manner seemed to suggest, to invite the Senator and Rosemary occasionally to dinner. But all other company was barred. 'Can't have Ginny getting overtired.' There was a scene early one morning when he strode into the stable yard and found both Ginny and Alex already mounted. 'Are you out of your mind, your stupid little bitch? Do you realize you could lose my grandson? Get down at once! Easy!' He gestured imperiously to the two grooms. 'For God's sake hold the damned horse! Get her down easy.' When Ginny was safely on the ground he turned once more to the grooms. 'If anyone in this stable ever again saddles up for, or helps Mrs McClintock, the whole damned lot of you will be fired. Mrs McClintock is *not* to ride!'

Then he turned to his son. 'And you – you're a worse idiot than I supposed. Can't you see the danger?' He was indifferent to the avid attention of the grooms and stable-boys.

Alex's tone was dangerously cold. He slipped from the saddle and gave the reins to one of the grooms. 'The mare is as placid as a stuffed rabbit. We had no intention of moving at more than a walking pace. The doctor recommends exercise. Come on, Ginny. We'll do our walking on our own two feet.'

After that, the atmosphere became increasingly charged. Ginny thought desperately of the months that still separated them from the birth of their baby and Alex's own birthday, when the trust fund would set them free. His father had set it up when his son had been born, and fixed Alex's inheritance for the year when he would have finished law school and joined the family business. It had been firmly established as an irrevocable trust, perhaps to please the Princess, and now, by good management of the trustees, had reached a sum that would make Alex completely independent. It was possible that Andrew McClintock now regretted that gesture. Perhaps it had been made in a mood of mellowness, when he had looked forward to a much larger family. But there had been only Alex. Ginny began to see in the gifts which Andrew McClintock showered on her the fear that possessed him. He dreaded a break with his son. After the incident at Prescott Hill, Ginny saw that Andrew McClintock made visible efforts to refrain from interfering in their lives. Now there were telephone calls alerting them that he would be coming to Washington. He would appear to take a deep breath and ask if they would mind his company at Prescott Hill.

On Andrew McClintock's orders a nursery was prepared both at the Massachusetts Avenue house and Prescott Hill. They were both stocked with toys Ginny did not have the pleasure of choosing. She looked at the tiny, exquisite baby clothes that arrived from Garfinkle's and Saks, and remembered, rather enviously, that Lucy had written that the sensible, practical layette they had bought for their first child would be doing nicely for the second. John Preston had a small private income, but in the army it did not do for a young officer to spend above the means of his rank. There would be no such economy practised for future McClintock children. There was no rank in the company which matched that of the only son and heir.

They went to Prescott Hill on a weekend late in March, when Ginny was six months pregnant. Andrew McClintock accompanied them. 'This must be the last visit here until after the baby's born. I want you near the hospital and the doctor in Washington. Can't risk you having the baby in that hayseed hospital they've got out here.'

Alex and Ginny made no open protest. They knew they had only to bide their time for another few months. 'It isn't worth your getting upset about, my love,' Alex said. 'Try to ignore him. Think of the baby. After all, I suppose he just has your best interests at heart.'

'My interests? It's his grandson's interests he's concerned about.'

She saw Alex off on his ride that Sunday morning with a little pang of envy. He leaned from the saddle to kiss her. 'I'll be back in an hour, sweetheart. Don't look so forlorn. It won't be long now. You'll be back riding beside me.'

She smiled. Her body was growing heavy, but it was Alex's child she carried, not his father's. She touched her fingers to her lips and waved him a kiss as he reached the arched entrance to the stable yard and turned back to look at her, as he always did. Why give him a sour face to remember as he rode? She walked slowly back to the house, and to the breakfast room. 'Soon it'll be over,' she told herself. She automatically assumed a bright smile as she entered the breakfast room, which was bathed in spring sunshine. After all, what difference did a few more months make?

'Good morning, Mr McClintock.'

He looked up from the newspaper. ''Morning, Ginny. How do you feel? Sleep well?'

'Never better. Perfectly.' Always her response, even on the worst days. She helped herself to two eggs and crisp bacon, a piece of corn bread, and watched him critically eyeing her plate.

She didn't begin to worry until she realized that Alex had

45

been gone almost two hours. She put on a thick coat and went to the stable yard, expecting to find him engaged in conversation with the head groom, something he often did as they went the round of the stalls and the horses. But he was not there and, seeing her, the head groom, Ned, came hurrying to her.

'Not back yet, Mrs McClintock. Expect he just went a bit farther than he planned. Always loves his rides, Mr Alex.' But as he saw her expression, he added, 'If you like, I'll get a couple of the lads to saddle up and go out to meet him. Tell him you're looking for him. Did he say which way he was going?' She shook her head. 'Don't worry, Mrs McClintock. Maybe Bold Boy –' that was Alex's favourite and most mettlesome horse, 'cast a shoe or went lame and he's walking home. Don't stay out here in the cold, Mrs McClintock. Go back to the house, and I'll ring through the minute he comes in.'

When Alex did not appear in the next half-hour, and there was no call from the stables, Ginny went to Andrew McClintock and told him. 'Why the hell didn't you say he hadn't come in?' His hand was on the telephone immediately, connecting him with the stables. 'Not in yet?' he roared at Ned. 'Then get every man into vehicles and start searching along the estate roads. Think of every place he could be. Damn it, why didn't you ask where he was heading? None of your business? I pay you to make it your business.'

The morning went leadenly. Andrew McClintock remained by the telephone. By now, though under protest, the county police were involved, and an ambulance and a doctor waited. Ginny had tried to dissuade Andrew McClintock from this action. 'Alex will be furious.'

'Let him be. He's no business to upset us, you, this way. Damn fool! In any case, I'm one of the biggest taxpayers in the county. Let the police earn their money.'

They found him face-downwards in a shallow creek in the part of the estate which was one of his favourite rides, and was heavily wooded. Bold Boy was wandering three miles away. A deep gash across Alex's forehead indicated that he had been struck by a low limb of a tree. His father's first reaction was an explosion of anger rather than grief. 'Damn fool! Horse must have got out of hand. Some damn thing startled it. Maybe a snake. Bolted with him – in timber like that. Shoot the damned animal! Oh, God damn it, Alex, you fool! You fool!' He suddenly became aware of the stricken face of his daughter-in-law, noticed that she swayed on her feet. He shouted to the butler. 'Get the damn doctor here.' Then he turned back to Ginny. 'Alex is gone, but don't think I mean to lose my grandson, too. You're not going to miscarry, or go into labour, you hear!'

When she came numbly out of the drugged sleep, Ginny was in the bed she and Alex had shared. Her hand went slowly, tentatively to the smooth empty pillow beside her. 'I love you,' she whispered.

The sound evoked a response from the other side of the room. Both the doctor and Andrew McClintock came to her, her own obstetrician from Washington. He applied a blood pressure cuff. Awkwardly Andrew McClintock took Ginny's hand. It was a gesture she had not thought him capable of.

'It's rough, Ginny. I loved him too.' She realized that the sharp face actually seemed etched in lines of grief. 'But you're a strong girl. You hang in here. We've lost Alex. Keep his child.' He no longer spoke of a son.

Ginny was not permitted to attend the burial at Prescott Hill. She was taken by ambulance back to Washington. The several doctors Andrew McClintock called in advised against more sedating drugs. 'They could affect the baby.' Her mother sat by her bedside. She stayed there when the doctors and even Andrew McClintock were forced to withdraw.

'I loved him,' Ginny said.

'I know you did. It was one of the most beautiful things I have ever seen in my life. You've had something rare and wonderful, Ginny. Try to keep a part of it. Rest. Above all, rest. Your father and I will be here. We won't leave you.'

Ginny was never aware of the extent of the battle which raged between her parents and Andrew McClintock, but later she guessed it. 'I won't have her turned into an invalid

47

in this mausoleum,' Rosemary had shouted at McClintock. She had at last begun to perceive the Washington house for what it seemed to Ginny, a sort of prison. 'She had a happy childhood at Pointerstown. Let her go back there. I give you my sacred word of honour that I'll never leave her side. Nearer the time we'll come back to Georgetown.'

In the end it was a compromise. Ginny went to Pointerstown until the end of her eighth month. Then accompanied by Rosemary, and a rather intimidated Lucy, nursing her second child, they moved into the McClintock mansion. Exactly on schedule the waters broke, the labour pains began. Ginny had a smooth ride to the hospital. With a minimum of fuss, and no drugs, she produced the grandson Andrew McClintock had so desperately wished for. She kissed his damp, very dark hair. 'My Alex . . .'

Thereafter, as she grew stronger, and spirit returned, Ginny began to perceive the struggle ahead. She must give Andrew McClintock his due share of his grandchild, but she had no intention of letting this child become his grandfather's possession. She would not permit him to repeat his father's lonely and privileged life.

She lived mainly at Pointerstown during the months after the baby was born, but she knew she could not do so for ever. Desperately Ginny began to look around for the foundation for a life which had no purpose except for the infant who absorbed her every moment. She had refused a nurse for him, to Andrew McClintock's fury. 'I want to look after him myself. I'm not incompetent.'

'Have you noticed what happens to women who shut themselves up with children, in this case, an only child? They become childish. What happened to that Radcliffe brat? I thought you were more intelligent than this.'

He was right, but she was loath to admit it. Where did she start to reform a life which no longer had Alex as its core and centre? She had spoken the truth when she had said to her father on the morning of her twentieth birthday that she would never love another man. She felt, she thought, not so much griefstricken, as totally empty; there was a hollow part of her that even the baby could not fill, would never be able to fill. She would place as much of a burden of love and possessiveness upon him as Andrew McClintock had placed on his son. She was in danger of repeating that mistake.

Eventually the child was christened. As he had on the night of her wedding, Andrew McClintock on this occasion decided to break his custom of isolation. He asked Ginny, quite humbly for him, if she would consent to a small celebration after the christening at the Massachusetts Avenue house. 'After all, this is the only grandchild I'll ever have.' Ginny could not refuse. He was called Lee Andrew Alexander McClintock.

A Supreme Court Justice was one of the baby's godparents; the First Lady was another. Andrew McClintock, himself a Democrat, always walked a fine line between the two parties, giving evenhandedly to each at election time. The godparents were as evenly balanced. There were godparents whom Ginny hadn't even met, names of such power in politics and banking and industry that they impressed even Rosemary. The reception was lavish and crowded, far more so than Ginny had expected. She saw Lucy struggling to get through the crush. She kissed her sister. 'Mr McClintock wrote personally and asked me to come. Paid my way, with a nurse for the children. I'm sorry I'm so late that I missed the ceremony. There was a mix-up changing trains in Chicago. Let me see him!' With difficulty Ginny managed to get the baby from the arms of one of his godmothers. Lucy stared down at him. 'Oh, Ginny, he's just the image of Alex, even this little baby face. He's . . . he's beautiful.' To Ginny's suprise she bent and softly kissed the baby's forehead. 'I hope you'll always think of me as his godmother—one of them. I'm not bad with children. And this one won't have an easy time of it.' It was an odd and strangely wise thing for Lucy to say. Not everyone would have predicted a difficult future for Andrew McClintock's only grandchild.

At the end of it Andrew gravely thanked her. 'You did very well, Ginny. I know it isn't easy for you, but I always guessed you'd come through it, not through it, but that you'd learn to live with it. And now I have another favour to ask of you.'

She braced herself for another of Andrew McClintock's favours. 'I've made some financial arrangements. Now don't look like that! Do you think that I'm going to allow the Senator to support my grandson for ever? He can't afford it, to start with.' He held up his hand. 'Hear me out. If Alex had lived a little longer he would have come into his trust fund, and he could have told me to go to hell, if that's what he wanted. I had planned to do that for all my children, if I'd had more. Well, as you know, the trust reverted to me, because Alex hadn't reached his birthday. Now I've set it up again for your Alex . . .' He slipped naturally into the name because Ginny always called him that. 'What I propose to do is to set up a trust for you –' Once again he held up his hand. 'Just let me finish. You will draw the income from it but may never touch the capital. It will be a very generous income, but it won't be so big that every fortune-hunter on this side of the Atlantic or the other will come calling. Of course, if McClintock's continues to grow, your shares will bring more income.

'I hope you will be sensible. The income from Alex's trust will also be available for use at the trustees' discretion. It will be used to house and clothe and feed him, and that also means you, as his mother and guardian. He will need nurses, and later, schools. He will need chauffeurs and riding instructors. Oh, yes, I know he'll ride, and do every damn dangerous thing a boy ought to do. He'll need a house . . . all of those things. Ginny, listen to me. Now, I don't expect you to live either with your parents or in this house. I know you and Alex hated it, and you planned to get out the day you got your hands on the trust. I expected it. It was the only red-blooded thing for a young couple to do. I would have despised Alex if he'd wanted to stay on here. I'm not asking you to stay here, but I'm not giving this house up. I'll continue to use it whenever I'm in Washington.

'What I'm asking, for the child's sake, is to consider a house I've looked at in Georgetown. Quite near your parents, but definitely not next door. You'll need your freedom from them, too. You can't live at Pointerstown. You've got to make a life of your own, and you sure as hell won't do that out in the boondocks. So . . . find a job, if that's what it takes to get away from the baby for a few hours a day. There are plenty of nurses to hire. I'd fix you up with a job at McClintock's in an hour, but I think you'd prefer to be more independent. Your father could put in a word for you in some government agency. Nothing too exacting, though you're a bright enough kid, I'll give you that. I want you to have some energy left over for Alex and a decent social life.'

'A social life! Alex's only been dead —'

'Damn it, I know! I didn't expect you to stick to those old ideas. Your life isn't over. I expect you to marry and have more children. Don't make the mistake I did.' He gave a half-laugh which was almost a choking sound. 'I guess you never thought you'd hear me say I made a mistake. I was in love with that damn Russian. She hurt me a lot. Hurt my pride. I didn't enjoy being cuckolded. So I refused her a divorce, out of spite I suppose. That meant I couldn't marry myself. I never found anyone I particularly cared to marry, but marriages, pretty good ones, have been made for convenience before.'

'So you expect me to make a marriage of convenience?'

'I said no such thing. I just said get out in the world. I don't ask you to forget Alex. I know that's not possible. I'm not such a fool as not to know you were really in love with him. If I'd thought for a moment that you were after his money, my money, I'd have stopped the marriage if it was the last thing I did. But so . . . Alex is gone. What's wrong with looking at other men? Washington is full of them. I may even emerge from my shell a bit, and naturally I'll expect you to be my hostess when I give a party. Young Alex has to have a future prepared for him. He's got to know other kids. By the time he's twenty he'll know everyone worth knowing in Washington and New York. Between us, I and the Senator will see to that. Now, what do you say? Start with the house, and a decent income, with the expenses for young Alex coming from his trust. The rest will happen when and if it does. Go and talk to your mother. Take her to see the house. Tell her no expense spared in furnishing it. Nothing like this . . .' His sweeping gesture indicated the grandeur of the McClintock mansion. 'Just in keeping with what the daughter-in-law of Andrew McClintock would be expected to have. We can't have anyone saying Alex left you penniless.'

'Alex left me his son.'

'Stubborn little bitch, aren't you? Well, you can't stop me taking care of young Alex financially. You can't deny me access to him. Any court would rule that he has the right to be brought up as my grandson should be. So . . . go and look at the house. Or find another, if that suits your pride. Don't be too stiff-necked, Ginny. Alex won't thank you for it later.'

She hardly realized it was Andrew McClintock talking. 'I always thought you . . . you disliked me. I was half afraid you'd try to take Alex away from me.'

'Well, I've never had an easy tongue. Never good at saying pretty things. Got it from my father, only he was worse. I suppose that's why the Russian left me. Jewellery and house and more furs than the Empress of Russia weren't enough. I guess she needed the pretty talk. Well, I'm talking plain to you, Ginny. Better think about it, girl.'

He won, as he was bound to. It all made such eminent good sense. When the Senator heard the details he said, 'I have to warn you, Ginny, that if you turned down this offer, you might find yourself having to prove to some judge that you weren't insane, in fact that you were a fit mother for young Alex. McClintock had been very clever. You'll have your income, a very generous one. Your mother would be delighted to do her housekeeping on a fraction of that. McClintock will own the house, the cars, all the rest of it, and Alex's income will pay for whatever he needs. He's giving you a lot, but not everything. Take it. As he said, your life isn't over.'

She accepted because there was nothing else to do. She applied for and got a job as one of the research assistants to the junior senator for Connecticut. He liked her Radcliffe background, he said, although she hadn't graduated. It was an unimportant job, and paid very little. It could easily have been arranged by her father without anyone ever accusing him of nepotism. But it filled her day, and it brought her among people and books. She raced home in the evenings to Alex. On weekends she went to Pointerstown with her parents and Alex, and the nurse. Some of the ice which seemed to have formed around her memories of Alex began to thaw; she found she could at last allow herself to think of him, to take out the memories and polish them like silver which has been put away and wrapped in green cloth, but which still remained silver. She rode and walked, and played with her son. He reacted to her as if he fully knew that it was she, and not the nurse, who was his mother. She went to her job cheerfully, dressed no better and no worse than any other girl in the Senate office building. She even started to make a few friends among the boss's staff, once they had got over their suspicion of her because she was Senator Jackson's daughter, and Alex McClintock's widow. Widow – the term had a strange feeling to it. Unreal. Apart from one remark from a girl sitting next to her in the Senate cafeteria: 'Aren't you kinda slumming it here?' there was little awkwardness. If she had to live in some nether country without Alex, this was as good as any.

Then came the time, almost a year after Alex had died, when Andrew McClintock called her. 'Get yourself a pretty dress, Ginny. Something that goes with the emeralds. I never really did throw a party for you and Alex, apart from that shin-dig at Prescott Hill. Pity he can't be here. But, anyhow, I'd like you to be hostess for a dinner I'm giving. Mostly just a bunch of old fogies like me, but I'll try to think of some who are more your age group. Pity you're so young . . . Never thought of it as being a fault before.'

She found herself accepting without resentment. Andrew McClintock had been surprisingly reticent. He came regularly to visit his grandson, but never without telling Ginny beforehand. Gifts were always brought, but he must have stifled the urge to fill his grandson's nursery with every stuffed animal in Washington. 'Great little kid, isn't he? Just like his father. I was always scared to tell Alex that I thought he was a great kid. Thought it might give him a big head. Best thing about having a grandchild is that you can't do all that much to influence him.'

Ginny was undeceived. She knew that Andrew McClintock would influence every step Alex made so long as he was alive, and after he was dead his money would continue the influence. Even the way he chose to leave it would constitute an influence. If his grandson showed, as he grew up, that he did not seem capable of controlling the empire that would be his, then it would be tied up in such a way that Alex would be rendered powerless to control or destroy it. He faced as formidable a future as his father.

When Ginny appeared early for the dinner party, Andrew McClintock waited for her in the library where they had all been when she told him she was pregnant. It still seemed a cold room, for all the richness of the leather-bound books and the flowers. It seemed empty without Alex. She had half expected what would happen, and it did. 'You look very handsome, Ginny. Green suits you. We should have someone do a picture of you in that dress.' He produced several new velvet boxes. 'Had them reset. You've earned them. You and Alex were right, that night. You were too young for them. Now you're a young mother, and you've grown up. From now on you keep them.' There was no mirror in the room for her to look into as he fastened the diamond clasp of the necklace. She fumbled as she screwed in the earrings, closed the bracelet. 'It's all too much. But I've learned not to argue with you . . . about some things.'

He gave what, for him, passed as a laugh. 'One day, we might get to understand each other. Well, let's go over the guest list again. You know you're here to work, don't you? A great hostess always works damned hard.'

Ginny was glad the Senator and Rosemary were there that evening as she took her place at the head of the long table. She and Alex had always dined alone in this great room, and she had never imagined how beautiful it could look in the full glory of lighted chandeliers, silver, candelabra, and the table, which had been extended to seat fifty, covered with linen and a low trail of red and white flowers. She had never seen the crimson and gold dinner service. Was this also a legacy of the Princess's reign? Self-consciously she fingered the emeralds at her throat. She wasn't ready for this, but Andrew McClintock was forcing her like a plant in a hot-house.

He continued to hold his dinner parties, and she continued to act as his hostess. It was as if the first one had been his way of declaring to the world that his daughter-in-law had emerged from her mourning, and with his full approval. The first big party Andrew McClintock had permitted to be written about in the newspapers, but thereafter the ban on writing about the McClintocks was back in force. He would entertain only in his own house and continued to refuse all invitations, though some now came to Ginny, and he advised her to accept them. 'It's time to get among people a little.'

She knew that her situation attracted attention, and that her hostesses strove to find eligible bachelors to partner her. Often she was partnered by her brother, Robbie, until he became engaged. She talked to the young men of the things she knew interested them. Since most of them were in government, the Washington political scene was their subject. It was something she had known all her life. And yet she found a sameness about these men, all ambitious, all striving to make it in a world in which her father had succeeded years ago, and, if they were in business, there was nothing any of them aspired to that could match what would naturally have been Alex's place.

The dinner parties Andrew McClintock now gave became smaller, more intimate. The talk around the table sometimes became general, but Ginny knew the real business was done during the drinks session before dinner, and the coffee and brandy afterwards. Only the very top people were asked to these smaller dinners; people whose standing could almost match McClintock's. Ginny heard and watched the nation's business and politics being shaped. She was not unused to it, being her father's daughter, but she had never before been an integral part of it. Over the weeks and months she began to comprehend the power of McClintock's vast interests. She was intrigued by how he could manoeuvre and persuade. Sometimes, much later, she would read in the business section of the papers of some new merger or power shift which had had its beginnings at Andrew McClintock's dinner table.

She had a new dress for each party, and McClintock continued to produce jewels he always said had been 'reset'. He gave her smaller pieces than the emeralds. She wore whatever he gave her dutifully, and insisted that they be kept in the safe at his house. He answered by having a safe installed in her house. 'I want you to wear them, damn it! You may play at being a little office girl by day, but you can't ever get over the fact that you're a McClintock.'

'Yes, I'm a little office girl by day. I wonder how long I'll be able to keep on? I don't think I'm exactly popular at work. People are polite, but no one ever asks me home to dinner, or to go to a movie.'

'Beginning to realize it, are you? I thought you would in time. You look more natural sitting at my dinner table than hunched over a typewriter.'

She noticed, almost right from the beginning, that one name, whether it was a large or quite small dinner party, was almost a constant on the guest list. Blair Clayton. 'Good man, Blair,' Andrew McClintock said off-handedly. 'And I wouldn't say that about just anyone. He works for – well, he doesn't really work for me. He came as part of the package when Clayton's Bank, New York, merged with McClintock's last year. He knew Alex well. I was glad to have him. Harvard and a good war record. He's as smart as they come. He's had a lot of experience in Europe. He's related to the Clayton Merchant Bank in London. They handle a lot of our foreign business. With the merger Clayton's also brought in a big pharmaceuticals business in Switzerland. It was an area McClintock's were weak in. His mother was English. Dead now. His father's retired. Ill, they say. He spends a good deal of time in London because of the family interests – interests that are now ours.'

'Aren't you going to tell me the rest of it?'

'What rest? What's there to tell?'

'Oh, that he's divorced, and there were no children. Aren't you going to point out that he's one of the most eligible bachelors either side of the Atlantic? Good family. Money that even Andrew McClintock doesn't sniff at. Charming. Delightful manners. Handsome, even. A touch of English class about him. Is he the one you've picked out for me? The only one who might remotely come near to Alex?'

'Hell, you'll make up your own mind. Perhaps he doesn't give a damn about you. How do I know? I just invite him because you're a pretty hard girl for a man to come up to. And he is a man, not a boy. I can't find people of his calibre every day. McClintock's needs him, and I wouldn't say that of many.'

'Am I supposed to marry him?'

McClintock gave a half smile. They were seated alone in the drawing-room after a group of a dozen guests had left. A late-night quiet had fallen on Washington. Ginny rose and took up her evening bag. She went to the mirror and ran her fingers along the slim, elegant little necklace of diamonds Andrew McClintock had given her that evening. It was exactly right for the occasion. The earrings were small and exquisite. They suited the simplicity of the dress she wore, the kind of simplicity achieved only at great cost. 'Thank you for these. I like them. I realize I'm a very pampered daughter-in-law.' She turned back to him. 'You haven't answered my question.'

'I don't have an answer, my dear. Marry him if you want to. Marry him if you can catch him.'

She pondered the words as McClintock's chauffeur drove her home to Georgetown. She pondered them as sleep deserted her that night. Blair Clayton was all the things Andrew McClintock had said. He was thirty-five, and his first marriage, to an English girl, was long behind him. He was one of the most sought-after guests for any Washington hostess, an ideal single man to balance the table, if one could get him. Ginny had only once encountered him at any of the dinners she had attended outside of Andrew McClintock's house. They had been seated together, and his talk, she remembered, had been interesting. It would have been surprising if it had not been. He was very different from the ambitious, eager young congressmen she usually encountered. He came from a world where he already had it made. He had time and enthusiasm for other interests, principally art. He had begun, some years ago, to collect Impressionist paintings. This he just mentioned in passing, as if he were unwilling to share with anyone what she guessed was a passion. His air of self-sufficiency would have been intimidating if she had been trying to impress him. The strange thing that her father-in-law had perceived as being the most likely to draw them together was the fact that neither of them seemed to need the other. There would never be the possibility that they would fall in love in the way each of them once had done. She had learned that his marriage had been a youthful affair, and the girl beautiful, rather wild, and unsuitable. Or, at least, she had been unsuited to the probity of Blair's merchant-banking family. She, like the Russian princess, had gone off with someone else, and Blair Clayton had been made to look foolish, and a failure as a husband. The divorce had been swift.

Ginny thought there might be some fellow feeling between him and Andrew McClintock on this subject, if either could bring themselves to speak of it. They suited each other, this young, rather enigmatic man, and Andrew McClintock. He was suitable in every way. But Ginny didn't seem to interest him. The evening when they had been dinner partners he had escorted her home, seen her to her door, and given not the slightest hint that he would have liked to be invited in for a nightcap. When he was a guest at the McClintock mansion, they were never seated together, because there were always older men who had to be placed on Ginny's right and left. As she finally drifted off into sleep just before the daily Washington bustle began, she thought that she couldn't much longer keep up the charade of the girl in the Senate Office Building. That had been a ploy of the Senator and Andrew McClintock to convince her that having married as she had, that sort of life was forever behind her. And she knew that there would never again be a love such as she had felt for Alex. She had been swept up in a relationship that had never had time to grow ordinary or stale. There had never been time for a quarrel, much less boredom. Alex had been the impossible prince, perfect, now forever beyond her reach. He could never be less than perfect. She had his child, and that was all. And that child would grow up, and would leave her. What exactly had Andrew McClintock said? 'Marry him if you want to. Marry him if you can catch him.' There was never again to be love's young dream. McClintock understood that; now she was beginning to do so. At times she thought she almost came near to liking her father-in-law. That was the measure of how much older she had grown.

In time she gave up her job with the Connecticut Senator. It had served its purpose. She offered herself to the various charities with which Washington was filled, and was given suitably junior and humble positions. She went even further and gave one day a week as a hospital volunteer. It was about then that Blair Clayton started to ask her out to dinner, or to be his partner at larger social gatherings. He was charming, agreeable, and still quite remote. She enjoyed his company, but did not greatly miss him when they were apart. Her thoughts did not stray to him when they should have been occupied with other things. In no sense did he compel and draw and enthral her as Alex had done. They circled each other coolly, as if sizing each other up, possible partners in a merger. Now Blair would kiss her when he escorted her to her front door, but it was almost a clinically exploratory kiss. She was pleased by it, but not greatly moved. Andrew McClintock's words continued to mock her. 'Marry him if you can catch him.'

They continued their careful appraisal of each other until Ginny began to weary of it. They were both being so careful, cautious, passionless. They both found each other good company, and that seemed to be all. Or was Blair afraid of making another mistake? Was she afraid of being trapped in what Andrew McClintock might have characterized as a marriage of convenience? Nothing seemed to happen between them, no spark was struck, until the evening they quarrelled.

It was a stupid quarrel, not even about themselves. They were dining at the new Hay Adams Hotel after attending a reception at the White House. Blair made some remark that seemed to Ginny to be disparaging of the attitudes of some Southern members of Congress. 'Just a bunch of good ole boys, rubbing each other's asses, while mentally the South stays just about where it was a hundred years ago.'

Ginny's temper flared at what she took not only to be an insult to the South, but to her father as well. She launched into Blair, accusing him of exemplifying all the greedy materialism of the North, the grasping instincts, the pushing attitudes. 'You all came down here and robbed the South. If we're poor and backward, it's mainly because of the Yankees!'

He laughed openly at her. 'My God, Ginny. Don't tell me we're fighting the Civil War again. You're talking just like your mother.'

She flung down her napkin and got to her feet before Blair had time to rise himself. The head waiter came rushing over, but he was too late to pull back her chair. 'And you, Blair,' Ginny said, 'you deserve what you got. A partnership with the son of one of the biggest, dirtiest carpetbaggers of them all – James Andrew McClintock!'

He was standing now. 'And your poor kid is his great-grandchild. Too bad, Ginny!' They were both aware that half the people in the dining-room were staring at them, delightfully amused at this public quarrel between the two who were thought to be the coolest, most reserved couple in Washington. There was no possible way the gossip columnists would not use this item, even if they didn't quote the names. Ginny left the dining-room, her cheeks flushed with rage, rage at Blair and at her own lack of control. She imagined the laughter, could almost hear it. The head waiter had gone ahead of her to alert the cloakroom attendant, and her coat was waiting. She half expected Blair to come after her, but he didn't. At a signal from the *maitre d'hotel* the the doorman whistled a cruising cab. Still Blair did not appear. She gave the Georgetown address, and when the cab reached it, she half expected that Blair would be waiting there. She took a long time finding the fare, and a longer time finding her key, but he did not come.

She waited all week for Blair's telephone call of apology, for the flowers that should have come, but nothing happened. He had insulted, by implication, her father; he had openly insulted her mother. Ginny still raged, but she had also begun to feel foolish. It was such a stupid thing to have quarrelled about, a war that was still being fought in the history books and whose outcome had been decided long before either of them had been born. She began to realize that their relationship, however distant it had been, had altered. It might be that they would not see each other again, except when Andrew McClintock's dinner parties brought them together. But the cool mould of politeness between them had been broken. They had been provoked into saying bitter, if stupid, things to each other. They had become friends who had quarrelled. She almost began to wish they had been lovers who had quarrelled. There was always the time-honoured path to reconciliation for lovers. But friends . . . perhaps they hadn't even been that.

The friendship only tentatively begun seemed over when Ginny scrutinized the guest list for Andrew McClintock's next dinner party, and saw that Blair's name was not on it. Pride almost demanded that she stay silent, but the need to know won.

'Blair?' Andrew McClintock answered off-handedly. 'Oh, he's been in Europe for some weeks. A lot of things need looking at there. He'll be busy for several months. I thought you'd know that. Or perhaps not. Heard you two had a pretty public wrangle a while back. I guess you're out of touch . . .'

Out of touch. That was precisely how it felt. Now that he was gone, beyond her reach, she wanted him back. He had left a vacant and empty place, some part of her she hadn't known existed. She tried to breathe life into the memories of Alex, and forget Blair, and found it could not be done. Should she write . . .? She put off writing for weeks, and the weeks became months. She did what she had to do in Washington, worked now two days a week at the hospital, went to Pointerstown with her growing child every weekend. Summer came again, and Alex was two years old. Andrew McClintock insisted on a large birthday party at his house. The young children and grandchildren of every socially desirable family in Washington were there. It began politely enough, with bows and curtsies being made, as taught at the dancing school, while the presents mounted up. It deteriorated into a kind of *melée*, in which the children all fought over Alex's presents. Orange juice was spilled, cakes thrown; the two candles on the birthday cake had to be relighted because someone other than Alex decided to blow them out. Andrew McClintock watched it all with grim humour. 'Look at them, Ginny. The rich at play. They'll do it with a little more finesse when they're older, but it'll be the same game. That is, for those who can afford it.'

Ginny heard from Andrew McClintock that Blair Clayton was back in New York. 'Smart man. Selling every share he owns in every publicly held company.' Andrew McClintock had been warning close associates, Ginny's father among them, that the Wall Street Market was over-valued and must crash. Some heeded his advice to sell, others did not.

Ginny didn't ask any questions about him. The time to write a letter or pick up a telephone and speak to him had long passed. Her pride had prevented a relationship that she now knew had promised a real fulfilment from developing. The quarrel had been for such a stupid reason. She had been spoiling for a fight and, having got it, hadn't had the guts to admit that her behaviour now seemed slightly ridiculous. She had watched her brother Robbie get married that summer with the bitter taste of envy in her mouth.

She was at Pointerstown on a Saturday in late September, a golden day which, when she had ridden that morning, had just the first crispness of autumn in it, when Blair came. She was in the nursery with Alex; her mother came in, breathing heavily, as if she had been hurrying up the stairs. Rosemary had thought it important enough to come herself, rather than send one of the maids.

'It's Blair Clayton, Ginny. He looks . . . looks strange. Ginny, don't go running like that.' She had never discussed

Blair with her mother, but Rosemary was not entirely without sensitivity in these matters. All of Washington must have at some time discussed the break-up of that promising partnership. Ginny tried to heed her mother's words, and she did not actually run down the stairs. But her nervous hand slipped on the handle of the drawing-room door, and it opened with a crash.

Blair turned from his survey of the lawns of Pointerstown. 'Still angry, Ginny? Are you going to tell me to leave?'

He didn't look so much strange, as different. Perhaps it was the clothes, casual though still impeccable. She had never seen him in anything but a dark suit or dinner jacket before. Perhaps it was the faintly quizzical furrow on his brow, usually so unperturbed. His gaze was more intense than he had ever permitted it to be with her before. She felt almost as if they were looking at each other for the first time.

'Want to come for drive? I have a quiet place to lunch.'

She nodded. They went out into the hall. She took a light coat from the closet; afterwards she realized it was her mother's coat. She sat silently in the car beside Blair, without gloves, hat, handbag or money. She hadn't told anyone she was going but her mother would have known. They drove for more than an hour in the direction of Richmond, and neither of them spoke. She had an odd sense of familiarity as they turned off the main highway on to a dirt country road. It was years since she had been here. Through the trees she recognized the chimneys of the house her mother had grown up in, the rather humble house built on the site of the great mansion, Wildwood, that had perished in the fires of the Civil War. Rosemary's brother had never married. That branch of the family had died out with his early death. The house had been sold. 'Here,' she said to Blair as he stopped the car. 'Here. You know what this place is?'

'Certainly I know. Your grandfather built it after the War. The War between the States, that is.'

'Are we starting that again?'

'I most sincerely hope not. We'll never finish it, you know. They'll still be fighting it out a hundred years from now, so

there's no sense in you and I wasting any more time over it.'
He was holding open the door of the car. 'Well, are you
coming in?'

She got out of the car slowly, staring at the old house, in
need of paint, a little run-down. She felt like weeping. 'I
thought you meant some quiet . . . well, a restaurant.'

'No, it had to be on my patch this time, Ginny. I'm sick
of seeing you at the other end of Andrew McClintock's table,
or at a cosy table for two with half a dozen waiters hovering.
If you really want to know, I loathe restaurants. They're
only fit for making business deals in.'

'This – this is yours?'

'Not exactly. It's for sale. I'm renting it.'

'You never said.'

'You never asked. Don't you think it's strange you never
asked where I went on the weekends when I was in Washington? What I did? Did you suppose I sat in the McClintock-
Clayton building watching the money tick over? I knew you
went to Pointerstown, always the perfect mother and dutiful
daughter. I wonder what you thought I did?'

She had no answer for him. They were in the hall now.
Some of the pieces of furniture she remembered as a child
were still there, a tall clock, a tatted rug. It all had a look of
homeliness she had never associated with Blair. They went
straight through to the kitchen. It had had a few improvements – a refrigerator and an electric stove, an ordinary
faucet instead of the pump handle she remembered at the
sink. It was clean and polished, but very simple. 'We'll have
lunch here, if that's all right with you. I don't like to have
help here during the weekend. There's a couple who live in
one of the cottages, I suppose they used to be slave quarters,
who look after the place. I just leave one big pile of washing
up, I'm afraid.'

'You spend your time here alone?' It had all seemed part
of their guarded relationship that she had never asked before.
But had it never struck Blair that he was the sort of man one
simply did not ask personal questions of? What a futile,
wasteful game of hide-and-seek they had been playing with
each other.

'Mostly.' It was the sort of answer she had expected. Half an answer. He was taking food out of the refrigerator and placing it on the big bare table. 'You remember where the cutlery is kept?' Automatically she moved to the drawers of the big dresser. Just as certainly she picked the strangely elegant glasses off the dresser shelves. Blair was laying out the sort of food that would have come in a hamper from one of Washington's best food stores. *Pâté de foie gras*, cold roast beef and chicken, peaches in brandy. He opened a bottle of Meursault and tasted it. He offered it to her. 'All right?'

'Perfect. You do things well, Blair. You realize . . . I've never seen you do anything before.'

'That's what wrong with you and me, Ginny. I've never seen you do anything either, except play the gracious hostess. You've never invited me to Pointerstown. I've never seen you play with young Alex. And yet everyone I know in Washington tells me what a wonderful mother you've been to him.'

'You don't mean that. What you mean is that my father-in-law says what a wonderful mother I've been.'

'Andrew McClintock barely mentions your name. He's too clever for that. He always meant us to find out about each other for ourselves. Or not at all. No one could ever accuse him of pushing you into anyone's arms. Last of all mine. Neither of us would have stood for it.'

She put down her glass. 'I've never been in your arms. I wonder what it's like . . .?'

'Do you want to find out?'

It had never occurred to her that she would ever make love in the bed her mother had probably been born in. Blair used the largest bedroom, but it had the same homely quality of the whole house. She lay in his arms beneath a quilt that might have been made by her grandmother. She forgot the strangeness of making love with a man who only in this last hour had ceased to be a stranger. She lost the sense of her whereabouts in the pleasure of exploring a body that had seemed so aloof. The cool, passionless relationship disintegrated. She felt a wild excitement. They moved together as if their bodies had known each other for a long time. Then

65

Ginny was spent and exhausted, lying quietly in his arms. Finally he spoke, and there was just an edge of coldness in his tone. 'I won't be a substitute for Alex, you know. I'd never have that. I'm too jealous. I would be marrying Ginny, not Alex McClintock's widow.'

'Alex is dead. I think I've mostly been dead until now. I've been afraid of you, Blair. You made me feel young and crass and yes, a little stupid. If I thought of you making love, if I thought of it at all, it was always smooth and perfect, and rather cold. Everything beautifully done, but without passion. I saw you as a fastidious perfectionist.'

'I am. And you, you are nearly perfect. A few little flaws wouldn't hurt. I was afraid, too. I saw no way to shake you out of that reverie you always seemed to be in. As if you were always with Alex. As if he'd never left you. Sometimes you seemed to be talking to someone else. I held back. I went away. I came back and wondered what I'd find. I told you I wasn't going to marry Alex's widow.'

'And I've told you he's dead, and I've only just come to life. Well, I had to find out, didn't I? And who said anything about marriage?'

'I just did.'

'Tell me more. I want to hear. I want to hear about us getting married. I'd like very much to hear about that.'

They didn't talk about it just then. Their bodies sought and found each other again, the need more urgent than talk.

It was dusk before she telephoned her mother at Pointerstown. 'I'm sorry I didn't say where I was going.' Her mother didn't ask where she was now. 'I won't be back tonight. Just didn't want you to worry. You don't mind giving Alex an extra kiss for me?'

'I'm happy to have him to myself to spoil for a little while. There's such a thing as being too good a mother, Ginny. Enjoy yourself, darling.' Sometimes Rosemary surprised her.

She went to the kitchen where Blair was making fresh toast for the *pâté*. The things he had laid out for their lunch were still on the table. He was opening a fresh bottle of wine. 'It should be champagne. But not even Blair Clayton is so cold-blooded he would think that far in advance.'

'It's strange, but since this afternoon I just can't seem to remember a cold-blooded Blair Clayton. That must have been someone else I was thinking of.' She raised her glass to him. 'Well, will you marry me, Blair Clayton?'

'If you'll have me, Virginia Lee Jackson McClintock.'

'Consider it settled. As soon as possible, please. And could we eat something now? I'm ravenous.'

He seemed to become younger as he talked. 'I'll be going back to Europe soon, Ginny. I suppose you can stand moving around a bit . . . it's all part of the job. You're taking on the other side of McClintock-Clayton. Much the same sort of moving about you probably would have done with Alex. London's important to us as a financial centre. I'll be spending quite an amount of time there. But I'm keen to develop the pharmaceutical business in Switzerland. We have excellent research labs in Switzerland, and a very good manufacturing plant near Birmingham. We've just acquired a good ordnance factory on the Mersey . . .'

'Ordnance?'

'Munitions, Ginny. Armaments.'

'I thought all that was over.'

'"All that" as you call it, is never over.'

'Then McClintock-Clayton is going in the direction of du Pont?'

'McClintock-Clayton may have passed du Pont quite a time ago. Your son's grandfather and great-grandfather have been and are financial geniuses, Ginny. I think I've learned a good deal, but compared to Andrew McClintock I'm a child.'

'Is there really that much money? I've never known.'

He took his time answering. He refilled her glass, put more *pâté* on toast, handed it to her. 'Eat. Yes, there is that much money. One of the reasons I was afraid of you. It all seemed too contrived. As if it was one more stroke of genius from Andrew McClintock. He lost his only son, so he was going to find the best possible stepfather for his grandson. Someone to look after McClintock-Clayton until young Alex was ready to grab it.'

'You don't believe that?'

'It's not your contrivance. I reserve judgement on Andrew McClintock.'

Later, when they were once again in her grandmother's bed, Ginny asked him, 'Why did you go away without telling me, and stay away for so long?'

'I had to go away. I keep telling you, it's part of my job. I was just working up to asking you if you wanted to come with me. Just pack your bags and bring young Alex, and come.' He laughed. 'And you had to blow it all with your stupid little quarrel. Look at the time we've lost. Your fault.'

'Well, I did say I thought you thought I was a little bit stupid. Let's stop wasting time.'

They were married in October at Prescott Hill. The house was bigger than Pointerstown, the occasion was bigger. Ginny was no longer the young, untried bride who had married Andrew McClintock's son. Now she was part of the company, as if her physical bond cemented the partnership between McClintock and Clayton. It seemed that everyone who had graced the christening of her son in Washington was present at Prescott Hill that day. She knew it would be difficult for many of them not to believe that this was Andrew McClintock's prescribed marriage of convenience.

She descended the stairs at Prescott Hill on her father's arm, perhaps too vividly remembering the day she had done the same thing at Pointerstown. But now she was part of Prescott Hill; it even belonged to her. It had been part of Andrew McClintock's wedding present to her and Blair. 'Oh, hell!' He had shrugged the matter off. 'I don't want the damn place. My father only bought it to annoy his stiff-necked neighbours. Might encourage you to come back from time to time. I wouldn't want young Alex to forget what he comes from.'

The ties were binding. She knew it was this gift, more than any money or jewellery, which had pleased her father. She was mistress of one of Virginia's finest *ante-bellum* mansions, and the name of Lee was once more graced in these surroundings. He took her to her new husband with pride, and, as his tears showed, with love.

The reception was splendid, the guests basking in the knowledge that they were in the place today that most of Washington society would like to be. It was more sedate than Ginny's first wedding. Young Alex circulated among the guests, forever bringing back the memory of his father and that other quickly arranged marriage. But it went well, and the guests enjoyed the wide porches and lawns of Pres cott Hill in warm October sunshine. The wedding had taken place at three o'clock. By five o'clock, as the sun began to dip, little shivers seemed to run through the crowd. They came back into the main rooms of the house, as if seeking company, reassurance. The Wall Street stockmarket had closed, and there were rumours, more than rumours, spread about by those eager to know the days results who had telephoned their brokers, of strange things beginning to happen on the stockmarket. The little spasm of fear was offset by more champagne.

They had the sort of honeymoon people had expected when Ginny had married Alex. They went to Europe occupying the royal suite of a great liner. The aspect of it that surprised people was that Alex came with them. Blair had insisted on this. 'We're going to be a family, Ginny. Alex never knew his father. I've had no experience of being a father. I hope I will with our children. But at this point, just about the worst thing I can think of is taking you away from Alex. He'll remember. Even if you think he's too young for thoughts like that. He'll remember, and hold it against me. We'll take him.' So Alex and his nurse had the adjoining suite, as they had at every great hotel they stayed at through the Continent. 'You're a little hick, you know,' Blair joked with her. 'Never seen the Mona Lisa. Never been to Florence. God, I didn't think they let you out of Radcliffe without having seen such things.'

And as they journeyed, the stockmarkets all over the world continued to tumble. Blair could joke with her about many things, but not about the stockmarket figures he saw.

'It makes no difference that we, personally, are not being hurt. This is a pure tragedy, brought about by our own greed. McClintock-Clayton is far richer than it was a year ago, and it will use the money well. We can always use money. The world is, well, Ginny, the only word is desperate. And I'll see the prices go much lower before I begin to buy again. And I'll be picking up for cents what I should have paid dollars for.'

Ginny thought of Andrew McClintock's advice to her father. She only knew from Rosemary's letters that he had partially acted upon it. 'We've come out all right,' her mother wrote. 'Though it rather galls me to know that we have McClintock to thank for it. So many of our friends have been so badly hurt.'

They visited the cities, saw the things he had promised her, and still he continued to do his business. By the spring of 1930 they had had their last week in Venice and moved to the villa on Zurich See recently bought by McClintock-Clayton for the convenience of the directors travelling there to do business with the new Swiss subsidiary. Their stay there was six weeks. After that the move would be to London, where he would introduce her to his English cousins and the partners and directors of Clayton's Merchant Bank. They planned to stay at Claridges, but all though the tour of the European capitals, and from Zurich, Blair was constantly on the telephone to the Clayton Bank about a house for them to rent or buy. 'Dammit,' he shouted one day on the line from Zurich. 'I can't set up house in a hotel! We have a child. Find something!' At last they, the anonymous people at the other end of the line, mentioned Seymour House. 'Sounds good. Put a reserve on it. We'll look at it the moment we get there.'

He turned to Ginny in explanation. 'It's right on Green Park. Absolutely perfect for you and the kids.'

It had just been confirmed that she was pregnant.

Chapter 4

Dena was the youngest of four children, the last of three girls. It seemed that once her father had a son, he wasn't very interested in what children his wife produced thereafter. Someone, well in his cups at a hunt-ball, said rather too loudly: 'Wonder if he even cares whose children they are!' It was as well Lord Milroy didn't hear him. However lightly he regarded his own infidelities, or the possible infidelities of his wife, he was the old-fashioned sort who would have enjoyed a knock-down, drag-out fight, with a horsewhipping at the end, just so long as the blackguard who had uttered the insult could be considered a gentleman in all other respects. In fact, he was relieved that he had only one son. There was precious little money to go with the title when his son inherited, and he fervently hoped that all the girls would inherit their mother's beauty, and thus marry and be off his hands. He looked at the splendid but decaying Tudor manor of rose-hued brick which would be his son's inheritance, and on which he had already spent the dowry his wife had brought with her. The dowry hadn't been enough, but then he had been in love, hadn't he? So he devoutly wished that whomever his son was lucky or foolish enough to fall in love with would have plenty of money. The place needed it. His son would need it. That he never thought that his son should marry without love was to his credit. Lord Milroy believed in love. It made everything possible, bearable. He regarded his wife fondly; if he hadn't loved her, how could he have had such an enjoyable time with other women? The most wonderful thing about his wife was that she never made him feel guilty. A rare quality, and one he prized highly.

They grew up, all four of them, in the happy chaos of that Tudor gem, Merton, just north of Oxford. It was not a great enough house to be considered grand, but it had enormous charm, which grand houses often lacked. There was a happy unselfconsciousness about it, and it seemed to instill that quality in those who grew up there. They were the children of an earl: the boy, Edward, was known by the honorary title of Viscount Garner, and the girls were Lady Ellen, Lady Julia and Lady Geraldine. Their father impressed on them that titles didn't count for very much: England was over-stuffed with them, and unless money accompanied them they were worth just that – titles. He was a remarkably unpompous man, their father. They all loved him, and he loved them in return, never mind the rumours that one or two might not actually be his own children. Of his son and heir he was absolutely certain. He had been very careful about that. As onlookers observed the almost absurd likeness between the Earl and the Viscount the thought of doubt became laughable.

There was much laughter at Merton. The Countess was a beautiful woman with a gift for friendship. She attracted all sorts to her house, not just her husband's fox-hunting fraternity. She was the daughter of a gifted artist, Guy Denham, who had been lucky enough to have made money from his art in his own lifetime, and was therefore a rarity. He gave a great deal of it to his only child on her marriage, and had known it would all be spent on that beautiful pile of a house into which she had married. In his Hampstead studio he painted portraits of the rich or the famous (some were both) for the money, and landscapes for the sheer joy of it. It was his landscapes which were most admired, and which he was loath to sell. He didn't care much about money, so long as there was enough to keep him and his wife in relative comfort, and provide his daughter with pocket money. While he painted his portraits, his wife would often play the piano in a room adjoining the studio. She was quite a clever pianist if one could overlook the little inaccuracies. What was a wrong note here and there, if the things sounded right? It was much the approach Guy Denham took to his portraits. A little flattery didn't hurt, as long as it didn't go too far. His landscapes were different. They were painted with love, and he knew there was no way he could flatter nature. So they were as true as he could make them. He laboured over them and for all their imperfections, not for all the money anyone could have offered for them, would he have changed a single thing about them. They were his statement, and he stood by it.

A lot of this feeling and his wife's musicality had gone into their only child. She was less romantic than her father, less vague than her mother. She had a smattering of their gifts. She chose the hapless Earl, and for a time she was in love and happy. She continued to be happy, while not any longer in love with him, but in love, temporarily, with other men. She enjoyed her life, wavering between grandeur and penury. She never knew what was in the bank. Their money came from the home farm surrounding the house, and from the rents of tenants on the estate. The Earl was an indifferent farmer, and didn't have the money or good judgement to employ a steward to manage the place for him. So they staggered from season to season, hoping for good harvests, for fat calves, for good grass. In good seasons he bought expensive hunters for his family, ordered more expensive guns for shooting in August on the moors of his friends in Yorkshire and Scotland. When he could he added to the collection of sporting guns and antique hand guns of which he was proud. All the family were excellent shots, as well as good riders.

For her part Lydia enjoyed the good times and took the bad as they came. When there was money she was often in London in the small *pied à terre* they had in Knightsbridge. She bought expensive clothes, went to and gave parties, visited her parents in Hampstead. When money was scarce she went on frantic economy drives. She dressed her daughters in clothes which were apt to come apart at the seams because she and Nanny ran them up – or cobbled them together – on a sewing machine she bought secondhand. What Lydia lacked in skill, she made up for in style. Fortunately as her daughters grew they were all slim and quite beautiful, and they wore the cobbled-up garments with such grace that no one bothered to inspect them very carefully. 'Lydia has such gifts' everyone said. Apart from bed, her

73

greatest gift was in the kitchen. She was an amazingly good and inventive cook, saving her husband the expense of a cook when money was short. She gave good dinner and luncheon parties. She taught all her daughters to cook, 'just in case, poor darlings, they don't catch a rich husband.' Nanny gave way to a governess, a nice, middle-aged lady, Miss Lightbody, who made up in usefulness what she lacked in teaching skills. It was she who taught the girls how to sew properly, and to knit. 'She saves us so much money,' Lydia would say. 'The cost of the three girls going to school, as well as all she does around the house. A treasure.'

The girls grew up cooking and sewing and chattering in French, and when the horsy atmosphere at Merton palled on them, it was always possible to go and stay with their grandparents in Hampstead, since the Knightsbridge flat was too small for them all, or because either their father or their mother might be engaged in a new flirtation or even a love affair, and the presence of three daughters might seem a bit intrusive. They didn't know they were an odd family. They so obviously enjoyed life, enjoyed the things they did together, that it almost escaped their attention that some people did not approve of the family.

Somehow money was scraped together, aided by 'loans' from Lydia's father, for a season for the two older girls. To save money they came out in the same year, protesting just a little. Lydia presented them at Court, in borrowed plumes and borrowed pearls. Their brother, Edward, to everyone's amazement, had managed to get a third-class degree at Oxford, which was more than anyone expected. To their further surprise, he went to an agricultural college, which no one had ever heard of, to try to learn something about farming. He was by far the most serious of the four children. No one knew where or how Edward met Verity, a girl who would inherit, with her twin brother, the fortune of their father, a steel and mining magnate. All Edward did was tell them that they were engaged. Lydia was delighted. 'How clever of you, darling. Such a sensible marriage. And Verity is a darling.'

Verity was, in fact, in Lydia's eyes, a mouse, and almost downright plain. But she worshipped Edward, and that was enough to overcome. They moved into the dower house of Merton and spent some of Verity's money on renovating it.

Ellen and Julia both married in the same summer, which saved Lord Milroy some money, as they had agreed to a double wedding. Ellen did rather well, marrying a young stockbroker whom everyone said was destined for great things in the City. Julia married someone who farmed great tracts of land, useless for anything but sheep, in the Highlands. A damp, old castle, romantically sited on a river estuary, went with the marriage. Julia looked forward blissfully to bearing the children of the glorious giant of a Scot, Douglas, she had married. 'I think,' Lydia said, 'we won't be hearing much of her again. It's all so remote . . . But she loves him.' She looked around her almost empty house with amazement. 'That leaves only my baby, Dena . . .'

'I think we must give Dena a really good season ,' Lydia said to her husband. 'The estate's doing quite well. Hasn't Edward turned out brilliantly? My father might let us have a bit more money. We could really do it in style this time. Dena is the best looking of the lot . . .'

Once again Guy Denham was forthcoming, though he warned Lydia it would have to be the last time. 'I'm getting arthritis in my hands, my darling. Can't go on flattering people much longer.'

Lydia looked at him in amazement. She saw that her father's eyes were faded, indeed what she saw was the beginning of the cataracts he had not told her about. She was filled with panic. 'I must do my best by Dena. A really lovely marriage. Get her settled before . . .' Before what? She wasn't going to die. The world would go on as it always had.

She prepared for Dena's season with more care than she had given to Ellen and Julia. In the end, both girls had made successful enough marriages, and Lydia believed that Julia would know happiness only in the Scottish wilds with her laird, but neither marriage had been the spectacular one Lydia had wished for. There were glittering matrimonial prizes, and Lydia wanted Dena to have one. Dena had inherited her mother's dark hair and eyes, and had that same almost iridescent complexion. She had Lydia's sense of style. Lydia bent her energies to ensuring that London would see her daughter for the beauty and charmer she was.

She arranged for Dena to share a coming-out ball with a friend, thus sharing the expense. She begged her father for yet another loan, telling him that this would be the last expense Dena would ever incur: she was certain to make a marvellous marriage. She did not realize that her father too had parted with one of his landscapes to meet the loan. Lydia presented her daughter at Court in May. In early June she was co-hostess at the coming-out ball. Although Dena's friend, Helen, was pretty, it was clear that London regarded Dena as a beauty. It was her night. Lydia watched her daughter in a blaze of happiness and pride. 'She is lovely, isn't she?' she said to her husband. 'Look at the men buzz around her. She'll have to cut each dance in half. Aren't you proud?'

Lord Milroy was proud but he was feeling rather tired. There had been so many balls in his life. Why should he see this, his youngest child on her night of triumph, as if through a tired haze? For the first time in his life he not only felt tired, but old. His head ached. He left the ball early, although he should have stayed on until the last.

The dawn had come, and the birds in Hyde Park were in full song when Lydia and Dena returned to the Knightsbridge flat. Dena moved in a glow of happiness. She felt ready for every single party the season could still offer. She was ready for every good thing that came her way. She hardly thought about getting married at the end of it. Marriage was a sober business, and she noticed it seemed generally to signal the end of a good time. She had only just begun to taste her good time.

A cry from Lydia brought Dena racing to her parents' bedroom. Her father lay crumpled on the floor, his eyes staring glassily at the ceiling. One side of his face was twisted upwards in a terrifying grimace. He saw them, tried to speak. 'Ahh . . .' Saliva ran down his chin. Dena wiped it with the hem of her ball dress. 'Oh, my God,' Lydia breathed.

The ambulance took him to St George's hospital at Hyde Park Corner. They hung over his bed for the next two days. He did not die in that time, as they had been warned he might, but he clung only fitfully to life. Dena thought of the night of her dance as if it had been in another existence. She looked at her diary and saw that these nights, when she took turns with her mother by her father's bed, she'd had two balls booked for each night. Between her presentation and her own party, she had been to a number of balls. Debutantes complained of being bored by seeing the same people every evening: Dena knew she would never complain, not if she could have it back again. Instead, there was only her father's poor, twisted face, his arm and leg which would not move, his tongue which could not frame words.

For the first time in her life she questioned the sort of existence they had led, all but dear, sweet, earnest Edward. There had been so much laughter and fun, but had they really cared about each other? Or had it been all one long lovely carefree charade? How could she look at her diary and mourn the balls she might have attended that night? Was Julia as selfishly wrapped up in her new baby as Ellen was absorbed in furthering her husband's career? Wasn't she, Dena, now wondering which of this season's debutantes was dancing with the partner she would have had tonight? They would all forget her, of course.

Lydia came into the quiet room. She looked weary. To Dena, impossible as it seemed to think of her mother that way, she suddenly looked old. 'What a shame, darling. All your good times spoiled,' she said in a low voice.

Didn't her mother realize that her husband could hear. Dena was sure he could. The eye on the unaffected side blinked, and she saw a tear begin to roll down his cheek. She stood up and wiped it gently. 'It's a shame about daddy.'

After three weeks they took him home to Merton. He was still speechless and helpless. Two nurses came daily from Oxford to care for him, and the night spell belonged to Dena. She learned from the nurses how to care for her father during those long nights. She performed intimate things for him that she knew her mother shrank from. Dena tried to

77

forget about the season and the fun she would have had. It was all over now. London would have emptied for the grouse-shooting season. She'd had invitations to country house parties. She had looked forward to being able to show off the skills her father had taught her. But her father would never raise a gun again, even if he managed to leave his bed. She felt ashamed at regretting the things she had missed as she regarded his helplessness.

He lingered in his stricken body until after Christmas. By that time, Dena knew how badly he wanted to go. She had almost ceased to think about what she had missed, was still missing. A deadly routine had set in. She might be here for years. She summoned up all her pity for him, to smother her self-pity. When the time came he was not able to frame the words of his farewell. Dena was half-dozing in the chair by his bedside. She didn't know what hour it was when she saw that he was trying to say something. His eyes were wide open, the good one focusing directly on her. Did he need something? She put her hand in his strong one, and felt a pressure. He uttered little, indecipherable sounds. What was he trying to say? Goo . . . Good? Good girl, or perhaps, good time? That would be like him. He gave up the struggle. Gradually the pressure on her hand eased. Perhaps it had been good-bye. It was some time before she thought of feeling for a pulse. If it fluttered at all, it was too feeble for her to feel it. 'Daddy . . .?' He seemed quite lifeless. She ran to wake her mother.

There were pleasant and flattering obituaries about him, hundreds of letter and telegrams. Very few people had a bad word to say against Charles Milroy. Julia and her husband came from Scotland, Julia again pregnant; Ellen and George came from London, but only on the day of the funeral. Edward had made all the arrangements. He and Verity had quietly taken over the tasks that might have been Lydia's and Dena's. For the first time Dena was aware of what an excellent woman Verity was.

The will was read, but it was a formality. The estate was entailed; it, the house and contents must go to Edward. They heard a new, unthinkable word – death duties. The estate had not had enough years of Edward's management to have recovered from his father's ineptitude, and there were heavy debts. It would take half Edward's lifetime to work them off, even with the help of Verity's money. Julia went back to Scotland, Ellen to London, both thankful that the problem was not theirs.

Edward offered to delay moving into Merton. Lydia would not hear of it. 'Darling, it's your duty. Your children must grow up here.' So Lydia, Dena and Miss Lightbody, who had managed to stay on as a companion and housekeeper, largely unpaid, moved into the dower house. It was more comfortable than Merton, but it was much smaller than Lydia was used to. She was restless and unhappy. 'I'll go up to London for a few weeks. See mother and daddy.' It had been agreed with Edward that the Knightsbridge flat would be kept on, for use by any of the family who needed it. 'It'll save money, I suppose, in the end,' he had said, but a little doubtfully.

Dena was hurt that her mother hadn't suggested that she go with her to London. Was she planning to restart one of her old affairs? Did she think she would be in the way? Dena hoped not. . . .

With Lydia gone, a silence fell on the dower house. Miss Lightbody seemed happy enough knitting things for Lydia's grandchildren, and rereading Jane Austen. Dena took charge of the cooking, but there was little interest in making elaborate dishes just for the two of them. By now she had faithfully answered all the messages of condolence which had come, but no one had written back to invite her to visit. Having started her season with a triumph, she seemed to have been forgotten. Sometimes she walked over to Merton, but Edward was always busy in the estate office or out inspecting something around the estate, when he wasn't driving a tractor. Verity was absorbed in her children, and with the difficulties of adapting to life in a big house with so little staff. The whole domestic atmosphere bored Dena. She wandered through the rooms that, even with the children about, now seemed empty. What had generated the life and laughter she remembered?

On a day early in April, out of boredom, Dena decided to go to a race-meeting over at Fealtham. It wasn't a big or important one, just one which at the little racecourse marked the beginning of the flat-racing season. Her father had been one of the stewards of the course. It was a run-down sort of place, a small stand and a group of wooden buildings for the jockeys and officials and some catering tents. She had almost no money to bet, and didn't know the form, so she used the time-honoured method of betting on names that struck her. *Debutante* was one name. It came in first, a truly dark horse, as she saw it paraded in the small winner's circle. She went to collect her money, and there in her hands was more than she had handled in her life before. She was aware that far greater sums had been spent on her by her parents, far greater sums loaned by her grandfather, but she had never had fifty pounds before of her own money. It was the first blaze of excitement she had known since the ball, a small stirring of life in the long months of pain and loneliness. In the members' bar, which she had infiltrated because they recognized her face and nodded her through, she bought herself a whisky, and with a tiny, but involuntary gesture, raised it. 'To daddy!'

'What are you toasting? A win? For your father? I didn't know they let little girls into places like this.'

She turned to face the man who had spoken. 'None of your business!'

He was handsome and relaxed. He merely laughed. 'Spoken like your father. Here – let me get you another one.'

'Who are you?'

'Can't claim to have been a friend of your father. Rather different ages. The same club in London. Now, let's see – you'd be Lady Geraldine? Right?'

'Do I know you?' in her iciest tone.

'Oh, forgive me, John Forley. I come racing quite often. But I don't remember seeing you around the tracks before. Lord Milroy was a steward here, wasn't he?' Somehow he had managed to get hold of a waiter in that crowded bar, and another whisky was being brought.

'He was. Sometimes he'd go to the big race meetings. He liked what he called "a flutter" . . .' Why was she speaking to him at all? He might be a member of one of her father's clubs, but that didn't make him a friend, or even an acquaintance. But he was the first person outside the family she had spoken to for weeks, and the first one who seemed to have a breath of life in him. She realized that he was quite attractive, in a dark, thin way.

'Well, there's going to be a big meeting at Newmarket next week. Can I take you?'

'Newmarket? That's miles away.' She had never been there. 'No. Sorry.'

'Of course, it would mean your staying overnight. But I'd make sure we'd be at different hotels.'

'I can't afford it.'

'It's on the house. It would be my pleasure to entertain you. Friends would be coming, of course. I wouldn't dream of your being alone, unchaperoned. Is there anyone you'd care to bring?'

Her mother was engrossed in whatever she was doing in London, and apparently didn't care what her daughter did. The only possible chaperone was Miss Lightbody. The idea was ludicrous. She laughed aloud, and although John Forley couldn't have had any idea what she was laughing about, he joined in. 'Is it so humorous? But race meetings can be fun. Newmarket's rather better than this.'

She didn't agree immediately. With a sense of bravado, she let him buy her another drink. She let him place two modest bets on the last two races for her, and hadn't the strength to hand back the modest winnings. He escorted her back to her car, not hers, but the one she and her mother and Miss Lightbody shared. 'Can I send a car for you next week, then? And whomever you bring with you.'

'Don't send a car. I won't be coming.'

She had a note from him the next day, detailing the arrangements. She tore it up. But the week hung heavily. There was no letter from her mother, and when she telephoned the flat, there was no reply. She tried telephoning after midnight, and Lydia answered. 'Oh, it's you, darling. I'm frightfully tired. Long, boring dinner. I'll ring you back in the morning.' But she didn't ring. Not for the whole week. Her mother, Dena reflected, seemed to have lost all sight of the ambitions she had once cherished for a brilliant marriage for her youngest daughter. How was she ever to meet anyone if she never went anywhere? In time, her mother might return to the person she had been, but the waiting was hard. She decided, without telling her mother, to go to Newmarket.

She never fully understood why she was drawn into John Forley's circle. She was younger than any of them, and far less sophisticated. She had no money, though she was well enough dressed. But she found she was drawn into a kind of group she had never encountered before. 'Do you think we're "fast", my dear?' John Forley said. 'Don't worry. Nothing will happen to you.' By this time she was beginning to wish something would happen. She telephoned her mother again, this time early in the morning, and roused Lydia from sleep.

'Oh, it's you, darling. Yes dear, Miss Lightbody said you'd gone to stay with friends. I'm afraid she's getting rather old and confused. She thought you were staying with my friends. Darling, I'm only half awake. Could you ring me back? Dying to hear about it all. Have a lovely time, darling . . .' '

After that, she accepted John Forley's invitation to come back to London with him. It seemed her mother didn't care what she did, so long as she didn't bother her. 'I have a little share in a nice, quiet hotel. It won't cost you a penny. Or me, so don't worry. Why not live a little? I heard you were marvellous to your father when he was ill. Such a nice man, your father. I think he'd rather like to think you were having a good time.' Perhaps it was because he used the word 'good' . . . the last word she had heard her father utter. Had he meant her to have a good time?

'I haven't brought the right clothes . . .'

'Too easy, dear girl.'

She was installed in a quiet, rather exclusive hotel, and John Forley made it clear he did not live there. But he took her on a shopping trip, assuring her that the clothes she selected cost next to nothing, because he owned a little piece of the dress shop. It was far from a shop. It was one of London's leading couturiers. 'But it's no trouble to do an alteration, Lady Geraldine,' the *vendeuse* assured her. 'You're almost as tall as the models, and slim. Just let out a fraction at the bust, and take a little off the hem . . . and this coat! Perfection . . . and of course you'll be going to the theatre. This dress . . . and Mr Forley's club . . .'

The matching silver lamé dress and coat swam before Dena's eyes. 'I can't possibly . . .' she said to John Forley.

'You'll look wonderful in them,' he answered. 'And don't worry. These places like to have their clothes shown off. A jeweller I know will lend you a necklace for tonight.'

That night they attended the opening of a revue of which John Forley was a backer. It seemed it would be a success, from the way the audience reacted. Dena was swept out of the theatre on John Forley's arm, and was conscious of the flashbulbs going off. Then they went to his club. She had thought it would be a nightclub, something like the Embassy. But John Forley was one of the few men in England who had a gaming licence. It was all very discreet and quiet and well-mannered. Tones were hushed as large amounts of money were bet. No one exclaimed on either winning or losing. Dena groped her way through the opulent rooms, and knew she was totally out of her depth. 'Who are you?'

'You don't know me yet, my sweet. You will. Sometime we'll get married. Very awkward that I'm still married. The bitch is sticking on a divorce, but she'll agree once I offer her enough money.'

Divorce was almost unknown in Dena's world. She had heard of affairs, infidelities, flirtations. But divorce was a serious matter, and most people did not go that far. All she knew about John Forley was that he had been at Marlborough and had a year at Cambridge before he was sent down. She wondered if he had been sent down for gambling.

'I hadn't thought of getting married. I shouldn't be here, shouldn't have done any of this.'

'Hush, my sweet. You're all right. I'll take care of you. Just trust Johnny . . .'

She telephoned her mother, thinking that if this time she

was either tired, or not at home, then she, Dena, had been cast adrift. Her father's will had made her aware of her position. No money. And if her mother didn't . . . But Lydia answered on the first ring.

'Oh, Dena, where have you been? I've been frantic. Those pictures in the papers . . . Dena, you can't be with that awful Forley man. Have you taken anything from him? Have you . . .? Oh no, I hope not. Not before you're married.'

'Would being married make it all right, mummy? I mean, being married to anyone? What did you and daddy . . .?'

'How dare you suggest such things! Your father and I were ideally, happily married. I won't see you ruined by this man. Don't you know he's married to a woman who'll never give him a divorce. You can't hope for anything from him . . . nothing that's respectable.'

'Did you care?'

'I didn't even know. I thought you were staying with friends.'

'And where were you, mummy? I telephoned you. I wanted to talk to you. I wanted to ask you . . .'

'Go back to Merton at once! On the first train. I can't imagine what you think you are doing. I assure you, Dena, if you stay with that man one day longer, you will be ruined.'

He was regretful, but polite. 'Well, we could have made it, given half a chance. I really have a thing about you, Dena. But chance wasn't with us, my lovely, and I'm a gambling man. You're too well brought up. My reputation would put off any decent family. Funny thing though, I really meant it. I'm much more than half in love with you. But we just didn't have time to see how it would work. Perhaps, after all, you *are* too young.'

He saw that she had a car to the station, and a first-class ticket. He insisted that she keep the clothes. 'After all, my dear, they've been worn, haven't they?'

'But the necklace was on loan,' she said, handing it back. 'It will probably be worn a thousand times. No one minds second-hand jewellery.'

An agitated Miss Lightbody met her at the station. 'Dear

child, I haven't an idea what's happened. Your mother's most upset. She's coming tomorrow.'

Nothing had happened. As Dena saw it, that was the trouble. She had been seen in the company of a man she now knew was regarded as undesirable, but who had treated her as gallantly as any gentleman could. Everyone, however, had assumed the worst. She had the name, but not the game. She thought the hypocrisy of it all sickening. What did anything matter now? No man would want to marry her. John Forley might have done, but he had probably spoken the truth. She was too young; she didn't understand that kind of man. But what kind of man would she ever understand? Who would understand her?

Lydia arrived. Almost for the first time in her life Dena found her irritable, snappish. 'What could have possessed you? Don't you know . . . ? He's not the kind of man a young girl is seen with. I suppose he tried to make love to you. Or did you make love?' Dena turned away, and refused to answer. 'Oh, well. It hardly makes any difference now. The damage is done. Don't you understand, Dena? One has to be married. Then it's overlooked.'

'That's a strange sense of values, mummy.'

'It's the only one the world understands.'

The laughter was gone, the gaiety. Her mother stayed for another two weeks, and then went back to London. Miss Lightbody took to accompanying Dena wherever she went, even for a stroll in the garden. She might have been back in the nursery, but the nursery had been much more fun.

Another season had begun in London, balls, parties. It now seemed remote. On her birthday flowers arrived. The card read, 'Regards, Johnny'. She cried, and then went over to Merton, and borrowed one of the beautiful Purdy guns her father had had made for the weight and size of his growing daughters. She enjoyed smashing the heart out of the target for an hour. Then she meticulously cleaned the gun, locked it away in its case, and left the money for the ammunition she had used. Everything had to be paid for.

Towards the end of the summer a letter arrived. It was from Helen, the girl she had shared the dance with. She hadn't remembered until now that Helen was a god-daughter of the Duchess of Marlborough. The Duchess had decided to invite her god-daughter to Blenheim for the weekend. Helen was to make up her own list of young people; they would mix with the Duchess's own guests. Dena suspected that this invitation to her was a gesture on Helen's part, or perhaps they all might be intrigued by the young girl who had flirted, perhaps too seriously, with John Forley. She had been to Blenheim before, as a child. Her father was regarded as a near neighbour, and her parents had often been there to dinner. The Duchess might pass over her name on the guest list, thinking of Helen's wishes first. In time the letter came. Defiantly Dena packed the silver lamé dress. She was not going to look like a debutante.

No-one could stand out against an invitation from Blenheim. She had telephoned Lydia, who was ecstatic. 'How kind of the Duchess! Have a gorgeous time, darling. Give my love to the Duke and to the Duchess, too, of course.'

Dena went through the ritual of the very grand country house party. It must have been one of the last places in the kingdom where they could still do it so grandly. She arrived on Friday evening. She wore one of her more demure dresses for dinner. No need to shock anyone so soon. She was seated next to a young man who was annoyed that he had not been seated next to Helen, and on her other side was a retired diplomat, who thought he would be wasting his wisdom on a child; so dinner was not a success. After dinner it was dull until the men rejoined them; Dena sensed a faint animosity from some of the women. She strolled to the billiard room after coffee had been served. A game was in progress, and she watched with interest. One player was very good. The game was quite swiftly over. 'Anyone else care to try?' No one responded, although the man was setting up the balls.

'Could I just have a shot? Not a game. I'm not good enough. But my father taught me. I haven't played since . . .'

Someone murmured. 'Milroy's girl.' The man handed her the cue with a slight bow.

'It's just a little practice . . .' But her hands itched to take the cue. She could have had no idea how appealing she looked as she bent and concentrated on the shot. But she did think that it was as well that she wasn't wearing the silver lamé. Her breasts would have fallen out of the bodice. The shot was a brilliant one, but she knew it was a fluke. There was a splutter of applause. A few more rather bored guests came in.

'Are all Milroy's children like this?'

'No. The son's a dead earnest dog. But he taught all the girls to ride and shoot. Obviously taught them billiards, too. Odd man . . . The two sisters are pretty, but only the one that married the stockbroker chap has any bit of dash. This one's the best. Spoiled it all by being seen around with the Forley man. Don't know why they keep him in the club.'

Perhaps Dena wasn't meant to hear the words, but they were heard, and they made her furious. She said to the man who had handed her the cue. 'Do you mind if I have a few more shots? It's been such a long time since I played, and I do love it . . .'

Perhaps her father's recent death lent her a sympathetic audience. Perhaps they were willing to believe that being with Forley had been a genuine mistake. Dena smiled at her opponent, and gritted her teeth. Then she played as if she had been an inspired angel, given a billiard cue for the first time. It was all chance and luck. She thought the man played down to her a little, set up some easier shots than he might have done for a male opponent. She did not do at all badly. In the end, of course, he won. But not hands down. There was much more general, and generous, applause at the end.

Flushed, she shook the hand of her opponent. 'Thank you very much for the game. I did enjoy it. I'm sorry . . . I know we were introduced before dinner, but I've forgotten . . . so many people at once . . .'

'Harry Penrose, Lady Geraldine. Thank you for the game. I see your father has passed on his skills.'

Dena wandered back to the women in the Green Drawing Room. 'Quite a triumph I hear, my dear,' the Duchess said. 'But then, your father was such a good player. He's taught you all sorts of things, I'm sure. I heard you were an angel

87

to him when he was ill. Dear Edward – how we all miss him. Always the life and soul of a party. So kind. And how is your dear mother bearing up? I hear she keeps herself quite busy in London.'

Dena realized she had been restored, if even by a tiny notch, into favour. Mentally, she made a note that even if she had to appear in the same dress for two nights, she would not wear the silver lamé. Let them think of her as a genteely poor debutante.

The next morning she appeared for the long, lavish breakfast which would extend through half the morning. The Duchess had a good chef, Dena observed, as she raised the lids of the silver dishes. One of the men who had witnessed the billiard game the night before came to help her at the sideboard. 'We're going to shoot some clay pigeons later. Sort of getting our eye in for the grouse. Care to watch?'

'Love to. My father was quite a good shot. He has – had – rather a good collection of guns. Some nice little antique pistols . . . things like that. But they're awfully tricky to fire. Not at all accurate.'

'Yes, I heard about Lord Milroy's guns. I expect your brother's got them now.'

'Yes. He's quite a good shot, too. Or was. He's so busy now with farming I doubt he ever gets a chance to use any of them. Daddy thought some of them ought to have been in a museum. But he didn't get around to making the arrangements.'

'Pity – may I give you some toast?'

The man Penrose was seated opposite her. 'Coming shooting? God help us if you're as good with a gun as with a billiard cue.'

'I haven't shot for a long time.'

'That's what you said last night.' He was very good-looking, she decided. Fair, English good looks. The bones of his face were finely drawn, but strong. He had firm, straight, rather bushy brows over eyes of a remarkably hard blue. Her mother possessed a blue topaz. His eyes were almost that colour and of that quality, and they now appraised her.

'You're a tease, Mr Penrose. My father was a country gentleman. Billiards and guns – they're just as usual as having dogs about the place. It was bound to happen that we picked things up from him. He didn't make much distinction between bringing up sons and daughters.'

He walked beside her as they went to the practice range – it was a full mile from the house. Blenheim Park was palely shrouded in mist. It was unnaturally cool for summer. The air was very still. 'Will we be able to see that target?'

'The young ones, with the best eyes, like you, will see it.'

'Are you so old, Mr Penrose?'

'Older than you, Lady Geraldine. I work in the Foreign Office, and while I'm old enough, I'm very junior there. Unless there's a revolution, I won't become very senior, I'm afraid.'

'If there's a revolution there won't be any Foreign Office. And this –' she glanced around and her gesture took in the peaceful beauty of the park, the misty outline of the great Palace behind them, the well-dressed little group walking towards the practice range. 'All this will be gone. It'll be like Russia. I wonder if they sometimes secretly wish they had the Czar back, and all the Grand Dukes and Duchesses. Life wouldn't be any more difficult than it is, and it would be much more colourful.'

'I must put that view to the next Soviet Ambassador I meet. But give them another few years. Then we'll see what they can do.'

'Don't tell me you're a Bolshevik, Mr Penrose?'

'In my job? No, but we have to try to understand them. Someone has to talk to them.'

'Yes. I suppose that's what diplomats are for. Talking.'

'Better than shooting.'

The clay pigeon shooting had been improvised, so no one had brought their own guns. There was a general examination of the Duke's guns, lifting and feeling for balance. Dena found one that almost suited her. Rather too heavy and long, but the smallest on offer. None of the other women had ever tried them.

89

'You first, Lady Geraldine.'

'That's not fair. I should have a chance to see who gets the range.'

'Well, I'll start you off . . .'

He did very well. The first clay pigeon went by, well clear of the shot. But he clipped the next one, and the third one disintegrated. Another man had his try, and did less well. The clay targets came very fast, as the game did, almost as erratically. One after the other, the men had their try; Dena put off her turn for as long as possible, so she was the last. Like many of the others, she missed the first, and caught the next two. They had another round. She watched them get the range, and feel more confident, while her own confidence diminished. Her gun kicked to the right; the second time around she allowed for the digression. Again two out of three. She was about to give up. 'Not a third time?' Penrose said.

'It's heavy,' she answered. 'Daddy had some lighter guns especially made for us girls.' His extraordinary blue eyes seemed to dare her. She called to the keeper that she was ready. Three clay birds rose in the air at random time intervals; she shot each of them into little clay fragments.

'Well done!'

'Bravo!'

'Lady Geraldine, I think you're a bit of a fibber,' Penrose said. 'You must spend all your time practising. Do you do anything else particularly well . . .?'

'Nothing.' She broke the gun, and handed it to one of the servants, feeling suddenly weak with relief. She retreated back into the group of women.

'My dear, how clever. I suppose you paint and sing, too. I remember . . . it's your grandfather, isn't it, who's the painter? Have you inherited his gifts, as well as your father's?'

The speaker was, apart from the Duchess, the *grande dame* of the party, the Marchioness of Penrith. She was dressed in tweeds that must have pre-dated the war, with the hem taken up a few inches. They suited her; she was elegantly thin, and she had once been a great beauty, and that still clung to her fine features.

'I can't really do anything, Lady Penrith. Our governess taught us to sew a little, and my mother taught us to cook.'

'To cook!' The Marchioness appeared to think that no one other than those who applied for that situation in the kitchen, as one of the staff, should have any knowledge of such things. 'What an extraordinary accomplishment! You will make some fortunate man a very good wife. I can hardly talk to my cook. She always has such clever explanations for why things didn't turn out well. If I just knew how to answer her . . .' She mused a little. 'Cooking and sewing . . . as well as guns and billiards. Being your father's daughter, of course you ride. Walk back with me, child. This mist, even if it is August, is getting into my bones. What a damnable climate we have.' They left the others, and started back to the Palace. 'Your mother's having a hard time of it, I hear. Misses your father dreadfully. I liked your father so much. Always such a kind man.'

'He was very kind. We all loved him.'

'Yes,' the Marchioness said, and then added. 'A lot of people did.' She changed the subject abruptly. 'You seem to get along well with Mr Penrose. Have you known him long?'

'We only met last night.'

'They say he's going to marry the Etchells' daughter. That should help him in his career. She has lots of money. Hasn't any of his own, poor man. Terrible handicap in the Foreign Service. But then, they're a brilliant family. His father, Sir Thomas, is Permanent Under Secretary at the Foreign Office. Great power in that job. Foreign Secretaries come and go, but the Permanent Under Secretary stays for ever. His uncle is General Sir Percival Penrose, one of the King's equerries. Harry's brother is really brilliant. Youngest Fellow ever at All Souls. I met him once. Very boring. He could talk only about his subject, which happens to be pure mathematics. Now Harry . . . he's got great charm, as you've noticed . . .' Lady Penrith's words streamed on. She would have made a great gossip columnist, Dena decided. She seemed to know the genealogy of every person in the house party, the state of their finances, their loves and hates, their prospects. 'The Penroses are related to the Cambornes. No money there either. They've got a derelict castle in Cornwall, and some worked-out tin mines. Descendants of *the* Camborne – the admiral. We've got a letter in the family archives from my late husband's great-grandfather, who served with Camborne. Apparently he was just as frightened as anyone else when it came to battle. But he could control it. That's what counts. I noticed you were very nervous when you started to shoot, and then you got very cool.'

'Or more frightened, Lady Penrith.'

'Almost the same thing. Fear is as good a spur as any. You're very beautiful, child. I expect every young man you've met has told you that. A pity about John Forley. Shouldn't have got into that situation. But then your mother should have been with you, shouldn't have let it happen. But everyone knows she's beside herself with grief. People will be understanding, you'll see – as the dear Duchess has been. Do you play bridge?'

'A little, Lady Penrith.'

'I suppose, she said drily, 'that really means you're a brilliant player. Just like the way you shoot.'

'Sometimes I'm lucky.'

'Well, let's hope it holds. Perhaps you'll be my partner this afternoon.'

'It all begins to seem like an obstacle course this weekend.'

'Well, child if you will come forward and do extraordinary things like playing billiards as well as any man and out-shooting good shots, you must expect to be tried. All the women will be dying for you to make a mistake. Some of the men will, too. They don't like women to be able to do anything. Well, riding's all right. And having babies. Being beautiful, but not too clever. Don't tell anyone you can cook. No doubt it's extremely useful, but it doesn't sound right. And don't encourage Harry Penrose.'

'*Mr Penrose!* Why, I've hardly spoken to him.'

'He's very taken with you, child. I can always tell. You've been in enough trouble over the Forley man. I wouldn't do to be seen trying to take Celia Etchell's future fiancé away

92

from her.'

'I've done no such thing! And you said they're not even engaged yet.'

'There you see! You are interested in him. Stay close to me, child, and get this weekend over. Don't do anything else spectacular, or all the women will really hate you. It's bad enough that you're so beautiful. They can't forgive you that, as well as being poor. Have you ever noticed how popular rich, plain girls are?'

At lunch Dena hardly dared address a word to either of the men beside her. Down the long table she was conscious of the gaze of Lady Penrith. But she was also conscious that Harry Penrose often looked her way. They were too distantly seated for any conversation. She looked along the table for Celia Etchell, but couldn't identify her. When Harry Penrose approached her when coffee was being served in the Red Drawing Room, she tried to avoid him by engaging her friend, Helen, in conversation. But Harry Penrose interrupted. 'We're riding this afternoon. Are you coming, Lady Geraldine?'

She was grateful to Lady Penrith. 'I promised to play bridge with Lady Penrith.'

'Oh, Lord, what a bore.'

'Well – what about Miss Etchell?'

'Miss Etchell doesn't ride. Fell off a horse once, and she's never got back on. Well then, I'll see you at tea.'

'He's rude, isn't he?' Helen remarked. 'Rude about Celia. Rude to me. He didn't ask if I wanted to go riding. I don't give much for his chances as a diplomat if he hasn't got ordinary good manners. But then he's very well connected at the Foreign Office. He knows everybody worth knowing. I suppose when you're as handsome as he is, there's a pretty good chance you'll be rather arrogant as well . . . Oh, there's Lady Penrith beckoning. I hope you're a good bridge player. She's a real demon.'

That made Dena nervous again. She thought she didn't play at all badly, but she kept watching the Marchioness's face for signs of disapproval. They won quite handsomely, but it was because Lady Penrith really was a demon player.

She was gracious to Dena over tea. 'Quite well done, child. For someone your age. There's far too much time for old women like me to spend playing bridge. But poor partners are such an irritation. You'll come along nicely, I think. Oh, here's Harry Penrose. Now, remember what I told you.'

Lady Penrith helped by engaging Harry Penrose immediately in conversation, that is, a series of questions fired at him about his present position, his prospects, where in the world he wanted to serve. He had just finished a tour in the embassy in Vienna.

'Not nearly as important as it used to be,' Lady Penrith observed, as if she knew the diplomatic service inside out. 'Now there's no Austro-Hungarian empire, we really don't need that big embassy there. Where do you go next?'

'Wherever I'm sent. It will probably be a hardship posting. We all have to take our turn. It can't all be Paris and Vienna and Rome. I'd like one day to have a stab at Moscow. A very interesting posting.'

'Speak Russian, do you?'

'I'm learning. A career diplomat has to. It doesn't do to have to use translators all the time.' The talk went on, and Dena slipped away, getting, behind Harry Penrose's back, an approving nod from Lady Penrith. It wasn't yet time to go upstairs to change for dinner. As a very junior and unimportant member of the house party she had been given a room with a view of the stables, a big room nonetheless, but not one to spend time in. So she went through the many State Rooms, glancing quickly at the pictures as she went, until she reached the great Library. It was already occupied by two older men, seated on each side of one of the two fireplaces, reading newspapers. They glanced briefly at her, decided to ignore her presence, as if she had invaded this male sanctum. The library was filled with books in cases with metal grilles. Dena didn't dare open one. She scanned the titles, wondering if any guest had ever borrowed a book. It seemed unlikely. She was flicking through some magazines on a central table when Harry Penrose came into the room. Again the two gentlemen by the fireplace rustled their newspapers, but said nothing. He came immediately to her side. 'They act as if it's a men's club.

Needn't talk to anyone if you don't want to.'

'Does that apply to women too? Do we have a choice?'

'Oh, I can see old Primrose Penrith has been getting to you. I'm not quite stupid. I read the signs. Is it your decision not to talk to me, or her advice? I just need to know.'

'Both. I've learned a little wisdom lately. Sadly. My mother says I've ruined myself. Perhaps this weekend will restore me a little. I don't want to do anything that will be talked about.'

'Why would that happen?'

'Because you're engaged to Celia Etchell.'

'Wrong. All surmise and gossip. I've never asked her, and I rather doubt she'd have me even if I wanted it.'

'She's an excellent catch.'

'When I get married I'll want far more than that.'

'Such as . . .?'

'Love.'

'As well as money?'

'Who said anything about money? I seem to have got along all right without it so far.'

'There's a bachelor talking. Wives and families cost money. I ought to know. I grew up knowing it. My mother and father were great at spending money they didn't have. I don't know why I'm talking to you about this. It's none of your business.'

'I'm very interested in everything you say. Here, sit down, will you? And never mind those two old fogies over there. Geraldine —'

'Dena. That's what my family calls me . . .'

They talked. Afterwards she was never sure of what they talked about. His family, her family, the places he'd been, the places he'd never been and wanted to go. He was an admirer of her grandfather's paintings, the landscapes. 'He'd like you for that. He always says, privately, that the portraits are the dogs he breeds in order to pay to feed the cats.'

'I think I'd like him very much.'

Eventually the two men folded their papers and left. They had not said a word to each other in the time they had been there. 'Probably the best of friends,' Harry observed. 'No need to say anything. But I've a lot to say to you.'

'We all leave tomorrow.'

'Tomorrow isn't the end of the world. Will you take a walk with me in the morning? We haven't taken a walk around the lake, or over Vanbrugh's famous bridge, which Capability Brown half-flooded. Before breakfast?'

She remembered Lady Penrith's warning, and started to say 'no'. The gong for dressing sounded, and his expression appealed. 'Please say "yes".'

She had everything to lose, and yet nothing. 'All right.'

They went upstairs to dress, and didn't exchange another word that night. In the morning, at eight o'clock, he was waiting at the entrance by the West Gate. It was pouring with rain, a chill, soaking, steady rain. 'Real English August weather, isn't it?' he said. 'I wondered if you'd come.'

'I said I would.'

They trudged steadily down towards the Grand Bridge, the statue of Marlborough on his Column of Victory gazing loftily on them. Harry held an umbrella over Dena. They looked back at the great Palace from the bridge. 'I don't know how anyone can bear to live here,' she said. 'It must be so depressing; nothing but great State Rooms and corridors. They've given up so much of it.'

'The splendour doesn't attract you?'

'No, not at all. We grew up in a house that isn't in the least bit grand, but we all enjoyed it. Everyone seemed so busy just enjoying living there.' She was too well aware of the history of the great Marlborough family. The present Duke had been obliged to cross the Atlantic to find a Vanderbilt heiress to restore its fortunes.

'Will you show me Merton? I've heard it's a beautiful house.'

'How can I show you Merton? I don't live there. And you can't stay at the dower house. My mother's in London.'

'If I found a friend who lived nearby could I come?'

'You're mad, you know. I'm not any use to you. I can't help your career. I haven't any money. You know what they're saying about me. All the worst things. It would be very much better if you paid attention to Celia. She would make you the ideal wife.'

'If you don't mind, *I* make up my mind about those sorts of things.' His tone and features expressed fury. He turned and walked away from her, apparently forgetting that he took the umbrella with him. She waited, standing on the bridge, until his figure vanished against the grey backdrop of the Palace. Then she followed along the sodden paths. Her coat and hat and hair were soaked by the time she reached the shelter of the building. She stood and had to ring to be admitted. A footman took her wet coat and hat, after she had shaken herself like a dog. His manner was sympathetic. 'I expect you'd like some breakfast, m'lady. It's still being served. We won't clear for an hour yet.'

She entered the dining-room. Harry Penrose was seated at the table. Three other people were present, all sipping their second coffees. Offering a brief 'good-morning' to them, she helped herself to coffee and a large breakfast. She seated herself as far away from Harry Penrose as possible. After breakfast she changed her shoes and stockings, and spent the morning walking with Helen through the great State Rooms, examining the portraits of the Marlboroughs, the busts, the ceiling decorations. It was August, but a chill hung on the place; or perhaps the chill had struck her the moment Harry Penrose had walked away and left her on the bridge.

Lady Penrith came to her when sherry was served before lunch. 'Child, you look wretched. Are you ill?'

'A cold coming on, I think.'

The shrewd eyes looked at her carefully. 'Nothing more serious, I hope.'

Lunch seemed interminable. Another guest was heading in the direction of Merton, and offered her a lift. She made her farewells to the Duchess. 'Remember me to your mother,' the duchess said. Her tone was a little less friendly than the day before. Perhaps they all knew about the morning walk.

Harry Penrose turned up at the dower house two days later. Miss Lightbody showed him into the drawing-room, and went to fetch Dena. She had explained to their guest that Dena had a streaming cold, and was resting.

Dena dressed and came downstairs. 'I'll make some tea, dear,' Miss Lightbody said. 'You go and entertain Mr Penrose. Oh, yes, I must bring some coal.'

Dena closed the door of the drawing-room firmly 'You're mad to come here,' she said by way of greeting to Harry. 'Nothing can come of it.'

He greeted her with a smile, as if he had not heard. 'You're looking terrible. I was so angry I forgot to leave you the umbrella. You can blame your cold on me.'

'You're mad to have come,' she repeated.

He shrugged. 'It's a free country. I couldn't think of a friend who lived nearby, so I'm putting up at the inn in the village. Quite a decent little establishment. Just the sort of place I would have chosen for a holiday in the country. I'll know pretty soon where I'm being posted. If it's some deadly spot in darkest Africa, I'll be happy to remember the peaceful English countryside – particularly in the rain.'

'You could have chosen a better place to view the English countryside. I hear Celia Etchell —'

He gestured irritably. 'It's not in order to keep referring to Celia. I thought that had been settled. On the bridge . . .' He sprang to his feet as Miss Lightbody rattled on the doorknob, trying to manage the tea tray in one hand. 'Do let me.' He carried the tray to a table. 'Is it all right here?' He went to close the door, and saw the coal scuttle. 'Shall I bring this in? A little more on the fire?'

Dena silently took the cup, crouching close to the fire, not seeming to care about her red nose and lank hair. Effortlessly Harry Penrose kept up a stream of conversation with Miss Lightbody. Finally he thanked her for the tea. 'I'm just having a short holiday. Perhaps a little fishing . . . Lady Geraldine promised that if I were ever in the area she'd show me Merton. I hear it's rather special.'

Miss Lightbody beamed. 'I'm sure Edward – Lord Milroy – would be delighted to have you fish the river. And Dena will take you over the house. And you must come to tea again.'

He refused to go away. Miss Lightbody telephoned Lydia in

London to tell her about the young man who had appeared from nowhere, and just simply hung around. 'Penrose . . . Harry Penrose? I know his father. Is there something going on?'

'Dena will hardly talk to him. But he keeps coming.'

Lydia sighed. 'I expect I'd better come and see what it's all about.' She came reluctantly.

'My intentions are perfectly honourable, Lady Milroy. I just want to marry Dena. She persists in turning me down. I'd be a little more patient, but I haven't time to be patient. My leave's almost up, and I'll be getting a posting from the Foreign Office any day now. That means going away somewhere. I'd like to marry Dena and take her with me.'

'Will you both,' Dena said, 'please stop talking about me as if I weren't here. I've told Harry, mother, told him and told him. It just won't work. He could do much better than me. I won't be any use to him in the diplomatic corps.'

Lydia bridled. 'That's too much, Dena. You're a beautiful young woman. Some nice young man will come along.'

'I'm thought to be a rather nice young man, just the right age for Dena, I should judge.'

'I had something different in mind for her.'

'You mean someone with money.'

'If you must put it like that, yes.'

'Well, I haven't any money to offer Harry either, Mother. You can't accuse him of being a fortune hunter. For all other people know, perhaps he's taking soiled goods!'

'Dena! There was never –'

'Well, at least give him credit for being the decent if misguided fool he is.'

'No one calls me a fool! Even if she is the woman I intend to marry.'

Lydia sank down on the sofa. 'Oh, for God's sake, someone pour me a drink. I've never heard of such madness. Both of you should be looking for someone else. Two penniless fools! You won't cut much of a figure in the diplomatic set on Dena's dress allowance.'

Harry poured her a large Scotch, and added only a dash of water. 'Don't you believe in love at all, Lady Milroy?

Dena told me she grew up in a very happy family.'

'Love? Oh yes. Love is wonderful. But money is very useful. It pays the bills.'

They were married very soon in the village church, with Edward giving his sister away. Julia and her laird came down from Scotland. Julia opened her eyes wide at the sight of Harry. 'But he's wonderful, Dena.' She hugged her sister. 'I know you'll be very happy. Look at Douglas and me . . .' She was pregnant again.

Ellen whispered to her mother. 'Poor things, they won't have two pennies to rub together.'

There was a small reception at Merton, just the families and closest friends. Harry's father, the Permanent Under Secretary, Sir George Penrose, eyed Dena sceptically. 'I wonder if she'll stand up to the life,' he said to his brother, the general.

'Of course she will. Probably be an outrageous success. I hear she's a wonderful rider, and a crack shot. I met someone who saw her almost beat Harry at billiards at Blenheim. That's where it all started, I suppose. Lady Penrith told me she's a natural at bridge, and coming from the old girl that means something. And she can cook! Imagine it! She can cook! Harry probably couldn't have made a better choice.'

Sir George looked at the general with equal scepticism. 'Perhaps she'd be splendid for the army. The diplomatic life is a bit different.'

Harry's 'hardship' posting was to Cairo, and it was no hardship at all. He would serve as a second secretary. The posting was not unexpected. Sir George, while serving his master, the Foreign Secretary of the day, no matter what his political persuasion, was a noted Arabist, and had encouraged his son in the study of the language, and the history of its people. Dena took all her cookbooks with her, and struggled desperately to take some tuition from Harry in Arabic on the voyage out. At times, when she was tired and the struggle with the language was too much, she just collapsed into his arms. 'It's no use. I'll never manage it.

Oh, my love. What a wonderful fool you are! Fancy marrying me! I love you so much, Harry. And I keep thinking how much better you could have done for yourself.'

'You're the fool. You just don't understand love at all.'

As soon as they arrived in Cairo, Dena bought rolls of silk that seemed ridiculously cheap, and wondrously beautiful, and sheer, fine cotton. She set about at once to make herself the clothes suitable for the climate, and to her position. Nothing grand was required, just what was suitable. She sewed the dresses on the sewing machine which had been a wedding present from the Marchioness of Penrith.

Their cook was very disturbed when Dena began, in her sparse Arabic, to ask him what was in the dishes he served. She tried to write it down. The cook took fright. Did the lady think she was being poisoned? 'Please, Harry, tell him my friends in England are all anxious to know the recipes.'

When she ventured to ask the same questions of the other wives in the diplomatic service and the army, there were mostly shrugs. 'I haven't the faintest idea. It's their business. One could never serve it back home.'

Her Arabic improved, though it wasn't expected that she speak anything but English and French. Her dresses were admired. She played bridge almost every afternoon. By this time no one was surprised when she asked about every new form of dish which was served to her. The other women had grown used to the rather tattered book she carried around with her in which she used to write all the ingredients and spices she saw used. She became popular in their small, enclosed foreign circle. She loved Harry. She loved Egypt. But she had come to understand that her life would be perpetual movement. No place would ever be a permanent home. She thought of her father and of Merton.

When she became pregnant, Harry insisted she go home for the baby to be born. 'It's almost unwritten Foreign Office policy, Dena, in places like this. The climate's very hard on women out here. And the hospitals . . .' He shrugged. 'Good enough, I suppose, but only in emergencies. If there were any complications . . . I very much want our child, Dena.

We've been married more than two years. I was beginning to think it would never happen.'

'You would like a son?'

'I don't give a damn. I just want you two to be safe and well.'

'So you see,' Dena had said to Ginny late that first night at Seymour House when they had started to tell each other about their lives, 'we really shouldn't have married. Neither of us has a penny except what Harry earns. I can't do anything to help him that way.'

'But you love him . . .'

'Oh, yes, I love him.'

Chapter 5

The two women had seen each other almost every day since that first meeting in the park. They had reached the stage of pregnancy where there was nothing to do but wait, and they waited in each other's company. The bare bones of their short lives they had told each other that first night were fleshed out, until there seemed there was nothing else left to tell, and yet they sought each other's company, as if, as trust and friendship grew, each became the safety valve of the other.

Dena discovered that for all the privilege the McClintock-Clayton money conferred, it did not carry with it the automatic gift of friendship. There were acquaintances in plenty, but Ginny viewed them with some scepticism; they all were wives of business associates of Blair's, or else were people to whom being on intimate terms with Blair Clayton's wife, and Alex McClintock's mother could bring advantage. She had been in London too short a time to have made friends outside that circle.

Out of politeness, Ginny invited Lydia to dinner at Seymour House on one of the occasions when Blair had come back from Zurich. Lydia, who had no particular axe to grind, hit it off well with them both. She was once again the forceful, vigorous woman Dena had described in her growing-up years, and she did not think it necessary that she should coddle Dena because she was in the last stage of pregnancy.

Lydia amused and interested Blair. 'I agree. These two mothers can well take care of themselves.' Blair had instantly realized the almost unique quality of the relationship which had so swiftly grown up between these two women, and was grateful for it. They appeared to give so much to each other, yet neither was a taker. He recognized Dena's appeal for Ginny. She was beautiful, and she had a great zest for living, for enjoying life; she was getting by on a diplomat's salary, but she had known people of great wealth since she had been a child, so what Ginny could command did not awe her. He thought it remarkable that she seemed so free of envy. He sensed the beginning of a genuine love and trust between the two, and in the world in which they both moved, it was a rarity. He smiled at them both, and encouraged the friendship.

For Dena, Ginny became the friend to whom she could talk about the Foreign Service with the sure knowledge that her confidences would never be betrayed. 'I don't think I'm a very good diplomatic wife,' she confided. 'I've never been good at kow-towing to people, and that's what wives and husbands too, I suppose, are expected to do in the Foreign Service. Until the husband becomes an ambassador. Then you can do more or less what you like, except to offend other diplomatic missions, or the host country.

'I doubt Harry will ever be made an ambassador, unless it's to some rather unimportant country. Lord knows, he's good enough at his job, everyone says that, but for one of the really top jobs, you do have to have some money. Until 1919 you had to have a private income to be accepted into the Foreign Office. I've heard of some ambassadors, career diplomats, managing to get along on what the Foreign Office pays, and it's hard work. It's not easy to serve very medium-quality wine to people who expect the best.'

'You look better dressed than most women I know, even in maternity clothes.'

'That's my mother again. She always did know what to do with the twist of a scarf.'

As she listened to what Dena confided about the social intricacies of the diplomatic life, always knowing one's exact place in the hierarchy, Ginny allowed herself to voice a few complaints she had in her turn about the boredom she knew and had known in the business world that both her husbands inhabited. Dena would not judge them as petty, or regard Ginny as a spoiled whiner; there was complete understanding that what each said was never repeated.

'Sometimes I've felt I'm so looked down upon,' Ginny

once said, knowing very well that Dena grasped her meaning. 'These men dealing in their millions, they've got it all buttoned up. They bow or kiss my hand or do whatever's appropriate to the country or place they're from. They're almost as good as their wives at appraising the cost of the dress I'm wearing, and probably better at valuing the jewels. I seem, sometimes, to exist only because I'm the mother of little Alex McClintock, on whom Andrew McClintock thinks the sun rises and sets. I'm valued because I'm married to the man who is the clever, skilful hand-selected partner who will hold the fort until Alex is old enough, and knows enough, to take over.

'Blair would like a son, but I find myself often thinking it would be better if this baby is a girl. There would be less conflict with Alex in the future. But then – we'll have more than one child, and one of them's bound to be a boy. They'll probably grow up to fight each other. Thank God Blair's so even handed. If any man can play fair between two rival heirs, it's he. Even with Andrew McClintock's weight on Alex's side . . .'

They speculated about the children to come, even laughed at the coincidence of having the same obstetrician and both being booked in at Portland Clinic. Dena's child was due a few days before Ginny's. But when the first labour pains gripped Dena a little after 2 a.m., three days earlier than expected, Lydia was absent for a weekend with friends in Wiltshire. Dena telephoned first her doctor, and then Ginny, in a mild panic. 'I'm taking a taxi . . . the contractions are quite far apart. I don't think I'll give birth on the way.'

Ginny's mellow voice soothed her. 'Well, I'll be seeing you at the clinic. My little fellow seems to be on the way a week early. I've telephoned Blair. There's a blizzard in Zurich. No planes. He's coming by train.'

'And Harry's ship isn't due in Southampton until tomorrow morning. I can't find the telephone number my mother left. Well, I always did muddle things up. I'm a little frightened, Ginny.'

'Don't be frightened. I'll be there, right beside you. What do we need anxious husbands for . . .? Listen, hold on where you are. It won't take five minutes longer at this hour of the morning for me to pick you up. The car's ready to leave now.'

So they had entered the clinic together; their doctor attended both of them. There were no difficulties, though Dena's labour was longer than Ginny's. Two girls were born within hours of each other.

Ginny visited Dena in her room, pushed in a wheelchair and holding her new baby. They both laughed, and both instinctively reached out to hold the other child. 'Who needs husbands?' Ginny repeated. 'They're almost twins, aren't they. Let's hope they'll be friends.'

Dena's telegram was delivered to Harry as the ship docked in Southampton. He came bursting into Dena's room at the clinic. He held her for a long time in an embrace which almost hurt, but which she would not break. At last he lowered her back on the pillows. 'You must think I'm an elephant! Oh, my love. I so much wanted to be here with you. A few hours too late. How are you? How is the baby? When can I see her? And who's the man hovering outside?'

Dena laughed and, recognizing the happiness in that laughter, Harry relaxed. 'You mean – I haven't got a rival? Unless it's our daughter?'

'No rival, darling. I suspect that would be Blair Clayton, Ginny's husband.' There had been time for letters to reach Harry. He knew about Ginny Clayton. 'Harry, if you happen not to care very much for Blair, which would surprise me, I'll expect the greatest diplomatic effort of your life. You must *appear* to like him. I am certain you will love Ginny.'

The two men met as they respectively watched their infant daughters fall asleep in the nursery. They recognized each other without introduction. 'A bit shattering,' Harry said, 'being a father for the first time. And I got here late.'

'Me too,' Blair answered. 'Same on both counts. You're Harry aren't you?' He extended his hand. 'Let's go and have a drink.'

Harry had thought he meant a pub, or a club, but Blair drove back to Seymour House. The drink extended to dinner. They got along well; no diplomatic effort was required by Harry. They talked of many more things than the new babies that evening, finding that in many ways their worlds interlocked. 'Our main business now, in these tough days,' Harry said, 'is to sell our country, its policies and its products. We have to be a lot more diplomatic than we used to be.' He looked at his watch. 'Must push off. I've burdened your marvellous hospitality too much.'

'Staying with Lady Milroy?'

'No, not yet. I expect I will be when Dena gets out of the clinic. But the Knightsbridge flat is pretty small. I think my mother-in-law would rather I didn't crowd her until it's necessary. So I'm on a sofa in my father's flat.'

Blair nodded. 'When they both come out of hospital perhaps you'd consider moving over here for a few weeks. For whatever leave you have . . .' He held up his hand. 'Oh, it would be a favour. I've got some negotiations at a rather delicate stage right now. Somehow bankers don't seem to understand that having one's first child is a pretty big event. I'm expected back almost immediately. It would be a favour. Could you come sooner, perhaps? There's loads of room. And there's Alex. This is the first time he's ever been without his mother. I don't want him to feel abandoned. And I learned today that Andrew McClintock is on his way. I would rather Alex weren't alone with him, or that Ginny were left to cope by herself . . .'

Harry had two weeks before he had to sail again. He tried to stifle his qualms about accepting so much hospitality. 'Won't Mr McClintock think that two, no, three spongers, have come to live with Ginny?'

'This is my house,' Blair said rather pointedly. 'He can think what he wants. If he has any sense, he'll know how fortunate Ginny and I are. People need friends. Particularly they need friends they know can't possibly benefit from them.'

Harry's bushy eyebrows shot up. 'Not benefit? I don't call taking weeks of your hospitality not benefiting. At the same time, I recognize that Lady Milroy's a bit past the age when she'd find being wakened by crying babies in the night a delightful experience.'

Blair held up his hand. 'Shall we agree that we're doing each other a favour? Remember, our kids met each other in the first hours of their lives. That has to mean something.'

Andrew McClintock arrived after Blair had gone back to Zurich. Neither Ginny or Dena were home from the clinic. McClintock gazed wearily at the stranger in his house – characteristically he thought of it as his house, even though it belonged to Blair and Ginny. A letter had waited for him at Southampton from Ginny, and a cable to him on board ship from Blair had alerted him to Harry's presence, but he still viewed the situation with some suspicion.

Andrew McClintock had had Harry Penrose's background fairly thoroughly researched in the short time available to him before meeting the man. There seemed nothing he could readily find fault in in the relationship between the two women. And Harry Penrose seemed a decent enough sort, a little happy-go-lucky for McClintock's liking, but there could be nothing for him to gain, financially, in a friendship with the Claytons. Diplomats got along by knowing the right people, of course, but McClintock was well aware that Harry and Lady Geraldine Penrose were no Johnny-come-latelies on the British social scene. But just for a moment Andrew McClintock thought that he could thoroughly dislike Harry Penrose when his grandson, Alex, was brought down to the library at Seymour House, and rushed instinctively to Harry. 'Uncle Harry! Come and see what I built—'

Harry turned him gently in the direction of his grandfather. 'Look who's arrived. Your grandfather McClintock,' he prompted the child. 'Come all the way from New York just to see you.'

Alex had an air of reserve as he approached his grandfather. It was six months since Andrew McClintock had been in London, and Alex didn't remember what he looked like. He seemed very ancient in the child's eyes. He much preferred Uncle Harry, who was good fun, took him to the zoo, took him up to Hatchard's to choose his own colouring books, took him to tea at Gunter's. 'No,' he said. 'He hasn't come to see me. He's come to see my sister.'

'Both, boy, both!' Andrew McClintock answered. He held

out his hand. It was not in his nature to embrace his grandchild. 'You're looking well. Shooting up, I see. Learning something, I hope.' He looked across the child's head at Harry Penrose. 'Isn't it time Ginny got a tutor for him? Can't leave boys too long with nursemaids, nannies, whatever you call them.'

'A little early yet, Mr McClintock, I think. Don't believe all they tell you about English nurseries being a hotbed of sissies. They have produced a few good specimens.'

'Including a few ancestors of yours, I hear,' McClintock rumbled. 'Very well then . . . so long as he's progressing . . .'

'If you've time, sir, I would suggest you come up to the nursery to see what progress we're making with a railway. It's almost got me beaten. If it weren't for Alex I wouldn't know my way round half the tracks.'

'Like that, is it? Well, so long as he's out of the teddybear stage . . .' Not for his life would Harry tell McClintock that each night since Blair left, he had put Alex to bed with his well-loved, well-worn teddy.

'Now I must go to this Portland Clinic place and see what sort of a daughter Ginny has produced for Blair.' He was unable to hide his satisfaction that the baby had not been a son. 'Coming? I have a car waiting.'

'I've been twice today, Mr McClintock. I think Ginny, that is, your daughter-in-law, would like a visit just from you.' He didn't mention that it was almost Alex's bedtime, and that he would rather put the child to bed with his teddy than visit the Portland Clinic in the company of this rather unpleasant man.

But he waited for the older man in the library, dressed for dinner, a modest Scotch and soda in his hand. Andrew McClintock came bustling in. Griffin followed immediately with a bourbon and water. 'Well, they both seem fine. Ginny was visiting with your wife, so I met her. Lovely-looking woman. You're a fortunate man. Got a fine-looking daughter too. Both children look well and lively. And the mothers get along as most people would wish loving sisters did.'

'You've just said a lot of things I agree with,' Harry answered.

'I took a chance on liking your wife. I respect Ginny a lot, and if she likes someone, I'm pretty certain I'll look at them favourably too. So I stopped at Asprey's on the way to the clinic. I telephoned and had them arrange to stay open a little longer. Two christening mugs – gold. Doesn't tarnish like silver.'

Harry gulped at his drink. 'I hope we can afford to insure it! Isn't that a little excessive, sight unseen?'

'Oh, I'll be godfather to Ginny's child. I thought you might ask me to be godfather to yours as well.'

Did the man know, Harry wondered, that he had just usurped one of the greatest privileges parents had to bestow? 'I'm sure Dena will be delighted. Are you staying on for the christening?'

'Well I figured you'd have to be on your way back to Cairo pretty soon, so the christening would have to be pretty soon. I'll probably stay.'

Harry thought that as large as Seymour House was, it might grow even more cramped than the Knightsbridge flat. 'Well, we'll have to get together our friends and relations in a hurry. I thought mothers needed a bit more time so they looked their best.'

'Oh, dressmakers can always rustle up something to make a woman look right . . .' Harry was conscious that in Dena's case, she'd probably be rustling up something on her own sewing machine, and then he remembered that it was back in Cairo. He decided to leave the matter to the women. He was already beginning to feel the heavy hand of Andrew McClintock, but he realized that what the man had just offered was as great a gesture of goodwill as he might be capable of making. Out of the blue, his little Rachel was to have a man of formidable power as a godfather. Harry thought he had no right to refuse that on behalf of his child.

So three weeks after they were born, Christine Clayton and Rachel Penrose were christened in the same ceremony in the Queen's Chapel of the Savoy. Harry's father and uncle and brother were there, and many assorted cousins, as well as friends from the Foreign Office. The Foreign Secretary

110

sent a telegram of congratulations and, as a gesture to the retired Permanent Under Secretary, was a godfather, by proxy, to Rachel. The Clayton family gathered, and a pair of rather grey Swiss gentlemen came to see the first child of their chairman christened: they themselves wondering why the Penrose family should be part of the affair at all. Dena was rather bewildered by all the people of the banking and finance world who gathered. Her mother and Ellen compared the two sets of christening gifts. Christine's were fit for a young princess, Rachel's just as numerous, but far more modest. No one knew how envious Ginny was of those gifts which were obviously handmade, and sent with love. Christine's represented money, and the power of the McClintock empire. But Andrew McClintock stood by the font as each child was named, and agreed to renounce the flesh and the devil in their names. Harry privately thought McClintock hadn't much use for the things of the flesh anymore, but that he might be capable of making a deal with the devil.

But still, Harry concluded afterwards, as he and Blair had a last self-congratulatory drink together, it had been a splendid christening party at Seymour House, and the two girls seemed well launched in the world. Dena had looked beautiful in a flowing silk dress which she had already made for herself in Cairo, knowing that a christening must swiftly follow the birth, if Harry was to be present. The Foreign Secretary might take a paternalistic interest in Rachel, because of her grandfather's long service with the Foreign Office, but that did not mean Harry would be granted indefinite leave. The rich and the influential mingled at that joint christening party, almost all of them taking note of the identical gold cups which were the gift of Andrew McClintock. And McClintock noted the guests on the Penrose side, and was well satisfied.

Harry was on a ship back to Cairo less than a month after he had arrived. Dena was to remain in London until Rachel was at least three months old. Against Harry's better judgement he agreed that Dena should stay on at Seymour House. He didn't like the amount of hospitality they had accepted from the Claytons, but he was aware of the closeness of the

111

two women. He knew she would not be nearly as happy or comfortable staying with her mother, and staying with Ellen had not even been suggested. He was conscious that the life Dena would live with him would be full of uprooting, and of partings. It belonged in the nature of his job. So let her enjoy Ginny's company for as long as possible. She was still rather nervous in handling her own child, and the nurseries of Seymour House, staffed by Nanny and two nursery maids, might give Dena the breathing space, the touch of confidence she now conspicuously lacked.

'Don't make it harder for her, Harry,' Ginny pleaded gently. 'She's a little bit bewildered. She'd be perfectly all right if you could stay with her . . .'

'That's the Foreign Service, Ginny. It's often going to be like this. This is one of the times when I wish I had plumped for a steady job in the City, like Dena's brother-in-law, and came home regularly to a nice settled existence in the stockbroker belt. All our children are likely to get out of the Foreign Service is a chance to learn a few languages. It isn't an easy life. I often wonder if Dena realized it.'

'She loves you,' Ginny said. 'She'll take whatever comes of that . . . including moving round the world. But just for these few months, let her stay here with me. I'd like it. Not even Blair and Andrew McClintock can create readymade friends for me. I believe I need Dena as much as she needs me.'

Harry made a gesture of submission. 'If only you weren't so blasted rich. I can't possibly keep up with what you've given us.'

'And I can't get over how Alex loves you, almost more than he loves Blair. It's having you here that's saved him from becoming jealous of Christine. Of course Blair's crazy about her, and Alex understands he's not Blair's child. But having Dena here with me will be a help. Alex suddenly has two mothers and two sisters to cope with. It just might be distraction enough in the first months to stop him realizing he's not the centre of the universe anymore. Of course he will remain the centre of Andrew McClintock's world.'

Harry smiled. 'Yes, poor kid. It's not an unmitigated blessing, is it?'

'Since you're one of the few people who seem to realize that, you can understand better why I'm anxious to keep Dena and Rachel with us for a while. Alex is going to meet, in his lifetime, many people who will want to know him just because he's the McClintock grandchild. He won't know many he can be as sure of as you and Dena.'

They were alone in the library. The light was fading over the park. Tonight was the last night for Harry in London. Tomorrow he would go alone to Southampton to embark for Cairo. In another week it would be Christmas, and he would spend it alone. He had carefully chosen his gifts for the three children, and wrapped them himself. He had entrusted his gift for Ginny to Dena, and the one for Dena to Ginny.

'Harry, I'm grateful to you. I never want to lose touch. Dena and I coming together that way has been one of the best things that's ever happened to me. I've got a sister, Lucy, whom I hardly seem to know. Dena's different. We chose each other. I hate the thought of her going all the way to Egypt. I know your life will take you to all sorts of places, but London will still be its centre. Blair and I will be to-ing and fro-ing across the Atlantic. Let's try to meet up whenever we can. I hope the next posting is nearer home.'

'If I make a mess of things, it's more likely to be Outer Mongolia.'

'You won't make a mess of things. Not you, Harry. Washington would be a nice posting, wouldn't it? Blair and I will often be in Washington. And New York. Perhaps they'll make you the consul in New York.'

'It's a little early for that yet, Ginny. I have to scramble my way up the ladder. But thanks. I'll work hard, even if it's just to make sure Dena sees you more often.'

Blair arrived back from Clayton's Bank in the City. 'You don't mind if I have an early drink? It's been a foul day.' He kissed Ginny. 'If I didn't know what sort of life I'd be condemning you to Harry, I'd ask you if you wouldn't consider a position with McClintock-Clayton.'

It was said only half in jest. Harry experienced a feeling that was more than alarm, as if in some insidious fashion the long arm of McClintock's had already begun to tighten its embrace. He shook off the feeling. All they had in common was the friendship of the two women, the births of the two little girls, the growing sense of comradeship with each other. Just the same, he had been glad to see Andrew McClintock depart for New York a few days before.

'I'll join you in that drink. And just be thankful that I haven't any head for figures. It could get to be an incestuous little group.'

They dined alone, the four of them. Harry thought he had never seen Dena more beautiful. But he sensed her sadness, and a little trace of panic now that his departure was upon them. He looked at tall, handsome Ginny. She wore a simple dress, and only her wedding and engagement rings. She never flaunted her jewellery.

'Blair,' she said, 'has just given me a beautiful gift. He's bought the place my mother grew up in in Virginia. It's just a little place. Mr McClintock gave us Prescott Hill, and he'll expect us to use it whenever we're in the States. But just let's think of my own little place, Wildwood. It will be your country house when you finally get posted to Washington. It would give us such pleasure . . .'

Harry had that uneasy feeling about the McClintock embrace again. But he replied like a diplomat. 'When I make a Washington posting, we'll be delighted, won't we, Dena?'

She had none of his qualms. 'Of course. What a lovely thing to look forward to.' Innocent, Harry thought. Still innocent.

She lay in his arms that night. It was still too close to Rachel's birth for them to make love, and the agony of that denial tore at them both. And it would be months before they lay together again. 'Oh, God, I hate your going. It's hard enough, but months. Harry, it will be so lonely. I didn't know how much I could miss you until I was on that wretched boat on the way back home.'

'You were better at home, my love. It's easier on the baby to have these first months of life out of that climate. She'll

114

get a good start here. Don't weep, my love. It won't be for ever.'

There were meetings and partings through the years. Ginny and Blair seemed constantly to travel between London, Washington, New York and Zurich. The winter following Rachel's and Christine's birth she came to spend a month in Cairo. She was accompanied by Alex, a governess, Christine and a nanny. The British Ambassador, knowing that the Penrose villa could never stretch to accomodate them all, offered a guest villa attached to the embassy. 'Really, it wouldn't do to have them staying at a hotel all that time. I've met Blair Clayton a few times. It's just a courtesy to his wife and family.'

It was a good month. Ginny took most of her meals with Dena and Harry. The two women and Alex travelled to the Pyramids. Ginny mastered the strange art of riding a camel. She relaxed in the gentle warmth of the Egyptian winter, and watched their children play together, Alex naturally their leader. The son of the First Secretary was brought over each day to join the group; he was almost the same age as Alex.

'I knew this would be the last winter I could come,' Ginny said. 'Alex will start school next fall. I'll have to spend most of my time in Washington. But we'll be in London all summer. We'll be expecting you at Seymour House when the baby's due.' Dena was then three months pregnant.

'Harry will have mixed feelings about my staying at Seymour House again. He worries about our being spongers.'

'I think Blair and I are the ones to decide that,' Ginny said crisply. 'We're not quite fools. You can't go to your mother's. Not Rachel and a nanny and a new baby in that little flat. You'd drive one another crazy.'

'There's room at the dower house at Merton,' Dena protested, but feebly. She longed for London again, for the safety and familiarity of her doctor, and the Portland Clinic. Harry gave way. So Dena was at Seymour House for six weeks before their second child was born.

The friendship between the two women seemed stronger

than ever. Harry had not imagined Dena as a good correspondent, but letters between her and Ginny had been frequent. He sensed that what Dena did not dare express openly in the close, gossip-filled society of Cairo, she had poured out to Ginny. And equally Ginny, in the highly-charged atmosphere of the very rich, of the business deals that hung on discretion and suavity, of poker-faced encounters, dared trust no one with her thoughts but Dena, who would gain nothing from what she might let slip. Harry thought he might have made small fortunes if Dena had cared to confide to him what deals McClintock-Clayton were currently engaged in, but it never occurred to her that such information might be useful or, if it did, she knew the trust placed in her, and never revealed it. He didn't know if she still remained totally innocent of what gains her friendship with Ginny Clayton could bring to them both, or if she cherished the friendship so highly she was determined she would never gain from it. He hoped it was the latter. She might be comparatively poor, but greed would never cause her to cultivate the rich.

Dena and Rachel slipped into the comfortable ritual of Seymour House in the last month of her pregnancy. Rachel and Christine once more re-formed the bond that seemed to have been forged the day they were born. Alex now had a tutor, at his grandfather's insistence, who seemed to enjoy his time with the three children as much as with Alex alone. He and Christine's nanny had several squabbles over domestic demarcation, but nanny did admit the young man was an excellent influence on the two little girls. Dena enjoyed her weeks of freedom, as her body grew heavier and slower.

Dena wore the maternity gowns from Ginny's wardrobe, enjoyed the dinner parties, enjoyed the company, relaxed into the sense of security she experienced with Ginny and Blair. 'It really is a holiday,' she said to them both. 'I'm so grateful.'

Harry arrived back a full week before the baby was born, bringing with him the news that their personal belongings were packed and were being forwarded. 'New posting,' he said cheerfully. 'Berlin. First Secretary.'

'It's because you're so fluent in that wretched German!'

Dena cried. 'How will I ever make progress with all those terrible long words, the meanings back to front?'

'I hope it's for a better reason than my German,' Harry replied, but he laughed at the same time. He added, mostly for Blair's benefit, 'I've a sort of special brief, to watch the progress of Russo-German relations. Keep an eye on what the press is saying in both countries, and keep my ears open in Berlin about what the talk is about Russia. I've been pressing ahead with my Russian – but I'm supposed to use these months of leave to take a crash course in it.'

Their second daughter was born in August, 1932. 'Are you disappointed, Harry? Another girl . . .'

'I can't have enough of my women. They're all so beautiful. I don't know that I'd enjoy the rivalry of having another man around.' This child had been born with Harry's distinctive eyes, the eyes that even in a young baby seemed to glitter rather than shine.

Dena kissed him. 'Diplomatic, always. I do love you.'

She was back at Seymour House quickly, surrounded by the comforts of the large but quiet staff, of silence, of the pleasure of nursing her baby, of playing with Rachel and Chris and Alex, but knowing the moment she felt weary she could leave them all and the new baby would be taken care of.

'It may just be coincidence, my dear,' Ginny said, 'but my father-in-law arrives in a few days. Of course, he's always coming and going – just as we are. He doesn't greatly care for hotels. I suppose that's why we have such huge houses everywhere. We always have to be ready for him.'

'Oh . . .' Dena said, a little frightened at the prospect of encountering Andrew McClintock. 'We'll move over to my mother's. Or better, we'll go to the dower house. Now that the baby's safely here, I don't mind.'

'Nonsense. You and Harry are our guests. I just have the faintest suspicion that Mr McClintock is coming because you're here. He'll want to be godfather again, you'll see. Do you feel up to a christening so soon? I just wish I had a baby to be christened with . . . What do we call her, besides Baby?'

It was a far less lavish affair, since the Claytons' English relations and the McClintock business associates did not participate. Harry and Dena felt almost obliged to ask Andrew McClintock if he would like to be one of the godparents. He might have been secretly pleased because there was, this time, no Clayton infant to be christened along with their child. As yet, young Alex had no male rival.

'I baptize thee Caroline Virginia Lydia . . .' Once again Andrew McClintock promised to renounce the flesh and the devil in the name of the pale, quiet infant, wearing the ancient Milroy christening robe. The christening had been hastened, mostly to accommodate Andrew McClintock's imminent departure for New York. Once again the christening party was at Seymour House, and all Harry's friends from the Foreign Office attended. Harry's father was there, older and a little bent. His brother's death during the winter had seemed to affect him more than Harry had expected it would. Harry's brother, Richard, was there, looking ill-at-ease at this celebration of a child's birth. 'He'll never get married,' Harry's father said. 'What woman could live with pure mathematics?' He said this to Lydia, who roared with laughter to a degree that caused most of the people in the room to turn to look at them. Lydia could thoroughly enjoy the birth of another grandchild, and the christening, because they caused her no trouble. She thought it was highly convenient that Dena and Harry should have such friends. By now, some of Harry's friends were firmly convinced that he and Dena had some special influence with McClintock-Clayton. But how could he? Everyone knew he had only a small private income and his salary from the Foreign Office. Such things didn't influence people like Andrew McClintock and Blair Clayton. Very few were prepared to consider that it all might hang on the unlikely friendship of the two women who rarely saw each other.

Harry worked every day with both German and Russian instructors. His German had been polished by his posting to Vienna, but to study Russian had been his personal decision. He worked until it was time for him to go to Berlin. He insisted on going ahead of Dena and the children, so that he could have their house and possessions settled before her arrival. After he had gone, Dena confessed to Ginny the sort of blank fright which fell on her in his absence. 'I always have the feeling that I'll never see him again. But he does love his job. He loves all the things that I think are so hard. I don't know at all how I'll get on in Berlin. The Germans frighten me. Everything there is so tense now. We all have to be so very careful of every mood and every word. All this talk about Germany rearming . . . Well, it's Harry's world . . . I have to go along with whatever comes our way.'

Dena remained in London until the day before Ginny was due to return to Washington. Alex was enrolled at school, and she had to be there with him. 'Berlin doesn't seem nearly so far away as Cairo,' Ginny said. 'Whenever Harry gets a long enough leave, you'll all have to come to Washington. Don't worry about the fare. Mr McClintock always has a suite booked on one of the Cunard liners. He doesn't mind who uses it, within reason. Of course, if he happened to need it himself, you'd be bumped off without any ceremony, or apologies.'

'How can we keep on taking so much?' Dena said. She was beginning to feel something of Harry's concern, but it was not so elemental. She knew only that their family had received more than they could ever return, materially. She did not share his sense that something all-pervasive had entered their lives in the form of McClintock-Clayton. She handled the gold christening mug, identical to Rachel's. 'I don't know why he bothers about us.'

'Perhaps he cares, just a little, about what Blair and I feel. Andrew McClintock can't buy people like you and Harry. He knows it. That makes you unique.'

'I've never thought of it like that. I suppose I'm very naive.'

'Stay that way,' Ginny kissed her goodbye at Victoria station, and Dena made the long train journey to Berlin with her two young daughters and a nurse, who seemed more frightened of going to Germany than she did. 'Never thought I'd do it, madam, like go to Germany .... My dad was shocked when he heard. He fought in the War.'

'We have to try to remember the war has been over tor a long time. We are at peace now. It can't ever happen again.'

She felt better about those words of bravado when they finally reached Berlin, and she was in Harry's arms. 'You look so well, my darling. God bless Ginny and Blair.'

'They have helped so much. But you, Harry . . . having you to come to . . .' She hoped it would go on for ever, their being in love. The babies might come, and interrupt things for a time. But they would be together again. Always. That was what she believed then, without knowing quite how much of this sense of wellbeing she owed to Ginny.

The house allocated to them was pleasant and spacious, and well-staffed. It was possible to feel that their time in Berlin would be pleasant, even when the frightening happenings of January and February 1933 swept around them. Adolf Hitler came to power, and the Reichstag was burned, a fire started by the Communists, the Nazis said. Harry warned Dena not to discuss events with her friends, or only in the most neutral terms. 'The servants, Dena, never forget they're always around. And we don't know where their loyalties are. One has to assume that some are Nazi sympathizers. Don't leave letters around. Try not to write anything that could be misconstrued.' So she wrote bright and conventional letters to her mother and Ellen and Julia, telling about the dinner parties she gave, the receptions she attended. She named the important political figures she met without giving any opinion of them. Only to Ginny did she confess disquiet.

I feel as if I'm always looking over my shoulder. In a way, Harry's interest in Russia makes him a bit suspect. There's a sort of uneasiness to life here that I never found in Cairo. I just have to be more careful. But sometimes I feel as if I want to turn my back when some fat Nazi in glittering uniform bows over my hand. I find I like the military much better. That's the old Prussian lot. They despite Hitler, but they can't do anything about him. That Nationalist Party have given him dictatorial powers. Harry says I'm not to worry, as we have diplomatic immunity. But sometimes I hardly dare open my mouth. And do you know, Rachel already knows as many words in German as she does in English. I expect she's inherited Harry's gift. I feel so stupid beside them both. I long to see you. To talk without being afraid . . .

In the summer Harry had leave, and they journeyed to London, where Ginny had brought Alex. Their reunion was almost without words. They hugged each other, and it was some hours before Dena felt able to talk. Nothing, though, inhibited the children. Rachel started shouting some order to Alex in German, and got told she was a little Nazi, a term she didn't understand. Neither did Alex, but he had learned it from his new tutor, and it sounded a good way to rebut Rachel's precociousness. She and Chris still treated each other like sisters. Christine's nanny was impressed.

Dena and Harry and the two girls went back to Berlin at the end of his leave. Dena felt refreshed, and needed to. She wrote to Ginny:

It's like going back into a sort of darkness again, though everything on the surface looks so lovely. Blonde, well-mannered children, in their pretty national costumes. Hefty giants of men in incredible uniforms at receptions. I have to do more entertaining now, and must step in when the ambassador's wife isn't there. I'm collecting German recipes, but it's all a bit heavy for my taste. The sausages are magnificent, and so is the beer. I have found a book of Rupert Brooke's poems, and I read 'Grantchester' when I feel particularly fed up.

The summer of 1934 Ginny and Blair, Alex and Christine came to Berlin to visit them. Once again the Ambassador, recognizing the importance of these visitors, stepped in. They were accommodated at the Embassy. The Ambassador hosted a dinner at which Thyssen and Krupp were guests. 'Industrialists should know each other.' Blair was invited to visit factories in the Ruhr, invitations which he accepted, and Harry was permitted to come along since he was technically

121

Blair's host. They would rather that the British diplomat had not been present, but what could anyone do when the women were so close? At the end of two weeks when they all felt that their lips had stiffened over the platitudes they had uttered, they went to the McClintock-Clayton villa on the Zurich See.

'What freedom,' Dena rejoiced. They took the children for trips on the lake and drives into the mountains. Switzerland was at its kindest: there was no rain, they saw the mountain peaks. Rachel got on well in the German-speaking cantons, though she complained that it all sounded different. She was indignant that she was better understood in English than in German. Chris was a little in awe of this twin of hers who spoke a different language, but Alex dismissed it. 'I'll bet my French is better.'

'It should be,' Blair said. 'You're three years older.'

Harry kept up with his Russian studies, but in Zurich he felt more free to seek out and speak with emigré Russians.

'Do you really feel compelled to read Dostoevsky in the original?' Ginny asked.

'I imagine Marx would be more Harry's target,' Blair observed. 'Though *Das Kapital* and *Mein Kampf* are both in German. A weird world we're living in. Andrew McClintock clings to the good old American tradition of expecting everyone to speak his language.'

'His language is money,' Ginny said. 'So many people speak that language.'

Dena and Harry and the children returned to Berlin to an atmosphere increasingly strained. In June a Nazi blood purge had seen the deaths of many party members said to have plotted against Adolf Hitler. In Austria the Chancellor, Dollfuss, had been assassinated. The word *Lebensraum* began to be heard. In August, after von Hindenburg's death, a plebiscite made Hitler the Chancellor. He retained the title *Der Fuhrer*.

Dena organized her life around Harry's activities, and tried to say nothing about what she saw happening around her. Apart from the fear and anxiety evidenced by some people, the majority of the Germans seemed proud of their leader; the humiliation of war began to recede. In March 1935 the Saar Basin was returned to Germany. After Hitler denounced the terms of the Versailles Treaty he signed a pact promising not to expand the German Navy to more than a third of the size of the British Navy. '*And now,*' Dena wrote to Ginny, '*Hitler has begun organizing a Luftwaffe. Purely defensive, of course, he declares. A frightful man called Goering is in charge.*' Considering the letter, she then scratched out the word '*frightful*'. Even with the letter going in the diplomatic pouch, she was afraid to express such views. She lived with the dread that some indiscretion on her part would cause Harry to be declared *persona non grata* in Berlin, and hurt his career. She dared not discourage Rachel's increasing use of German as her everyday language, but she sent to London for children's books in English and helped Rachel to read them. She kept telling them both stories about life in England, an idealized life she admitted, so that they should not think this was the only world they would know.

By spring Harry knew that his term in Berlin would be finished by the summer. He was given three months leave, and it was hinted that Moscow would be his next posting. This could not be confirmed until after he had left Berlin. Dena heaved an enormous sigh of relief and wrote at once to Ginny.

The day after Dena's letter went off to Ginny, a letter arrived from Washington. Somehow the McClintock-Clayton network had obtained this obscure piece of information about Harry.

Friends in the Embassy here have just found out that your tour of duty in Berlin is ending this summer, and Harry has quite a spell of leave due to him. Why not come to us? We'll be at Prescott Hill all summer. It'll be rather hot, but not worse than Cairo. It would make a change for you all . . . would even be a chance for Harry to get his eye in on a place he's bound to be posted to sometime. I'll expect you. Don't let me down, please. For more reasons than one, I'd like your company, and I don't think I should travel right now. At long last, there's going to be another Clayton child.

They spent a week in England, staying at an hotel in London, and spending a few days at the dower house. 'That's quite enough of family,' Dena said, and Harry didn't dispute it. They booked second-class on a Cunarder, but when they arrived in Southampton, they were met by a junior purser, and taken to a suite in First Class. There was an adjoining room for Rachel and Caroline and their young nursemaid. 'Compliments of Mr McClintock, sir. He hopes you'll be comfortable.'

Dena looked at the rooms clothed in flowers. 'I don't know if we should accept, Harry. But it's hard to give up, and he'd probably think we were very churlish.'

He was uneasy himself, but decided there was nothing he could do without upsetting both Ginny and Andrew McClintock.

'Since it's inevitable, my love, I think we'd just better lie back and enjoy it. One doesn't get close to Andrew McClintock and not expect to feel his hand somewhere. I wonder what sort of favour he'll eventually ask of us? God knows, there's nothing I can think of we could give.'

They had five days of the sort of luxury neither of them had ever experienced before. They had stayed at houses of the rich, but the experience had been nothing like this. 'One could get too used to it,' Harry said. He chose the most modest wines he could find on the list, fearful of the bill, but at the end of the voyage, when he asked for it, it was refused. 'Mr McClintock's instructions, sir.'

'I can't accept that—'

The look on the head steward's face was enough to warn him: 'If I have to choose between insulting you and insulting Mr McClintock, sir, you know where the choice must be. I'm sorry, sir. He's one of Cunard's best customers.'

The same treatment continued all the way down to Washington. A private coach was reserved for them on the train. 'I suppose we'd better just accept that we're guests of what in Europe we'd call royalty. This is the way things are done.'

'I like it,' Dena said. 'I could do with quite a lot of royal treatment.'

'Will it spoil you for ever, darling? Do I have to worry that some American millionaire is going to take you from me?'

'I wouldn't worry. What I have to worry about is that someone may take you from me.'

He took her hand. 'Then neither of us has any worries.'

Ginny met them at Union Station in Washington, Alex and Christine with her. There was the usual exchange of how much the children had grown, the now almost ritual coming together of Rachel and Christine. Now, although a year had passed, they were old enough to know each other. The word 'Twins' was once again used. Alex hung back, until Harry put his hands on the boy's shoulders. 'You're not too old or grand to welcome back an old uncle, are you? What are we going to be doing this summer, eh?' Alex started to rattle off a list of things he had planned for Prescott Hill. For Ginny and Dena the embrace was long and emotional. 'It's such good news about the baby . . .'

They spent a week in Washington, seeing the city, attending the dinner parties Ginny and Blair had arranged for them, making the obligatory visits to the British Embassy. Harry was greeted warmly by old colleagues in the Foreign Office. 'I expect you'll be here with us pretty soon, old boy. Know the next posting yet?'

Harry had been instructed not to speak about it until much closer to the time. 'No. Our masters in their wisdom have chosen to keep me in suspense. But I always fear Outer Mongolia. It would be rather hard on Dena and the children.'

'Paris would be nice,' Dena said ingenuously. She had shared the news only with Ginny and Blair. The distance of the posting made the time together more precious. During that week Ginny and Blair gave a dinner party at which the British Ambassador was the guest of honour. 'Guess where we got the first news about your being given long leave?' Ginny said.

Andrew McClintock also gave a dinner party for them, to which Ginny's father and mother, other members of the

Senate, and business leaders in the capital were invited. 'Everyone's dying to come,' Ginny said. 'This will be the first party he's given.' Andrew McClintock had bought a house for his own use at Dupont Circle, just along Massachusetts Avenue from what was still known as the McClintock mansion. 'He's torn down the Fifth Avenue house in New York, which was built for Alex's grandmother, and put up an apartment block. Being him, he's reserved the two top floors for McClintock-Clayton. That principally means him and us . . . and whomever he cares to invite. I assume that means you and Harry among others.' The Dupont Circle house was hardly less large or·less grand than the mansion he had left. 'Such a pity. All that for just one man. I wish he could have brought himself to marry again. But who would put up with him?'

They moved to Prescott Hill, Ginny, Dena and Harry, the four children, Alex's tutor, nanny and the nursemaid Dena had brought. Blair would visit on weekends. Andrew McClintock would visit whenever he took it into his head to come. Dena was enchanted by the house. She moved through the huge rooms, with their high ceilings and fans slowly moving the hot air. She examined the paintings, the antique furniture, the chandeliers. 'I never thought it would be possible to put together something that so perfectly belonged in this setting. It says at once it's American, apart from some of the pictures. Mr McClintock's father . . .'

'Mr McClintock's father was very rich, Dena. He was rich a long time ago. He just wanted to show the impoverished Virginia gentry at the end of the War what real money would do. He hired and bought only the best, what he was told was the best. I doubt he would have known himself. He hardly ever used the place. Some strange revenge on the South for being so uppity. Well, I think you'll like my *little* piece of Virginia just as much. It's simple and homely, and very Southern. The one Blair bought for me, where my mother grew up. The one I promised you and Harry as a country place when you're posted here.'

They visited Wildwood, and many other places through the summer. Dena and Harry grew knowledgeable about the battle grounds of the Civil War. 'Just look,' Ginny advised them. 'I don't want you to start taking sides. Blair and I almost blew up over the Civil War – who was right and who was wrong. We weren't the first to do that, and we won't be the last. Just look, and don't say anything. Virginia is so very nearly the North, and yet so completely the South, it's wiser to say nothing. Particularly to our neighbours.'

The weeks sped by. There were parties at the weekends, eagerly attended by families attached to the British Embassy and other members of the Washington diplomatic corps. They came mostly to lunch and brought their children. There were parties on many levels, which Andrew McClintock seemed to enjoy, because he was often there. They used the swimming-pool, rode, lazed in the deep shade of the oaks in the heat of the day. Dena discovered that a practice range existed, and she went through the gun cases eagerly. Blair maintained his guns in excellent condition, but he protested that he didn't get enough time to practise target shooting. 'I'm rusty myself,' Dena said. 'Haven't done any shooting since . . . well, for a long time.'

'Watch out,' Harry warned Blair. 'She's a crack shot. She's beaten some very good men at shooting and billiards. And you can see how she rides.'

'The products of a misspent youth,' Dena said sweetly. 'And I've learned that in the South ladies don't talk about such things and they're really not supposed to know about them. Well, riding's all right, I . . . I guess.' She added the last, and then laughed at the expression on Blair's face. 'Well . . . Harry's not the only linguist in the family.'

'It just sounded so funny with an English accent.'

Alex seemed to enjoy lording it over the three girls, though Rachel offered him more opposition than Christine. 'She's too used to being bossed around by him. Does him good to have Rachel stand up to him.' Caroline hardly dared open her mouth in Alex's presence, she was so in awe of him.

He was now eight, and king of everything he surveyed. Insidiously, he was beginning to know his position. 'I can't keep it from him for ever,' Ginny said. 'His grandfather treats him as if he were already grown up, and into his

127

inheritance. That sort of attitude is catching. Within reason, what Alex wants he gets. He'll always be the only grandchild of Andrew McClintock. Even if this one's a boy, he won't be a blood relation to my father-in-law.' The coming child was precious to her and Blair. 'I was beginning to think there never would be another Clayton child. We all need him . . . Blair and I, Alex and Chris. For so many reasons, we need him.'

Dena noticed how carefully Ginny paced herself that summer. She would walk to the stables to see them saddled up and off on their ride, but she never mounted herself. She exercised daily, often with Dena as a companion; she gently lapped the pool the number of times prescribed. She rested, and stayed rigorously within the advised diet. She glowed with the beauty some women have in pregnancy. The neighbouring families came to visit, all the women exclaiming on how well Ginny looked. 'You're good for Ginny, Dena,' Blair said. 'I wonder if it's possible for you to stay on . . . well, that's asking a lot.'

'When the posting's official, we'll talk about it. It's obvious that Rachel and Caro are thriving. As I am . . . Oh, so wonderful not to feel always under scrutiny. The good life, Blair, can be very seductive. But I can't say or any of us are suffering yet.'

From time to time Andrew McClintock came out to Prescott Hill to spend a night. 'I hope Ginny's not overdoing it. I suppose she ought to have another child, though, myself, I think two's plenty. At any rate, I like to see how my godchildren are doing. Coming on fine, I'd say. That Rachel's going to be a handful someday. Smart as a whip. We'll have to see she goes to the right schools. I don't mean the fashionable ones. The right ones. Don't like to see brains wasted. I wish Chris were as smart. Do you notice she does everything Rachel tells her to do? And Rachel's not all that much impressed with Alex. Given that he's a hell of a good-looking kid, and about twice as smart as he ought to be, that's saying something. Of course his father, my Alex, was brilliant. And Ginny's no slouch. Radcliffe. You don't get in there just on pretty manners.'

'You have a remarkable family, Mr McClintock,' Dena said.

He stared at her for a moment, then broke into genuine laughter. 'Damn me, young woman, if I don't know when I'm being put down. You and Harry . . . you don't come from such bad families yourselves. Come to think of it.' He mopped his face with a silk handkerchief, and sipped his bourbon. 'Go on, talk away. I like pretty women who aren't stupid.'

'How kind of you, Mr McClintock. I must try harder.'

Finally the official word came from the Foreign Office of Harry's posting. He was to be First Secretary and Chargé d'Affaires in Moscow. Telephone calls came from his friends in the Embassy in Washington. 'Really thought you were being posted here, Harry. Moscow's a tough job the way things are now.'

Now that it was official, Dena experienced her first fears. 'I was so relieved to get out of Berlin, I hardly thought of what Moscow would be like. It'll be . . . well, different, won't it?'

Harry nodded. 'Moscow's a tricky assignment. It's such a closed society. Still so suspicious of the West. It's a challenge, Dena. But . . . well, it's not going to be very easy for you and the girls. I mean . . . everything's so restricted. You'll be assigned housing, of course, and just about everything else. But it will be housing reserved only for foreigners. You'll shop at approved places, take the children to the approved parks, to play only with other children of the diplomatic corps. You won't ever be able to know any other Russians. You'll meet them at receptions and that's all. We're just about tolerated there. We can't put one foot over the line. The women, I'm told, find it very claustrophic.'

'But it's good for you, Harry?'

'I have to assume so. At least it's not Outer Mongolia.'

Her lips twisted in a smile. 'It's that obsession with Russian you've always had. You see, if you'd been a fool and just stuck with French, it would have been Paris. But then, I knew I wasn't marrying a fool. When do we go?'

'I go early September. That's the end of my leave. I should be in place by mid-September. Look, why don't you do as

Blair suggested to me. Why don't you and the girls stay with Ginny until the baby's born? It would help Ginny, I do believe. It would be an extra break for you. The older Caro is before she has to make that long journey, the better.'

'Yes. The journey. Whenever I think of Russia I think of winter, and those interminable train journeys. Those Russian novels . . . I'd better start rereading them.'

'Stay here with Ginny,' he urged, suddenly conscious of a sense of desolation in her. 'And stay a while in London and see your family.'

'You don't sound as if you want us to come.'

'I know you'll come. You'll be comfortable enough, but it will be an isolated life. Make lists, and buy anything you think you'll need. Even the shops for foreigners may not be well stocked. As for me, well, Dena, I've been convinced for a long time that important things are going to happen in Russia. A country as big as that, beginning to modernize, a huge population. It bears watching very closely. I didn't enter the Foreign Service just because it was something my father had done. It means something to me, Dena. In some small way I may be able to help shape events, shape something that will be to our advantage. Russia and Germany will turn to claw each other some day. If I can help our side at all . . .'

'And which will our side be?'

He turned away the question. 'Wars make strange bedfellows.'

'And will there be war?'

'It's the job of people like me to try to stop that happening.'

'If that happens, could we be caught there?'

'I'd never let you and the children be caught there.'

'And you, Harry?'

'Don't worry. I'll never be in danger. I'm quite a coward.'

'You're quite a fool, too.' She stood up and put her arms about him. 'Why weren't you a stockbroker? Life would be so much more predictable.'

'And we'd be bored to death.'

'Sounds quite nice, being bored to death rather than being scared to death.'

130

'You don't want to go? Even at this stage, I could put in a request for something else.'

'And get a black mark? Not for me, you won't. Besides, I might learn a little Russian. Certainly Rachel will. It can't be a total loss.'

'God love you.' He kissed her very tenderly.

'God does love me. Look whom He gave me for a husband.' She straightened herself briskly. 'Well, we'd better get dressed for dinner. And give Ginny the good news that she's going to have house guests for the next few months. I hope she really meant it when she talked about my staying on . . .'

Ginny's reaction was both fear and gratitude. 'I've known, of course, but until it was confirmed I kept hoping it would be somewhere closer. Moscow sounds so distant, and so . . . so foreign. One hears such stories . . .' She broke off. 'But nothing can happen to you. Thank you for staying, Dena. It's hard to say how much I hoped you would, and yet I couldn't press too much. Blair has to go back to London next week. He'll only be away a few weeks, but still . . . the baby's awfully important to him . . . to us both. I don't know why I feel so worried . . . after all, I've had two already.'

Harry went to Washington for a few days, getting his final instructions about Moscow. He would stay in London for a week for further briefing. He returned to Prescott Hill for a final weekend. 'Just as well you're not coming immediately, Dena. By the time you arrive I'll have most things sorted out. One will have to expect that the servants will be spying on us. As if there will be anything to spy on. But when we want a private – or what the Foreign Office calls a "sensitive" conversation, we'll have to take a walk in the park.'

'God, it sounds terrible.'

'It won't be so bad,' Dena said. 'We'll get leave.'

'Of course,' Harry said. 'Dena and the girls can go back to London every summer if they want to.'

'Then I'll be there,' Ginny said. 'We'll have wonderful reunions. You'll have to meet the new baby . . .' Her brow wrinkled. 'Perhaps Mr McClintock knows . . . oh, he's sure to know someone in the American Embassy.'

131

'Don't worry. In Moscow, the foreigners get to know each other in a hurry.'

He left Dena and Rachel and Caroline at Prescott Hill. 'I'd prefer that you didn't come all the way to New York with me, Dena. Let's not have a protracted farewell. It's only a few months, after all . . . I'll feel better about doing it this way.'

So he went. The first tinge of autumn touched the country around Prescott Hill. Ginny made plans for their return to the Massachusetts Avenue house. 'It's a pity to have to go. The fall is so beautiful here. There's such a marvellous smell in the air. If we could stay a bit longer, you'd get a bit of hunting.' But Alex was attending school in Washington, which was about to reopen, and Andrew McClintock was already starting to fuss Ginny about being too far away from her doctor. 'I don't see why he's worried. He has his grandson.'

'Oh, Ginny, he's not as bad as that. It's just, I think, that he has to feel he has control of the lives of the people close to him. In fact, I think he's really very fond of you.'

'Then God help me if he wasn't! If I get frightened at all, Dena, I get frightened that something might happen to me, and that Alex would be left in his hands.'

'My God, Ginny! That's mad! There's Blair! He'd never let Alex be taken away from him. Besides, what can happen to you?'

What happened they didn't know: Ginny had no fall, no strain. Dena first knew when she was wakened by the housekeeper. 'Please, Lady Geraldine, Mrs Clayton's asking for you. I'm afraid . . .'

The local doctor came at once, and by early morning the gynaecologist had arrived from Washington, sped there by one of Andrew McClintock's chauffeurs. McClintock himself arrived there about an hour later. Dena waited for him in the hall. 'I'm so sorry, Mr McClintock. Ginny seems to be all right, but she's lost the baby. It's heartbreaking—'

He cut her short rudely, as if he didn't want to hear anyone's sentiments. 'Damn fool! Has she been doing something she shouldn't? I've told her . . . She damn nearly lost

Alex with her silly carrying on. I'll go and talk to her.'

'Have some breakfast,' Dena took him firmly by the arm and steered him towards the dining-room. 'Blair's in London, as you know. He doesn't even know about it yet. It's not an easy thing to put into a cable. And I'd wait a bit before telephoning. Let's just be sure Ginny's all right . . .'

'That's what I intend to find out. Right now!'

'No, you won't, Mr McClintock. No! Ginny has to be quiet. Just about the last thing she needs is a visit from you.'

'Why, you—'

'Just say it! Interfering bitch! I don't give a damn what you call me. I stayed to be with Ginny. To give her any help I could. At the moment, the wisest thing would be for her to do as the doctors say, just rest. You can't give her back the baby. Oh, for God's sake go and have some breakfast! You'll find the doctors tucking into theirs very nicely. Ask them all the questions you want. Just don't bother Ginny.'

For one of the few times in his life, Andrew McClintock obeyed someone else's directive. He went in to breakfast with the doctors. Later in the morning, when they had gone, he spoke to Dena. 'It was very bad, wasn't it? She's had a bad time. They say there may have to be some – what did they call it – "corrective surgery". Whatever the hell that means.'

'It means, Mr McClintock, that Ginny's had an incomplete miscarriage. In fact, she's still in pain. They are taking her to Washington for a D and C – that's a dilation and curettage. She has a slight fever.'

Andrew McClintock seemed to back away from too detailed medical information. As with many men, matters to do with a woman's health seemed to baffle and annoy him.

'Whatever they think is best. But you will stay, won't you? Until Ginny's back on her feet. Mentally, as well as physically. They told me . . . well, they told me it would have been a boy . . .'

'Trust you to know that, Mr McClintock. I've already agreed to stay on. I'll stay as long as Ginny needs me.'

He was quite humble. 'Thank you. I've already written to

our Ambassador in Moscow. Telling him what a fine man Harry is, and what a good friend . . .'

Dena tried to restrain her anger. 'That Harry is trusted by his own Foreign Service is enough. I don't think he needs recommendations from you.' She had flared up because of worry over Ginny, and tiredness. He took it quite well.

'With your permission I'll just slip in to say goodbye to Ginny. I'll be seeing you both in Washington.'

The same afternoon Ginny was moved by ambulance to Washington, where what the doctors called 'minor surgery' was performed. 'At this stage we have to be sure everything is . . . clear,' the surgeon told Dena. 'She had a raised temperature, which indicated infection.'

Dena was with Ginny when she regained consciousness. 'I messed it up, didn't I?'

'Nature messed it up this time, Ginny. There'll be other times. You have two healthy children. No reason why there shouldn't be more.'

Ginny stayed in hospital more than a week. Dena thought the doctors were being over cautious: she managed to waylay one of them, the young assistant to the leading gynaecologist who attended Ginny. He had guessed, despite all the attention being lavished on Andrew McClintock's daughter-in-law, that this was the one friend she trusted. 'We're being careful, that's all. It was quite serious. We suspect an infection of the fallopian tubes. Of course this doesn't mean she can't have other children. There's a chance that fertility will be diminished . . . But she's still a young woman. Plenty of time . . . When her temperature's steady for a few days, she can go home. But don't expect her to be too perky. She lost a lot of blood. and there's the inevitable depression . . .'

So it was Dena who took Alex to his first day in his new grade at school. She came back to the hospital to Ginny. 'We needn't ever be afraid Alex can't cope. He marched in as if he owned everything in sight.'

He returned that afternoon with the beginning of a black eye, and an unrepentant attitude. 'There was a bit of a fight. Some kid called me a Yankee carpetbagger. I don't know what a carpetbagger is, but it didn't sound right. So I socked him one, and he socked me! They told me if I didn't behave myself, I couldn't come back. Suits me fine!'

Rachel and Chris and Caroline gathered to examine his injuries. 'You look like a pirate,' Rachel observed. Chris said, 'Does it hurt?'

He gloried in their attention. 'The other guy hurts worse!'

Blair arrived back only in time to see Ginny home from hospital. 'I should never have left,' he said to Dena.

'It could have made no difference, Blair. It just happened. We'll both take care of her now.' He said little, but his anguish was evident in the clouding of his eyes, the stoop of his shoulders. He spent long hours by Ginny's bedside, sometimes talking, reading papers, sometimes just slipping into a doze. Dena left them alone while he was there; it was their time of mourning for their lost child.

Ginny's spirits and health returned slowly. Blair went to New York, and hurried back to her. 'He will always be on the go,' Ginny said. 'I'd be with him all the time if I could. But the problem will be the children. I think Chris could be all right with a governess for a few years, but Blair thinks Alex should be in school. I can't bear to think of him having parents on the other side of the Atlantic. Mr McClintock is adamant that Alex must go to school in the States. Understandable, of course.'

'That's a worry for us, too,' Dena said. 'Rachel will be in a special school for the children of the diplomatic corps when we get to Moscow, but there will be constant change.'

'What a pair we are,' Ginny said. Then she reached out and lightly touched Dena's hand. 'Thank you,' she said. 'There is no one else I would have wanted around at this time. No one else Blair and, yes, my over-zealous father-in-law would have permitted.'

Dena did not let Ginny's hand slip from her grasp. 'I often think back to that meeting on the bridge. Thankful it happened. I've got a best friend. I'm part of an American family. I never expected that.'

Gradually Ginny lost her pallor, her listless air. 'Blair and I will just have to try again for another baby. They gave me a "possibly . . . quite possibly" verdict at the last examination.

135

Now I'll have to help you get ready for Moscow.' She looked at the list Dena had been making, and picked up the telephone. 'No sense in your rushing around to shops. So much of this is routine.'

Blair insisted on accompanying Dena and Rachel and Caroline to New York and on board ship. 'I don't know how to say "thank you." There's no other woman Ginny could have tolerated near her at this time.'

The thought comforted Dena. It was a rough and slow crossing of the Atlantic, but made easier by the fact that once again they occupied a suite booked by Andrew McClintock. Apart from the things she had bought herself, there was an extra trunk. 'Not to be opened before Christmas,' Blair instructed.

She saw Lydia and Ellen in London, but didn't try to make the journey to Scotland to see Julia. 'My dear,' her mother said, 'she can hardly get her head up from all those children. I think they've lost count . . . It must be the bracing Scottish air. I can hardly bear to go there. The place smells of milk and babies, with a nice little mix of sheep and goat. When I think of my beautiful Julia lost in those Highlands . . .'

'So long as she still loves her Scot . . .' Dena replied.

'And you're rushing back to your Harry. If I'd been you, I'd have stayed out the winter in Washington.' She looked around Dena's bedroom in Seymour House. The house had been made ready for their few day's stay in London. 'Do you think we could just peek into that Christmas trunk? It looks so intriguing . . .'

'No! Ginny would never forgive me.' Dena was dressing to pay a visit, with Rachel and Caroline, to her grandparents in Hampstead. She found them older-looking than she had expected, but her grandfather still retained a dash of his vitality. 'I think they'll have to drag the brush out of my hand before they can put me in my coffin, child.' He no longer attempted portraits. 'I'd only disappoint my sitters,' he said. So the stack of landscapes grew, painted now from memory because he could no longer make his field trips into the country. They had become more impressionistic as his eyesight dimmed. But he refused to sell more of them than

136

was strictly necessary for his needs. 'They'll be far more valuable, Dena, when I'm dead. Don't let your mother sell them all in a bunch, will you? One at a time will bring more money. I rather hope . . . well, I flatter myself, perhaps, but I hope my grandchildren will like some of them enough to want to keep them.'

'Of course we'll keep them.'

After a long, tiring journey over a snow-covered Eastern Europe, they arrived in Moscow. Harry greeted them, bundled in a long coat and a fur hat. It was Christmas Eve. 'The best Christmas present I ever had in my life.' He scooped up Caroline in his arms, but Rachel had become too tall for him. 'You're growing up beautifully, upstanding like American trees. The Virginian air seems to do you good.'

'I'm taller than Chris, and she gets it all the time.'

The apartment was just as Harry had described it: large, lavishly and heavily furnished in bad taste, but warm, and staffed with maids who greeted Dena with some suspicion (why had this wife been so long apart from her husband?), but they embraced the two girls with delight and a show of real affection. 'They love children,' Harry said. 'You don't have to worry that they won't be well looked after.' The apartment block housed only members of the foreign diplomatic corps. 'You'll find life comparatively easy, except for doing without things they just don't import. Foreigners have it much easier than the Russians. Our own special shops, the pick of the food, anything you want, within reason. But they'll read your post, and listen in on your telephone calls. There's no getting around it. They just suspect the whole of the outside world is trying to undo the Revolution . . .'

On Christmas morning Harry gave her, among other presents, a pair of fur-lined boots of the softest leather she had ever handled. 'I took a pair of your shoes – I suppose you never missed them – and had them made to size. You'll need them, darling.' There were boots for the girls also, as well as dolls dressed in native Russian costumes. They were enchanted with the novelty of it all, and now that their weariness from the journey had worn off, they demanded to go out and play in the courtyard of the apartment block,

137

where, between the swept paths, the deepest mounds of snow they had ever imagined had been piled up. 'We'll open Aunt Ginny and Uncle Blair's trunk first.'

They had forgotten about it, but they fell on its contents with delight. Games, books, toys, it all seemed endless. And for Dena there was a coat of Russian sable, with a matching hat. They examined it, she and Harry, not knowing quite what to say. The note from Ginny was contrite:

> If you've obeyed instructions, you're opening this in Moscow, too far away to scold me. Please don't and don't be stuffily English about accepting it. Everyone knows about those Russian winters. It was Mr McClintock's idea. I said you wouldn't want to accept it, and typically he said: 'And what can she do about it when she's in Moscow? Damn fool if she throws it out the window!' How like him, but as is often the case, he's quite right. I just hope it didn't land you in any trouble with the customs people.

Harry, who by now was able to judge quite well the quality of Russian sable, murmured, 'We could probably have got it for half the price here, or less with foreign currency, but when would we be able to get together even half the price? Wear it and be warm, darling. That's what they meant it for. And jolly thoughtful of them, too.' There were other presents, more modest. A desk set for Harry. 'I wouldn't dare display it at the embassy. The ambassador would think I was imagining myself in his job.' Some silver serving dishes for Dena. From Blair there was the addition of a twelve place setting of silver flatware to add to the small collection Dena had started when they had married. Such things were part of the little store of treasures diplomatic wives collected, and were carried from posting to posting. Harry gulped when he saw it. 'I wouldn't like the ambassador's wife to see it . . . I suppose the Claytons just can't imagine a dinner for less than sixteen.' Dena's china service had also been added to. 'They're very kind,' Dena said. 'And they do know the diplomatic world. We can always say we inherited them. No need to say they're brand new.' She especially prized a set

138

of copper saucepans and pots lined with silver. They were in the last of the boxes they unwrapped. 'Oh, Harry . . . how wonderful! They're absolutely the best things to cook in. And they last for ever.' Harry looked at the array spread about them. 'McClintock was right. What can we do? Throw it all out the window? It's difficult being friends of the rich, Dena. They know we can't match these sorts of presents. But what can we ever give them?'

'I'll find some of those Russian dolls you got for the girls. Maybe there'll be some Russian version of lead soldiers for Alex. Of course it doesn't match. But we didn't ask for all this. All we give them is friendship.'

'Do you think that's so easy?'

'With Ginny and Blair, yes.'

The long Russian winter went through its inevitable cycle. Dena found Moscow oppressive, in a different way from Berlin. Their lives were so circumscribed, the weather formidable. Her letters to Ginny were her only outlet.

I can't imagine this place without snow. I see those old women shovelling snow on the streets and in our own courtyard, and it breaks my heart. I understand fully now what defeated Napoleon. And yet, when we go to their parties, nothing is too much. Endless food and drink . . . I wonder we survive it.

She made acquaintances within the diplomatic corps, and Rachel and Caroline played with their children.

We're a very polyglot lot here. It's very good for their languages, but Rachel is starting to ask for some Russian lessons. It amazes me! Just like her father. I suppose it's understandable, but I feel most comfortable with the wives of the American legation. The British are a bit stiff, and there's no getting away from the fact that Harry is Chargé d'Affaires. So I'm more relaxed with the Americans. I can talk a little about my Virginian family.

When Dena reported Rachel's demand for Russian lessons because she was frustrated at not being able to talk to people

139

in the street, Harry said, 'Well, she'll just have to learn a bit from me. My Russian's getting rather good.' The embassy provided a tutor in Russian for Harry, and he studied conscientiously and enthusiastically. 'The ambassador has me with him at all the important interviews now, just as a sort of check on the interpreter. Otherwise, I'm doing the usual hack duty . . .'

Dena noticed, however, that Harry was always at the ambassador's elbow at the many receptions they attended, and never far from him at the dinner parties, though protocol dictated the seating. She gave her own small dinner parties, inviting members of the diplomatic corps, and experimenting with Russian dishes which were new to her. Her recipe book filled up. But Russians could not be invited to these parties. 'They wouldn't accept,' Harry advised her. 'Couldn't. We can't go into their homes and they won't come into ours. We can only meet them at these grand affairs they give. But go on doing what you're doing, my love. You know, you have a great reputation with the diplomatic corps. They all wonder how I managed to persuade such a paragon to marry me. The most beautiful woman in Moscow. Did you know they say that? You serve the best food, have the loveliest, most polite and gifted children. If I dared tell them you rode like a Tartar, and shot like a – well, I can't think who are reputed to be the best shots – I don't tell them about the copper, silver-lined pots. I just say you come of an extraordinarily gifted family.'

Dena wrote it all to Ginny. As in Berlin, she was her safety valve. They had agreed their letters would be discreet, that no criticism of Russia would be implied or written. She filled her letters with details of Rachel and Caroline, and, in reply Ginny's letters read as if she were a housewife in a very ordinary suburb of Washington. She did not even use headed writing-paper. She wrote of Alex's progress at school, that Blair had been 'travelling' again; she sent the crayon pictures Chris made for Aunt Dena. '*When will I see Rachel again?*' she wrote laboriously. '*I bet I'm better at riding than she is.*' Little slips like that gave away the privileged but to Alex and Chris the ordinary background of their lives.

'Don't worry,' Harry said to Dena, 'and don't imagine the powers that be in the Kremlin don't know that our two daughters are goddaughters of that arch capitalist, Andrew McClintock. It sometimes amazes me that the Foreign Office sent me here . . .'

'Me too, Paris would have been more appropriate. If only you hadn't learned Russian.'

'Then I'd better not start on Turkish . . . I don't think you'd find Ankara very comfortable.'

They gratefully welcomed spring to Moscow, watched the mounds of snow melt in the courtyard, and in the sidestreets. Watched the ice break on the river. The first buds appeared on the trees. Gradually the winter-browned grass on the parks was uncovered. The day Dena saw a small clump of daffodils about to bloom she found tears in her eyes. She began to plan for the summer ahead, for Harry's longed-for leave. *'We're coming to London,'* she wrote to Ginny, *'and I'll never complain of the British climate again.'*

First Caroline and then Rachel went down with measles. Dena nursed them through anxious weeks, watching the symptoms of fever and spots come, and eventually fade. She had been warned to watch for complications, and dreaded their appearance. Eventually the two girls recovered, but they were listless and pale. Rachel complained of headaches; she was bored and irritable. Dena took them, into the courtyard, to sit in the sun, and when they were stronger to the park. Both of them seemed little interested in playing with other children; even Rachel's span of concentration on her books was short. Caroline was often in tears. The summer heat began to close in on Moscow. Dena dreamed of the soft English countryside.

They're all right now, but still weak and out of sorts. We just can't think of taking them on that long train journey back to London. It's exhausting even for adults. So we'll go to St Petersburg, Leningrad. It should be cooler there. It's one place we're allowed to travel to.

The bad news came in two heavy, swift blows. Harry's father died in the autumn of 1936. It was impossible for

141

Harry to get to London in time for the funeral. His brother, and other friends, sent all the obituaries. There would later be a memorial service. The Foreign Secretary wrote a personal note of condolence.

I knew him quite well, of course, years before I held this post. One of the best, most upright men I've ever encountered. Many Foreign Secretaries have reason to be grateful for Old Spade's help and advice, whether they acknowledged it or not. In my opinion, one of the greatest servants the Foreign Office ever had.

'Old Spade,' Harry repeated. 'I always wondered where he got that nickname. Meant to ask him. Perhaps he didn't know himself. So many things one forgets until it's too late to ask.' His father had been a distant figure in his childhood; his mother had died when the two boys were young. An admired figure, but one perpetually immersed in work. 'I'll have a hard time living up to his reputation in the Foreign Office . . .'

He did not attend the memorial service. It was too far to go, and it was a period when the ambassador planned to be absent from Moscow. The Foreign Office was showing a marked interest in the dispatches Harry was writing. They often went out with the ambassador's signature, but the real authorship was generously acknowledged. The Foreign Secretary had asked that they should be sent to him routinely, and the more important of them were sent on to be read by the Prime Minister.

Winter closed in again on Moscow, and Dena saw its coming with a sick heart. It was not just the weather which oppressed her. The tension in the country was almost palpable. There had been many rumours within the diplomatic corps of arrests, secret, and usually in the dead of night; contacts in the Kremlin were inexplicably and suddenly missing. The news of a great purge broke on the country in August, with the public Trial of the Sixteen, charged with organizing a secret terrorist centre under the direction of Trotsky. They were found guilty, and shot. Alleged confessions implicated others. A period of savage terror began in September. NKVD officers arrested, interrogated, and then shot thousands of people, or sent them to labour camps. Even Dena's servants grew silent and nearly hostile, because they had contact with foreigners. To have family or friends abroad was reason to fear detention. A purge hysteria gripped the country. Neighbours denounced neighbours, and even their own families. The ambassador came back quickly, and Harry went on writing his dispatches, compiling the story of the terror he saw all around him. In January 1937 came the Trial of the Seventeen. Again elaborate confessions, and executions. Leading party members seemed paralysed by fear of Stalin and the NKVD. Even to protest was to be seen as guilty by association. Harry wrote of the horror, and tried to conceal its worst excesses from Dena. But down to the lowliest clerk, the diplomatic corps knew what was happening. They seemed to crowd together more closely, as if seeking comfort and a sense of protection. But they spoke little, because that was too dangerous.

Along with the spring of 1937, when even the Red Army were caught up in the purges, came the news from Harry's brother, Richard, that their second cousin, Perry, had been killed climbing in New Zealand.

He got engaged last year but, being Perry, travelling and climbing was always more important. He didn't get around to getting married, so of course there wasn't an heir. The estate's entailed, so it and the title go to you I'm afraid Harry. Tough luck. As I see it, that tumbledown ruin of Tresillian is a rotten inheritance. There are a few farms which go with it, but the rents from the tenants barely pay the taxes and keep the roof on the place. In my opinion it would be better to tear it down. But as it was the Admiral's birth place, you might find a lot of opposition to that. I'm sorry to load this on you, Harry, but I'm selfishly glad it's your pigeon rather than mine. The solicitors will give you a fuller picture. It would be a help to them, I think, if you could arrange a visit pretty soon. But one hears things are pretty hot over there, and I don't suppose it's too easy for you to get away . . .

'Perry!' Harry murmured, in some shock. 'Why he was younger than I! Why the hell didn't he get married and have a son? Why me? Of course, my father was next in line. I didn't give Perry a thought when Father died. Why should I? There was a generation out of step somewhere. My father certainly never expected to inherit. I had only one visit there. They only ever used the place in summer. Great old tower perched practically on a cliff top. The house starting to fall into ruins, even then. A few farms, some worked-out tin mines, or uneconomic at any rate. Dena, we'll try to avoid using the title.'

'Why? With the Admiral in the background, it's rather hard to avoid. The name is Camborne.'

He sighed. 'Well I just don't like the fact of having a title when I'm working in the Foreign Office. Doesn't do to upstage one's ambassador. Of course you never outrank your ambassador diplomatically. But outsiders don't always understand.'

Inevitably word spread through the diplomatic corps. The wife of the American first secretary, who knew she could joke with Dena, asked: 'Are you Lady Camborne now?'

Dena lit a cigarette, trying to mask her agitation. 'It would be easier to inherit a title if some money went with it. I suspect we'll continue to be poor as church mice. But people will expect something a bit better from us.'

She wrote a guarded letter to Ginny:

It's rather a volcano in one's life. Harry's father dying was bad enough, but this development has been sprung on us. I so much hope, Ginny, that you and Blair are in London during the summer. There's a chance Harry will get leave, though things are difficult here. Some time he has to get to this Tresillian place. Things have to be looked into. We don't know . . . Well there it is, my dearest friend. We just don't know. I need you.

Rather the way I needed you that evening on the bridge.

In June they left Moscow as the purge of the Red Army gathered fury. They began the long journey to London. Ginny and Blair greeted them there. They sank into the haven of Seymour House, the children became re-acquainted with one another. Christine had an English governess, Alex had an American tutor. They had all grown and changed, but the old alliances were re-established.

Harry had only a month's leave. He spent many hours with his solicitors. At his request, Blair attended some of the meetings. 'After all,' Harry said, 'you're the lawyer.' The facts of the estate were becoming plain. There was little indebtedness, but little income. The dreaded words, 'death duties' were heard. 'They will amount to very little, Lord Camborne. The house and lands are not very valuable in their present state. No income comes from the mines. There's a potentially valuable china-clay pit, but in these times the product isn't wanted. No pictures or anything else of great value to sell, unfortunately. Farming is depressed. Some of the farmers are well behind on their rents. Should we put eviction notices on them?'

'Good God, no! Give them whatever chance they have these days.'

'There are inevitable expenses, Lord Camborne . . .'

'Well, let the roof fall in. Do you think if I'm sent to Outer Mongolia it will help me sleep easier at night knowing I've taken the roof from other people's heads. We'll manage . . .'

The principal solicitor looked alarmed. 'Outer Mongolia, Lord Camborne? Surely not . . .'

'A family joke. Don't worry. It might only be Liberia.'

So they had some days of what Dena called 'freedom' in London. 'I can't describe,' she said to Ginny, 'how wonderful it feels to be able to speak again. To say almost anything.' They had spent most of that sunny afternoon out in St James's Park. Now it was time to go back for tea. The children, the governess and the tutor were ahead of them. Both involuntarily paused at almost the centre of the bridge over the lake, gazing towards Buckingham Palace. 'Best of all, to be able to talk to you.'

So they all travelled down to Cornwall in two cars. The children were excited at the thought of adventure, of a castle, a real castle, by the sea. Harry and Dena viewed the visit with hardly disguised apprehension.

Chapter 6

1

Isa experienced appehension. She had never known anyone to live at Tresillian. There had been only brief summer visits when she had been too young to go and help there. It had been, for more than the past ten years, a empty house on its height above St Just. Now there would be the new Lord Camborne, with a wife and two children. But they had been told by the solicitors to expect two more guests, Americans, with their own two children and a tutor and a governess. Isa's hands twisted in her apron with nervousness. She had never known an American before. And what would the new Lord Camborne be like? She went on a round of final inspection of the rooms. The best she and her cousins had been able to do was to see that they were clean, the beds well aired, the towels laid out. She hoped the old boiler would supply the demands for hot water. Wherever possible she had brightened the dark corners with flowers. She could do nothing about the stains on the ceilings, the smell of damp that would not be driven out of some places. Every fireplace was laid ready to put a match to. The pantry was full of her baking: bread and pies and pasties. There was ham and chicken and several kinds of local cheese. Soup waited to be heated on the iron stove. She didn't know what time they would come.

They arrived about six on that bright summer's evening. It was very calm; no cloud moved in the sky. The tide was on the ebb, and it would be hours before it began its vicious swirl around the Tresillian Rocks. Waiting in the kitchen, their tea finished, Isa and her two cousins heard the sounds of the cars outside. But Livy, who had been waiting at the bend in the drive, dashed in by the stable-yard door. 'They're here!

They've come!' The three women rushed out to help with the baggage. Livy, overtaken by a new experience of shyness, hung back. Bully, curious to know what the sudden fuss was about, had ambled out to investigate. Livy grabbed Tubby to her for comfort, and sat in the big wheel-backed chair by the stove, trying to pretend the sounds of the strangers' arrival did not disturb or even interest her. But she licked dry lips and knew the feeling of resentment. Her kingdom had been invaded. Her castle had been taken from her.

She heard their voices. There seemed to be so many of them. She heard racing footsteps on the stairs. The light voices of children, the deeper voices of the adults. For Livy the castle had never resounded to so many voices before; she knew its secret voices, the whisper within it when the light summer breezes blew, the deeper, harsher notes when the gales found the breaks in its fabric. But this . . .? This sounded like an alien invasion.

She heard a strange voice, deep, throaty, an accent she had never heard before, even among the summer visitors.

'Harry, Dena.' A woman's voice. 'This is magnificent! But what are you going to do with it?'

The answer came in a lower tone, doubtful, a little dismayed. 'I don't know what we can do with it. We didn't want it. It just came.'

There, Livy thought, they didn't want it. They would go away. Eventually they would go away, and she would have it back to herself. She hugged Tubby more tightly. 'They won't take it from us,' she said to Tubby, fiercely.

It was inevitable that they would invade the kitchen. The children had raced around on the second floor, then clattered down the back staircase, and came out on the little hallway that led to the kitchen. Their headlong rush was halted as they encountered and sta ed at Livy. She took them in quickly. A tall boy, dark, very good-looking, two girls about her own age, though the dark one looked as if she were already striving to overtake the boy. And then a younger blonde one, with extraordinary blue eyes. Bully had come padding into the kitchen, having lumbered up and down stairs, trying to keep track of all the newcomers; Isa had to

148

introduce him to each one of them, so that he was reassured that they rightfully belonged here. He trotted silently to Livy's side, and squatted with a loud grunt.

Livy, Bully and Tubby all stared at the strangers. The youngest one put her thumb in her mouth; the dark girl snatched it out again.

The boy said, 'Who are you?'

'Olivia.' It was the first time she had ever used her own name fully.

'Do you live here.?'

She nodded. 'Yes and down there.' She jerked her head in the direction of the town.

'Well,' he said, 'come and show us the rest of the place. Everything—the secret rooms, the dungeons.'

'How do you know there are secret rooms?'

'Because . . .' the boy answered, 'because places like this, castles, always have secret rooms. They have to!'

Gently Livy dropped Tubby to the floor. Bully rose, prepared to accompany her wherever she went. 'I'll show you then,' Livy said, with a faintly proprietorial air. There were things she knew which they did not and there was the treasure-house of Cornish legends which her father had related to her. She reinforced her slight authority by saying, 'But there are two places you must not go.'

'What are they?' the boy demanded. 'Why not?'

'You can't go into the Tower, and you mustn't go down to the Tresillian Rocks. They can kill you.'

The youngest looked as if she was going to cry. Her thumb moved back towards her mouth. 'I don't like this place. I don't like dungeons and secret rooms.'

Livy felt sorry for her. She looked tired and a little grubby. 'The dungeons are only the cellars. There are only a few cubby holes, not really secret rooms. The Tower's only dangerous because it's falling down. And the Rocks are only dangerous when the tide turns. You can get caught down there. It isn't as if there was a dragon, or anything.' She held out her hand to the little girl. She didn't realize then that Caroline was only a year younger than she. 'Come on, I'll show you.'

149

That night the children ate in the kitchen for convenience, watched over by Christine's English governess, Miss Bonner, and the young American college man who was called Alex's tutor, but was a sort of companion to him for the summer only. They had their pre-dinner drinks, seated at the table with the children. The little group was hungry, and quite tired. They ate whatever Isa put before them. Although Livy had eaten earlier, with her mother, they evidently expected her to sit down with them. She did. The boy, whom she now called Alex, fed pieces of ham and chicken to Bully and Tubby. 'You're not supposed to do that,' Livy said, 'but I expect it's all right, because it's your first night here. You have to watch Bully. He'll take everything you've got.'

'I never saw a dog like Bully before.'

'He's terribly ugly, isn't he?' Caroline said.

'Don't be rude,' her sister Rachel admonished her.

'I wish I had one like him,' Christine said. She looked rather wistfully towards Miss Bonner, hoping the hint would be passed on to her parents.

'He was a little puppy when he came to the town with my father,' Livy said. 'That was before I was born.' She added, with pride. 'My father was a poet.'

Isa watched her child being absorbed into the little group; no strain seemed to exist between them. There were no barriers. Even in those first hours she seemed to cross the line from the town into Tresillian as if she had been born here, as if indeed she were the princess of this castle. For the first time she could remember since Oliver Miles's death, Isa heard Livy laugh. She silently blessed this little crowd of tired, hungry children; she would give every skill she had and every waking hour to make it the sort of summer she already sensed these two families sought: a summer of peace and careless freedom.

Dena and Harry, Ginny and Blair sat in the library after the children were in bed and Miss Bonner and the young American had withdrawn. They could hear the distant crash of the sea against the Tresillian Rocks. The last of the long

150

summer twilight had almost gone. No one switched on a light. The shabbiness of the room was masked, its beauty shone.

'Wouldn't you just know it of a place like this?' Harry asked. 'One goes through it and disturbs the ghosts, and then finds in the kitchen the widow and child of one of England's finest poets of this century.'

'Beautiful woman,' Ginny observed. She almost yawned; it had been a long journey. The sea air made her sleepy.

'And a very good cook,' Dena added, 'if dinner was anything to go by.'

'The child will be even more beautiful,' Blair said. 'What eyes. Like the sea.'

'I'd say our kids are lucky having her,' Harry said. 'Well, I'm going to bed, if I can remember where our room is. You'll have to overlook the deficiencies, Ginny. Rusty old baths and clanking loos. A bit of damp here and there . . .'

'And a magnificent house. Spectacular scenery. Fresh, fresh air. We all need it, I think.'

Harry had less than three weeks of his leave left. Blair would return to London in a few days, and come down as many weekends as he could manage. Harry had decreed that Dena and the girls must stay for the whole summer. 'You need the break. The children need this sort of holiday to set them up for the Moscow winter . . .' Ginny and Alex and Chris would remain until it was time for Alex to return to Washington for the opening of school. Almost two long idle months stretched before them. A summer of ease. For Dena the spectre of Moscow began to drop away. A summer of freedom and contentment.

2

For Livy it was a magical summer. She could almost forget her longing for her father in the excitement of these new friends. They accepted her without question among them. Alex was naturally dominant; the only boy among them, and ten years old, but Livy was there as a counterbalance,

151

because this was her country and they the strangers she could introduce to it. Rachel was in a hurry to grow up, eager for knowledge and experience; Christine was her softer counterpart, more reliant on her mother and Miss Bonner. Caroline, although only two years younger than her sister and Christine, seemed, at five, to be determined to cling to the vestiges of her babyhood and the privileges it gave her. 'She hasn't even been to school yet,' Rachel said, with a touch of scorn. 'And she doesn't know any Russian. Won't even try to learn.'

Every day Livy begged from Rachel a few words in Russian, and tried to memorize them. 'Haven't you got any Cornish in exchange?' Livy shook her head, ashamed.

'Not many people speak Cornish now and my father was English.'

Through Livy they were beginning to understand the difference. When they went down to St Just, Livy was greeted in every street, and it seemed there were many doors where she could knock and be welcomed. She brought them all with her—Alex, Rachel and Christine, Caroline, and Miss Bonner and the American, Mr Aimes. Pasties were handed out, not because they were Lord Camborne's children and guests, but because they were Livy's friends. They learned the names Tregenna and Trevallas and Penhale, all cousins or aunts or uncles of Livy. In one of the little shops that catered to tourists, Mr Aimes found some volumes of Oliver Miles's poetry, and became a devoted admirer. With permission, they all visited the studios of some of Oliver Miles's friends, but Thea Sedgemore and Herbert Gardiner were the favourites, and Thea's sculpture intrigued and fascinated them. Blair and Ginny came to look and admire. Blair bought two of Herbert's pictures, and rather diffidently commissioned a piece from Thea. 'Something to go out on a big expanse of lawn at Prescott Hill. Something not too esoteric for a Southern house, but not what anyone's expecting.' He knew the then experimental nature of Thea's work. He shrugged. 'Who am I to tell you? It will be what it will be. I'll be proud to have it.'

The children loved, as Livy always had done, Thea's

garden. They swarmed all over her sculptures. 'I wonder how she puts up with them,' Ginny said to Dena.

'I think she's Livy's godmother, not that that explains her tolerance . . .'

On fine days (they were becoming aware of how fickle the Cornish weather could be) they piled into Ginny's car and made expeditions to some of the great and largely secret places of Cornwall. They drove on Bodmin Moor, picnicked by Rough Tor, saw the sunlight shine through Trethevy Quoit, fantastic mounds of great stones, balanced one upon the other, evidence of something man-made that had slipped from mind centuries ago, places of pagan worship. Never having had the use of a car, Livy had never before seen these places, but she had heard them spoken of. Even her childish recounting of the Arthurian legend was stilled as she gazed in awe at the great stones.

'How did they ever get them there?' Alex wondered. Neither Miss Bonner or anyone else could offer an answer. It was lost in time.

'Be sure you remember them,' Harry said. 'Not everything has an explanation. Not readily available, that is. My brother once came here and figured out something mathematically about the sun on Midsummer's Morning. I didn't understand it.'

Livy became totally, for that summer, part of the family. Often she forgot they were really two families, they melded so completely. Lord Camborne departed for London, and then on to Moscow. Rachel brought out an atlas and showed Livy exactly where the train journey would take him. 'We'll be going back in September . . .' The thought made Livy sad. With Alex she traced the route to New York that his ship would take. His mother and Christine would go with him; they might be, Ginny said, coming back to London during the winter. 'Mr Clayton comes and goes a lot,' she explained to Livy. 'I try to stay with him.'

Livy was learning a great deal from these children, as well as giving to them. For two hours a day, lessons, in a more formal style, went on. 'I have to earn my keep,' Mr Aimes said sheepishly. 'I don't have a degree yet . . . but Mr

153

McClintock wanted . . . well, let's just say he didn't want another woman with Alex. Seems to think there are enough around.'

So they sat together, the five children. Miss Bonner had the first hour, Mr Aimes the second. She read to them from English history and gave them spelling lessons. Mr Aimes was majoring in American history at Princeton. Livy heard of things and places she had never known before, and probably wouldn't have heard of if she had not been among them. She sensed that it was something far beyond the dame school. She listened avidly. Then one day Miss Bonner read a poem none of them understood. 'It is by an English poet. His name is Oliver Miles.'

Livy seemed an essential, a binding part of that small group in those, for her, enchanted weeks. There were two cars, a small, rather rusty affair Lord Camborne had bought second hand, and a long, serviceable vehicle which belonged to the Claytons. They all referred to it as 'the Rolls'. Miss Bonner, like many before her, was smitten with the Arthurian legend, and the story of Tristan and Iseult, and wondered if they weren't one and the same. They went searching for Arthur's seat; they visited likely and unlikely places, they went back to the stone monuments on the moors. Livy advised them, 'If the stone has a hole in it, like the Men-an-Tol, the wisest thing to do is to crawl through it nine times against the sun.' They did so. In such things as the monuments, they began dimly to perceive the origins of Thea Sedgemore's sculpture. They gazed at the pillar, seven feet high, half a mile from King Mark's fortress, Castle Dor. The words inscribed there, translated, read 'Tristan lies here, son of Mark'.

They realized that the country was dotted with the ruins of the chimney stacks and engine houses, ivy-covered, of the tin and copper mines. In the nineteenth century Cornwall had produced most of the world's tin and copper. Dena pointed to the ruined stacks on the headland across from Tresillian. 'What a pity they're not economic now. We'd be rich.' She looked again at the house. 'They must have been rather rich then, to have built such a place. A pity the roof

154

leaks. We might have rented it. We still haven't decided what we should do with it. Harry says the entail can be broken . . . but it's a long business, and he hasn't time to go into it just now.' His first letter had arrived from Moscow. It contained little but trivial news. Dena knew what it did not say. The newspapers carried only scanty news of the purges of the Red Army and Navy, but she knew the storm of terror still raged.

Blair had gone to Zurich and then on to New York. They were alone. 'It's like old times,' Ginny said. 'Just you and I.'

'Old times and a parcel of kids.' Dena replied. 'Does it seem so very long ago to you, Ginny? I mean when we met on the bridge? I don't feel much older, but I look at the children and I know I must be. I wish I felt more . . . more mature.'

'You will . . . but only when you're much older. By that time people will be telling you how young you look. That's when you'll know you're not young.'

Livy felt a responsibility, along with her mother and two Tregenna aunts, for looking after the family. She was dismayed at the state of 'the Rolls'. To her it was a beautiful thing, and badly used. Lady Camborne called it a shooting brake, but Livy didn't know what that meant. The vehicle was muddy, and the carpets inside needed sweeping. One morning, while her mother was cooking breakfast, Livy started about the task of sorting out the piles of gumboots and fishing tackle, sweeping out the pieces of broken biscuits and hard crusts of bread, the remnants of their picnics. These she simply threw into the air, and watched as the seagulls swooped and dived for them. Then she went and brought a pail of water, and started washing off the worst of the dried mud. 'Livy! What on earth are you doing? No one told you to do that!'

Livy blushed. 'I wasn't doing any harm, Mrs Clayton. It just seems such a pity. It's a beautiful car. My mother says it's the best car there is. I don't like to see it dirty.'

Ginny squatted down beside her, and looked directly into her face. 'That's all right, Livy. I'm not angry. Just so long as you wanted to do it yourself. No one told you to do it?'

'No, no one told me to. I just wanted to . . .'

Suddenly she felt Ginny's arms about her, hugging her fiercely. 'Oh, what can I say? I wish my two selfish little monsters would sometimes have thought like that.'

'They're not selfish. They share everything with me. Alex lends me his books, even though he knows some of the words are too hard for me. But the pictures are beautiful. And Chris gave me the most beautiful jumper the other day. My mother says it's cashmere. I never felt anything like that before. It was all right for her to give it to me, wasn't it?'

'If she wanted to give it, I'm very pleased. Get Alex to help you with the hard words. Now come in to breakfast. I'm starving.'

Livy replaced the boots and the fishing tackle. Ginny poured the water out of the pail. She took Livy's hand and led her through the stable yard back to the kitchen.

'Two hungry women, Mrs Miles. We wondered if we could have a piece of toast before breakfast? Livy's been working so hard.'

'I hope she's not bothering you, Mrs Clayton.' Livy had gone out to the stillroom, where the milk and butter were kept. 'You're all very good to her. I hope she doesn't put herself forward. It's difficult, hard, you see, for her to know just where she belongs. She's found that some people come to St Just to see the house where her father lived. She doesn't understand the difference between things, that her father was, well, famous, in a way, and that I'm only an ordinary woman. Her father—'

'Livy is precious to us all, Mrs Miles. Our children are lucky to have her for a friend. We're all lucky to have her. She's been fortunate in both her parents.'

Isa put her head down, and banged the big iron pan on the stove with unnecessary force. 'I'll have the bacon going in a second, Mrs Clayton. I hear the rest of them coming downstairs. Livy! What's keeping you? Help make the toast, now.'

As their last week at Tresillian began, Andrew McClintock arrived about noon one day, driven by his chauffeur. 'I hope you don't mind,' he· said, with a perfunctory gesture of courtesy. 'I took the precaution of booking a room at a hotel in Penzance, but you look as if you might have a few spare rooms here. Thought I'd look in and see what my grandson and goddaughters were up to this summer. Quite a collection of them I have now.' He was strolling around the unkempt grounds, and had reached the foot of the Tower. He pointed his cane at it, and to the steep path that led to the cove below, now uncovered by the low tide, and revealing the vicious fangs of the Tresillian Rocks. 'I hope you're very careful. It would be possible to lose half of them in one little accident between these two decorative amenities.' By this time they had all come out to greet him. He stared around at them all. 'Well, I must say, this place seems to agree with you. You all look healthy as . . . well, now, who's this?' He pointed his cane at Livy, who then shrank back.

'It's Livy,' Alex said. 'She lives here with her mother. Her father is . . . was . . .' He struggled for the right word, '. . . a famous poet.'

'Ah so you're the one.' As always, Andrew McClintock had been well briefed. 'The child of the Cornish legends. I wonder if Iseult had red hair. All Celts, of course . . .' He seemed to gazed off into the distance, beyond St Just, into the greyness of the place where the Irish Sea and the Atlantic met. Then he turned. 'Well, don't just stand there. Am I to stay the night here, or not?'

'You'll have a room and a bed, just as soon as Ginny and I can get it ready for you,' Dena replied. 'We can't expect Mrs Miles to do everything and the other women would just get flustered if we threw them out of routine. Lunch will be ready soon. I'll get Chris and Rachel to lay another place.'

'Homely,' he remarked. 'Good to know the girls are of some use. I suppose you, boy,' he poked Alex's cheek. 'I suppose you're having a whale of a time, with all these females to boss around.'

'Livy doesn't let him boss us around,' Chris said. 'She tells him what's what.'

'Oh, I'm glad to hear it, young woman,' Andrew McClintock said. 'You don't have your red hair for nothing.'

157

So far, Livy had not uttered a word. She had heard, of course, of this grandfather, and godfather. They all spoke of him with a suggestion of awe. She backed away, and then turned and ran to the back door of the kitchen.

'He's come,' she said to her mother. 'Alex's grandfather. He has a big stick, and he scares me . . .' She usually took her meals with the other children, but this day she refused to go into the dining-room until Alex came to fetch her. 'Grandfather wants to know what's wrong? Does he scare you?' Alex leaned towards her confidentially. 'He'd like to think he did. He likes to scare people. So you'd better come . . . just to show you're not scared.'

Livy combed her hair, made sure her hands were clean, and joined them in the big dining-room. The children hardly spoke during the meal, constrained by the presence of Andrew McClintock. This was the meal they always took with the adults. Breakfast was in the kitchen, and so was their evening meal, which, under Isa's supervision, was an unrestrained affair. Andrew McClintock took his time over the soup and the steak and kidney pie. He drank appreciatively the best wine that Dena could find in the cellar, mentally breathing a prayer of thanks to her dead cousin, Perry, for having laid down a few cases of good quality wine. They finished with peach pie and clotted cream, and a Somerset cheddar. Andrew McClintock lingered over the last of his wine.

'My compliments to Mrs Miles,' he said. 'One of the best meals I've had for a long time.' He looked directly at Livy. 'I hope you inherit your mother's talent.' And to Chris and Rachel and Caroline he said, 'And you lot had better pay attention. It never hurts to be able to cook.'

'Lady Camborne is teaching us some things,' Livy said, 'and my mother's learning them too.'

'Ah, yes. Our *cordon-bleu* chef,' Andrew McClintock said. 'Be sure you don't leave those copper pots behind in Moscow. Too good for the Bolshies. They were my idea. I like women with pots and pans and sewing machines. Now all you kids get out of here. And be careful. Be careful around that damned Tower and don't go down into that

158

cove.' He glared at Ginny. 'You didn't tell me there were such damn dangerous things about.'

'To live is to take chances, Mr McClintock,' Dena said.

'So it is, Lady Camborne.' He used the name with mock deference. Like all the others, he called her Dena. 'Now tell me – yes, I will, thank you,' he said, as Ginny offered more wine. 'Now tell me . . . Just how did it happen that Harry came to be Lord Camborne? Rather mixed up family history, isn't it, and desperately short on male heirs. Hopeless ruin of a place he inherited, but the title can't hurt him . . .'

In the early evening, while the adults had their drinks, the children gathered in the kitchen for their supper, thankful to be with Isa rather than face Andrew McClintock again. 'Are we really all his goddaughters?' Caroline whispered. She had not dared open her mouth in his presence. Livy came in age between her and Rachel and Chris, and that summer Caroline had come to trust Livy more than she did the other girls. To her, Alex was almost a distant god, to be obeyed unquestioningly.

'All of us. But Alex is his grandson,' Rachel said. 'That's different . . .' She turned to Livy's mother. 'Mrs Miles, what exactly does a godfather or a godmother do?'

'Why, child, they take care of you. They see that you love God, and fear the devil. But there really isn't any devil. Just the one you make yourself.'

'If there isn't any devil, where is God?' Caroline asked.

'All about you. In the sea and the sky. In Livy's father's poems. In Rachel and Caroline's great-grandfather's paintings. In Mr Gardiner's paintings. In Mrs Sedgemore's work. Go into Mrs Sedgemore's garden one day and watch the rain run through those sculptures that some people say are heathenish – and that's where God is.'

'I'll go,' Alex said. 'I'd like to meet God.'

'You won't meet Him, Master Alex. If you're lucky you'll see some of His creation.'

'I think my grandfather believes he created almost everything in the world.'

'With all respect, Master Alex, then more fool your grandfather.'

159

The next morning Andrew McClintock appeared in the kitchen long before anyone but Isa was stirring. 'May I share a cup of your tea, Mrs Miles?' He seated himself at the long, scrubbed kitchen table, as if this were the greatest banqueting hall to which he had ever been privileged to be invited. 'A lovely room, but a bit primitive. Marvellous how you manage that stove.' He eyed the freshly-baked bread, the dough she was kneading for the pasties which were always in demand from the children. Silently she poured tea for him, using a good cup, and placed milk and sugar by his hand.

'I think you'd rather have coffee, Mr McClintock, but I don't make it until Mrs Clayton comes down to breakfast. The coffee beans come from Bath, and I grind them fresh. She's always said she likes the way I make it, but then Mrs Clayton's a kind lady.'

He was very direct, as always. 'And your child, Mrs Miles. What's to become of her?'

She looked at him, half fearfully, half hostile to his question. She did not like the fact that he had so rapidly gone to the heart of her secret worry. 'What's to become of her? Why, she'll grow up, just like any other child.'

'Will she? She's not quite an ordinary child.' He pushed back his chair and rose. 'Well, Mrs Miles, it was very kind of you to allow me into your sanctum. That was an excellent meal last night . . . I'm thinking of staying another day. What will there be for dinner tonight?'

She flushed with pleasure. Last night she had made veal in saffron sauce. 'We've always used garlic, but Lady Camborne got the saffron. Makes a treat, doesn't it? Tonight, well I'm making a chicken liver *pâté*, as Lady Camborne taught me, and there's lobster. For lunch there's stargazy pie . . .'

'Stargazy pie? and what might that be?'

'Oh, that's pie with grilled pilchards with their head sticking out the sides, I suppose looking at the stars, if you like . . .'

'Well . . . I'd be interested to try it. Imagine . . . stargazy pie . . .' He wandered out into the stable yard. If she hadn't believed that Andrew McClintock wasn't capable of laughter, she would have thought she heard him chuckle.

160

The next morning he was back in the kitchen, asking for tea. 'You rise early, Mrs Miles.'

'Always have, Mr McClintock. Always plenty to do. And I do enjoy the early mornings in the summer. Lovely time to do the baking and get started on lunch . . . It's nice to hear the birds. I have a little garden in our cottage in the town. I leave the door open so I can hear them.' Bully had come to stand gazing up at Andrew McClintock, and was eventually rewarded with a piece of fresh-baked bread piled with the rich Cornish butter. 'Oh, there, you do spoil him, Mr McClintock! He's had a wonderful summer, with all the children. All the extra bits and pieces they slip to him. He loves all the company. Always has been a dog for company. Got it from my husband, I suppose. My husband loved people . . . loved to talk . . .'

Her shyness left her as Andrew McClintock sat there, sipping his tea. He asked her many things about her life, her husband's life. She laid out the simple story of her brief years with Oliver Miles, and the thread of love was a shining strand woven through it. 'Never did understand how he came to take to me. I didn't have education or anything.'

'You have a great deal, Mrs Miles. Your husband was a very fortunate man . . .' He gave the last of his bread to Bully, and for a moment ran his fingers over the heavy folds of that dark, mournful-looking muzzle. Then he got up. 'Thank you, Mrs Miles. You have made my stay most enjoyable. Stargazy pie . . . I will remember that.' For him it was an awkward moment. He was accustomed to tipping lavishly, but he was less skilled at giving. 'Anything I can do for the child . . . anything. May I offer my thanks?' He left an envelope on the table.

Except for Oliver's insurance policy it was the largest amount of cash Isa had ever had in one piece in all her life. She stared at it, torn between the desire to rush after this rather domineering stranger and hand back his money, and the knowledge that to do so would insult him, would negate the friendliness of his visits to the kitchen. She looked at the money, and knew that it would pay for at least another year at the dame school for Livy, and perhaps more. It would

161

buy coal and replenish her larder with tea and other expensive items. It would buy books for Livy. She brushed away the tears that threatened. She tried to imagine a world where it was possible to give away so much money, and failed.

3

As suddenly as they had come, they were gone. The two cars were packed up, and they left. Livy kissed Rachel and Chris, hugged Caroline to her desperately, shook Alex's hand, all in a state of disbelief. Of course she had known that they must go, but hadn't been able to visualize the reality. They couldn't be going, and leaving her behind. But they were going, Lady Camborne, Rachel and Caroline back to Moscow; Mrs Clayton, Alex and Chris to Washington, with Miss Bonner and Mr Aimes. She started to thank Lady Camborne and Mrs Clayton as her mother had taught her to do. 'Thank you for a wonderful summer,' she managed to get out, 'and all the other things . . .' The disbelief and woe in the face of the child moved Ginny. She squatted and hugged her. 'Next time we come back to London you must come and visit us. You're old enough to travel on the train by yourself if your mother speaks to the guard. I'll write . . .'

Dena held the bright red head against her. 'I wish we could take you with us, little one. It's just too far, and you'd miss your mother, and Bully and Tubby . . . and everything . . . We'll probably be here next summer . . .'

They didn't mean any of it, Livy thought. They were only saying these things because it was time to go. She had lived through all these people this summer, learned from them, shared her little knowledge with them. Her world had expanded, and now it was closing again. They wouldn't come back. Hadn't Lady Camborne said right at the beginning that they had never wanted Tresillian? Livy felt that she was being lumped with the discarded clothes and toys and books they were leaving behind.

Dena bent to kiss the child, and she could see the tears that brimmed in her eyes; she wasn't surprised when Livy

162

broke away, and ran towards the stable yard and the sanctuary of the kitchen. It would have been too much to expect her to stand and watch the cars drive off. Dena had the sick feeling of leaving behind a loved and loving dog, who does not understand that the parting would not be for ever.

That night Isa counted all the money Dena and Ginny had given her, extra to her wages. She added it to the pile Andrew McClintock had thrust on her. It would be an easy winter. Livy would have new clothes and go to the dame school, she would have all the books she needed. She would have a warm room to study in. She would live as Oliver Miles's daughter should.

The two Tregenna cousins had been paid off, but a young man, Austell, would keep up the vegetable garden, and tend the trees in the walled orchard. Isa would come up to the castle every day, to clean and air, just as she had always done. There was some promise of continuity in all this, some hope that, after all, the families would return. But she could not forget the eyes of her child, and the supper which all Isa's coaxing and commands could not induce her to eat. Sensing that this would be a hard and silent evening, Isa had baked Livy's favourite cake, and Livy would not touch it. She had the look of someone deserted and betrayed. She looked almost as she had done after her father's death.

'I'm glad we're going,' Livy had said fiercely as they went back down the hill to St Just. Isa carried the two suitcases, Livy carried Tubby, and Bully walked beside them. Each day Isa would bring down some of the books left behind for Livy. Isa lighted the first fire of the autumn in the kitchen of the little cottage. Livy sat on the stone in the garden by her father's bench until the sun had dipped behind the high wall. Then she went to visit Thea and Herbert.

Through the window, Thea observed the child's face as she wandered through the garden, stopping by each of the sculptures, touching one or two which were her favourites. 'She thinks her world has collapsed,' she said to her husband.

'To a degree, it has,' he answered. 'I wonder if they ever will come back?'

He went to the door and opened it before the child could

knock. 'Welcome back. We wondered how long it would be before you came to see your old friends . . .'

The tears that had threatened during the two days since the families had departed suddenly burst in a torrent. Herbert held her wiry little body close to him, and tried to comfort her. 'I'll never love anyone again . . .'

Thea gave her a small glass of sherry, and persuaded her to have a few mouthfuls of soup and bread. Livy fell asleep lying across Herbert's knees before the fire. He wrapped a rug about her, and carried her back to Isa. 'Broken hearts do mend,' he said, 'but there's no use telling her that just now.'

By the time the Camborne family had reached Moscow, by the time the Claytons were back in Washington, the dame school had reopened and Livy was once again absorbed. She seemed deliberately to seek to put the memory of the summer behind her, as if it had been a dream not to be repeated. She started to take some interest in the books Isa had brought down from Tresillian. Isa watched, and her confidence grew that Livy would be all right. She had begun to think of what she must do when Livy had outgrown the dame school. Where would she find the money to send her to the sort of school she should have? It would be away from St Just and it would cost much more. She didn't even know where Livy should go. Isa placed all her faith in the wisdom and friendship of Thea and Herbert. They would advise her. If it came to having to raise some money as a loan, with the cottage as security, Herbert would surely advise her how to approach the bank. Isa hated the idea of the security of this little cottage being threatened, but Livy must have whatever was necessary. She lay awake at nights, missing Oliver, thinking and scheming years into the future.

Almost three weeks after the families had left Tresillian, a letter with a Cunard crest on the envelope, and an American stamp arrived for Livy. Isa watched the child's face carefully as she handed it to her. 'It's from Alex!' Livy read its brief contents slowly, savouring each word. 'He wrote it on the ship . . . He hates the thought of going back to school. He says he had a wonderful summer, and thanks us both. He says he misses us . . . Tresillian . . . St Just, you and Bully and Tubby. He misses me!' That evening she read its one brief page over and over, and went to sleep with it under her pillow. Much later there came notes from Moscow, a fairly lengthy one from Rachel, a short one from Caroline bemoaning the fact that she had to start at the school for the children of the diplomatic corps.

There were Christmas cards, handmade from Rachel and Caroline, splendidly decorated and sparkling ones from Alex and Chris. In February came the letter from Mrs Clayton to Isa.

We will be in London for a few weeks in March. I hope, Mrs Miles, that you will allow Livy to come for a short visit. If you are agreeable, my husband's office will make all the necessary arrangements.

Livy glowed with happiness. 'She meant it!'

The ticket, first-class, came, with money 'for expenses'. Herbert drove Livy and Isa to Penzance to take the early morning train. Bully also came to say goodbye, to mark the momentous nature of the journey, the first Livy had ever taken by train. Not trusting the buffet car, and not wanting to cost Mrs Clayton any unnecessary money, Isa had made up a package of sandwiches and fruit. Thea had made Livy a present of a new coat, and a skirt and jumper; Isa had provided patent leather shoes and what she thought of as a 'party' dress. Livy listened to all the instructions, and could hardly breathe with excitement. She had a large label attached to the lapel of her coat with her name and address, and Mrs Clayton's. Herbert tipped the guard to keep an eye on her.

At Paddington Mrs Clayton and Chris waited for her. 'Oh, you've grown!' Chris said. 'Don't you look nice! You've got some new teeth! So have I!' In the middle of the station, while the porter waited with Livy's bag, Chris insisted on showing the new permanent teeth.

'Are you tired, little one?' Ginny asked, for the first time seeing the child away from her native place and sensing both her excitement and bewilderment. 'What a long day you've had. Never mind, we'll soon be home.'

The car that waited outside the station was much grander even than the one Mrs Clayton had brought to Tresillian. Livy tentatively touched the pale grey upholstered seats, wondering if she should even sit on them. Chris chatted away, and Mrs Clayton pointed out various things as they drove by. Livy was too excited and tired to take in much of what was said. They drove past a building which Mrs Clayton told her was St James's Palace, and then almost immediately arrived at Seymour House. Mrs Clayton had to hold Livy's hand as they ascended the steps. Tresillian was much bigger, but Livy had an instinctive impression of grandeur here. She had never seen a butler before, nor had any idea of what the two young men in some sort of uniform were supposed to do. One carried her shabby suitcase, which had belonged to her father, up the stairs of a great marble hall. Suddenly Livy desperately wanted to go to the toilet. She had been afraid to use the one on the train. She managed to whisper her need to Mrs Clayton. 'Chris will show you . . .'

They didn't go upstairs, but to a cloakroom for ladies on the ground floor with velvet curtains and carpet, embroidered towels, and small, marvellously-scented pieces of soap in many different colours in a cut glass jar. The room was lighted with two small chandeliers. The flush of the toilet was silent and smooth. These were the sort of things Livy thought existed only in fairy stories, except fairies never went to the toilet. When they came out, Ginny looked at Livy's pale face, with two hectic spots of colour in the cheeks. 'You need tea, my dear, and then bed, I think . . .'

They had tea in the library. It was not as large as the library at Tresillian, but again touched with the sense of luxury and splendour. The cakes weren't any better to eat than those her mother made, but daintier and iced in many different colours. The sandwiches were wafer thin. Mrs Clayton waved away the white-gloved footman who came to serve them, knowing that his presence would petrify the child. 'I brought some of my own food,' Livy volunteered. 'Mother sent some things for you . . .'

166

'That's very kind of your mother. She shouldn't have . . .'
At last Livy got the words out. 'Where is Alex?'

'Alex is at school, Livy. I thought you knew that. He's at his school in America. Just outside Washington. He boards there. We're only here for three weeks, and then we go back. Alex can't leave school in the middle of the term. That's why we have Miss Bonner for Chris, so she can travel with her father and me. But eventually Chris will have to go to school, too.' She was astonished as tears began to roll down Livy's cheeks. Instantly she was at the child's side, holding her. 'Why, Livy, whatever's the matter?'

'Still in America? And Lady Camborne and Rachel and Caroline are in Russia. She showed me how far away it is. I never thought families weren't with one another all the time.'

'Only lucky families stay together all the time, Livy. If we didn't come over here, Chris and I, Mr Clayton would have to be alone, don't you see? But don't worry. We'll all be back at Tresillian this summer. Everyone, even Lord Camborne. He gets a short leave, and they're all coming back to England. Alex has his long holidays. We'll all be together. Don't worry.'

She thought the child's face had never looked so beautiful, in its weariness and relief.

In the next four days that Livy spent with them, Ginny witnessed a metamorphosis. Blair, who was with them only briefly in the evenings, recognized it. 'She's never struck me as being a child to pity. Back there, in St Just, she was like a little princess. But she's just burst out of her chrysalis like a butterfly. I'm afraid she'll be utterly exhausted when she gets back, but have you ever seen anyone enjoy themselves so much? Almost makes me wish I were back there at her stage, and having it all sprung on me for the first time.'

Words tripped over themselves as Livy tried to explain the wonder of what she was seeing and experiencing. Lessons with Miss Bonner had been suspended for the period of the visit. She was always with them, but Ginny found time to accompany them on most of their expeditions. Livy's excitement and happiness were not to be missed. They did the usual things, which were not usual at all to Livy, the

167

changing of the guard at Buckingham Palace, the Tower where the awesome Crown jewels were guarded, the shops, the zoo. Livy gained a false impression that everyone in London lived close to several palaces, and had parks outside their doors. Ginny took them shopping. Books, some toys, a new suitcase to take them back in. Livy was now just about as tall as Chris. For them both Ginny bought identical clothes. 'It really should be Rachel, because she's Chris's twin,' Livy protested. Ginny was careful to buy only clothes which would be useful in St Just, but the quality was something that Livy was only beginning to comprehend. They had tea in beautiful places where orchestras played. For Livy, it was growing beyond a fairy-tale. 'How shall I ever tell my mother and Thea and Herbert?' she asked Blair, when he came upstairs to visit them before they went to sleep. Blair didn't disillusion her by saying that Thea and Herbert knew all about it. The happiness on the face of the child bemused him, but he realized that this was, for her, the beginning of the loss of innocence. Never again, he judged, would any occasion be so filled with wonder.

Livy waited impatiently for the summer, applying herself to her books, so that she might earn if not praise then not scorn from Rachel. There was another note from Caroline. *'Everyone here seems frightened of something. I don't know what. They always stop talking whenever any children are around. Mother can't wait to get back to England.'* That reassured Livy. There was a note from Chris. *'We'll be coming over a little bit before Alex gets out of school. Mr Aimes can't come this year, so there'll be someone different.'* It was full of promise for Livy. Finally the day came when Isa packed the suitcases again. Herbert drove them up to Tresillian, with Bully and Tubby and all the books Livy thought she wanted with her. Isa's two cousins were re-engaged to help out. Extra linen and towels had arrived from London, sent by Mrs Clayton, so that there needn't be the fearful scramble to get them laundered as there had been last summer. Austell was proud of the vegetable garden, and the orchard. Isa made arrangements for daily supplies of fish, crab, lobsters, mackerel, pilchard when they could get them. They didn't know exactly when anyone would arrive, but just that they were coming.

They came separately this time. First there was Lady Camborne, with Rachel and Caroline, driving the same shabby little car, which had been garaged at her grandfather's Hampstead house since last year. They had stayed longer in London than first intended. Dena's grandmother, Marcella, had died during the winter. They had stayed a week with the old man, trying to comfort him, trying to help organize his life. 'There's nothing he's willing to change,' Dena told Thea and Herbert when they shared dinner with her that first night. 'He's over eighty, and he can hardly lift a brush anymore. It's sad to see him alone in that big house and the studio out there in the garden is crammed with landscapes he's almost forgotten about. But he won't leave.'

Livy marked the subtle differences a year had made in Rachel and Caroline. Caroline appeared to have grown inches; her chubby, baby face was giving way to a childish prettiness that promised beauty. Rachel seemed far more grown up than she had been a year ago. She was thin and spare and dark, with a sharply intelligent face. She fingered the books Livy had in her room rather disdainfully. 'My Russian's improved, and so has my French and German. That's one good thing about going to a diplomatic school. Everyone's chattering away in different languages, and the teachers have to be up to scratch. Father insists on Latin as well. He's become very fluent in Russian now.' She seemed somewhat aggressive, sometimes truculent, a little mistrustful of Livy at first, as if she thought her too much in command at Tresillian. She insisted on having a room to herself. 'There are enough rooms, goodness knows. Perhaps I'll share when Chris gets here . . .' But over supper in the kitchen she relaxed somewhat, approaching the camaraderie of last summer. 'It's strange in Russia now. Lots and lots of people have been put on trial and shot. And they've sent thousands away to labour camps. Everyone's very frightened. The diplomatic people aren't involved, unless one does something or goes somewhere one shouldn't. But they wouldn't put you in a camp. They'd make you leave.'

'I don't like Russia much,' Caroline confided in Livy and Isa. 'Caroline is a cry-baby,' Rachel said. 'She's only learned a few words of Russian, just things to say to the servants.' The difference between the two girls was now more marked. Rachel ambitious, determined to forge ahead, determined to be right in everything; Caroline much softer, getting her way by smiles, and, as a last resort, by tears.

'I'm glad to be back with you,' she whispered to Livy on the way up to bed. 'Sometimes I don't like Rachel.'

Then Ginny and Blair and Chris arrived. With the presence of a man, the household seemed to take on better shape. Alex was on his way by ship, accompanied by a tutor. 'It's a polite name for a sort of bodyguard,' Blair said to Dena. 'He's too young to be on a ship by himself and, when I'm not here, I feel easier in my mind about all the kids having a man around. This one's called Matt Boyd, and he's mad on sailing, so we'll be hiring some sort of craft for the summer.'

Harry would be the last to come; he had less than a month's leave. Blair stayed at Tresillian until Alex and Matt Boyd arrived. Livy hung back in the kitchen with Isa when she knew Alex was expected. Even as she heard the commotion of the arrival, the sounds of reunion, the greetings, the laughter, she did not come out to join them. Isa did not urge her to go. For all the kindness of Lady Camborne and Mrs Clayton, there still remained the fact that Isa worked in the kitchen at Tresillian, and Livy had to be invited to join the families. Only Bully felt free to go out and join in the welcome. Livy thrust her head into a book, and kept Tubby clutched close to her, as if she were readying herself for disappointment or a rebuff.

It did not come. In a short time there came a quick, light knock on the kitchen door. Livy looked up, shifted, and Isa thought she was about to flee through the scullery and out the kitchen door. But Alex had come in, followed by a tall, broad-shouldered, pleasant-looking young man. 'Hello, Mrs Miles. I'm very glad to see you again. I wanted to introduce Matt Boyd. He's been reading your husband's poetry all the way over on the ship. He had to borrow his copy from my grandfather. Mr Miles's poetry is hard to find in the States.'

As Matt Boyd shook Isa's hand, Alex turned to Livy. 'Well, what sort of a welcome is this? The dame school certainly doesn't teach you very good manners. Has the cat got your tongue? Can't you even say "hello"? Matt, this is my friend, Livy. When she's not struck dumb, she's quite good company.'

Livy closed the book, put Tubby down and advanced towards Matt Boyd. 'How do you do? I'm very pleased to meet you. I hope you have a very pleasant stay in Cornwall.' It was all said in the best dame-school manner.

Alex hooted. 'Did you notice she said Cornwall not England, Matt? They all think, down here, that England stops at the Tamar River.'

Livy's instinct was to embrace Alex. Instead she held out her hand. Her heart was almost too full to speak to him. He had grown taller, the more sharply defined features were more handsome. He even looked a little foreign with his black hair and dark grey eyes; his face was deeply tanned. 'I'm so glad you're back, Alex. Mother and I have missed you, all of you,' she added quickly.

Caroline put her head around the door. 'Oh, there you are, Livy. Mrs Miles, Mother said we're one place short at the table.'

'Well, Miss Caroline, well, it's Livy's place I left out. I wasn't sure with all the extra company . . . Mr Boyd and Master Alex . . .'

Dena now stood beside Caroline. 'I know it's an awful crowd for you to feed, Mrs Miles, but I know we'll all eat magnificently. Livy will have her lunch with us, as usual, and all the children will have their supper here in the evenings . . . just as before. It lets the rest of us relax at dinner without all that chatter.' She gazed around the big stone-flagged room, the shining pots, the sun that streamed through the windows, the old iron stove from which Isa produced such miracles. 'It's just as well we came. Harry was right . . .' She added, more briskly, 'I'll show you to your room, Mr Boyd. You're in your old room, Alex. I suppose you can remember

171

where it is?' They followed her from the kitchen. Isa and Livy heard Matt Boyd's Bostonian accent.

'What an absolutely marvellous house this is, Lady Camborne. Alex said it was "special", but one doesn't expect English castles to be, well . . . just as they're supposed to be . . .' Their voices faded away as they went upstairs.

Livy bent and picked up the cat again, hugging it so fiercely it struggled in protest. 'Oh, Tubby, I do love you!' Isa knew Livy might just as well have addressed the cat as 'Alex'.

The summer fled away; they were absorbed in the same activities as the previous year, except now, on particularly fine days, they took the small fishing vessel Blair had made a contract for and spent hours on the water. Matt acted as additional crew to the two fishermen who owned the boat, and as instructor and general lifeguard to the children. He made them all wear life jackets, much to Alex's anoyance. 'I bet I can swim better than you,' he said to Matt, but he did as he was told.

'This must seem pretty tame to you, Matt,' Blair offered, 'after racing skiffs.'

'Anything on water will do, sir. I'm pleased to be out with real professionals. I'll bet these two' – the men were vaguely related to Livy – 'have weathered more gales than I've had hot dinners.'

For the first time they saw the Tresillian Tower and the Rocks from the sea. 'A beacon of hope and homecoming,' Matt said, 'and a death-trap.'

Other times they all went off to the usual picnic sites. The weird rock monuments had to be shown to Matt; they found deserted and calm coves where it was safe to swim. At low tide, under Matt and Miss Bonner's supervision, they were allowed down the cliff path to the wet, firm sands around the Tresillian Rocks; gazing upwards at the jagged heights towering above them, they scrambled over the bare bones of ships which had met their ends there. Matt carried a whistle with him and when he blew it, after consulting his watch, they scrambled up the cliff path and waited there to watch the fearful tidal race of the sea back into the land and the Rocks.

Watching, during these weeks, Isa saw Livy expand in height and breadth and social ease; she also grew in knowledge, grabbing, like an eager gull, at whatever came her way. Isa was aware of what a world opened up for her child through all these people.

Blair continued to come at weekends, and at last Harry arrived, weeks later than expected, and with his leave cut short. He would have a bare ten days there before he had to start back to Moscow. He had driven down from London with Blair, and his mood was bleak. Livy stared at him in puzzlement and wonder; she had never seen, could not have imagined, the usually smiling, light-hearted Lord Camborne in this mood.

He faced his wife, his friends Ginny and Blair, Thea and Herbert that night after dinner, when the children were in bed, and Matt and Miss Bonner had tactfully retired. 'It's rather bad news for you, Dena. The Foreign Office strongly advises me that it would be most unwise, in fact dangerous, for you to go back to Moscow with me. Under no circumstances will they let the children go there. I suppose that really applies to you too, as you wouldn't leave the girls alone.'

A cry of distress came from Dena; her face was deathly white. 'But they, the Russians, won't do anything to us. Not the diplomatic corps.'

'Well, we wouldn't be sent to a labour camp. But you surely know that war is likely any time. It's touch and go. The way Hitler's annexed Austria – the claims against Czechoslovakia. The Russians are half-convinced that we're going to continue to appease Hitler, and that we're selling them out. They don't know whether Hitler will turn against France and Britain, or against them or both if it seems possible to bring it off. It could mean a very hurried evacuation if he turns east. Hardly enough time for even the very fleet of foot to get out. Certainly no time to have to worry about the safety of wives and children. It's one of those times in the Foreign Service that we all start earning our keep, and wives and children find life very disagreeable.'

They talked late, talked about the perilous state of European relations, talked of the great show trials, the brutal purges in Russia. Harry talked of the scant details of the camps, administered by GULAG, which had seeped through to him. Dena looked appealingly at Blair, hoping to hear a contrary opinion of what lay ahead for them all.

'We're very close to war,' Blair said. 'It will be a miracle if we avoid it. And I don't see how it can be avoided for ever. So far as I see it and read it, Hitler means to conquer Europe. Whether Russia is sooner or later on his list depends on how much is handed to him on a platter. Our factories are geared to their highest production level, and we're adding new plant. If there is a European war, it is only a matter of time before the United States must come in, no matter what isolationists in Congress may say.'

The hope died in Dena's face. 'Have you any idea how long . . .?'

Harry shook his head. 'No one can say when I'll be free to come back – or when it would be safe for you to come to me. We must just accept . . .'

She got up and went over and poured a brandy. She busied herself getting glasses for the others; the decanter rattled lightly against the rims of the glasses as she strove to control her shaking hand. Some measure of control was back in her voice as she turned to face them.

'Well, we must just hope. The girls and I will go back to London. There's plenty of room in grandfather's house, and I think he'd be glad to have us there. I can get Rachel and Caroline into school . . . and wait. I just wish . . . well, never mind. If what you both fear is going to happen really does happen, plenty of people are going to be wishing for things they can't have.'

The blackness of the mood of the first evening lasted all through Harry's short leave with them. He took part in all the activities, went sailing and picnicking, and insisted on telling Rachel and Caroline himself that they would not, this time, be coming back to Moscow. Dena had not wanted him to shadow these days they had with him with that knowledge, but he overruled her. 'How will it look to them? That I just went away and deserted them. They're old enough, well, Rachel is, to understand why you can't come with me. I never want them to think I went off, left you all and didn't seem to care.'

'You make it sound,' Dena said faintly, 'as if it could be a long time before we see you.'

'I don't know, my darling. No one knows.' Their love-making had a sense of desperation and farewell. Dena found it impossible, as she lay in Harry's arms, as she heard the tide boil over the Rocks, not to let silent tears break from her. There was no war yet, but a threat of war. 'Oh, God,' she prayed with childlike simplicity, 'don't let there be a war.'

It seemed to Livy that they went earlier that year. Harry's leave was up, and Dena went alone with him to Penzance to say goodbye. He simply kissed his children as they lay sleeping one morning, and was gone. Bully, lying at Livy's feet, gave a soft growl as he heard the engine start up and then, when Livy's hand soothed him, went back to sleep.

It was time for Ginny and Chris and Alex to go back to Washington; it was time for Dena to go to London and inspect the school at which she had enrolled Rachel and Caroline.

There was not the uncertainty in Livy's heart this year as she saw them go. The Cambornes would still be in England, and, if the war that everyone now talked of came, they would be back at Tresillian to escape the air-raids that everyone feared. But as Ginny and Chris and Alex left, she wondered if she would ever see them again. If that threatened war came, they would surely never cross the Atlantic again. Always in the years that followed, whenever she thought of separation from these beloved friends, she seemed to hear the remote, small noise of a car engine starting in the early morning, and Bully's low growl.

She was back at the dame school, and already feeling much older than the other girls of her age because she seemed to have lived so much in that summer.

Livy felt a shock of bitterness because it was only in September, not so many weeks after they had all left, that

Mr Chamberlain came back from Munich after meeting Hitler and announced 'Peace in our time . . . peace with honour'. So there was to be no war, after all, Livy complained to Herbert. They had all rushed away for no reason.

'They had to go, in any case, Livy. But now you can feel sure they will be back next summer.'

Privately Harry wrote to Blair and to Dena: *'They see it here as the complete sell-out. They think Chamberlain just wants to see Germany and Russia slug it out, while the West has peace. We are deeply mistrusted here.'* In March that year, 1939, Hitler invaded Czechoslovakia, and announced that he had taken Bohemia and Moravia under his protection. *'It is exactly as the Russians expected,'* Harry wrote.

During that winter Dena forced her grandfather, against strenuous objections, to go through the stacks of landscapes in the studio and select what he considered the best, to be sent down to Tresillian for safety, in the event of war. 'There won't be any war, Dena,' he said, as he muddled indecisively among the canvasses. 'What do you want to keep?' she demanded. 'What do you like the best?'

'I don't know,' he wailed. 'I'm too old to be pushed around like this. How can I possibly choose? It isn't necessary.'

Dena told him of what precautions Blair was taking. His collection of Impressionist paintings had been moved for safekeeping to a remote place in Wales, as had Seymour House's silver. Folding wooden shutters had been fitted to all the windows to try to minimize bomb-blast. He had stopped short, though, of sending away the contents of his magnificent wine-cellar. 'I'll be in and out of here all the time, whatever happens. I'll need a shot of booze to keep the chill out!'

To Livy's surprise they all came that summer, all except Harry, who could not leave Moscow. Dena, Rachel and Caroline arrived as soon as school was over; Ginny, Blair and Chris came a week later, Blair for a fleeting visit, Ginny, Chris and Miss Bonner to spend the whole summer. Alex, and, once again, Matt Boyd, were on the way. . . .'

'Honestly, Ginny,' Dena sighed. 'I don't know why you all bother, when you live in such luxury in other places. Alex

176

must have lots of school friends he could be having the time of his life with.'

'Trying to get rid of us?' Ginny laughed. 'Never worry about Alex. He wouldn't come out of politeness. He's coming because he wants to, and not even his grandfather could stop him. War hasn't actually been declared yet, so there wasn't much Mr McClintock could do to stop him coming, but it wasn't for lack of trying. Sometimes I wonder if Mr McClintock really ever concedes whose child he is!'

Tresillian fell into its by now almost accustomed routine. Livy welcomed everyone joyfully. The Tregenna cousins were begging Isa for a chance to switch places now and again so they could enjoy, even at second hand, life at the castle. Blair sent lavish stores of spirits, wine and brandy from London. Whole cases of tinned food, at which Isa looked askance, arrived from Fortnums. 'Is Blair trying to tell us something?' Dena asked. 'This looks as if he's preparing for a siege.'

What disturbed Dena more than anything, in the midst of people making preparations for war, while hoping for peace, was the arrival from Moscow of their household effects. Crate by crate they came, sent through the agents for the Foreign Office. The silver, the china, the copper, silver-lined pans. 'He couldn't have spelt it out more clearly, could he?' Dena said to Ginny, as she unpacked them. 'Harry obviously expects the worst. He doesn't want my lovely things to be lost. I'm glad I brought the coat, even though I thought I was coming only for the summer last year.' She had clung to the Russian sable, refusing to leave it behind in Moscow. 'It could be stolen,' she explained to Ginny. 'How could I have ever looked you in the eye again?' But she finally broke into tears as she pulled from one of the crates the fur-lined boots Harry had had made for her. 'He obviously expects it to be a long war.'

Andrew McClintock arrived, unannounced as before. 'I'm sorry if I inconvenience you. But I know there's plenty of room here.' Blair was then in Switzerland, and hadn't even known of his coming. 'Thought I'd get my eye in on what preparations you're making.' This he addressed to Dena.

'Of course, all our family will be in America. But this, naturally, is the place for you to be when the shooting breaks out.'

'We're not certain of that.'

'Well, I am. I'm trying to suggest that you all, you, Dena, Rachel and Caroline, come over to us in Washington. I'm going to suggest the same to Mrs Miles, her and the child.'

'You're mad,' Dena cried. 'This is the only place I'll ever have a chance of seeing Harry. God knows, there's enough distance between us now. I can't add the Atlantic as well . . .'

Andrew McClintock put the same proposal to Isa when he joined her for tea early the next morning. 'You could have a wonderful position in any of our households. The child could have the right schools. No fear of bombing . . . you'd lack for nothing.'

Isa shook her head. 'You're very kind, sir. I would say "yes" for Livy, but it would break my heart to see her go. And there's something else, Mr McClintock. Livy belongs here. No matter what you gave her, I think she'd be unhappy away from here.'

'But have you thought that England could be conquered by Hitler? Have you thought what that would mean?'

'Livy will stay, as most of the rest of us will do. England will not be conquered, Mr McClintock.'

'You are stubborn, but I admire you. Yes thank you, Mrs Miles. I'll have more tea. And some of that bread . . .' The kitchen still fascinated him, the smells, the atmosphere. He continued to give Bully pieces of well-buttered bread. He always ran his hand along the drooping folds of the dark muzzle.

'You're about the only person besides Livy, Mr McClintock, who does that. Bully mightn't stand it from most people.'

'They both show good sense.' It was an aspect of Andrew McClintock which few people ever saw. 'Well, think it over, Mrs Miles. You may see it differently when war really comes. Just send me a cable. Anytime. I'll see that you and the child have transportation on an American vessel. America still has a little breathing space, but not too long. Don't wait until it's too dangerous.'

He left an envelope fat with notes. She saw it, and wondered if the large sum of money indicated that he did not expect to be back at Tresillian for a long time, if ever. The farewell gesture, the offer to bring Livy and her to America, shook Isa as no other presage of war had so far done. She had taken it for granted that if war should come, she, like all the others, would stay, and would win.

After Andrew McClintock's visit a special van was sent from Harrods. It contained all the things he imagined they might go short of: blankets and soap, hot water bottles and bedsocks. Wine and tinned ham. Whisky, gin, champagne.

'What on earth would the champagne be for?' Dena said to Ginny.

'Well, that might be to celebrate peace.' As they noted some of the other contents, the whole load seemed to have been made out by a quartermaster. There were shovels and trowels, garden hoes and rakes. Austell examined them appreciatively. 'Fine quality, my lady. Things like this could go awful scarce if it comes to a war. And we'll be asked to grow all we can. I was thinking I'd better start breaking extra ground, so the hard part's done if you have to look after it yourself . . .'

Andrew McClintock had even enquired about the guns that had belonged to Harry's father, and had been sent to Tresillian for storage after his death. There was a stock of ammunition to suit each one. 'Am I supposed to pot rabbits with them, or hold off the enemy?' Dena examined the tins of corned beef and stew. 'I suppose if it comes to it, Mrs Miles could wrap a bit of pastry around it and call it a pasty . . .'

Blair joined them briefly. He had just flown from New York on the new commercial Pan American flight across the Atlantic, which had refuelled in the Azores, and delivered him to Lisbon. The flight had taken twenty-six hours. 'Damn shame. It ought to be coming directly to London. Will be, I suppose, when the diplomats stop arguing about landing rights . . .' It was good to have him among them; his presence was reassuring, even though he brought no news of comfort. They knew about mobilization in France, in the cities of Britain they had started to issue gas masks and prepare air-raid shelters.

'I think it's almost time you and Chris and Alex went,' Blair said to Ginny.

Calmly she shook her head. 'I have the choice of not leaving you, Blair. You can't make me go back to Washington. I know you'll be spending more time in England than anywhere else, no matter what happens. Your job with McClintock-Clayton is this side of the Atlantic. That's where I intend to stay.'

He was disinclined to argue with her at this moment; it might need the first air-raid to convince her. 'We'll see . . .'

He inspected the stores which both he and Andrew McClintock had sent to Tresillian. 'One thing we both forgot,' he said as Dena closed the heavy oak door on one of the cellars. 'Padlocks. Things will vanish when there are shortages. I'll send down a box as soon as I get back to London. Must remember to do it at Seymour House, too. I think you could stand an extra supply of tools – hammers, nails, screwdrivers, flashlights and batteries.' He began making new lists. Dena could only stare at him in dumb wonder, trying to fight her panic.

Early in August Blair returned to Tresillian and said he could spend perhaps a week with them. A light heat lay on the countryside, hardly a breeze stirred. Matt Boyd shook his head about sailing. 'We'd never make it out of the bay without power. Power isn't much fun.' They decided on a picnic at one of the usually deserted coves a few miles along the coast, a place that abounded with rock pools and was safe for swimming. At the last minute Rachel and Chris decided against going. There had been an argument that morning between Dena and Rachel; Rachel objected to going back to the school they had attended last year. 'I should be moved up an extra form and I know they won't do it. If I started at some other place they'd put me in a higher form, I know they would. Even Miss Bonner says I'm ready . . .'

'There is no other school,' Dena replied, exasperated, and wished Miss Bonner would mind her own business. 'It's far too late to make those sorts of arrangements. It's so unfair on Caroline . . .' Rachel had gone off in a sulk. She withdrew from the picnic party, and Chris decided to stay with her.

Blair dismissed the whole episode. 'Let her get over it, and if Chris wants to join the revolt, then she can just stay behind. I'm not going to have my day ruined by a pair of sulky kids. Rachel will have sweetened up by dinner time.' Dena agreed with him, wishing Harry were there to deal with Rachel's demands; his word held far more authority than hers. She sensed that part of Rachel's dissatisfaction was itself engendered by Harry's absence. It troubled all of them.

As a gesture of their independence Rachel and Chris had taken their own picnic lunch out into the orchard. Isa supplied everything she could find in the pantry that they particularly liked. Pasties were Rachel's favourite. She put in a stone bottle of her own brew of ginger beer, and some chocolate cakes, peaches and plums. She made it a real picnic by putting in the basket a tablecloth and napkins. Let them play at being grown up; the real thing would come soon enough. She saw them disappear behind the high wall of the orchard.

Her cousins had finished their day's work, eaten lunch with Isa, and disappeared down the hill towards St Just. A deep quiet fell on Tresillian. Tubby was curled in a patch of bright sun on the window sill; Bully lay by Isa's chair as she drank the last cup of tea in the pot she had made for lunch. The lunch dishes had been washed; it was some hours before she need start preparations for the children's supper, and the adults' dinner. She sipped, and thought over the events of the summer. Had she made a terrible mistake in not accepting Mr McClintock's offer to have her and Livy in America? It would, she thought, have been a wonderful opportunity for Livy; for her it would have been a nightmare to be separated from the only life she had known. But was it also very selfish? She would have to think about it carefully. Mr McClintock had not closed the offer; it had been she who had closed the discussion. It was unthinkable to Isa that Livy should be in danger from a war or from a conqueror. But the questions were endlessly asked in the newspapers delivered daily to Tresillian. Why should there be a war, she wondered? Hadn't they had enough of it? She mostly thought of Oliver's ruined, tortured lungs. The war poems, after much rereading, began to make more sense to Isa now that another war was being discussed. But surely they'd never do it, not again?

The thoughts, swirling in her head, tired and worried her. These days she was unusually tired, but she shrugged at the thought. She was organizing and running a large household, a position of trust which was generously paid. It was worth whatever effort she put into making these people comfortable and well-looked after. She liked to give them pleasure. What did it matter if she was a little tired at night? It was natural. When she did drift into sleep it was with the thought that she was discharging her responsibility to Oliver Miles's daughter with all the strength that lay in her.

'Mrs Miles . . . *Mrs Miles*.' She had dozed off in the big chair by the stove, thinking of Livy. Beside her, Bully had been snoring; now he was on his feet, barking. It was Rachel's hand, not Livy's, which shook her. 'Please come and help. It's Chris, down at the Rocks. She's twisted her ankle – or something. Maybe sprained it. She can't put it on the ground.'

'Child!' She was instantly awake, every sense alert, as if it had been Livy Rachel had spoken of. 'Find Austell! We'll have to carry her up.' She raced through the stable yard, and started for the cliff path. Her first reaction had been of mild fright, concerned that Chris was alone and hurt. Then the instinct as old as the race of fisherfolk from which she sprung asserted itself. She knew, as well as she knew the day from the night, the turning of the tides. It was an instinct born of a hundred generations of families who had lived with and by the sea. She possessed no watch and didn't need to look at a clock. The tide had turned, and was now racing back in across the sands of Tresillian Cove, turning faster than any man could run, rushing in to cover all but the tips

182

of the notorious fangs. She reached the top of the cliff path. Rachel had started to follow her. She paused for just a second. 'No! Find Austell! Quickly!' Rachel turned back to the walled garden. With half her mind Isa prayed that Austell hadn't taken this time to find a shady place to have a quiet afternoon cigarette. From behind those high walls he would hear nothing of their shouts.

Halfway down the cliff path, sometimes stumbling but trying to move cautiously because she feared to fall herself, she saw the little speck out beyond the farthest of the Rocks, the Needle Point itself. The child was crawling towards the path, but not apparently with any sense of urgency. Lost in the heat mist of this August afternoon, the tide snaked up its channels. Only from above could it be seen. Isa saw and knew it too well. She couldn't swim, few of the fisherfolk could swim, but even if she could it wouldn't have made any difference. No one could swim in the currents which the flowing tide created about the Tresillian Rocks. She ran, not calling to the child but saving her breath. Why frighten her? She stumbled to the end of the cliff path, and thankfully found the firm, wet sand under her feet. She paused only a few seconds to pull off her shoes. She waved now to the child crawling along the sand. 'I'm coming . . . coming . . .'

Even when she reached Chris she did not warn of the tide racing towards them. Panic could undo them both. She dropped down on her hands and knees beside Chris. 'Pull yourself up on my back. Can you manage that?' As she felt Chris try to straddle her back, she also heard an exclamation of pain, as the twisted ankle took some weight. 'Easy, child, easy.' She reached around and tried to help what now seemed an unchildish weight on to her back. 'Put your arms around my shoulders. Try to hold on with your knees. It's just piggy-back, child. Hold on tight.'

The weight staggered her as she slowly tried to rise from her knees. Perhaps in a now-realized sense of panic, Chris's grip had shifted up from her shoulders, so that her hands caught at Isa's throat. 'Down a little, child. I can't breathe!' But the arms stayed obstinately there. Isa put her own arms back around under Chris's buttocks and tried to heave her upwards, tried also to drag some air into her own lungs. She began to run. Ominously, under her bare feet, she felt the first touch of the tide. On the race towards the sands, twisting between the rocks, it lapped her heels. She knew she could never beat its speed. The Rocks themselves were unclimbable, certainly not with the weight on her back. She had never imagined that taking a breath could hurt so much, that knees and legs could feel so weak. Even on that hot afternoon, the touch of the water was cold. It was deeper now, gaining on her. It was now lapping her heels; it had reached her ankles. The sand softened with the water, and shifted under her. Her toes and heels dug into it, and she ran more slowly.

But surely she had won. There was Austell, shoes flung off, running towards her on the little space of sand left. Without wasting a word, he took Chris off her back, just holding her in his arms, and turned back to the cliff path. Isa paused to heave a great, refreshing gulp of air into her anguished lungs. It was all right. The water now swirled about her calves, but she knew it was all right. Lightened of her burden, she struggled through the water, trying to run but knowing that she would make it in time.

Austell was ahead of her, and had gained the place on the cliff path above the high water mark. He turned back to look at her, freed one hand of his hold on Chris to give a half-wave, acknowledging that he knew she was all right. And she was. She reached the bottom of the cliff path, grasped the rough holds in the rock to help herself on the way up. When she knew she was clear of the high water mark she paused to rest, waving to Austell, who was now at the top of the cliff and had put Chris gently down on the grass. Bully rushed down to meet her, his long tongue hanging out, panting, washing her face in a frenzy. 'Good, Bully, good boy. It's all right now, boy.' She was thankful his own instinct had not permitted him to follow her down on to the sands. His ungainly body would have been swallowed by the tide.

She took her time going up the rest of the path. She could look back now at the sea and almost smile. It had been cheated of its victims. But it didn't make any difference to the sea. It had claimed so many in the past; it would claim so many more.

At the top of the cliff path, where Austell waited for her and Rachel knelt by Chris, she first felt the real pain. It was not the pain of struggling for breath. This was deep and overwhelming. It dug cruelly into her chest and side and arm, furled itself around her neck, gripped her more tightly than the pull of the tide. She was aware of the mist-clouded sky, the sound of the sea, and Bully's frantic licking of her face. She was lying face-upwards, but darkness seemed to descend on that hot August afternoon. She began to feel cold as well as pain.

Rachel's frightened voice sounded close to her ear, but she could not see the child's face. 'Mrs Miles! *Mrs Miles*!' Bully started to bark; the tone carried panic and fear, and yet it strove to will her back to life and to movement. Every other sound faded but Bully's voice. She died there on the cliff above the Rocks, while Austell raced to the telephone to bring a doctor. After a time, Bully's barking changed to an anguished howl of despair.

The news passed like a shock wave through St Just. She had been so young, and no one had guessed she might have been ill. She had never complained, never seen a doctor. It was generally accepted that the Tresillian Rocks had taken yet another life. They brought masses of flowers to her funeral, the sort of simple flowers Isa liked. The little Methodist chapel where she had worshipped was packed, and many had to stand outside. But they carried the coffin to the graveyard of the Anglican church at the top of the hill, to lay her beside her husband, Oliver Miles. The townspeople sorrowed for Isa Miles, and worried about the future of the child, Livy. One of Isa's brothers, Alfred, came to see Dena and Ginny and Blair at the Castle, where Livy still stayed. 'Of course we'll take in Isa's child, Lady Camborne.' He mainly addressed his words to Dena, as Lord Camborne, who was the master of Tresillian, was too far away to be able to make any decisions in this matter. Alfred was a little afraid of the Americans. 'Of course, Livy must come and live with us. We're humble people, Lady Camborne, as you know, and my sister married a gentleman, but we know our duty, and we'll take good care of young Livy.'

'Let's think about it a little,' Dena answered, wondering what Harry would have counselled, and yet at the same time knowing. 'I'll tell Livy what you've said, and I'm sure she'll thank you. But I won't say anything just yet. The poor child is dazed, as your cousins must have told you. She sits with Tubby in the kitchen, and Bully won't leave her side. She doesn't cry. It would be a help if she would. None of us can reach her. She comes to the table with us, but she hardly eats at all. It's hard to know what to do. Please leave her with us for a while. The children are all her friends. They may break through to her sooner than any adult.'

The man had nodded and gone away. The next to come were Thea and Herbert. They knew well enough what Dena, Ginny and Blair were feeling. Isa had saved Chris's life; but the disobedience of both Chris and Rachel had been responsible for that killing dash across the sands. Useless to tell themselves it might have happened at any time, for any other reason. It had happened when it did, and the moment and the guilt would stay with them all for ever.

'Leave Livy with us,' Herbert said. 'Alfred's a good man, a kind father, but the family's not . . . well, Livy has gone beyond them. They have too many children as it is, and fishing's a precarious livelihood. She'd want for nothing with us, you know. We'd see that she went to the right school when the times comes – when she's outgrown the dame school. Good lord, we've known her since the day she was born. The cottage could be rented, I dare say. It should be kept for her, in case she wanted it in the future. We wouldn't like to see Oliver's cottage sold. It would always be there for her, her own little rock to cling on to.'

Blair listened to it all, and his mind raced into the future. He had, in his times here, observed them both closely, this distinguished pair, the sculptress and the painter. Whatever gifts Livy might have would be fostered and nurtured, and she need never leave the place where she had been born. she would still be among her own people. But . . .

it was an objection he had to phrase very carefully.

'Mr and Mrs Gardiner, it's very generous of you. Livy and Isa couldn't have truer friends. And I'm certain she would have everything she needed. But have you considered the age gap?'

'More than considered it. We're old enough to be her grandparents. But still, we think we can give her some years of love, a sense of security for a while. Until's she's a little older.'

'Then why not let her stay with her young friends here? With Alex and Chris and Rachel and Caroline?'

Thea protested swiftly. 'But you don't stay here. You go your separate ways.'

'She could come back to London with us,' Dena said. 'Go to the same school as Rachel and Caroline. I'm certain I'm saying just what Harry would say . . .'

Blair cut in. 'But why shouldn't she stay with Ginny and me? We have a house in Washington as well as London. There's Prescott Hill. She would have everything Chris has. Mrs Gardiner, do you think Ginny and I can ever forget that Livy's mother saved Chris's life? That effort probably caused her death. She might have had many more years of life. No one can be sure. But she saved Chris. No one can argue about that. We owe a debt we can never repay.'

Thea looked doubtful. 'With all respect, Mr Clayton, don't you think you perhaps can give Livy too much. You live on rather a grand scale . . .'

'We don't,' Dena put in quickly. 'Livy would be part of our lives, too. She's just the right age, between Rachel and Caroline. Caroline adores her. She'd still have Chris and Alex as friends. A whole, ready-made family, two families.'

'And Livy,' Herbert observed, 'thinks Alex is some sort of god. Between you, you have great power and influence and money. And I think you really do care about the child. It would be hard for anyone to say "no" to all that on Livy's account. Coming to terms with her mother's death will be easier, I think, if she's with other children.'

Blair said carefully, 'Perhaps we're all being a bit presumptuous in this. Aren't we rushing this decision a bit? No one's

187

asked Livy yet what she wants. Her mother's only been buried two days. God knows what the child's thinking. We have some weeks yet. Alex doesn't go back to Washington until the end of the month. And Ginny will be staying here with Dena until it's time for the girls to go back to school. She could either go to school with them, or share Miss Bonner with Chris. It would be a natural thing just to take her with us to London.

'We think we should leave it to you,' he said to the Gardiners, 'to explain the alternatives to her. She's known you all her life. She loves and trusts you. Perhaps she'll just want to stay here with you, in her familiar world. Perhaps she'll want to come with us. Let her decide in her own good time what she wants to do but I think she should be told now that she's loved and wanted. We can't take away her grief. We can let her know that she's not been abandoned. But we shouldn't hurry her.'

He added. 'Will you talk to her? It will come best from you. Just make sure she understands there's no need to rush her decision . . .'

Herbert nodded. They went to talk to Livy, who sat in the kitchen in the big chair, Tubby in her arms, Bully at her feet.

In the end the decision was made for them all.

The signing of the non-aggression pact between Germany and Russia was a signal that the partition of Poland would begin, and Britain would honour its treaty to protect Poland. Conscripts were called up, and the evacuation of children from the large cities was begun.

Dena went immediately to London, and by bullying and persuasion managed to get her grandfather to pack two bags and return to Cornwall with her. He was installed in Livy's cottage. Lydia, her mother, refused to budge from London. 'There'll be things for me to do here, if we're bombed. I'm not quite helpless.'

A peremptory telephone call from Andrew McClintock decided Alex's future. His grandson was not to be trapped in a country at war. He and Matt Boyd would return on the first American vessel which could accommodate them. 'Alex is not going to school in England. He's an American, and he's going to grow up as one. You make what decision you want, Ginny, about where you stay. You wouldn't be the first woman parted from her husband by war. But that's your choice. Personally, I think you and Chris would be better off, far better off, here in the States. Blair has to stay, I know. The company needs that. He'll be of great and important service to his country, and to the British, in London. But I have some say about what happens to my grandson. Have him on that ship, Ginny, or I'll set every lawyer in creation on to you and Blair. The boy has a right to be removed from danger. Don't force me to fight you in law.' He had received the news of Isa's death. He added in a gentler tone. 'Try to persuade that Livy child to come over here with him. I'd be glad to take her . . .'

Ginny shouted angrily, 'Not even you, Mr McClintock, can just take a child. Do you want to take her away from everything she's ever known, and break her heart completely? She's staying with us, right here.'

In consultation with Blair by telephone Ginny had decided that she had no course but to follow Andrew McClintock's instructions. 'He would go to law, the old devil. He'd get a court order tomorrow on the grounds that I was placing Alex's life in danger by keeping him here. I'll have to let him go. Blair . . .'

'You and Chris should be going with him. It isn't safe, Ginny. It just isn't safe to stay.'

She said quite firmly, 'I told you before that I'm not leaving as long as you have to stay. When will I ever see you? And Chris stays with me. I'm not turning her over to Andrew McClintock.'

'If you don't go now, in a little while it may be too late. When America comes into the war, there won't be any neutral ships to travel on.'

'The argument's over, Blair. I'm staying. I'll take my chances.' Her heart ached over the separation from Alex. But he had a core of toughness that would withstand domination by his grandfather. He had been stoical at their parting. 'I'm proud of you, Mom – staying on.'

He did force an agreement on her that she would remain at Tresillian with Chris. 'Half the kids have left London, Ginny. You can't bring a child here.'

Upset and frightened, Ginny saw Alex go. By the time he was halfway across the Atlantic, Britain had declared war on Germany. Finally Livy, who had not cried since her mother died, wept in Ginny's arms. 'It's over, isn't it? Nothing will ever be right again. We'll never see Alex again. My mother . . .'

'You'll be all right here with us, Livy. We'd never let any harm come to you. We're all staying, and one day Alex will be back with us. Just wait and see . . .'

Chapter 7

1

It was as well, Dena and Ginny acknowledged afterwards, that they did not know how long the wait would be. They were ashamed to admit it, or to complain, except to each other, that the most wearing factor of the years between 1939 and 1945 was tedium. They both experienced fear for the safety of those they loved, they knew tragedy, but it was the waiting, with little knowledge of what the ending would be, that most wore on the nerves. They suffered a sense of helplessness in the face of great and terrible events. They were small, totally insignificant cogs in the great wheel of the rolling war.

As soon as her grandfather was installed in Livy's cottage, Dena took Livy to visit him alone. He professed himself comfortable there, Livy's Tregenna relations came in each day to cook and clean, to make up fires, to comment on the war and bits of local gossip. Thea and Herbert came often; he enjoyed talking with them. It was a link back to the old life in London. He could no longer paint. He didn't try. Livy's visit to him forced her to the first adult decision of her life. Guy Denham wanted to discuss the matter of the rent.

Livy was shocked. She looked from Dena to Guy Denham, and then at the floor. 'I couldn't take rent, Lady Camborne . . . Mr Denham. That's awful! I'm living in your house. You don't charge me anything. And you feed me and look after me. Well, there's me, and Bully and Tubby . . .' Her voice seemed to crumple, as did her face. 'My mother would never have wanted you to pay, Mr Denham. It's an honour to have you. She and my father would be ashamed of me if I took any money.'

Guy Denham held up his hand. 'Then, dear child, we

won't discuss it any more. Oliver Miles has a worthy daughter. Your mother, ah, how her family loved her. I shall be as happy here as anyone rooted out of a familiar nest at my age can be.' Dena knew that by comparison to the large Hampstead house and the big, bright studio, the cottage on the narrow street was very confined indeed. 'I love the garden. On sunny days I even try to take up a fork and do a few weeds out of their prime. What a hand and eye your mother had. I love all this great cheerful confusion. A real artist she must have been . . .'

After that, Livy often went to visit him alone, or took Caroline with her. 'I can hardly believe,' he said, looking at Caroline's golden beauty, 'that I am a great-grandfather.'

Without Livy's knowledge, after consulting with Dena, Guy Denham had opened a savings account at the bank into which he deposited a monthly rent. 'The child will need it, one way and another.'

Everyone had expected air raids on London and the major cities almost immediately. But none came. What came was a rush of evacuee children, sometimes with their mothers, but mostly without. Tresillian got twelve of them, mostly from the East End of London. They had the toughness of city children, and almost universally a thorough dislike of the countryside and Tresillian itself. They swarmed over the place without much supervision. They had their ration books, a few clothes, and that was all. Dena begged the Ministry to put a fence around the Tower and to block off the cliff path down to the Rocks. The Ministry had other things to worry about.

The children were enrolled at the local St Just school, which was bursting at the seams, as was the dame shcool. The dame school though, offered to squeeze in Rachel and Chris and Caroline, but Rachel refused on the grounds that she was too advanced for what they could offer. Miss Bonner, a month after the outbreak of war, joined the WRAAF. Rachel calmly set about organizing a school of their own. She commandeered the room next to the kitchen, which would have been a housekeeper's room in better days. It had a fireplace and a pleasant view to the gates of the walled garden. It was small enough to keep warm. This she established as her own kingdom from which the evacuee children were barred. An undeclared war existed between the four girls and the rest of the children.

She and Ginny tried to cope as well as they could, with help from whomever of Livy's aunts could spare the time. They worked in the vegetable garden, thankful that Austell had prepared the ground for them. When they could spare time, one or other of them put in some hours with the girls, checking exercise books, hearing vocabulary and spelling. Dena took on the cooking. They acquired a pony and a small trap; Ginny's Rolls was never used because it consumed too much petrol. It was the job of the girls to feed and care for the pony. There were constant arguments with the evacuee children about who was allowed to ride him, when he wasn't needed for journeys down to St Just for shopping.

In the evenings, after the children had been fed and superficially washed, when the squabbling had finally stopped, the pillow fights died down, the grumbling subsided into what sometimes were tears of homesickness, Dena and Ginny sank, exhausted, into chairs in the kitchen, the one room they could keep warm, the place where everyone ate. Dena hoped the old stove would hold up to what was now demanded of it. Isa was desperately missed as a presence, as well as a person. 'I just know she would have been able to calm this lot down,' Ginny said. They shared cigarettes and a carefully measured tot from the whisky store Blair had sent, grateful now for it in a way they had never before imagined. They worked on the ration books, trying to devise ways of stretching the 'points' as far as possible. There was a tug of conscience about which of the precious stores in the cellars they should allow to the evacuee children, and soon the struggle was given up. 'Might as well share as cheerfully as possible. I'd be too ashamed to see our four have jam on their bread, and the others nothing. We really can't allow a "below the salt" mentality to start.'

As the winter wore on and there still were no air raids, and therefore the reason for living the kind of life they did was not compelling, Dena said to Ginny. 'God, Ginny, what

193

on earth are we doing here? Isn't there any way out . . .? Can we spend the whole war marooned here, looking after other people's brats? If only . . . well I'm ashamed to say it, but I don't care for my war duties at all. But why don't you and Chris get away? Mr McClintock was right, you know. You'd be far better off in Washington. You could ginger up the local Red Cross group, and get parcels of food and clothing flowing here. People would think you were a saint. What none of them will ever know is how boring all this is. And to remember now how I used to think the diplomatic service was a bit of a bore. What I wouldn't give now to get all dressed up and go to a diplomatic reception.'

'I'm not going back, not yet. I just can't think of leaving Blair here. I feel guilty about sneaking up to London now and then to see him, guilty about leaving you here to cope. I see those notices plastered all over the railway stations "Is this journey really necessary?" But Blair's bound to be here more than he'll be in Washington. I have to spend some time with him, share his life as much as I can . . .' She had come back from the latest brief visit to London with the kind of glow that always followed any time spent with Blair.

'Blair thinks war is only a matter of time.' In Washington Blair had urged on McClintock-Clayton further expansion of armament and aircraft factories. He left the financing of this to Andrew McClintock and his directors. The message he had to deliver in Washington was, 'Just get the money how and where you can. But expand. Don't imagine, if Hitler gets all of Europe, he's going to stop there. To save our own skins we'll have to fight in Europe and probably in the East.' This did not go down well with the isolationist thinkers, of which Ginny's father was one of the most prominent. But during a short meeting with President Roosevelt, Blair got encouragement. He told this to Ginny in the few days they spent together before he packed her off back to Cornwall. He had almost given up trying to persuade her to return with Chris to Washington. 'It would give me some peace of mind if you both were there . . .' he pleaded.

To this she always shook her head. 'When will I ever see you? How often will you be in Washington?'

To Dena she added, 'What chance do I have of a baby if I never see Blair?' That silenced Dena's protests also. She finished her cigarette before she spoke again.

'You could send Chris back . . .'

'And leave her to be brought up by Andrew McClintock? I don't think so. I could send her back and stay in London with Blair. We could both be killed in a raid, and she'd have no one.'

'It doesn't look as if there are going to be any raids. It all seems so unnecessary, all this evacuation fuss. I don't think Hitler ever means to try to invade.'

That was the opinion of many people. One by one the evacuee children were sent for by their parents. Tresillian experienced some measure of peace at last. Dena and Ginny looked about them in some bewilderment. 'I'd forgotten what quiet was like.' As if pulling them out from the corners to which they had retreated, they found their own children again. Rachel was proud of what she had achieved in organizing their own 'school', but she was reaching the end of her ability to lead the others further. 'We've all kept up, but we need more books, more of everything. I've been teaching them some Russian. I wrote a letter to Daddy a few weeks ago in Russian, just a note. And the censor sent it back! Livy's getting on very well in Russian. She learns very quickly.'

Isa's death had profoundly affected Rachel. She was unable to forget the terror of that day, her fear for Chris, her horror at watching Isa die before her eyes. She had made a special effort to try to compensate Livy since then, and knew her efforts were meagre compared with Livy's loss. Dena and Ginny had seen her change: her once exclusive preoccupation with Chris had now been extended to the two younger girls. It was she more than any of them who had put up the barricades against the evacuee children.

'Sometimes,' Dena said, 'I have a lot of sympathy for the way Rachel feels. Oh, hell, this stupid war . . .'

By May it had ceased to be either phony or stupid. The Germans suddenly invaded the Lowlands, and they were back on the old ground so bitterly fought over during the

195

last war. But this time, no one bogged down in Flanders mud. In June the British Expeditionary Force was retreating towards Dunkirk, and trapped. At Tresillian, and everywhere else, they waited, almost holding their breaths, as the incredible armada of little ships, the absurd armada, lifted the army off the beaches. Most of them got home. A 'little England' spirit developed. 'We will fight them on the beaches . . .' Churchill declared.

'What with?' Ginny asked. She had been on a quick visit to London to see Blair. Once again she had refused to return to Washington. 'Blair is going to be more in Europe than the States. As an American he can still move around. But I can't go everywhere with him. I have to make a choice of one place or the other. I believe it has to be England. Chris is safe down here . . .'

'Chris is safe unless there's an invasion . . .' Sometimes now they thought the unthinkable, spoke the unspeakable.

Alex's letters came regularly, and were cheerful – perhaps deliberately so, as if he tried to assuage her sense of guilt. She blessed him silently for the courage he both displayed and imparted to her. Ginny's father, the Senator, wrote demanding that they both return. *It's time to pull up the drawbridge. England, like the rest of Europe, will go down. But no one can touch America.* He had become the complete isolationist, very outspoken in the Senate, and he had a considerable following throughout the country. He was no longer an obscure senator, but a figure of power and a symbol of opposition to Roosevelt's views. Not only was he concerned for Ginny's and Chris's safety, but he didn't like the idea that his own daughter was publicly defying his opinions. It might have been different if she had been relatively obscure. But she was married to the McClintock-Clayton dynasty. Staying on in England brought unwelcome publicity. In the American press she was pictured as either a fool or a heroine.

'Can't they understand that I want to stay near Blair? In a war, most women don't have a choice.'

There was no need to elaborate further to Dena. The separation from Harry was beginning to take its toll. It was nearly two years since they had last been together. Her body longed and ached for him, her ears needed his voice, his laughter, her eyes wanted to see the tilt of his head, the sudden flash of wicked humour in his eyes. She needed him to take away the everyday boredom of their lives, even though now they knew their lives might, ultimately, be in danger. She tried not to let her sense of disenchantment, of boredom with the mundane routine of her life at Tresillian, appear in her letters. She did not find it exciting to hoe the vegetable garden or watch the cabbages grow, to feed the poultry. She sometimes took the children in the pony trap up on to the moors and tried to bag a rabbit or a hare to add to their meat supply. It in no way resembled the shooting parties of hers and Harry's youth. They acquired a cow, for milk, and that further tied them down, as someone had always to be on hand to milk it. Livy took on this task. She was guilt stricken about Bully and Tubby. She had seen pictures of a bishop blessing a gathering of people and their cats and dogs when the air-raids had seemed inevitable; they were being put down so that they might not die of hunger, or turn savage. 'Bully and Tubby are eating food, Lady Camborne. Perhaps . . . perhaps they shouldn't be allowed to.' Her voice quavered miserably. Dena's heart was wrenched by the thought that the child was offering to give up her last link with her parents. 'The country expects sacrifices, Livy, but not the life-blood of its children.' She knew she was speaking in a very childlike way, but that Livy understood. 'Keep Tubby and Bully. We all need them. There's always enough fish . . . and you notice that Bully's not complaining about eating it when I doctor it up a bit . . .'

Of such details were her letters to Harry made up. She tried not to feel resentful, not to express her frustration when others faced danger. But she thought he was probably having a much better time than she. She knew his work was necessary, that his presence in Moscow was important. They needed every scrap of information about the state of mind of the Russians, how well armed and prepared they were, whether they might actually throw in their hand with Germany if the reward were a large slice of the countries to the west of their borders. As they had carved up Poland, they might decide to carve up Europe. They had signed a non-aggression pact; their relationship might be formalized as allies. While that possibility remained, so did the importance of the diplomatic mission in Moscow. But, Dena thought, diplomats would still congregate; the vodka would still circulate. With the wives and families gone, there remained the Russian girls, the clever ones, who spoke excellent English and French. The interpreters, the secretaries, the drivers. The thought make Dena shiver a little. What happened to marriages which had to be lived apart?

The problem of someone to teach the girls was solved by the Foreign Office and Harry. Retired two years before, having spent her life moving from one department to another until she was one of their best all-rounders, at one time assistant to Harry's own father, Bess Bromley had come to the Foreign Office with a double first from Oxford. Harry sent a colleague to search her out.

'Why should I go to Cornwall?' she replied grumpily to the suggestion that she might become a teacher-companion to four young girls, even if two of them were Harry Camborne's girls.'I don't much care for children. They bore me. The country bores me. I have arthritis and, besides, I don't know any geography. I was always stupid at algebra . . .'

'Bess,' said Harry's friend, 'you can't tell me you speak six languages fluently and don't know anything about their country of origin? Forget the algebra. They can manage without it for the moment. Do it for Harry. You always liked him . . .'

'Well, since you put it that way, I'll try it.' She packed her bags with ill-grace; from her large library she selected the books she considered would be useful, though they would have appeared on no school list, put her cat in a basket, and got a train to Penzance. Dena and Ginny were both there to meet her. 'I'm not going to like it, I'm sure . . .'

'Very likely not,' Ginny said. 'Perhaps we're not going to like you. But then again, you never know.' She was carelessly cheerful, determined that this woman would not dominate them all. They had tea in the kitchen at Tresillian, Bess

Bromley sizing up the girls. 'I hope none of you is stupid. I can't abide stupid people.'

'Why don't you try us?' Rachel said sullenly. She was almost sorry to be relinquishing her semi-official role as instructor to the others. She didn't see why this irascible old woman had to come. Her father was interfering unnecessarily. And yet Rachel had about come to the edge of what she could teach herself without guidance. The thing she most feared about the war was that she would emerge from it untutored, not ready for what the world offered. 'Did you really get a double first at Oxford? That's what I'd like.'

'I did, young lady. And to get that you have to work very hard. This is good jam. We don't get jam in London anymore.'

'Mother made it. She's a very good cook.'

'That will make a pleasant change for me. I can't boil water.'

Her immediate decision on whether or not to give the plan a trial seemed to rest on her cat, Timmins. He was released from the basket, and everyone waited. He and Tubby looked at each other, Tubby's tail swishing, determined to show that she ruled this particular roost. Timmins seemed to take after his mistress in temperament. With studied indifference, he selected a place near the stove, sat down and washed his face. His stance seemed to declare that he didn't give a hoot about the opinions of other cats, or for large bulldogs either. Bully approached him, sniffed him thoroughly. He put up with it for a minute or two, then gave the dog a light cuff on the muzzle, but with his claws sheathed. Bully did not retaliate. 'There, that's settled,' Bess said. 'Timmins will stay.'

She went to inspect the 'schoolroom' and the books. Then she immediately wrote out a long list of required grammar and text books for Foyle's. 'It appears I shall have to try to make sense of algebra again,' she said. Dena wrote to Harry:

Bess is a rather fascinating addition to the household. She has Rachel firmly under her thumb, and yet feeds her ambition, ambition for what I'm not sure even Rachel knows. But Bess won't let anything go undeveloped. If I had been thinking of a dear motherly soul retired from the Foreign Office, I have been rudely undeceived. She can be quite a Tartar, but she's never a bore. And she just happens to think that Oliver Miles is rather more than a minor poet. Her cat has Bully and Tubby routed . . .

This was all there was to write about. How dull the letters must seem in faraway Moscow. As the summer advanced and there still was no bombing, Dena's thoughts began to turn towards London. Once or twice she and Ginny discussed a return there, especially after Ginny had come back from a brief visit to Blair. 'Yes, Blair would like us there, all of us, even Bess and Timmins. He'd like our company. But he insists it isn't safe. He's so busy, and he looks so tired, and there's only Griffin to look after him, and one cleaning woman who comes when she can. The place looks very neglected, and Griffin is no cook. It shocks him to see me in the kitchen, but he has to permit it. We could make life much better for Blair. But he keeps on saying "Wait!" Dunkirk was a lucky accident. We got the men out, but nothing else. The country's so short of everything, munitions, arms, planes. Don't you remember what Churchill's been warning us about for years? Well, the ability to fight a war barely exists yet, Blair says. The first line of defence has to be the Air Force. Blair believes Hitler won't hang back much longer from invasion, and how the Air Force performs will settle it all. I shouldn't be repeating these things. Blair shouldn't even talk about them. Bad for morale . . . as if a lot of people hadn't figured it out for themselves. Yes, he'd like us there, but he still says ''Wait!'' Something's going to happen . . .'

So they were far away when the Battle of Britain was fought out in the skies over the south-east corner of England beginning in July. Dena realized she must have been mad to think of returning to London. Belgium and France had fallen; how could anyone assume that Britain would not? They seemed to hold their breath as every day the tallies were released of British and German fighter planes destroyed. Almost no one but the Cabinet and Fighter Command knew how close they were to defeat, how few the numbers, how stretched the resources. Churchill came close to disclosing it when he said, 'Never in the history of human conflict has so much been owed by so many to so few.' For the Germans the real Battle of Britain began in August when Hitler ordered the Luftwaffe to destroy Fighter Command as an essential prelude to invasion. They failed. So Goering sent four hundred bombers, heavily protected by a fighter escort, to raid London. Again and again he sent them. Blair spent his nights in the heavily fortified shelter constructed in the cellar of Seymour House. Griffin spent most of his nights in his new and double role as an air-raid warden. A letter from Harry.

My darling, I'm sick with fear for you all. If invasion comes I shall never forgive myself that I did not insist that you all go to America or Canada.

'As if I would have gone,' Dena commented to Ginny.

Bess got the news that her flat had been bombed and totally destroyed. 'Well, there it goes. All I really care about is the books . . .' She sat with Ginny and Dena in the kitchen on the night she received the news, drinking some of the brandy from the precious store. 'Well, they would have sent me away now, if I were still alive. No one wants old helpless people in a bombed city. So you're stuck with me, me and Timmins.' She looked at them morosely. 'I hope that's not all bad news.'

'Delighted,' Ginny said briskly. 'Dena and I might learn a little Russian too.'

'Not such a bad idea. We might be fighting the Russians one day . . .'

Letters from the Senator to Ginny now became furious.

I find your behaviour inexplicable. Get out while you can! You have a son here, and a daughter who may be

201

trapped in a country which is invaded. Why, they've even bombed Portsmouth, and that's not so far away from you.

Andrew McClintock's letters were calmer. Ginny showed a recent one to Dena. 'If it weren't an entirely wicked thought, I suspect Mr McClintock isn't altogether unhappy about my absence. He has his grandson to himself and his influence. He mightn't even mind my getting killed.' Dena protested, but Ginny said calmly, 'I wouldn't put any thought past Andrew McClintock where his own interests were concerned. I gave in about letting Alex go back only because I believed his threat about the lawyers. He would have found a way of taking him from me, I haven't a doubt. The battle – and the scandal – would have hurt Alex more than the separation.'

But with what Andrew McClintock was able to arrange, they had many luxuries denied other people, such as soap and tinned meat, sugar and biscuits, articles of clothing. 'I'm almost ashamed to take them. When I think of what people are going without . . .'

'Don't be ridiculous,' Bess snapped at Dena. 'Take what's sent, and be thankful for it. Do you want the children to be cold?' She was fingering the pile of sweaters which had come in one parcel, the hanks of wool. 'I suppose he assumes they're all about the same size. And he knows you're good at knitting. You haven't had much of an education but at least you can knit and sew . . . very useful.' Somehow Blair had had time to seek and find a sewing machine, and it was now at Tresillian. Dena sighed as she looked at it. Once this skill had given her the advantage of being able to whip up dresses that did nicely at an embassy dinner, and pretty muslin things for the girls. Now she must turn to making good sensible skirts from the lengths of tweed Andrew McClintock sent, or turning the collars and cuffs of blouses, or letting down hems as the girls grew taller. One of the first things she made was a tweed skirt for Bess, who needed it. 'Never fussed about clothes,' she muttered. 'Never thought I should have brought all I possessed with me.'

With the bombing of the big cities, once again the stream of evacuees came. This time there were fourteen at Tresillian, but Dena and Ginny were better able to cope, to impose some discipline. Somehow Bess's presence had a calming influence on what seemed a multitude of new faces, new personalities. Long years at the Foreign Office, spotting and often covering up the mistakes she saw young men make, had given her an aura of authority, which was recognized by these obstreperous, but often bewildered and homesick children. A few words from her could bring order at the kitchen table where they all ate their meals, but she was also good at discerning the shy and the frightened, those who might be bullied by the others. She had dealt with bullies in her time before. It was her task to administer the sweet ration; the bullies got short measure from her. Although she professed not to like children, she pitched in and helped Dena and Ginny to run this strange household.

All through the second winter of the war the raids on London and the other big cities continued. Blair would no longer permit Ginny to come to Seymour House. He himself was not often there; he travelled constantly between the ordnance factories, made his way once to Washington to demand more supplies, travelled to Switzerland again. He never told Ginny when he was making one of these journeys; it was better that she did not know and worry. Neither would Lydia consent to leave London. She gave her days to Red Cross work, and most nights to fire watching, ready to report where the incendiary bombs landed and alert the fire brigade. Dena realized she was absolutely in the midst of the Blitz, and she refused to come out of it.

By April the Germans had invaded Greece and Yugoslavia, and Rommel had encircled Tobruk. It was then, in one of the last major raids on London, that Lydia's flat was hit. She was on fire-watch and escaped, but returned in the April dawn to find the Knightsbridge block all but demolished. She sent a telegram to Dena, and was on the next train to Penzance. When she arrived at Tresillian she still had grey plaster dust in her hair and her Red Cross uniform was shabby and worn. Dena helped wash her hair, drew her a full bathtub of water, which was a luxury none of them had had for a long time, and saw her to bed. She came down to the kitchen and confessed to Ginny and Bess. 'I've never seen her like this. She's aged so much . . . she looks so frail, and yet she's determined to go back. She says she's very experienced now . . . and she's needed.'

But Lydia stayed a full three weeks, staying in bed late, visiting her father in St Just when the days were fine, talking with them by the kitchen stove at nights. They learned something of what the Blitz was like from the eyes of someone whose responsibility it had been to cope with it.

Dena made her skirts and blouses, knitted two cardigans, even had a not very successful try at making her a coat. Lydia took what Dena gave her and didn't seem to care that they weren't very smart. 'That's what's so hard to take,' Dena said to Ginny. 'I've never known her not to care what she looked like before . . .'

By early May the worst of the raids seemed over, and Lydia went back to London. She wrote from a small, cheap hotel in Pimlico.

The doctors say I must rest a while longer. What a bore.
I think I may impose myself on Verity for a few weeks.

The mention of doctors troubled Dena. 'She didn't say anything about seeing a doctor.'

'She's worn out,' Bess said. 'As anyone else would be.'

With the end of major raids, once again most of the evacuees departed. Once more peace fell on Tresillian. Since it was June, Bess had decreed that there would be lessons for only a few hours each morning. 'You're due for summer holidays,' she told the girls. She confessed to Dena and Ginny, however, 'The fact is that I'm only two chapters ahead of them in mathematics.'

Dena prepared an outdoor picnic dinner for them all for Midsummer's Day. They ate it in the orchard and stayed together talking, watching the very last of the sun's glow disappear in the western sky. Livy sang a song in a Cornish dialect, something mournful, as if of far-away things. She wasn't able to translate the words; it was something she had learned by rote from Isa. Dena thought of Harry, in the heat of the Moscow summer. Ginny had brought three bottles of champagne from the cellar, and glasses for them all, even the girls. 'Just a taste. I've a feeling we're supposed to be doing something pagan and witchlike tonight, or rather, at dawn. Up at the stone monuments on the moor. I don't feel like waiting until then.'

'Neither do I,' Bess said, holding out her glass.

In the dawn of 22 June Germany invaded Russia. By 12 July, the Anglo-Soviet Treaty of Mutual Assistance was signed, and Dena felt as if a trapdoor had been slammed on Harry. They would never let him go now. They were allies of Russia, and Harry was now considered a Moscow old hand. A sense of cold despair entered her heart. The letters from Harry had grown painfully brief. He enquired lovingly about her and the children, he tried as far as he could to share her wartime. But he could say little or nothing about himself or what he was doing. With the logical side of her, Dena knew this was necessary. But they were beginning to seem like letters from a stranger. It was now almost three years since she had seen Harry. She looked very often at his photo to remind herself of what he looked like, and yet she knew in this time there would have been subtle but noticeable changes. She strove hard to conjure up the sound of his voice. It was becoming harder.

On 1 September Edward telephoned Tresillian. 'I'm sorry, Dena, it's mother. She just slipped away last night.'

'What do you mean? Slipped away?'

'She didn't tell you? Her heart wasn't in good shape. The doctors had warned her. They wouldn't let her back into the Red Cross . . .'

Dena understood. 'No, she didn't tell me. She just said she felt tired. I'll go and tell grandfather. I'll get the evening train. I'll be with you in the morning.'

Ginny urged her to stay on after the funeral. 'Not at Merton. That's no holiday now. But there hasn't been a big raid on London since May. Stay at Seymour House. Griffin would be delighted to see you. There's a good stock of canned food, and Blair's cellar still yields some lovely wine.

But don't mope about at Seymour House. Look up some of your old chums. Dig out some of Harry's friends at the F.O. Blair would take you about but I think he's just about on his way to Washington. I'll telephone Mike Goodrick. He's senior military attaché at the American Embassy. A good pal of Blair's. I think he could do with some company. He lost his wife about a year ago. She was a lovely person, sweet, gentle. Mike's rather that way himself. I think he misses her terribly. You might cheer him up. He might cheer you up. For heaven's sake, Dena, don't come rushing back here. Without the evacuees, it's almost like a holiday. It's more than time you had a break. I've felt so selfish, always dashing up to see Blair and leaving you to cope. Do stay on.'

'I might,' Dena murmured.

Everyone crowded into the little car to go to Penzance to see her off, even Bess and Bully. 'Take your time in London,' Bess said to Dena. 'Don't worry about anything here. I'll keep pounding something into these young heads. A lot of good it'll do them, though. Never got me anything except a Foreign-Office pension.'

'My mother . . .' Dena was surprised at how her throat seemed to close as she uttered the words. It was impossible to believe yet that the vibrant, once-lovely woman was gone. She had made their childhood so joyous and carefree, she had taken such a delight in living. 'My mother,' she started again, remembering how it had all been, 'used to say when we were young that men didn't much care for clever girls.'

'In many ways, your mother was right,' Bess said.

'I'm clever,' Rachel said, 'and I'm going to marry the most brilliant man in the world.'

'Who's that?' Chris asked.

'I don't know yet, stupid. How can I know until I get to the right age and I've looked around?'

Dena found the one she was most affected by leaving was Livy. She was aware that Livy looked stricken, graver than the other children. She had insisted on Bully coming with them, although they could hardly squeeze him into the car. 'But Livy – I'm only going for a few days.' Perhaps Lydia's

206

death had brought back too painfully the memories of Isa's death.

'I know. But I'll miss you terribly.'

She waved to them as the train pulled out – the four young girls, Bess, Ginny standing so tall, with the long blonde hair blowing, Bully with his head raised, the mournful bulldog face having the look of not knowing what all the fuss was about. Dena fixed the sight of them in her mind. They were her world. She had them to come back to. As the Germans advanced ever closer to Moscow the unthinkable thought that she might never see Harry again had begun its insistent rapping on her consciousness. She had this little group to hold on to. And she would.

2

Something seemed to snap inside Dena when she had her first sight of London as the train approached Paddington. Reading and hearing about it, seeing the pictures, did not tell the story. The dust of the bombed and devastated buildings swirled in the air with every slight stirring of wind; there was the smell of charred wood. Dangerous buildings had been pulled down, and the rubble lay piled high above their basements. Others beside them were shored up with timber beams, looking as if they too would soon come crashing down. It was a long wait for the Oxford train, and she shared the time with two other women, both of them seeming too tired and absorbed in their own thoughts to talk much. One of them asked her where she had come from. When she answered 'Cornwall', the weary face assumed an expression that was both envious and angry. 'Had it pretty easy down there.'

Edward met her at Oxford. They embraced briefly. He carried her bag, and enquired about his grandfather. Dena was shocked at how worn he looked. His shoulders were hunched. Since he was a farmer, his was a reserved occupation and he had not been permitted to join up. He seemed to regard it as a stigma which he bore with what grace he could. He took her to Merton, and to Verity's kind, gentle welcome. 'She didn't suffer, you know,' Verity said to Dena. 'When I took her breakfast, she was just lying there, looking so peaceful. There didn't appear to have been any struggle.'

'Did you know,' Edward said, 'that she was going to get a George Cross?' It was the award instigated by the King for extreme heroism among the civilian population. 'Seems she went into a burning building where she knew someone was ill. Brought them out through the smoke. She always checked on the people in every street on her route. She was only supposed to be a fire-watcher, but she actually worked as an air-raid warden. They all knew her, loved her I suppose. It will be awarded posthumously now. Someone will have to go to the Palace to receive it.'

'I didn't know,' Dena said. 'She never told me.'

Ellen arrived, somehow managing to look smart and polished. Now that the worst of the Blitz seemed to be over, she had moved back to London to be with George. Her children were with friends in Wiltshire. Julia came. She looked almost as careworn as Edward. Her beautiful Scot, Douglas, had joined up and left her in charge of those thousands of hilly acres and the grazing sheep. She managed to keep it going with the help of old men, who could scarcely struggle through the snow drifts at lambing time. Douglas was fighting in North Africa. 'He'll do something stupid,' she said to Dena when they sat quietly by the fire, 'and go and get himself killed and win a medal. I have five children, Dena. I can't imagine going through life without him.'

They saw their mother laid in the ground beside her husband the next day. It seemed unreal to Dena. They, her children, hardly seemed to know each other now, and had only the bond of these dead parents.

They all, Dena thought, were retreating into their own private world of worries and preoccupations. They had to live the war and survive it, somehow. She read the newspapers carefully in the train on the way back, and the maps showed ominous movements of German troops towards Moscow. Leningrad was almost cut off. Where was Harry? There would surely be an evacuation of the diplomatic corps from Moscow? But how would they get out, and where would they go? The doubt grew stronger in Dena that they would in fact survive the war.

She crossed to St James's in a taxi. The faces she saw were tired, and no one seemed quite clean. Parts of streets were blocked off, choked by rubble. The parks and squares looked grim under a mantle of soot and ash, zigzagged by the mounds of air-raid shelters. She wondered why she hadn't returned at once to Tresillian. What consolation could she find in this place of destruction? Panic seized her momentarily. Was it truly the end then? Would they all die or be conquered? The feeling that she would never see Harry again grew stronger, settling in her heart like a stone.

At Seymour House she rang the door-bell, which hadn't seen brass polish for months. Griffin greeted her warmly. Ginny had telephoned him to expect her. 'A pleasure to see you, m'lady, though I'm sorry about the circumstances of your visit. May I offer my deepest sympathies on the death of Lady Milroy.' She nodded her thanks. Griffin took her bag and led her into the marble-floored hall where grit crunched under her feet.

'Things are different, Griffin.'

He answered, quite matter-of-factly. 'Yes, m'lady. The world's gone mad.' He was gratefully interested in the eggs and butter she had brought from Tresillian, the fresh vegetables Verity had given her. 'We've had a few near-misses in the raids, as I expect you've noticed. These old places, they rain dust and mortar if they're shaken. Myself, I think if Seymour House survives this, when we've won the war, it will almost have to be put back together brick by brick. If there's an air-raid warning, you'll have to go to the cellar. There are mattresses and blankets down there. It gets very stuffy in the summer, and damp in the winter. But still one mustn't grumble. It's better than sleeping in the underground stations, or the shelters out in the parks. The smell, m'lady . . .' Dena could remember that the smell was what her mother had complained of most.

Griffin handed Dena a set of keys. 'I'm sorry I won't always be on call. I have my regular duties as an air-raid warden. Last winter and spring when it was very bad, I was on duty every night. I always wondered when I turned the corner if I'd see Seymour House either burning or in ruins. I trust the young ladies are well, m'lady?'

'Very well, and lucky to be out of this.'

'I agree. No place for children. No place for anyone, I'd say. But we can't all leave, can we? A city has to keep going.'

He was wearing a grey cotton jacket, with a knitted vest underneath, and a shirt which was fraying at the collar. The only part of his dress which resembled the model butler Dena remembered was the black tie and striped trousers, but both were shiny from wear. If it were possible in a man such as Griffin, he actually looked unkempt. But he was not young; he was not used to cooking and washing his own clothes.

She unpacked in the big guest bedroom, with a bow-fronted window looking out on the park. She would not stay long. Already she was acutely conscious that, in other days, her first thought would have been to telephone her mother. The sense of hurt and loss was more keenly felt now than when she had seen her mother buried.

She telephoned the Foreign Office and managed to reach Percy Thompson. She knew he had fairly recently returned from Moscow, because Harry's last letter had reached her through Percy. They had both known him quite well in Moscow, and Dena had liked him. It was puzzling then to hear the note of almost false brightness which came into his tone when he learned the identity of his caller. 'Why, Dena! How lovely to hear from you. I thought you were safe in the depths of remotest Cornwall.'

She sensed at once that he was not as pleased to hear from her as his words implied. She told him of her mother's death, listened to his automatic words of sympathy. 'I'm just really here overnight, a few errands, and then back to Cornwall. How is Harry?'

'Harry? Oh, Harry . . .' as if he had never heard of him. 'Very well, last time I saw him. Very busy. He's considered one of our experts, you know. Always huddling with the ambassador. Of course, one doesn't see too much of other

210

people, except those in one's own section. It's all work now. Good old life's gone, Dena.'

'Don't tell me there are no more parties? I really can't believe that . . .'

He didn't bother to answer. 'Look Dena, I've got to rush. Got a meeting in a few minutes. What about lunch tomorrow? The Ritz? One o'clock. The building's still standing, but don't expect too much of the food.'

She took a short walk in the park that afternoon, going up the same path she had walked with Ginny when they had first met. She hadn't the strength of mind to go back to the bridge in St James's Park. Too many memories of happier times would greet her. The park railings were gone, but she glimpsed the Royal Standard flying over Buckingham Palace. People walked in the sunshine of an early autumn afternoon, not looking about them as she did, perhaps too well used to the altered aspect of the city which she found so depressing. Half of St James's Place, near Seymour House, had disappeared. From Queen's Walk she could see right through to St James's Street. The fire weeds were tall in the gaping basements. The beech hedge was still in place, its leaves just beginning to turn to their winter russet; it was covered in the grey dust of the city and needed pruning. The first crisp leaves had fallen from the plane trees. Unhappy, not wanting to see more, she went back to Seymour House. It was strange to be letting herself in. Griffin had heard her, though, and came up from the kitchen.

'I expect you'd like a cup of tea, m'lady. The library's still in use, but we've closed the drawing-room, the dining-room and the morning room. There's a telephone message for you. From a Colonel Michael Goodrick. At the American Embassy. He said to telephone at any time. He's working late . . .'

She now wished Ginny hadn't contacted her friend, Blair's friend. No doubt he would feel he was required to take her out; she felt like doing nothing now except getting back to Tresillian. But she did telephone, and a voice rather like Blair's answered. 'I'm so glad you called, Lady Camborne. I admit to being very curious about Ginny and Blair's friend. When may we meet?'

211

They arranged that he would call for her at Seymour House the next night. 'I'll probably be going back to Cornwall the next day . . .'

'I'm sorry to hear that.'

She rang off, feeling the smallest prickle of excitement. How long had it been since she had been invited out to dinner? She hoped she would like Colonel Goodrick, and could report to Ginny that she had had a pleasant evening. She cooked and ate a solitary dinner, this being one of Griffin's nights as warden. She telephoned Ellen, but made no arrangements to see her. She tried telephoning some other old friends, when they could be reached. They sounded like Ellen, tired and querulous. They congratulated her on what an easy time she was having down in Cornwall. London was dreadful; they would go if they could. In some cases, strange voices answered the telephone. Her friends had left, and other people had taken over the flat or house. A number of times, the telephone gave an unobtainable signal, which surely meant the place had been bombed, and the friend had moved away or died. She went to bed miserable and depressed. She wished once more that she had gone straight back to Tresillian. At least there, with the young faces about her, there was reason to hope, to hope there might be some future, that peace would come. That she might see Harry again. The bed felt huge and empty, and she had never felt so alone. She wept for her mother, for that vibrant life ended, it seemed too soon. She wept for Harry, who could be in grave danger. At last she admitted she was weeping for herself.

The lunch next day with Percy was not a success. He was brisk and hurried her through it. They had a token sherry before he whisked her through to the diningroom. Its golden splendour was still intact, but the tableclothes had little darns in them. The price of the meal was restricted to five shillings by law, but the price of the wine was astronomical. The food was well enough prepared, but meagre. The service was poor, because there were too few waiters, and none of them was young. Percy took up what was now becoming a familiar theme: how lucky she was to be spending the war in Cornwall. Things didn't, he admitted, look good in Russia.

212

He didn't think they were well prepared, not nearly enough military equipment for the battles they must fight, almost no provisions for the civilians. 'But there are so many of them, millions upon millions, and I think Stalin would be prepared to sacrifice every last one of them. They're still so suspicious and fearful of foreigners. They'll take a fearful revenge on the Germans if they ever get the chance and there's always the Russian winter. If Hitler can't clear the whole thing up before the winter really sets in, that could be his trap. As it was Napoleon's . . .'

She was acutely aware that he was shying away from the subject of Harry. 'To be quite frank, I didn't see much of old Harry in the last months. He's very much involved with the ambassador. It's all very high level stuff. So it's quite some time since I've actually seen him. I was ordered out by the first return of a British convoy from Murmansk. We don't, in these days, go in for farewell parties and all that sort of thing. I'm not permanent in London, either. I'm on a ship in a few days' time, and I don't have to tell you I'm not allowed to say where I'm going.'

She began to be irritated by him. Why had she never before realized that he was smug and pompous? 'Don't worry about old Harry,' he said, as if she were a child. 'He's always known how to take care of himself. Of course, no one knows who'll be left behind to mind the shop now that things are so bad there . . .' That was all he had to say. The war had messed up so much. 'I often wonder if we'll ever get the pieces together afterwards . . .'

'Do you ever wonder if there will be an afterwards?'

His eyes seemed to bulge with shock. 'Look here, we don't go around saying things like that. It doesn't do to think that we mightn't win. Now, if the Americans would just come in . . .' She listened to a long lecture on the selfishness of the Americans, why they had to save Europe in order to save themselves. He looked at his watch. 'Sorry, Dena. Got to rush. Lovely to see you. No, do finish your coffee. And don't worry about old Harry . . .'

He was gone and she asked the head waiter, who remembered her from all the times she had come here with Harry

213

when they had been on leave, if there was any brandy. He looked around the rapidly emptying dining-room. 'For you, m'lady.' He brought and poured it himself. It looked like a thimble-full in the bottom of the glass. 'And how is Lord Camborne?' Head waiters never forgot titles, she thought.

She sat over the cognac until she was the only person left in the dining-room. Something was wrong about Harry. Percy had never been a good dissembler, which was why he probably would never get beyond second secretary in any posting. But he had always been cheerful, and had seemed, in those long ago days, a good friend, someone to be counted on. There was something he didn't want to say about Harry. She didn't for a moment believe that they had hardly crossed each other's paths; the Moscow diplomatic corps wasn't that large, even if they were now in different departments. She swirled the last of the brandy in the bottom of the glass, wondering, as she had more than once wondered, if Harry had been unfaithful to her during this long separation. She didn't doubt that he still cared about her, but the physical separation had been . . . hard. Hard on both of them. Would she, given the opportunity, given the desire, have taken a lover? She couldn't answer. There had been no opportunity; she had never been tested. Fidelity was a common casualty of war. Communication between them had grown thin, strained. As the Germans closed in on Leningrad and Moscow in these last desperate days, she wondered if she ever dared judge Harry, no matter what had happened. She felt the pincer claws of defeat close about her. The last of the brandy tasted bitter. It hadn't been very good to start with.

She went to the ladies's room to ready herself for an appointment with Oliver Miles's publisher. This was what she had not told Livy, but it was one of the reasons for her staying on in London. She tried to put aside the haunting question of Harry on the walk down to the address near Charing Cross.

Mr Venables apologized for his cramped and untidy office. 'We got bombed out in Pall Mall. We're sharing this space with Wyndham's. Sharing everything, really. Secretaries, filing cabinets. Occasionally our manuscripts get mixed up. We have hardly any editors left. Even the women have joined up, working in intelligence and so on. But there's not much to publish. Only the authors too old to be on active service, and those who've already been invalided out. I expect there'll be a great spate of memoirs after the war. Boring old generals who'll endlessly refight their battles. What I hope for is a crop of fine young novelists. The war will have some great stories in it, eventually.'

'You really think there will be an end to it, then?' Dena asked. 'That you'll be publishing generals' memoirs and perhaps another *War and Peace*?'

'Why, bless you, yes, my dear.' He called her that quite naturally, as if she had been his daughter. 'It's a touch-and-go situation, skin of our teeth sort of thing. But we haven't quite lost our teeth yet. Hitler's fighting on two fronts, three, really, counting Greece. If he doesn't win in Russia soon, he won't win anywhere.' He said that in the face of the fact that the Russians had been annihilated at Smolensk and Kiev, that they had evacuated the Karelian Isthmus, that it had just been intimated in the newspapers that the Germans had occupied Estonia. He had a simple and heart-warming faith in ultimate victory that was very different from Percy's official view. 'We'll be hearing something pretty good soon from America, I believe. Something good. That great country, headed by a great President, will not let us down. That was the reason for the signing of the Atlantic Charter. Our two great leaders, Churchill and Roosevelt, don't go to all that trouble to meet just to have a hand of bridge. Maybe they played a little poker but that's what leaders are for.'

Immediately, Dena felt better. 'Then there's something I've come to suggest to you.'

He leaned forward, interested. 'Tell me.'

It had been Ginny's idea, and Dena said so at once. She knew that Mr Venables was aware of the position of Mrs Blair Clayton, and the power of the McClintock-Clayton consortium. 'It's about Oliver Miles's poem, *This England*.' Among all his poetry Oliver Miles had written only one long narrative poem. It was very different from the rest of his verse, in content and style. Venables had published it, with only very modest success.

'I did it only because I admired his other work so much. He didn't really care whether I published it or not. He thought it was pretty poor stuff. Almost doggerel. He wrote it when he was convalescing after he got his dose of gas; poor man, you could say he was convalescing for the rest of his life. But then he was sharing a room with another officer who couldn't see the sense in anything Oliver wrote. He said it didn't rhyme. And why didn't Oliver write something that told a story. Almost as a joke, Oliver dashed off *This England* in a few weeks.'

Dena had read it several times. 'I think I'm rather like his officer friend. I loved it.'

'It came out at the wrong time. It was just after the war, and people wanted to forget the war. Perhaps, if it had been a novel . . .'

'Supposing it were republished now? It's a great and inspiring story of two families in that war. Don't you think it might help people remember they managed to win that one? The American family – that could touch a lot of chords. Mrs Clayton has written to her friend, Helen Sampson. She is willing to record it. Andrew McClintock will put up the money for that.' Helen Sampson was an English actress who had had a remarkable career on both sides of the Atlantic; she was currently starring in a Eugene O'Neill play on Broadway. In the theatre, her name was magic, almost a guarantee of success for any vehicle she appeared in.

'By Jove,' Venables said. 'Has she really? That would be a remarkable coup.' He pursed his lips then. 'It's a bit of a gamble . . . Even with her recording it, would the BBC put it on?'

'I believe they would. I think they'd jump at it. I feel the Ministry of Information would push it. Patriotism . . . and all that.'

'It's a question of getting paper. All publishing these days depends on paper. We could sell the most awful rubbish if we could get the paper . . . it would mean allocating resources I had earmarked for other things . . . Care for a cup of tea, Lady Camborne? Let's talk about this . . .' The tea, brought by an elderly secretary, was terrible, weak, without sugar.

To Dena it tasted better than the cognac at the Ritz. She felt her spirits and her hopes rise. Perhaps it wasn't all over yet. There must be more like Mr Venables left, those who hadn't given up.

He was getting excited. 'We're modest, quiet publishers. Most publishers who do poetry are. It would be wonderful to have a really big best-seller.' Then he grew morose. 'Perhaps we're not the people to do it. There are some big guns in publishing who'd jump at the chance to do something connected with Helen Sampson. People with publicity departments. Of course, *This England* has been out of print for so long the rights should have reverted to Oliver's child, as his heir. We normally require six months' notice, but that's a formality we would waive. I'd hate to fumble a chance like this when it would mean so much to Oliver's child.'

Dena thought he was too nice to be in business at all. 'Do you think you could fail if you had the resources of McClintock-Clayton behind you? Those people know all about public relations and promotion. They sometimes spend small fortunes to be sure they don't get any publicity. It would be quite easy for them to reverse the process. Venables has published every poem Oliver Miles wrote, and all of us know you've made little or no money from them. Do you think it would be right if some other publisher took this from you?'

He stood up abruptly and went to the window, which was criss-crossed with paper strips to try to hold it together against bomb blast. He was staring at the Charing Cross Hospital. Dena saw his hands go up to his face; was it possible that he was trying to brush aside tears?

His voice, when he began to speak, quavered at first. 'I would give my soul to do it, successfully.'

His tone strengthened as he began the familiar words.

This royal throne of kings, this sceptred isle,
This earth of majesty, this seat of Mars,
This other Eden, demi-paradise.
This fortress built by Nature for herself

Against infection and the hand of war,
This happy breed of men, this little world,
This precious stone set in the silver sea,
Which serves it in the office of a wall,
Or as a moat defensive to a house,
Against the envy of less happier lands,
This blessed plot, this earth, this realm, this England.

Now Dena's own hand went up to brush the tears from
her eyes.

She walked back joyously to Seymour House, going along
Pall Mall, wondering which of the bombed-out buildings had
once housed Venables, Publishers. Venables, who had loved
Oliver Miles and his poems. She thought of Oliver's wife,
Isa, who had died saving Chris. It was a gamble they had to
win.

Griffin greeted her cheerfully. 'I've fired up the boiler,
m'lady, so you can have a bath. And flowers have come from
Colonel Goodrick. I truly didn't think there was a florist left
who was able to deliver. Almost like old times . . .'

It was indeed almost like old times. When Dena came
downstairs, the flowers were arranged in a beautiful glass
bowl. There was champagne in a silver cooler and caviar in
a silver dish. It was Griffin's gesture to 'old times'. Dena had
almost begun to believe they might return again.

3

It wasn't at all like loving Harry, the way Dena fell in love
with Mike Goodrick. Then she had been so young, and
Harry had courted her without considering a refusal, had
defied the expectation of a much more advantageous marriage. He had been courageous, and very sure. There had
been no threat to their personal future together, no cloud
hung over them. And she had loved Harry with the very
special beauty and blinding passion of first love. During their
marriage she had sometimes flirted, but always had been
faithful; it was unthinkable that she could seriously care for

anyone other than Harry. But those were the innocent years, the years when she had believed that nothing could take Harry from her: not war, or death, or love of another woman. The doubts about all three things were now strong in her.

Her feeling for Mike Goodrick was very different. She encountered him at a time when her fears were uppermost, when she felt the blow of her mother's death most keenly, when she half believed that nothing, not even love, could survive this war. This tall, gentle, almost shy man was very unlike Harry. He had good looks that were not flashy; she saw dark eyes under dark brows, an almost tentative half-smile. Even as he smiled his face seemed to register pain. She had the sense that he had not smiled often or easily in the year since his wife had died. 'It's very good of you to spend some time with me, Lady Camborne. Ginny's very lucky to have you for a friend . . . She told me about your mother's death. I'm sorry. I don't say that tritely . . .'

She nodded, and accepted what he said. While they drank the champagne and put little scoops of caviar on toast, she found herself talking a little about her mother, about her parents. 'They gave us a marvellous childhood. I shall always be grateful for that.'

Afterwards she could remember no conventional conversation as was normal between strangers. They hadn't talked about the weather, or the difficulties of life in the bombed capital. For the moment the difficulties did not seem to exist. He drove her to the Savoy in an official car. He wore civilian clothes. They talked of the coming alliance of Britain and the United States, but not in a superficial way. Dena had the impression that Mike Goodrick very rarely bothered with what was superficial.

'Are you allowed to say this? About an alliance? Do you have inside knowledge?'

'No, just a gut feeling. It's something that has to be. America will have to commit herself fully and totally. If she doesn't, Hitler will win.'

The pleasure of the evening departed for Dena. She felt it again, the near-certainty that they all were doomed, either to death or to life under a loathsome regime. She found herself talking about Ginny's father, the Senator, and his isolationist views, his belief that Europe was finished and that America would and should draw up the bridge across its moat. 'Could he be right?'

'Never,' Mike said firmly. 'He's forgotten the Japanese.'

The evening fluctuated between hope and despair. She liked him so much. She wanted desperately to believe all he said that was hopeful for the future. It was a small miracle to her that he believed in a future. In turn he listened to every small and seemingly trivial thing she wanted to say, things that had seemed too unimportant to write to Harry. She talked about Tresillian, and how they lived there now; about St Just, and how Livy's family helped them, about her grandfather, and Thea and Herbert. He heard about the dreadful, awesome Tresillian Rocks. She told him the story of Isa and Oliver Miles. The story of Livy; how Isa had died. Even of Bully and Tubby. She was almost ashamed of the way it poured out. But Mike's eyes, his whole attitude led her on. Finally she told him about Mr Venables and their plans for *This England*.

'You'll do it,' he said. 'You and Ginny and Mr Venables. And let's not forget Andrew McClintock. Now, there's a man who hasn't a sentimental bone in his body. Why did he decide to do this?'

'Twice, very briefly, he visited Tresillian. He met Isa and Livy. The combination is magical. For whatever reason, he's doing it. I don't question why. I'm just grateful.'

He drove her back to Seymour House. Dena used the key Griffin had given her. The wooden shutters and blackout curtains were closed on every window. A single light burned in the hall, a dusty chandelier.

On a silver tray Griffin had left out a bottle of very fine old brandy, and two glasses. 'We're obviously meant to have it,' Dena said. 'Blair has always kept a marvellous cellar. One part of the tragedy if this great old house got a direct hit would be that some fabulous wine would go with it. The silver too shouldn't be here.' She wondered why she was rattling on, talking for the sake of talking. He accepted the brandy she had poured. Silently they toasted each other.

There had been something unspoken between them all evening. She knew that he was grieving for someone he had loved. Until now she had not had the courage to speak what she thought she must say.

'Ginny said your wife died about a year ago.'

'Yes.' His tone was so low she hardly heard him. He sipped his brandy, and she wondered if he would say another word. Had she blundered terribly?

'I'm sorry. Perhaps I shouldn't have . . .'

'No. That's all right. I'm glad you said it. People avoid the subject. I wish they wouldn't. I loved her. She was beautiful and sweet and gentle. I don't want the memory of her shut away. It was terrible to watch her die slowly. It was breast cancer. Like all women, she thought she had been mutilated. I found the sight of her both touching and sad, and I loved her even more because of what she had suffered. It hurt her very much when she realized that in spite of the operation she was going to die. She said she would rather have died whole. I found it impossible to reassure her that what had been taken away didn't matter to me. I wanted her alive, no matter what. She was very brave in the end. She even sent our two children to live with her parents, so that they wouldn't have to see her go down. It was painfully slow, and she kept struggling to live. She wanted to stay with me, with us. She wanted to see the kids grow up. They're still living with her parents. I went over to visit them this last summer, during their holidays. I hate it without her. I feel totally inadequate to make up for what they're missing.'

Dena was silent, looking down at her glass, feeling his pain and the pain of the unknown woman he had loved. She thought of breast cancer, and the familiar shudder of fear that all women experience could not be repressed. He saw the shudder.

'I'm sorry. I've talked too much. It's hard never to be able to mention it because people would rather not hear.'

'I'm glad you did, that you like me, trust me enough to want to talk about it.' From a new knowledge that had only slowly come to her, she added, 'Everyone should be allowed to grieve.'

'I like you very much. I could talk to you about anything. I see now very well why Ginny loves you. She said you were very special to her.'

She told him then about the meeting on the bridge in St James's Park and their friendship since. He finished his brandy and rose. She went with him to the front door, switching off the light before she opened the black-out curtain hung across the door. The night was dark, the full moon was still dreaded as an invitation to the bombers. She felt his hand on her shoulder. His head bent towards her, and he kissed her very lightly on the lips. 'Thank you. Thank you very much . . .'

She remained there on the steps until the car, with its two little slits of headlamps, disappeared in the direction of the darkened Palace. Down the street she heard the sound of the sentries' feet in their rhythmic pounding of the pavement. Her lips felt his kiss, light as it had been. What had it been? A farewell? Would she ever see him again? She went upstairs to a bed emptier than it had ever been before.

She saw him again and again. He telephoned early the next morning. She had raced into the telephone in Blair's room before Griffin could pick it up downstairs. What was she hoping for? They agreed to meet at a restaurant in Soho. There had been an unspoken agreement between them that he would not call for her at Seymour House. It seemed to Dena a frighteningly long step to have taken in the space of a few hours. She found she was nervous when she greeted Mike. She realized that compared with most women she was remarkably unpractised in this sort of meeting. What worried her more than anything else was that Mike might think exactly the opposite. And yet, how to convey it to him?

He said it for her. 'You don't usually do this, do you? One evening out because Ginny arranged an introduction is all right. But two nights in a row worries you?'

'Does it show so much?'

'Yes, and I have to confess to being so old-fashioned that I like it.'

It was the most personal exchange they had all through

dinner, but Dena could feel the tension mount between them. There were often silences, and they would then both begin to talk at the same time. Dena wondered what was wrong with them, adults who had lived for a long time in a sophisticated world acting like inexperienced adolescents. She smoked his American cigarettes between courses, something she had never done before. He talked a little about his job, the part of it which was safe to talk about, he talked about life in the army, the house he still had in Alexandria, Virginia. 'Don't know what to do with it. I keep it because if I sold it the kids might think I was selling *their* place, their mother's place. In a way, I think, they blame me for not keeping their mother alive.'

'That's very hard on you. I expect you've all been hiding from the fact that she's dead, and now you know you have to face it. All of you.'

'I faced up to it more realistically last night than I ever have before. It wasn't true what I said about people not wanting to know or to hear. I didn't want to talk about it until I talked to you. I think I'd almost turned against women because one of them, unintentionally, without ever meaning to, caused me great suffering. Suddenly, last night, I liked women again. Specifically, I liked you. It's a good feeling. A marvellous feeling. I've come back into the world.' He looked at her directly. 'I've got some brandy back at my flat. Not quite as good as Blair's, but passable. Will you come?'

She knew exactly what the invitation meant, and he didn't attempt to disguise its meaning. The war, which had meant long periods of dullness and waiting, now produced one of its great accelerations. There was not time to ponder and think, no time for a gentle dalliance to grow into something stronger. The leisured ways of peace were gone. The sense that they all were doomed returned strongly to Dena; Harry was slipping away from her. She might never see him again. If the future did not exist, she would have the present.

'Yes,' she said, and knew that she had consented to love him; she had consented to life.

At first he was an almost diffident lover. She knew at once that he had been with no other woman since his wife had

223

died, and that the physical longing in him was as great as her own. The furnished flat near the American Embassy was as impersonal as these places always were, but it became a haven to Dena that night. She found that the thought of Harry drifted away as she lay in Mike's arms. His first diffidence left him as the physical passion caught them both up. 'Beautiful . . . wonderful, Dena. How can I have been so lucky? Do you like me . . .? It isn't that you feel sorry for me?'

'I've never been unfaithful to Harry before. I wouldn't be here if I only felt sorry for you, if I only liked you.'

'Do you really believe two people can fall in love in one single meeting?'

'Is there any other way? Is it planned and arranged? Is it something that can happen gradually? Maybe . . . when there's time. But war doesn't give one time or too much of it. When you said you were going away . . . back to Washington.'

'I could stay. If you wanted me.'

She put a hand over his lips. 'Let's not look that far forward. For me, this hour will do. Let's just live this hour.'

They saw each other every night. She telephoned Tresillian and enquired from Ginny about the children. Was everything all right? Was Ginny bored, was there too much to do?'

'I haven't time to be bored. And I'm glad you're taking a little break. It makes me feel less guilty about all the times I've been up to London to see Blair. He's still in Washington and probably will go from there to Switzerland. I don't know when. Why don't you stay on a bit longer? Since there's no bombing at the moment you should be quite safe. I hope you're enjoying yourself a bit, Dena.' They talked about Dena's interview with Mr Venables, and Ginny gave her the names of the people at McClintock-Clayton she should contact so that the promotion plans for *This England* could start. 'Andrew McClintock has sent the word from on high. All we have to do now is sit back and watch the professionals at work. Did Mike Goodrick get in touch?'

'Yes. We had dinner. I liked him so much. He's a really

marvellous man. But still so sad about his wife . . .' She was lying to Ginny for the first time, lying by omission.

'Yes, he would be. He's the sort. But I'm glad to hear he gave you a pleasant time. You've probably helped to bring him out of his shell a bit. Make him take you out again. It would do you both good.'

Dena felt the sour taste of deception in her mouth. 'Yes . . . perhaps I'll give him a ring. He's very charming. Courtly . . . like Blair.'

They talked further about the chilling news from Russia. 'I've heard nothing from Harry. They're starting to evacuate a lot of the population of Moscow. I heard from someone in the Foreign Office that anyone who can get a railway ticket east is leaving. Nothing specific about the diplomatic corps, except plans to retreat to some place called Kuibyshev. It's all such chaos, no one really has any definite information, at least none they're willing to pass on to wives. There have been air raids since July, but not too bad.' She did not dare add, because the news had come secretly from Mike, that Roosevelt and Churchill had decided that a top level meeting was required to reassure Stalin that he would have the aid he needed. Lord Beaverbrook was to represent Churchill, and Roosevelt would send Averill Harriman. There was disagreement between the British and American embassies about the survival of the Soviet Union. 'I have an awful feeling,' Dena added bleakly to Ginny, 'that Harry will end up somewhere east of the Volga. I don't think diplomatic immunity will mean much if the Germans take Moscow . . .'

Mostly for the sake of appearances, Dena and Mike once more went through the charade of Mike calling formally at Seymour House, of the champagne and caviar ritual which seemed to give Griffin so much pleasure. Once again they dined at the Savoy, but they did not return to Seymour House for brandy. Mike's bachelor flat was their sanctum and retreat. Once they were inside its door the world was shut out. Dena cooked meals for them to eat alone. They lingered over their wine. Ten days lengthened to two weeks, and spread to three.

'I'll have to go back,' Dena said. 'I can't leave Ginny there

225

at Tresillian alone any longer. I've run out of invented friends I'm supposed to be seeing and reasons to stay on in London. Even seeing dear Mr Venables doesn't require that much time. The girls expect me back. This it it, Mike. I have to go.'

'And what about me? Does this end it? I can't believe this has just been a distracting interlude to you. A little light relief in the dullness of war.'

'You know I love you, Mike. You know it!'

'And Harry?'

'Harry isn't here. That's the trouble. I haven't seen Harry for more than three years. I don't know what he feels any more. The letters seemed so strained . . . so distant. He's grown away from me. He says nothing. And I can't put a finger on what is missing, there's just a sort of flatness. He's almost formal with me. I'll know when I see him. If I ever see him . . .'

'Dena, will you marry me? You must have thought about it. You know how much I love you. I never expected to feel so alive in my life again. You've brought me back to life. I live through you. I want to marry you.'

'What about Harry? The children? You're free, Mike. I'm not.'

'This can't be final. I don't believe it. Can you fall in love for three weeks, and then say it's over?'

'It has to be over. Now that it's come to this, I finally know it. I've been drifting from day to day, living just to see you. I've forgotten my responsibilities, my promises. Now I know that it has to stop. I must go back tomorrow. If I stay any longer, then I'll stay for ever.'

'Then stay. Stay with me for ever. I love you so much, Dena. Harry . . . Harry doesn't exist for me. I know I shall love your daughters, because they are yours. Harry would never stand in the way of them being with you. I'd be very good to them, Dena.'

'Stop it! This is madness. I can't break up our lives because of three weeks.'

'Think about it.'

'It can't be, Mike. Put it down to a temporary madness on

my part. Blame it on the war. Think anything you like . . . No, not that! Remember that I love you. When you think of me, remember that I love you. I always will.'

'If you mean that, you will stay.'

She got up and began to dress. 'Take me back to Seymour House, please Mike. Please . . . Tomorrow I'm going back. I won't be seeing you any more. And this hasn't been a flirtation. Or a distraction. It is love. Part of me will always be with you. Three weeks out of my life, and part of me will always be with you.'

He drove her back to Seymour House in silence. His kiss in the doorway was firm and possessive. 'I don't believe it.' It was not a kiss of farewell.

She was packing the next morning when she heard the sound of the doorbell, and then a more than ordinarily profuse greeting from Griffin. It was Blair, she thought. There had been some change in plans and he had come to London instead of Zurich. Then the voice became clearer, the running footsteps on the stairs. It was Harry who opened the door. They looked at each other for a moment, almost transfixed. 'My God,' she said, 'it's you!'

His arms were about her, his lips on hers. 'Dena! I didn't imagine you could be here! I cabled Tresillian . . . Never expected to find you here. What luck! . . . what incredible luck!'

She drew back a little from him. 'How did you get here? I mean . . . well, I thought you'd be part of the evacuation from Moscow. I wondered . . . it's been so long since I heard from you, I wondered if you were even alive. Of course, the Foreign Office wouldn't tell me anything.'

'I was held in Moscow to help with the Beaverbrook-Harriman talks with Stalin. I flew back through Tehran with Beaverbrook. The FO wants its own report, apart from what Beaverbrook will tell No 10. I'm supposed to be carrying all sorts of personal demands from Stalin to Churchill, and through him to the Americans.'

'Demands . . . for what?'

'What do you think? Munitions. Guns. Tanks. Planes.

They want it all, and a Second Front too. Oh, damn it, Dena, let's not talk about these things. I'm not supposed to, as you well know.' He held her back from him. 'Just let me look at you a minute, my love. You're different. Older . . . more beautiful. I love you.'

She broke the thrust of his arms and sagged against him. 'Sometimes I thought I'd never hear you say those words again. I thought you were lost, gone, swallowed up by Russia. I thought we were going to lose the war, and it would be the end of everything. I've been afraid. A coward. You have right to be ashamed of me. I've let you down.'

'I've never heard such rubbish! Everyone's afraid. And with reason. We're tired and stale, and the whole thing's one damn long grind. If you didn't have doubts, you wouldn't be human. You're very human, Dena, my beloved darling . . .'

They drew apart because Griffin had come into the room with Harry's baggage. 'I just took a chance that someone might be at home here at Seymour House, and there might be a bath going. I've been in that blasted airplane . . . well, I can't count the hours. Is there enough hot water for a bath, Griffin, or shall I do with a wash? I think I may be seeing the Foreign Secretary today.'

'We can manage a bath, m'lord. After all, it isn't every day someone gets back from Moscow. Sometimes I had my doubts, the way things are going, that we'd ever see you again. Shall I get some breakfast going for you, sir?'

'I was afraid to ask if there was anything to eat. I'm starving.'

'I've been hoarding the eggs her ladyship brought up from the country . . . A pleasure, m'lord.'

When he had gone Dena said, 'And you'll probably get his ration of bacon as well.' She went into the bathroom and started running the bath. It would take most of Griffin's supply of hot water, but it would be given gladly. Her hands shook as she busied herself getting towels ready, helping Harry unpack. 'Got a clean shirt?'

He reached out and touched her hand. 'What is it, Dena? Aren't you pleased to see me?'

'Pleased? You can't imagine! It's a bit of a shock. I was

getting ready to go back to Tresillian, and I thought you'd be in Russia for ever. Perhaps lost to me . . .' She had started to search for clean underwear for him, but her hands faltered. 'Harry, I've been at Merton . . . and Ginny insisted I stay on here for a while.'

'Merton? Dena, there is something wrong!'

She told him about Lydia's death. 'The family's broken apart, Harry . . .'

He held her quietly, his hand stroking her hair; he murmured small endearments, made soothing noises as if he had picked up one of his own daughters who was frightened and disturbed. 'This family hasn't broken apart. We'll be together always, dear heart. I'll try never to leave you alone again. Oh, Dena, it's been so long. Cruelly, long. Just let's get these next few days over, my darling, when I have to report to the FO. We'll stay on a bit. Have some time together alone. It can't make up for three years of being apart, but I want you to know that I'm with you, and I'll never leave you. I never did . . .' He paused. 'I'll telephone the girls, but we'll have just a little time alone . . . they won't begrudge us that. Ginny will understand . . '

Griffin knocked. 'M'lady, it's Mrs Clayton on the telephone. I've switched it through to the master bedroom.'

'Thank you, Griffin. Harry, you'd better take that bath while it's still hot, or at least warm. It's a luxury, my dear.'

'Don't I know it! Give my love to Ginny. Hurry back.'

Ginny's tone was both excited and anxious. 'Dena, there's a cable from Harry.'

'I know. He's here! He's just arrived. He's in the bath.'

'Wonderful! I was afraid he'd come straight down here, and you'd miss each other.'

'Almost did. Ginny, Harry says he'd like to spend just a couple of days here before coming down to Tresillian.'

'Oh, yes! You both deserve some time together . . . enjoy yourselves . . .' They exchanged news briefly, Dena asked about the girls; she had less to say about what she herself had been doing. three weeks was a long time to spend in London alone. She was lying to her friend, and sick with guilt about it. 'Harry send his love,' she finished.

Quickly Dena dialled the American Embassy, and asked for Mike's extension. She was lucky enough to find him at his desk. 'You're staying,' he said, his tone jubilant.

'I'm staying for a few days. Harry's just come back. We'll be going down to Tresillian, and I'll be staying there. I won't be seeing you again, Mike.'

It was some moments before he replied. 'You're sure? You're absolutely sure?'

'Absolutely sure.' Casting aside the caution she had always exercised when speaking to him on the embassy switchboard she added, 'I love you,' and then hung up.

It was over. She went back to hear Harry splashing and singing in the bath.

Harry spent most of the day at the Foreign Office. He looked tired when he returned to Seymour House, his face drawn in uncharacteristic lines of fatigue, lines which had not been there when Dena had seen him last in 1938. She was waiting in the library for him. Griffin had closed the shutters and curtains against the chill of the early October evening. Dena had refused the festive champagne and caviar Griffin had wanted to put out, but she had gone and bought flowers for the library and the table in the housekeeper's room where they would have dinner. She had spent her unused ration coupons for the past three weeks on a small piece of steak and some kidneys, and made a pie. She had paid a fortune for some fruit from Fortnums, and had made a *pâté* from what scraps were in the refrigerator. She didn't feel she was robbing Griffin. There would be plenty left over. Griffin had beamed over the preparations and produced Scotch and an outstanding claret from Blair's cellar. He had spent his own ration on a piece of Wensleydale. 'It's a lovely dinner, m'lady. Perfectly English, and a lovely change, I'm sure, from all that Russian stuff.'

Harry flung himself gratefully into a chair, and accepted the Scotch she poured. Griffin had managed coal for a small fire. The shutters and curtains kept out the noises of the traffic in The Mall, the faint footfalls of the people on Queen's Walk. There was a very deep quiet in the room.

'Thank you, my love. I was getting a bit tired of vodka.'

'How did it go . . . today?'

'Today? Well, it was all rather a rush. I was summoned first to brief the Foreign Secretary, and then we were called to Number 10 to see the Prime Minister. Beaverbrook had been there before me. Essentially, we had the same story to tell. I was carrying dispatches from the ambassador. The Foreign Secretary had already seen them. Churchill knew what to expect. Guns and more guns are what the Russians want. More than food. I had an awful feeling, Dena, as I listened to Stalin in Moscow, that he was thinking if he could get enough food and the other necessities for the army, he didn't really care what happened to the civilian population. He is making tremendous demands. He's well briefed. He even pointed to me at one stage in the discussions and began to demand that my friends, McClintock-Clayton give Russia the priority when they're allocating war materiel.'

'You warned me about what they knew a long time ago . . . about the girls being goddaughters of Andrew McClintock.'

'So I did. What an age ago it seems . . . that first Christmas in Moscow. Well, we'll be needing everything Blair can squeeze out of his factories. We and the Russians. The trouble is America will pretty soon need all they have for themselves. Ginny's father and his disciples haven't managed, after all, to pull up the drawbridge. I think, whether they like it or not, they'll be dragged in.'

He slumped back in his chair, the Scotch almost untouched on the table beside him. 'God, I'm tired, Dena. It isn't just the plane journey. The worst thing is that I'm tired of the war, and we're not even halfway to winning it. God knows what's going to happen in Russia. The Germans seem unstoppable. Leningrad's cut off. They'll soon have reached Moscow . . . I suppose I was lucky to have been ordered out. Some part of the British mission will have to stay on, no matter how far they have to retreat. The only thing I can think of that Stalin has on his side is the millions of troops and civilians he can afford to sacrifice. That . . . and the winter. But let's not deny the Russians their courage. The stories coming out of Leningrad . . . Almost unbelievable heroism . . .' His voice faded; he sipped his drink.

'How I've dreamed of this,' Harry went on. 'Just to be back in England. Even a battered England. As hard as it is to comprehend what has happened to London, there still are places like this where one can breathe. Can have a little peace. Do you mind if we don't go out tonight, Dena? If there's just a bit of bread and cheese in the house . . . and I could write Blair an IOU for a bottle of wine . . .'

'I think we can do a bit better than that. I've been making preparations all day. And Griffin has given us his cheese ration. And he's brought up a bottle of claret you'd hardly believe. Positively insisted that Mr Clayton would be hurt if you didn't have the best. We're dining at home, Harry.'

He smiled wearily at her. 'You are my darling, wonderful Dena. Thank God for you . . . and Ginny and Blair. Thank God for the Griffins of this world. Thank God for what's left of England.' He held out his glass, and she took it silently and went and refilled it.

'I think, if you don't mind, we'll spend just tomorrow here, Dena. I'll have to go back and talk to a few people at the FO, and find out what's on their minds for me to do. I have a couple of weeks' leave. Suddenly, I can't wait to get back to Tresillian. To see something utterly untouched by war.'

'It isn't quite the same. But the differences aren't that noticeable. It's all slow, and gentle, and most of the time the war seems very far away.'

'That's part of the dream. That's what I want.'

They ate supper without Griffin attending them; Dena wondered if it were truly one of his nights on duty, or if he was being his usual discreet self. 'There hasn't been a raid for weeks, not even an alert since I've been here. Perhaps that's why I stayed. Too much of a coward, and too comfort-loving to spend my nights in the cellar.' She wished then she hadn't said that. Harry hadn't asked, except in very general terms, where she had been spending her nights. Not even a day had gone by since his return, since her final parting with Mike, but she was beginning to feel the tight drawing of the web of deceit about her.

They shared a brandy in the library, over the dying fire, before going to bed. The image of Mike was in this room, like a spectre. A little uneasily she thought about her own readiness to have a brandy with Harry in the library after dinner. In other days she would have been eager, in fact impatient, to go to bed with him. They went upstairs slowly.

It should have been a joyous reunion. It failed. Harry held her in his arms as if he never would leave go of her again, but that was all he did. She felt him stiffen and grow hard against her, waited, holding her breath, almost, for him to enter her. But he dropped away. He released his hold on her, and rolled over on his back. 'Oh, God, I'm so sorry, Dena. So sorry. Just too damn tired. Been thinking of this moment for days. For years . . . Forgive me, my love. Tired old Harry . . . must be getting old.'

She kissed him. 'Of course you're tired. What does it matter? We have the rest of our lives. What's one night? One doesn't get over three years in a few hours. We have to search a little, Harry. Find each other . . .'

'Yes, my wise love. Seek, and find.'

The next night they walked up to the Ritz to dinner. He had spent the whole day again at the Foreign Office. 'They've got something cooking for me. I think they mean to attach me to the Private Office.' The Private Office was the office of the Foreign Secretary. 'If so, it's a promotion. But I don't know that I'll be able to take a desk job much longer, Dena. It would mean resigning . . . oh, well, there's plenty of time to think about that. Two glorious weeks of leave . . .' He listened with enormous pleasure to the plans for *This England*. 'My clever girl.'

'It was Ginny's idea. And Andrew McClintock's money and pull. Mr Venables said he's had extraordinary co-operation from the Ministry of Information. They say it's right up their street. Or perhaps McClintock-Clayton has made them see which street they should be taking.'

After dinner she was surprised when he suggested they go over to the Century Club for a drink. 'I think I'm still a member. I think I might even be able to get around the dance floor. I just can't get used to the fact that I'm out of

233

Moscow. I keep looking around to see who's following . . .'

They danced, and Harry drank too much, and they stayed too late. Dena realized she also had drunk too much. They walked back to Seymour House by the light of a new moon. Would the full moon bring bombers? They still came, in an almost haphazard fashion, to continue to disrupt the life of the big cities. Why these thoughts, when she should be thinking only of Harry. They were silent during the walk. Were they nervous, she and Harry, who had never known a moment's tension together? She recognized her own nervousness. Was that what Harry sensed? Nervousness and guilt? Had she welcomed him less than whole-heartedly? She strove mightily to put Mike from her thoughts, but he was there, a silent barrier between them. She was almost on the point of telling Harry about him, but knew this was not the hour or the moment.

They went to bed with less show of eagerness than the night before. And once again they failed. Harry sighed in the darkness. 'It's no good, my love. I'm useless to you.'

'Why? Is it me! I don't attract you? Sorry, that was a terrible thing to say. You're just tired. We've been apart for so long. I feel like . . . well, as if I didn't know what to do. As if I had become middle-aged, and not caring so much. Harry, I do care . . .'

He put on the bedside light and reached for the cigarettes on the table. He lit one, and lay for some minutes silently, drawing on it, not looking at her. 'Give me one, please.'

He handed her his own, and lit another.

'I'd better tell you. I have to tell you. It's not something I can keep from you for ever, but I thought . . . just a few days . . .'

She didn't want to hear what she sensed he was about to say. Some part of her already knew it, and her own guilt recognized his.

'Don't.'

'I must. It's very important. I can't live with you until I tell you.'

'I think I know. You had . . . someone . . . someone else, in Moscow?'

234

'It must show. Of course it does. I'm riddled with guilt. I loved you with every part of me, Dena, but, God, we were separated for so long. What a wretched excuse. No excuse at all. Millions of men and women will be parted for the whole length of the war and will still be faithful, no matter what. But I wasn't. I felt lonely and fearful . . . I was a coward in the worst sense. I deserted and betrayed you.'

'You came back.'

'Yes. I came back. I came back because I knew I had to. I went to the Ambassador and told him. I was becoming a security risk. I had myself sent back –'

'*Security risk!* My God, Harry! What did you do? What sort of woman was she?'

'Innocent, I think. It never occurred to me in the beginning that she might have been a set-up. We came together so naturally I couldn't believe it had been contrived. I prided myself that I understood the Russians . . . but will anyone ever understand them? I believed she loved me . . . perhaps that's too strong a word. We liked being with each other. We were alone . . . just a bit fearful. Wondering if there would be any future. I never thought of a future with her. It was always with you, Dena. And she, well, she knew there could be no future with a westerner.'

'Was she . . . pretty?'

'I won't denigrate her. She is beautiful. Quite different from you, Dena . . . but beautiful. Comes of a line of intellectuals . . . a brilliant interpreter. Her father had a high standing in the Party . . . which is why they trusted her among the diplomatic corps. I'm not aware that I ever told her anything I shouldn't have. We're allies, after all. But what did I say to her I wonder? What might I have let slip? The smallest scrap of information can be pieced together with other scraps to make some sort of whole. In the beginning, I didn't see it. I didn't realize . . . And then I knew it could all have been set up. I ran from her because I'm a coward. I ran before it could become serious enough to warrant blackmail. I deserted her in the end and at the same time I betrayed you. All I can hope for in redemption is that I

235

haven't yet betrayed my country. If I did . . . I didn't intend to. So, Dena, that's the rotten story I have to tell you. I don't know whether you will keep me. I don't know whether the Foreign Office will keep me. But I had to tell you . . . as I had to tell the Ambassador. I can hardly bear to live with myself. I can't live a falsehood with you.'

'And she . . . what is her name?'

'Sonya Dimitriyevna.'

'What did she think? How did she take you . . . going?'

'I don't know. Once I had told the Ambassador, I couldn't get in touch with her. It was as if someone within our own embassy had passed the information and yet I thought only the Ambassador knew. Was the embassy bugged? My telephone? All our telephones? When I tried to contact her, she just wasn't there. Not at her apartment. Not in her office. A wall went up. That sort of wall in Russia is impenetrable. I tried to tell myself that she had been evacuated, but somehow I couldn't believe she would go without some word to me. The Ambassador didn't seem to view the matter very seriously, called it a peccadillo. Perhaps other people knew about our affair . . . and didn't regard it seriously. The Ambassador knew I wanted to go at once, but he asked me to stay on while Harry Hopkins was there, sent by Roosevelt, and for the talks he'd arranged between Stalin, Beaverbrook and Harriman. So when the talks were over I left. Feeling ashamed, sick, cowardly. Feeling worse than I've ever felt in my life.'

'Would you have told me eventually?'

'Fair question. I hope I would have had the guts to do it. In time. I hoped it would be a good homecoming. I hoped my shame wouldn't be so evident. I was unable to help Sonya . . . for all I know I may have endangered her. Now I'm useless to you. And yet . . .'

'And yet?'

'And yet . . . I do love you. I've never stopped loving you. You were never out of my mind when I was with Sonya.'

She rolled over and raised herself on her elbow, trying in the dimly lighted room to fathom his expression.

'But you cared for her?'

His features twisted in anguish. 'I have to say it. Yes, I cared for her.'

'I'm glad.'

'Glad!' He stubbed out the cigarette abruptly, himself sitting up to try to study her face.

'If you hadn't cared for her, it would have been very bad for both of us. Just casual sex . . . I wouldn't want to know about that. I wouldn't want to condone it. If you felt something, just some tenderness, some love, then I understand. I understand better than you imagine.'

'Better than I . . .?'

'Yes . . . just imagine. In these past three weeks while you've been going through the agony of knowing you had to leave, of not being able to find her, having to tell the Ambassador. Knowing that you might be ruining your career and possibly destroying her . . . well, during the past three weeks I haven't been blameless either. It's been a lonely time, Harry. More than three years . . . not that that's an excuse. There was something I began to sense in your letters some time ago. Something wrong . . . not quite a coldness, but as if you were holding something back from me. Yes . . . I did consider the possibility that you might have a mistress. I couldn't blame you. It seemed as if the war had engulfed us. We were being swept away from each other. My mother dying was a blow I hadn't been prepared for. It shocked me. I felt empty and hollow. Defeated. I began to understand what your isolation must have been like.' She lay down again, and put her head among the pillows. Her hand reached out to pull him down to her. She didn't try to embrace him, just laid her cheek against his shoulder. 'I thought I'd never see you again. I thought we were all done for. With half of my mind I still believe that . . . there's such a long way to go in this war, and I'm not sure we'll make it. So . . . when I met Mike . . .'

She told him all of it, up to the last telephone call. 'I won't ever see him again, Harry. I had said that to him the night before you came back. I meant it. I was packing to go back to Tresillian, and he was going to ask for a posting back to Washington. Yes, we cared too . . . about each other. His

237

wife really was gone, but I just imagined I'd never see you again. What does it do to us, Harry? Loneliness and tension, and all the time wondering . . . always wondering. We can't be the only ones who feel this way. It must be happening all around the world. Men and women snatching what little comfort they can, something to salve the loneliness, the waiting. A sense of pain that the other person can never drive out. And the guilt. We have to forgive each other, Harry. If we don't, who will? Is there a God to forgive us? Or does He just tell us to forgive each other . . .'

'You needn't have told me. I wouldn't have known. Not the way you can tell about me . . .'

'I would have told you. I would have told you in a thousand ways. Guilt has a way of speaking for itself. It would have spoken for me, if I hadn't got there first.' She began to weep.

'Don't my love . . . don't weep. You're my precious, beloved Dena. You're the most important thing in my life. It was to save this love, much more than to save myself, that I went to speak to the Ambassador. The thought that I might lose you was far worse than the prospect of what might happen to me. Yes, he did call it a peccadillo, and he didn't see that he was obliged to report it to the FO. But I knew I had irrevocably harmed you. I just pray that somehow I'll redeem myself . . . win back . . . Oh, Dena, I do love you.'

'But I'm glad you cared about her. You wouldn't have been Harry if you hadn't . . .' They talked more, saying the same things over and over to each other, words of love, of forgiveness, of trust restored. Their voices grew fainter, lower, the pauses longer; they held each other like children, clutching each other for comfort and reassurance. Eventually Harry felt Dena's body relax completely, her breathing grew deep as she slept. He wondered, as he lay awake, hearing the first stirrings of the city, the first twittering of the birds in the trees beyond the windows, if in her last moments of wakefulness she had thought of this man, Mike, her love for three brief, lonely, frightened weeks. As he now thought of that beautiful, clever enigmatic woman, Sonya, the one who might or might not have been set to entrap and betray him.

Their lives had almost been blasted apart. They lay in each

other's arms, seemingly with forgiveness and trust restored. But he knew that they were passing through a crisis, and that they would have to grope their way back to each other. But when they came through it, if they came through it, they would both be changed, altered. They each had known a fire; he hoped that they had not been burned out.

In the morning they went down to Tresillian by the early train. Ginny met them, joyous at Harry's return. 'And I'll be leaving you at the end of the week. Blair's going to be back in London.' The welcome from the children was rapturous, even Rachel breaking out of her shell of reserve to greet her father. Harry wondered if they also, like Dena, had come to believe that they would never see him again. 'How you've grown! I shall have to get to know you all over again. How are you, Bess?' He embraced, rather awkwardly, his old colleague from the Foreign Office.

'Well enough. Eating better than I've any right to expect. Hope I'm doing some good with these children. But you must never blame them for a blank spot with mathematics. I didn't promise you everything, you know.'

It was Livy who touched Harry most deeply. She managed to pull her chair closest to him in the hour when they sat in the kitchen before dinner, the adults slowly sipping their Scotch to make it last, the children drinking a watered-down elderberry wine in honour of his homecoming. Harry was aware that Livy's gaze seldom left him; it was the first time he had seen her since Isa's death, and that loss, as well as the years in between, made her seem to him more grown-up than she should be. Dena busied herself at the stove. 'I've done nothing really useful for three weeks. It's time I took my turn . . .' Harry guessed that she was pleased to have the activity, pleased to have the crowd about them. The silences on the train had been long and thoughtful; forgiveness there had been between them, but reconciliation was still something to be won. Harry looked at all the faces about him, the altered faces of the children, Rachel and Chris, the 'twins' of Dena and Ginny's friendship, his lovely soft gentle Caroline, Livy with eyes like the sea fixed on him as if she could not have enough of him. Bess smoked frugally, her experienced, old face revealing little, but she seemed content enough. He knew she was restraining herself from bombarding him with questions about the Foreign Office, about the old colleagues, most of all about the Moscow station. He dreaded the questions when they would finally come. He looked at Ginny, her fine, handsome features glowing in the dimness of the kitchen, and then again he turned back to Livy. For once Bully did not snore at her feet; it was as if he too knew that this night of Harry's return was an occasion. He moved his head from side to side, as if he strove to follow the conversation of the speakers. But he was deaf, and the haze of cataracts was growing across his eyes. Dena had told them all of the plans for reissuing Oliver Miles's *This England*. It seemed a light of hope in those darkest days. Harry thought that the dog almost knew what was to happen, as if he lived again at the mention of his master's name, although he probably could not hear it.

For just a moment a silence fell on the whole group, as if they were catching their breaths for the next onslaught of talk. Harry seized the moment. He raised his glass, moving it to include the circle gathered at the table, Dena and the cats by the stove.

'I can't tell you how many times I was afraid I'd never see you all like this again. I can hardly believe I'm back . . .' Then he was ashamed of what he had said. It was not the business of the only man in the group to confess to fear or uncertainty. Their world did not allow the possibility of defeat. They had not experienced loneliness. Then he knew that what he had said had been for Dena alone. She turned from the stove. Her hand went to the glass on a nearby table. Without any of them noticing it, she raised it silently to him. By very small and diffident steps, they reached towards each other.

Ginny went off at the end of the week. Harry had almost two more weeks' leave, and then he would return to London. 'I hope I'll be there for some time,' he answered to Bess's probing. 'On the Russian desk. Have to put the experience to some good use.'

240

They went visiting in St Just, to Dena's grandfather, to Thea and Herbert. The town seemed crowded, though the summer season had long ended. 'A lot of them have been bombed out. Some just don't want to go back to the cities. It's a great relief to have Bess. The school's terribly overcrowded. No one so far has bothered to question her qualifications to teach. They're just glad not to have to accommodate four more pupils.'

A little of summer lingered into these autumn days; gardens were touched with the cheerful glow of chrysanthemums. Dena and Harry spoke little as if afraid to break the fragile loveliness of those days. They never spoke about the events which had jolted them apart. Slowly, they worked their way towards another relationship, because the old one had gone and something must take its place. They went on long walks; there was no petrol for venturing far from Tresillian. Bess had excused the girls from lessons for the term of Harry's leave. Livy did not come with them on the walks, or the picnics they took. She accompanied them just to the gates. It was always then that Bully sat down firmly. He had come as far as he could. 'I can't leave him, you know,' Livy had said to Harry. 'He hasn't got very much longer.'

Harry was dumb in the face of the child's precocious wisdom. 'I suppose,' Dena said softly, 'when you've seen both your mother and father go by her age, you recognize these things. Sometimes she almost frightens me. She knows too much . . .'

'Livy is a Celt,' Rachel said. Her face had become, Harry decided, not exactly pretty but very arresting, full of sharp planes and angles, poised on a lovely long neck: she had Dena's dark hair and eyes. Her intelligence was as developed as Livy's intuitive understanding. They made a strange contrast; they could have been at loggerheads, but they were not.

'What do you mean by that?' her father asked.

'Oh,' Rachel said vaguely. 'They see things. Sometimes Livy's a thousand miles away. She's out there, somewhere in the sea. She could be a good scholar if she didn't let her mind wander so much . . .' Somehow, Harry thought, sweet pretty Caroline and Chris, who should have been Rachel's equal, paled beside these other two.

Less than a week after Ginny had gone to London, Harry was wakened at first light by a gentle knock on the door. Dena still slept, so he went quietly to open it. Livy stood there, barefooted. She looked at him with the face of a stricken adult. Harry put his finger to his lips, stepped into the passage, and closed the door behind him.

'It's Bully,' Livy said. 'He's snoring, but I can't waken him. He just seems to be . . .'

Harry went to her room where Bully was stretched on the bed. Tubby lay curled in her usual place on a cushion on a chest. The old dog's efforts at breathing were strenuous, but did not seem painful. Livy slipped back into bed, wriggling until her lap lay beneath the old head. Very softly she stroked the dog's forehead. 'Would you open the window wide please, Lord Camborne.'

'Why, Livy?' An October mist hung on Tresillian, and blotted out the sea; the room was chill.

'So he can get away. He wants to go. It won't be long now. I'm sorry if I disturbed you, Lord Camborne. I didn't want to be alone. It won't be long now . . .'

He tucked the blanket about Livy's shoulders and about the dog, and added an extra quilt which had slipped to the floor. He slid under the quilt himself, his back against the headboard, held the child closely but gently, stroking the bright red hair as she stroked the head of the dog. There was a sense of shared grieving between them. In the silence of the next hour, he thought of his two beautiful women, Dena and Sonya. He wondered if Sonya were lonely and alone. Or if their adventure had been contrived and cynical on her part. He wondered if Dena's lover had been able to give her something that he, Harry, had never given. He recalled the lives of Livy's parents, their love story. He knew that he held the child because she realized that the last living part of her father was slipping from her.

Her voice invaded his thoughts. 'He's gone, Lord Camborne. I know he's gone. I think you should close the window.'

Unwilling to believe that the animal had truly slipped away, just as she had predicted, he felt over the soft loose folds of skin. Bully was still warm, but he no longer breathed. He touched the dark, mournful muzzle in a lingering farewell. 'He was an old fellow, Livy. He helped your father and your mother and you through some bad times. All he wanted was for you to love him. And you did.'

'We did.' As if exhausted, she slipped from under Bully's weight, stretched herself out, one arm lightly laid on the heavy neck. She fell asleep almost instantly; probably she had not slept all night, Harry thought. He could not leave her to wake alone. He was still there, propped up in bed, his feet in the folds of the quilt, when Rachel came. She knocked quietly, and opened the door. 'Oh, you're here! Mother's been worried. She knew you hadn't dressed.' Her gaze went to Bully, and the sleeping Livy. 'Oh . . . oh! Bully . . . Bully's gone!' She let out an anguished cry. Harry was amazed to find that it was his reserved, self-contained child, who wept unreservedly for Livy's dog.

Harry dug a grave, and they buried him that morning among the trees in the little orchard. He did not consider the occasion morbid. The dog was due the courtesy of the love he had given and received.

The next morning Thea trudged up the hill, bearing a beautifully shaped and polished piece of basalt. 'I knew I was keeping it for something special. I knew one day it would find its right use.' She had chiselled on it the words: *Bully. Beloved friend of Oliver, Isa and Livy*. Almost indiscernible on the bottom right hand corner of the stone were her initials: *T.S.*

After the others had gone back to the house, Harry stayed to ponder it, admire its beauty. One of Britain's foremost sculptors had fashioned a headstone for a dog.

The leaves of autumn, blown by a light wind, were already gathering about the stone. It was more than two years since the war had begun.

Harry and Dena edged tentatively closer. Their words came more easily; they touched each other, his hand often sought

243

hers. In bed they held each other as they had first done, for comfort, for reassurance. They never tried to make love, they bided their time, afraid to break the fragile bridge which grew between them, afraid to speak of but yet not willing to deny the other person each had loved.

It was the last evening of Harry's leave. He and Dena sat alone in the kitchen. All the children were in bed, and Bess had left them to their conversation. Harry had brought out cognac, and they each had a small glass. They could hear the wind outside gathering strength; by morning it could be a fullblown autumn gale.

Dena looked down at the richly-coloured liquid in her glass. 'I suppose I shouldn't have too much of this from now on. They say it's not good for a baby.' She raised her eyes and looked at him directly. 'I'm almost certain I'm going to have a baby, Harry.'

The movement of his hand towards her, as it rested on the table, was infinitely slow. 'It's Mike's child.' A statement, not a question.

'It could only be his. Harry, we will have to divorce. I couldn't . . .'

'Why divorce? What lunacy that would be! You will have a beautiful child, and I will regard her as mine. You're my wife, Dena. Unless you want to change that. Unless you want to tell Mike Goodrick, go to him. Is that what you want?'

'To leave you, Harry? No! To force myself on him? I'd rather be alone . . .'

'I will never let you be alone, Dena. Never. You're my wife. I love you. That has not changed. Unless you want to go. I wouldn't try to hold you if you wanted to go. But I won't willingly let you go.'

'But . . . another man's child? Can you take that, Harry?'

'I can take whatever is necessary to keep you.'

'Could you love such a child?'

'Try me. Just give me a chance. She would be your child, Dena. Can't you understand what that would mean to me? I would love and cherish her. Keep her . . . hold her . . . your child . . .'

'You talk as if it is certain that it will be a girl. Suppose it's a boy?'

'Well . . .? What difference would that make. I'm just used to thinking about girls.'

'As your acknowledged son, he would inherit a title. Something he would have no right to.'

'Good God, Dena, do you really think things like that matter now? All that sort of thing is over. It's part of the world that blew up in our faces. Oh, I suppose the forms will go on for some time, but the fact is that titles just don't matter. All they do is get you a seat in a restaurant. As little as that. No more. It will become totally unimportant.'

'Then you don't care . . . boy or girl? You don't care?'

'All I care about is to keep you. I care about that, and to keep the girls, and whatever other children we may have. We may have other children, Dena. Other sons, if they come. It would all be part of keeping you. Of working for forgiveness. I cannot believe that we don't love each other any more.'

'And . . . the other? Sonya?'

'I cared about Sonya . . . but I never pretended to her that I didn't love you. Mike's child . . . my child . . . what does it matter? Another child is going to be born into this world where madmen are trying to ensure that no children will ever live safely and happily again. Have your child, Dena, and for God's sake, let us love and cherish it. This is the only way the world can go on.'

His hand, which had lain only lightly on hers, now gripped it. 'Come to bed with me, my dearest wife. Let's celebrate this new life. Let's make it ours, completely . . . shared . . . whatever is mine is yours. Whatever is yours is mine.'

They consummated the pact that night, swiftly, eagerly, passionately. Making love seemed to possess a meaning it had never had before. They did not attempt to banish the remembrances that stood behind them. But they had once again established the pre-eminence of each other. Once more they were first in each other's memory and in love.

Dena felt very calm and unafraid as she saw him off the

next morning. 'For the first time I'm beginning to think that we will win. That it isn't the end. Now it's more than ever important to live.'

He kissed her. 'Live in order to love me, in order to give life to our child.'

4

Ginny returned to Tresillian when Blair went back to Washington. 'Every time I go up to London Blair reminds me that he's in Washington almost as often now as he's in London, and that Chris and I would have been a lot more comfortable and safer there. And yet he understands that I wouldn't have wanted that. In this way I've experienced a little of what he's experienced. The war hasn't made us strangers, as it might have done. The war and what he's doing in it would have to look very different viewed from Massachusetts Avenue and Prescott Hill, than from Seymour House and Tresillian. Being here has kept us closer . . . we've shared. That will matter very much when it's all over.'

Harry had immediately been absorbed into the Private Office of the Foreign Secretary. 'It's quite important,' Dena explained to Ginny. 'There are no precise rules of who gets selected to work so closely with the Private Office. But it *is* the hub of the FO.'

Harry had politely declined accommodation at Seymour House. 'That's carrying hospitality a bit far, and Griffin has quite enough to do.' He shared a flat with a colleague whose family had also left London. His letters to Dena indicated that the work was heavy; there seemed no limit to the hours they worked. But he wrote almost every day, often in the early hours of the morning, his eyes burning with fatigue, a precious whisky saved up for this moment.

I need the refreshment that the thought of you and the children bring. I can't express to you how much I want this child. She will be the most perfect, the most beautiful, the most desired. I dream of our child as I dream

of you. I hold you both in my arms. I kiss you tenderly.
Be well, be safe, my two loves . . .

Dena could not remember such letters from Harry before.

And yet, with all the expression of his love, his joy at
being near her, though there had never been time to make
the long journey down to Tresillian since he had returned
to London, she realized that a feeling of discontent and
restlessness nagged at him.

I know the job's important, and that someone must do
this work, but I don't know how long I can stick it here.
Other men are fighting, and I sit at a desk. I'm forty-one
years old. Not too old, surely, to serve, to serve in some
other way, where I feel I'm doing more than writing
briefs and trying to see into the mind of Stalin from a
distance.

Dena tried to soothe him with her comments on the
importance of his work, how much his experience was
needed, but she felt she accomplished very little.

'I know what he wants to do,' Dena said to Ginny as they
washed up the last of the dishes after the girls and Bess had
gone up to bed. She had put the kettle on the stove for a
cup of tea, a nightly ritual. 'He wants to join up. He wants
to get close to some fighting, even active service, though I
suppose he'd be considered a bit old for that. It would mean
resigning from the Foreign Office. And just hoping they'd
take him back after the war. Of course, the awful irony
would be if he joined up, hoping to see some action, and got
landed at a desk in Intelligence in Whitehall . . . I wish he
could stay in England just a little longer, though.' She was
spooning tea leaves sparingly into the big brown pot. She
placed the cosy on it and left it to brew. She turned back to
Ginny. 'I'm going to have a baby in June.'

For a moment Ginny's hands clenched the arms of the
chair; her mouth opened slightly. 'Oh . . . oh, how wonderful!' Then she was on her feet, reaching out to embrace
Dena. 'I'm fiercely envious, but I'm so happy for you and
Harry.' She added, 'Have you told Harry?'

'Oh, yes, just as soon as I suspected.' Dena gently disengaged herself from Ginny's arms and turned to pour the tea. After she handed the cup to Ginny she said, 'Harry knows it's not his child.'

The cup clattered down in Ginny's saucer. 'Not . . .?'

Dena sat down opposite and told her. Ginny listened without interrupting. Expressions changed on her face as Dena talked – worry, surprise, sympathy. 'I hardly know what to say. I introduced you to Mike . . .'

'It's possible that it could have happened with someone else, but I don't think it would. Mike and I seemed to need each other so badly. I had a terrible feeling I'd lost Harry. He'd lost his wife. Two more casualties of war, Ginny. Apart from Harry, if I had to pick a father for my child, I would have chosen Mike. And you are the only person in the world who will ever know this, besides Harry. Mike will never know it. I don't plan ever to see him again. I had made up my mind about that before Harry got back.'

She reached for a cigarette. 'If anyone bothers to count, the baby may seem two or three weeks premature. You will be the only one who knows for certain. Don't be sorry you introduced us, Ginny. I'm having a child, and Harry already loves it dearly. There's no question that he'll accept it as his own.'

Ginny reached for, and lit a cigarette. 'You know, you didn't have to tell him. Women have faked these things before.'

'I would have told him, whether or not there was a baby. I've never had an affair before, Ginny. I don't expect there'll be another one. If I'd kept it from Harry, it would have seemed a sordid little thing. As if I hadn't cared about Mike . . .'

Ginny nodded. 'I think I understand your reasoning. Crazy as it might sound to most other people.' Suddenly she rose and went to the cupboard where the drinks were kept. 'A shot of whisky in your tea . . . it'll help you sleep.' She settled herself again in her chair, took up her cigarette. 'I'll have to take extra good care of this baby, and of you. I feel as if it's partly mine . . .' She smiled across at her friend. 'So early in June you'll have a baby who should have been born a few weeks later. I'm first on the list as a godmother.'

'Thank you. Thank you . . .'

Dena had known that she would tell Ginny at some point about Mike's baby. What Ginny would never hear from her was the story of Harry and Sonya Dimitriyevna.

By the end of November Dena had told Bess about the baby. Bess's lined face had stretched in a smile. 'Good for you! It's what Harry needs most. He's been away too long. I've seen how it affects men when they've been sent to troublesome places where their wives couldn't go. Best thing that could have happened . . . Perhaps you're both hoping for a boy, but all I can say is, if it is, you'll have a very spoiled baby on your hands. Think of all us females clucking over him. Mind you, I've never been one to cluck over babies of either sex. So long as they're clean and pretty and don't cry, I can tolerate them. But I'd like to see Harry have a son. He was always one of my favourite young men when he started at the FO.'

'I'll have to tell the girls soon,' Dena said. 'Better to tell them before I begin to show.'

Bess snorted. 'Well, they've seen kittens and puppies born by now. They've seen countless babies born down in St Just. No mystery there.'

Early in December the three women sat as usual in the kitchen before going to bed. Bess had made tea, and had taken up her book again. She had found many books in the library at Tresillian to delight her. They sat sipping their tea, waiting for the late news. A December gale had torn at the coast for a full twenty-four hours, and was now starting to abate. They all hated the gales, not because of the wind itself, but because it brought closer the knowledge of the battle waged unceasingly on the Atlantic between the German submarines and the Atlantic convoys bearing the lifeline of supplies to Britain; it became all too possible to imagine the men in open boats. The Tresillian Rocks took on a greater menace. Dena's hands worked almost automatically at her knitting. She was becoming skilled at unravelling

249

sweaters which had become too small for the girls, rewinding the wool, and re-knitting them slashed with stripes of another colour. Anything of a light colour was knitted for the baby. As she worked on these small garments, she often saw Ginny's eyes on her wistfully. Harry had been right; a baby was an act of defiance against the powers of evil and darkness which threatened to overwhelm them.

The announcer's voice broke into the programme.

We bring you a special news bulletin. This is Alvar Liddell reporting.

The BBC had adopted the practice of having their announcers identify themselves by name, so that in the event of invasion, the people would know by the familiar voice that they were receiving the news from an official source.

It has been confirmed that today, Sunday, 7th December 1941, at approximately 7 a.m. Pacific time, a heavy force of Japanese fight-bomber planes attacked the American naval base, in the Hawaiian Islands, Pearl Harbor. Widespread damage was inflicted, with the loss of a number of capital ships and, it is feared, a heavy loss of life. News is still incomplete, and a definite statement from Washington is still awaited.

They listened, but their stunned brains had hardly comprehended the news. The radio had returned to the dance music it had been playing. Dena put down her knitting and stared at Ginny. Then without any selfconsciousness, she rose and went to her friend. She bent and kissed her. 'I don't know what to say. It's so terrible! It means . . .'

'It means war,' Ginny said calmly. 'In a few hours we will have declared war, if it hasn't already been done, against the Axis powers. We always knew it would come.' Her lips twisted wryly. 'And the Japanese were talking peace while they were getting ready to attack.' Her thoughts had already turned to her family. 'Blair . . . no, he'll never see active service. Too old, even if they'd let him go, which they won't. There's Robbie . . . and Lucy's husband, John. The last letter I had from Lucy was from Pearl Harbor.'

'It is the beginning,' Bess said. 'A terrible beginning for America. I suspect the losses must be very great if they're announcing them so early. But it's also the beginning of the end. Whatever way it came, it could not be anything but tragedy. I'm sorry, Ginny. Truly sorry. America's sacrifices have just begun. But the whole world has need of them.' She pulled herself heavily from her chair. 'I'll go up now. Good night.' She looked directly at Ginny, and then she said something that for her was strange, because she was not a religious woman. 'God bless you, and bless your country.'

They stayed alone in silence for a while. Ginny paced the floor a few times, restive. 'I feel so far away . . . Robbie will join up. John's already in the middle of it. I wonder if they'll send Lucy back to the mainland. Pray God none of the family was hurt. I wish I were with them . . . Most of all I wish I were with Blair.'

Suddenly she dashed down to the cellar, and returned with a bottle of champagne. 'Don't think I've gone mad. Or that I don't care. I intend to sit up until there's some more news.' She wrenched the cork from the bottle, careless that the shaken wine frothed over. She swiftly filled two ordinary tumblers. 'I don't toast the dead. God knows, there'll be grieving in the States in the next few days as people begin to hear whom they've lost . . . But I toast victory, Dena. Victory in a fight my father thought should never happen, but Blair always knew we had to fight . . .' Tears began to slide down her cheeks. 'Victory . . . and death. It always costs so much.'

Ginny read Blair's letter many times.

It has happened as we thought. We shouldn't be separated any more than we have been before, except that I can't any longer travel as a neutral, and access to Switzerland will be more difficult. They've given me a fancy uniform, and a sort of Department of Defense address. You can address your letters to Colonel Blair Clayton. But essentially I'll be doing the same job as before. The censor won't let me say what . . .

251

Ginny knew that it would be the business of McClintock-Clayton. It would be armaments, war materiel, planes, huge quantities of drugs and medical supplies. Part of the tragedy of this tragedy was that McClintock-Clayton would grow richer.

Stay where you are, my darling. I'll be crossing the Atlantic almost as often as before. Probably now by plane.

The censor struck out the next two lines. Even Blair Clayton had to learn a caution he had never known before.

Dena wondered what Mike Goodrick might be doing, where in the world he would be. The war had now taken on a global scale, and they were all its hostages. As if he knew her thoughts, Harry wrote.

We have so many people in our minds, so many scattered all over the world. It will come right some day. God knows what will happen to us all before then, but it will come right. It must.

By February he was at Tresillian. He had not written and telephoned that he was coming. 'I had to face you with the news myself. To write would have seemed cowardly, dodging your pain and worry. I'm resigning from the FO, Dena. It's the only way I can get into the services. Of course they won't guarantee my job back when it's all over. How can they? I saw the Permament Under Secretary and talked it over. All he could say was that if he were still around when I came back, the FO would view sympathetically my application to be taken back. So I'm doing what everyone else has done. Just going out into the unknown, and hoping there'll be something to come back to. But I'll be able to look in the eyes the men who have gone out and risked everything. I'll be with the FO for about another month, till they get someone in my place, or load my work on to some other poor chap. Then it should be about three months trying to learn how to be a soldier. I've applied for the Cornwall King's Own. It isn't a fancy regiment, but I think I might feel as if I belong, at least a little. I'm a bit old for tough fighting, and I haven't

252

an ounce of experience in leading men, so I expect I'll be attached to someone's staff. Not much chance of glory there, but better than a desk in Whitehall . . .'

'I knew,' she said. 'I knew you'd do it. I can't say I'm happy about it, but I can't say I want to stop you. I have to be able to look you in the eyes when this is over, too.'

Harry was in the last month of his training on Salisbury Plain when Dena's son was born in the last week in June. She had vaguely mentioned the middle of July as the time for the birth. Only the doctor, Ginny and Harry knew differently. Dena called Ginny very early one morning in June; Ginny drove her to the cottage hospital in St Just just as the sun was beginning to touch the town. 'Remember how we sat up on Midsummer's Eve last year? and that day the Germans invaded Russia . . .'

'Stop thinking about war, and start timing the contractions,' Ginny said reprovingly. 'You're supposed to think about peace at a time like this.'

Dena gave a half laugh as another contraction seized her. 'All I can think of is that it hurts. Just as well one forgets in between babies or one would never have another one . . .'

But the labour was swift and quite easy. Dena had been astonishingly well during the whole pregnancy, and the baby was large and healthy. Ginny held him when he was less than half an hour old. She tried to banish the envy from her heart as she looked at Dena's radiant face. She gazed for a long time at the beauty of the child, who had dark eyes, and already long dark hair. She looked at the perfectly formed little body, gently played with the fingers, which groped blindly, but strongly, already exercising the new sense of tactile feeling. 'He's utterly beautiful,' she breathed. He gave a little cry, which was almost a laugh, as if he were pleased to find himself in this different world. But as she looked at this large, strong infant, she wondered how many people who remembered the date of Harry's return from Moscow could believe he was premature. Bess might do some counting, but she would never say anything. The rest of Dena's family would not see the child until he was past the stage when they might wonder. That this was Harry's child was a pretence she would support wholeheartedly; not even Blair would know.

'I must get a message through to Harry,' she said. 'I didn't telephone while you were in labour. Why let him worry unnecessarily? Now I'll be able to tell him he had a beautiful, healthy son. I'm glad that, at last, between these two families, Alex will have a little competition. What a pity there's a whole fifteen years difference in their ages . . . Alex will be more like his uncle than his brother.'

Ginny, Dena realized, was already lost in the fantasy that this child was partly hers. She watched as Ginny struggled between envy and desire. For just a few seconds she wished that this child could have been Ginny's. Then she looked back at her son, listened to the little noises he made, and the sense of maternity and love repossessed her. She would gladly share this child with Ginny, but he would be hers in a most personal and special way. He would never know his real father. That thought was sad, but Harry would never allow him to feel the lack of a father. She already knew that Harry would appear to favour this child because he finally had a son, but the truth would be that Harry would love this child with more devotion precisely because he was not his own. When Ginny was gone, she kissed the baby's forehead and whispered. 'I hope you don't disappoint him. I hope you give him happiness, my little love.'

After three weeks Harry's basic training was finished, and he was given leave before getting his orders. He had applied for overseas duty. Blair had just got back to London and, despite the work that awaited him, he decided to go to Tresillian also. He could, and did command an army staff car, and he picked up Harry in Wiltshire on the way down to Cornwall. Harry wore a captain's uniform. 'It all feels so bogus, but if I'm going on to someone's staff, they can't have a forty-two-year-old second lieutenant.'

'Same here,' Blair said. 'They only made me a colonel so I could pull a bit of rank. I hardly remember one end of a gun from the other. I must be the most untrained quartermaster in the American Army.'

'Some quartermaster!' Harry commented.

Their talk moved on to the baby. At Andrew McClintock's command, Asprey had produced another gold christening mug. 'We might be able to melt them down when we run short of cash,' Harry said cheerfully.

'I hope Ginny feels all right about the baby. She's been so desperate for one herself. I don't think it's going to happen. What are you going to call him?'

'Livy wanted to call him Tristan, but we all had to rule that out because he'd get hell all his life from that. I don't think any boy would like to be called Tris. So she came up with Mark, after King Mark of the legend. She's determined that the Tristan-Iseult thing will be in there somewhere. I don't know why we're all listening to Livy, but we are. She's convinced that the baby was born just to give her a brother and he's the only one to have been born in Cornwall, so she's got some weight in that argument. Dena's agreed to Mark, I've suggested Thomas after my father and Blair after you. And Ginny tacked on Henry so I wouldn't be left out.'

The baby was christened in Truro Cathedral by the bishop. Ginny held the baby, and she and Blair, promised solemnly, in the name of Mark Thomas Henry Blair to renounce the flesh and the devil.

There was a simple christening party at Tresillian, with hand-knitted bootees and shawls from the Tregenna family, one single beautifully carved and polished stone from Thea, and a small, very abstract landscape of the bay of St Just from the baby's great-grandfather. Guy Denham could now hardly see the famous view, his hand could hardly hold the brush. He had begged canvas and paints, which were difficult to get, from Herbert Gardiner, who gave them gladly, as well as a small painting of his own. Mark lay in the cradle which had been Livy's, and received the adoration of the guests, but particularly from the four girls whom everyone already regarded as his sisters.

But Andrew McClintock did manage to reach out and touch the child. A telegram was delivered at Tresillian while the party was in progress, as if he could somehow control the Post Office even in time of war. It was addressed to the Honourable Mark Thomas Henry Blair Penrose. It read:

'*Welcome to the family. Andrew and Alexander McClintock.*'
'Curse the man,' Ginny muttered.

The day that the Honourable Mark Thomas Henry Blair Penrose was christened was also the date of the first reprint of Oliver Miles's long narrative poem, *This England*. It had been announced in the newspapers, and on the BBC, that Helen Sampson would read it immediately following the nine o'clock news. At Tresillian they listened, as did half the nation. Apart from those who made their way to the pubs in the black-out, or had night-duty, there was little to do in war-time Britain except read or listen to the wireless. Most listened to the wireless. The simple telling of the story of two families, British and American, interwoven with the brutal tragedy of the Great War, as they still called it, had a stunning effect on this nation once again at war, and once again with an American ally. The next day the bookshops sold out, and Venables was besieged with orders. All their valuable paper stock had gone into that reprint, with the hope that Helen Sampson's reading would send it on its way, and win a respectable audience. Frustrated in their attempts to buy the slender little book, the demands began to come into the BBC for a repeat of the reading. That was done, on morning and evening programmes. It went out to the Commonwealth, which in turn demanded copies of the book.

A bewildered Mr Venables wrote to Dena.

It is the most marvellous success! We cannot keep up with the orders. I have appealed to the Ministry of Information to help with the supplies of paper. McClintock-Clayton have also put pressure on in certain quarters. In this hour of our peril, it seems the nation responds to this poem of Oliver's almost as it does to Mr Churchill's speeches. It is ironic that Oliver regarded this as just a bit of versifying, not dignifying it with the name of poetry. My fervent hope is that it will lead more people to read what he regarded as real poetry. Just pray, my dear Lady Camborne, that we get our paper! We don't need now to advertise. The book sells itself.

I hope the child, Olivia, is well and thriving, as I'm sure she is under your care. How happy I am that, at last, in whatever form, her father's work has received popular recognition.

When Dena showed the letter to Ginny, Ginny immediately telephoned the McClintock-Clayton London offices. She knew that Blair had already flown back to the States – he now used the quicker but no less hazardous means of crossing the Atlantic. He could usually get space on a military aircraft, a long, cold, uncomfortable journey, but many times quicker than by ship. Ginny relayed the brief message of urgency to Blair's secretary, confident that additional pressure would be put on the Ministry of Information to allow paper to Oliver's publishers as a matter of national importance. And so it seemed to have become. Several times Helen Sampson's reading was repeated, and people began to know bits of the poem by heart. The necessary paper came through, and as many copies as Venables could print were snapped up. It even appeared on the railway bookstalls, where commuters bought their morning paper. Whether or not it was a pure invention of the McClintock-Clayton publicity machine, word appeared in a national newspaper that a copy of *This England* had been seen in the Prime Minister's private sitting-room at No 10 Downing Street, and at Chequers. The race to obtain a copy was on.

It was as well, Ginny and Dena concluded, that Livy was not living in her father's cottage, or even with her Tregenna cousins in St Just. There was little travel in those days of war, and few tourists. But word spread that the poet had died in a small cottage in St Just, and on Sundays or whenever people on their holidays or on leave could make their way to the town they came to search for the house. Dena's grandfather was constantly having to answer the door to strangers.

Dena arranged for one of the Tregenna women to be there, at least in the afternoons, during the whole summer, so that her grandfather could be spared the intrusions. The Tregenna women took on the task gladly, with the same willingness as they looked after the old man himself; it was now a matter of pride to them that such a man had lived in their town, and married their Isa. Letters began to arrive addressed to Livy, simply as 'Oliver Miles's daughter, St Just, Cornwall'. Stacks of others were forwarded from Venables. Ginny tried to sharpen up some rusty typing skills but she was unable to cope. They placed an advertisement in the local paper for a secretary-typist, and specified the reason. From all the nearby villages came offers of help, not so much from typists who wanted to be paid, but from women who volunteered to dispatch handwritten replies to those who wrote, if just the postage would be paid. Most of this Livy remained unaware of. They made a point of listening whenever the Helen Sampson reading was rebroadcast, and Ginny took the precaution of placing the two copies of the first edition which Livy possessed in the vault of the local bank. She thought about putting the rest of Oliver Miles's publications there also, but she hadn't the heart to take them from Livy, though, as a precaution, they remained locked in the library. Mr Venables wrote:

I'm hoping that when the paper shortage eases, we will eventually be able to reprint all of Oliver's work, as it surely deserves. At the moment, it is more than we can do to keep up with the demand for *This England*. I'm sure this phenomenon would both have pleased and annoyed Oliver.

A letter came from Andrew McClintock.

Well, we did it, didn't we? Fine publicity machine, and *This England* is just enough of a tear-jerker to please the masses, much as the thought might horrify its author. Well, I am negotiating with Pyramid Press for its publication in the States. Oliver Miles has never been published here before, but the Helen Sampson reading has created a demand, and we haven't been subtle in exploiting it. I have my lawyers keeping a sharp eye on things. No one will steal the copyright. Just for this one time I won't be charging my usual agent's fee for acting for the child. And I won't let anyone steal her money, either.

Dena laughed when she read the letter. 'Can you imagine Mr McClintock acting as anyone's agent? We must keep this letter. Some day Livy must have it.'

When the first royalty cheque arrived Livy was bewildered. 'That's an awful lot of money, isn't it?' She couldn't conceive that money in that quantity even existed. It bore no relation to the small sums she could remember her mother had earned for the years she had cleaned and cared for this house. 'Now I'll be able to pay you . . .'

'Whatever for? What do you have to pay for?' Dena was stricken that Livy had even thought of such a thing.

'Well . . . everything.'

'Just let me put it in the bank for you. We'll all have a big think about it when the war's over, and you're able to go off to school somewhere, the sort of place your mother and father wanted for you.' She put the money in the account her grandfather had opened in Livy's name so that he could pay the rent on the cottage.

And while *This England* became a much-loved, much-quoted poem, and the infant, Mark, began to emerge as an individual, while Bess continued to press the girls hard at their languages, and even harder in mathematics, of which she showed a formidable grasp, even though she disclaimed any interest in the subject, the war rumbled on. Soon after Mark's christening, Harry had been posted abroad. It took some time for his first letter to reach Dena. *'Back at the old stand,'* it read, *'and I have a wonderful boss.'* 'That has to mean Cairo,' Dena gasped. 'So he must be on Alexander's staff. He should be useful. He speaks Arabic, and has a good knowledge of the country. When they do meet up with the Germans . . . well, perhaps he knows too much about them.'

The newspapers did not present a cheerful picture. The Germans had taken Sebastopol, and had reached the Don. The battle of Stalingrad had begun. Ginny's brother, Robbie, was reported missing. They learned from the Senator that Lucy's husband had been wounded at Guadalcanal. Verity wrote that Julia's husband, Douglas, had been killed in the Western Desert. Dena sought to find words of comfort for her sister, knowing that there could be little for Julia, isolated in her Highland castle.

The girls anxiously traced and thumb-tacked the map of North Africa, as the battles raged. The letters from Harry were regular, but he dared say little. There came the first stirrings of good news. In October the battle of El Alamein began. By early November the papers headlined '*Axis troops start retreat from El Alamein.*' Churchill and Roosevelt met in conference in Casablanca in January, and later that month the 8th Army entered Tripoli. In Russia the tide turned. The Germans surrendered in Stalingrad. A hope they hardly dared express began to dawn. The Russians recovered Kursk and Rostov. It was not, however, all good news. March 1942 was the worst month of the war for Allied shipping losses in the Atlantic. They read the fearful total of forty-three ships sunk in the first twenty days. They stared out across the Atlantic from Tresillian with awe and fury, conscious of the toll it had taken. But by May the Germans and Italians had surrendered in Tunisia. By Mark's first birthday United States troops had landed in New Guinea.

Anxiously they read the news of the Allied invasion of Sicily. Harry was still with Alexander's staff. By the end of July Alexander had moved his quarters to a site south of Syracuse. Then came a letter from a fellow officer written for Harry from Palermo.

Silly fool was sent forward by General Alex to carry messages to Patton. He wasn't supposed to do a thing but just press on. Instead he got himself involved in a little action, and ended up pulling someone from a burning tank. Bloody thing was about to explode. So the idiot disobeyed orders and didn't mind his own business, which is the General Staff's business. He'll either be court-martialled or they'll give him a gong. He's a bit burned about the hands and he's got a whacking great burn on his bum, which is why he's lying on his stomach and can't write. Silly bugger. But he's cheerful, and sends his love to you all. When he reeled off all the names and showed me the photos, I just thought I'd go and visit this harem when it's all over. Lost my wife in the London blitz. Pity the girls are just a shade too young.

Ginny was relieved, but mystified. 'What's a gong? It sounds a bit obscene.'

'Slang for a medal,' Dena said.

Later, when Harry could write, he told them that he had been recommended for a Military Cross.

I don't in the least deserve it, and General Alex was furious or so I'm told. But there wasn't anything else anyone could do. It was so instinctive. But for the time being, until I can sit down without yelping, I'm in a backwater. General Alex's headquarters have left me behind. Funny how everyone calls Montgomery 'Monty' and Alex is always General Alex. He's that sort of man. The next leap is to Italy, and we'll need all his genius for that.

'Thank God he is out of it for a while,' Dena said.

Blair was at the Quebec Conference when the South-East Asia Command was set up under Mountbatten. The summer gave way to autumn. 'Russians recover Smolensk,' the papers announced in late September. By early November they had retaken Kiev.

From London Blair telephoned. 'I've learned that Harry has been taken from Alex's staff, and is going to be helping out at the Tehran Conference. It seems they need everybody who ever had any dealings with Stalin, and someone who even begins to understand what's on his mind. The Russian Bear is starting to show its claws. When he produces his figures of the millions of dead, who's going to say he can't have what he wants . . . I wish I could get down to see you, Ginny. Isn't possible just now . . .'

After the Tehran Conference Harry seemed to be constantly on the move. He never said in his letters where he was, or what he was doing, '*The usual business*,' he wrote to Dena, *'but this time I'm in uniform. I got the totally undeserved gong.'*

'That means he's being a diplomat again, but in the Army,' Dena said. 'Well I hope its keeping him very far away from trouble.'

The RAF raids were hitting Germany very hard, now, but what the newspapers were not so free with was the news that the Germans, now aided by radar, were hitting Bomber Command. The Americans proposed daylight bombing, and then produced, along with the British, a Mustang fighter capable of long-range escort for the bombers. Mark had not quite reached his second birthday, running as a change from walking, starting to frame coherent sentences, learning from all the people who surrounded him, when the Allied invasion of the mainland of Europe began. At Tresillian, when the news came after months when all their coast line had seemed one enormous army camp, that the invasion had finally begun, they toasted Mark's birthday a little early.

There was a hurried telephone call from Harry in London. 'I've been, sort of, seconded to Eisenhower's staff. Sort of dog's body. Can't say any more. I might get to France.'

As the Allies advanced through France the V1 and V2 bombs began to land on London and the south-east of England. Thea came to Tresillian one morning with news telephoned from friends in Hampstead. Guy Denham's house, his studio and many streets around them had received a hit. Everything in a site of about an acre had been demolished. It was a wilderness of rubble.

Dena went down to St Just. Her grandfather sat in the little kitchen-sitting room, his face curiously calm. 'We all have to make our sacrifices, and so many have. They've lost sons and husbands, brothers and lovers. They've lost their wives and sisters. All I lose were my landscapes. It's little enough.' He sighed. 'I'm so old, Dena. It hardly seems to matter. Just take good care of those you've got at Tresillian.'

The next morning, very early, one of Livy's aunts appeared at Tresillian. 'I just couldn't telephone the news, Lady Camborne. It's your grandfather. He couldn't be woken this morning when my sister went as usual to make his breakfast.

Such a nice old gentleman . . . but so old, Lady Camborne. I expect when he heard about the pictures all going up with the bomb, he just lost heart. Yes, I suppose you could say he just lost heart.'

Guy Denham was buried in the Anglican churchyard in St Just. Ellen came from London, and a harassed-looking Edward from Merton. He had spent his war doing the work of two men, and feeling bitterly ashamed of his civilian status. Guy Denham's will left all the landscapes which Dena had insisted on his sending to Tresillian to Dena, '. . . in gratitude for these years of devotion.'

As the V1 and V2 rockets landed on London, once again the tide of refugee children came; once again Tresillian took its share. Dena and Ginny almost lost count of how many there were. The children filled the rooms long disused, they scrambled over the stones at the base of the old Tower, raced among the Tresillian Rocks at low tide, and no warnings would keep them in bounds. Resignedly, Dena snapped the locks back on the cellars and the library, and she and Ginny spent most of their time trying to devise ways to stretch their small rations. Most of the children were noisy and boisterous, but under a sort of bravado the women sensed hidden memories of hideous bombings, and a lasting fear. Some were sullen and apathetic, grumbling, moving listlessly, feigning boredom to hide their fear and grieving. Some had lost fathers in the war; some had lost mothers and brothers and sisters in the bombing. 'Whatever I feel about them,' Ginny said, 'the sight of them breaks my heart.'

The invasion in France pushed on; winter gave way to spring. In March the Allies over-ran the last of the V1 and V2 rocket launching sites, and the bombing was over. The evacuees departed. They looked around, suddenly finding each other in the new peace of the old house. 'God strike me dead if I ever complain again,' Bess was heard to mutter.

And in the first days of April Roosevelt died. '*I don't think this man Truman can handle the job*', Ginny's father wrote. His son, Robert, was still missing, and the Red Cross had not so far been able to locate him in any prisoner-of-war camp. Ginny knew the sadness that pressed on her father, but more especially on her mother. *'She's not well, and the worry over Robbie, the uncertainty, doesn't help.'* Through she never said so, most particularly not in letters back to her parents, Ginny believed her brother was dead.

Mark was approaching three years of age, when the Red Army moved into Berlin and Hitler committed suicide. Harry was pushed forward as quickly as possible to the British sector of Berlin; he had skills that could be used. He could now write freely of the horrors of a starving Germany, picturing for Dena the destruction of the places where they had lived and worked and walked, where the girls had played. 'Thank God he's survived,' was all Dena could say, over and over. 'Thank God.'

The 8th of May 1945 was proclaimed by Churchill and Truman as Victory in Europe Day. From Tresillian they went down to St Just and joined the celebrations there, bringing bottles of wine to share with Livy's family. For Thea and Herbert Ginny brought an especially fine bottle of brandy. 'I've been saving it for something special. I expect there won't be anything more special than this.'

Blair came down to Tresillian as soon as he could manage. He was just back from Washington, and he was loaded with tinned hams and fruit and butter. They had their own belated celebration. Ginny touched his face tenderly. 'No more worrying every time you cross the Atlantic. No more fear that one, last stray bomb will get you . . . I expect we can breathe again. Begin to take up . . . well, not exactly where we left off.'

'I advise you all,' Blair said, 'to stay put, at least for this summer. London's uncomfortable and difficult. Seymour House has survived, but we almost have to prop it up, it's been so badly shaken. The heating system's given up. The only hot water I get is what Griffin can boil on the stove. I'll get it all in order as soon as I can . . . that is, as soon as I can get building permits. Fortunately, it has historic value, and we maybe allowed to do necessary repairs quite soon, in case it just falls down of its own accord.'

Ginny travelled to London and waited patiently until there was space on an aircraft, cold and cramped, to take her to

New York, where she travelled on to Alex's prep school in Rhode Island. Their meeting was unchronicled except in the joy in Ginny's face when she returned two weeks later. 'He said . . . he said I did the right thing by staying in England. He'll be here as soon as it can be arranged.'

Harry was part of the British team when Churchill, Truman and Stalin met in Potsdam, an outer suburb of Berlin. He brought back photographs of the leaders at this conference, with himself in the background, as there were photographs of him with other members of Alexander's staff. In the early days of August the man Senator Jackson had thought too small to follow Roosevelt in the presidency gave orders to drop Japan the atomic bomb, whose success had been revealed to him while he had been in Potsdam. It had been calculated that to invade Japan could cost a million lives. He chose the other option, and the world gasped in awe at the enormity of the decision.

'This is it,' Ginny said. 'Finally, it is the end.'

On 2nd September the Japanese signed an unconditional surrender. On the next day, six years after the war had begun, a cable came from the Senator. When Okinawa had fallen to the United States forces in June, one of the prisoners, without dog tags, suffering from amnesia which was the result of a head wound, was believed to be Captain Robert Jackson. He was now in Hawaii. Ginny sat in the kitchen and wept. 'I always believed he was dead.'

Blair came down to share her joy in the news, though the celebration was low-key. He had brought the best food and wine he could find from London for their time of celebration. They put the big dining-room back into use, and Dena brought out a yellowing linen tablecloth, and decked the table with flowers. Blair and Mark, in his highchair, were the only males around the table.

'A sort of early Thanksgiving,' Blair said, raising his glass to them all. He studied the faces of the women; Ginny and Dena were older, but in some fashion more beautiful. Bess's face was sombre. She spoke of no plans for herself. Then he came to the girls. Incredibly Chris, his little Chris, and her twin, Rachel, were almost fifteen; Livy was fourteen.

Caroline was thirteen. They all had begun their womanhood during these years of war. Chris had an appealing, fresh beauty which would develop; Rachel was oddly attractive in her rather sharp way. She would be an acquired taste, like olives, which Blair liked. There was glorious Livy, the full beauty of her mother joined to her father's poetic, dreaming mind. And little Caroline, she of the angelic face, with Harry's golden hair and strange blue eyes; Mark was so much like Dena, dark haired and browed. Except that his eyes were brown, instead of dark grey; he looked, Blair thought, just a little bit as Alex had looked at his age.

As if Blair's thoughts had been spoken aloud or that she was prenaturally sensitive to these things, Livy said, 'Now all we need is to have Alex back. And Lord Camborne. When will we see Alex, Colonel Clayton?' She was still remembering the boy who had left. Blair, who had seen him on each visit to the States, wondered how they would adjust to the transformation from boy to young man.

The December days were growing shorter, and the house was feeling the bedevilment of its draughts in the winter winds when Blair sent word that Seymour House was again habitable. 'Don't expect it to be exactly as it was before. That's going to take some time.'

Ginny said to Dena. 'I'm not going to leave you here.'

'Why not? You know we can manage . . .' But the little car that had served them before the war had rusted almost to the point of uselessness. The house would seem appallingly empty; the flat in Knightsbridge had vanished.

Ginny took the decision for them all. 'Come on. We're going! All of us. There's plenty of room at Seymour House. Yes, you too, Bess. We can't put the girls in school until we've sorted some things out . . . and we can't let them run wild. Yes . . . Timmins too. The lot . . . Now everyone start getting things ready. You have two days. Then we're all going to pack into my car. Livy! Don't look like that! You'll be back again. Lots of times . . .'

'I didn't know I was coming.'

Ginny clucked with impatience. 'Don't be silly. Do you

suppose for one moment we'd leave you? You have a family. You belong with us . . . Lady Geraldine and me . . .'

'Can I take Tubby?'

'Silly girl. He'd have a hard time looking after the house by himself.' They engaged some of the Tregenna women to care for the house. After Burma had fallen it was learned that young Austell was among the thousands who had died there. There were other young men straggling back into St Just, glad of any work they could find. So the garden and orchard would be taken care of. 'Just don't think about it,' Ginny said. 'Get packed.'

It was an acutely uncomfortable journey back to London, they and the baggage and the two cats squashed into Ginny's Rolls, for which she had to beg a new battery. Boxes of books and other belongings had been sent by rail. A beaming Griffin greeted them at Seymour House. 'Now I really believe the war is over. You'll excuse the deficiences, Mrs Clayton. We've accomplished a great deal, but things are still hard to come by. It will be some time before we're allowed to paint anything. The curtains and loose-covers look terrible . . .'

'We won't complain, Griffin.' He had aged since Dena had last seen him. The sight of him reminded her acutely of the times when he had laid out champagne and caviar for her and Mike Goodrick. His clothes looked a little better than, at that time, but still dated from before the war. The difference was that he had been able to engage some staff. There was as yet no housekeeper, but there was a cook and two maids, and even a young man he was training as a footman. A small squad of cleaning-women came in daily. 'It's all I can do to keep them from drinking up all our tea ration.'

By right of long service, he inspected all the children. 'Goodness me! Which of you is which? Now, let me see. Miss Christine, and Miss Rachel grown so tall. Little Miss Caroline . . . and Miss Livy. No one could mistake that hair. And here,' he lingered over the small boy, 'is Master Mark. Why, Mrs Clayton, doesn't he remind you of Master Alex when he was that age? Master Alex is a grown man now. Mr

Clayton has shown me his pictures . . .' He was courteous to Bess, knowing what a part she had played in their lives, but dubious about the cats. 'I'll try to arrange for one of the carpenters to make some sort of little door in the kitchen door . . . If you'll show them the way. I do hope they won't go wandering off in the park.'

'Timmins wouldn't be so foolish,' Bess snapped. 'He's a town cat. But I wouldn't answer for Tubby . . .'

'I will,' Livy said, fiercely defensive. 'I'll go with her every step.' She glared up at Griffin. 'She won't make any trouble. She's been . . . fixed. Besides, she always knows where to come for her meals.'

'Ah, yes, the meals. Well they don't have animal rations. But I expect we'll manage.'

They spread themselves out over the house, the girls finding the rooms they wanted. Rachel and Chris were together, Livy and Caroline paired off. Ginny found Bess unpacking her bag in the smallest of the rooms on the nursery floor. 'But, Bess, you can't be up here! There are plenty of larger rooms downstairs.'

'This will suit nicely. It's good and high. I can see above the trees. All those years at Tresillian . . . I've quite forgotten how closed in London can seem.'

Ginny lingered in the doorway. 'Bess . . . you won't be leaving us again, will you? I mean it's been so long. You're part of the family.'

Bess answered with her usual reservation. 'While something needs pounding into those thick young heads, I'll be here. Or in St Just. I rather fancy a little place of my own there. I have my pension, you know. I won't live on charity.'

'Whoever thought of such a thing? Now don't get your stiff neck up, Bess, just because you're cleverer than the lot of us put together.'

Bess gave what passed for a smile. 'Just so long as you remember that I'm cleverer than the lot of you put together.'

In the last of the daylight Bess and Livy were seen escorting their cats around the boundaries of the garden. Griffin's nose twitched as they went through the kitchen, but he said nothing. Things were very much changed since before the war, he reflected. And would, he thought sadly, stay changed. They would never go back. Even people like the Claytons would never go back to what they had been.

Ginny made enquiries through the American embassy, and through the Red Cross, about a number of friends they had lost touch with during the war, wondering now if they were alive or dead. Gradually the information came through. She was able to tell Dena, 'Mike Goodrick's all right. He was wounded at Anzio, but he's all right. He's a General now.'

Dena nodded, turning her face to her friend. They were walking in St James's Park, heading back to Seymour House for tea. Inevitably the memories of their first meeting were revived. The lamps had just been lighted on Queen's Walk. 'Thank you. I would never have dared make enquiries myself. I wouldn't have seemed fair to Harry. I'm thankful he's safe. I hope . . . I hope he can be happy.'

By Christmas life began to seem more as it had once been. Parcels arrived by the dozen from America. Andrew McClintock sent crates among the regular shipments of goods which were meant for industry, to be delivered, eventually, to Seymour House. Nor did Griffin scruple now to deal on the black market for food. 'No men are risking their lives to bring in butter and meat,' he protested to Ginny. 'If the money's available . . . I beg your pardon, Mrs Clayton, but I think you've been too long in Cornwall. You've forgotten the ways of the city. I have my suppliers. They make a living finding and selling these things. Where's the harm? It isn't as if you and Colonel Clayton haven't contributed to the war effort. The King should be pinning a medal on the Colonel . . .'

Ginny gave in, and let him do as he wanted. She and Dena revelled in the luxury of not having to cook, hardly even having to mend clothes any more. There were few coupons to buy new clothes, and Ginny refused to allow Griffin to deal on the black market for them. But no one could stop the flow of packages that came from Andrew McClintock, and from Ginny's parents. Since the girls were so much of an age, what didn't fit one fitted another. There were underclothes and nylon stockings and sweaters. Dena still wore the sable coat, and gratefully. From somewhere in the cellars where he had stored them, Griffin produced Ginny's startling number of fur coats. The girls all had new coats sent from New York. For the first time Livy saw the label Saks Fifth Avenue. She could hardly believe the riches that unfolded. She often talked of the magical days she had spent here in Seymour House before the war. Mark was now wearing a remade version of the red wool dressing-gown Ginny had bought for her then.

Silver reappeared about the house as an everyday item. 'It's all been stored in vaults,' Blair explained. 'And some bits we kept here; you know, there are cellars under the cellars here. Maybe one of the advantages of having an old house.' The beautiful, glowing Impressionist pictures had been brought back from the storage place in Wales. Blair rejoiced in them, as he rejoiced in the house being full, in the lights burning in every window with the curtains drawn. 'Now I believe it's over . . .'

They decked a tree for Christmas in the great marble hall, and everyone pretended, for Mark's sake, that Santa would make his way unerringly through the network of chimneys. Mark was used to the myriad chimneys of Tresillian, but he worried that Santa would get mixed up with all the chimneys of the houses he saw about him. Livy had to show him that Seymour House stood independently of other house. He tried to count the chimneys of St James's Palace, but it was beyond him.

'They took pity on me,' Harry said as he stood unexpectedly in the hall of Seymour House on Christmas Eve. 'I just went to Templehof Airport in Berlin and waited until they had a plane going this way. I have three days . . .' He swooped Mark up in his arms. 'You've become a man while my back was turned.' Mark looked bewildered. He didn't know this stranger. Dena had to explain to him that this was the 'daddy' they were always talking about. 'I'm sorry,' Harry said, 'I've come with no presents. Nothing for any of you. There isn't so much as a potato to spare in Germany, and, if there were, I'd give it to the nearest child.'

As Ginny kissed him she said, 'I'd hate it if you'd come laden. Can't you imagine what a Christmas present this is for all of us?'

Dena lay quietly, thankfully in his arms that night. 'There never has been such a wonderful Christmas present for me.'

They were ready with the sherry glasses almost empty, the ceremony of opening presents over with, the joy of seeing Mark breathlessly, unbelieving, explore what Santa had managed to drag down the chimney for him, ready to sit down to Christmas dinner, with the plum pudding made from ingredients sent over from Washington, with two fat geese Griffin had procured from sources Ginny had stopped asking about. They had waited until after the King's Christmas broadcast, the first in peacetime. 'Now I finally understand the word privilege,' Ginny said, looking around them all. They knew she did not mean the good things spread about them, but the fact of simply being alive and together.

Instead of Griffin coming in to announce that dinner was served, they heard a minor commotion in the hall. Griffin flung open the doors of the drawing-room and, before he had time to say a word, Andrew McClintock appeared. He walked with a cane, more dependent on it now. Behind him came a tall, very dark-haired young man, slenderly built but with the hint that the already broad shoulders were going to fill out. He had been beautiful as a child. He was not less so now, though his features had sharpened and matured. He looked around the room, and then went to his mother. 'Alex!' Ginny began to weep as he held her. 'You said you'd come – I couldn't hope it would be for Christmas.' Tall as she was he lifted her slightly off her feet in a gesture of boisterous celebration.

'I didn't think we'd make it. This has to be the best Christmas ever . . . there'll never be a better one.' Six Christmasses they had spent apart, but, as she knew, Alex did not resent his mother's choice to remain in England. He fully accepted the importance of Blair in her life; perhaps he was also wise enough to be thankful that he wasn't the only male on whom she focused. His affectionate gaze, his hugging, laughing greeting also showed to some of those

271

who watched that he knew she had also taken the decision not to live out the war under the shadow of Andrew McClintock.

'Damn me!' Andrew McClintock said, 'can't anyone get me a drink? No, I don't want any of your sherry. Brought over my own seventeen-year-old Scotch. It kept me alive on the plane. Never been so cold in my life. We had six planes loaded with drugs for Germany setting out, and I just decided to hitch a ride for Alex and myself. Told them to drop us off in London. They had to refuel in any case. Look, Blair, this is something we've got to look into seriously. People are going to want to go flying all over the place. We've got to make it more comfortable for them . . .'

Alex was going from one to the other, greeting, kissing them all. 'Well,' he said, looking around the girls, 'haven't you all turned into a bevy of beauties . . .' He shook Harry's hand. 'We didn't expect this pleasure, Major. Thought you were locked up in Berlin . . .' As at the time of his return to Tresillian that last summer before the war, Livy again felt unsure of where she rightly belonged. Alex took some time greeting Mark. 'Hi, fella. Hope Santa Claus brought some good things for you. We ran into him at the airport. He's just getting ready to go back to Lapland. Had the reindeer all hitched up. He said there were a few things he forgot to drop off with you, and he asked us if we'd mind doing it for him.'

Livy had her last sight of Alex fixed in her heart: this handsome, assured young man was someone she did not know. But there was no kitchen to retreat to now, no Isa to shield her. She kept retreating from Alex. At last he stopped talking with Mark, and there was only herself.

'And Livy . . .' He bent and kissed her. 'I always knew you'd turn out beautiful. I've never forgotten your mother.'

Dinner was delayed for another half hour while the presents which Andrew McClintock and Alex had brought were opened. Again Livy hung back, and Alex came to her last. 'I was going to mail it . . . but this way's much better.' She tore the wrapping off a morocco bound copy of *This England* stamped with her initials. 'I've got my own copy. I hope you'll sign it. Not quite like having your father's autograph, but almost as good.'

She stared at it, struggling against tears. 'I have some of his books that he signed. He signed some specially for me before he died. He said it was all he had to leave me . . . I'd be proud to give you one.'

'That's too much, Livy. They're yours . . . especially yours.'

'He would have liked me to give you one. I want to give you one. You can't refuse.'

Before the day was over she had selected one volume of her father's poems, and underneath the inscription her father had written, she wrote Alex's name, and signed it: 'With love, Livy.' And to Andrew McClintock she gave one of the first editions of *This England*. 'You made it all happen, Mr McClintock. Because of what you did for *This England* a lot more people are starting to read my father's other poetry. I wish it had happened before he died.'

Andrew McClintock accepted the book gravely, and with unusual gentleness. 'Why, thank you, young lady. It's very generous of you to share this with me, knowing how you must treasure it. I'll take great care of it. I wish I had been able to see your mother again. A splendid woman. We'll be expecting a lot of you in the future, the child of two people like that.'

Livy knew he meant the words kindly, but she also knew that he had begun to include her as a member of these two families, which family in particular she was not sure. And because of that, much would be expected of her, as he had warned. Andrew McClintock did not bestow his patronage lightly. She was pleased, and yet she felt the beginning of a burden placed on her. She began to understand how Alex must feel, the only grandchild of such a man. How much more would be expected of him in the future.

Andrew McClintock moved from Seymour House to the Ritz the day after Christmas. 'You've got a full enough house,' he said to Ginny. 'In any case, I like to have a bit of peace. I'll leave Alex with you.'

The next day, before Harry was due to return to Berlin,

Andrew McClintock made a formal appointment at Seymour House. 'Just the adults,' he said tersely to Ginny. 'I don't need to see any of the children.' He sat in the library with them for an hour, arguing his case, or rather simply stating it, as he didn't seem to think the case required argument. As a result, as soon as he had left, Dena was on the telephone to Thea and Herbert.

'Can you possibly come up, Thea? On the night train if you can manage a sleeper. Harry has to leave no later than tomorrow evening, and we have to discuss some things. This time Mr McClintock really seems to have lost his mind. He proposes to adopt Livy . . . yes, I said adopt!'

The Gardiners arrived weary and crumpled the next morning. 'I've brought all the papers,' Thea said grimly. 'Let's rout the old dragon for once and all.'

They faced Andrew McClintock in the library only a few hours later. Thea let him read the last will and testament of Iseult Miles. 'It's properly drawn and witnessed. It appoints Herbert and me as executors and trustees of the estate, and while it doesn't appoint us as Livy's guardians – after all, Isa never expected us to outlive her, the will was just something to see that no one took the cottage and the other bits and pieces from Livy – the document would certainly carry a lot of weight with a judge. It is our opinion that you would be a totally unsuitable person to adopt Livy. In the event that you pursue this, we will take steps to adopt her. If the judge thinks we are too old, and we are too old, but you are older, then the natural adoptive parents should be, would be, Harry and Dena. She has lived in their house for years, she is midway in age between their daughters, and a close friend of theirs. They treat her as their own child . . .'

'Treating someone as your own child is different from acting as a parent. Why didn't they take these steps before? Have you thought of what I can give the child?'

'Only money,' Thea said shortly. 'Why this? Why now?'

'The child interests me,' he said, as if that was all that mattered. 'I sense she is gifted. I was impressed by her mother. Think of the life I could give her.'

'I am thinking of it. It's no life. If you think any English court would hand her over to you just for the asking, to take her to another country, to live with an old man . . . why, Mr McClintock, I expected you to be more intelligent than this.'

'And what about us?' Ginny said. 'I remember we had this discussion years ago, after Livy's mother died. We, Blair and I, wanted to have her. We love her. Her mother died saving Chris's life. Don't we stand a chance?'

'I cannot believe that any judge would not look favourably on an application from me,' Andrew McClintock said. 'After all, it isn't every day that an orphan child . . .'

'Are you going to say that it isn't every day that a poor little waif is taken in by one of the richest men in the world? I don't think that would weigh very heavily, Mr McClintock. Livy was born in St Just. That is her natural place. Between us we can certainly ensure that she will be sent to the right schools, and that without touching her little bit of capital which is building up, oh, yes, I'm aware of it, from the sales of Oliver's poetry which you made possible. That has been placed in a trust and no one can touch it, except Livy when she reaches majority. We have not been negligent. We may have been a little careless about adoptive formalities, given the fact that Livy was living happily and well among children of her own age, getting an education, living as normally as any child can live during a war. They can be started at once. And will be. Go home, Mr McClintock. There are some things money just can't buy. Don't be a foolish old man.'

Andrew McClintock's mouth dropped open slightly as he gazed at Thea. Then, to everyone's amazement, he began to laugh. 'Well, you are a shrew, aren't you, Mrs Gardiner! I can just hear you telling some sympathetic judge what a terrible old man I am. And of course my lawyers would remind him of the bohemian life you and your husband led before you settled down into middle-aged domesticity. About your daughter who doesn't really care to see you. I wonder how he would view the whole thing. We could make quite a case of it. But I don't think we will. It would damage the child.'

'I'm glad you've remembered Livy's interests at last,' Thea said.

'I have only Livy's interests at heart. I could give her a great deal. More than money. Is this child forever to remain a shuttlecock between all of you? She ought to know where she belongs.'

'With us.' the words were said almost simultaneously by Harry and Blair.

'There! You see! You can't even agree on that. Where will she be? I'll be watching, you know. I'll know exactly how she's treated. I'll know where and when she goes to school, and with whom. If I discover any evidence of neglect, I'll see that it is remedied in law.'

Thea leaned forward. 'What exactly is your interest in Livy? She's hardly more than a child. Only been out of Cornwall once before . . .'

'My interest? I've told you. She is an interesting child. I think that, eventually, she and Alex might make quite a pair.'

Ginny gave a gasp of outrage. 'You're arranging their lives! Alex is only a boy and Livy's barely in her teens. You're already thinking . . . why, it doesn't bear thinking of! What does she mean to you? I would have thought you would have had some much better dynastic match in mind for Alex, someone of family, or money, preferably both.'

'Alex needs neither. He has that. Livy is more likely to make him the sort of wife he needs. I won't want him marrying some spoiled brat. I married that sort of woman, remember. A brat of noble birth, but a spoiled brat nonetheless.'

'Let Alex make his own mistakes,' Ginny said bitterly. 'You've played God once too often. Blair and I must now withdraw our offer of adoption, because that would bring Livy too much into your sphere.'

Andrew McClintock used his cane to raise himself from his chair. 'Well, I don't appear to have done the child much harm. At the very least I've made you sentimental, negligent fools realize where your duty lies. This child is nobody's child until someone makes her theirs officially. Do something about it, or I will. Good day to you . . . Blair, I'd be glad if you would accompany me to the hotel. I'm returning to

Washington tomorrow, and there are things we need to discuss. Ginny, I expect we'll be seeing you in Washington very soon. It would be nice for Alex to see something of his mother, and I think it's time Christine began to know her own country.'

Thea slumped back in her chair. 'Is he always like that! Could he possibly have meant it about Alex and Livy?'

'Not for a moment,' Ginny said. 'It's more like a warning to us not to make any such plans, or allow Livy to dream of them.'

'Still,' Dena said, 'he has woken us up. We have to do something about Livy.'

'Do exactly as I said,' Thea replied. 'Herbert and I will apply for adoption. And then we will, if that's what you want, leave her with you. I have no intention of taking her away from her friends.'

'Nor I of letting you,' Harry said. 'Well, we must never let Livy know that she nearly was the subject of a right, royal battle. Wouldn't it have looked wonderful in the press? The poor little poor girl – or almost poor. And I think if we'd given him half a chance, the old devil would have gone ahead. He enjoys a fight.'

'Don't you think it's time we asked Livy what she wants?' Herbert said. 'We've been putting this off since her mother died.'

Ginny felt stricken, remembering Livy's doubt when the move to London had been decided. 'We'd better do something. She's got to know she's not going to be cast aside. You know perhaps we've misjudged Mr McClintock. He's capable of having created this whole storm just to make us realize how careless of Livy's feelings we've been. We have to make her understand, once and for all, that she is wanted by all of us. She has utter and complete trust in you both, Thea and Herbert. If you tell her what we plan . . .'

'Then we'd better start planning.'

Livy lay awake that night while Caroline breathed deeply in sleep beside her. It was all decided. She would have Thea and Herbert as sort of legal parents, she couldn't quite make out how this was to be arranged. But they would guide her and help her and they would always be there, in St Just. And she would stay with the families. In her own mind the families were inextricably entwined. But she would never be without them. Under this one roof, this night, were gathered all the people she most loved. In her mind she ticked off the list. Tubby snored at the foot of the bed, pressing against her feet as she always did. There was Caroline beside her. And Rachel and Chris. Colonel and Mrs Clayton. Lord and Lady Camborne. Little Mark. And Bess. And, finally, there was Alex.

The arrangements had been explained to Bess. 'Well child, I'm very glad it's been sorted out and properly. Not everyone has two, no, it's really three, families. And always remember, if you fall out with all of them, there's Bess to come to.'

Livy knew that night what it was like to feel rich.

Chapter 8

1

Thea Sedgemore took her time over her tea in the kitchen of their cottage in St Just. It was early; it would be an hour and more before the winter's light touched the garden, longer before it would be light enough to go to the studio. But she had been wakeful, thinking about yesterday's work and the day's work which lay ahead. The stone was gradually shaping into something which almost had the sense and the life she strove for, and yet it continued to display a character of its own. It was the unending compromise of her life and work: what she could see in the stone, and what the stone itself would yield.

They had never left St Just after the war. She loved her studio and her garden; Herbert was content to work in his studio a few doors along the street. Blitzed and shattered London had never attracted them back. It was 1952, and she was close to sixty; Herbert had crossed that line. The work of the war years and the years that followed had brought a wider recognition to them both, but it sometimes dismayed her to realize that she was now the more famous. Herbert didn't seem to mind; he was quietly proud of the recognition she had received. The work that once had been thought so controversial was now accepted, and in some quarters much admired. Galleries from all over the world had bought it. People were talking of her as they did of Henry Moore, but Thea knew that she would never match that gigantic talent. But she was happy, more or less satisfied with what she created. A body of work lay behind her; there was more to do, much more, as much as her strength and her hands and her imagination would bear. She was aware that it was dangerous for any artist to become smug, but she gazed into the burning coals and counted herself a fortunate woman.

The knock on the door was urgent, and it startled her. The light from the room could be seen from the street outside, but who would be coming at this hour? She felt a chill of premonition as she hurried to open it.

Bess Bromley stood in the street outside. She, like Thea, was still wrapped in her dressing-gown, her hair uncombed. After the war Bess had returned to St Just, and she now rented Livy's cottage over on Water Street.

'Bess!' Thea held the door wide.

'Just heard it on the wireless. The King's dead. Died last night at Sandringham.'

Thea stood for a moment, shocked by the news. Then the chill of the February morning struck her. She gestured Bess inside, and went immediately to pour her a mug of tea. 'That poor girl!' there was no need to speak her name. 'Twenty-five is very young to be queen.'

And around them others had begun to learn the news. The bell of the Catholic chapel had begun to toll, a single mournful note. This was followed shortly by the different sound of the bell of the Methodist church, and this in turn seemed challenged by the yet different note of the bell of the Anglican church, which stood at the top of the hill and whose little steeple was the first thing the fishermen saw as they approached St Just from the sea. Thea was reminded that the young woman of twenty-five who last night had become queen, was also now the head of the Established Church.

The unofficial, unusual bells had wakened Herbert. He came downstairs, eyes still half closed in sleep, his hair standing on end, his dressing-gown fitting his thickening shape like an old droopy skin. They told him the news. He pondered it in silence for a time, poured himself a mug of tea, and then went to the beautiful old Welsh dresser that graced this homely room. He took out a bottle of fine brandy, and laced his own tea and Bess's and Thea's. 'What a rotten job to be saddled with at her age.' He raised his mug. 'Well, good luck to her.' And then, surprisingly, because he was prone to declaring himself an atheist, he raised his mug and added, 'God save the Queen!'

Within a few minutes the telephone rang. It was Livy. 'You've heard the news? Isn't it sad? He was so young to die and she's so young. Bess is with you? Good . . .' It was typical of Livy that she had telephoned. She would soon be twenty-one, and Thea and Herbert's guardianship would end. Except for summers at Tresillian, she had seen little enough of them in the years since Andrew McClintock had forced them to legalize her position; but she had never been far away from them either. Letters had come, written regularly and with ease, as to dear friends. She had shared her school experiences, her life at Oxford, the pains and pleasures of falling in and out of love. Thea was convinced that Livy had never been truly and passionately in love. In that case there probably would have been silence. Livy wrote with glowing pride of the exhibitions of Thea's work she had seen, often having seen particular pieces begin to take shape here in St Just. She had attended every one of Herbert's exhibitions at his London dealers, though he himself now never bothered to attend. She had written from Washington, New York, Paris and Zurich, wherever her relationship with the two families, the Cambornes and the Claytons, had taken her.

Immediately after that Christmas when Thea and Herbert had started adoption proceedings, all four girls had been enrolled in a school in the south of England noted as much for its exclusivity as its excellence. If the headmistress had any doubts about accepting Livy, they were swiftly dispelled. It was natural that she would be glad to have the daughters of Lord Camborne, and the daughter of Blair Clayton, who in his quiet way was known to have been so influential in aiding the war effort, and who spent more time in England than he did in his own country. The headmistress was aware of the humble background of Livy's mother, but that point was far outweighed by the fact that she was also Oliver Miles's daughter, a girl of startling and, even at this early age, almost ripe beauty and, the headmistress guessed, a quick, sensitive, intuitive intelligence. Thea and Herbert's rather scandalous past was now left well behind. They were respected artists. Even in a world where traces of the snobbery still remained, there was still no question that Livy would not be accepted at that school. Looking at them all, the two sets of parents, Thea Sedgemore and Herbert Gardiner, even Bess Bromley, the four girls themselves, each different yet a part of a whole, the headmistress knew that she must take all or none. None of these people would allow them to be separated. The headmistress acted as if such a thought had never crossed her mind. She had never encountered quite such an assembly before.

So Livy had continued to share the lives of the two families. She had the same clothes, the same uniform and found herself accepted by the same people because those who did not accept her, or who tried to snub her, found a ready snub in return from one of the other girls, all except Caroline, who did not seem to know how to snub anyone or to give a rude retort. Rachel sometimes despised her younger sister because she was soft, given to tears. Most other people loved her on sight, the classic English beauty, soft lips and her father's distinctive blue eyes, her mother's profile, the perfect chin and neck.

All of this seemed to slip through Thea's memory in the brief time she spoke with Livy on that February morning. In embracing Livy, she had taken them all into her life, even Alex and young Mark, who trailed so far behind all of them. In her memory it was always summer at Tresillian; they were all gathered there, even Harry and Blair, who came and went with bewildering speed. The voice on the telephone seemed to bind them more strongly. A death in the family. Thea guessed that that was how much of the nation would regard this morning's news.

'Will you be coming up to London, I mean, for the funeral? I suppose it'll be in about a week. There has to be time for everyone to get here.'

'Gracious no, Livy. The King won't miss me!'

'I wish you would. We'd all like to see you.'

It occurred to Thea for the first time that Livy must be speaking without knowledge of the others' plans. 'Where are you now, Livy?'

'At Oxford, of course.'

'Then how do you know what the others will be doing?'

282

'I just know they'll all be there. Except Alex, of course. There'd be plenty of room for you at Seymour House.'

'How do you know? You haven't consulted Ginny.'

'I just know.' It was true. Livy, who belonged to no one, now belonged to them all, and over the years her confidence had grown so that she could suppose with the certainty of a member of the family that some arrangements could be made. 'We'd all like to see you and Herbert and Bess.'

As they brewed a second pot of tea, a call came from Ginny. 'How sad it is! He was too young to go.' She spoke from Seymour House, and echoed Livy's thoughts, without being aware that Livy had already spoken to them. 'You'll be coming up for the funeral?'

'What are we supposed to do at the funeral?' Thea demanded. 'We'll see and hear enough about it. You and Blair will be busy enough, I've no doubt.'

While Thea cooked the full breakfast which Herbert always demanded, and which he relished now more than ever because rationing was easing, a call came from Dena in Paris. 'I've had such a time getting through. All the lines are engaged, naturally enough. You'll be coming up to London, won't you? Such sad news. I do feel so sorry for her . . .' She said much the same as the other. 'We'll see you in London,' she concluded.

They ate their breakfast in their dressing-gowns, and the telephone continued to ring. Friends, mostly from London, commiserating, as if it were indeed a death in the family. Bess finally went home, and Thea had her bath, and let the telephone ring. Later that morning she called at Bess's house, and together they climbed the hill to Tresillian. Bess moved with some difficulty now, one hip arthritic, which she was unwilling to admit. Their conversation was disjointed. Together they recalled the war years, and the years since, the years when the country had tried to pull itself out of the ravages of war. Both Harry and Blair had been heavily involved in the administration of Marshall Aid, though in different ways. 'I suppose Harry bargained for as much as he could get, and Blair wanted to give it all. But still I do think . . .'

'They were not,' Thea observed drily, 'between them entirely responsible for how it all got shared out.' After the war Harry had been kept on longer in the army than he had bargained for, because his skills were useful in the tricky business of administering Berlin between the four powers. Eventually he had been given back his job in the Foreign Office, and found that those who had stayed out the war there were generally senior to him. He had headed the department concerned with liaison with the Americans, which inevitably involved him in the administration of the Marshall Plan. It was generally supposed that his friendship with Blair Clayton, and the connection with Andrew McClintock, who had been an enthusiastic promoter of that plan, had landed him this special job. He made frequent, quick visits to Washington, and it was noticed that he was sometimes summoned to 10 Downing Street, along with the Foreign Secretary, for conferences with the Prime Minister and heads of various industries. If they could not actually summon Blair Clayton or Andrew McClintock, there was always Harry Camborne who could carry their messages. And he did. 'Harry's been lucky in his career,' Bess said with the authority of an old hand. 'The war held him back a bit, but his ambassadors generally have liked him. But still, I hear he's always worked brilliantly and very hard. There's no doubt he'll make ambassador some day, unless he does something stupid.'

As if in preparation for that, he had been transferred from the American desk at the Foreign Office to Head of Chancery in Paris. He was in that post now, and Dena was filling the role of diplomat's wife with the skill she had learned over the years.

Thea and Bess wandered that day in the walled garden of Tresillian, noting that the early daffodils had already come into bloom, pausing, as all of them always did, at Bully's headstone. Bess, who had her private doubts about Thea's kind of art, preferring the more traditional, had always liked Bully's stone. Her cat, Timmins, and Livy's Tubby were buried in the garden of Seymour House Neither of them had long survived the move to London.

'There's so much of us here,' Bess said, as they gazed at Bully's stone.

In the days that followed, by newspaper and by the dim, flickering pictures on the television set, Thea learned of those who were assembling to mark the passing of a king. She studied the pictures of the young Queen being greeted on her return from Kenya – where she had paused on her way to Australia, only to be summoned back to London – by the Prime Minister, Winston Churchill. But one picture above all haunted Thea. In the Great Hall of Westminster, where the King's body lay in state, three women had appeared briefly at the top of a small side staircase to pay tribute, all their faces screened by a mourning veil, but the features in profile quite distinct: Queen Mary, the King's mother, Queen Elizabeth, his widow, and the young Queen Elizabeth, his heir. The picture gripped Thea's imagination. Somehow, someday, it might be possible to carve out of stone an impressionistic ideal of that tableau: the three queens. She sighed, and let the idea pass. Better leave it to the photographers.

On the day of the King's burial, she and Bess went, as if by common intuition and consent, back again to the walled garden of Tresillian. They picked the fully opened daffodils, and laid them where most of the townsfolk had laid their tribute, at the War Memorial. Herbert surprised them by attending the service at the Anglican church. That night they shared dinner, and Herbert's best wine, and their memories of those they always called 'the girls', or, encompassing them all, 'the families'.

That same day most of the Camborne and Clayton families were gathered in London. Harry and Dena were in the Abbey for the funeral service, by right of his being a peer of the realm; Blair and Ginny were there as invited guests, an invitation which acknowledged Blair's constant and distinguished service to Great Britain before and during the war and his continued service thereafter. There were many who might complain that McClintock-Clayton had made a great deal of money from that war, but it was never denied that Blair himself had headed that war effort, and worked unsparingly, and often in danger to accomplish what he had done. It was rumoured that after the war he had been offered the ambassadorship to the Court of St James's, and had refused.

Andrew McClintock, also in the Abbey that day, was there as a courtesy, acknowledging his brief tenure of the office which Blair was said to have refused. For a short time during Truman's presidency he had held the post of American ambassador to Britain. He had done it almost in a joking spirit, more or less to oblige the President until someone younger and able to give more service could be found. The post had always required a great deal of money to support its occupant. Andrew McClintock had shown that, even ceremonially, he could fill that need. All he required of his President was that he shouldn't ask him to be a diplomat. So for a few months he had enjoyed his position, poured money into the refurbishment of Winfield House in Regent's Park, the Ambassador's residence, very often importing by the plane-load the necessary materials which were still scarce in Britain. He had left behind him some beautiful antique furnishings, and a few very choice pictures. He had bowed out gracefully when his successor had been appointed. He had been surprisingly popular at Buckingham Palace, and with his staff, mostly because he had no pretence of knowing the job, and left the diplomatic side of it in the experienced hands of his aides. He sometimes commented to Ginny, who had acted as his hostess during those brief months, that he didn't know what his father would have made of all this hob-nobbing with kings and queens. Not very subtly he reminded her that when his father had arrived in Washington he had been labelled by the Southerners as the biggest carpetbagger of them all.

The four girls, Rachel, Christine, Livy and Caroline were jammed into a high window of the Home Office, overlooking the route the funeral cortège would take along Whitehall to Paddington Station, where the coffin would be borne by train to St George's Chapel, Windsor, for burial. Mark, not yet ten years old, had begged Harry to get him leave from school

286

to come up to London for the occasion. His headmaster had not been pleased by the request, but it was difficult to refuse when backed up by a similar request from the former American ambassador, who said he would send a car for Mark, and that the boy would be back at school in time for evening prayers. It was well known that Lord Camborne spoiled his only son outrageously, that he was the only male in that coterie of Camborne and Clayton girls, if one did not count the McClintock-Clayton heir-apparent, Alex, that darling of fortune, blessed by brains as well as good looks, a graduate of Harvard Law School, a Rhodes Scholar, and presently preparing himself at Harvard Business School for the McClintock-Clayton empire he would inherit. The head-master knew all this, and he bowed reluctantly to the wishes of these two families, and so Mark, thrust ahead of the four girls, stood on tiptoe for a glimpse of the place where the cortège would pass. He felt no particular grief for a king he had hardly been aware of, though there was the inevitable curiosity about the young woman who would take his place. What pleased Mark was that he had beaten the wishes of his headmaster; he liked neither his school nor his headmaster. He thought his father was about the only acceptable adult male he knew, with the exception of Blair Clayton. He was already painfully aware that he had not inherited Harry Camborne's charm and brains, his easy mastery of whatever he touched. Mark had his own gifts, mostly those of an athlete, but they were not the sort likely to make him a star in the Foreign Office. He knew, even then, that he was bound to disappoint. He wished he didn't have to disappoint his father.

'Here . . .' It was Livy putting a thick telephone book under his feet. He smiled at her. He seemed to have been brought up by these four young women in ways his own mother had never been able to accomplish. Of them all, he loved Livy best. He knew it was wicked not to love his mother more than the others, but he felt a strange constraint with her, almost as if he did not belong to her. She was far more critical of him than his father was, expecting more of him, forever exhorting him to better things, greater achievements. Perhaps his sense that he would inevitably disappoint sprang from this. She was never harsh, but he knew that she was hurt when he failed to live up to her expectation. 'Never mind, old chap . . .' was all his father ever said. 'Better luck next time.' It was always his father he appealed to when he wanted something, his father or one of his sisters. But before he appealed to Rachel or Caroline he would ask Livy or Chris. It had struck him at quite an early age that his great luck was in knowing the women he did. 'Aunt Ginny' was almost as beloved as Livy. When there were problems, she listened and did what she could. It seemed strange to go through Aunt Ginny to reach his own mother. He removed his eyes, just for a time, from the bit of Whitehall he could see, waiting for the first of the cortège to appear, to gaze at the faces around him.

Caroline, the youngest, was closest to him in age, but still distanced by too many years, Caroline, whom most people described as 'sweet' before they mentioned her obvious beauty. Even Mark could see that she was beautiful, even if she was his sister. Was there anything more to say of her than that? He didn't know. She hadn't tried university, as the others had. She had dabbled for a few months in a secretarial course, taken a Cordon-Bleu cooking course, and finished neither. She did little odd jobs: sometimes she acted as a sort of social secretary and general dogsbody to either his mother or Aunt Ginny, flitting happily between London and Paris; she did very junior work in some charities, she went to a great many parties. Then he looked at his other sister, Rachel. Although he didn't quite understand the nature of her accomplishments, she was always described as 'brilliant', and after that came 'a striking-looking girl'. She had attended Girton College, Cambridge, and had achieved a double first. Now she was at some place called the London School of Economics, and as studying something mysterious to Mark called political science. He didn't know what she proposed to do with what she learned, but he had gathered that the LSE was a place of 'brilliant' people, and therefore appropriate to such as Rachel. Chris, who so much resembled Aunt Ginny with her patrician good looks, her tall, lithe figure, that mane of wonderful hair, had left after her first year at Girton, where she had gone with Rachel; she had spent the next year 'idling away her time', as the formidable Andrew McClintock had described it. She painted a little, had taken further voice lessons, everyone said she had a lovely singing voice, more piano and dance lessons, and without telling anyone, had auditioned for the Royal Academy of Dramatic Art, and had been accepted. She was learning to be an actress, something no one in the family had ever been. As a gesture of independence, immediately after her twenty-first birthday when she had gained control of a large trust fund, she had bought a mews house in expensive Belgravia.

'Little monkey.' Livy whispered beside him. 'Trust you to get away from school.'

'It doesn't make much difference. There weren't going to be any classes today, just a long service in the chapel and everyone being very mournful. No games . . . I'd rather be here.'

Sometimes Livy felt more like his sister than his real sisters. She always seemed to remember his existence when it slipped the minds of the others. She was in the last year at Lady Margaret Hall at Oxford. The choice had been her own. 'I just like Oxford,' she had said when the question had arisen. 'After all, my father was at Christ Church.' Mark came to see that it had been her own particular bid for independence, to do something different from the others. Livy was quietly proud of the fact that the royalties from her father's work, now carefully husbanded and increased by the personal supervision of Andrew McClintock himself, had paid for the expensive school she had attended, and paid her way to Oxford. She could afford to dress well, though she didn't seem to care much for clothes.

They had all had their seasons, but only Caroline had attached any importance to it. Rachel, Chris and Livy saw it only as something to be got through before other, more important things could be begun. Seymour House had been bedecked for balls, the garden lighted, the marquees festooned with flowers. Caroline's ball had come last, because she was the youngest, and she seemed the only one of the four who really enjoyed it. She had stayed in London all through June and July, attending every party she had been invited to, and there were often several on the same night. She had delighted in the attention of her partners, and, in her demure way, had become a delightful flirt. Mark had privately thought it all a great bore, and he noticed that the other girls had escaped to Tresillian as soon as possible, not even staying out the length of their own seasons. Aunt Ginny and his mother had made a very special effort with Livy's coming-out dance. It had been more lavish than the joint party shared by Rachel and Chris, the decorations had been more elaborate, her dresses more numerous than the other girls'.

Livy was the ward of Thea Sedgemore and Herbert Gardiner. Because he had grown up with those so much older than he, Mark was precociously knowledgeable for his age, though not academically outstanding. But even he realized there was much yet to learn about the tangled relationship between these two families. He liked Thea and Herbert very much – they were almost as indulgent of him as his father. He was glad they were Livy's parents, though very soon, when she was twenty-one, she would be free even of this bond. Mark wondered what it would be like to be free, to have freedom, and even the little money Livy could command. It seemed like heaven to him, and a very long way off.

Privately, Mark thought Livy far more beautiful than his sister, Caroline, and that she should be the one to make 'the great marriage', if that was reckoned to be such a wonderful thing. But Livy married would be somewhat removed from him; sometimes, when he thought deeply about it, he wished Livy would indeed stay at Oxford, reading her books, and that when he was old enough she would marry him. That way he would have her for ever. His summer memories of Tresillian were always bound up in the memory of Livy. She had driven him to many of Cornwall's secret and enchanted places, shown him ruins to which were attached wonderful stories. From her he had learned the legend of Arthur, and the story of Tristan and Iseult. He knew it had been Livy who had given him the name of Mark, that tragic king. But always his most persistent memory of Livy was of being sprawled on the grass reading, or just staring ahead, and always she was in the same place, just near where the cliff path descended to the notorious Tresillian Rocks. How many times had he sat there with her, watching the tide race and rip its way among those jagged teeth until only their murderous tips showed. The wind blew through her red-gold hair, and her greenish eyes seemed to see beyond the rocks, as if she waited for something, a ship perhaps, but a ship of another time, something an ordinary person like himself would not be able to see. Sometimes he felt jealous of that vision she seemed to see. He wanted Livy all for himself.

Her hand was on his shoulder now. 'They're coming.' The people at the back of the room, who had been talking quietly, now moved to the windows, pressing against Mark. The windows were opened, so people could lean out. He heard the muffled drums, the solemn music. When the gun carriage – escorted by young sailors because the King had been a sailor, followed by his royal brothers, and his son-in-law, the sailor husband of the new Queen, and then the mass of the great Europe and the Commonwealth – passed beneath them, Mark glanced swiftly up to Livy's face. He saw the tears that brimmed in her eyes. He hated to see Livy sad. He took her hand in his.

The girls and Mark walked back across the Park to Seymour House. Griffin had retired; the new butler, Knox, admitted them. Slowly the others trickled back. Ginny and Blair were first, since they had been near the back of the Abbey. Then came Harry and Dena. None had bothered to try to have a car pick them up, the congestion was too great. The last of them to arrive was Andrew McClintock. He was unable to undertake the walk across the park, and had had to wait irritably for his own car, in the long stream of others, to pick him up. 'Damn nearly froze to death,' he said, stamping his cane with unnecessary force on the marble floor. 'All very well, this pageantry and pomp, but it's damned inconvenient when you're my age.'

'Come now, Mr McClintock,' Rachel said, as she went to pour him a whisky. 'You know you're just as sentimental as the rest of us, and you wouldn't have missed it for worlds.'

'And what about you, Miss?' McClintock said, as he took the glass. 'Aren't you just dying to see the day when it's all swept away, the monarchy, the House of Lords, the lot?'

'All in good time, Mr McClintock. We'll do it by democratic process. Revolutions are all very well, but it's putting the pieces back together when it's all over that's difficult. I'd rather see it taken down, the stones numbered, and it all put back in a more equal fashion. I've never cared for pyramids, with just one person, or a few privileged ones at the top.'

'I knew, even before I opened the door, that it would be Rachel on her soap box again. That's about what you were saying, dear girl, last time I saw you.'

For an instant the room seemed frozen, before the exclamations came, but above the cries of 'Alex!', and the murmurs of pleasure and surprise, his grandfather's voice was clearly heard. 'And what, sir, are you doing here? Has Harvard nothing more to teach you? Do you imagine you know it all?'

Alex was careful to kiss his mother and Dena, to shake hands with Harry and Blair, before he confronted his grandfather. 'Can you resist the pull of history, Grandfather? I squared it with the Dean, who said it was all right so long as I was back next Monday morning. I think he rather envied me. He's an Anglophile himself. I'd made sure there was a seat on the plane. McClintock-Clayton can be very handy at times. I suppose you have a seat permanently booked, don't you?'

'But you got here,' Livy said. 'How did you manage to get into London from the airport? Traffic's been very restricted since midnight.'

'Thumbed a ride,' Alex said. 'Went as far as the chap and his family were going. They decided to get as close to Paddington Station as possible, so I stayed with them. We squeezed through the crowd, and managed to see the coffin transferred from the gun carriage. They, the family, were pretty mystified by the American who'd come all the way just to see it. I actually invited them all back here for a cup of tea. They had offered to share their sandwiches but I had to say "no" because I could have wolfed the lot. When I said where I was going the chap suddenly got all formal. He's with Barclay's . . .'

'The English know their place,' Andrew McClintock said. 'I hope you didn't mention Clayton's bank.'

'If I had, that would have put him off me for ever. I just pretended I was a poor student.'

'Some poor student who can afford to cross the Atlantic on a whim,' Livy commented. She stood beside Alex, and thrust a glass of Scotch and a plate of sandwiches into his hands.

'Thank you. Lovely,' Alex said, accepting the offering as if he had known someone would give it. 'You can't imagine how I've been dreaming of this all day.'

'Which?' Rachel demanded. 'The food or the company?'

'Both. Wanted to be here with you. I wish I could have made it sooner. I just knew you'd all be here, even you, Mark. Did you run away from school, or were you expelled?'

'Neither,' Andrew McClintock growled. 'And you'd better eat up, young Mark, because I promised your headmaster you'd be on your way from here just as soon as the traffic started to clear. The car will be waiting when Cady's had something to eat.'

'It was very good of you to arrange it, Mr McClintock,' Mark said. 'You know, sir, if you hadn't telephone the head, I don't think it could have been wangled. His giving in because Father asked would have seemed like favouritism.'

'These chaps know what side their bread's buttered on. After all, I did give the school a new science laboratory. No doubt they'll be looking for something else now.'

Mark looked uneasy. 'Well, sir . . . whatever. It was jolly nice of you. I was rather scared to telephone your office.' He glanced at Harry. 'I didn't think my father would approve . . .'

'I like a lad with a bit of initiative,' McClintock said. 'You were better here today than hanging around school singing hymns. It's better to be at the centre of things. This is where it's all happening. At least for today.'

'Then you must thoroughly approve of my being here,' Alex said.

'I don't know that I go that far. But now you're here . . . Well, it was a good show.'

'Oh, Mr McClintock.' Chris had never advanced beyond that formal address even though she was Alex's half-sister. 'I thought I'd be the only one to say such a thing.'

'Place the right value on things, Chris,' McClintock said. 'The Coronation will be a better show. If the British haven't got much else left in the world, they've still got their pageantry.'

'Mr McClintock!' Ginny protested. She had never ceased to call him that. No one could imagine her calling him 'father'. 'Is it very polite to say such a thing in the presence of one of His (oh, no, it's Her now, isn't it?) Majesty's diplomats?'

'If that's the only undiplomatic thing Harry's ever had said to him, then he's still wet behind the ears. Diplomats are made to be insulted, and to frame suitable insults in return. Isn't that so, Harry?'

'We prefer to think we pour oil on troubled waters, but you're just about right. The diplomatic insult is a nicety it took me a long time to learn. Of course, we're all the best of friends at other times.'

'Well . . .' Blair rose slowly to his feet. 'I'll let you get on with the insults, and I'm going upstairs to get out of these glad rags, and try to soak the cold out of my bones in the hot tub.' He went to Mark and held out his hand. 'Glad you made it here. The day wouldn't have been complete without you. And having Alex here just put the finishing touch to it.'

'Oh, yes, sir. It's super he made it.' Mark had a fondness for Alex, which he tried to play down, but couldn't. 'Sir,' Mark said as Blair turned to go, 'if my father can't get away, and you're free to come, I wonder if you could manage to get down to school for a cricket match when the season starts. They're trying me out for the second eleven. I'm a bit young, and some of the chaps don't like it. It'd be a bit of support.'

'Let me know the date,' Blair answered. 'I'll be there.' He waved vaguely at all the others in the room. 'See you all at dinner.'

For a moment an awkward silence hung on the room. They all knew that it was one of the penalties of Harry's job that he was so often absent from the country when some of the seemingly trivial, but important things in his children's lives occurred. It wasn't so bad for the girls, because they always had had each other's support, but Mark trailed behind, and seemed too often forgotten.

'You might have asked me,' Andrew McClintock said drily. 'One good turn deserves another. If it's a good day I wouldn't mind stretching my old bones out in the sun. I'll expect strawberries, and something more in my sandwiches than watercress.'

Mark flushed with pleasure. 'Oh, would you, sir? The head would be very pleased . . . I mean, I'd be very pleased if you came, but you're very busy.'

'So is Mr Clayton. He works far harder than I do these days. If I'm in the country, invite me. See if I don't get there. But not if it's one of your freezing English summer days.'

'Mark,' Dena said, 'I think it's time you went down and asked Knox if Mr McClintock's chauffeur is ready to take you back. It doesn't do to abuse privilege, you know. And the poor man's already had a long day, having to be at the Abbey so early.'

There it was again, Mark thought. He had hoped to linger for at least another half hour, enjoying the warmth and the food, revelling in the sense that he was part of this group, this very special group. But here was his mother, prompting and urging him to do the right thing. He would have taken a bet that Mr McClintock's chauffeur wouldn't have minded a while longer of food and company and probably a tot of whisky after his long vigil as close to the Abbey as he had been permitted to park.

Typically, while Mark made the round of the room saying his farewells, starting first with Andrew McClintock, thanking him again, kissing all the girls, Ginny was gathering up sandwiches and cakes and wrapping them in a linen napkin. 'Just in case you miss supper,' she said when she kissed him. There was far more than he could eat, and he knew he was intended to share them back at school while he recounted the spectacle of the day. He kissed his mother, and offered his hand to his father. Harry's smile had warmth in it. 'Sorry to be packing you off, old chap, but your mother's right.' He moved with him towards the hall.

Mark once again silently vowed that in future he would try harder to do the things that pleased his father. He would try harder with languages, even at the cost of time on the sports field. And yet he knew that in some areas where his father excelled, he was already doomed to failure. The odd thing was that his father didn't seem to mind.

Both Dena and Harry came with him to the car; he elected to sit beside Mr McClintock's chauffeur, Cady, in the front, not in solitary splendour in the glass-partitioned back. The car which had come for him that morning at school had been an ordinary car; this was Mr McClintock's own Rolls. That meant that the old gentleman, which was the way Mark always thought of him, meant to stay at Seymour House for dinner. Or perhaps he was staying there for a week, or for however long he would be in London. Mark was still confused about the arrangements the two families made. He never knew until the last moment where he was supposed to go when the holidays came. Tresillian and Prescott Hill and the big villa on the shores of the Zurich See were part of the summer ritual. At half-term he sometimes went to spend the three days with his father and mother in Paris; if Aunt Ginny were in London, he went there, and she always managed to find time to spend with him.

He was already familiar with the embassies of Great Britain in Paris, and of the United States in London. With fascination he had watched the bustle when an important dinner party or reception was being prepared. He had made friends with chefs. The pastry chefs always seemed the most ready to give of their results, believing that all young boys like sweet things. Mark had even made overtures to the *chef de cuisine*, and was not always rebuffed. Perhaps for them it was a novelty to find someone of his age who was interested in what they did, what the outcome of the long labours would be. The one person he had learned never to go near when a dinner was in progress was the *saucier*. An instant's distraction could mean a sauce ruined, and the wrath of God heaped on his head. His mother, sometimes apologizing for his poor French, explained that he spoke excellent 'kitchen French', since all the language of the kitchen was in French, even in England. 'Very limited,' Dena once said. She didn't know the stock of good French profanities he commanded. One time, in the brief months when Mr McClintock had been ambassador, he had spent an afternoon in the chef's room at the Residence, and had learned for the first time the magic names of Escoffier, Carême, La Varenne. The chef had found him reading recipe books, and had been amused and interested. 'I'll take you one night to a big restaurant, a good one, where everyone is ordering something different. These embassy dinners are rather boring. The menu is set beforehand, and all you have to do is to see that it is hot and ready to serve at the right moment. The good restaurant – everything comes at once. Meat, fish, vegetables . . . a different way of preparing, a different sauce. Not to wonder, young sir, that we sometimes swear at each other, and maybe, if things go wrong, fling a pot. But the customer must never know. Oh, yes, maybe I'll take you. But never tell the ambassador. It's not really fitting . . .'

The chef had never had time to make good on that promise, or had thought better of it, but Mark by then had learned where to go when he wanted to see the excitement of an embassy lunch or dinner in progress. He never hung about on the stairs, as other children did, but insinuated himself into the kitchen. This was permitted to him, even in Paris, though strictly he had no right in the embassy. He knew the back way in, the guards recognized him, and so long as he kept quiet and out of everyone's way, his knowledge of 'kitchen French' gained him acceptance. He began to read his mother's and

Aunt Ginny's cookbooks. So far no one had noticed that, if they were short of help in the house, or it was late at night and the staff had gone, his eggs benedict or skilfully prepared and presented sandwiches were better than any of the girls could produce. It was always assumed that one of the girls had produced them, and no one made any comment. It was a secret he preferred kept. It was one thing to be good at athletics, but poor at maths; the last thing he could have admitted at school was that he liked cooking. His tall, lithe body, big for his age, carried no spare weight. He liked to prepare food, but to eat little of it, especially what was presented at school. He even liked to sample the dregs of his father's wine or port glass, and decide whether his mother had made a good choice to complement the evening's menu.

Mark looked at their two faces as they bent to bid him goodbye, his mother's faintly worried. 'You will try hard, won't you, darling? I mean . . .' She meant that she wanted him to measure up to almost impossible standards, to be sportsman and scholar and charmer, and yet self-effacing. She wanted desperately for him to be like his father, Harry. He wished he could, but thought it impossible. He took Harry's hand again. 'Thank you for arranging for me to come up today, sir. I had to make Mr McClintock think he had done it, but the head really would have let me go because you had asked.'

'Quite right, old man. You did the right thing. Mr McClintock has been very good to us all. I would never want you to suck up to him, but good manners never hurt. He's earned a bit of respect. Well . . . take care of yourself, old chap. And maybe I'll be able to make it to a cricket match. Have fun, if you can. I don't remember ever having much fun at school myself, but there were one or two good spots.' Harry didn't like to say that when Mark reached Eton in a few years' time, his early years there were likely to be hell. Why frighten the poor kid? He stood with Dena as the car moved off, and they saw Mark roll down the window to wave to them. They waved back, then slowly climbed the steps of Seymour House. 'He'll work out all right. Don't worry, Dena.'

'But I do worry. I want him to be everything . . .'

He pressed her arm. 'He isn't ten years old yet, my darling. You must give him a chance . . .'

She didn't answer. Never once in the years since Mark's birth had Harry treated him in any fashion but as a son. Never once had he thrown back at Dena the knowledge that Mark was not that. It was almost too saintly, Dena sometimes thought. Her guilt would have been easier to bear if Harry had even once upbraided her for that infidelity. But then, there was his own infidelity to recall. Why, she wondered, couldn't they have been more like her own parents, who had smilingly indulged each other's affairs, taken nothing seriously except their abiding affection for each other, and the knowledge that their son, Edward, was truly the heir. There lay the worst rub for Dena. Always between them lay the knowledge, unspoken since that time long ago at Tresillian when she had told Harry she was going to have a baby, and he had said he would always claim it as his own. She shivered slightly, and Harry's arm was around her as they re-entered the hall of Seymour House. 'It's been a long day, darling. Perhaps it's time we went and followed Blair's example of a hot bath . . .'

After they had bathed, secure in the knowledge that they wouldn't be disturbed for some time, they crept into bed, grateful for each other, grateful for the love passionately and eagerly given and taken. Dena sensed that the sight of Mark among them had strangely affected them both. They had witnessed the funeral ceremonial of a king: they had experienced a sense of mortality, and wanted now to reaffirm life. Dena wondered what it would have been like if she had ever conceived and borne a son of Harry's – how far could his generosity towards Mark have extended then? It was as well, perhaps, that that had never been tested. When Harry slept briefly in her arms, unaware that she kissed him gently as he slept, she thought of the Russian mistress who might now be dead. After the war they began to learn something of what had happened to those who had consorted, even if it might have been under orders, with their Allies, who had now become their enemies. She thought of Mark's father, thankful that he had survived the war, and yet always hoping that their paths would never cross again. Mark's father lived, and didn't know he had a son; and Harry, who might have longed for his own son, brought up the child of another man.

Dena moved quietly as she dressed for dinner, wanting Harry to sleep as long as he could. At times he worked cruelly long hours; she welcomed any break he could get. She wakened him with a kiss before she went downstairs. She made her way to the drawing-room where the girls' voices were raised in an excited babble. The door of the room was open and she paused there, unnoticed, and took in the scene. Andrew McClintock had changed into a dinner jacket, but Alex had changed only his shirt and tie. He probably had come with only one small bag, and might be gone the next day. Ginny wore an informal, but long dress. All the girls unconsciously, Dena guessed, grouped them-selves about Alex. They all talked of the day's events. All except Blair, who seemed quite content to sit and sip his whisky. But Alex, who had been only on the outskirts of this day's ceremonial, talked more than the others, and they listened. They always did. He would always lead them, in one fashion or another, always be important in their lives, no matter how different the directions they all took. He was the older brother for them all. Dena thought of Mark, speeding off into the grey afternoon, to the bleak school supper which would be supplemented by Ginny's cakes and sandwiches. She thought, with sorrow, of the baby boy whom Ginny had miscarried. If the child had lived, he could never have been a match for Alex, but he would have been a counterweight. If he had lived, he might have been a friend for Mark, separated from him by only a few years. If he had lived, Blair would have had a son, and the eyes of everyone in this room might not have focused on Alex.

But the attention of everyone was not focused on Alex. Blair had noticed her, and quietly risen to go and pour her a drink. He raised his glass to her. 'Well, Dena, our flock have grown, and soon they'll all be on their way, whatever way they take. Alex's is predestined, of course, and lucky for him he's able to stand up to it. Little Caro, well, she'll be engaged and married in no time. The rest, it's a toss-up how they'll turn out. I catch myself at times wishing they were all young again. I missed so much of their young years because of the war. I wish I could make everything plain and straight for them, make it all effortless, as it seems to have been so far for Alex. But they're all in for some tumbles. I suppose that's inevitable . . .'

'Yes, inevitable, Blair.' Dena smiled gently at him. How dear and wise he was, and yet at times like this hopelessly impractical, almost sentimental. She had understood years ago that Blair had welcomed and encouraged the friendship between these two families, the bonding of their children, as much as Ginny had. For all the money and power that lay with the Clayton name, Blair had always made it seem that it was Ginny and he who were most complimented by their friendship, they who were eternally in the Camborne's debt. Useless to remind him of the favours they had had, their many stays at Seymour House, the use of their transport, their servants, their other homes. Blair treated the whole situation as if she and Ginny had been born sisters, and this was the large family for which he had longed.

Her eyes went to the one who belonged to none of them – to Livy. She stood slightly behind Alex, who was seated on a sofa next to his grandfather. The faces of the other three girls were fixed on Alex, and perhaps it was only Dena, Blair and Ginny who read Livy's expression.

'I wish she didn't care so much about him,' Dena said quietly. 'I hope she isn't going to be terribly hurt.'

'Does she care so much? They all treat him as the big brother.'

'Since the day he first walked into the kitchen at Tresillian. She's argued with him, disagreed with him, learned from him and loved him. She's not his sister, Blair . . .'

2

The next morning Caroline had breakfast, grapefruit and coffee, in bed in the room she was sharing with Livy. 'I feel

301

lazy, and I want to look rested at lunch.' By the time Livy got down to the dining-room, Chris was the only one at the table. She had stayed overnight at Seymour House; the mews house was only half-furnished, and she drifted in and out of her parents' house as if she still lived there.

'You may have noticed,' Chris said, 'that the library door is firmly closed. McClintock, Clayton and the heir apparent are all in conference.' Livy poured coffee, and came to sit beside Chris. Chris added, 'I think it's a pity Alex never had any choice about what his future was to be. Just as well he's got the brains and temperament that it takes. Supposing he'd been flighty, like his Russian grandmother. Suppose –' she laughed, 'Oh heaven help us, suppose he'd turned out to be an idiot! Or he'd wanted to be a painter? Imagine what that would have done to Andrew McClintock's plans. But I think he's had his moments of fun. The news from a couple of Radcliffe girls I know is that he's hot stuff on the Harvard scene. But then, why wouldn't he be? He's got the brains to keep up with his classes, and the looks to drive any girl wild.'

'And a fortune to make him a most interesting prospect to any hopeful mother,' Livy said. 'You'll have to watch out for that yourself, Chris. Even dreamy actors and artists know when there's money around.'

Chris bit down on the cold toast. 'I don't intend to be a meal-ticket for anyone. I'll be in love as many times as I want. But I mean to be an actress. A successful actress. I'm not sure that goes with being a wife, or a mother.'

'I wish I could feel so certain of something. Can you really see your way so far ahead?'

'I'm twenty-two, and I'm not certain where life is going to take me. But I mean to make the decisions. I'm a whole lot freer than Alex.' As if to change the subject she said, 'When are you going back to Oxford?'

'Tomorrow. I suppose I should go back today. But I have only one essay to get ready over the weekend. The exams are in June. I probably won't get my head out of a book until then.'

Chris's brow wrinkled momentarily. She had always felt

that leaving Girton that first year had been a mild disgrace, when Rachel had sailed so brilliantly through. 'Oh, you'll get your first. And then what?'

'I just said I don't know. I just need to get over this hurdle first. But I might take up Aunt Ginny's suggestion that I get a really good grounding in shorthand and typing, perhaps a bit of bookkeeping.'

Chris slammed down her cup. 'You can't be serious! You'll have a first in English from Oxford, and you're going to be a typist. It doesn't make sense. What a waste!'

'Not when you think about it. I might find a job in publishing. But women still have to creep through the back door. Aunt Ginny suggested I might come to Washington and do a course there. Sh thought of a job in the Senate or the House, but I'd have to have a work permit for that. Maybe there'd be a chance with the British embassy or the BBC. Women are moving ahead much quicker in America than here, Chris. All sorts of possibilities . . . but there's no need to rush into a decision . . .'

Chris nodded. 'Have you thought about writing?'

Livy's face closed, grew tight. 'Because of my father? No. Writing's not something you think about. It's something you do, if you have to. The world is full of scribblers, unprofessional scribblers. I don't intend to join their ranks.'

'And the world is full of unemployed actresses.' Chris took time to put some butter on her toast. She nibbled at it delicately. 'Does it frighten you, Livy, thinking about what one could be, or might be? Most people, most women, don't have any choice. They don't have any saleable talent. They don't have any money to buy them time to think. The choices are mostly made for them . . .' She finished her toast. 'Well, if I don't show up for class this morning, I'll be kicked out of that. And I shouldn't have had any butter on my toast.' She stood up and patted her perfectly flat stomach. 'Can't afford to get fat . . .'

'Idiot!' Livy said. She half rose from her chair and pulled Chris's face towards her to place a kiss on her cheek. 'I probably won't see you until the summer. Think of me slaving away. And I'll think of you learning your lines and painting scenery and singing and dancing and working yourself half to death. What's the matter with us, I wonder? I don't know what Rachel's after, either. Why can't we be like Caro? We all know what she wants.'

Her kiss was returned. 'Good luck. Good luck to both of us. I sometimes wonder if Caro isn't right. She's almost certain to get what she wants.'

When Chris had gone, Livy sat alone in the dining-room. Then she realized how late it was, and that Knox would want to clear the room in preparation for lunch. She poured another cup of coffee, and went into the drawing-room. A fire had already been lighted. Livy sat down with her coffee. She looked appreciatively at Blair's lovely pictures. Everything in this house bore the stamp of Ginny and Blair; she had come to love it. It occurred to her, as she sat there in the quiet, with the low drone of the men's voices coming from the library, that so long as she had her room at Oxford, she possessed her own little world. And after her exams, when she packed her bags and her books and the few bits and pieces she had collected, what then? Where would she go? She would have to find some place of her own. Rachel had her tiny bed-sitter in a cheap house in Pimlico, cooking on a gas ring, and sharing a bathroom with ten other people, determined not to cost her father a penny more than was necessary until she was ready to take a job and become independent. Chris had her three-bedroom mews house in smart Belgravia, and had to ask no one for money. Caro moved between Paris and London, making herself useful in return for food and accommodation. All of them spent their summers between Tresillian, Prescott Hill, Paris, and the McClintock-Clayton villa in Zurich. It was a pattern they had fallen into after the war, and until recently none of them had questioned it. Livy had known that her fares across the Atlantic were paid from her trust fund. How did Lord Camborne manage the money for Rachel and Caro and Mark? Once Lord Camborne's appointment in Paris had come, they had given up the flat in London; there was now nowhere for them to stay except at an hotel or Seymour

House. Livy knew that Ginny always insisted that it be Seymour House, but she realized that this hospitality was still accepted with a slight sense of unease. They tried to reciprocate by making Tresillian available to anyone who wanted to come, and anyone who wanted to bring friends. They often spent Christmas at Prescott Hill where sometimes there had been snow, clean and white, making the paths among the firs and the spruces and the cedars mysterious and enchanting. She recalled with utter clarity the crunch of snow under her boots, their breaths misting on the cold, sharp air, on the morning Alex had walked her the long trek and shown her the place where they had found his father's body, a place now garlanded with icicles.

'It's not morbid,' he said, half apologetically. 'It's part of the long history of Prescott Hill. I wasn't born then, and I never knew him. All I ever knew was my mother and my grandfather. It was a relief when Blair came along, and then Chris. It would have been better for all of us if my mother had been able to have another child . . .'

'Does it bother you, Alex, that you're the only male around to inherit all this? I don't mean the money. Your grandfather expects so much of you. Blair loves you, but I think he feels life would be easier if you had a couple of brothers to share the responsibility. It's almost a curse that you're so bright. If you'd been a fool, no one would have expected much of you.'

'Would you want to be a fool, Livy? Even if it meant an easy life? When I was at Oxford,' – he hardly ever referred to the fact that he had won what money could not buy him, a coveted Rhodes scholarship – 'I took the time to go to visit the place where my great-great-grandfather was born. I've only ever told my grandfather, and now you, about this. I'd traced him back to a little slum house in Edinburgh. He'd been a solicitor's clerk when he decided to emigrate to America. He was dirt poor, and even his family thought he'd made a big advance just by getting himself into that position with an Edinburgh solicitor. They were Highland crofters, and proud of it, even if they had only porridge and oatcakes to eat and their own illegally distilled whisky to drink. I

305

stayed the night with the only McClintock family I could find in that village. They hadn't any idea in hell who I was, or if they could even believe that my name was McClintock. They certainly hadn't ever heard of McClintock-Clayton. They gave me the best they had. Afterwards I tried to let them know that we could arrange for the son to emigrate to the States, and that there would be a job for him. But they wrote a painfully polite note, saying he'd rather stay on the farm. The farm, I may tell you, was what's known as a 'hill farm', land on the mountains that will carry only sheep. It's damned hard work, out in all weathers. You know what the winter's like in Scotland.

'So that's where I'm sprung from, and I'm proud of it. I'm not asking for an easy coast through life. If my efforts have to be with bankers and money men, then so be it. But I often think about Jamie McClintock, who has all the decisions made for him by nature. If the weather's too rough, he loses lambs. In the future, if I make the wrong decisions, I'll lose millions. And I won't be able to blame anyone but myself. So, no, I wouldn't choose to be a fool, just for the ease of it. Because I know what it feels like not to be a fool. I wouldn't change, even if the burden and the price has to be McClintock-Clayton.'

He would carry the burden well, Livy thought. And he'd never blame anyone else for the mistakes he made. The thought of how calmly he faced his future pulled her back to the thought of her own. Did Aunt Ginny's suggestion of Washington draw her because Alex would be there? She decided that she had better thrust the thought aside for a time. When Oxford was done with, when she'd had her healing time at Tresillian, she would know better what she should do. Try not to put your heart on your sleeve, Livy, she warned herself. And yet how not to remember the special times like the time when he had told her in Washington, early in January, just before they were all to go back to London after Christmas at Prescott Hill, that he wanted her to be up and ready to drive at five the next morning. 'I'll have them fix sandwiches and a vacuum flask,' was all he said. 'Dress warmly.'

He had driven her through the darkness, hardly speaking, refusing to answer questions about where they were going. The late winter dawn was nearly breaking when they reached the Back Bay Wildlife Refuge. He parked the car, and they moved towards the edge of the water on one of the marshy coves. As the sun rose she saw something she had never before imagined. A stick snapped beneath her foot, and thousands of long white necks rose in unison, the sun blushing them faintly with pink. 'Whistling swans,' Alex whispered. The whisper carried over the cold blue water. They rose, seeming to run on the water, their great wings stretched, heads and necks arrow-straight. The whistle-like blasts from the long windpipes shattered the dawn silence. 'They say a swan mates for life. If one dies, the other remains alone.'

'And sings before dying?' Livy whispered. They had stayed an hour, watching them land and take off. 'Pretty soon, about late February, if you come here, you can hear them begin to get restless, begin to talk about getting going. By March they're on their way back to the Arctic.' He had driven her back, and, as if by common consent, they had never mentioned the trip to anyone. That night, after dinner, he had driven her to the Lincoln Memorial, had let her see, for the first time, what the solitary, lighted figure, frozen in a majestic melancholy, was like when no other person stood on the long steps to that temple abode. They had walked around in the cold winter's night, and read the words inscribed about him, the unforgettable words.

'I suppose it's my way of trying to thank you for showing me what Cornwall is, more than beaches and pretty villages.'

These were the only things that made her think there was something as yet unspoken which linked her to Alex, things, feelings which had to be left alone to grow, or perhaps to wither.

'Brooding on the King, or worrying about the exams, Livy?' He stood in the door of the drawing-room, looking at her, and she had been unaware of his presence.

'A bit of both, I suppose.' She quoted softly. '"To me, and to the state of my great grief, let kings assemble". I

307

wonder if the Queen thought that yesterday.'

'Yesterday I kept thinking that she's only a year older than me. I'd hate to be landed with that job. With grandfather and Blair around, I've got a few years to find my feet.'

'But you and she were both brought up to inherit an empire,' Livy said. 'I predict that while hers shrinks, yours will grow.'

'That sounds like Rachel on her soapbox. Don't do that to me, Livy. Look, I've only the rest of the day here. Back on the plane tomorrow. What shall we do to celebrate? I haven't talked to you for a long time.'

'Life's busy, isn't it? The way we all come and go.'

'Well, we have to try to make sure we spend time together this summer. Tresillian, a few weeks at Prescott Hill. Yes, we must make sure Mark gets to Prescott Hill this summer.'

'The kindest thing you could do for Mark would be to drive down and visit him this afternoon. I know he was disappointed he had such a short time with you yesterday. You're a sort of hero to him, Alex. He suffers a bit from being a late-comer. Quite often he's an afterthought with us. We remember to let him tag along, but only at the last minute.'

'Right! I'll borrow a car, and we'll go down. I suppose they'll let us take him to tea without getting permission first? In the meantime, I'm taking you to lunch at the Ritz. Have you got something gorgeous to wear to visit Mark? I can remember when I was at school I always wanted my mother to turn up looking . . . well, looking like a queen.'

Livy got to her feet quickly. 'I'll do my best.'

She raced upstairs to the room where Caroline was trying on one outfit after another, and discarding them in turn. They were almost the same size, Caroline just fractionally shorter than Livy. Despite the fact that clothing was still rationed, Caroline always dressed well; she didn't scruple to bed or plead for whatever could be brought from America. Ginny always found her a grateful recipient of her cast-offs. Caroline had inherited and developed Dena's skill with a sewing machine. 'How else can I manage?' she had retorted when Rachel had accused her of wasting her time. 'I don't propose to go around dressed like you!'

So she offered to Livy a suitably stylish suit of a kind of heather pink, set off with a pink velvet beret, both of which had come from Ginny. 'Isn't it divine?' she said. 'I wish I had the right sort of brooch to lend you for it. Make it sort of Highlandish.'

Livy surveyed it doubtfully. 'Do you really think . . . I mean . . . *pink*, with my hair?'

Caroline signed with an air of exasperation. 'You just don't understand what chic is. Everyone's been saying for centuries that red-heads can't wear pink – or red, for that matter. But just look at yourself! It's a rule made to be broken when you have your sort of complexion. Is Alex taking you out? That's lovely. I wish he'd take me out, but I'm afraid I bore him to death.' She was giving her hat a final adjustment; the fragrance of her perfume made her seem more flower-like. 'You'll be going back to Oxford tomorrow? Keep on writing to me, Livy. I love to hear from you, and I'm ashamed of the babyish nonsense I write back. Oh, and keep the suit. Aunt Ginny's just given me a gorgeous one that needs only a bit of alteration. Borrow my grey coat. It goes beautifully with the pink. There's some perfume in the top drawer. Take your pick. Aunt Ginny gives me all her left-overs. Sometimes, there's half a bottle there. It's just her way of being nice. How can we have been so lucky as to have someone like Aunt Ginny and Blair in our lives?'

'Thank your mother and father,' Livy said. 'Not all the rich are generous with friendship, or love.'

'Don't I know it!' Caroline waved from the door. 'Have a good lunch.'

Livy was careful with her make-up, and still doubtful about the pink velvet beret. She had a horror of the thought that, with her hair, she might be thought to be imitating the pre-Raphaelite school if she wore anything outstanding. Perhaps Caroline was right. There was a difference between being flashy and being chic; she wished she felt more sure of which was which.

Alex waited in the hall. He inspected her carefully. 'Marvellous! Only you would think of that colour.'

'It comes by courtesy of your mother, by way of Caro.

And she forced me to have the courage to wear it.'

'It becomes you. Or you become it. A touch of dash, or a touch of the poet. You'll be the loveliest woman at the Ritz.'

But she wasn't. When they entered the dining-room Livy instantly saw Caroline seated at a very prominent centre-table. They waved distantly to her. They were given one of the favoured window seats, with a view over Green Park. 'Who's that with her?' Alex asked.

'I think that's Lord Osborne. Lord Bolton's heir. He's something in the Foreign Office. A junior "Permanent" something. I don't think he gets sent overseas. He might end up as someone important like Permanent Under Secretary – like Lord Camborne's father.'

'Well, I wouldn't expect our Caro to be out with the dustman.' Alex's tone sounded uninterested, but through the meal Livy saw that he often glanced towards Caroline's table. She thought how much he resembled his grandfather in certain ways. He was quick and discerning, and he always wanted to know as much as possible about the people he encountered, knowledge giving him an advantage; he, like Andrew McClintock, liked to be forewarned and therefore forearmed. 'He's quite a bit older than Caro, isn't he?'

'About ten years. I suppose he's about thirty. What's wrong with that? Do you expect her to be enchanted with spotty-faced youths? She's so beautiful herself. His father's distantly related to the Royal family. I suppose he must be, well, he might be a second cousin to the Queen.'

'Good looking,' Alex conceded, 'but arrogant, and a little effete. Needs a good dash of sturdy blood injected into that family, I'd say. Still, what does it matter? Is he courting Caro?'

'How would I know? She goes out so much. She never talks about anyone in particular. Caro likes a good time, and the people who can provide it.'

Alex turned his attention back to his food. 'Well, all we can say about our dear Caro is that no one is ever going to marry her for her money, since there isn't any.'

Livy put down her knife and fork. 'Alex! That's a disgusting remark. Can't you even imagine that people might fall

310

in love money or no money. After all, Caro's parents did.'

'I've nothing against love. It's good if you can find it. Not everyone's that lucky. Think of my Russian grandmother.'

'Think of your mother and father. Think of your mother and Blair.'

'Yes,' he assented. 'The world's full of fairy tales, isn't it? And it's full of people who do things for money. Now come on, eat up. And don't dally around with dessert. If we're to get down to Mark and have time for the kind of cream tea he's going to expect, we'd better be moving . . .' Carefully, he didn't look towards Caroline and her escort again. He gave the same distant wave from the doorway as they left the room. He was probably, Livy thought, as much aware as she that Caroline's escort might have liked to be introduced to the McClintock-Clayton heir. In the world in which Alex moved, titles had little meaning. He already had his own.

They drove down into Hampshire in a Rolls which had to have been borrowed from McClintock-Clayton. Alex was a fast driver, but skilful, not taking chances, but never hanging back. He half apologized for the car. 'Apart from wishing that my mother would come to the school dressed like . . . like a queen, I always wanted Blair to come in a showy car. Small boys are like that.'

'There were all the war years when you didn't see your mother . . . all the time she stayed in London and at Tresillian. Did you ever mind that, Alex? Did you think she didn't care? Were you ever jealous?'

'I confess to all those emotions. I've always been half-jealous of her love for Blair. Chris, as a half-sister, doesn't bother me. I'm very fond of her. She isn't a threat. But during the war I seemed to belong to my grandfather. He made all the decisions, or most of them. If it hadn't been for Blair so often showing up on the scene, reminding me that I had a mother and a stepfather, I might have given up on the whole family, and gone my grandfather's way. But my mother wrote wonderful letters, many of them. She made me feel and understand the reasons why she stayed. And yes, to give my grandfather, the old devil, his due, he never

311

seemed to want me to forget I had a family. And that didn't just mean Mother and Chris. He was as eager to have the Cambornes in our lives as my mother and Blair were. I think he was beginning to understand that children brought up alone are often at the risk of thinking they really are the only people in the world. The one thing I'm positive of is that he was determined that the McClintock heir wasn't going to be sacrificed to a bomb, or an invasion, or even the chance that he didn't get to the right schools.'

'They must have been lonely years though, Alex.'

'Sometimes I remember that they were. But the Old Man kept them filled and busy. He told me to invite anyone I wanted to Prescott Hill or the Washington house, or the New York place. We had good summers, I remember. Horses, swimming, but always some damn tutor or bodyguard hanging around. I always had a few hours of lessons, even during the holidays. And always, of course, the weekly report to write to my grandfather on what I was doing, how I was comporting myself, what girls I seemed interested in.'

'At that age? Even Mr McClintock couldn't have been that cynical.'

He glanced at her. 'Don't you believe it. The Old Man knows men, and boys. And how early we get interested in girls. He didn't want me creating any disasters with the pretty daughters of my hosts, or the local girls around Prescott Hill.'

Livy stared straight ahead. 'I take it he's let you off the apron strings. There can't be any more tutor-bodyguards hanging around.'

'He knows better than to try, the old devil. But still . . . when I got a bit older, I could see his point. There were some girls I might have gone too far with, and ended up married at eighteen. That wouldn't be according to plan.'

'And what is his plan for you? Are you expected to marry the richest girl from the best family in America?'

He laughed. 'Come to think of it, I'm damned if I know what plans he has in that direction. He just doesn't talk about it. He hasn't even made any hints. I go out with whom I please, and he doesn't ask about it. Of course, I'm pretty sure he's fully informed about each and every one of my dates. Someone totally unsuitable would be crossed off the list very quickly.'

'Supposing you fell in love with . . . with someone totally unsuitable? Would you defy him, Alex? Would you go ahead and marry her, and tell him to go to hell?'

They were approaching the massive pillars and open iron gates of Mark's prep school, whose fees Livy knew Harry could hardly afford, before Alex answered. 'Never thought about it much. I've been in love, sometimes for as long as two weeks. I've never met someone I thought I couldn't live without. Marriage is a hell of a business, Livy. I'm getting a good education in the business of McClintock-Clayton, but the business of marriage is still a pretty foreign country to me. Yes, I do think about the marriage of my mother and father and a pretty unlikely thing it was, too. They didn't have time to fall out of love, and they stuck out against the disapproval of my mother's family. That must have shaken my grandfather. To have a marriage with so much money involved questioned . . . And then there was the unlikely event of my mother and Blair really falling in love, even though the Old Man wanted that marriage very badly. It could have been a formality. But it hasn't been. I began to understand that during the war, when she elected to stay close to him. That taught me a lot. I began to understand that it's possible for two very rich people not only to fall in love, but to remain in love. But I always think that my mother and Blair would have made it together – no matter where fortune placed them.'

'If you know that, then you know a lot.'

Alex drew the car up in front of the grey pile of buildings which comprised one of England's foremost prep schools. Only the well-born, the rich or the talented attended this school. Sometimes, but rarely, the three things came together.

'But you know it, don't you, Livy? And your father knew it and your mother. Even dear old Bully, God love him, knew when he was with quality. I'm proud to think that my grandfather recognized that in your mother. He's quite often reminisced about those breakfasts he had in your mother's kitchen. He never found the right description for her. All he ever said about her was that she was a "rare woman". And once he added, "fit for a poet". My grandfather doesn't have much time for poets, since they don't make money. But something about this situation struck him as different. Perhaps it's as well he never met your father. Perhaps, at his age, he fell romantically in love, for those few days, with your beautiful mother. If the poet hadn't got in the way . . . well, who knows? It's just a fantasy I have.'

Livy couldn't reply. She had never before thought of Andrew McClintock in that light. Was it possible he had ever loved? But once, disastrously, he had loved a Russian princess. Perhaps he understood, knew, more than she ever gave him credit for. Perhaps . . .

Alex came around and opened the car door. 'I expect you to put your best face on encountering Mark's housemaster. You have to play the elderly aunt . . . but I also expect him to fall in love with red hair and a pink cap. I hope there's a good place nearby where we can take Mark to tea.'

For a second she held his hand. 'It's good of you to take this trouble, Alex. I think perhaps you can understand what it will mean to Mark – you taking the time to come and see him.'

'I know. I would have liked beautiful aunts to drop in to take me to tea when I was at school. It was the one thing the Old Man wasn't able to provide.'

Mark was allowed two hours off, with the promise that he would be back in time for prep. His housemaster, not quite approving that Mark had had the day before off to attend the funeral, was somewhat reluctant; but Livy pleaded that Alex would be flying back to New York the next morning, and he was like an uncle to Mark.

'I knew he'd fall for the pink hat,' Alex said triumphantly, as they drove to the staid seaside resort nearby, to the hotel Mark told them served the best teas.

'He didn't fall for the pink hat,' Mark objected. 'He fell for Livy.' He was exultant over their unexpected appearance and his hours away from school. He was too often left behind, Livy thought. But what else could Harry and Dena do? They had to conform to the system of their times. Prep school was ordained, as was Eton, just as it had been for Harry.

She noticed he ate sparingly of the cakes and sandwiches provided. They had a favoured table close by the fire in the big lounge of the hotel; the atmosphere was mellow. Mark obviously basked in Alex's company. 'Here,' Alex said, 'aren't you going to eat a bit more? I thought they gave you pretty awful food at school.'

'It is pretty awful. Stodge, really. But I was just remembering the cakes and sandwiches Aunt Ginny gave me last night. They were super. I shared them around . . . I was lucky to be away yesterday. All the chaps wanted to know what it had been like. The funeral, and everything . . . All they did was read books and attend chapel. Someone said it was just favouritism because I had a whole flock of relatives in the Abbey. Well, not all were relatives. Mother and Father and Uncle Edward . . . And Aunt Ginny and Uncle Blair, and Mr McClintock. Someone made book on who had the most relatives in the Abbey . . . I didn't win because half of them weren't actually related.'

'What nasty little snobs you all are,' Livy said, but she said it lightly. It was the system. It still prevailed, even though it was thought that Britain had undergone a social revolution. This little band of boys, whether they actually liked each other or not, would know each other all their lives. They might go on to different public schools, but they would meet and mix later in life; there would always be that exclusivity about them. It was the same system into which she had been thrust. Her mother's humble origins would be overlooked because she was the protégée of the Cambornes and the Claytons. She knew that Mark's standing at school had been raised just the tiniest notch because he had been allowed to attend the funeral yesterday, and because today Alex McClintock, trailing his air of Oxford and Harvard, his prowess at sports, his grandfather who had been an ambassador, had come down especially to visit him. Alex had been right, even the car would have been noted, and the way she was dressed. It wasn't fair, but that was the way it was.

They drove back quietly, in the early winter darkness, Mark having said a fervent thanks to Alex. 'Poor little blighter,' Alex remarked. 'He's got so many years of hell to get through yet. I've only just started to feel that I've come out of it myself. From his end, the tunnel looks endless. I've always imagined it wasn't so bad for girls, but I could be wrong.'

'Not so much was expected of us. And the four of us always being together, that made a huge difference. I never felt alone. But I could have cried to see Mark shaking hands with you, and looking as if he might never see you again.'

'I know. I'll come to Tresillian as early as I can this summer, and I'll get Mother to arrange for us all to be at Prescott Hill together.'

'You might find that Caroline and Rachel and Chris have other plans. But I wish they could go on for ever, those summers when we were young.'

'Dear girl, you have a little way to go before your fortieth birthday, and all is lost, including your sweet youth.'

'Alex, stop teasing.'

'Well, don't expect me to take that nonsense about "when we were young . . .". The talk was light-hearted all the way back to London. But Livy did feel both old and young, young and inexperienced beside Alex, old with the feeling that so much that was precious was slipping away too fast.

That very feeling was there in the house when they returned. Dinner was early because Harry and Dena had a flight back to Paris that evening; they wore their travelling clothes, and no one else had dressed. 'I must say, Livy,' Caroline greeted her, 'you looked smashing at lunch today. Toby kept looking at you, and I was quite jealous. And he was quite miffed that he wasn't introduced.'

Alex, with his small bag already packed, was relaxing with a whisky. 'He ought to keep his eyes on his own date. Do you like him, Caro, or was he just someone to go to lunch with?'

'I go to lunch with almost anyone who asks me, so long as I don't positively dislike them. How else is one ever to learn who's interesting and who's a bore?' She laughed at Alex. 'I keep a very open mind.'

'And a very full engagement book,' Dena remarked.

'I suppose you go only to the very best places?' Andrew McClintock asked. He had already announced his intention of being on the plane with Alex in the morning. Again Livy experienced the sensation that too often her world flew off in too many directions.

'Why not, Mr McClintock? One is just as likely to meet the love of one's life at the Ritz as at the London School of Economics.'

'Is that what you're looking for, Miss?'

'What else is there for a girl, Mr McClintock? For a girl like me? Rachel has brains. She could follow Father into the FO. By the time she's sixty, they might even be appointing women ambassadors. But there won't be anything like that for me. All I can hope for is . . . is, well, the love of a life, or a reasonable facsimile thereof.'

'Will you know it when it comes?' Alex asked.

'I hope I do, Alex. And I hope that was a serious question.'

'It certainly was serious. I hope I'll know it too. I was just wondering if you had any tips.'

'Me give you tips! You've probably broken more hearts than you can count.'

'None that I'm aware of.'

Livy sipped her sherry, and said nothing. The banter continued between Caroline and Alex, and Livy was uncomfortably aware that Andrew McClintock's eyes were upon her most of the time. If her heart wasn't broken it was because she believed that her time with Alex had yet to come. She knew that she had imagined herself in love several times, and as quickly discarded the feeling. She wasn't impervious to the attentions of other young men, and had enjoyed them, but there was always the figure of Alex in the background. They were both coming to turning points in their lives. In June he would be finished at Harvard Business School, she would be finished at Oxford. His future at

317

McClintock-Clayton was predestined, but what he would do with his life personally was not. She waited for an indication that she might have a place in it.

But he was making plans. As they went into dinner, he said to his mother, 'I hope you can fix dates for us all to get together this summer. A few weeks at Tresillian, and then at Prescott Hill. I'll try to get here as soon as possible. Will you be able to come to Washington, Lady Camborne?' For some reasons he had never called her 'aunt' as Chris did.

Dena did not immediately answer. She waited until the soup was served, and Knox and the footman had left the room momentarily. She looked across at Harry. 'Are we allowed to say anything yet?'

'It's all in the family. I imagine you can all be discreet. By the summer I'll be posted again, and this time it's Washington.'

A little gasp of excitement came from Caroline. 'Ambassador! – you've been made ambassador!'

''Fraid not, my darling. That will have to wait a little. There are a few good men ahead of me, and Washington's our most important post. But I'll be minister in charge when the ambassador's not there. Mind you, Washington has five ministers at the Embassy. It's a step towards Ambassador, but the Foreign Service being what it is, I may never be Ambassador to Washington. Our chap there at the moment is pretty good at his job. They're not going to kick him out for me.'

'It's the most wonderful news, just the same,' Ginny said. 'I'll have you for neighbours. I must see that everything's in order at my grandmother's little house, Wildwood. I've just been waiting for an excuse to redecorate and modernize it a bit. It's one of Blair's and my favourite places. Blair actually rented it one time, before we were married.'

Livy saw their eyes meet fondly across the table, and she noticed that Andrew McClintock raised his wine glass to his lips quickly, and drank. She fancied he was trying to hide a smile. Why did the mention of Ginny's grandmother's old home amuse him, or was it the fact that he might have engineered Blair's renting it? McClintock was capable of any sort of plotting. But when he spoke it was to Harry. 'Glad to hear your news. Yes, I suppose an ambassadorship is the next move, but it probably won't be Washington for a few years. They'll break you in in Paris, or a tamer place, like Denmark. Or why not Moscow? You've had very useful experience there.'

Harry seemed to hesitate a moment. 'I'd resist Moscow if I could. Dena wasn't happy there before. It's a difficult posting. I rather hope they'll put me in a place where I can continue to be a Moscow-watcher rather than the man on the spot. Well, we'll see –' He broke off as Knox and the footman brought in the next course, and started to clear the soup bowls. 'At any rate, it will be a nice reunion in Washington this summer. And we'll try to make it to Tresillian first . . .'

Livy experienced a feeling much like panic. It was all rushing ahead too fast for her. She needed time to catch up. She wanted them all static just for a while, just for a little longer. The approaching summer was looming too quickly, and too much was going to happen. With a rapid movement she reached for her wineglass, missed the stem, and knocked it over. She looked at Ginny apologetically. 'I'm so sorry, Aunt Ginny. It was dreadfully clumsy of me.'

'It certainly was,' Alex said cheerfully. He was seated beside her, and had risen and was mopping up the spilled white wine. Knox approached and laid a clean napkin over the damp place, and offered another one to Alex.

'Don't look so stricken, Livy,' Ginny said softly. 'It's not a catastrophe.'

At that moment, when all attention was on Livy, Andrew McClintock's glass also fell, and once again wine flooded on to the table. 'It's these trembling old hands,' he said. 'Sorry, Ginny.' Everyone, Livy thought, must have known that his action had been deliberate. But how had Andrew McClintock known of the momentary sense of panic and fear that had possessed her? She looked across at him, not knowing whether to be grateful or annoyed. How did he manage to insinuate himself so shrewdly into all their lives, to know them so well that he could read their emotions so readily?

'Are you two playing games?' Alex asked. 'If this is some new kind of game, I doubt it will be very popular with hostesses.'

'Livy and I don't play games. But we do have quite a few things in common. Don't we, Livy?'

She was forced to answer. 'Yes.' But all she could think that they might have in common was a shared need of Andrew McClintock's grandson.

When the main course was served, and their glasses had been filled with red wine, the old man raised his. 'Well, here's to our next meeting-in Washington, I expect. Let's hope both Alex and Livy cover themselves in glory from their exams. We'll have to start thinking about your future, won't we, young Livy?'

'I think a year off mightn't be a bad idea,' Ginny said. 'What's the hurry about deciding what to do? Livy's never been certain, like Rachel, that she was going to be either a political journalist or a politician.'

'I disagree,' Andrew McClintock said. 'The young can't afford a year, any more than the old can. I don't approve of just messing about. It gets to be a habit.'

'Oh!' Caroline said. 'You are a bit hard on we less-than-brilliant ones, Mr McClintock.'

He looked along the table as if he had hardly seen her before. 'Oh, well, I've never been very interested in the less-than-brilliant ones. I hope you make your way very well, young lady, but I won't lose any sleep over it.'

Harry looked at his watch very deliberately. 'Sorry, Ginny. We're running a bit late. I think we really must go. Ready, Dena? Caro, when do we see you back in Paris? Or has Ginny got some things for you to do for her?' He made his goodbyes around the table, and Andrew McClintock received only a perfunctory handshake.

Chapter 9

1

Spring broke over the spires of Oxford, and Livy hardly noticed. She cycled to the library, working on her revision, and at night dreamed of the exams, in which she seemed able to write nothing; only a blank sheet of paper stared back at her. Her tutor remarked sharply that she was losing weight and looked too pale. 'There is such a thing as taking exams too seriously, though in the academic life that attitude hardly exists. Why don't you go and punt on the river with some nice young man?'

'Because all the nice young men are doing exactly what I'm doing, cramming for finals.'

Another being, someone Livy barely recognized, also lived for the time when finals would be done. She lived for what seemed almost unobtainable, the months of summer. She lived for what Alex had promised; the weeks at Tresillian, the weeks at Prescott Hill. They would be the prize for all the work, the wearying hours of study. Pass or fail, she would have the summer. Alex had promised that.

Yet nothing worked out as it had been promised. The first hint came from Caroline, who had gone back to Paris after hanging about in London for some weeks after the King's funeral. She wrote to Livy:

Mother's so busy getting ready for Washington that I doubt she'll have time to get to Tresillian. I don't think Aunt Ginny will be back in London before the summer, so I expect we'll have to give Tresillian a miss this year. I'm helping mother all I can. She has a big round of farewell dinners to give, and attend.

Rachel wrote that she didn't think she would come to Tresillian that summer.

There's still so much to do with this paper. I'd like to get in another couple of weeks at the British Museum. I don't really want to go to Washington either, but there are lots of things I'd like to look up in the Library of Congress. I'd rather like to get a feel of the place. Blair and Mr McClintock have so many political contacts. I'm hoping I might get a job there for a while once I've got my degree here.

With typical thoroughness Rachel had prepared for every eventuality by learning typing and shorthand. Chris had been offered a small part in a summer stock, and wouldn't be going to Tresillian either.

If we get a long enough tour, I won't be coming to Washington. I can hardly believe I'm actually going to be on the stage, even if it's only a tiny part.

There was, though, no letter from Alex. Livy assumed he was as busy as she preparing for his exams, and she tried to put the thought from her mind, but an anxious letter arrived from Mark:

Alex has written that he can't come to Tresillian this year. He says he has too much to do. But he still expects us at Prescott Hill. I don't suppose, now, you'll want to go, either. I'll miss going. I don't think people should make promises they don't mean to keep . . .

Just before she began her exams in May, Livy wrote to Mark. The silence from Alex had hurt and bewildered her, and she was angry at the offhand way he had appeared to let Mark down.

I'll meet you in London just as soon as the holidays begin. We'll have a little time at Tresillian together, and then we'll go to Washington. The others can do as they like. I want to see Thea and Herbert and Bess. I'm going to have my twenty-first birthday then, and that's where I want to spend it. Will you come?

A telegram reached Livy the morning of her first paper, just before she set off for the Examination Schools, dressed in the black and white which was *de rigueur* for all examination candidates. '*Thanks a million. Good luck, Mark.*' A scribbled note had come from Dena.

You're a darling to take Mark to Tresillian. It means so much to him. I hope the exams aren't too terrible. Harry and I are thinking of you, dearest. We'll see you soon in Washington.

Livy felt lonely and rather frightened as she cycled off to the Examination Schools. But what had she expected? That they would all come and hold her hand? Rachel had needed no such cosseting when she had achieved her first at Cambridge. With finals over, she felt dazed and weary, and she packed her belongings with the knowledge that she would never come back to Lady Margaret Hall. First, second or third-class degree, she didn't think her future was as an academic. But she was too tired to think just where it might lie. Perhaps she would let it all go, wait until the results were in. She thought longingly of Tresillian. She wanted to lie in the orchard near Bully's gravestone, she wanted to walk in the sun-warmed streets of St Just, to hear herself greeted by her Tregenna cousins as one of them. She realized she was homesick.

She and Mark had one night's reunion at Seymour House; they were served delightedly by Knox, who was glad to have something to do. 'The staff tends to get idle when Mr and Mrs Clayton aren't in residence,' he complained. After dinner Mark went downstairs to thank the chef, and ask the ingredients of the fish sauce. 'I think Aunt Ginny should give Knox and the chef a spell in Washington. It would be like a holiday for them. They get bored and stale just looking after each other. They'd come back with some new recipes and some new ideas.'

Livy thought it an odd thing for a young boy to say. 'Are you interested in how a house is run? I mean the catering, and all that?'

'Certainly I am. I've seen enough of what mother has to do keeping her end up in diplomatic circles. It isn't just butlers and cooks, it's laundry and fishmongers and butchers.

323

All the best chefs go to the market themselves, almost every day. They like everything fresh.'

Livy told him that was the tenet by which her mother had lived. 'But there wasn't much choice in St Just. You made the best of what the fishermen and farmers brought in that day.'

They were welcomed at Penzance by Thea and Herbert and Bess. Thea had wanted them to stay at her house, but Livy insisted on Tresillian. Dena had written to the Tregenna women who now took care of it, and beds were made up and fires lighted. They drove up the hill, and the castle made the same dramatic impact as always. Now the ruined Tower was silhouetted against a sea which had its high summer evening sheen upon it. The house was decked with flowers, the windows open to the sweet air. Livy felt her fatigue slip from her, her sense of alienation from the world disappeared. She was back in the place she most loved, surrounded by those she loved, and who loved her. There had never been any other home, only here and the little house where her father had taught her to read, and her mother taught her the homely virtues and demonstrated what it was to love a man.

They had lobster *bisque* which Thea had made, and a *bouillabaisse* which held almost every sort of fish available that morning in St Just. They finished off the beautiful burgundy Herbert had brought with cheddar from Somerset. Mark sighed in satisfaction. 'I think I must be in heaven . . .' That night Livy slept with the window fully open to the breeze from the sea, and the distant sound of the waves on the Tresillian Rocks. It was the first night for months in which she hadn't wakened, roused by fear and apprehension. For good or ill, the examinations were over. The warm sun wakened her next morning. It was nearly ten o'clock.

Sara Tregenna was busy in the Great Hall when Livy came down. 'It's just the same as always,' she said to Livy. 'You begin at one end of this house, get through it, and start again. Just like your mother did . . .'

'An omelette?' Mark suggested, when she entered the kitchen.

'Oh, I don't think I'll bother. I'll just make some toast.'

'But would you like an omelette? Plain? Ham? Cheese?'

'You're going to make it?'

'Certainly I'm going to make it.' He was cracking eggs into a bowl with one hand. 'Can you manage three eggs? There are dozens in the pantry.'

'With a little bit of everything,' she said, to tease him, and found that he took the challenge quite seriously. He chopped ham and a shallot, grated cheese, all the time watching the toast he was making, and served her with coffee, which she thought was the best she had tasted for a long time. She said so.

'I expect when you're cramming for exams you don't notice what you're eating. I ground the coffee beans and of course the water and the cream here are wonderful.' She watched him handle the big old iron pan with ease. The omelette was delicious.

'Always the test of a cook, that's what mother says.'

'Did she teach you?'

He shrugged. 'Oh, I just sort of picked it up from watching. That's one of the things I like when we go to France. They take the food seriously. And when they know you appreciate it, they let you in on things. The *chef de cuisine* at the embassy—'

'You know him?'

'Yes. He doesn't mind my hanging around the kitchen so long as I don't get in the way. He pushes me into scrubbing the vegetables sometimes, and chopping them. I just watch the pastry chef and the *saucier*, and I'm careful not to get underfoot. At least I used to. I rather suspect they're not going to let me into the kitchen at the embassy in Washington.'

'Well, I'll look forward to some interesting meals . . .'

He looked slightly alarmed. 'Look, I'm not that good. Just a few simple things. Mother's always been a marvellous cook, and she told me your mother was, too. Rachel doesn't even notice what she eats. Heaven help the man she marries. Caro's pretty fair, but I always think she does it because she thinks it a useful thing to be able to do, not because she

325

wants to. Chris is a bit like Aunt Ginny. She can do a few things well, and she likes things beautifully served; that's the theatrical part of her. But, you see, there's always been all that money, and she knows there'll always be someone around to cook for her.'

Livy was both amused and a little disturbed by this judgement of their characters based on culinary skills, or lack of them. 'You've left me out.'

He smiled. 'It's hardly polite to say it to your face, but you're pretty fair when you put your mind to it, but half the time you're off in some other place. The French would know right away that you weren't *serieuse*.'

'I intend to be very unserious for the next two weeks. Ham and cheese sandwiches or maybe I'll be industrious and make us a batch of pasties.' Suddenly the memory of her mother was strong and very real, the many days they had sat in this kitchen and eaten pasties for lunch. The sun flooded the kitchen, but the ghosts were everywhere. She almost fancied she could see Andrew McClintock seated at this table.

'You've slipped off again,' Mark observed.

Livy smiled. It didn't matter. Whatever happened it would be all right. Their wonderful summer had begun, the promised summer of ease and delight. And in a few weeks she would see Alex.

The two weeks sped away. They had picnics and dinners with Thea and Herbert and Bess. They walked the streets of St Just, and selected presents to take to Prescott Hill. Thea gave Livy a painting, framed, but originally made on a piece of torn canvas. 'It's by a man called Alfred Wallis. A primitive; shows great talent. He died in the Penzance poorhouse. I thought Blair might like it.' Livy selected a beautiful brown pot from the studio of Bernard Leach. The whole of St Just seemed filled with people who were painting or making pots or trying to write books. Mark gave her a present of a beautifully bound book. It had no title, and when she opened it, the pages were empty. 'It's for you to write in,' he said. 'I imagined you might write some poetry.'

'I'd be afraid to. It's too beautiful to spoil.'

'You'd never spoil anything, Livy.'

Their plane tickets arrived from Blair Clayton's office, bringing the American prospect closer. 'I almost hate to go,' Mark said, 'and yet I'm dying to see them all.' Dena had written that she was settling well into the house the embassy had provided.

It's a charming house – quite large. Well, we are expected to do a good deal of entertaining. Caro approves. The staff is all coloured, and very pleasant and cheerful. I suspect I'm going to enjoy myself quite a lot. Of course, Ginny is everything. Just knowing her in Washington is something, but to be introduced as a best friend, well, it works wonders. The marvellous thing is that it's true. I can't imagine life without Ginny.

Livy shared the letter with Thea and Bess. Thea looked at Mark. 'I suppose you know that Ginny just got your mother to the hospital here in time. You were practically born into her arms. I think if Dena could have given you to her she would have . . . she wanted a child so much.'

'What a pity I wasn't twins,' Mark answered. 'They could have shared me.'

Two days before they were to leave was Livy's twenty-first birthday. There were presents from everyone. From Herbert a painting, from Thea a sculpture which she placed in the walled garden of Livy's cottage, a small sculpture which seemed to belong precisely where it was placed. 'Bess can look after it for you . . .' She laughed as she said it because she knew very well that Bess had never wholly approved of her work. There was a worn, but beautifully-bound copy of the *Odyssey* in Greek from Rachel. 'Fancy her remembering. How kind . . .'

'She obviously expects you not to forget how to read it,' Bess said. Her own present was a book. 'I can never think of anything else.' She had gone to great trouble and expense over it. It was a nineteenth-century copy of Cornish legends, illustrated by an unknown artist in the pre-Raphaelite style. 'I've had an antiquarian bookseller looking out for something like this for two years. It turned up only a few weeks ago.

Otherwise I'd have been reduced to giving you a scarf, which you'd go and lose.'

They feasted that night in Thea and Herbert's house. 'You must be with us, dear heart,' Herbert had said. 'This is the day we give you away to the world. You belong to yourself now, Livy, but you know we're always here.'

They remembered many things over the beautiful wine he had provided. They remembered Oliver and Isa and Bully. Bess remembered the guarded meeting between Timmins and Tubby. Telegrams had come from Washington, *'We'll have a gorgeous party here for you, darling.'* On Livy's right hand there glowed Andrew McClintock's present, sent by special delivery the day before. *'Don't believe that bunkum about opals being unlucky,'* said the note that accompanied it. *'Just remember that it looks like the sea around those nasty rocks of yours.'* It was a rounded opal, of a very dark colour, surrounded by tiny diamonds. 'A black opal,' Thea had marvelled. 'It must be very valuable. And to think I imagined that man hadn't a poetic thought in his head. It is the colour of the sea in some lights. I imagine it's the only stone that can't be faked.'

Mark had read up on opals in Bess's encyclopedia. 'It probably comes from a place called Lightning Ridge in Australia. All the best ones come from there. It suits you, Livy.'

Livy regarded it with some misgiving. Apart from a single strand of pearls Ginny and Blair had given her for her coming-out party, it was the only piece of jewellery she possessed. Her mother's wedding ring was locked up in the bank in St Just. She had never seen anything quite so beautiful. The jewels that Ginny wore on grand occasions were dazzling, but the fire and flash of the opal was endlessly fascinating, its differences revealed in every movement of her hand. 'I hardly dare wear it,' she said, as the candle on the dinner table seemed to draw yet more colour from the stone.

'You'd better wear it,' Mark said. 'Or Mr McClintock won't give you anything else.'

'Mercenary little animal, aren't you?' Bess remarked.

Mark grinned. 'Not really, Aunt Bess. I just want everything beautiful for Livy.'

They left two days later, met by a representative of McClintock-Clayton, who saw them to the small company-owned plane which would take them on to Washington. Caroline was waiting for them at the airport with one of Ginny's cars and a chauffeur. Livy thought her greeting seemed a little restrained, though she kissed Livy, and again wished her a happy birthday. 'We were planning a little party . . .' she said as they went to the car. Livy was too tired and too hot to give much thought to why Caroline had said 'were'.

Caroline waited until they were settled in the back seat of the big car; the windows were down to get the warm rush of air in, but the sliding glass panel between them and the chauffeur was closed.

'Things are a bit at sixes and sevens,' she began. 'It only happened two days ago, and we didn't want to spoil your birthday; well, I mean, we didn't want to startle you by sending a cable. Since you were going to be here so soon, Mother thought it better to wait, and then you could have all the details.'

'What details?' Mark demanded. 'What's happened? You make it sound like something serious.'

Caroline made a faint attempt at a laugh. 'Well, it is always serious when someone gets engaged. Marriage is supposed to be serious.'

'Who's engaged? You?'

'No, not yet. I'm not so lucky. It's Alex. Two days ago he announced he's going to marry Nancy Van Isler Winterton. Out of the blue, just like that!'

The buildings along Pennsylvannia Avenue seemed to fade into a blur for Livy. It was the heat, of course. Why did they all waver together? And yet, in the rush of the hot air through the windows, she felt strangely cold.

'Who's she?' Mark said.

'Well, I wouldn't expect you to know, but everyone in this town and a few other places in America certainly does. She's the daughter of . . .'

Livy hardly heard the words. She could almost have recited

329

the litany herself. It was a famous name in America, and beyond. A great fortune had been made in railroads, steel and meat-packing by Henry Winterton. He was probably this girl's grandfather, or great-grandfather. The Van Islers owned vast tracts of land on the Hudson River, and their fortune had begun with the trading of furs from Canada. They had diversified, and now had offices on Wall Street, and owned blocks of down-town Chicago and San Francisco. They were the majority stockholders in a private bank, which brought them into immediate contact with McClintock-Clayton. Often the two firms had worked together to finance the same projects. But the name of Winterton was better known to the world outside finance for the art collection they had put together at the end of the nineteenth century. Most of it was now on permanent loan to the National Gallery in Washington. It hardly even mattered what this girl, Nancy, was like. She was an obvious choice for the heir to McClintock-Clayton.

'Well, it sounds all right,' Mark said. 'Why are things at sixes and sevens? Was it so unexpected? After all, Alex was going to marry someone.'

'Of course he was. And she seems ideal. But for some reason Mr McClintock is dead against it. No one's supposed to know but Aunt Ginny. He's done everything but threaten to disinherit Alex. No one can understand why. Why should he possibly object to her? She's a stunning-looking girl.'

'Oh, do be quiet!' Livy said. She hardly recognized the strangled tone which came from her throat. 'It's far too hot to argue about these things. Who ever knows why Mr McClintock does anything? At times he's as impetuous as a silly little girl.' She looked at the opal on her finger, whose beauty had become a familiar and loved part of her life in these brief days. 'When you're old and rich and powerful, as he is, you don't like people making their own decisions. One day Alex would . . . would marry. Did Mr McClintock expect to choose the bride?' She tried to laugh, and the sound was harsh and strident. 'Alex has just exercised the same prerogative as most men. What's the fuss?'

The fuss was in her own heart. She stared resolutely ahead

at the buildings which still seemed to waver before her eyes, and willed her mind to clear, and her senses to stop reeling.

Caroline turned huffy. 'Well, I was only trying to explain. Everyone would be celebrating, except that Mr McClintock is in such a state. The Wintertons don't understand why he should object . . . Aunt Ginny and Blair are trying to put a good face on it, but everyone knows it needs the Old Man's blessing—'

'Don't call him that!' Livy snapped. 'He's Ambassador McClintock! Mentally, he can still run rings round men half his age!'

'We are touchy, aren't we! Of course Nancy is just the sort of girl one would expect Alex to marry. She had a couple of years at Vassar, though I don't think she graduated. She's got all the right connections, and all the money.' Here Caroline paused, and sighed. 'Lucky girl!' She added, more reflectively, 'Alex doesn't give me the impression, though, of having fallen head over heels. He goes around with that same self-assured smile, and lets the Old Ma – the Ambassador, carry on. There's not a thing he can do to stop it, not any real objection he can make.'

'Are they going to be engaged for ever . . . until Mr McClintock changes his mind?'

'Mr McClintock is hardly being consulted,' Caroline said, almost with relish. 'It's up to Nancy Winterton's parents to arrange the wedding, which is going full-steam ahead. The wedding's probably going to be in late August. Alex gets his office at McClintock-Clayton after Labor Day. Naturally, no one expects him to have flunked at Harvard Business School. That just wouldn't be our bright, brilliant boy, would it?'

'You make him sound such a prig,' Mark objected.

'He isn't a prig,' Caroline said, after a moment's reflection. 'It's just that he's so . . . so . . . Well, he always does get it right, doesn't he? No wonder Nancy Winterton's parents don't want to let him slip. I suppose you could say he's America's most eligible bachelor. I'm not as up on these things here as I am in England.'

'Snob!' Mark howled, and laughed at the same time. The car was turning into the small forecourt of a neo-colonial house in a street off Massachusetts Avenue, the avenue where most of the embassies were situated, and where the McClintock mansion was one of the few remaining private homes. 'I say, things are looking up a bit! Father's flat in Paris wasn't nearly as grand as this.'

'That's because Paris keeps everything on the inside,' Livy said, glad to have something other than Alex to talk about. 'You don't show off in Paris.' She had found her voice, and she knew already that there was a bitter edge to it.

The chauffeur had opened the door for them. Mark ran around to help unload the luggage. Dena was starting down the steps of the house. 'Buck up,' Caroline whispered. 'I thought I'd better let you have all the news and get it over with. Put a smile on your face, for heaven's sake!' Little Caro, Livy thought, whom some people considered not very intelligent, but who displayed moments of uncomfortable perception.

'Thanks, Caro. You're a sweet girl. I sound like a bear but it's just I'm so hot and grubby and tired . . .' Her words were cut off by Dena's embrace.

'Darling! Happy birthday. We're sorry we weren't all together to celebrate it. But we'll make it up to you . . .' Her arm remained about Livy's shoulder as they walked up the steps. Mark seemed almost forgotten, though Dena did turn at the top of the steps and extended her free arm to him. 'How you've grown! My goodness, it must be inches. We'll have to go shopping tomorrow to get you something decent to wear. Poor love, you must be suffering in that heavy suit.'

They were swept on into the hall of a handsome, simply but elegantly furnished house. A black butler in a white jacket was beaming at Livy and Mark. 'This is Thomas,' Dena said. 'He's been very good to us. He's helped us so much to get settled.'

'It sure is good to meet you,' the man said, and white teeth showed in a smile of genuine pleasure. 'You surely do have handsome children, Lady Camborne.'

'I'm not Lady Camborne's child,' Livy said, a little defensively. She still felt shaken, and the words were more tart than she had intended. She was sorry when she saw the smile fade, and the dark eyes grow more wary.

'She just belongs to us all,' Dena said. 'We're very lucky to have Livy. Mrs Clayton and I fight over who's to have her.'

The smile returned, though more cautiously. 'Never did see such beautiful red hair in my life,' Thomas said. 'And pardon me, Miss Livy, if you think that's too forward.'

'Of course not.' Livy exerted herself, and found she also could smile. 'It's very kind of you, Thomas . . .'

'What can I bring you, Miss Livy . . . Master Mark? Iced tea? . . . Iced coffee?'

'Iced tea,' Dena said quickly. 'We'll have it on the back porch. Then you can both go and have baths or showers. The house has everything. Best equipped house we've ever had in the Foreign Service. And having Ginny so close by is heaven. I feel very spoiled. And now very complete that you two are here. Rachel promises she'll come soon.' She led them through to the back porch, which was shaded by the floor of the porch above, and by densely leafed trees. The garden was mostly paved in bricks, with large shrubs set among wandering paths. 'It's not a large garden, but just right. We sit out here at night, and the patio's nice for entertaining.' The whole place, Livy noticed, had just been hosed, and the bricks gave off a refreshing smell of damp from the moss between them. She sank into a wicker chair with a chintz cushion, and let the talk flow over her. She found herself responding automatically to questions about the exams, about Thea, Herbert and Bess. About Tresillian. Her opal was exclaimed over, and Mark quoted what Thea had said about it. Iced tea was brought and little cakes and sandwiches, for which Livy had no appetite.

'I'm sure Caro's told you the news about Alex,' Dena at last ventured on the subject. 'Everyone was rather stunned but it is a very good match. She's a lovely girl, and she seems terribly in love with Alex. He kept it all very much to himself. But then, he's always been dating someone . . .'

'Oh Mother, Livy's sick of hearing about the whole thing

333

and the virtues of Nancy Winterton. I'm sure all she wants is a bath, and to flop into bed . . .'

'Of course . . . of course . . .' Dena' said. 'I'll take you upstairs, and help you both unpack. You'll be sharing a room with Caro, Livy, just like old times. I thought I'd better keep a room free for Rachel when she comes. You know how prickly she is when she can't have a place of her own . . .' She was leading them back through the house, and up the wide curving staircase. Livy was aware of flowers and pale curtains, polished bare floors, and a few good pieces of furniture. 'I wonder if it's just possible that Ginny might have some of Alex's old summer clothes tucked away in the attic . . . just until we can go and buy something for Mark. We're invited for dinner this evening, but only if you feel up to it, darlings. Ginny said she'll quite understand if you just want to rest . . .'

Livy glanced at Mark's eager face. He loved the glories of the McClintock mansion, loved the fine food and wine. 'Of course we'll go. A bath and an hour's sleep will do just beautifully.'

But she lay and tossed in the soft bed, which seemed hot even though an air-conditioner thrummed in the window. Dinner with Ginny and Blair. And probably with Alex. Perhaps with Nancy Winterton. Mentally she stiffened herself. Better to get it over with. Better to see what Alex in love was like, and to know, finally and for ever, that he would never be in love with her.

Alex in love, Alex about to be married, seemed no different than the Alex she had always known. He kissed her cheek, gave her a hug. 'Great to have the exams over with, isn't it? I'm sure you came through covered in glory. Livy, this is Nancy. Nancy, by this time you know Livy's about the best thing that ever happened to my family. Livy's the only person I know who's ever had three families fighting over who'd have the privilege of taking care of her. What we were really fighting about was having the privilege of her taking care of us.'

She was, as Caroline had said, beautiful. She had an

elegant, patrician face, a tall, finely-boned body. She looked at Livy with cool blue appraising eyes, and must have long ago decided that this family favourite should be cultivated.

'I'm delighted to meet you, Livy. Of course I've heard so much about you and seen your photos. I've read your father's verse. He's a very fine poet. Everyone says so. I've been bragging to my friends that I'm going to know Oliver Miles's daughter, so I hope you'll back me up.' As she spoke she slipped her arm through Alex's; the gesture was at the same time possessive and clinging. It said it all for Livy. *I have him.*

Apart from the rage of anguish and longing in her heart, Livy immediately felt clumsy and badly dressed. Why hadn't she got her head out of the books long enough to know what sort of clothes were being worn this year? She realized that she must have been wearing this dress since she was eighteen, and it no longer suited someone who had come down from university, and had turned twenty-one. It certainly did not have the sort of elegance which might be expected of someone Alex McClintock would marry. But what did it matter? He wasn't going to marry her. She could have come dressed in a school hockey tunic, and no one would have noticed. She smiled, and knew that the smile was false, and could do no better.

'Congratulations, Alex!' she managed to say. 'You really have found the American Beauty! It seems everyone was surprised, but then you've always kept your secrets well. I understand the wedding's going to be quite soon . . .' She heard her own voice babbling on, and the replies. The Wedding would be in late August. Here in Washington. 'Alex is being awfully mean, and very conscientious,' Nancy said. 'He says that everyone gets back to work right after Labor Day, so we'll have only a week or so at my parents' place at Bar Harbor as a honeymoon. I'd hoped it would be a month in Europe . . . but . . .' She looked up at Alex. 'The Master has spoken. Duty, and all that. Europe will have to wait until next year. Of course, my parents have been taking the whole family there since we were kids. I have three brothers, Livy. Did anyone have time to tell you that?'

335

'Ambassador McClintock, madam,' the butler announced.

Andrew McClintock stood in the doorway, his weight resting lightly on his stick. Ginny hurried forward to greet him.

'Hope I'm not intruding, Ginny. I guessed you'd be having the young folk together tonight. I always feel I have to make a bit of an effort for Livy, since she's the only one of the brood who isn't my godchild.'

Grateful for being delivered from the agony of trying to talk with Nancy Winterton, Livy went towards him. 'Mr McClintock, how can I possibly thank you!' She held the ring on her hand up for his inspection. 'It's utterly beautiful. Thea said she had not imagined you a poet, but now she knows it.'

For the first time ever, he leaned forward and placed a dry kiss on her cheek. 'Good to see you, Livy. The stone reminded me of the sea and your mother. When I saw it I said to myself, "Those damned rocks!" But they're there, and we can't pretend they don't exist.'

In turn he greeted the others, last of all Nancy, who seemed to hang back a little, still holding on to Alex's arm. Livy had as yet heard nothing of any presents Nancy had recieved from Andrew McClintock, but she was more than conscious of the size and beauty of the sapphire ring Nancy wore on her left hand. On his twenty-fifth birthday Alex had taken control of several trust funds set up for him when he was born. The ring on Nancy's finger displayed his new independence.

Harry arrived, looking hot and tired, but his greeting to his son and Livy was affectionate and warm. 'My God,' he said, looking at Mark and echoing Dena, 'how you've grown!' Mark had been hastily fitted out with a light suit which Ginny had kept from Alex's teen years; it was only slightly too large for him. Harry embraced Livy, and kissed her. 'Dena's planning a little party for you next week. We just had to fit it in between other commitments.' He accepted a whisky from the butler gratefully. 'Even in summer the diplomatic round doesn't stop. Every new nation that's become independent and takes a seat in the UN has to have

336

its national day, and woe betide the embassy that's not represented at senior level. Especially if the new nation happens to have been one of our former colonies. The Ambassador must have a liver of iron. You'll like him, Livy. He's promised to look in on our little party for you if he can possibly manage it. He and Lady Halliwell have been very kind to Dena and me. You've been around the diplomatic life long enough to know that one's Ambassador can make all the difference in life. If he's friendly, and his wife likes your wife, you've practically got it made.'

'Don't make it sound so easy,' Andrew McClintock said. 'You know very well that since Burgess and Maclean slipped out from under the noses of your security people, all you British have had to work twice as hard to convince us here that you really can be trusted. I've never known the "special relationship" to wobble so much.'

'It'll take us years to get over that one,' Harry confessed wearily. 'You know what they're calling all members of the Diplomatic Corps now, no matter what country they're from? Spies and salesmen. That's what we're reduced to.'

Blair's arrival halted that line of discussion. There was the ritual greeting of Livy and Mark. 'So you're a grown-up woman now, free to do as you want.' He kissed her, touched her face fondly. 'Welcome back.'

'I hope,' Andrew McClintock remarked to Livy, as Blair was being served his drink, 'now that you're independent, you'll continue to honour McClintock-Clayton with your business. I shall hope to see you in my office, young lady, and we'll review your portfolio. Naturally, you're quite at liberty to dismiss me now as your business manager if you think I haven't been doing a good job . . .'

Livy laughed; it was almost true laughter, the first she had been able to summon since she had heard the news about Alex. It was a well-known fact, almost a family joke, that Andrew McClintock himself still supervised the portfolio of stocks he had bought for her when the royalties from *This England* had started coming in in what had then seemed to Livy quite unbelievable sums. Since then she'd had an allowance from the trust, and her expenses had been paid.

337

To this day she didn't know the value of the portfolio. To question Andrew McClintock's judgement on any financial matter was unthinkable. 'I must warn you, Ambassador –' she frequently gave him that title, though in a democracy he was not strictly entitled to it since he no longer held that post, because she knew he secretly delighted in it. 'I've been taking a correspondence course on managing trusts. It's called "Widows and Orphans".'

'For an orphan, Livy's got the biggest damn family I've ever known,' Alex said.

When the butler announced dinner, they began to move across the hall to the dining-room. Andrew McClintock offered Livy his arm. 'To honour your birthday, young lady.' Livy had been aware that Ginny had rushed to rearrange the setting at the dinner table. Never in the long years of her marriage to Blair had Andrew McClintock given up the habit of treating whatever house Ginny happened to be in as his own. He still expected a place at dinner or lunch whenever he chose to arrive. For Alex's sake, for the sake of peace, Ginny had never complained. Sometimes Livy thought she would have made an even better diplomatic wife than Dena. Andrew McClintock moved automatically, by long custom, to the seat at Ginny's right hand. Livy found herself on Blair's right, Nancy Winterton was on his left. As they began the *vichyssoise* Nancy was eagerly telling Blair her latest news. 'We've found this darling house in Georgetown . . . daddy insists on giving it to us as a wedding present . . . mother and I will be racing to get the bare essentials of furnishing into it before the wedding. We have to have a place of our own . . .'

Glancing down the table, Livy saw Andrew McClintock's face darken. He didn't much care for the fact that he had not been consulted about this decision, and that someone else's money would pay for it. Just for this special evening, Mark had been placed on Ginny's left. The big McClintock voice, which had not diminished with age, boomed out, drowning Nancy Winterton's words. 'You're looking fine, young man! But only average marks at school, I hear. Still, you've time to pull up.'

'Everyone isn't as clever as my father,' Mark said, defensively. 'But I'm doing all right in sport. You never did come to watch any cricket, sir.'

'No time, young man. No time. But I'll get to it yet. Maybe when you're at Eton.'

'Shouldn't worry too much about the marks, old son,' Harry said mildly. 'Average is about right. I can remember my father telling me he almost wasn't accepted into the Foreign Office when he applied. One of the big-wigs who interviewed him said, "Good Lord, man, you got a first from Balliol." That nearly ended it right there.'

'You got a first from Balliol, Harry,' Dena said.

'And is that where you're headed, young man? Are you going into diplomacy too?'

Mark wriggled uncomfortably. 'I doubt it, sir. I don't think they'd have me. Now if I were Rachel . . .'

'Rachel is a socialist,' Andrew McClintock said sourly. 'I wouldn't be at all surprised if she isn't a damn commie. The Foreign Service wouldn't have her.'

It was, Livy thought, a typical dinner with Andrew McClintock. She wondered if he had truly meant it about going over her portfolio with her. Until now, the fact that she was twenty-one had scarcely impressed her with the fact that she would control her own money. The first thing she would do, the very first, when she got some money, would be to go out and buy some clothes. She would take Caro with her, and rely on her advice. And she'd buy Caro something too; Caro had always shared what she had with Livy.

The dinner ended at last. Livy felt that her smile, her false smile, had been stretched to the limit. Harry's car had come to pick them up, but Livy said she would rather walk the short distance. 'I'll go with you, Livy,' Mark said. There were protests about them going alone. 'It's only three minutes,' Livy retorted. 'We both need to stretch our legs and get a little air . . .'

Something in her manner made the objections stop. Alex was driving Nancy back to her parents' home; he waved distantly from the driveway. Dena and Harry's car went off, Caroline giving them a wave from the back seat. They walked

339

down the short driveway to the entrance on Massachusetts Avenue. A large dark car waited there. They heard the imperative knock of Andrew McClintock's cane against the window. His chauffeur opened the door.

'Now, see here, I can't have you wandering around at night. Any special place you want to go, or do you just want to drive around? I don't sleep very well most nights. Going to bed is often a waste of time.'

His tone was almost gentle, comforting in a way. Livy didn't argue, just climbed on to the large back seat with Andrew McClintock. There was plenty of room for Mark. She felt the fatigue of the long journey wash over her, the strain of trying to keep a smile fixed on her face, the endless questions answered, the polite questions asked, trying not to look at Alex too much, and yet afraid of being seen avoiding him. Not wanting to look at the loveliness, the desirability of Nancy Winterton.

'One place. If you don't think it's stupid, sentimental.'

'I don't make judgements until I know. Where?'

'Abe's House, I mean, the Lincoln Memorial. I like it best at night. So beautifully lighted. No people about.'

'A hero, is he? Well, I wouldn't quarrel with that.'

He sat in silence while they drove to the Memorial. He waited while she and Mark climbed the long flight of marble steps. As always, the brooding figure moved and inspired her; once again, together, but soundlessly, she and Mark read the words inscribed on the inner walls of the monument. Mark was now old enough to understand more fully their meaning. He took Livy's hand as they went slowly back down the steps to the waiting car. Suddenly, Livy was crying.

Andrew McClintock's voice was quiet, but precise. 'You care a great deal about him?'

She groped for a handkerchief, and was offered his own silk one. 'Yes – a hero – to me, at least.'

He tapped his stick on the glass, indicating to the chauffeur to drive off. 'Anywhere else? The Jefferson Memorial?'

'No – just this one place. This one man . . .'

Harry was waiting for them on the steps of the house. 'We

340

were worried,' he said. 'I didn't realize that Mr McClintock
. . .'

'She's tired. They're both tired. Just a little journey to
visit a hero. All young people should have heroes. Just don't
believe in them too much.'

The car drove off into the leafy darkness.

Harry closed and locked the door. Dena stood by the
staircase in a dressing robe. 'I guessed he had taken you
somewhere. I saw the car waiting as we left. Darlings, you
must both be so tired . . . It was too much . . . this evening.'

'I loved it!' Livy said. 'Thank you, Lady Camborne. Thank
you.' She kissed the other's soft cheek. And then mounted
the stairs, not quite sure where she was going, getting used
to yet another strange room in another strange house. Diplomats, she thought, did they ever know where home really
was?

Caroline greeted her sleepily. If she noticed from Livy's
eyes that she had been weeping, she said nothing. 'Father
was just about to call the police. Fortunately, Mother is
much calmer about these things. I must say the Old Man, I
mean, the Ambassador, really makes a fuss of you . . .' She
kept on chattering as Livy undressed and cleaned her face
with cold cream. 'We've just got to get you some clothes. You
haven't, I suppose, got any money left from your allowance?
Well, I suppose father might make an advance on mine . . .'

'There's some money,' Livy said vaguely.'I don't remember how much. I've had my head in the books for so long, I
haven't bothered . . .'

'Right,' Caroline said. 'In the morning we'll go shopping.
There's the party mother's giving for you next week. You'll
need something for that. And then the Wedding. You'll have
to be beautifully turned out for that!'

'Yes. Yes, the Wedding.' For once Livy wished she wasn't
sharing a room with Caroline. It would have been so much
easier to have let the tears come. 'What did you say . . .?'
she asked.

'I said,' Caroline repeated, 'where did you go? I thought
you looked half dead at dinner, and who could blame you
after that journey. Did you just drive around?'

341

'No, we went to the Lincoln Memorial. Mark and I like going there.' She hoped no one would ever know that it had been Alex who had first taken her there at night.

'What a strange pair you are! At times I think he acts more like your brother than mine.' As Livy got into the second twin bed, Caroline shook off her sleepy air. She left her bed and went and placed a kiss lightly on Livy's cheek. 'I'm so glad you've come. I've missed you. I hated being the one to break the news to you this afternoon but someone had to.' She switched off the bedside lamp.

Was it so obvious, Livy wondered. Did they all guess? Did Alex know? It was humiliating, and it hurt, but he had never promised or even hinted at anything more than their brother-sister relationship. She tossed restlessly; the air-conditioner thrummed. It was the sound of the city, not of the sea. She thought of the Tresillian Rocks, felt the opal ring which she wore, even at night. She thought of the tide receding, exposing the Rocks; she thought of the tide rushing in, covering the wet sand. Alex had gone, slipped away from her like the tide going out. Now she might weep, but tomorrow she would put on another face. She would sleep, and tomorrow some of the hurt would have washed away. She had to believe that.

The next morning Caroline examined Livy's bank statement with a knowledgeable eye. 'Dear, Livy, I know Mr McClintock wouldn't want you to be a spendthrift, but I'm sure he intends you to use your allowance. It looks to me as if you haven't bought a thing for ages . . .'

'I probably haven't. Somehow, I didn't seem to need it. One doesn't dress at Oxford.'

'Didn't you ever have any boyfriends? Weren't you taken out? I can't believe you lived like a nun.'

Livy replied testily. 'Of course there were boys, men, they call themselves. Undergraduates. But all those clothes Aunt Ginny insisted I have for that stupid season. I just kept on wearing them.'

'Oxford's finished, Livy. This is the real world. And it's run by men who like pretty, well-dressed women. With this,' she tapped the bank statement, 'we'll have a feast for you. I know a place where the model dresses are sent, just a little shop-soiled. All one has to do is have them dry-cleaned. Will you let me have father get this worked out in dollars, and then we'll go and shop?'

'Only if you'll take a commission. You've got to have at least as much as I spend.'

'That's outrageous!? I could use a few things, but you've got to be completely fitted out. We'll both get dresses for your party next week. Just as well father's in the Diplomatic Corps. We'd never get pounds changed into dollars otherwise. Though I suppose Mr McClintock could arrange it in a second . . .'

Livy hadn't even thought of that. She had come to America with money in her bank account, but no way to change it into dollars, since the restrictions on exchange were still in force. Always before she had taken what was offered, and never thought of the money. She had taken the houses, the cars, the planes – everything that flowed from the McClintock-Clayton sources, from the influence of the Cambornes. She had taken everything, and had even wanted their most prized future – she had wanted Alex. She felt naive, unsophisticated, a fool. 'Manage it somehow, Caro. Yes, I think it's about time I started to get out into, what did you say? the *real* world.'

2

Dena gave her party for Livy, a reception which lasted for two hours, followed by a buffet dinner. Livy was greeted and congratulated by people she vaguely recognized from other years, other places. Had it been Washington, or Prescott Hill, or Zurich, or London? The diplomatic faces were mixed with the McClintock-Clayton faces, and she grappled in her memory for their names. She wore the present that Dena and Ginny had devised from both families, an intricately wrought but slender gold necklet, set with a single diamond at the centre, and two small single diamonds as

343

earrings. She hated to think of what it had cost, hated to think that half of the gift had come from Harry's hard-pressed income. 'Oh, do stop fussing,' Caroline had said as they dressed. 'A twenty-first birthday is special. Rachel had her present, and Chris had hers, and I shall have mine next year. Believe me, Aunt Ginny can drive a hard bargain with her jewellers for these small pieces because of what the Claytons spend with them on her important ones.' As Livy had observed the elegance of the dresses they had bought at a marked-down price, she began to realize how many of these tricks there were to be learned about what Caroline called the *real* world.

The garden was lighted, and smelled sweetly of some night-blooming plant, a three-piece ensemble played, though there was no room to dance. The British Ambassador, Sir George Halliwell and Lady Halliwell came, and stayed twenty minutes. 'Very nice,' Caroline said. 'He can hardly ever get to anything that's private. Too many official occasions.' But Livy was beginning to realize that the McClintock-Clayton name was a valued connection into the highest reaches of the American establishment. The attendance was more than Dena had anticipated. 'Just about everyone who said "yes" has come. That doesn't often happen.'

Livy could see that although she was congratulated by everyone on her birthday, almost as many took the opportunity to congratulate Alex and Nancy on their engagement. The Wintertons had given a small family party on the announcement of the engagement. It was their style to play these matters discreetly. The wedding, so soon to follow, was the big event, and apart from the announcement in the newspapers, there had been no other celebration. But Nancy walked the rooms on Alex's arm, and many eyes went to the sapphire ring. Her mother and father, and two of her three brothers were present. 'They're here because of Mr McClintock and Aunty Ginny and Blair,' Caroline said, slightly waspishly. 'They know how fond everyone is of you. I think they're a bit miffed that Mr McClintock isn't exactly jumping for joy. They think Nancy's just as big a catch as Alex.'

'Then they're perfect for each other, aren't they?' Livy

said. 'I don't know why any of us should fuss. It's their business. Come on, Caro, I'm going to have another glass of champagne. It feels like a champagne night to me . . .'

She carried her glass and went to the sofa where Andrew McClintock sat. 'Don't you think Caro was clever to find a dress that went so beautifully with the opal?' It was a silk taffeta, shot through with greens and blues.

He eyed her critically, carefully. 'You make the dress,' he said. 'I wish your mother could have seen you.' It was said rather gruffly, as if the words were dragged out of him. She became conscious of how seldom he paid anyone an outright compliment.

'Thank you for remembering her. Particularly this evening.'

'I never forget her.'

She was learning to put a soothing gloss on the ache in her heart over Alex. Remembering the kitchen at Tresillian where Andrew McClintock had sat at the big table and talked with her mother, she remembered again how far these people had carried her with them into their world. She would not have been the only one to fall in love with Alex McClintock, and, despite Nancy hanging on his arm, she guessed that she would not be the last to love him. That she had not captured this greatest prize in their little circle was not to be wondered at. She had been given so much. No one but Alex could have given that, and he had not chosen to do so. She drank her champagne, and smiled; the smile, she knew, was becoming freer. She was learning very well how to keep it fixed there.

She accepted congratulations and many compliments; smiled and even laughed, and realized how few people asked her what she would be doing now that Oxford was behind her. It was expected, she thought, that now she would simply enjoy herself, enjoy the charmed circle of the Cambornes and the Claytons. In time she would make a good marriage, not perhaps a brilliant one, but a good one. Wasn't that what every girl wanted? And that old man sitting on the sofa, hands clasped about his silver-headed cane, could make the crucial difference.

'I think,' Livy said to Caroline when it was all over, 'I

drank too much champagne. I never remember a party at Oxford like this.' She peered doubtfully at herself in the mirror as she removed the necklet and earrings. 'I hope I don't look too awful tomorrow. I have a luncheon engagement with Mr McClintock.'

'I know exactly what to give you,' Caroline said. 'But I don't think you'll have a headache. It was vintage champagne. Uncle Blair's contribution to the evening.'

The next day, a few minutes before twelve forty-five, Livy presented herself at the headquarters of McClintock-Clayton, a building that more resembled a family mansion than a place of business. She was aware that there were bigger, more modern offices of McClintock-Clayton further along the Avenue, but Andrew McClintock preferred to do his business in this place where it had started. He liked a hushed and dignified atmosphere. The entrance hall, which she had to ring to be admitted to, was all marble and carved mahogany, with some beautiful pictures placed where they received the light from the central dome above the winding marble staircase. If there were typewriters and telephones about, she heard none of them. As she was being shown to the directors' dining room by a butler, she glimpsed only one woman on the stairs, wearing the almost inevitable black dress with white collar. It was as she imagined the interior of a small, very rich, very private Swiss bank would be. She realized now why Caroline had fussed about what she wore, the dress discreet but sophisticated, the hat borrowed from Dena, the immaculate white gloves, worn even in the heat.

Andrew McClintock waited for her alone in that large room. Evidently the other directors, including Blair, had been advised to have their lunches elsewhere that day. She was offered sherry, and McClintock nodded his approval when she chose the driest. Lunch was simple, and beautifully served. Their talk was general, mostly about Oxford. He was fond of recalling with pride that Alex had been a Rhodes scholar. But it ranged into other topics, politics, the economic state of Britain. She felt as if she were being shrewdly examined; he wanted to discover if she had done more with

346

her three years than read poetry and write essays; there was Caroline's real world, which was clothes and a social life, and there was the McClintock world, which was knowledge and power.

In his office after lunch he showed her the contents of her portfolio. It was bewildering to her, confusing. 'Haven't learned to read these things yet, have you? Well, you must, or someone will try to steal from you. But here's the end figure. I've had copies made, so you can take one and study it, see exactly how it's all arrived at.'

Livy stared at the figure to which he pointed, without much comprehension. It was a much larger sum than she had imagined. She could remember the royalty cheques that had come after *This England* had been published. Since that time, with Thea and Herbert's approval, they had gone directly to this trust fund; she had hardly thought about it except to be grateful that it had paid for school and university.

'It might have been more,' McClintock said. 'I feel it should have been more. But it's been very conservatively invested. But I did get you in on the ground floor of some very worthwhile enterprises. You must read up on them. Any time I was tempted to take a risk, I remembered Thea Sedgemore and Herbert Gardiner. They're not such naive fools that they wouldn't have spotted the places where I'd put in my own money to cover up where I'd lost some of yours. Of course it's taken the dips and swings of the market, but none too wildly. I haven't topped it up. I knew their pride, and eventually yours when you came to see it, would never have stood for that. In fact, it's been a little hobby of mine. I've looked at it at night as a sort of relaxation like playing chess, or doing a crossword puzzle. It was quite refreshing to deal in small sums in a rather simple way.'

Livy was scanning the pages, trying to gather the overall picture of what he had made of the money over the years. 'That's like the king saying he doesn't mind going into the kitchen and giving a little stir to the soup now and again.' She tapped the pages. 'You're right. I'm not good at reading these things, and there's quite an amount to read. But I can't see where you've charged any commission. Don't all professional managers do that?'

He allowed a slight smile to appear, then pinched it back. 'I told you it was a little hobby. I can hardly charge you for that, though I respect your reasons for asking. If it's wounded your pride, then I'll see an adjustment is made.'

'Pride, Mr McClintock! Pride! How could I display it with you in circumstances like this? You said it last night. If my mother could see me now . . . not as I was last night, dressed for a party. If she could see me in this room, talking to you like this. This is something to be proud about! If it has given you a little amusement, a little relaxation to look after the small affairs of an unimportant girl, then I'm not too proud to accept the results. Now, tell me what to do with it.'

'Leave it with me. I'll still enjoy playing about with it. I'll consult you, of course. From now on I expect you to read the financial papers, as well as the art pages. Take what you want from it, but there's not enough to go mad with. Something tells me you won't. If I continue with the conservative policies I've applied in the past, you'll never be rich by the standards of the really rich. But you won't starve either. You get rich only if you're prepared to take big risks, and that also gives you the privilege of losing it all. I don't think that sort of risk-taking is in your temperament, not where money's concerned, though I imagine you'll take many another kind. To live is to take chances, Livy. You'll take them.' He tapped the papers on his desk. 'Just don't let anyone take away your bit of independence. It gives you the right to follow whatever path you think you must take. The child of two such parents would hardly play it safe. You have many choices ahead. If your father had had even this little source of money, he might have lived ten more years and written more poetry. But then, your mother would never have been at Tresillian, and I would never have known her or you. I can't make your choices for you. Though there are those who say I manipulate others' lives. I have, but only when I've seen clearly it was for their good. That sounds arrogant, doesn't it? As if I play God. I'm not always able to do it. I'll help you where I can, for as long as I can. But in the end yóu must make your own way. Just try to remember that no one and nothing must take this little bit of independence from you.'

'I'll remember it. It's like having the little house my father bought. If there were a million dollars in this . . .' She indicated the portfolio, 'I would never sell that house. Never! I always have it to go back to. I don't think my life is going to be spent in St Just, but that place is my rock. I'll hold on to it.'

'I'm glad to hear you say so.' He rose, and she knew the interview was over.

'How can I thank you?'

'Just try not to disappoint me.'

Before he put his hand on the doorknob he paused. 'I suppose you . . . I suppose you . . . like everyone else, are wondering why I'm not showing great enthusiasm for this marriage Alex is making. According to all I hear and read, this is exactly the sort of marriage I would have arranged.'

'It's none of my business.' She said the words tersely. She was learning to cover the hurt, but her strength in this direction could not be severely tested; it was still too fragile. 'I have no right to ask of you why you think certain things anymore than you have of me.'

'Well, I'll tell you gratis. It won't cost a cent, and I don't want any confidences from you in return. I haven't said these words to anyone but Alex, when he belatedly came to see me with the news, and I had met the girl, this Nancy. It is a very predictable marriage, as everyone seems to imply, exactly the sort of one I might have manipulated and encouraged. Money marries money. Beauty marries beauty. What could possibly be wrong with that? The girl is wrong, that's what's wrong. I had them alone to dinner the day they became engaged. It was a long dinner. I encouraged them to stay late. I tried out every mean trick I could to make her reveal herself. Wherever I pressed, I found nothing. Conventional ideas, conventional behaviour, up to now. But she's greedy and spoiled. A spoiled brat. A beautiful spoiled brat. That kind likes to spend money, it doesn't matter whose it is. They relish position, and demand a good time, all the time. They're not capable of taking a bad blow, or a reversal of fortunes. They'll drop one thing when it becomes hard or unpleasant, and go on to the next. Beautiful, superficially educated and, in the final analysis, empty. I would have expected Alex to have better judgement. I wonder about the children of this marriage. I don't think it's a marriage fashioned to last . . .'

'And yet, and yet, you married the princess. Was that good judgement?'

He paused, and she thought he would not reply. 'Only you would have said that. It was one of the worst mistakes of my life. And Alex will make his own. I'm powerless to stop him in this case.'

'I wish you hadn't told me this, Mr McClintock. What's the point of it?'

'I really don't know, young lady. But there are times when you remind me so much of your mother. We had some good discussions, your mother and I. She had an innate wisdom and understanding. A strong woman, and a loving woman. A fit wife for a poet. I shall never forget her.'

A secretary waited to take Livy downstairs. McClintock formally offered his hand. 'You study what you've got there. Remember what we've talked about. And indulge me in my little hobby. Goodbye. See you at the Wedding.'

They moved to Prescott Hill – Caroline, Livy, Mark and Ginny. On weekends Harry and Dena came and, always rather late on Friday nights, Blair. Alex came and went, usually without notice; he resembled his grandfather in this habit, and Livy thought Ginny was infinitely patient with it. He would show up with a good-natured, rather lazy smile, and another place would be laid at the table. Livy noticed that although Ginny's grandparents' house, Wildwood, was at the disposal of Harry and Dena, it was seldom used. She imagined that the spaciousness and luxury of Prescott Hill were hard to resist, the ever-waiting servants, the lack of fuss. It might also be, Livy thought, a matter of money. The loan of a house was not enough: it had to be staffed, there were endless extras of time and money to be expended. She had realized even in that brief time how hard Dena worked to help Harry during the week in Washington. Prescott Hill must have seemed a haven of ease and luxury to her, especially when it was constantly urged on them by Ginny and Blair.

Those were languid days at Prescott Hill. They swam and rode and played tennis when the heat of the day was gone. It was wonderfully peaceful, except at the weekend, when Ginny seemed to hold open-house. The dining-room was nearly always filled, and tables set up on the wide, shady porch. People wandered in and out; some called Livy by name, and she struggled to remember theirs. One Saturday Sir George and Lady Halliwell came to spend the night; the next weekend the Swiss Ambassador came to Sunday lunch. The world of the McClintock-Clayton empire continued even through the supposedly relaxed weekend. Livy was beginning to comprehend to what a degree diplomats, even at the highest level, had become salesmen, as Harry had joked.

Rachel arrived, spent a few days in what she called 'idling', and then borrowed one of Ginny's cars to drive to Washington every day to work for some hours at the Library of Congress. 'Lazy lot,' she termed them all. She was up early in the morning, swimming, and they wouldn't see her for the rest of the day.

Alex refused to get drawn into the preparations for the Wedding. 'I'll attend the rehearsals, and that's that. I'll be at the church on the appointed day, at the appointed hour. Let Nancy have her bridal showers and fuss over her trousseau. That's her business. I'm damned if I'm going to bother about what colour the flowers should be!'

Chris had arrived in Washington the day before, and Alex had driven to Prescott Hill with her. Nancy had asked Chris, as Alex's half-sister, to be one of the bridesmaids, and Chris had politely declined, pleading that there was a chance that the show would be held over for an extra two weeks. It hadn't happened, but she had been in no hurry to cross the Atlantic. 'Oh, there's some good-looking loafer in the company who's keeping her there,' Rachel had said. 'If it weren't for the wedding, I doubt she'd be coming at all.' But she was there at last, and had slipped easily into the lazy routine of Prescott Hill.

'You're selfish,' Chris said to Alex. 'You're supposed to support the nervous bride.'

'Nancy's the least nervous bride I've ever laid eyes on,' Caroline said. Most weekends Nancy came to Prescott Hill, and when she was there a strange constraint seemed to fall on the group of the four girls and Mark. 'I wish she'd stay away,' Mark said once, after Nancy had appeared and broken up a tennis coaching session he was having with Alex.

Ginny rumpled Mark's hair affectionately. 'We'll all have to learn to do without him. He's going to be married and have his own home and his own set of friends.'

'I expect he'll be so grand he won't want to know me,' Mark said. 'Well, I don't want to know Nancy, that's for sure.'

'Aren't you,' Ginny said, 'being just a bit mean and possessive, the four of you, and Mark as well? Alex is his own man. This isn't Tresillian. You're all going your separate ways. You're grown up too.'

'Which only leaves me, trailing behind,' Mark said. 'I can't wait to be grown up.'

'All in good time. Perhaps rather too quickly,' his mother said.

It came to the last weekend before the Wedding. Nancy had not come, nor had Alex. His presence for rehearsals and the eve-of-wedding parties was demanded. Harry would not arrive until the next day, Saturday. 'They've had an exceptionally heavy diplomatic bag,' Dena told them when she arrived alone. 'He could be at it all weekend. The Kremlin's making noises again . . . the Foreign Secretary's always on the telephone . . . Who's coming this weekend, Ginny?'

Ginny sighed. 'Mercifully, no one. I suppose they've all decided to give us a break before the Wedding. I can't help feeling selfishly glad that it's Mrs Winterton and not I who's had all the arrangements to make.' She looked at the faces of the four young women about her, 'but I expect you lot will keep Dena and I busy when your turns come.'

'Not me,' Rachel said. 'Not me. It'll be a registry office, and a breakfast of fish and chips, and a telegram to you all after it's over.' For once she was laughing, laughing at herself. 'Of course, the poor man doesn't know it yet. I haven't informed him.'

'I pity him,' Mark said, 'whoever he is.'

'Brat!' She pushed him playfully. 'Come on. Time for a swim before we change for dinner.' She caught Mark's arm and pulled him to his feet. 'Don't sulk because Alex is leaving us. It had to happen one day. I expect he won't entirely drop out of our lives. Come on. Race you to the pool.' The three other girls followed, but not running.

'Rachel can be unexpectedly kind when she remembers to be,' Ginny said. She is very clever, isn't she, Dena?'

'Look who she's got for a father. She'll end up a Member of Parliament. In her time it's just possible there'll be a woman Prime Minister. No doubt she's got the strategy all worked out.' She refused Ginny's offer of a drink. 'I think I'll just go and stretch out in a bath before dinner . . . Washington was so hot, and I had to give a lunch for the wives of three MPs who are over poking their noses into what shouldn't rightly concern them.'

'Let me have a tall drink sent up to you. You can sip it in the bath.'

Dena touched her friend's hand lightly as she rose. 'You must be the most thoughtful . . . the kindest woman in the world. I still can't get over my luck at having you for a friend. And keeping you. You'll never desert me, Ginny, will you?'

'Why ever should I?'

'I don't know . . . sometimes I have the oddest fears. Nothing to put a finger on. Sometimes a shadow . . .'

'No shadows . . . Not any more, Dena,' as if she were drawing too close to what should remain unspoken. 'Off you go. I'll send Lilia with your drink, and I think I'll follow your example. I don't think Blair's going to get here in time for dinner.'

Dena turned back as she was about to go upstairs. 'Don't you think it's strange that Mr McClintock's not been down

353

here since . . . well, since Alex became engaged? I can't get used to him not arriving, unannounced, and expecting everything to be ready.'

'The time isn't up yet,' Ginny answered. 'For all we know, he could show up this evening. Thank heaven I have angels for staff. Sometimes I don't know how they stand it.'

Because, Dena thought, they were paid about twice the normal wage, and because they could quickly call in women from the families who farmed Prescott Hill's many acres as tenants. Slaves had now become tenants, and some had been modestly successful. But a call from the Big House always brought an instant response. The 'old days' were not entirely gone from Prescott Hill.

Someone had arrived, Dena thought, as she lay in her bath. She heard the sound of a car, and a low murmur of voices. It could not be Andrew McClintock, more fuss and attention would have attended his arrival. She heard the voices of the girls on the stairs, and Mark's, when they returned from their swim. She luxuriated in dressing slowly and carefully, sipping the long lime and ice drink Lilia had brought, just lightly laced with rum. She did her face, and for once had time to examine it. The lines that were appearing did not unduly trouble her. She knew that many people regarded her as a very attractive woman. But the years were slipping past. She was forty-four. She wondered what she would feel at fifty, at sixty. She brushed the thought aside. That was eons away. Perhaps she wouldn't care. Was that one of the consolations of age? She applied scent, and finished her drink. She carried her glass downstairs with her, and left it on the hall table. The house was quiet. There was a little hum of activity from upstairs, the sound of bath water and showers being run, occasionally the girls called to each other through their open bedroom doors.

She stood in the doorway of the large drawing-room, which had changed little, except for new curtains and chair-covers, from the days when Andrew McClintock's father had bought it and refurnished it as the finest country mansion in Virginia. Mark must have showered quickly and, not having to fuss with hair and face, as the girls did, he had come down before

354

any of them. It was growing dark, but no one as yet had switched on a lamp.

Mark's voice reached her. 'I've never been to the Pentagon, General. Uncle Blair always promised me he'd arrange a visit, but he's so busy and I hate to bother him . . .'

'It would be my pleasure, young man . . .'

Dena's hand gripped the doorframe. The voice was unforgotten through the years. She had known that sometime in Washington she must encounter him, and she had always hoped that the occasion would be a gathering large enough that their meeting would be brief and superficial. But here . . . at Prescott Hill. It was impossible that Ginny had arranged it deliberately. She would never be capable of such cruelty. In the dim light she saw only the outline of them both seated on the sofa, Mark and the man who was his father. She tried to slip back into the hall, but Mark caught the movement. 'Mother? This is General Goodrick. My mother, General.' They were both standing. She was forced to move forward.

'General Goodrick . . . how nice to see you again. We did once meet, Mark, briefly, during the war. Before America came into the war, that is. Since then, the General has covered himself in glory. Is it three or four stars, General? I'm bad at remembering these things.'

'I had what they call a "good" campaign in Italy, Lady Camborne. And then there was Korea . . . the Pentagon has to have its quota of four stars. You know what the military's like.'

'No, I don't, really.'

She blinked when someone switched on a lamp. Blair's voice was behind her. 'Why on earth haven't you helped yourselves to a drink? Dena, you know Mike, I think. I just caught him today on the hop. Ran into him in the Pentagon where I was doing a little selling job. We haven't seen each other for . . . well, it's been a couple of years, hasn't it, Mike? I said this was our quiet weekend, with no one staying, and insisted on his coming along.'

'What Blair doesn't seem to realize when he says there's no one staying is that he's got almost permanent house-guests in the Camborne family, General. It really shames me to think how often we're here . . . almost as if we're part of the furniture.'

'Ginny always did have marvellous taste in furniture,' Mike said. 'I didn't expect you to be here, though I did hear that Lord Camborne had been posted to Washington. It's been a pleasure to meet your son . . .'

Nothing of any consequence was said; the talk flowed on . . . the Pentagon, Korea, the wedding. Blair sank wearily into his chair after he had been given a drink. Dena had insisted on pouring them to give herself something to do, a reason to turn away from Mike Goodrick's scrutiny. For herself she poured a stiff Scotch, and held it in both hands to try to steady their trembling. She had always feared the return of her nightmare of guilt if she should ever again encounter him. When Harry's appointment to Washington had been announced, she had hoped General Mike Goodrick would have been posted to Germany or some base on the other side of the United States. She had feared the friendship which existed between Blair and Ginny and Mike Goodrick, but yet Ginny had never said that she knew he was in Washington. But Ginny wouldn't have said. If he had sometimes been a guest in the Clayton house, as now seemed obvious, Ginny had never mentioned it. Oh, God . . . something inside her prayed for release. It had been an unwitting blunder on Blair's part; he couldn't know . . . Ginny would never have told him. Dena looked at the two figures seated on the sofa, both with dark hair and brown eyes, but Mark had her features, still blurred by a childish roundness. Mike had aged in the same way she had, but an amount of grey had appeared in his hair; the lines around his eyes spoke of being out in the weather more than she, and he could have been five or six years older than she. She didn't even know how old her son's father was. She remembered his last desperate plea to her to come to America with him; she remembered the final telephone call. She remembered too much. She remembered the part of her that had loved him, had clung to him in those days when she thought her world was falling apart. A selfish, greedy love perhaps, but it would always remain with her. The outcome of that love now sat beside him on the sofa.

The girls came downstairs, and there was a round of introductions. Caroline now poured the drinks, brought Blair another one. Although she seemed to need it so badly, Dena could hardly raise hers to her lips for fear of spilling it. She retreated behind the buzz of conversation. She heard that the General had just returned from a tour of duty in the NATO countries, travelling to its farthest reaches, to Iran and Turkey. Mark gazed at him as if he were some latter-day Marco Polo.

Ginny came down last. She went to Mike directly. 'I'm so sorry I wasn't down to meet you. Blair didn't tell me until he got here that he'd brought you. It's marvellous to see you, Mike. It's been too long . . .'

Dena imagined that even the girls must notice the forced pitch to Ginny's voice.

'I have the most wonderful wife,' Blair said, smiling with mock complacency. He leaned back in his chair, a man looking supremely content, his eyes scanning the whole group. 'I forgot to telephone her . . . that's what happens when you have a Ginny to look after you. If I had brought a whole regiment unannounced, she would fit them in. I just said "family" to Mike, Ginny. I keep forgetting we're such an extended family.'

'You're very fortunate,' Mike said. 'My two are grown and gone.'

It seemed an endless time to Dena before they went in to dinner. She was grateful that the length of the table separated her from Mike, and the talk of the girls covered her silence. As the only male guest besides Mike, Mark had been seated on Ginny's left hand, opposite Mike. There was a good deal of conversation between them; Mark seemed to be asking the General a lot of questions in a very uninhibited fashion. But then, Mark had never been a shy child. Ginny's voice, whenever Dena caught its tone, still sounded strained and false.

After dinner, as the others moved towards the library, Ginny held Dena back. 'I'm so terribly sorry. I wouldn't

357

have done this to you for anything. I didn't even know Mike was back in the country, and Blair didn't tell me he was bringing him.'

Dena shrugged, and managed a smile. 'That's what happens to those who are too hospitable. You'd take the world in, and Blair knows it. I'm just sorry I've caused . . .'

'Don't! Don't, Dena! It's agony for you. Do you want to make some excuse and go back to Washington? I can say, oh, say anything. Say Harry called. Some VIP has shown up. Anything . . .'

'No . . . it's happened. I knew it could happen any place in the world. Once I knew he'd survived the war, I thought I'd be bound to run into him somewhere. Some reception. Some dinner party, in some country. But I didn't expect it to be here – and with Mark. No, I'll stay. I have to. I can't run away. I can't leave Mark here with him, alone. I doubt he even suspects, but still . . . I can't leave. But I must telephone Harry. I must tell him. And then I'll come back and have coffee. I don't dare let Blair think anything's wrong.'

Harry was not at the embassy, but she reached him instantly at their house. She knew he was working at his desk. 'Camborne,' he answered.

'Harry . . . I have to tell you, Blair has brought an unexpected house guest. Do you remember a name, Harry? From more than ten years ago. Do you remember a Mike Goodrick. Now General Goodrick.'

He paused only momentarily. 'I remember. Do you want me to come to Prescott Hill, Dena? Would it help you?'

'No, don't come unless you're free of work. Unless you would normally have come. Harry, I've never seen him until this evening. I swear to you, Harry . . .'

'No need to do that, my darling. Don't you think I know. I love you Dena. You're the most precious thing I have in life. I love you, and I love our son. *Our* son, Dena.'

'I love you,' she answered. 'Good night.'

Then she went downstairs and accepted the *demi-tasse* of coffee from Ginny. 'Just spoken with Harry,' she said in a clear voice, so that everyone could hear. 'He's overloaded.

He'll be working all day tomorrow, and if he's sensible he'll sleep through Sunday.'

'Good for him,' Blair said. 'I thought he was looking a bit done-in lately.' He turned to Ginny. 'Will Mrs Winterton have a fit if we add one more to the guest list at this late stage? It isn't every day we have a wedding in the family, and I'd love Mike to be there . . .'

Harry did no more work that night. The papers he had been working on lay untouched on his desk. He sat motionless for a long time, thinking, remembering. He thought of Dena, there at Prescott Hill, with the father of her son. His heart grieved for her; he breathed a humble prayer that Mark would not be touched by the anguish that must now rack her. He wished he could reach out and take her hand, somehow comfort her. He shared her agony, but there was a particular agony of his own which he had never shared, dared not share, with her. He remembered his return from Moscow in that October when it had seemed that their world might succumb to the conqueror, his retreat, on orders, from chaos and near-defeat. He unlocked a drawer of his desk and took out a sealed envelope, which bore his signature across its seal. Then he went into the drawing-room, switched on a single lamp, and poured himself a drink. He sat down and slit the envelope. The first photo was grainy and rather blurred, but it was distinct enough for its purpose. He remembered too well the day it had come to him. He had been working past his normal hour at the Paris embassy, not long after his appointment there. He had just been beginning to put his papers away, to lock up those which were sensitive. The phone had rung, and the duty officer for the night had told him an envelope addressed to him and marked personal had just been received at the front desk. 'Shall I have it sent up, Lord Camborne?'

'I'm just on my way out. I'll pick it up.'

He had read it there in the foyer of the embassy, under the gaze of the night porter. An envelope with only his name typed on it, and inside a typed message. *'I will be at Fouquet's for the next hour. You are expected.'* He would have ignored it; ministers of the British embassy did not keep appointments with unknown correspondents. But the final words jolted him, '*I'm sure, after all this time you would like news of Sonya Dimitriyevna.*'

In a daze of wonder and fear he had walked out into the wet Paris street, dismissed his chauffeur and car, and headed towards the Champs Elysées, and Fouquet's.

It had been an autumn evening, and chill. No one sat at the outside tables. He had entered uncertainly. Why such a public place except that it lay on his route home? When he entered, a man seated at a table stood up. 'I've ordered coffee, Lord Camborne. I was sure you'd come.'

Harry sat down at the small table. He had never seen the man in his life before. 'What do you want?'

'Just to pass on a little memento.' The man handed over an envelope. It contained a photo, grainy, as if it had been blown up. He recognized Sonya, though she was older and thinner: hers hadn't been a face to forget. But she looked prematurely worn, and her eyes were deeply sunk into her head. With her was a child, a girl of about five or six, whose childish features resembled Sonya's and also, or could he in guilt and anguish imagine a likeness that did not exist, resembled his own when he had been that age. She was blonde, like Sonya, like himself, and had light-coloured eyes, either blue or grey, which he couldn't tell.

'A family portrait for your collection. She's still alive, and so is your daughter.'

'Where did you get this?'

'You cannot seriously expect me to tell you that. I am simply a messenger. Of no importance.' For the first time Harry looked at him closely. Heavy set, with an accent which could have been German, or Dutch. 'We will be in touch. They've watched your career with deep interest all these years. They feel the time has come when you may be of some service to them. They are sure you would want to protect the wellbeing of those you left behind. You would like them to continue to live, wouldn't you, Lord Camborne?' The man rose. 'The coffee has been paid for.' He left and Harry sat at the table, staring at the photo, staring,

staring. Finally a waiter asked if he would like fresh coffee, a hint that the table was needed. Harry got up and walked out into the damp night.

That night he had carried the picture with him, and after Dena had gone to bed he studied it again as he drank a brandy. As he studied it now. He looked long, also, at the second photo, which also had come to him in the Paris years. Sonya again, in a much clearer photo, the lines on her face much deeper than they should have been. The child was with her, but it was no longer a childish face; good clean features which hinted at beauty to come, blonde hair, light-coloured eyes under well-defined brows. The expression in the eyes tormented him. The child was afraid. She had been instructed to smile, but it was the smile of a puppet. If ever he had seen an old face in a child, this was it, the expression, despite the smile, wary, defensive. She would be the same age as Mark. He relived every second of the agony of seeing those faces, of learning of his daughter's existence.

He had done what he could for them; he had played the game that had been demanded of him. He had fought to keep them alive, and he was tangled in a web of deceit and subterfuge which threatened at times to strangle him.

He poured another drink. Except for the noise of the air-conditioners, the house was absolutely quiet. He thought of Dena there at Prescott Hill, confronted with the man who had briefly been her lover. And he thought of that cheerful precocious child, Mark, whom he loved more, perhaps, than he would have loved a son, whose face had never worn, probably would never wear that expression of fear and wariness in the eyes of the girl in the photo. Mark, unknowingly, had tonight met his father.

The weekend seemed interminable to Dena. She wished now she had urged Harry to come, and yet she could not inflict on him the cruelty of being forced into close proximity with the man he knew to have been her lover, who was the father of her son. As she thought about it, she realized that she and Harry might have been judged by many of their friends to be amusingly old-fashioned. But Harry had more than condoned an infidelity, as well as confessing his own. He had brought up and loved a child who was not his; he and she had drawn closer because of it. She could look at Mike Goodrick now and understand, remember, why she had loved him. She looked at Mark, and she looked at his father, and she knew that honour had not been besmirched. She had been loved by two men whose natures were essentially honourable. It was she who felt unworthy.

The weekend was filled with activities, despite the heat. A sense pervaded them all that after the Wedding there would once again be a dispersal, and they tried to be together as much as possible. Even Rachel deserted her books. She splashed around in the pool with Mark, rowdily trying to duck him. It was so unlike Rachel that Ginny commented on it. 'All I've ever seen her do here is lap the pool, as if exercise were the whole purpose, and there was no pleasure in it.'

'Rachel finds it hard to take pleasure in a world that's filled with pain,' Blair said. 'Her socialism is still in the idealistic phase. One day she'll have to settle for what can be done by slow degrees, and know that the whole task can never be accomplished. There will always be inequalities. I wonder has it ever occurred to her that it isn't fair that she's so much brighter than most people? She belongs to a natural élite. If she could renounce her Camborne name and all her other grand relations and contacts, she would. But she'd still shine through like a bright penny.'

They were having a barbeque lunch by the pool. Chris chewed a spare rib, and said wistfully, 'It would be wonderful if father could sometimes talk about me as he did just then about Rachel. He thinks everything I do is a joke. To be an actress . . . the Claytons don't do things like that. And I can't starve in a garret to prove I'm serious. The trust money is there; when I can use the principal, I could even be a producer and still not outrun it. I could even be successful, and he'd still think it was a very second-rate thing to be doing. The only one who wouldn't think success a joke is Mr McClintock. He's always admired success, no matter how it comes.'

362

'Your father isn't like that, Chris,' Livy said. 'I think your biggest problem is that you have an awful lot to live up to in your mother.'

Chris put the rib back on her plate. 'Yes . . . I know it. Kind, loving, calm . . . generous in every way. One could go on and on. Every good attribute you can think of, she has. No faults. That's impossible to live up to. I can't even try.'

Livy felt impatient. 'Oh, for God's sake don't give me the poor-little-rich-girl act. Do what you have to do, and just do your best. We all fail, one way or another. Even Aunt Ginny. She manages to play her failures pretty close to her chest. I don't see any, but she must have had them. But don't ask me, when you're only twenty-two and have barely started out, to feel sorry for you.'

Chris stared at her. 'You're right. That's in the worst possible taste. I wish I didn't feel so . . . so uncertain. Not sure which way to turn.'

'Look around you,' Livy said. 'Do you think any one of us is certain? Even Rachel, who seems to have her life so under control. We're all here together. It might be the last weekend. One or other of us might be together in the future, but will we ever be together in the same place at the same time? Alex has already gone . . .'

'Yes, Alex has gone, and Nancy will never belong. Never quite belong.'

'We've been too exclusive, all of us. Tresillian, all those years together. It hasn't been all good, not now that we're out in what Caro calls the *real* world. When my mother died, you all closed in around me, so that in some ways I never missed her . . .' Livy stopped. Her mother's death, even her name, could not be mentioned in Chris's presence. Only she and Rachel had been with Isa on the cliff top when she had died.

'And that's something I can't live up to, either.'

Chris put her plate down on a table, and ran back towards the house.

'Now what's biting Chris,' Caro asked. She got up from the chaise where she had been lying, and approached Livy. 'You two were so intense, I thought you must surely be solving the whole world's problems.' She really was beautiful, Livy thought. Perfection in body and face. Her swimsuit outlined the curves of her body, and there was nothing to fault, no disproportion, no bulge; nothing too much or too little. 'Chris is so full of artistic temperament you'd never think she was the daughter of a banker. Lives on her nerves.'

'Don't you imagine Uncle Blair lives on his . . . it can't be easy to sleep at night when you've got millions . . . possibly billions of dollars to make decisions about. I think Chris is every bit Uncle Blair's child . . . though she'll never make a banker.'

Caro's laughter eased the tension that lay on Livy. 'No, that's one role I can never see her playing.'

That afternoon Chris and Rachel battled each other on the tennis court; for a little time it was as it had always been – friends and protagonists. Then, the match over, and Chris having beaten Rachel narrowly, they went off to swim in the pool which was now deserted. Rachel lapped with determination, as if there were no time to be lost; Chris mostly floated on her back, watching the sky, watching the shadows of the trees creep slowly across the water. When she pulled herself out of the pool, the heat was still there, and yet she felt a chill. She remembered what Livy had said. 'The last weekend . . .' It couldn't be, and yet they all knew their world was breaking up. It had to.

Dena sought to work off her restlessness, the sense of fear and apprehension and guilt which lay on her, by taking Mark to the target range in the late afternoon. All day she had fought off the impulse to telephone Harry and beg him to come to Prescott Hill, and so far she had resisted the impulse. If she could just last until dinner time, it would be more bearable. She could get through the evening, and leave directly after lunch tomorrow. It had been an edgy day, and she had been grateful that Mike had not sought her company alone; he had been part of the group, and his talk had been for them all. He had never again alluded to their war-time meeting in London; he had treated her precisely as he would have done if they had met only once before. She was thankful for his understanding.

Mark chose his gun carefully. He had grown used to the array of guns at Prescott Hill, and ever since Dena had begun to teach him how to shoot, he had used the guns made for Alex as he had grown up, hand-made guns from Abercrombies, almost as good as the guns her father had, Dena thought. There always seemed to be one which exactly suited his height and reach. They walked in companionable silence to the target range, Mark pleased to have his mother to himself. The range was well away from the house, and was at the far end of the grove of cedars which stood around the guest cottages where Ginny had told her she and Alex's father had spent the first night of their marriage.

Dena enjoyed the target practice; in her effort of concentration she could almost forget her guilt and misery. 'Was Grandfather a really great shot?' Mark asked. He was doing very well himself, though his form was a little erratic.

'He was superb. Why do you suppose I'm so good?' Dena answered lightly. She never minded when Mark asked about Lord Milroy. It was safe to answer questions about that grandfather. When it came to the subject of Harry's father, Dena was carefully vague. 'I never really knew him, darling,' she always answered when Mark asked about him. 'He was so distinguished and very clever. That's where your father gets his flair for languages.'

'I think I would have got on with Grandfather Milroy better,' Mark had once said. 'At least I can ride and shoot and do some of the things he did. I would have been a big disappointment to my grandfather Penrose. One of the masters at school once said after I'd turned in my Latin paper that my grandfather would have disowned me. I didn't have to ask which grandfather . . .'

They moved in closer to the target and had a little period of practice with a revolver. It was the first time Mark had ever handled one. Dena showed him how to sight, and the stance of holding the gun with two hands for steadiness. 'Mind you, if you ever had to use one seriously, there wouldn't be much time to get into this beautifully correct position.' He used it rather nervously. 'Sorry, I don't seem to get the hang of it.'

'Never mind. I hope you never need to use one. Strictly speaking, we shouldn't have borrowed it from the gun case. The licence is in Blair's name. I just wanted to see if I still could use one. Father had a pair of duelling pistols. They were beautiful things, but they weren't beautifully balanced. I'd have hated to have fought a duel with one of them.'

'May I come near? Is it safe?' Mike Goodrick walked slowly from the direction of the guest cottages. 'I had no idea, Dena, that you were such a crack shot.'

'You should see her at billiards, General,' Mark said. 'My father says he fell in love with her across a billiard table at Blenheim Palace.'

'A suitably aristocratic setting for a pair to fall in love. I was there once during the war, when it was taken over by MI5. I'm sure it must have been very grand indeed in the pre-war days. The abiding impression I have is of its size. I'd have hated to live there.'

'My grandfather Milroy lived quite near there,' Mark said. I went hunting near there once, General. I managed to keep up, even though I only just managed to cling on, especially over the fences. Sort of shut my eyes and hoped the mare knew what she was doing. It turned out I was in at the kill, and because I was the youngest, they gave me the brush and blooded my face. I didn't ever hunt after that, but I was too much of a coward to tell them I thought it was an awful way to kill a fox.'

'You're not war-like then?' Mike said.

'No, sir. I suppose, you disapprove of that.'

'Not in the least. I joined the army, and stayed in the army because I hoped we'd never have to fight a war. Just be there as a deterrent. Well, it turned out we had to fight. I hope we never have to again . . . once this business in Korea is over.'

'How did such a pacifist get to be a general?' Dena said coolly.

'The army needs men who know how to fight, and are

willing to fight, when necessary. We aren't all hawks because we're soldiers.'

'I'm glad,' Mark said. 'I don't like fighting, but I've had to do my share of it at school. I expect everyone does. I don't like people who try to bully me. I'd never let anyone bully me, except a prefect, who had the right to. I don't like prefects either.'

'You've got a bit of a rebel on your hands, Lady Camborne.'

She set Mark to picking up the spent shells. Before the guns were put away, they would be carefully cleaned. It was a hard and fast rule.

'We, Harry and I, would almost prefer it that way. Who wants the perfect conformist?' Mark was now out of earshot, walking ahead of them. Mark never did anything slowly. His walk was lithe and graceful. He carried the two guns they had used, empty of bullets and broken, as he had been taught. 'He's not brilliant academically. Very average, in fact. But he's a natural athlete. Sometimes I think that's the only reason they keep him at his school. He does tend to get into scrapes. He's due to go to Eton in a few years. He won't like that either.'

'Then why send him?'

'His father and his two grandfathers went there. I suppose it's a good enough reason.'

'If he were my son—'

'He is *my* son, Mike.'

'He could be mine. I sensed . . . I asked him his birthday.'

She was suddenly furious and afraid. 'Why don't you mind your own business? Harry came home then. I told you that. He'd been away a long time. Mark is the natural outcome of that reunion.'

'Not as I count it.'

She stopped and faced him. 'You will believe it! He was premature by a couple of weeks. Ask Ginny. He was practically born into her arms.'

'No, Dena, I won't be asking Ginny. And I won't be interfering. I won't set out to cultivate Mark or to make anything special of him. I'll treat him just like any other

367

young boy. I'm headed back to Korea, so I won't start messing around in his life. But I'll go on believing he's probably my son. He could be my son. But I don't intend to disrupt anything, or upset his life. It's set in its pattern. The Penrose-Camborne pattern. I can't change that. But I wonder will he really fit the pattern.'

'Harry knows about . . . about us,' Dena said. 'I told him. I told him as soon as he got back.'

Mike nodded. 'Yes, I believe that you told him. Your honesty was one of the reasons I loved you. You were never a sham, Dena. And I've gone on loving you, loving that memory. Oh, it probably could never have worked. Being you, you'd have been too racked with guilt. And you'd never have left your girls. But I did love you. At that time I was so desperate to have you I could have persuaded myself that anything was possible. It would please me to know that Mark is my son.'

'He is my son,' she repeated. Her tone had softened. 'You're very kind, Mike, and I have my own good memories. There was never any one else, Mike. No one but you and Harry.'

They didn't speak again while they walked back to the house. It was almost dark when they reached it. Dena went to the gun-room to replace the revolver, and help Mark clean the guns. Mike accepted Blair's offer of a drink before he went upstairs to shower and change. There was the usual exchange of voices from the girls' rooms and the call of the cicadas to break the stillness of the summer night.

Dena left the next day immediately after lunch. 'I must get back and see that Harry has a proper dinner. We have no staff on Sunday.' Blair and Mike Goodrick would leave early the next morning. Ginny and the girls and Mark were staying until Thursday. On Saturday Alex was being married.

'See you at the Wedding,' was all they said as they parted.

Alexander McClintock and Nancy Van Isler Winterton were married at St John's Episcopal Church. The Winterton mansion had added a marquee to its large garden, in case of rain.

But it did not rain, as it had the night before. The storm cleared the air; the day was sunny, bright and sparkling. It all went as perfectly, Livy thought, as she watched the ceremony and attended the reception, as any perfectly scripted and rehearsed production should. They were the most handsome, the richest, the most blessed by name and fortune. The perfect couple.

They departed in the traditional style, with rice and old shoes tied to the car. At the National Airport the McClintock-Clayton aircraft would take them to Bar Harbor in Maine for their brief honeymoon. After they left, the crowd at the reception started to dwindle. Livy and Caroline joined up with Rachel and Chris. Across the wide marble hall their parents talked with the Wintertons, who were in a self-congratulatory mood. After all, it had all gone off perfectly.

Mark joined the four. He had, for a while, attached himself to General Goodrick, whom they had, for the first time, seen in the splendour of his full-dress uniform. Mike, after a time, gently steered him away. 'Will someone beg a glass of champagne for me,' Mark said. 'I've already had one from each waiter I could find, but they won't give me more than one. General Goodrick was a sport. He got me one.'

Caroline started to giggle. 'Are you drunk, Mark?'

'I don't know. I've never been drunk before.'

'Well,' Chris said, 'come with me. I'll see that you get another. I could stand one myself after this dreary affair.'

'What do you mean, dreary?' Caroline protested. 'It was all just beautiful.'

'I agree. Beautiful and utterly predictable. Boring,' was Chris's verdict. 'Come along, Mark. At least you and I can enjoy ourselves.'

Livy and Rachel looked at each other. 'Let's go home,' Rachel said.

'I don't think I will just yet,' Caroline said. 'Sometimes one just picks up the best men at the scrag end of the party. I'll just take a look around.'

'She'll find someone,' Rachel said as she and Livy got into a taxi. 'She'll go out to dinner, and she won't be home till one o'clock.'

Livy folded into the seat of the taxi. She had drunk far more champagne than she ought; she had nearly choked on the tiny nibble of wedding cake she had tasted. It would not have done to have refused it. She had kept smiling through the reception, and agreed with what anyone had said. And how many times had people she'd never seen before remarked to her, 'Aren't they a wonderful couple?' and she had agreed.

She hadn't seen Alex for a week before the wedding. He had given her a perfunctory kiss, the same kiss he had given to all the family lined up to see them depart. She thought of the flight in the privacy of the company plane. She thought of the house she had never seen in Bar Harbor, waiting, welcoming. A little exclamation of pain escaped her.

'What's the matter?' Rachel said. 'Too much champagne? Mark's going to learn tomorrow that a champagne hangover is the worst kind.'

'My feet,' Livy said, finding an explanation quickly. She slipped off her shoes. 'They're killing me. The shoes are too tight.'

'Well, they do match your dress.'

'Of course they do. Caro chose them. What's a little matter of a case of aching feet so long as the shoes match the dress?'

Livy lingered another week with Dena and Harry; they had one more weekend at Prescott Hill. 'Mercifully quiet,' Ginny said. 'I don't know how Mrs Winterton feels, but just being mother of the groom was almost too much. I wonder how I'll manage when Chris gets married.'

'I doubt you'll have any managing to do,' Blair commented quietly. 'I think Chris will arrange her own wedding . . .'

Already it was different. Rachel had departed, back to London, with a promise from Ginny's father that any time she wanted a job in the Senate Office Building, she had only to ask. Caroline had accepted an invitation to spend the weekend at the country house of someone she had met at the wedding. 'Our dear Caro never misses an opportunity,' Dena said. 'Well, good luck to her.'

They had the luxury of three days together – it was the

Labor Day weekend. Alex would soon be back with his bride, settling into the newly decorated house in Georgetown, and the office one floor below his grandfather's. Livy decided she would be gone before he returned. Her mood of despondency was lifted by a cable from Thea. *'Congratulations. Results published. You got a first.'* They had a quiet celebration. No one had yet completely recovered from the wedding.

She went to pay a farewell call on Andrew McClintock. Instead of seeing her at the office, he invited her to his house on Dupont Circle. They had a formal dinner together, plain food, supremely well cooked and served. 'I won't offer you champagne,' Andrew McClintock said. 'I imagine you've had enough this week. Instead I've got something special. You won't often encounter it. Romanée Conti. From a four-acre vineyard which the Rothschilds, whose land is only a dirt track's width away, would give their collective souls for.' He carried on, not waiting for her comment on the wine. 'Now you've got your degree, what will you do?'

'I'm flying back with Mark, who has to be at school next week. Then I think I'm going down to St Just. To sleep and read and eat my head off.'

'So long as you don't eat your heart out.'

'I've no intention of doing that. I need a little time. A month or so. Then . . . well, I just might do as Rachel did. I might take a crash course in typing, shorthand and bookkeeping. All the dull, traditional skills women have to have before they can get a job. Now that I've got a degree in English, I really wonder what I'm supposed to do with it.'

'You should have thought of that three years ago. However, you've done an amount of growing up. I doubt whether you'd have made a scientist or a doctor, given the people your parents were. All right. Go ahead with your courses. Won't be wasted. We always need bright young women at McClintock-Clayton.'

'Patronage, Mr McClintock . . . nepotism. Aren't you afraid of them? Perhaps I don't want that.'

He carefully cut his roast beef. 'Perhaps you don't. I'm glad you've retained me as your broker, though. Let me

371

know if there's anything I can do. I don't care to force anything on you. I don't expect I'll be over there before the summer. I let Blair do most of the travelling now, as you've noticed. Of course everyone will be there in London next summer. I'll be pulling all my little ambassadorial rank to make sure I'm in the Abbey. Wouldn't miss the Coronation for anything. Now there's a young woman with a job to do. Inherited, like Alex's. Nepotism . . . patronage . . . can't really escape them. So I'll see you at the Coronation.'

Chapter 10

1

Livy did not go back to St Just to the orgy of sleep, eating and reading she had told Andrew McClintock she would indulge in. During the long plane journey back to London with Mark, she pondered the future, and decided to postpone it no longer. She knew she would be no more certain of what she should do at the end of six months of idleness than she was now. She would take the first, the logical, step. She would take the course in typing, shorthand and bookkeeping. When that was finished, she would look for a job. She would try to forget her o)session with Alex; she would look around for the many other men there were in the world.

As she formulated the future it seemed sensible and possible; but her inner feeling told her that the plans were dull and prosaic. But only by such prosaic means could she move forward at all. At the moment it didn't seem to her that she would be capable of shutting Alex out of her heart. But she would have to try.

Unexpectedly, Rachel had borrowed a friend's small car and met them at London airport. 'Of course Aunt Ginny offered the usual grand chariot, with chauffeur, but I was afraid one of my friends might see me in it, and think I'd gone over to the enemy . . .' Sometimes Rachel could laugh at her own political attitudes. 'I'm sorry I can't have you to stay, but it's only one room and, really, a bit of a slum. So we're accommodated at Seymour House for the night, otherwise Mark would have had to go straight back to school. I telephoned Knox, and he's delighted to have something to do, and I think he's laying on something rather special as it's Mark's last night. You're staying on there for a while, aren't you, Livy?'

'Just until I can find something of my own. Aunt Ginny wouldn't hear of my going to an hotel.'

'No I couldn't see her letting you do that. She has to be one of the kindest, most generous women in the world.'

'Your mother,' Livy said, 'is just as generous, and just as kind. The only difference is that she doesn't have the Clayton money. I'm sure she'd give it just as readily.'

'You're right,' Rachel answered. 'One does tend to take one's parents for granted. I did telephone Chris, sort of hinting she might come too. But I think she's pretty heavily engaged with the current love-affair, and so I didn't suggest you stayed there instead of Seymour House. If it's a live-in love-affair, you'd be rather underfoot.'

Knox greeted them with evident pleasure. They luxuriated in the beautiful rooms of Seymour House, enjoyed the food: artichokes with *sauce au berre*, sea bass in pastry stuffed with lobster mousse, and a towering mound of profiteroles with chocolate sauce; Knox served a Chabis Grand Cru, and a Pouilly-Fuissé. They all declined a dessert wine. Mark leaned back and sighed with satisfaction. 'It will last me the whole term.' When Knox had left the room he leaned towards the other two. 'I hope Knox wasn't going overboard a bit with those wines. I mean, as butler, he has to account for everything.'

'Don't worry,' Rachel said. 'If Aunt Ginny said you were to have dinner here, she meant the best, wine included. I'm so glad I didn't invite you round to my dump for baked beans on toast.'

Mark went downstairs to talk to the chef. 'Monsieur Jacques, Jacques,' they heard him call. Then he broke into rapid, rather ungrammatical French. When he returned, Knox had served coffee in the library, and was offering liqueurs. Mark shrugged. 'Oh, what the hell! Tomorrow's banishment. May I try some chartreuse please, Knox.'

Rachel stayed the night at Seymour House, and early the next morning she drove Mark back to school; Livy went with them. Mark was rather silent on the journey. 'Just live it one term at a time,' Livy said, trying to console him.

'Yes, and when I've lived out this lot, there's Eton. And

374

that's going to be hell. The first year, at any rate. I'll have to fag for some bloody tyrant. I just hope I'll make the grade in sports quickly enough so the hell won't last too long.'

Neither Rachel nor Livy had any defence for the system to which Mark unwillingly bent. But when he took his bags, his tennis racquets and cricket bat from the car, he gave them the grin of a scrappy urchin. He couldn't be seen to embrace them. 'Trouble with this prison is that they don't give you any time off for good behaviour.'

'Since you hardly ever behave well, it wouldn't make much difference,' Rachel said. 'Good luck. We'll get together at half-term.'

On the drive back Livy told Rachel what she planned to do. 'I was going to indulge myself with a few weeks at St Just, but I feel if I go down there, it would be months before I could drag myself away. I'd better just plunge in. Suddenly, it's very strange. No one's making any plans for me, or telling me what to do. Of course I'll have to find a flat.'

Rachel made little comment, but she nodded approvingly. 'Yes, you do have to make your own life now. It comes as a bit of a shock.' As she dropped Livy back at Seymour House, she said, 'Try to find somewhere to live as soon as possible, no matter how grotty. Seymour House can become a frame of mind. Aunt Ginny would love you to stay here for ever.'

For the next week Livy was lapped by the luxury of Seymour House, and the attentions of Knox and Jacques. Tentatively she telephoned some of the girls she had known at Lady Margaret Hall who lived in London. None had been special friends, since there had always been the strong ties that bound her to Rachel, Chris and Caroline. But she realized that having a few acquaintances around was also part of the new life. She did not invite them to Seymour House. She thought that would be pushing hospitality too far, even though she knew Ginny would have urged it. But she asked advice about finding a flat, about secretarial courses, made plans to see them when she found a place of her own.

During the days she haunted estate agents, and walked

375

shabby streets looking for TO LET signs. She concentrated on the area below Victoria Station and on towards the river. Rachel's bedsitter was in Pimlico, and while Livy vowed she wouldn't camp on Rachel's doorstep, the thought of being somewhere close to her gave some comfort. At last she found a top-floor, self-contained flat, unfurnished, which itself was a miracle in this housing-short city, overlooking Vincent Square. It was in a row of tall, bomb-shaken Victorian houses, which had gaps where a house had received a direct hit or had been burned out. It was a shabby house and needed paint and repairs, and the owner wanted key money for the flat. Livy bargained a little, and finally settled on it. It had a large, south-facing living room, higher than the tops of the trees in the square, a large bedroom, and a much smaller one. It contained a rather crudely converted kitchen and bathroom; there were gas fires for heating. Amazingly, there was a telephone, standing on the floor by the big windows. Livy bought a bottle of champagne, bread and cheese, two cheap glasses and plates, and telephoned Rachel.

'I don't believe it,' Rachel said, as she surveyed it. 'I suppose by now you know how hard it is to find anything unfurnished. They can charge double the price by throwing in a sagging bed and a few orange crates. This is heaven . . .' She gazed out over the square, the playing fields for Westminster School. 'It must cost the earth.'

Livy confessed about the key money. 'I haven't been spending all the allowance I had when I was up at Oxford, much to Caro's horror. I thought I'd blow it on this and finding a bit of furniture. The furnished places I looked at were so depressing.' She felt awkward. She hadn't ever seen Rachel's bedsitter, but she could imagine it. 'You know Mr McClintock has looked after the money my father's books have earned. Really most of it came from *This England*.'

Rachel waved aside the explanation. 'Don't apologize. You know I make a big thing of socialism. What I'm talking about is money made by exploitation.' She sat on the floor, cut cheese and put it on the bread, wiping up the butter with radishes. 'I wouldn't doubt there must have been a bit of exploitation in whatever stocks Andrew McClintock bought for you. But there was no exploitation in what your father did. It was earned by the sweat of his brow. Your mother too. You deserve every penny of it.' She looked around her again, at the light, bare room. 'It may seem heaven to me, but by the standards of a lot of people I know, it's a rather modest heaven.'

Livy laughed and relaxed. 'Thank God you said that. I was almost afraid to ask you over.'

'Oh, don't pay too much attention to my grizzly-bear act. It's mostly a façade. I wouldn't turn down this heaven if it were offered to me.'

Livy smiled and basked in Rachel's approval. It wasn't often she won it.

That night at Seymour House she wrote to Andrew McClintock, describing the flat, its cost, what expenditure she expected to make on the bare necessities of furnishing it, what the secretarial school would cost, what she expected her living costs to be. The answer came by cable. '*Approved. You don't seem to be going mad with the money.*' He couldn't apparently resist the last little twist: '*I think you may afford the odd bottle of wine, but not Romanée Conti.*'

She had telephoned Thea about what she was doing. 'Dearest girl, go ahead,' Thea had answered, 'but I wish you'd taken just a few weeks here with us. We do miss you. Try to come at Christmas. I'm a bit worried about Bess. She doesn't seem well. Stubborn old thing won't tell us anything, but I suspect it's her heart. And the arthritis isn't any better.'

Livy had also written to Dena and Ginny to tell them about what to her was an exciting development. She spent a week painting the flat completely white, making lists of what she needed, looking around the shops in which most things still seemed to be in short supply and of a quality described as 'utility'. Utility it would have to be, she decided. She found a handyman who put up bookshelves made of green, unaged timber, which she knew would warp and sag. Her books and records and the few things she had collected came out from storage in Oxford. Then Knox told her of the cable he had received from Ginny. 'I'm to go through everything that's

377

"spare" in the way of china and glassware. You know, Miss Livy, Mrs Clayton buys her dinner services in large numbers of settings, and glassware by the dozen. Inevitably some things get broken. If the pattern can't be repeated, Mrs Clayton orders a new service. The box rooms are full of odds and ends, more than enough to start you up. And she has instructed me to look over the furniture stored in the attics and basement. Of course, no one threw anything away during the war, but when Mrs Clayton refurbished the house . . . well, there's quite a number of items to choose from.'

Livy found herself with rugs and a sofa and easy chairs, a mahogany drop-leaf table, more china and glasses than she needed, oddments of cutlery from the kitchen. Jacques went through the stocks of pots and pans and decided which he could do without. 'Mrs Clayton has provided the very best from America. Those I must keep here. But there are some of quite good quality, a little bent handle here, or not quite steady bottom. But good enough . . .' They were, Livy knew, much better than she could have bought, at whatever price.

She accepted everything, and wrote a grateful letter to Ginny. And yet there was the smallest sense of frustration. She would have liked to buy her own things; she would gladly have managed with much less. But she realized the foolishness of this, as well as the hurt a refusal would have caused Ginny.

· The day she moved in Jacques came over and helped her prepare the food for a party. Three girls she had known at Lady Margaret Hall were coming and bringing men friends; Rachel was coming and bringing two men and another girl from the LSE. Because the kitchen was so small, Jacques had prepared most of the food at Seymour House: leek, onion and potato soup, boeuf bourguignonne, pastries. He helped Livy with the selection of the wine. 'I understand, Miss Livy. Nothing expensive. But there are some very nice little wines . . .'

They shared a glass together before the first guests arrived. Livy looked at the still rather bare white-walled room, decked now with flowers, and glowed with pleasure. She had made tiny Cornish pasties from a recipe of her mother's, to be eaten in the hand. Jacques tasted one, and nodded his approval. 'You won't starve, Miss Livy.' He raised his glass to her 'Santé! Happiness! Cheers!' Far below someone pushed the bell beside the name Miles. Livy leaned out the window and saw Rachel and three other people down on the pavement. She tossed down the key. They had five flights of stairs to climb. She turned back and smiled at Jacques.

'My first party. How can I thank you?'

His answering smile had a twist of sadness in it. 'I am starting to feel a little more than middle-aged, Miss Livy. You know, I came to England after the war to make a change. My wife died while I was in a prisoner-of-war camp in Germany. There was nothing left to go back to. It does me good to see someone young just starting out. To help a bit . . .'

The room filled up. Jacques stayed to help serve the soup and boeuf bourguignonne, and went around pouring the wine. One of Rachel's friends remarked, 'I never knew anyone who had a housewarming party where there weren't enough chairs, but there was a *chef*! Please, dear Livy, I've only known you an hour, but I beg you to invite me again.' They stayed until after midnight. At first Livy had played the records everyone played those days: 'Hello Young Lovers', 'People Will Say We're In Love'. Then someone found the pile of records Livy usually kept for her own listening. They drank the last of the wine listening to Schubert's 'Death and the Maiden'.

Caroline wrote from Washington.

> The flat sounds lovely! How nice to have a bit of independence. Is there a bed in the spare room? Beware! You may have a visitor.

The letter rambled on; she was helping her mother with secretarial work, having some dates – Chris had tried out for some Broadway parts. Toby Osborne had written to say he was going to spend his leave from the FO in Washington, sort of getting a look at operations there. Caroline was generally supposed to show him the sights.

Ten days later Chris was at Livy's door with flowers, wine and *pâté* from Fortnums. She inspected the flat carefully. 'It's great, Livy! Your own place at last! I'm so sorry I missed the housewarming. The New York things looked so promising that I couldn't not try out for them. Well, as you know, I didn't get either of them.'

A bed had been put in the small room, and Livy had found faded curtains and a matching bedcover in one of the box rooms at Seymour House. She had bought a utility wardrobe and painted it white. 'This will do for you when your own flat's crowded out with other people.' Chris made no mention of the love-affair which Rachel had said kept her engrossed; perhaps it was over, or it had never been.

'Don't tempt me,' Chris said. 'I might take you up on it. I've got two almost complete strangers staying at the moment. Friends of friends. I can hardly get into my own bathroom.' She carefully examined the two water colours Herbert Gardiner had given Livy. 'They're quite beautiful, aren't they – and of the places you love best.' A view of St Just from the height of Tresillian, and of the Tresillian Tower. She spent a long time looking at a small piece of sculpture Thea had sent, a bluish stone with brass wires strung in an intricate web through the hollow in its centre. Livy had found a special table for it. 'My Lord, Livy, how are you going to insure it? Her pieces are bringing big prices now.'

'I thought of that. She says it's still under the insurance policy of all her "works in progress". This looked very "finished" to me.'

Mark came at half-term. By then Livy was well into her shorthand and typing course. He rushed to the small bedroom and flung himself on the bed, whooping, 'Free! Four days! What are we going to do, Livy?'

'What do you want to do?'

'Well . . . sleep late in the morning. No alarm clocks and no bells. If you could afford a good dinner . . . I've saved as much of my allowance as I could. Oh, and of course I'll have to see Rachel and Chris.'

'They're coming to dinner tonight. I've phoned Seymour

380

House. Chef Jacques is expecting you. We will have dinner there tomorrow night. He'll let you help prepare it . . . but of course you'll have to get there early to do that.'

'At dawn, if I have to.'

They sat around Livy's table that night, eating the ragôut of lamb Mark had helped prepare. Livy had splurged on two bottles of Châteauneuf du Pape. Candles were lighted. Deep red curtains were drawn against the autumn light. The room, with Herbert's pictures and Thea's sculpture, looked, Livy thought, quite beautiful. Somehow the mood of Rachel and Chris didn't quite match what she thought she had created. Rachel seemed more than usually abrupt, although she enquired in detail about everything Mark was doing at school, good and bad. Chris seemed abstracted, rather far away, though not distant. She talked to Mark in a soft, dreamy voice. 'How you've grown! You'll be as tall as your father, taller, I think. You're going to make a very handsome man one day, young Mark.'

He looked embarrassed. 'Oh, shut up, Chris! You might make a slip one day and say something like that in public.'

'We're not "public", I suppose,' Livy said.

'You're family. That's different.'

'There's a revival of *A Streetcar Named Desire* on,' Chris said. 'I think I'll take you to it, Mark. It's time you started to see something . . . something of the world.'

'A little raw, isn't it?' Rachel said. 'For Mark I mean . . .'

'Mark is growing up,' Chris answered, and won a look of gratitude from him. 'I don't know how young boys learn about sex, but it might as well be from a master.'

'I'd say Tennessee Williams was the wrong kind of master. Of the wrong persuasion.'

'All Mark has known is the perfectly gentlemanly love his father displays for his mother. There is a raw, brutish kind. Just sex. No love. It's as well to understand the difference.'

Rachel departed early. 'I've a meeting,' was all she said by way of explanation.

When she had gone, Chris lighted up another cigarette. 'I hear our Rachel is following Frazer Campbell around to all

381

his political meetings. Sort of sitting at his feet. He doesn't seem to mind it.'

'Frazer Campbell is so left-wing he could almost be described as a communist.'

'And what is Rachel, under the skin? But it's not her politics I'm complaining about. We're all used to that. It's Campbell. He's sort of picked her up as a young protégée. He likes her adoring manner.'

'Who's Frazer Campbell?' Mark asked.

'A very left-wing Member of Parliament. He's shadow Chancellor of the Exchequer. He comes from a rich family who made their money in whisky. He uses his money to finance whatever cause is radical enough for his taste. He represents a rock-solid Labour constituency in Glasgow where they seem to forgive him for having money. I suppose because it was made in whisky. He's very powerful in the Labour Party. It's not impossible to imagine that one day he might be Prime Minister.'

'And what's that to do with Rachel?'

'It may have nothing to do with her, or it could have a lot. Frazer Campbell is about forty, young for a politician but too old for Rachel. And he's married with two children.'

'Oh, Rachel wouldn't get involved in anything like that.'

'Wouldn't she? It's been known to happen before. Rachel, when one stops looking at her as a sister, is a very striking-looking woman. She has the sort of face a camera loves. Those beautiful cheekbones, the jaw line. I've often thought she should be the one who's trying to be an actress. And Frazer Campbell is just about the age to have his head turned by someone Rachel's age who thinks he's a great man and a hero.'

'I wouldn't like Rachel to be . . . to be hurt,' Livy said quietly. 'Since he's married.'

Chris shrugged. 'All of us are going to be hurt, one way or another. The press would make a dog's dinner of this, though, if there were ever any suggestion of a divorce. But I shouldn't think he'd have to worry about his constituency. They'll go on electing him for ever.'

Mark stirred uncomfortably. 'Rachel mixed up in a divorce? I hope it doesn't happen.'

382

Chris reached out and tousled Mark's hair affectionately. 'Don't worry. It happens all the time. People fall in and out of love. They get hurt. They heal. They pick up and go on.' She got to her feet. 'Now I think I'll go back and try to get some sleep. An early dance class in the morning. I'm just hoping my lodgers haven't decided to have a party.'

'Why do you put up with it?' Mark demanded. 'All those people sponging off you?'

'That's the theatre, kid.' She put on her coat. 'Thanks for the dinner, Livy. I'll get tickets for the three of us for Saturday night. I doubt Rachel will want to come. I'll telephone. Right? See you for your "do" at Seymour House tomorrow night.'

As they washed up Mark said, 'They're not such friends as they used to be, those two. Remember when we used to call them "the twins"?'

'Even twins grow apart. They were bound to develop different interests.'

'It can't be true about the Campbell man. Rachel wouldn't do that. She'd be too proud, for one thing.'

'Sometimes pride is the first thing to go when a person falls in love.' Into Livy's mind flashed a vision of Alex. 'Falling in love isn't very rational. And when it happens to a girl, a woman, like Rachel, it can be pretty devastating.'

'I wish I were older,' Mark said. 'I wish I didn't trail so far behind all of you.'

'You'll be old soon enough.'

The next night Chris was already at Seymour House when Livy arrived from the secretarial school. She was smoking and an almost empty glass of whisky was on the table beside her. 'Mark's all of a dither. Jacques is taking it all very seriously, and he's made Mark do the whole meal himself. He came and poured the drink under Knox's supervision, and presented it to me on a tray. What's the game? It looks to me as if he's training to be a major-domo at someone's embassy. Rachel's telephoned that she can't come. No doubt it's that damn Campbell man. I do think she could have given the kid this one night. He's on his own often enough, poor devil. But Rachel would think that was just one more thing wrong with our class system. Packing the kids off to school . . .'

'It's part of the diplomatic system too. Mark's got caught up in both.'

'Yes, I suppose he has. We were lucky, weren't we? There were always the four of us. Shall I ring for Butler Mark to pour us both another drink?'

Mark served the whole meal himself, dashing between the hot plates on the sideboard and his own place at the table. 'Of course Chef Jacques supervised everything, but I cooked it myself.' A good clear consommé, beef Wellington, a selection of vegetables. 'Jacques let me off the pudding. He made it himself. He doesn't think I'm quite up to lemon soufflé. But I had to wash up after him. I've been working all day!'

'Pretty good,' Chris said. 'I've had a lot worse at the best restaurants. What are you planning to do with all this cooking, Mark?'

He shrugged. 'Don't know. Just a hobby. Most people have hobbies, don't they? I just sort of picked it up from mother. You can't play cricket and rugger all the time, can you?'

'Well . . . there are books,' Livy said.

Mark ignored her. 'Pity Rachel couldn't come. I suppose it's that Campbell man.' In one day, Livy thought, he had absorbed and digested this information, and now could put on a casual air about it. Was he preparing himself for the gossip that might come, steeling himself? 'I'm looking forward to *Streetcar*, Chris. I've been talking to Jacques. He once spent a few months, just after the war, in New Orleans. He was a *sous chef* at a big hotel there. He told me a lot about it. The city and the play.'

Such a lot of growing up he had done in this time, Livy thought. He was able to grasp the concept of *Streetcar* before he had seen it, as he had grasped the concept, the very thought of Rachel and Frazer Campbell.

'Will you excuse me,' he said. 'I couldn't make the coffee beforehand, or it would be undrinkable. May I pour some brandy in the library while you wait?'

'Some kid,' Chris said when he had gone. 'He's tall, athletic. He's going to be an incredibly handsome man. If he goes on at this rate, he'll know how to handle any social situation by the time he's twelve. He'll be so suave at eighteen people will think he's forty. But will there be a kid inside him, still?'

Mark went back to school, and Livy went on with her classes. It surprised her when she discovered that she liked the bookkeeping course the best, though the typing and short-hand were the essentials. Bookkeeping led her to take an interest in the financial pages of the newspapers. She kept checking her portfolio of shares against the quoted prices. 'Becoming a regular capitalist, aren't you,' Rachel said.

'You know, Rachel, some of the things you say are so predictable, they're almost boring.'

She didn't see as much of Rachel as she had hoped to. 'I'm busy. The LSE doesn't tolerate dilettantes.' She was studying political science, and it seemed to Livy a very gloomy subject. Livy attended many parties at Chris's flat, but never encountered Rachel there. 'We're all too frivolous for her,' Chris said, shrugging. 'Did I tell you I've got a small part in a play? Not much more than a walk on, just one scene that's worth anything. But it's a chance . . .'

Livy went out occasionally with one of the men friends Rachel had brought to her first party, Joe Simmons. He was quite boastful of his working-class background, of his struggle to get to a grammar school on a scholarship from a Yorkshire textile village, of his winning a place at Oxford. 'It would have been harder before the war. They didn't take you if you didn't have the right accent.' Livy noticed, though, that he had ironed out the Yorkshire burr in his own accent, and it would be difficult now to place him, by speech, in any social stratum. He was frankly curious about her relationship with the Cambornes and the Claytons. Particularly he was interested in Andrew McClintock, the history of the family, his position in Washington and on Wall Street, his interest in Livy herself. 'You're a sort of protégée of his, aren't you?

385

Although what Oliver Miles's daughter needs from a man like McClintock I can't imagine.'

'What,' Livy said coolly, 'kind of a man do you suppose he is? He doesn't eat little girls for breakfast.'

'No, he just swallows companies and factories and the lives of all the people who work there. The smartest thing Andrew McClintock and Blair Clayton ever did was to sell before the Wall Street crash, and buy back shares for pennies . . .'

'Since you seem to know all about him, and most of that is just speculation, then I don't have to answer your questions.'

'Oh come off it, Livy. You can turn so damn cold at times. Of course Andrew McClintock is a subject of interest and speculation. Every buccaneering tycoon is. But if my interest offends you, we'll drop the subject.'

'Yes, do.' Livy went to change the record on the player. She hunted through her collection for the Mozart clarinet quintet. When she had put it on, she turned to find Joe close behind her.

'I agree,' he said. 'Why waste time when you're with a beautiful girl. You intrigue me, Livy. Are you still a virgin? I find it hard to think a girl like . . . am I allowed to find out? We could turn out to be very good for each other. Don't you like me just a little bit?' His arms were around her too tightly, and she fought against them. She'd had encounters like this with young men before, but never one so determined, nor had any approach been so distasteful. Why had she invited him here? He had probably construed it as an invitation to her bed. She felt his groping hands on her breasts, and with a mighty heave she pulled herself away from him.

'I think you'd better leave, Joe. I'm sorry. I seem to have given you the wrong impression. A few kisses don't make a love story. I don't sleep around, Joe.'

He said contemptuously, 'I see you belong in the great brigade of the teasers . . .' He was gone as soon as he could pick up his coat. She heard the angry slam of the street door five flights below.

She sank down on the sofa. 'Oh, Alex . . .' she sighed. 'Why did you have to put such a hold on me? Why can't I manage other men?' Then she lifted her head. 'What am I moaning about,' she asked aloud. 'I'm not sure I ever liked Joe Simmons. Was it just to have someone to go out with? Am I afraid to admit that I'm alone and sometimes lonely?'

The next week she met a young man, handsome, articulate, ready with his smile. 'I think your father was a wonderful poet. Trouble is, he didn't write enough.'

She found herself, in the midst of the hubbub of the party at Chris's, telling him a little of her father's last years, the slow ebb of his energy. He listened to her with an engrossed expression. 'It makes the poetry all that much better for me. He's about the most anti-war poet we have. Did you know he's been taken up by the anti-bomb lot? They read his poetry at their meetings . . .'

'Do you go to those meetings?'

'Just as a spectator. Come on, let's dance. I hear this is the last party Chris will be giving for a while, at least for the run of the play. Early nights and exercise classes and voice coaching are the rule now.'

'And what do you do?' Livy asked, after he had questioned her about her present life.

'Me, oh, I'm in the City . . . sort of.' He took her back to Vincent Square in a taxi, saying goodnight formally on the doorstep. He asked her to a concert and dinner the next week.

The seats in the Albert Hall were good, but not the most expensive; the Italian restaurant in South Kensington was modest but served excellent food. So far he had struck just the right note with Livy until in the middle of dinner she realized she was once again being questioned about the business of McClintock-Clayton. 'What on earth would I know about it?'

'I understand you're very close to the families, both McClintock and Clayton. You stay with them often enough. You must know something about what they discuss. There are rumours that they're about to try a take-over of I. B. Amman, the Swiss firm.'

She was angry. 'Hadn't you better ask Chris about that? After all, she's the Clayton's daughter.'

'Chris hasn't got two ideas in her head about high finance.

'If I did know, I wouldn't tell you. Is it your business? Are you trying to get inside information for your . . . your firm? Who do you work for?'

He shrugged. 'You're not quite the pushover you appear to be. Perhaps Old Man McClintock taught you a thing or two about holding your tongue.' He gestured helplessly, and smiled that ingratiating smile. 'Well, I could but try. Actually, I work on the financial section of the *Post*. A little inside information would have been a scoop for me. You see, I'm confessing all. But that wasn't why I asked you to dinner, Livy. You're a stunning girl. Really . . . I don't suppose you'd like to give a little item about your staying with the Cambornes in Washington last summer. I could do a favour for our gossip columnist, and in turn he might do a favour for me. Nothing nasty. Just a bit about how the Cambornes and the Claytons and the Old Man live, especially about the Old Man. They say it's almost impossible to get inside his house.'

'Which is precisely why no one who ever goes there talks about it. Shall I have my half of the bill? I don't think I've given you value for money.' She had risen. He rose also, his face flushed.

'Journalists are always treated like scum by people like you. The dinner's on me, Livy. And I promise, if you'll ever let me see you again, I'll never mention the names Camborne, Clayton or McClintock. Livy Miles is really all I want to talk about.'

But when he rang again a week later she told him she was going down to Cornwall for Christmas, which was the truth. 'Perhaps in the New Year . . .' She knew she would never see him again. She was beginning to realize that she would now begin to pay the price demanded for the love and loyalty of those two families. The Oxford years now seemed so innocent, and she still seemed so naive. This was Caroline's *real* world, and she handled it badly. She felt like pouring her heart out to someone, but could not bring herself to admit how easily she seemed to be taken in. Strangely, it was in one of her letters to Andrew McClintock, in which she generally reported what she was doing, that she wrote, without explaining why the knowledge was dawning on her. *'I begin to understand why the rich stay together, and tend to mistrust outsiders. They feel safer that way.'* Let him read into it what he liked. No doubt he would read plenty.

2

Mark came with her to St Just for Christmas. Chris's play was due to go into rehearsal in the New Year, and she seemed to cling to London and the company as though she feared that if she left she would be forgotten, and the precious past slip away from her. Dena had written understandingly when Livy had told her of her intentions, the need to see Thea and Herbert and Bess. Mark had made his own decision not to fly to Washington. Livy hadn't been sure how this news had been received by Dena and Harry, but they made no protest to her. Dena wrote:

> We will miss all of you. It seems so strange not having any of you about except Caro. As you can imagine, her party schedule is formidable. She's quite a belle here in Washington!

'I'm glad we're going to St Just,' Mark said when they met at Paddington Station. She noticed he carried a second suitcase filled with books. 'I promised father I'd try. It's really for mother. She minds so much if I don't do well. I really don't know what she expects of me. It isn't as if I'll be following father into the FO.'

Livy soothed him, and ordered the best wine on the list in the buffet car. 'I wouldn't start worrying about it yet. There's a lot going to happen before you need to make any decisions.'

'I don't worry but Mother does.' He nodded his head appreciatively as he sipped the wine, and the steward of the buffet car, since Livy had tipped him heavily on the way in, decided to turn a blind eye to the fact that a minor was drinking wine.

They were received lovingly and joyfully by Thea and Herbert. They were shocked by the appearance of Bess. She seemed to have shrunken, and her face had a greyish tinge. She struggled out of her chair by the fire in Thea's house to greet them. 'Don't pay any attention to the infirmities of this old crock. Arthritis is getting to me. Just plain old age. I can hardly bear to think of how many years it's been since the Foreign Office pensioned me off.' She was obliged to look up at Mark. 'Lord, how you've grown. Filled out a bit, too.'

'Can't play rugger if you're a flyweight.' Mark kissed her without embarrassment. Like Thea and Herbert, Bess was one of the figures he had first become aware of, teachers and friends, all of them, whom he had loved. 'I'm so glad we came. Mother seemed a bit put out when I wrote her, but I reminded her of how long it's been since I saw you all. And she's so busy at this time of year. Those endless diplomatic parties . . . I'm too young to go to them.'

'From the way you look to me, old man,' Herbert said, 'you'd easily pass as being old enough, or nearly. But we're honoured that you decided to come here. It's pretty dull beside all those Washington attractions.'

'It's good of you to have us,' Mark replied. 'I feel . . . I feel at home here. That's the trouble with the diplomatic service. The family never has a real home. If it weren't for Tresillian and St Just I'd feel a real nomad. No one in their right mind would think of school as being a home. I'm sorry for the chaps who have to stick it out there during the holidays. I've always got you . . . and St Just.'

Herbert looked pleased. 'Always remember it.'

They feasted their way through the holiday season. Livy and Mark went to visit her Tregenna cousins. Through marriages, the family circle grew wider; they included the houses of the Penhales and Trevellas as places where they would be welcomed. At last the close-knit families had come to believe that Livy would always be a part of them, and whatever fabled and exotic existence she lived elsewhere, she would always sit by their hearths and share their meals.

Even the little ones lost their shyness when they saw their mothers comfortable in the presence of this stranger who was Aunt Livy to some of them; the older ones had called her mother Aunt Isa. They all cherished the story of the poet who had walked into St Just with his puppy bulldog on a lead, and married one of their own.

Every day Mark and Livy walked up the hill to Tresillian; sometimes they took a picnic lunch there with them, and lighted a fire to sit by when they ate it. The walled garden was in good order, hoed and ready for the spring planting of vegetables. The apple crop had been good, Thea said. Every year the garden was prepared in case the family – which family, Camborne or Clayton, was never specified, since both were thought of in the same way – should decide to come for some part of the summer. If no one appeared, the vegetables and fruit were shared out among Thea and Bess and the Tregenna families. Harry paid the small wage of the gardener gladly, acknowledging how well his family and the Claytons had been looked after by the townsfolk during the war years. The house was clean and tidy, well aired, but, as Dena had predicted, cold. At Harry's request, Livy and Mark thoroughly inspected the ceilings of the attics, looking for the telltale stains or leaks. There were many. 'Father will have a fit,' Mark said. 'He can hardly afford the few repairs that have to be done very year, never mind a whole new roof, which is what it needs.' Apart from the walled garden, the rest of the grounds grew more overgrown. The lawns were rank with weeds, and the rhododendrons encroached ever more on the twisting drive. The wind above the Tresillian Rocks caught their hair, and stung their eyes. As always, Livy glanced down at the opal. How strange that Andrew McClintock had so perfectly caught the mood of this place in this gift. 'Do you still see them coming, Livy?'

'Who?'

'The Vikings coming down the Irish Sea? Do you see Tristan and Iseult on the boat, and King Mark waiting for them? Rachel always said you did.'

Livy smiled faintly. 'When the mist comes in, it's possible to see all sorts of things.'

They spent a good deal of time with Bess, sometimes talking, sometimes just sitting in companionable silence. Mark often took his books to Bess's house to study, knowing that just his presence pleased her. There was nearly always one of Livy's cousins in the house, cooking, cleaning, making cups of tea. 'They're very good to me,' Bess said. 'Since this arthritis got me so badly, there's always one of them to come and see to things. They pass the word around, you see. If one can't come, another does.' The little cottage which Livy owned had been modernized to some degree. There was now central heating, and a new bedroom and bathroom had been added on the ground floor at the back, since Bess found climbing the stairs so difficult. It had been squeezed in with great ingenuity between Livy's house and the next, without taking space from the garden. 'The garden's the thing I love most, here,' Bess said. 'On good days I can go and toast my bones in the sun, and all the aches go – at least for a few hours.' Livy could remember how her father had sat on that same garden seat; the same rock, which had been her seat, had its fresh coat of whitewash every year. Bess had insisted on paying for the additions herself.

'I'm very pleased about your first, Livy,' Bess said. 'As your old teacher, I rather wished you had stayed on at Oxford but then, the academic life's a bit arid unless one is absolutely cut out for it. The Cambornes and the Claytons have shown you something different. But you're on your own now, and you'll make your own decisions.' She raised a tea cup to her lips with a hand which trembled with the effort. 'Sometimes at night, when I can't sleep, I think of you all, how it was when we were all up at Tresillian. I remember when I first came I thought it was the end of the earth, and I didn't think I could stick being away from London. It turned out very different. In my old age, I was given a family. Even now I have Thea and Herbert with me every day . . . I'm a fortunate old woman. I just wish I could stay around a bit longer to see how you all turn out. I'd like to know what happens.'

Livy stayed in St Just for the whole of Mark's holidays, and was lectured on her return to the secretarial school. 'You'll have to make up time, Miss Miles. We pride ourselves on turning out the best product, and you won't receive a diploma from us until we are quite satisfied you are fully competent.'

Livy knew Andrew McClintock would not have approved of over-long holidays. *'You're damned right. I don't approve,'* he wrote back. She often wondered why she felt obliged to write such things to him, but she did, and her letters always received prompt answers.

But still, Thea and Herbert and Bess deserved a visit, and it must have done young Mark a power of good to be there with you all. There's nothing for him here except these damned parties. Everyone goes to parties these days. In my day, you just got on with the job. Which is what you ought to be doing now. How can I keep a spot warm for you at the Clayton Bank if you don't come out of that place with flying colours? And if you don't think a bank's a good place for a future poet – if that's what you're thinking of – remember there's a kind of poetry in reading a financial statement. Good or bad, it has to end up the same on both sides. A nice rhythm.

Only Andrew McClintock could have written that, Livy thought. She didn't like the implication of the job at the bank, but she did admit, secretly, to liking the balance sheets to work out properly. A mathematical nicety, rather like the mathematical perfection of a Bach fugue.

In late January Caroline was on her doorstep. 'I couldn't miss Chris's debut. Father gave me an advance for the fare. Aunt Ginny will be here tomorrow. But I thought I'd rather stay with you than at Seymour House. I thought your place would be cosier and, in any case, Aunt Ginny is going back to Washington right after the opening. Pray God Chris gets some good notices. The Ambassador thinks it's outrageous that she's gone on with the notion of being an actress. In his opinion she should be marrying someone in banking, starting a family and generally being a copy of her mother. He doesn't know our Chris.'

'Aunt Ginny is the last person who would want a daughter to be a copy of her. Chris has a tough row to hoe. To be on the stage you're supposed to struggle. And everyone knows she could probably buy and sell the producer. Her hardest job is to make anyone believe she's serious.'

The next night Ginny came to dinner at Vincent Square. She looked beautiful, Livy thought. Even the lines that were appearing around her eyes and mouth only lent depth and character to her face. She studied the little flat carefully. 'Livy, congratulations. It's exactly the sort of thing I dreamed of when I was your age, or a bit younger. I've really been sent by all the family to inspect. I shall be able to give them a very good report. Especially to Mr McClintock. I've been instructed to make sure that you're eating properly, that the place is clean, and the area decent. In short, that everything is up to scratch. I haven't an idea what Mr McClintock has in mind for you, whether it's the bank or the general McClintock-Clayton companies. I don't know whether you're supposed to go into pharmaceuticals or publishing. He seems to want you to be ready for everything. It isn't easy, Livy, to have Andrew McClintock breathing down your neck. I know. I lived that way for years. I still don't know whether I ever measured up. And these days, I really don't care.'

She still cared, Livy thought. She was beautiful, warm, elegant. Her years had given her great poise. She was in every sense the lady who should have married Andrew McClintock's only son. She had seen pictures of that only son, seen his physical beauty. He had never grown old. He had never had time to make mistakes or reveal weaknesses. After such a person, Livy thought Ginny had been extraordinarily lucky to find and marry Blair Clayton.

They went together to the first appearance on the London stage of Blair Clayton's only child. It was a swift, rather brittle little comedy, imported from New York. Chris had only minutes in which to make her impression, but they were important minutes. They attended a party for the cast afterwards, waiting for the newspapers and the reviews. 'We should have gone home,' Chris said. 'I don't think I can bear to read a bad review in front of all these people.' Various members of the press clustered around her. 'They're waiting for the poor little rich girl to take a pratfall,' Chris whispered to Livy and Caroline. It was noticeable how much attention was paid to Ginny, especially by the producer and the playwright, who had come to London for the opening. 'Of course it's the money,' Chris groaned. 'They're hoping I'll be a success, and that mother will become stage-struck. They think they've got a ready-made angel on a string.'

'Mr McClintock wouldn't like it,' Caro said.

'Don't worry. No member of my family will ever put up money to buy a part for me in anything. I'll either make it, or fail, by myself.'

The reviews came, and were almost good. The stars were praised, and the arrival of Christine Clayton was welcomed. One critic said:

A sharp, bright new talent, perfectly cast for this part; we look forward to seeing what she will do with the larger roles that will undoubtedly come her way.

Ginny telephoned Blair with the news. The producer thought the play might run six months, and, with luck, make some money. The playwright vaguely mentioned something he had in mind that might suit Chris perfectly. 'A lead role, Mrs Clayton.' Chris tried to freeze him out. But the afternoon papers, in the gossip columns, talked of her debut, and, inevitably, in each one of them there was a picture of Chris and Ginny together.

'I'm sorry, darling,' Ginny said to Chris. 'It should have been totally your night. But I just couldn't help coming to be with you. I'm proud of you. I just can't stay out of sight because the papers will print items about us both. Blair would so much like to have been with you to celebrate. But he's working on some deal now that's keeping him at the desk about fourteen hours a day. And then, too, he knew if he came, there'd be even more speculation that somehow we'd put money into the show. That we'd bought the part for you.'

'I know,' Chris said. 'I know exactly how daddy feels.' For the first time she showed them a bracelet he had sent to her before the opening, a slim gold band, studded with small diamonds. Inside, where no one but Chris would ever see, was inscribed *'With love to my first-night girl. Dad.'* By ten o'clock the next morning a cable had come from Andrew McClintock. *'Understand congratulations are in order. But don't let it go to your head.'*

'The usual blend of sweet and sour,' Chris commented. 'But I'm amazed he cabled at all. I'm not his grandchild, and I'm in a profession he disapproves of. But, of course, if I can make a success of it . . . Success is McClintock's bible. If you're a success, everything's forgiven you.'

Ginny hugged her. 'Try not to mind what he says. He's an old man, used to dominating people's lives. You're young, Chris, and you'll choose your own way.'

'I hope the play's still running when he comes over for the Coronation. Perhaps he'll come and see me . . .' There was just an edge of wistfulness in her tone. She was no blood relation of Andrew McClintock, and there was no reason why she should try to please him; yet he had instilled that feeling in them all. Perhaps only Rachel had truly escaped. Rachel had not attended the first night or come to the party afterwards. 'I'll get around to it sometime,' she said. Livy considered her either thoughtless or downright cruel. The twinship seemed to have split apart with a vengeance.

Caroline stayed on after Ginny had returned to Washington. 'Mine's a three-week economy fare. Can you put up with me for three weeks?'

'Stay as long as you like,' Livy said. 'You've no idea what it feels like to be able to offer any of you a bed, even if it isn't exactly luxury accommodation. Something of my own . . . I'd like your company. Temporarily, I'm off men and I can only practise shorthand and typing so many hours a day.'

To her disappointment, Caroline was seldom there in the evenings. 'Oh, I'm just catching up on friends I haven't seen for a while.' But when Livy took telephone messages for her, they were mostly from Toby Osborne. But when the telephone rang at six o'clock one morning, she knew it could not be Toby Osborne, or anyone else calling for a social reason. She lifted the receiver fearfully.

Thea's voice. 'Livy, I'm sorry. It's Bess. A stroke yesterday afternoon. Fortunately, your cousin Nell was with her. She's been staying in the house since Bess had a bit of a turn about three weeks ago. We got her to the hospital right away, but it was a massive stroke. There was really nothing they could do. She slipped away just about two o'clock this morning. We're grateful it is this way, Livy. You know how outraged Bess would have been to be totally dependent.'

'I'll come down,' Livy said.

She went to wake Caroline. They made tea, drank it sitting over a gas fire, and there were tears. 'I remember what a gorgon I thought she was when she first came to Tresillian. I was terrified of her. And then I began to realize what she added to our lives there. And when I got to school, I realized what a superb teacher she had been.' Caroline spoke in a mournful whisper.

They put in a call to Washington, and Harry answered. He listened carefully to the news. 'Dear Bess. She's been such a wonderful friend. Here, Dena's awake.' Livy only remembered then that it was only about two o'clock Washington time. She and Dena talked briefly. 'I must come over,' Dena said. 'I don't think I ever adequately thanked her for what she did for us all . . . one always leaves these things too late.' A few more words exchanged with Harry, and Livy hung up.

'About eight o'clock I'll have to telephone Mark's housemaster. God I hate Mark getting the news this way.' Her mind was filled with the practicalities, telephoning Thea with the news that Dena was coming, that she and Caroline would be on the night train. Telephoning Rachel and Chris. The sadness, the sense of loss had hardly begun to dawn. She tried to imagine her cottage unlived in, empty. It had housed her father and mother, then Dena's grandfather, then Bess. For all of them it had been a haven, a refuge. For the first time in many years it would be empty. She knew she wanted to leave it that way.

'I have an idea,' Caroline said. 'Let's get dressed quickly and dash out and hire a car. Let's drive down and see Mark ourselves. Maybe they'll let the poor kid off classes for the morning. Maybe they'll even be decent enough to let him come to St Just with us.'

So Mark was summoned from his class to the house-master's study. His face was fearful as he entered. 'What's wrong? What's happened? Is it Father . . . or Mother? Someone has to be dead.'

They told him. He averted his face from them, went to stand by the window looking out on the playing fields. 'She was such a decent old bird,' he said. 'I'm glad it was over quickly. I could see at Christmas that she was afraid she'd become totally helpless. She once said something about being a burden.'

The housemaster refused Livy's plea to allow Mark to come to St Just with them. 'Miss Bromley was not even related. I have had no specific request from Lord Camborne. You have to understand, Miss Miles, that if I let Penrose go, there'd be no end to it. Nannies, old retainers, third cousins . . . there'd be a death every day, and the boys would take advantage of it.' His manner clearly implied that Bess Bromley was not of sufficient importance to rank Mark's attendance at her funeral.

'Bloody old snob,' Mark said as he went back to the car with them. 'If she had been the Duchess of Somewhere, he'd have found a reason for my being there. Listen, give her flowers from me, will you?' He gazed at both of them; he had grown so much his eyes were now almost level with Livy's; his wrists jutted awkwardly from his too-short jacket. But they were muscular wrists, made that way by cricket and tennis and gymnastics. He showed inches of sock below his trouser cuffs. 'I don't mean just to put my name on flowers from the family. I want flowers specially from me. I've almost spent my allowance for this term, but I'll pay you back . . .' He drove to the school gates with them. 'Damn decent of you to come down to tell me. I don't think I could have stood hearing it from that old snob. A Miss Bromley, he would have called her. A Miss Bromley . . .'

He waved to them until the car was out of sight, and took his time walking up the long drive through the playing fields. When he knew he was absolutely secure from anyone's observation, he leaned against one of the oaks which lined the drive. He dashed the furtive tears from his eyes. 'Decent old bird,' he said aloud, telling it to the oak.

Livy and Caroline arrived in Penzance the next morning; Thea and Herbert met them. They were mostly silent, their grief voiceless. 'I'll miss her terribly,' Herbert said, hesitant at first. 'Got used to hearing that tart and knowing tongue laying about the world in general, and politicians in particular.' When they got to the Gardiners' house a cable from Dena waited them. *Ginny and I flying together tonight. Wednesday. Car will drive us down. Expect us Thursday evening.* A weeping Chris had telephoned the Gardiners twice, and telephoned again after Livy and Caroline had arrived. 'I just can't come down. I don't dare be out of the show a single night unless I'm on my death-bed. Oh, God, that was a stupid thing to say. It sounds so awful when Bess . . . I wish I could be there.'

'Bess would have understood,' Livy reassured her. 'You're a professional now, Chris. She would expect you to behave like one. She was proud of you.'

'I made a bit of a mess of things last night,' Chris confessed. 'Couldn't really concentrate after the news about Bess. The director happened to be around, and he told me my timing had been off.'

'Then don't let it be off again tonight. That would disappoint Bess.'

Rachel telephoned and asked briefly about the funeral arrangements. Her call was so brief that Herbert, who had answered the phone, hadn't time to tell her that Dena and Ginny were expected. Herbert came away from the telephone puzzled and slightly angry. 'I would have expected more from Rachel. It was Bess who fostered every gift she has. If it hadn't been for Bess, Rachel wouldn't have been ready for whatever world she seems bent on conquering . . . Well, I suppose that's that. There's only Bess's sister in Harrogate, and she's too old and unwell to travel. The two nephews . . . one in Canada and one in Australia. They didn't even exchange Christmas cards.'

Ginny and Dena arrived late that night in a car belonging to

McClintock-Clayton. They were weary, and grateful for hot baths. Herbert told them the arrangements for the funeral, which would be the following afternoon. They drank a brandy around the fire in Thea's living room, and then Livy and Caroline went over to what Livy still called in her mind 'Bess's house'. Her cousin, Bridie, had waited up for them. The fire blazed, the house was fully lighted, there were the early spring flowers of Cornwall all over the little house. 'I couldn't let you come in to an empty house. Not the first time . . .'

They were wakened the next morning early by a loud knocking at the door. Livy struggled into a dressing gown and went down to answer it. Rachel stood in the street; the taxi driver who had brought her from the train at Penzance was holding her bag. 'I didn't want to disturb Thea at this hour. We stopped at one of your Tregenna cousins to ask if you were staying here. I guessed it would be here.'

She paid off the taxi, and Livy pulled her into the kitchen, putting the kettle on the stove, ready to make tea. 'Cold? I'll have some breakfast ready in a few minutes. We didn't expect to see you here. You might have told us. One of us would have met the train . . .'

'I didn't want the fuss,' Rachel said, bluntly. 'And as for my being here, why not? Bess wasn't exclusively yours.'

By this time, alerted by her sister that Rachel had stopped at their cottage, Nell had arrived. She took over the breakfast preparation from Livy. 'I'll just light the fire in the dining-room. Have you cosy in no time . . . though with this heating Miss Bromley put in the fire's a bit of a luxury. But she liked them.'

Livy told Rachel about Dena's and Ginny's arrival. 'I heard it from your cousin. I must go over and see mother as soon as it's a decent hour.' Rachel looked pale and weary; Livy wondered if she bothered to eat properly, or remembered to. She had sat up all night on the train. When Nell put down the bacon, eggs and grilled tomatoes, the rack of toast, Rachel fell on them as if she hadn't eaten for days. 'I telephoned the florist here yesterday. I hope Bess didn't say she didn't want flowers, because I've ordered some.'

'We all have,' Caroline said. 'We're just assuming she

wouldn't mind. Even Mark's sent his own flowers. She didn't say anything about where she wanted to be buried, but she was Church of England, so she's being buried up there on the hill. She wasn't religious, you know, but the rector used to come here often. He liked to talk to her.'

'So did everyone with half a mind,' Rachel said.

She finished her breakfast in silence. 'I'll have a bath and go over and see mother and Aunt Ginny.' She hesitated. 'Where is she, Bess, I mean?'

'The coffin's already in the church. It's been there over-night.'

'So I can't see her.'

'I don't think Bess would have liked that,' Livy said.

'You never thought of what *I* might have liked.'

'You didn't tell us. You didn't even tell us that you were coming.'

'Of course I was coming. Didn't any of you realize that!' Her tone was angry rather than hurt. She slammed the door of the dining-room.

'One can't ever guess it right with Rachel,' Caroline said.

They saw her buried that afternoon. A chill wind blew at the top of the hill, but the churchyard wore the sheen of small spring wild flowers. It would have been enough for Bess, Livy thought, just those tiny wild flowers of the Cornish earth. But her grave was massed and heaped with other, more exotic flowers. Not just from the three families, but from those in the town no one would have expected to send. There was even an official one from the Foreign Office; that would have been at Harry's prompting. No one had expected the crowd which gathered.

'How good they are,' Dena murmured to Livy. 'Somehow I never thought of Bess having so many friends.'

Bess's solicitor had asked if he might come to the Gardiner house after the burial. 'Just a formality, Mrs Gardiner. The will is very simple.'

They gave tea and biscuits and cake to anyone who had wanted to stop at the house to pay their respects, and Herbert offered whisky 'to drive out the chill' he kept saying. But at last they were all gone, all but the families. The solicitor read through the preamble rapidly. 'It's the usual thing about her just debts and the funeral expenses. A few bequests to charities. To paraphrase it, she has left the remainder of her estate to be divided equally between Miss Rachel, Miss Caroline and Master Mark Penrose, Miss Christine Clayton and Miss Olivia Miles. Miss Olivia is to have the contents of the cottage and all Miss Bromley's personal effects. Miss Bromley called me in recently to go over the will again, and she disclosed the amount of her estate at that time. I estimate that each of the five principal beneficiaries will receive something over five thousand pounds.'

Thea gasped. 'How did Bess ever put together that amount of money? We thought she had only her pension.'

The solicitor explained that Bess had inherited a small amount on her father's death. 'That was many years ago. She invested it quite shrewdly. As I understood from the way she spoke of it, she never cared about spending money on anything but books, all of which she lost during the war. Her needs were few and simple. You must remember that by the time she retired from the Foreign Office she had reached quite a senior rank, although, being a woman, no one thought of her as actually having a career.'

'I don't want to take it,' Rachel said. 'It doesn't seem fair. I can't bear to think that Bess might have done without something she needed to save money for us. What did we do to deserve it?'

Herbert's tone was sharp. 'Bess did without nothing she really wanted. Do you think Thea and I would not have noticed that – would have stood for it? Bess said it herself. In her old age she had a family she never expected to have. Do what you like with it, Rachel. Give it to the Communist Party, if you must. Or an old cat's home. But you can't give it back to her.' He added, as if out of patience with her, 'All I can say is, "Try to enjoy it, if you know how to." That's what Bess meant it for.'

They stayed another day, trying to hold together what they all knew was another splitting, another parting. Their group was growing larger, and yet shrinking. For the four girls, one of the props of their young years had gone. Livy and Caroline went to the churchyard and collected the cards from the flowers which had been sent. There were costly red roses from Andrew McClintock, and a small, but exquisite spray of primroses and violets with the words, *Bess, lovingly, Alex*. He would have had to telephone London to arrange that, Livy thought, showing it to Caroline. 'I'll answer them all,' Caroline said. 'Every one of them. It's about the only sort of thing I do well. It's the very least I can do for Bess.'

That afternoon Ginny and Dena and the three girls walked up to Tresillian. Ginny was wrapped in a fur against the cold wind; Dena's sable had begun to show wear and it was now the lining of a black wool coat. They spoke little as they moved through the silent rooms. Then they went to the walled garden, and stopped by Bully's headstone. 'I don't think Thea will make a stone for Bess,' Ginny said. 'She never really did approve of modern sculpture. It's amazing she and Thea were such friends.'

'Even Bess could have her blind spots. I expect we all do,' Dena murmured. Then she added swiftly, 'I wish Mark were here. If I'd just thought, well, Harry would have telephoned and insisted. I have to say it, and I'm his mother: I'm often guilty of forgetting Mark. I wonder if he'll ever forgive me?'

None of them attempted a reply. Ginny just took her friend's arm and led her gently from the orchard. Their arms stayed linked together as they descended the overgrown drive, and the town came into view.

They all ate dinner with Thea and Herbert that night, and some plans were discussed, the summer and the coming Coronation. 'I don't think I can be bothered going up to London. They say it's all going to be on television . . .'

'I shall expect you at Seymour House,' Ginny said firmly. 'You can watch it in comfort in the house, and then dash along the street to St James's Palace when the procession comes into view. I believe Blair has already made a commitment to some space that overlooks the processional route. I insist. Mr McClintock, of course, has his suite at the Ritz,

403

and he'll enjoy it all hugely. All the girls will be there, and with luck Chris's play will still be running. With all the visitors in London there should be packed houses. Blair will be able to see her, and perhaps Mr McClintock will.' She turned to Caroline. 'When are you coming back to Washington? I miss you in more than one way. The girl I've got as a temporary isn't as good on the telephone or at answering letters as you are. Somebody said to me the other day: "Where's that high-class English accent that used to answer your personal phone?" It's as snobby having an English secretary as having an English butler.'

'You could have ten of each, Aunt Ginny,' Caroline protested, but she was pleased. It seemed to Livy that Caroline was surprisingly humble. She had once said to Livy: 'I haven't got anything but looks . . .' Now she said, 'Could I just hang on here a while longer? Toby Osborne has asked me to spend a weekend with his people at their place in Northamptonshire . . .' She looked around the table, as if reaching for a reaction. 'I'd like to go.'

'Toby Osborne?' her mother said. 'Has he got serious about you, Caro? He seemed so . . . well, so detached when he was in Washington. As if he were looking the field over.'

'He can afford to,' Caroline answered. 'All he has to do, really, is lift his finger.'

'I don't like the sound of Toby Osborne,' Herbert said.

'Toby Osborne is one of the really good examples of what the hereditary peerage can throw up in the way of arrogance and insensitivity,' Rachel said. 'But one day, unless we tear it down, he will take his father's seat in the House of Lords, and have the right to vote against and delay and generally mess up the bills we pass in the House of Commons.'

'Well,' Thea offered, 'that's about as good a speech as I've heard from someone who *isn't* in the House of Commons, and whose own father is an hereditary peer.'

'I can't help what father is, but one day I intend to be in the House of Commons. And maybe Bess's money will help that. She never liked politicians, but she knew I was bound to get mixed up with them.'

'Well, I'm glad you're seeing some sense about why Bess

left you the money,' Herbert said. 'Now, before I forget it, Livy, do you want us to do anything about renting the cottage? It would bring a very good price in the summer, but I.'

She shook her head. 'I couldn't bear strangers being there, touching my father's and my mother's things. The things that Lady Camborne's grandfather left there. All Bess's things, especially the books. There's Thea's sculpture, and the little landscape that Lady Camborne's grandfather painted for Mark's christening. No, it wouldn't do. I'll be down to stay there from time to time. I like to think of it waiting. My cousins will take care of it for me.'

Herbert nodded, pleased with her answer. 'So will we.'

They drove up to London the next day, going straight to the airport. Chris was there, waiting for them, looking at her watch. She had a taxi waiting, knowing she had to be at the theatre well before the curtain rose. Rachel asked if she could have a lift back in the taxi. 'I have a meeting,' she said. Ginny and Chris talked for a while, kissed and parted. Livy and Caroline remained until the flight was called. Ginny and Dena had automatically been shown to the VIP lounge. 'That means,' Caroline said, 'that McClintock-Clayton have paid for mother to fly first class. It's just like the days when they used to travel by ship. There was always a McClintock-Clayton suite.' She settled back in the comfort of the Rolls which would take them back to Vincent Square. 'How I'd love mother and father to be able to afford to do that themselves . . .'

As they threaded their way through the traffic back towards central London, Livy ventured a question. 'Tell me to mind my own business, Caro, if you want. I wondered . . . are you serious about Osborne?'

'Question is, is he serious about me?'

'Do you love him?'

'I like him. He's much nicer once you get past what Rachel calls his arrogance. It's only a mannerism. He's . . . he's . . .' She fumbled for words, lost them, and lapsed into silence.

'Would you marry him, Caro, if he asked you?'

'Yes!' The word was uttered with fierce emphasis. 'Certainly I'd marry him. I'm not like the rest of you: brilliant, talented, full of ambition. I've got only a face and a body. And he has lots of money. God knows, he could marry almost anyone he fancied. Somehow, he fancies me, I think. If his parents don't turn thumbs down on me, I think we may be engaged. And if we are, I'm going to push for a quick wedding.'

'Caro . . .'

'Oh, Livy, don't you turn against me. I'm doing the only thing I know how to do. I think I'm making a good marriage. What else? What else can I do?'

The chauffeur took them to Vincent Square. They climbed the five flights of stairs in silence. As they mounted each flight, Livy recognized that it was precisely this situation Caroline sought to escape; she was doing only what her own good sense told her was right. Caroline did not look forward to a life of climbing five flights of stairs to a small flat.

Caroline waited nervously through the next week. Three times she went out to dinner with Toby Osborne. 'He's nice. He takes me to the most divine restaurants – last night he invited his best friend, Percy Leathbridge, and his wife, Triss, to have dinner with us. I was being looked over, Livy. I know. It's nerve-racking. We're good friends, but he hasn't said a word that I could construe as an invitation to marriage. I suppose that will depend on what his parents think of me. He's the only son.'

Livy didn't say so because it would have hurt Caroline, but she didn't think much of the sort of man of his age who would wait on parental approval before he said anything of love. If indeed there was love. Whenever he came to call for Caroline, correctly toiling up the five flights of stairs, drinking a polite sherry before setting out to dinner, he didn't strike Livy as a man in the grip of passion. Looking at the loveliness of Caroline, Livy failed to understand how anyone could spend so much time with her and not appear to delight in her presence. He was a certain Foreign-Office type who would never leave Whitehall. He would serve faithfully, and anonymously. One day he might be Permanent Under Secretary, and very few people would ever know his name.

Caroline went for the weekend at Lord Bolton's Northamptonshire estate; the country seat of the Boltons' was one of England's best-known stately homes. She returned pleased, but faintly subdued. 'He asked me. He telephoned father to ask permission. It's all settled. They'd like the wedding to be before the Coronation, because everyone will be so busy celebrating that and the Boltons don't want to be overshadowed. So it will be early May. We're going this afternoon to the jeweller to choose a new setting for the ring. There's an enormous great ruby that Lady Bolton produced. I would have preferred a sapphire or a diamond, but I couldn't really say "no". There was even some talk about having the wedding in Northamptonshire, but I wriggled out of that. I'm afraid I presumed on Aunt Ginny's generosity by saying I was sure the reception could be at Seymour House, and it would be so much easier for our friends to attend a wedding in London. The announcement will be in *The Times* on Thursday. There's so little time to get ready. And so much to arrange . . .'

'Caro, what's the matter? You don't seem happy.'

'Happy? Of course I'm happy. It's what I wanted, isn't it? I'll be a good wife to him. We'll have a lovely house, and beautiful children. I'll make a good hostess. I didn't think when we were growing up all over the place that the diplomatic service would teach me how to please people. But I think I pleased the Boltons. They value their connection to the Royal family very highly. It wouldn't have done for Toby to have married someone like . . . well, like Rachel . . . or Chris. No one flamboyant . . . or different. Someone rather ordinary but acceptable, like me.'

Livy felt like weeping. This beautiful girl, glowing with life, who thought of herself as ordinary but acceptable. Who was not in love with the man she would marry, nor he with her. She felt tempted to try to dissuade Caroline, and knew she couldn't. At this moment what Caroline seemed to need was the security of money. What would happen if she ever awakened to a passionate love for another man? What if a storm of that kind should strike her? There was a basic coldness and calculation on the part of both of them in the arrangement. Livy could think of it only as an arrangement, something Caroline could grow out of and regret. She had never been truly in love, nor could she contemplate what she was now determined to do. If only Caroline showed just a little sign of happiness or even excitement.

She collapsed back into the sofa. 'What a relief!' That seemed to express the depth of her emotion. 'Thank God for Bess's legacy. It will pay for the wedding and my trousseau. I won't have to beggar father for that . . .'

Livy had a worried letter from Dena, which she concealed from Caroline:

> I don't much like it. I don't much care for Toby. I tried while he was in Washington to point out to Caro the things I think he lacks and what he had too much of. But she wasn't listening. And, after all, what is there to object to? He is a very eligible young man, and will do well in his career. There isn't a single thing to point to against him. I'll be the delighted mother . . . Of course Ginny has insisted on our having Seymour House for the reception. They're all coming over – the Ambassador, Ginny and Blair, Alex and Nancy. I have spoken to Lady Bolton by telephone. She is very busy on the guest list. I'm afraid it will be very long. I hope to God they don't manage to snare one of the Royals. That would be too much. I hope they're all far too busy with Coronation plans . . .

But Dena had very little to do with making the plans and what was done had to be by post with the occasional telephone call.

Caroline took it all in her stride. 'After all, it's about all I know how to do.' She consulted with Lady Bolton and Toby about the guest list; she made arrangements with the Dean of St Margaret's and settled on a Saturday early in May. She bullied the printers into rushing through the invitations. She sat up late at night addressing them by hand in her beautiful italic script. She needed no advice on selecting her trousseau; she bought with a sharp eye for price and value. When she settled on the menu for the reception she managed to balance nicely its cost and its effect. She sought the help of Knox and Chef Jacques on which champagne to order. She did it all with such swift efficiency that Livy thought she was more like a person hired to do the job, rather than a young woman about to be married.

'The date's so close to my twenty-first birthday that we won't have to have a party for that. There'll be so many parties around the time of the Coronation, no one will notice . . . we'll have just a week in Venice for the honeymoon. Have to be back in good time for the Coronation. Of course the Boltons will be in the Abbey . . . Toby has been offered a few good windows along the route. It's just a matter of picking which group of people we want to be with.'

In the middle of Caroline's preparations, unnoticed because Caroline was totally absorbed in them, Livy took her final test in shorthand, typing and basic bookkeeping. She had reached very good speeds in both skills, and the bookkeeping was judged quite satisfactory. She walked back to Vincent Square in the early spring sunshine, her thoughts deliberately unfocused, absently noting that the trees were budding, and would be fully in leaf when Caroline was married. Just as last summer, after her finals at Oxford, she had once again come to a time of decision, and was shying away from it. This time there would be no escape into another situation in which she seemed merely to mark time. The secretarial course had been interesting, but not challenging. to have finished it was merely an anti-climax. Caroline looked stricken when Livy told her she had finished the course. 'Oh, God, I've been so selfish. Up to my eyes in my own affairs, I never thought about it.'

'It's not terribly important. I would have thought it odd if you had noticed. Not when you're on the verge of getting married.'

Caroline was caught up in the details of the marriage ceremony, the reception. She gave no impression of a girl wandering in the blissful vagueness of someone in love. 'Now that I'm free, I can help a bit with preparations.'

'Not a lot to do now except check the acceptances against the regrets, so I have a final number for the caterers. It's going to be a squeeze. All father and mother's people had to be asked, and the Boltons' list was huge. I thought that with Toby and father both being in the Foreign Office, there would be a lot of duplications, but they're different generations. And of course there are all the people serving overseas who won't be able to come, but who had to have an invitation . . .'

Dena arrived from Washington, expecting the sort of chaos which surrounds most weddings, and was taken aback to find so much already done. 'Why, Caro, you really didn't need me at all! I feel so guilty, leaving all this to you . . .'

'Mother, darling . . . aren't you pleased I can do it? It was you who trained me. If Toby weren't rich, I think I'd rather like to be hired out to "arrange" things. I've enjoyed it. You must come with me tomorrow for the final fitting of the wedding-dress. I hope you like it. Quite demure . . .'

'Knowing you, I'm sure it's lovely and exactly right. Just think, I have two daughters, and I'll never have a hand in choosing a wedding-dress. Rachel will get married in any old thing that comes to hand, I know.'

She was staying at Seymour House; by now, Harry had almost given up protesting the Claytons' hospitality. 'He'd love to have some tiny place in London just for us, so we needn't always seem to be on the "take" from Ginny and Blair. But with the expenses of keeping Tresillian from falling into an absolute ruin, and very gradually paying off the death duties from Perry's estate, and even Perry's father's estate, there really isn't a hope of that yet . . . He keeps talking about breaking the entail, and perhaps finding a buyer for Tresillian, but he's done nothing about it yet.'

The very thought of it tugged at Livy's heart. She couldn't imagine life at St Just without the knowledge that Tresillian was there to visit, to live in, to keep on loving. 'Let me give you another scotch,' Livy said quickly.

Dena was having dinner with her alone. Toby had come

to take Caroline to the theatre; he had been quietly correct in his enquiries about Washington, Ambassador McClintock, the Minister, as he called Harry, the members of the embassy staff he had got to know. 'I wish there were just a little excitement going on between them,' Dena sighed. 'I'd like to see just a little spurt of passion in those cool eyes. Toby gives me the impression that he's weighed everything up very carefully, and Caro won on points. The only thing she hasn't got is money, and he doesn't need that.'

'But Caro does,' Livy said. 'They might make a perfect match.'

Andrew McClintock arrived, settled himself in his suite at the Ritz, intending to stay there until after the Coronation. He refused accommodation at Seymour House, saying it would be too crowded, but he felt quite at liberty to present himself there as he always had done, unannounced. Thea and Herbert came up from Cornwall, but stayed at the Cadogan Hotel. Harry arrived; Ginny and Blair arrived. The rehearsals took place at St Margaret's. 'It's all going so smoothly it's almost a bore,' Chris said. 'Rehearsals are supposed to go haywire. Caro seems to have us all on strings. Whoever thought she'd turn out to be such a genius as an organizer? I don't detect even a hint of first-night nerves. It's unnatural.'

Presents arrived, and were unpacked and displayed in the library at Seymour House. Caroline had registered her preferences with the General Trading Company, and she purred with satisfaction that she had a complete dinner and crystal service. Andrew McClintock had given her a whole silver flatware service, the Boltons a Georgian silver tea service. 'Probably one of the old ones they didn't need,' Chris remarked, 'like Caro's ruby.' Mark sent a copper chafing dish. Livy sent a vacuum cleaner, since it was one of the items on the list not filled. Ginny and Blair sent a whole range of Steuben vases and bowls from New York. Dena had brought one of her grandfather's landscapes from their house in Washington. 'We can't compete with the Boltons,' she said. 'But it's something money can't buy.'

In spite of the preparations for the Coronation, the press took an extravagant interest in the wedding. It was popular and very suitable. It seemed just a welcome prelude to the great events, and the national rejoicing which would follow early in June. Caroline floated up the aisle on her father's arm, a visionary creature shimmering in ivory silk. She walked back on the arm of Viscount Osborne just as calmly. The four bridesmaids followed, but few eyes went to them because Caroline had put them into the shade, even the beautiful young actress, Christine Clayton. The combination of the elements of class and money and fame were irresistible to the press.

'And how's the most beautiful bridesmaid?' Alex's voice sounded behind Livy. He and Nancy had arrived only the night before. They were staying at the Ritz to avoid the crush of the bride and her bridesmaids dressing at Seymour House. Livy hadn't yet spoken a word to him, but had been acutely aware of him seated in the church behind the Ambassador, Dena, Ginny and Blair. Juggling with the realities of the complex affairs of McClintock-Clayton, instead of the theories he had encountered at Harvard Business School, seemed to have suited him, or was it marriage? He seemed as smoothly at ease as ever, but there was that extra degree of confidence about him. He had worked in an office close to his grandfather for nearly a year, and still appeared to be his own man. Livy sighed, and pretended it was one of fatigue. She wished she could get away from him; she wished it would never be necessary to see Alex again. She had long ago realized that in the matter of Alex, she had not been a good loser. Her sharpened eyes had dissected Nancy, and there was no fault to be found with her, not in appearance. She joined Alex now, as if she had some antenna out in the crowd, following his progress, knowing to whom he spoke.

'You look lovely, Olivia,' she said. 'How clever of Caroline to choose dresses that suit all the bridesmaids. Hard thing to do. I think you must be the favoured one – red hair is difficult to dress . . .'

'Caro has always liked blue.'

412

'So I see. From the dinner service. I hear the ruby is a Bolton family heirloom.'

'I remember a girl with red hair who wore a pink velvet cap,' Alex murmured. Livy found the colour flooding her face, and inwardly cursing him for remembering such things, and in front of Nancy.

'What?' Nancy asked. Alex shook his head, as if he hadn't said anything. 'Obviously the Ambassador knows she likes blue. Besides that enormous service of flatware I've just spotted among the presents, the Ambassador has given her a table inlaid with lapis. I recognize it. It comes from his Washington house.'

'My dear, Grandfather can give Caro anything that comes into his head. He is, after all, her godfather . . . He made her cut her teeth on gold.'

'Then a little of it must have rubbed off', Nancy said. 'I understand that . . .' with a little nod of mock apology to Livy, 'this is rather a golden marriage for Caroline. She won't have to worry any more about money. Must be quite a relief for her parents . . .'

'Nancy!' Alex took both her arms and turned her around. 'Now why don't you go and get yourself some champagne, like a good girl. And try to behave yourself. You had your wedding last year. Looking for another one?'

Nancy shook off his hands. 'Oh get . . .' She paused. 'Look, here she comes! Exciting, isn't it?' The excitement was not about the bride, but the progress of a Royal duchess through the crowd. Although Americans were not supposed to curtsey to royalty, Nancy's was deep and proper as the duchess passed.

'Come on,' Alex said to Livy, 'let's get out of here.'

'Where?'

'Out in the park – easy, just go through the usual gate. There's a security man on it, but he knows me.'

'Like this?'

She indicated her long blue dress, the widebrimmed hat, his morning dress of grey coat and striped trousers. 'Why not? The park's free.'

A little dizzy with excitement, and at the same time feeling

413

some resentment, Livy followed him from the marquee. On the way he lifted two glasses of champagne from a tray. They passed through the gate on to the walk that led down to The Mall. Livy was conscious of many stares, sometimes a faint cheer of merriment. They walked together, sipping champagne. 'Don't pay any attention,' Alex said. 'They just think it's all part of the preparations for the Coronation . . .' They reached The Mall, and then turned back. Alex sometimes raised his glass to one or other of the crowd who had turned out on this fine May Saturday afternoon, numbers of them clustered beyond the iron railings outside the garden of Seymour House, gazing at the wedding guests who strolled between the house and the marquee.

'You know it never could have worked for us, Livy.'

'Worked? What do you mean?'

'We couldn't have married. It wouldn't have worked. It was what my grandfather wanted. I wouldn't be manipulated. Neither would you. Not everything can be arranged to his liking.'

'Oh – go to hell!' Livy handed him her empty glass, and indicated to the security guard to open the gate. Before Alex could move, she clanged it shut, and hurried to the marquee. She immediately picked up another glass of champagne and almost downed it.

'Steady on.' It was Mark beside her, looking impossibly grown up in a hired morning suit. 'That's meant to be sipped.'

'Might as well be drunk as the way I am,' Livy replied.

3

After the wedding, Livy returned to St Just with Thea and Herbert. She stayed in what she still thought of as Bess's cottage, going through all Bess's things, distributing to her cousins Bess's clothes. Thoughtfully she went through the small but choice library Bess had started to build once she knew her cherished one in London had gone in the Blitz. There was little of a personal nature left: all the left-overs of girlhood, the photographs, the class groups, the pictures from Girton where Bess had been an outstanding student had all gone in the same bomb blast. If outsiders had gone through these things they might have believed that Bess's life had begun and ended in St Just.

Harry had persuaded Dena that there was no need for her to return to Washington with him for these few weeks, so she came to St Just to stay with Livy for some days. She looked around the cottage thoughtfully. 'Who would have expected Bess to be so domestic?' The curtains and sofa covers had been recently renewed; the new bathroom on the ground floor had the novelty of a large, tiled shower stall.

'It was because of her arthritis,' Livy explained. 'So much easier for her than climbing into a bath.'

As always, they went up to Tresillian. Dena saw for herself the ominous stains on the sloping ceilings of the attic rooms.

'It all terrifies me,' she said. 'Once we start, there'll be no stopping. I know he has the worst bits patched up every year, but that's all they are, patches. I'm sure there's dry rot in some of the floors. We just daren't investigate that.'

She smiled at Livy as they sat across the fire they had made, eating pasties and drinking coffee from a thermos. 'Here I am, talking to you as I'm not able to talk to my own two daughters. Ellen came to the wedding, did you see her? and we had hardly two words to say to each other. Julia never leaves that Scottish hermitage. Rachel frightens me, she's so intense. And Caro is too much like me. I see all my faults reflected in her.' She gave wistful sigh. 'Well, Livy, you will have to be the daughter of my old age. The one I can talk to. It's almost like having another Ginny . . .'

Dena left after three days, and Livy missed her. She went to her Tregenna cousins and made arrangements for Tresillian to be opened and made ready for whatever number of guests would arrive after the Coronation. 'Lady Camborne thinks Mr McClintock, the Ambassador, might come down. I know you'll have everything ready. If there's going to be a big crowd, Mrs Clayton's chef will come down and cook. I don't know what he'll make of the kitchen and the stove. If he makes anything of it. Of course he'll need help . . .

and all the fresh vegetables and fish you can find. But it will be very informal. Just a sort of homecoming. Probably just the family.'

'Does that mean Alex and his wife?' Nell said, using the name from long familiarity. 'And Caroline and her new husband?' They had pored over the wedding pictures Livy had brought down.

'I don't know. Whoever comes . . . comes.' She prayed that Alex would not come.

When Livy got back to London, there was a message from Andrew McClintock informing her that he would like to be invited to dinner. She telephoned the Ritz and protested about the stairs, the size of the flat. 'What?' he shouted at her. 'Do you think I can't climb a few stairs? What have you got there that you're hiding?'

'Nothing, Ambassador.' She was raging, but she kept her tone cool. 'I'll be delighted to entertain you whenever you're free.'

'This evening then. I'll come at seven-thirty.'

Which gave her, she thought, not even time to slow cook a decent *boeuf bourguignonne*. She got a taxi to Harrods, thinking how her mother would have been able to devise a superb meal from almost anything she saw in the food halls. She settled on asparagus, blessing Jacques for the tall pot he had given her in which to cook it; her whole meat ration, not used in St Just, went on two supreme Scotch beef tournedos. She would bake potatoes in their jackets, and unashamedly offer him Harrods best strawberries with cream. He couldn't expect her both to entertain him and cook an elaborate dish for him. The wine posed a different problem. She bought flowers extravagantly.

There was no question that she would throw down the keys. She was waiting on the steps when his car drew up, and went to greet him. 'Well . . .' he growled at her. 'You ran away from London pretty quickly after the wedding.'

'I thought I was due a holiday,' she replied. 'I stayed on only because of the wedding.'

He had nothing to say as he climbed the stairs. Halfway

416

up he stood for a while and rested. 'Oh, don't let this fool you. I'm not done for yet. A little shortness of breath.'

He examined every part of the flat with the thoroughness which in anyone else Livy would have regarded as rudeness. He sniffed in the bathroom as if he expected to smell bad drains. 'Don't know how these old places stand it. They were jerry-built in the Victorian era, and then nearly shaken to bits during the Blitz. Well . . . the American word for all this is quaint, a word I detest, and which Alex's wife uses when she can't think of anything more fitting.' He peered at Thea's sculpture and Herbert's pictures. 'You're rather grandly set up in art.'

She expected him to ask for scotch, and was rather nonplussed when he asked her to mix him a martini. She gritted her teeth, used all the ice her small refrigerator was capable of making, thrust a glass in the little freezer compartment to chill briefly, and added only a hint of vermouth to the gin. 'Olive or onion, she enquired.

'A twist of lemon,' he replied. He lifted the glass to her, then tasted, suspiciously. 'Not bad,' he conceded.

They ate the asparagus with butter: she had not dared try hollandaise in case it went wrong. She served him chablis. 'The kitchen and I are not quite up to *haute cuisine*,' she said as she brought the steaks to the table, with the potatoes and a salad which she was not quite sure he could digest. He attacked it with relish. 'But I hope the wine will make up for deficiencies.' He peered at the label on the bottle of burgundy after she had tasted it, and then filled his glass. 'Romanée Conti. You said I'd never find it. Well, I did. I telephoned every wine merchant I could find in the better places in London, and finally found someone in St James's with a few bottles he was willing to part with. I bought just one.'

For the first time a smile flickered over his features. 'I like people who take trouble.' Over the cheese they finished the bottle between them. He moved away from the table and went to sit on the sofa.

'Well, I hear you finished up pretty well in that secretarial course. What now?'

'I'm thinking.'

417

'That's what you said a year ago. You're a year older.' He waved his hand to dismiss her protestation against time wasted. 'All right you have a degree in English which will get you nowhere. You can take shorthand and type. You know that a balance sheet ought to balance. That's just the beginning. You never needed the English degree. You'd absorb that sort of thing through your pores, being the daughter of your father and your mother, too, for that matter. Oh, I know she didn't have much formal education, but to hear her speak one knew she knew. So what will it be? Law, economics?' I hope you don't think of being a teacher or a librarian. Neither would suit your temperament; in any case, it's a waste. What's it to be then?'

'Are you still keeping that seat warm for me at the Clayton Merchant Bank?'

He looked at her for a long time. 'Is that what you want?'

'Would I ask if I didn't? You made me independent, you remember, Mr McClintock. And Bess's legacy has helped. If I wanted to, I could just go on taking courses in this and that. Or I could retire to St Just, and pretend to write poetry. But I wouldn't shame my father by trying that. I could go to Venables and ask them for a job. Sometimes women get to be more than secretaries in publishing. Would I learn anything about banking if I went in as a secretary?'

'It depends. It depends on how keen you are. You wouldn't be a teller, because private merchant banks don't have them. It's a man's world, Livy. You'd find it hard to get past taking letters and answering the telephone. Finance is about the hardest world for a woman to crack. You might find after a year that you wanted to leave and take a degree in economics so you'd have more clout. Even that isn't any guarantee. I can open the door for you. I can't do more.'

'Then open the door. I won't disgrace you. And if I find I don't fit, then I'll apologize and go.'

As he went slowly down to his waiting car he said, 'You made a very pretty bridesmaid. Are you thinking of getting married?'

'I would never have asked for a place with Clayton's if I were.'

'Merchant banks are strange places, Livy. One of the first things you'll learn is discretion. People will think you know everything because you work there. You must learn not to talk.'

She laughed. 'Mr McClintock, you needn't worry. I've already been tried that way.'

He nodded. 'I expect you have.' She stood on the pavement, waved at the departing car, and received a languid wave of the silver-topped cane in response. She stood in the sunshine of the late May evening a long time after the car had disappeared. Across the road on the Westminster playing fields the last overs of a cricket match were being played before the light failed. She wondered how long it had been since Andrew McClintock had toiled his way to the top-floor of a 'walk-up'.

On Coronation Day it rained. Very early in the morning Livy walked from Vincent Square to Seymour House. She had to cross The Mall before the processional route was closed. She threaded and pushed her way through the crowds who had sat or lain all night on the pavements. They were dense, wet and cheerful. Policemen held open just a few crossing points. If she had tried now to take her place in the crowds there would have been little point. Some key spots had been staked out for days. She saw the unfamiliar sight of the big outside broadcast TV vans parked at their special places. The newspaper headlines blared the news; EVEREST CONQUERED! A fit coronation present for a queen.

Seymour House was jammed with people. There were hot trays spread with breakfast dishes. Thea and Herbert greeted her delightedly. 'Didn't think I could get caught up in all this stuff at my age,' Herbert said, 'but here I am.' Ginny had rented TV sets for all the principal reception rooms. In black and white the cameras panned over the crowds on the pavements, gave pictures of Buckingham Palace, the odd quick shot of a peer or peeress in full robes hurrying on foot to the Abbey. She was just in time to see the departure of Dena and Harry in their ermine-trimmed robes – Dena in the white dress she had worn for her presentation at Court, and the robe her mother had worn for the Coronation of King George VI. Harry wore the rather faded red ermine trimmed robe the last Baron Camborne had worn at the King's Coronation, and his ancestor at the Coronation before that. They both carried their coronets, which they would not place on their heads until the Queen had been crowned. Ginny was dressed in stiff cream silk, Blair in morning dress. The police cleared a space for the cars through to St James's Street. It would be many hours before they would be back at Seymour House.

Alex was beside Livy. 'How about some champagne?'

'For breakfast?'

'It's a champagne day.' Nancy, it seemed to Livy, deliberately kept away from them, but there were so many people in the house it could have been purely accidental. 'I hear you're going into Claytons. I wish you weren't. You're deliberately putting yourself under the Old Man's nose. Why not break free?'

'Perhaps I don't need to. It isn't a soft option, going into Clayton's. He'll know every move I make, and I'd better be good.'

'You're damned right.' Then he strolled off.

They cheered with all the people on the streets when the first pictures of the coaches and cavalry escorts leaving the Palace appeared on the TV screens. Glasses were charged with champagne. Cameras panning the Abbey once picked up the face of Dena, waiting with the peeresses, separated by the aisle from the peers. They looked but could not see Ginny and Blair. The ranks of distinguished visitors were scanned, and there was Andrew McClintock. Everyone shrieked and whistled. 'Never thought I'd be proud of the old buzzard,' Chris muttered beside Livy.'I hear he went to dinner with you. He hasn't been to see the show yet.'

A strange silence fell on all of them as the ceremony in the Abbey began. They saw a slight, small, pretty young woman walk down the long aisle, her train borne by eight maids of honour. Everyone stopped drinking the champagne. They saw her beauty in the simple white linen gown

420

in which she was annointed with the holy oil. The most sacred moments of this religious ceremony were screened from the TV cameras. But the cameras were present when the crown was placed on her head by the Archbishop of Canterbury. The cry rang out through the Abbey *Vivat, vivat, Regina!* Peers and peeresses held their coronets above their heads and then lowered them, some askew, some fitting, some not. 'Long live the Queen!' Herbert shouted from the back of the crowd around one of the TV sets. Glasses were being refilled again. People wept when the Queen's husband knelt before her and swore 'life and earthly loyalty' and in their numbers they came, each rank of the peerage represented, to swear the same oath. And then the young woman walked from the Abbey bearing the heavy sceptre and orb, her head held straight under the weight of the crown. 'Damned if I mightn't become a monarchist,' Herbert said.

At the moment when the return procession, travelling in a light drizzling rain, came near to St James's Palace, the guests at Seymour House dashed to the corner where Blair had rented the first floor of an office building, put in scaffolding with planks so that everyone could have a view, and from there they watched the unfolding spectacle: heads of state, kings and queens, princes. Then came the state coach bearing the young woman and her husband. There was a rumour that some mechanical device had been placed in the coach to help her support the weight of the sceptre and orb. Beneath the heavy crown she bowed and smiled. The crowd went wild. Many wept openly.

'How can she stand it?' Chris whispered. 'It's the best theatre I ever saw, and if I were she, I'd be crying my eyes out.'

'Which you are,' Alex said. He carefully wiped the mascara from beneath Chris's eyes. 'I'll have to explain to Nancy that it's *your* mascara.'

They trailed back to Seymour House, and once again the champagne was poured. 'Will we ever see it again?' Alex wondered aloud. 'Will she be the last? I think I have a tough job, but I don't envy her hers.'

421

Caroline and Toby had pushed their way through the dispersing crowds from the place where they had watched the procession from a window of Toby's club in St James's. 'Wasn't it wonderful?' Caroline demanded. 'Just thought we'd look in, since it's so close. The Boltons are giving a party, once they get back from the Abbey, but that could take hours. I'll bet it's a mess, all the cars trying to find their passengers . . .' Eventually Ginny and Blair, Dena and Harry arrived back, having pushed their way through the crowds on foot.

'The Ambassador will have to wait for his car. It's too far for him to walk with these crowds. I'll tell you,' Harry said, 'I felt a fool marching along in these robes. But everyone's in such a good mood, it really doesn't natter. Dena and I raised a few cheers.'

The party at Seymour House flowed on. Everyone kept hoping for just one more appearance of the Queen and her family on the balcony of Buckingham Palace. Harry reappeared in an ordinary suit, and Dena in a day dress. They went swiftly to the buffet tables. 'I'm famished,' Dena said. 'Some people in the Abbey were very cunning. They must have sewn pockets inside their robes. I saw tiny little sandwiches, and more than one pocket flask. I wish I'd thought of it. I was cold.'

Rachel appeared just as Caroline and Toby were leaving. 'I watched it on TV. I didn't feel like camping out.'

'You should have come here, and you could have watched and seen the procession live,' Caroline said. She was eyeing her sister. 'You do look nice, Rachel. New outfit . . .'

Rachel seemed to have gone to unusual trouble. The dress and coat matched, a deep blue which set off her dark good looks. She smiled tentatively at Caroline's compliment, but there was a slight air of dejection about her. She looked younger and more vulnerable than Livy had seen her for a long time; Livy guessed that she had been at some all-day party, and had dressed for it. Perhaps Frazer Campbell had been among the company. But now she was alone, and on this day of national celebration she hadn't be able to face the bedsitter in Pimlico. She had turned, like a child, to the place that had always been home to her in London.

Mark greeted her enthusiastically. 'Rachel, you look great! Here, have some champagne.' Livy thought Mark had had rather too much champagne himself. He had spent the day glued to the TV set, and in running up and down steps helping Knox and Jacques and the maids replenish the buffet tables. There was a TV set in the kitchen, so he had missed very little. It amused Livy to see that he was not only tolerated in the kitchen but actually encouraged. He had learned early to cross that most difficult of barriers in this society, the class one. The staff treated him with amused indulgence, and more or less let him do what he liked. He was staying at Seymour House, so he would be at the party until the very last guest departed.

At last the Ambassador arrived, and was greeted by a round of applause. He looked rather taken aback. 'I almost stopped at the Ritz, but the chauffeur said he thought he could push through to get here. Ginny, I've sent him down to the kitchen. He's as cold and hungry as I am.'

Swiftly Mark rushed to place a small table near the Ambassador's chair, while Knox covered it with a pale yellow cloth and napkin, and laid it with silver. 'Will you let me pick you some things from the buffet, sir?' Mark asked. Knox had come forward with a tall glass of champagne, which the Ambassador waved away.

'The only thing that will get the cold out of my bones is a nice dram of malt whisky. The Glenlivet please, Knox.' He knew perfectly well that Blair's bar would stock almost any brand he cared to name.

Mark sat beside him while he ate, asking what it had been like in the Abbey. 'Damned uncomfortable,' was the reply. 'If it hadn't been for the honour to my country, I would have preferred to be here.' Everyone knew perfectly well that Andrew McClintock had been present in the Abbey only to be able to talk of it later.

'When do you go to Eton?' the Ambassador asked Mark when his first whisky had been downed and refilled, and he had taken the edge off his appetite.

'Year after next, sir.' He added, a little defiantly, 'I'm

423

doing better with my marks, sir. I promised mother . . . but I'd rather play cricket.'

'Compromise, boy, compromise. That's how it's done. Nobody gets all they want.'

'No sir . . . expect not, sir. Shall I bring you some more salmon? Or there's very good roast beef.'

Nancy had come to the Ambassador's side. 'Let me get it, Mr McClintock.' She hurried away before he could speak, and Mark seemed wary of butting into what was not his territory. He watched Nancy as she moved along the tables which still looked perfectly and freshly stocked, as if people had not been eating from them, on and off, all day long. 'She's . . . she's very beautiful, sir. I mean, Mrs McClintock.' It was a slight shock to Livy to hear Nancy called that. Nancy . . . Alex's wife . . . there hadn't been a Mrs McClintock since Ginny had married Blair.

'Yes,' the Ambassador said drily, not caring who heard him. 'My grandson's wife is perfectly beautiful. She's well bred, well educated, though that hasn't given her much in the way of wisdom. The only other thing that's wrong with her is that she isn't pregnant. I imagine she's afraid of spoiling her figure.' He downed the rest of his whisky.

Feeling a little shocked, Livy moved away. She didn't want to hear any more, didn't want to make conversation with Andrew McClintock. It had, on the surface, seemed such a cruel thing to say. Alex and Nancy had been married for less than a year. She told herself to understand him, to understand his age. His father, and then he, had built a great business, an international name. So far, there was only one McClintock to inherit it. Blair had no sons and so long as he remained married to Ginny there would be none. There were Clayton nephews, but they did not bear the name McClintock, nor were they any blood kin to the Ambassador. The dynastic streak in men, she reminded herself, trying to find some charity towards Andrew McClintock, could still run very deep. She felt slightly sickened by it.

People were starting to leave. Out in the park, though, the day was far from ended. People had moved away from The Mall and now spread all over the park. Picnics had been

424

going on for hours, and, from the sound of it, there had been more than hip flasks to keep out the cold and the damp. Livy found her coat, decided she wouldn't disturb Ginny in her conversation with a group of guests, and went to let herself out.

'Here, let me walk you home,' Alex said. 'It could be a bit wild out there . . .'

'It's a long way.'

'That couldn't suit me better.' Had he overheard Andrew McClintock's remark? Whether he had or not this time, she didn't doubt that, in one way or another, he had heard the same sentiment expressed before. He took her arm and marched her through Milkmaid's Passage into Queen's Walk. It was thronged and noisy, and litter lay deep on the usually immaculate path down to The Mall. There was still a press of people around the Victoria Memorial outside Buckingham Palace, still calling for the Queen, though all but the most optimistic must long ago have given up hope that she would appear on the balcony yet again.

'She must be terribly tired,' Alex shouted to Livy through the noise. 'I hope they gave her a good strong whisky and let her put her feet up.'

They were caught in the slow procession of people making their way to Victoria Station. 'Give us a kiss, luv,' a young man shouted to Livy. As she dodged him, and Alex's arm came protectively about her, a wild hoot of laughter went up from his companions. 'Long live the Queen!' one of them shouted.

When they got to Buckingham Gate, Livy pulled Alex aside. 'It'll be quieter this way, and quicker.' They were jostled once again, as they crossed Victoria Street, by the flow of the crowd heading to the station. The walking was easier, but Alex still kept his arm about her. They came to Vincent Square. It was comparatively quiet, though there was still a trickle of people making their way to the bridges leading to the South Bank.

'This is it,' Livy said, stopping before her house.

'Aren't you going to ask me in?' He glanced up at the sky, held out his hands to feel the rain on them. 'Everyone else has been here, even my grandfather.'

425

She shrugged. 'If you feel like a climb.'

'If my grandfather can make it, I think I can.'

She tried once more. 'Won't they miss you at Seymour House?'

He shrugged. 'Let them miss me.' Nancy's name was not mentioned. They climbed the stairs in silence. He looked at the flat carefully, as everyone else had done, but slowly, and with care. 'This is the first time I've ever seen any place you've created for yourself, Livy.'

'I didn't create it, really. It's all made up of odds and ends, mostly given to me by your mother out of the attics and basement of Seymour House. And there's Thea and Herbert's contribution, which one doesn't see every day of the week. The plumbing's fairly primitive, and the kitchen barely adequate . . . however, as they say, a small thing but mine own.' Her defences were down. She had never imagined Alex in this place, had never thought of him here with her, always he seemed in the far-off land of power and money. But she had certainly thought of him, oh, God, how she had thought of him. She added, 'Just because it's Coronation Day I put a bottle of champagne in that tiny refrigerator. Shall we open it?'

He took the cork out with the ease of long experience. She watched him, remembering the wines she had tasted first at Tresillian, then in Washington, at Prescott Hill, in Paris and Zurich, remembering all the things she had learned from these mixed families. With glasses from Seymour House brimming with the good vintage, they hesitated before the toast.

'The Queen's had enough today,' Alex said. 'Let this one be for you and me, Livy. Here's to us, and to hell with the rest of them.'

She made no reply, but drank.

They sat on the sofa, and the twilight of the long English summer's day, when it had rained and a Queen had been crowned, began to close in. Occasionally there was a renewed cheer of revelry. Looking across the Square, they could tell where the parties still continued. 'What a lot of bottles there'll be to collect tomorrow . . .' Her voice was soft, slow.

Was she getting drunk? There had been champagne from early morning; she had not expected to share this last one with Alex. She knew what she had recognized in Rachel's expression; the need not to be left alone at the end of this day.

'Alex . . .' She turned towards him.

His expression hardened. 'Don't go into Clayton's bank, Livy. Don't you see what's happening? The Old Man just needs to keep his hands on you. I was born to it, but you can escape. Get free, Livy. This family can crush you. You can still go . . .'

'Suppose I said I didn't want to go? Suppose I said I'd be grateful for whatever came my way. Don't you understand, Alex? I can't let go. You're the first man I've ever invited to my bed.'

He put down his glass. 'Which is a very good reason for my refusing.'

'You can't refuse me, Alex. I love you.'

He pulled her to him. 'Oh, Livy . . . why did you say that? I've loved you for so long. But I thought it wasn't right for us. I didn't want to be manipulated . . . used, by the Old Man. I didn't want you used. You have always been a free spirit, much more than I could ever be. I couldn't pin you down, like some beautiful butterfly who was meant to fly and live out its short life. My sweet, darling, beautiful girl . . . I could never have married you and forced you into that mould in which I have to live. You weren't meant for those sort of things, Livy. You were meant to create . . . to be free to create.'

'Come to bed, Alex.'

For those few hours, until the dawn broke, she had what she had always desired. At first painful, then sweet. The pause of exultation, then rest, refreshment and passion renewed. She dreaded the first light, the sound of the birds in the trees of the square. She held Alex sleeping in her arms, not wanting to sleep herself, lest one moment of his presence, his loving, be lost.

He went early, when the light showed the littered streets, the dropped flags, the bunting that sagged from a day's rain.

427

'We will never do this again, my love. I can't ask it from you . . .'

'Ask anything. I'll be there.'

He held her closely, burying his head against her shoulder, against the old red wool robe she had worn since she had grown tall enough to inherit it from Ginny. 'I'll never ask for this privilege again. I can't hold you, Livy. Escape . . . get away! Don't be tied by me or my family. But remember this one thing, this most important thing. I didn't just make love to you. This has been a declaration of love. I do love you.'

She listened to his footsteps on the stairs. She leaned out of the window; he closed the street door very softly. She watched him as he made his way, avoiding the strewn bottles, out of the square.

Chapter 11

1

Some of them made their way to Tresillian after the Coronation. The Ambassador, Ginny and Blair travelled down by car. Dena and Harry had preceded them to make sure everything was ready; Livy and Mark went with them. Rachel said she would be too busy to come this year, Chris's play was still running. Caroline promised that she and Toby would 'find time' to spend a few days there. There were a number of American friends and diplomatic colleagues expected. There was still a sense of festivity around them. But Alex had announced that he had to return to Washington, and he and Nancy had stayed on in London only one day after the Coronation.

Mark and Livy slept at her cottage to make room for other guests, and to ease the burden of the housekeeping. But very early in the day they were up there to help in whatever way they could. Mark spent all his time in the kitchen, washing, peeling and chopping vegetables under chef Jacques' direction, standing anxiously over the sauce just before serving. Livy helped Knox with the laying and clearing of tables, stripping and remaking beds for the new arrivals with her Tregenna cousins. There was a constant air of bustle about the house, and for the first time since the war there was no shortage of food and the wine cellars had been replenished. The American guests were enchanted with Tresillian, overlooking the scarcity of bathrooms with good humour. There were many photographic sessions in groups as people came and went. Once, one guest who was only a slight acquaintance of Ginny's, but who had been invited at the Ambassador's request because he was an important contact of McClintock-Clayton, left, along with his tip to Knox and

Jacques, something extra for 'that nice young assistant chef'. Mark was very proud. Throughout those hectic days he had worn chef's checked trousers, a white jacket and neck scarf, loaned to him by Jacques. He ate his meals in the kitchen with Knox and Jacques after the guests had finished.

Blair and Harry could spent only a week there before returning to Washington, but Ginny and Dena had to remain for as long as Andrew McClintock wished to stay, and he seemed in no hurry to depart. The weather was warm and golden, the breezes light, the bay of St Just sparkled, and the fishing fleet brought in prodigious catches. Almost every day the Ambassador was driven down to St Just, and there he called on Thea and Herbert and stayed to take tea or coffee with them. On these occasions he was always accompanied by Livy. When he wished to rest during their wanderings of the narrow St Just streets, they sat in her cottage, or Livy knocked at convenient doors, and they invited themselves and the Ambassador in to visit her cousins. They sat in well-used kitchens, often with enchanting views of the bay. He ate endless pasties, possibly because he liked them, or from politeness, or both. He never failed to say, 'Livy's mother gave me the first one of these I ever tasted. I never forgot it.'

He became a favourite with the struggling artists of the town. Livy suspected that he often bought what his own taste dictated against, and once the pictures were back in Washington, they would be consigned to the attics. He discovered the potter, Bernard Leach, and bought seriously and heavily of his work. He persuaded Thea that a large piece she was working on would look splendid in the secluded garden at the back of his house on Dupont Circle, and he promised that after he died the piece would go to the Corcoran Gallery. He genuinely enjoyed Herbert's pictures and bought many of them. 'It will save you the trouble and expense of going through your gallery. Those fellows always cheat the artist. I haven't room to hang them all, but sometimes I'm stumped to think of a present for some very special client. You don't mind if I spread them around a bit . . .?'

Herbert shrugged. 'Do what you want. I never quarrel

with a patron. I'm glad to have them off my hands, and not to have to have another exhibition this autumn.' The Ambassador enjoyed sitting in the garden, surrounded by the sculptures and the semi-tropical plants that grew there, listening to the bamboos rattle against one another in the light breeze. He also liked to sit out in the little garden where Oliver and Livy had sat. He was often silent and ruminative. 'I miss your mother,' he once said. 'I never saw her down here, of course. But now that I've met your family I can picture her . . .'

And then, at short notice, he left. 'I've spent two weeks of idleness,' he said. 'Any more of it and I shall forget how to work.' He offered dry lips to brush the cheeks of Ginny and Dena. 'I'll see you in Washington. You ought to shut off the guests, and have a few quiet days.' He shook hands with Mark. 'You've done well, young man.' To Livy he said, 'They expect you at Clayton's on 1st September. If I were you I'd start practising your typing and shorthand again. I have recommended you, and I don't expect you to let me down. Work hard, keep your ears and eyes open, and your mouth shut.'

Dena and Ginny stayed on another week. Caroline and Toby had visited briefly at the time when the house had been most crowded. 'Trust her to come when her presence will be most felt,' Mark said sourly. 'She made sure it would be when Mr McClintock was here, and the most important guests. She'll make a good diplomatic wife.'

Caroline had announced, 'I'm pregnant, already. Isn't it disgusting?' But she had laughed happily as she said it, knowing it was what her husband's family wanted to hear. And she had the pleasure of seeing a swift expression of jealousy touch the Ambassador's face.

Finally Dena and Ginny left; Knox and Jacques went with them to look after them at Seymour House. Mark and Livy saw that the house was in order, and Herbert came in his car and took away all the left-over food, and distributed it among the Tregenna families. Livy and Mark settled down in her cottage. Too much of the summer had gone by for Mark to go now to Washington. He was quite happy to stay

431

where he was. 'I feel underfoot there, and rather useless. The only fun I get is when Mother gives a party, and I dress up as a waiter . . .'

'Are you serious about it, this cooking business?'

He shrugged. 'Can you see my mother allowing me to train to be a chef? I have to slog my way through Eton. And after that there are two years' National Service. I think mother's counting on Eton and the army to knock a lot of this nonsense out of my head. What she doesn't understand is that I *enjoy* it. She did it from necessity, and it's been jolly useful. I don't think she can imagine anyone making a living out of it.' He gave her his sudden, flashing urchin's grin. 'It's all very well for me to dress up and play *sous chef* to Jacques. Imagine the shock she'll get when she goes to someone else's party and finds me passing around the *hors d'oeuvres* – and being paid for it. Father's all right. He knows I'll never make a diplomat.'

He spent the rest of the summer hanging around the fishing-boats in St Just, helping to unload the catch, mending the nets, cleaning the decks. He was accepted by the men of Livy's family in the way he had earlier been coddled and loved by the women. Livy borrowed Herbert's car, and they drove up on to the moors, and spent hours walking. They were sometimes drenched by Cornwall's fickle weather; they shared good meals and wine in Livy's cottage. Mark was lean and fit, and wanted the summer not to end. 'I hate to waste this good life by going to school,' he sighed.

They returned to London, to Livy's flat in the last week in August. Mark trailed around with Livy while she bought the sort of clothes she thought would be suitable for Clayton's Merchant Bank. Caroline joined them on the shopping expeditions, giving advice. 'Simple . . . simple . . . keep it simple,' she advised. 'But good quality. The skirts mustn't ever bag in the seat. Never wear cashmere in the office, or the girls will think you're showing off. Save it for weekends. Good quality lambswool, and a fresh blouse every day.' She advised a Burberry: 'No one could object to that.' And then she insisted on a bright red winter coat. 'We can't have you too sombre.' She forced Livy to buy a black velvet suit with a ruffled white blouse.

432

'What for? I couldn't wear that to Clayton's.'

'Well,' Caroline said coolly. 'I do expect you'll be going out some evenings, won't you?' She had found her usual sources of slightly-used model clothes. 'This pewter silk. It would wash out most women, but with your hair, you'll be a knockout.'

Livy looked at it all, and remembered Caroline's lectures of such a short time ago. 'Apart from the evening things, it isn't much different from what I wore at Oxford.'

Caroline turned her sisterly attention to Mark. 'Mother left me money to buy you some new clothes for school. She decided that at the rate you're shooting up, you'd disgrace us all if you went for another term in those old things. And you've grown out of your shoes again . . .'

'I can't help it,' he said.

'No, my love,' Caroline replied cheerfully. 'All the Cambornes are tall. No one would want you a runt. And father left something extra. He noticed your tennis racquets and cricket pads had seen their best days.'

Mark beamed. 'Trust father.'

On the last night before Livy joined Clayton's Merchant Bank, Caroline gave a small dinner party. To their surprise Rachel had agreed to come, and when she appeared she was smartly dressed. 'You see, you can do it when you try,' Caroline said. She was glowing in the flush of her pregnancy, and seemed pleased with life.

Chris had had Livy and Mark to lunch. 'Isn't it wonderful how the play goes on and on? But I must start to look around. If I go on in this part much longer, I'll be typecast as the pert ingenue for the next ten years. I have a tentative link with a New York agent. That might produce something . . . Livy, I just don't understand your taking this job with Clayton's. It's really putting yourself in the trap . . .'

Livy shrugged. 'Oh, it's just to get a bit of experience. I'll be the lowliest of the low there. The new girl . . .'

Chris shook her head. 'There's no way they won't know that Mr McClintock put you there. I think you're in for a miserable time. And God help you the day you decide you've

433

had enough, and opt for something else. The Old Man will never forgive you.'

Mark insisted on accompanying her on the bus to the City on the morning she started work. 'It's a bit like the first day at school . . . you're glad of someone to go to the gates with you.' But he left at the bus stop nearest to the bank. 'I'd better not go any closer. Someone might recognize me from one of Aunt Ginny's parties.'

She went past the heavy oak doors which would not open until ten o'clock, and round to a side entrance. She had already had her initial interview; she gave her name, and stated that she was starting work with Mr Edwards. She knew very well that Mr Edwards was almost as new to the house of Clayton as she, and a long way from a director's desk, if he ever made it. She was in her place ten minutes before he arrived. She had his mail laid out, everything opened except that which was marked confidential. Today, there was nothing confidential.

'Good morning, Miss . . . Miss Miles.' He read through the mail briefly. 'Well, shall we start?' He dictated several letters; she knew she would have to look up the addresses. She knew she would have to ask the help of the girl who had been his secretary, and had now moved up. She learned where the ladies' room was, where she could get a sandwich at lunchtime. She knew she was expected to make coffee whenever it was demanded; she learned that she had to do many things for Mr Edwards which did not strictly come under the heading of secretarial duties. Mr Edwards was distant and polite, and in the first weeks she knew that she was learning very little about banking.

She also knew that there was a certain distance between her and the other secretaries of about her rank. Somehow the word had got around that her job had been 'arranged', and there was some hostility and resentment. She had been sad on the morning when Chris called in her car to take Mark to school at the opening of the new term, and sad to find the flat empty that night. Who needed her now? Not Mr Edwards – any junior would have done for him. Not Claytons. She fought against a wave of loneliness, arguing that

434

in any job it would have been the same. But they had all warned her. Only Andrew McClintock had wanted her in this position. And Andrew McClintock was far away, and wouldn't lift a finger to protect her from any blunder she might make.

After a few weeks she began to relax a little, accepting that banking was a mystery she would be initiated into only slowly. Sometimes she looked at the great marble hall which was far beyond the reach of Mr Edwards at this time. It was tall and pillared, and had a beautiful staircase. Except for the few desks spaced about, and the uniformed commissionaire, it could have been the entrance of a great private house. Occasionally she was sent with papers from Mr Edwards to the office of one of the directors, never to the inner office, just to the secretary, who, besides a good carpet and velvet curtains, nearly always had a mahogany desk. Usually the papers were received with a swift nod; sometimes the secretary's eyes followed her with a certain curiosity. She told herself that in time they would forget about Andrew McClintock in her background. In a year she would not be the newest junior; perhaps she would have a different boss. Mr Edwards was decidedly slower at dictation than the secretarial school had led her to believe, and they were mostly routine letters she could have written herself. She settled into a pattern, and gradually the other girls began to accept her, to speak to her as they passed in the corridors. 'Pretty boring, isn't it?' one of them said one day at lunch time. It was the first time anyone had ever asked her to join them at the nearby sandwich and coffee bar.

'Yes,' Livy agreed. 'I thought . . . I thought somehow it would be more exciting.'

'Not at our level it isn't, or our bosses' level. It's only up there, where they're dealing in their millions that you ever see any excitement. By the time you get there as a secretary, you'll be middle-aged. You've noticed, haven't you? No young chicks up there. Wouldn't be the image of the House of Clayton. You know that, don't you?'

'Beginning to.'

The girl smiled. 'You're not deceiving anyone, you know.

But, any rate, you started where everyone else does. Mr Edwards arrived only a few months before you. He's not sure he'll make it through the first year, either. Myself, I know I'm not going to grow old with Clayton's, or even middle-aged. As soon as I can find someone decent to marry, that's it! We're only drudges, you know. Sort of glorified tea-ladies.'

Livy nodded, knowing that in certain particulars the girl was right. But she continued secretly to read the *Financial Times*, struggling to understand even the nomenclature, not really understanding much of the reasoning behind all the dealings that were written about. The financial press seemed to contradict itself and one another, in every other article. Buy this, sell that. No guarantees. After two months she knew that the way forward was not by the secretarial route. She would stick it out a year, finding her bearings, and then she might have to try for a degree in economics. That would be the only graceful way to bow out of Clayton's, the only way not to infuriate Andrew McClintock. But she was beginning to understand that it was not his anger she feared, but the fact that she might be disappointing him. They had grown closer in those days in St Just. She remembered his last words to her. She didn't want to disappoint him. There had not been a letter from him since then, but she had not expected one. She could not look for more favours when he had already given so many. Some of them were hard to bear, and she was fully aware they were given with the expectation of a return.

The demand for a return came sooner than she thought possible. On a dark, wet November afternoon, just after lunch, the phone rang on Mr Edward's desk, indicating an in-house call. 'Miss Miles . . .?' he said. 'This phone is not available for personal calls for Miss Miles.' He was pompously indignant. 'Who? Oh . . . oh, yes sir. At once, Mr McClintock.'

His face was a rather sickly colour. 'It's *Andrew McClintock! Here!*' He handed her his own phone, and she was obliged to lean over his desk as she listened.

'Ambassador?' she said.

'You're needed. We've arranged a flight for you to Washington tonight. A car will take you from the bank, now! Ginny and Dena will need you.'

'Mr McClintock what's . . . why am I needed?'

'The company plane left Pittsburgh about four p.m. yesterday afternoon, ahead of a snowstorm. It never reached Washington. It's vanished. Alex and Blair were on board.'

'Oh!' She could say nothing more; she felt limp and sick, deathly cold, as if the life blood were draining from her.

'You hear me? You must come at once.'

She struggled to get the words out. 'I'll come.' The connection was broken. Mr Edwards had risen to take the phone from her hand, but she let it slip and it struck the desk.

'Miss Miles . . .' At the door of Mr Edwards' office stood one of the senior directors of the bank, someone so elevated that Edwards had barely spoken to him before. 'A car will be ready for you in a few minutes, Miss Miles. We are arranging everything, at Mr McClintock's request. The driver will take you to your . . . your address to let you get your passport, and to pack what you need. You'll have to be quick. The flight leaves in about three hours.'

'Yes, sir.'

He stepped aside to let her pass, detaining her for just one moment. 'Please give Mrs Clayton and Mr McClintock my deepest sympathy. It is a terrible blow . . .'

Strength had seemed to flow back into her. She did not believe what the message implied. She answered sharply, almost savagely. 'They're not dead yet! Not yet! . . . sir!'

At Washington she was escorted through immigration and customs by an immigration officer. Both the British Embassy and McClintock-Clayton had cleared the way, since her visitor's visa from last year had expired. It was very early in the morning, Washington time, and five hours behind London time. Dena was waiting for her, her face a bleak and drawn mask. 'No news,' she said as she embraced Livy. 'We're going to Ginny's house. Mr McClintock and Nancy are there. We've been in touch with Chris. There's nothing she can do, of course. We couldn't locate her at the time Mr

437

McClintock telephoned you . . . I suppose she could have been on the same plane if we'd reached her in time. But Mr McClintock asked first for you. He hardly seemed to remember Chris . . .' Dena held Livy close to her in the darkness of the car. 'They've been missing two nights now. No news . . . no hope, really.'

Livy noticed that the bare branches of the trees still held a faint covering of snow, but it had been swept clean from the roads and sidewalks.

'The Allegheny Mountains run between Pittsburgh and Washington, don't they? Part of the Appalachian range? Was the storm much worse in the mountains?'

'They always are. The pilot filed a flight plan to take them through the Cumberland Gap. The weather was coming in from the north-west, behind them. I suppose they assumed they'd beat it. Then it got to blizzard conditions. It's tapered off, but it's still snowing lightly in the mountains. No visibility. Oh, my God, poor Ginny. I think she's always been afraid when Alex and Blair flew together in that light plane. But it has happened all the time since Alex started working for the company. He had to be in on everything . . . being groomed to take over some day from Blair . . .' She paused. 'What am I talking about? What am I saying? Unless there's some miracle they're both gone. Mr McClintock refuses to believe it. He thinks they've just put down at some little local airport, and that the storm has taken out the telephone lines, that they'll show up. The newspapers are carrying the story already . . . as if they are dead.'

'I don't believe it, either,' Livy said. The pain in her was anger, fierce and hot. Alex could not be dead, or she would surely know. The invisible bond between them would have snapped; his physical presence would have been wrenched from her heart. And Blair, kind, gentle, infinitely generous and loving, Ginny's husband, Chris's father, would he have left them? She had not so much certainty about Blair. His personality, a *persona* almost, seemed to waver at the edge of her consciousness, almost a wraith-like figure which came and went through a mist of seeing, and then not seeing. Her mind's eye held the image of the mist that settled over the

Tresillian Rocks, their jagged peaks appearing and disappearing. Somewhere Alex clung on, but Blair might have been pulled out with the tide. She shivered violently. Dena drew her closer.

'Try to be strong for Ginny's sake. She's so quiet. Almost withdrawn. She and the Ambassador just sit there, waiting for the telephone to ring. Of course it rings, but there's never any news. Nancy broke down a few hours after the plane was reported missing. Hysterical. The doctor gave her some sort of knock-out pill. The Ambassador wanted her out of the way. You were the first person he sent for . . .'

'He said I would be needed. I didn't quite understand. But it's better here, with you. I don't know how I could have stood it waiting alone in London.'

They had reached the McClintock mansion on Massachusetts Avenue. For a brief time the car was stopped while the big wrought iron gates were opened. Livy blinked in the sudden blaze of camera flashbulbs. She saw men calling questions at them, but did not hear the words. As the car drew up to the house, the door was opened. Ginny appeared at the top of the steps. She folded her arms about Livy, held her, as if seeking strength. 'Thank you for coming.'

Their coats were taken, and Livy's small flight bag, which was all she had time to pack, was taken upstairs. Ginny led them to the library. Andrew McClintock sat in a high-backed chair before the fire, his hands clasped about the head of his cane. He raised his head as she entered. His expression was one of both rage and near-despair, defiance against the fates which might have delivered this unspeakable blow. 'I don't believe it,' he almost shouted to Livy. 'No! I don't believe it. They'll have been forced down somewhere, and they'll be in touch as soon as someone gets to a telephone. Those hillbillies out there, they don't have telephones . . .'

Ginny turned away in anguish; Livy knew she didn't want to hear such talk. She could not endure this hope sustained in the face of odds so enormous. But still she waited by the telephone, waited for the final message.

'Chris is coming,' was all she said. 'She's on tonight's flight . . .'

Livy refused breakfast. The butler had brought fresh coffee and placed a tray of sandwiches where someone might be tempted by them. Ginny poured a brandy and gently forced it into Livy's hand. 'Just a sip.' Silence then settled heavily on the room; there was nothing to say.

Livy tasted the brandy and found it bitter, but its warmth immediately reached her stomach. She drank some coffee. Then she began quietly to circle the room, unwilling to look at the despairing faces of Ginny and Dena.

This had always been her favourite room of the great McClintock mansion, and she knew it was Ginny's also. Ginny had once told her that it was here, during one of Andrew McClintock's unexpected visits, that she had told him and his son that she was pregnant with Alex. There was the smell of old leather and wax. Many of the books were collectors' items. Livy had spent many fascinated hours among these books; they greeted her like friends. At the end of the long room a carved Jacobean strecher table was spread with open books and paper maps. The books were atlases; the papers were large scale maps of Pennsylvania, Virginia and West Virginia. She looked at them for some time, and the feeling that had tormented her through all the long sleepless journey from London returned. Her finger traced a line between Pittsburgh and Washington, the route through the Cumberland Gap which would have been the logical one for the pilot to have taken, the one he had filed. The maps were dotted with the names of small towns, most of them would be barely more than hamlets. The area would be heavily wooded, as well as mountainous.

Andrew McClintock's gaze had followed her. 'Don't bother looking. They'll tell you nothing of what's out there.'

She put down the brandy glass. Her hands twisted together as she stared at the maps; she felt the familiar shape of the opal ring. She gazed down into its depths, and the vision and the feeling of the Tresillian Rocks was very strong. The finger which bore the ring felt both burning and cold. She reached out and touched a place on the map. 'Mount Davis,' she said. 'It's quite plainly marked.'

'The highest point in Pennsylvania,' Andrew McClintock

growled. 'Of no particular significance. Dozens of small peaks in that range. They could be anywhere.'

'No,' Livy said. 'That's where they are. I feel it. I'm sure of it . . .'

'What makes you so sure?'

'I don't know,' she said. 'No reason I can give. Just that something draws me there. It's not just a mark on a map. It's . . . it's *alive!*'

'You're talking nonsense, girl. It's that damned Celtic streak in you. You're tired . . . imagining things. Better get some sleep.'

She walked away from the table, and went to one of the tall windows which looked out on to the garden of the mansion. It seemed uncountable hours since she had boarded the plane in London. Perhaps her instincts were totally wrong, dulled by fatigue, or perhaps sharpened by it. She pulled at the cord which drew back the heavy curtains. The winter morning was now fully light. This side of the house was screened from the cameras at the gates. What they saw in the first light of the day was the glimmer of sun.

Andrew McClintock picked up the telephone beside him. Whoever answered expected his call. 'The weather's cleared? Cleared up in the mountains? The search parties will be going out? Take people with sharp eyes and binoculars to have a good hard look at Mount Davis. Promise those hillbillies any amount of money if they can spot something. But don't call off the searches in any other place. Rouse whole townships, if you have to. These people don't have anything else to do, in any case. And they know the mountains . . . Tell them there's a reward – a large reward.'

Ginny persuaded Livy to go up to bed. She took a shower and lay down, wearing one of Ginny's nightgowns. But there was no rest. Every nerve in her body was wakeful and alert. She closed her eyes and saw endless wooded mountains, hardly more than high hills, but empty, with the leafless trees showing the snow-cover on the ground. By now, since the weather had cleared, other small planes would be scouring the mountains; even the pilots of the commercial flights would be watchful as they came towards Washington from the west. Somewhere, someone must see something.

After two hours she got up and dressed, and went downstairs, again to the library. At first she thought it was empty. But the fire burned brightly, and she smelled fresh coffee. A tray had been placed by the Ambassador's chair, and a cup was half filled. Toast lay wrapped in a napkin nearby, but it was untouched. Then she saw the Ambassador standing near the windows, gazing at the garden. The day was brilliant, bright and sunny. The snow had dripped from the branches of the trees.

'There's been no news?' She hardly needed to ask. The house would have rung with it if there had been.

'No! and it's thawing, damn it! I suppose it doesn't matter, since they've had so much snow up in the mountains. But if it thaws, it makes it harder to spot anything unusual.' As if he had sensed her presence, the butler appeared and poured her coffee, again offering her something to eat. She realized that she was hungry, having been unable to eat any of the meals offered during the Atlantic crossing, yet knowing that just now she could hold nothing down. She went close to the fire for warmth. The figure at the window seemed diminished, shrunken; he leaned heavily on his cane. Livy sank down in the chair opposite the Ambassador's. Her body felt leaden, weighted, heavy. She was not now so firm in her belief that Alex was alive. Something in her – hope, spirit, sureness – was dying.

The telephone rang. She leapt to her feet, and then remembered Andrew McClintock's presence. He moved towards it more quickly than she had ever seen him move before. 'Yes . . .? Yes . . .! Well, don't hang about. Investigate it. But don't let up on the whole search. This could turn out to be nothing. Get them moving!'

He put down the telephone, and looked at Livy. 'They have seen a gash in the woods near the top of Mount Davis. A plane is going in to take a closer look. If they spot anything, a party will set out. We can only hope they make it before dark.'

442

They gathered around the table for lunch: consommé and a soufflé were served, but little eaten. Nancy appeared, looking dull and apathetic; she said nothing to anyone. Harry had come down from the embassy, not with the hope of news, because any would be instantly telephoned, but to lend some support. The inspection by a light plane had confirmed the wreckage near the top of Mount Davis; the rescue teams were now making their way up on foot. There were no roads in the area to facilitate them. 'Rachel telephoned,' Harry said. 'It's been on all the radio bulletins, and in the first editions of the papers. She telephoned Mark at school, and she went to see Chris off at the airport.' They picked over their lunch quickly, and returned to the library for coffee. By now Livy realized that this phone had been connected directly to whomever was co-ordinating the search. Any calls from the press or from friends were being taken on other lines by one of Andrew McClintock's secretaries. The house was eerily silent.

It was growing dark before the news came. Their vigil had been almost unendurable. The telephone rang, and Ginny sprang to answer it, but a gesture from the Ambassador forbade her.

'Yes . . .?' His peremptory tone faltered. 'Yes . . . I hear. Take great care. A plane has arrived? Where is the airstrip? Are they able to take off in the dark? Doctors and nurses on board? A doctor went up with the search party . . . that's good. Yes, here to Washington, of course. Have everything necessary waiting.' He hung up.

For a second he closed his eyes, his face the mask of an old, old man. 'Tell us! – for God's sake tell us,' Nancy screamed at him. She had rushed to him and clutched his shoulder, shaking him as if he were a child. His face hardened, and he brushed her hand aside with surprising strength. 'Behave yourself, girl! You've had your hysterics!'

He walked to where Ginny sat. 'Alex is alive. Burned. A leg and arm badly hurt.' The hand he placed on her shoulder was gentle and sought to comfort. 'I'm sorry, Ginny. My dear Ginny, I'm most deeply sorry. Blair didn't survive. Nor did the pilot. We can only hope that Alex . . .' He dropped

443

his hand. 'There is hope. He's young. They have to bring him down slowly by stretcher. The doctor has done what he can . . .'

Ginny's face was so blanched that both Livy and Dena rushed to support her. But she brushed them aside, and walked wordlessly from the room.

Once again Andrew McClintock picked up the telephone. It was instantly answered. 'Take care of any press matters. Tell them only what you must. We would like peace in this house until Alex is back in Washington.'

Almost absentmindedly he accepted a glass of brandy from Livy. Dena had quietly followed Ginny upstairs; she would watch over her, Livy knew. There might be words those two women could say to each other in private that would never be spoken before others. Tears could be shed, and no one else would witness them.

Andrew McClintock looked at Livy. 'You knew . . . how did you know?'

She shook her head. 'I didn't know. Just a feeling. They would have looked at Mount Davis in any case . . .' What she did not tell him was that coldness was growing in her; she experienced the cold of that blizzard Alex had endured, exposed on that mountain for two nights. The coldness was also the chill of feeling his life ebb away through the weeping agony of his burns. Perhaps the dullness that now lay on her was because he had been given morphine against the pain that the journey down the rough mountain by stretcher must cause. Perhaps the numbness was because he no longer lived. She saw, too vividly, the blackened swathe cut through the trees, the burned wreckage. Blair dead, the pilot dead, perhaps by now Alex dead. But while even the faintest spark of warmth remained within her, she continued to believe that Alex still lived. She touched the Ambassador's hand lightly. 'I think he will live . . . I'm almost sure . . .'

Nancy shrieked at her, 'How dare you think like that about Alex? What do you know? Why should you know more than I? I'm his wife.'

'Then behave like his wife, with as much dignity as you can scrape together. I don't want any tearful faces for the

444

press at the gate when we go to the hospital. I advise you to go to your room and wait. On no account intrude on Mrs Clayton. You'll be called when it's time to go to the hospital. There are some calls I must make. Livy will assist me.'

Nancy faced him briefly, her face twisted with fury. 'It would serve you right if he died, you cold-hearted old bastard. He's the last thing you've got, isn't he? You don't give a damn about my feelings, do you?'

'Quite frankly, I don't. I actually doubt you have any, except fear of what may happen to you. You wouldn't want a disabled husband, nor one whose burns might make him hideous. Perhaps I judge you too harshly, but time will show that. Please leave us.'

The silence of the house was shattered as Nancy slammed the door with all her strength. The Ambassador took a long breath; he seemed to force his body to straighten.

'We must think about who must be informed. Too soon to trouble Ginny about details. We still don't know that Alex will survive. This double blow to Ginny . . . she will bear it bravely if it must be. But I fear for her.'

'Alex will live.'

'For the time being, Livy, I must believe you.'

The newspapers bore banner headlines. Blair Clayton was dead, and the heir to the McClintock-Clayton empire was on the threshold of death. There were pictures of the wrecked plane, interviews with those who had gone up the mountain. There were pictures of a weeping Nancy and the anguished but stoic features of Ginny. They were permitted only to look through a glass partition at Alex. A glass cubicle beyond the door where nurses and doctors donned sterile clothing sought to protect him further from infection while his terrible burns were treated. They saw little but a swathed face, an arm and a leg. The doctors were not yet certain that they would not have to amputate the leg. 'But that,' one of the surgeons attending Alex said to Andrew McClintock, 'may be academic. He could well die from the burns before amputation is necessary.' Some doctors, Livy thought, were very

445

brutal. Why torture the old man with that thought? Andrew McClintock did not relay that information to Ginny.

Livy went to meet Chris at the airport. There was no way to avoid the photographers. Chris had received the news on the plane, and had had time to adopt Ginny's stance. Chris had never looked more like her mother as Livy met her at the bottom of the steps from the plane. Customs and immigration formalities were waived. Everyone knew who Christine Clayton was.

Before the funeral, Rachel surprised them by turning up at the McClintock mansion with Mark. 'We had to come. I had the most almighty row with the housemaster to get him away, but I was determined that this time he wouldn't be left out. I had to lie like a trooper about father telephoning and demanding that he come. I even said Alex was asking for him.'

'Good for you,' Harry said. 'We need all the help we can get. And if Alex should be lucid enough to recognize people, I'd like him to get a glimpse of this ugly mug.' For a moment he permitted himself to hold Mark closely. 'Good to see you, son. I'll back Rachel up in every word she said.'

Mark looked stricken. 'I feel almost as badly as if it had been you, father. I don't know how Aunt Ginny will stand it. Not the two of them . . .'

'There won't be two of them,' Livy said firmly. 'Alex will live.'

'I don't know where Livy gets her information from,' Harry said, 'but I intend to keep on believing her.'

They buried Blair very privately, while Alex still fought for his life, drifting in and out of consciousness. Messages and telegrams poured in from all over the world, from all kinds and degrees of people. 'Blair made so many friends,' Ginny said softly, as the cables mounted. She and Livy and Dena read them all. 'I think this must be from one of the gardeners at the Zurich house. Blair got his boy a place in college . . .' It was placed alongside a message from Korea from General Mike Goodrick, and one from the President. There was a long cable from Caroline to Ginny. She was now five months pregnant and had been advised against flying and the long journey to Washington. *'There was no one like him,'* the cable concluded. *'The dearest friend. Another father to us.'*

The burial was almost secret, to keep the press at bay, arranged hurriedly with the pastor of the little Episcopalian church near Prescott Hill. Members of the Clayton family had come from England. Livy recognized the senior director of the bank who had come to Mr Edwards's room as the message from Andrew McClintock had come through. The flowers were few, because people did not know where to send them. Later, the Ambassador said, there would be a memorial service. Unspoken was the thought that, before that could be arranged, there might be another funeral.

Livy held Mark's hand all through the burial service and on the drive back to Washington, and he did not try to break from her. 'I'm glad he's buried here. It seems more personal. He gave us such great times at Prescott Hill. I wish it could have been Tresillian, but Aunt Ginny and the Ambassador wouldn't have wanted that. Tresillian was the first place I can remember seeing him.' It occurred to Livy then, as it must have occurred to Rachel, that during the long wartime absence of Harry, Blair's occasional appearances at Tresillian might have caused him to assume a father's role in Mark's life sooner than Harry did.

It was a time of terrible waiting. For the first few days the words from the doctors seemed always the same. 'If he survives the night . . .' The nights turned into days. 'With serious burns, it's a matter of being able to keep enough fluid in the body . . .' He had lost three toes and two fingers to frost bite; the state of his leg was still worrying the medical people, but he was not strong enough to withstand an operation.

Although she could never speak to him, Livy observed him often through the glass panel in the sterile room. 'He's getting stronger,' she told the Ambassador. 'He's fighting so hard. He will live. I'm certain now.'

'I still keep on believing you,' he said. 'Though I don't know why I should.' He had not left Ginny's house, though

447

Livy and Rachel and Mark were now with Harry. Dena remained with Ginny, sharing her hours of vigil at the hospital. They had a room on the floor below Alex, where they slept fitful hours but were always within call. Nancy had returned to her parents' house. Mrs Winterton often accompanied her daughter to the hospital. 'She shouldn't really come,' Mrs Winterton said, 'since she can't speak to Alex. It just distresses her to see him this way. If he's to go, it would have been kinder if he had gone like Mr Clayton, quickly, in the crash. This long drawn-out agony . . . sometimes I wonder if doctors really know what they're about. Prolonging suffering . . . it's so upsetting for Nancy. She's always been a highly-strung child.'

'I imagine it must be rather more upsetting for Alex,' Livy said. She had just come from a session of watching through the glass panel, watching for slight movements in Alex, watching how the doctors and nurses reacted towards him. Nancy spent very little time watching by that panel.

Now Nancy said to Livy, 'Why don't you go home? I mean, go back to England, back to that little fishing hole you came from. You're not wanted here. Alex is my husband, and he doesn't need you.'

'I'll go when Aunt Ginny and the Ambassador say I should go. It's none of your business.'

'It certainly is my business. You all still think you own Alex, don't you? Your exclusive little group. Well, Alex is mine, and not even Andrew McClintock can take him from me.'

'All Mr McClintock wants is Alex's life.'

After that she and Nancy did not speak, hardly glanced at each other if they chanced to pass in the hospital corridor. Livy kept her vigil by the glass panel just as long as she wanted to, and Nancy's presence did not drive her away. Once she saw Nancy retreat before her. Nancy did not like to look through the glass panel. She was often in tears.

At last the long waiting paid its dividend. A nurse and a doctor had just finished replacing a dressing, a very delicate and time-consuming task which must have placed great stress on Alex. But before he succumbed to the pain-killing drugs

448

his eyes opened wide, and he seemed to recognize Livy's figure beyond the two glass doors. He managed to raise his uninjured arm in a brief salute. Joyfully, she responded. When he had seemed to fall back into sleep, she raced down to the next floor and woke Ginny and Dena. 'He waved to me! I'm sure he recognized me! He waved!'

She took a taxi to the McClintock mansion, where the Ambassador was still staying, and gave him the news. He grunted, and his whole body seemed to sag with relief. 'Go back to him when you can. You seem to do him good.' He was alone in the house because Chris had returned to London. Rachel and Mark had also gone back. She realized it was now two weeks since they had begun to watch at the glass panel of Alex's room. Andrew McClintock had been bitterly critical of Chris's return to London while Alex's life was still in danger. He had hardly comprehended that she had begun in a new play, *Tempo*, in a strong dramatic supporting role only three nights before the news of her father's death. Unless she returned to it, her understudy would be replaced by some better-known actress. 'What does it matter?' he had said when Ginny tried to explain the situation to him. 'It's only play-acting! She could buy the show if she wanted to!'

After three weeks Alex came out of his isolation room, and they could see and talk to him for short periods. A major operation was performed on his leg, and there were still many operations to go through, many skin grafts in the future, further surgery on his arm and leg. One side of his face and head was still covered in bandages. Livy hardly dared to think of what they would see when they were removed. No one had yet told Alex he had lost his left eye. She spent short periods with him, always making sure Nancy was not already present. Once Nancy had opened the door of Alex's room when Livy stood beside the bed; she had frozen for a second, and then hurled the flowers she carried at Livy.

'For God's sake why don't you go back where you came from?' The door had swung closed.

'Don't tell me my dear wife's jealous?' A lopsided smile appeared on his pale lips. 'Stay a bit, Livy. Don't let her scare you off.' His good hand reached out to her. 'You know,

449

I thought a lot about you when I was lying up there beside the plane.'

They now knew the general facts of what had happened, the snowstorm that had swept into the mountains with appalling speed and ferocity, the battering the plane had taken, the wild swinging of the compass, the total lack of visibility. The radio had gone out, and they had been alone in their world of white, shrieking, roaring nightmare until the plane had ploughed into the mountainside. Alex had regained conciousness many yards from the burnt-out fuselage. He had been aware only of the searing impact, the immediate explosion of the petrol tanks. What remained when he was able to open one eye was the shell of the plane, black against the falling snow. He had crawled to it, able only to pull himself with one arm and push with one leg. He had called to Blair and the pilot, and there had been no reply. Later, between periods of unconsciousness, he had become aware of their charred bodies still within the fuselage. He had crept into the wreck, for some protection, taking the ragged remains of two seat cushions to cover a part of his body, burying himself as deeply as he could in the snow. 'I'd always heard that if you just let yourself go to sleep when you were too tired and too cold to hold on any more, you didn't feel anything. But I kept on waking and hurting. It was so cold, and I was burning. I woke up that morning, and it was bright sunlight. I wasn't dead, but I couldn't move. Couldn't sit up. I remember the terrible thirst. The only good thing about the snow was that it melted in my mouth. I don't even remember the rescuers getting there, not their actually arriving. I didn't hear anything. I suppose someone gave me morphine, because I don't remember much about coming down the mountain on the stretcher . . .'

'Don't talk any more, Alex.' She didn't tell him about the burning sensation in her hands, which had also been cold. But the Ambassador had told him of her insisting that the plane had gone down on Mount Davis. 'It was obvious, wasn't it?' She had shrugged it off. 'It's the highest mountain, and not too far off your set course. I just pointed it out.'

'The Old Man thinks you saved my life.'

450

'That's rubbish.'

'Strange, isn't it though, that your mother just knew there wasn't even a minute of spare time to get Chris up above the tide? . . . The Old Man keeps remembering . . .' He grew tired, and drifted off into a drugged sleep. Livy bent and brushed his dry lips with hers, kissed the uncovered eye. Then she picked up the flowers that Nancy had thrown, and laid them neatly on a table.

That night she and Dena and Harry had dinner with Ginny and Andrew McClintock. The Ambassador seemed to cling to Ginny. He now spent a few hours each day in his office, but had not yet returned to his own home. Dena and Harry were expected each night for dinner, along with Livy. The rest of the world was excluded.

'I think it's time I got back to Clayton's,' Livy ventured. 'I just hope they've kept my place. I did write to Mr Edwards . . .'

'They know better,' Andrew McClintock said. 'No one would dare fire you in these circumstances. I've seen to it. What's your hurry?'

'I think, Mr McClintock, that you don't realize how difficult it is to be an employee and a . . . well, a protégée. I'm between two worlds.'

'You were needed. I sent for you. The rest of it is none of their business.'

'I think,' Ginny said gently, 'that you have to let Livy get on with her life now. She's given us enough.'

He was displeased, and remained silent through the rest of the meal. The next day he moved back to his own house. Ginny's face wore a look of painful concern when his car had taken him away. 'I suppose he thought I was saying that I should be left to get on with my own life, too,' she sighed. 'What a waste! The old man and I living only a few blocks apart in houses far too big for us. Living just with the hope of being able to help Alex recover, to get back to some sort of normal life, and that job rightly belongs to Nancy.'

'A job I don't think Nancy is very eager or able to take up,' Dena observed. 'She seems to shrink from him. Perhaps

451

if you did stay, Livy? Alex always seems brighter when you're there.'

'Which is perhaps why Nancy doesn't do very well with him,' Livy replied. 'I've got to leave.' she looked in turn at each of the women. 'Do I have to say any more than that?'

Ginny nodded slowly. 'I understand. You must go. I'll say goodbye to Alex for you. Come back in the summer. Things will be different then . . . come back and spend time with me at Prescott Hill. I need company. The right company.'

'I haven't got months of holidays any more,' Livy reminded her. 'With all the weeks I've taken off, I wouldn't dare ask Clayton's for holidays so soon.'

'Why don't you chuck the wretched job?' Ginny said quickly. 'You know you're not going to get anywhere as a secretary. Unless . . . unless you marry, they'll let you moulder there until you end up a tight-lipped secretary of uncertain age looking after the chairman of the board . . .'

'I've got to give it a year. When Mr McClintock arranged it, I knew he wouldn't be pleased if I didn't give it a go.'

'Well,' Ginny said, 'you're damned if you do, and damned if you don't. He's furious with you for going back just now.'

Livy tried the next day to make an appointment with him to say goodbye. The answer from his assistant was that Mr McClintock would be in conference all day.

She let Ginny make her farewell to Alex. 'He'll think I've deserted him,' she said to Dena, 'but you both know why I have to go.'

Harry and Dena went to the airport with her. 'I wish you would stay, dear heart,' Harry said, 'but I know you can't. Come to see us when you can.'

'Won't you be coming to Tresillian this year?' Livy asked. 'Won't you be coming when Caro's baby is born?'

'It's . . . it's uncertain,' Dena said. 'I don't want to leave Ginny. If she would come . . . if Harry got some leave. But it will depend on Alex. He isn't halfway through the operations yet. All the skin grafts . . .' She shivered slightly. 'I hate to think of what he will look like when all the grafts are done. A mutilation . . . to one of the most handsome men I've ever seen. A mutilation . . .'

452

'He'll still be Alex,' Harry reminded her. 'And he'll need friends who can face him and not turn away.'

Livy returned to Mr Edwards, tried to make sense of what the temporary secretary left to her, and knew she would find it difficult to stay even the year she had set herself. Mr Edwards was patient and sympathetic. 'What a terrible ordeal for poor Mrs Clayton and for Mr McClintock. Do you think that young man will ever be able to return to his desk?'

'In time, Mr Edwards. Alex can't be idle. But no one yet knows how badly his arm and leg are affected. He used to be such a great athlete. However, when I last saw him, there was nothing wrong with his brain.'

'Miraculous how he survived at all. Two nights and days on that mountain in the snow . . .' The details of the crash were almost as well known to the most junior clerk in Clayton's Merchant Bank as to the members of the board. No chairman had been elected to succeed Blair Clayton. They all seemed to be waiting on word from Andrew McClintock, who appeared in no hurry to indicate his preference. They functioned as they always had; decisions were made, but always with the thought that Andrew McClintock could veto them. Uncharacteristically, Mr Edwards confided in Livy. 'Everyone up there –' He nodded towards the ceiling, indicating the offices of the high and mighty, 'seems afraid to proceed with anything major. Mr Clayton had always approved the big ventures, and beyond him, there was Mr McClintock. They say . . . they say no one can get any answers from Mr McClintock these days. Of course, he's an old man . . . Perhaps he's thinking of stepping down.'

'Mr McClintock,' Livy said firmly, 'will not step down until Alex is ready to take his place. There will be no interim emperors of McClintock-Clayton.'

For once Mr Edwards's shy eyes looked at her fully. 'That's what you think, Miss Miles?'

'I know, Mr Edwards.'

Livy endured the months at Clayton's Merchant Bank, living on the letters from Dena and Ginny, feeding off every scrap of information about Alex's progress. He had taken the fact of the loss of his left eye stoically, and even joked, Dena said, about the black patch which covered it. The loss of the toes had not yet troubled him, but the fingers were visible, and, even on the left hand, difficult to become adjusted to. It was less easy to joke about his appearance.

Dena wrote:

> The burn marks are still very vivid. They say in time they will fade, but his face is really destroyed. His leg is much better. He is walking on crutches, which I imagine is very painful to both his leg and his arm, which has to take the weight. Poor Alex! I never thought I'd find myself thinking that of him. He had everything in the world . . . now that he's out of hospital he has gone to his grandfather's house, because that has a lift in it. He can't manage the stairs in the Georgetown house. Nancy is still living with her parents. She goes every day to see Alex once she's sure Mr McClintock has left for his office. She and Alex have lunch together, I understand. Alex can't use his hand well enough yet to cut his food. She does it for him, and at night Mr McClintock does it for him. Of course there's a nurse with him, helping him to bathe and dress. Nancy doesn't have to do any of that. Nancy refuses to meet Mr McClintock. There must have been some terrible row between them.

There were sad letters from Ginny.

> I seem to lack the courage to live without Blair, but I know I must live for Alex. So I just take it as he does, one day at a time. I am, I'm afraid, very demanding of Dena, but she is such a wonderful support. Alex is driving himself too hard, and I don't know how to stop him. It will be better when the elevator in the house is ready and he can come here, and better yet when he

can go to Prescott Hill. And yet his presence is the prop of Mr McClintock's life. I hate to take him away.

From Alex himself there was no word, although it was his left hand which was affected, and Livy knew very well he could have written if he wished. She wrote brief notes to him, not revealing as much as she knew of the circumstances of his life. She was glad to have the Easter visit to St Just to write about.

Mark does most of the cooking, and I am shamefully lazy. We go up to Tresillian every day, and meet the ghosts of ourselves at every turn. What a long time ago it seems since you walked into the kitchen and took over all our lives.

Because she was writing a joint letter with Mark she dared to add, '*We all miss you very much.*'

. On Easter Monday they had a telephone call from Toby Osborne, as excited as Livy had ever heard him. 'Caro's had a baby boy. Both very fit and healthy. I've cabled her parents.'

Mark and Livy went directly from the train to the hospital to visit Caro and the baby. She was radiant, and the baby was a bawling, lusty scrap of humanity. 'Well, what a relief! At least if we have all girls after this, I'll have performed my dynastic duty. But he is rather gorgeous, I think. No, of course Mother shouldn't have come trekking over here. I had a lovely telephone call from them both, delighted to be grandparents, and that the baby's so well and strong.' She beamed upon a world in which her place was now secure.

Mark talked gloomily about going to Washington for the long summer holidays. 'It'll be nice to see father and mother, but I don't like Washington much. Perhaps, though, we'll be at Prescott Hill, but that will be so changed now. I'd really much rather go down to St Just.' This was to be his last term at prep school, and Eton was ahead of him. 'I'll hate it. They'll expect me to measure up to father and grandfather . . .'

Mark eked out his last term, and Dena made arrangements for him to come to Washington. He was to have a week in

London with Livy before he travelled, and the highlight of the week was his being one of the godfathers to Caroline's baby. Dena had sent money for new clothes, anticipating that he would have grown out of last year's. Chris and Livy went shopping with him, taking great care over the suit which he would wear to the christening the next Saturday. Then Chris treated them to lunch at the Mirabelle, where she was well known. 'There's talk that they'll take *Tempo* to Broadway if Equity lets us in. There must be some way I can get an Equity card, since I'm an American. The show's run much longer than anyone expected, but we've only a few more weeks before we'll have to close. Broadway in the fall would be good.'

'Then you can spend some time in Washington after the play closes here.'

Chris looked uncomfortable. 'I know I should go and see mother and Alex, but I can't quite face it. I still really haven't grasped the fact that father's dead. He just seems to be on one of his long business trips. If I saw Alex, the way he is, I'd have to face the fact that father died in a terrible way. I'm not sure that I wouldn't resent the fact that Alex lived and father didn't.'

'You're a coward,' Mark said very plainly and soberly.

She looked at him without anger. 'You're dead right. A coward is what I am.' She paid for the lunch. 'I'll see you before you go. Don't hold this against me. I'm just not ready yet to face what I should face. It's easier to get up there on the stage and pretend to be someone else.'

'Poor Chris . . .' Mark said on the bus back to Vincent Square. Livy knew the remark had nothing to do with money. For that moment Mark had not only bridged the gap in age that separated him from the four women, but he seemed ahead of them in some respects.

They were invited for a drink to Rachel's new flat in Dolphin Square. The modern building had been built just before the war, and was the largest block of flats in Europe – with an inner garden the size of a city square, a small shopping arcade, a swimming pool, squash courts and a restaurant. Rachel had graduated from the London School of Economics, and had already taken a job with the Trades Union Congress, as a research assistant. 'I felt,' she said, 'that with the job, and a bit of an assist from Bess's legacy, I could afford to get out of that slum.' The flat had only one room, overlooking the river. 'But at last I have my own kitchen and bathroom. It seems an unbelievable luxury after sharing a bathroom with about ten other people of dubious habits.'

The light and the view of the river were what Rachel cherished most. Mark explored all the other features of the vast place with interest. 'She might have given us a meal,' he said, as they walked back to Vincent Square. 'It's a much better kitchen than you have. It must have taken a bit of pull to get an unfurnished flat in there. I expect it was the Campbell man. He'll use it as his little *pied à terre*. Nice and handy to the Houses of Parliament.'

'Mark, I shouldn't forgive you for saying that, but I have to.'

'I know . . .' he said gloomily, 'it's not written about in the newspapers yet, but it will be. One of the boys at school made some remark about Campbell and Rachel. He seems to be related to Campbell's wife in some way. I gave him a bloody nose, and he shut up. I hope it was before he had blabbed it all over the school. Well, who cares? I've left the place now. I just hope she sees sense. It wouldn't do for an MP to get a divorce and marry her.'

They attended the christening in the church in which his parents had been married of Henry Ian Mortimer Percy Osborne. Andrew McClintock was a godparent by proxy; he and Mark were the only ones of the eight godparents who didn't have a title, but Livy reflected that one day even Mark would have one. 'Well,' Mark said, 'I expect Caro roped me in because I haven't done anything terrible yet, and she had to have one of the family. Rachel wouldn't do, or Chris. And you aren't family, Livy. Mr McClintock is there because he's her godfather, and can send a handsome cheque as well as the same gold christening mug. Naturally, they didn't expect him to attend. He won't be leaving Alex's side for a long time. But still a useful name to have among the godparents.'

'Mark, you're the most awful little cynic. Caro is very nice to us, had us to dinner to see the baby . . . what more can you expect? She's married, a mother, and busy.'

'I still think you should have been one of the godparents. If the crunch came, I'd bet you'd be the only one who'd do something.'

But he enjoyed the reception at the House of Lords. He drank champagne with the best of them, and passed on the food as 'quite good'. He had borrowed from his father to give the baby a present: a set of beautiful lead toy soldiers almost a century old. Toby Osborne was thoroughly approving. 'They just perfectly fit in with mine,' he said. 'Adds nicely to the collection . . . The child already has enough teddy bears.'

Andrew McClintock's gold christening mug was prominently displayed. People Livy only vaguely remembered from Caroline's wedding came to ask about Alex's health, and sent good wishes. 'Aren't you something in the City?' one young man enquired of Livy. 'Something in Clayton's Bank? We must get together sometime. I'm with Dunston, Firburn.' It was a well-known firm of stockbrokers. Unlike the man who had sought information from her about Clayton's, Livy didn't think he had an ulterior motive. She gave him her telephone number without much enthusiasm. 'No,' she answered his query, 'I'm not planning to be away this summer. Just a few weekends in Cornwall. I took rather a lot of time off before Christmas.'

He nodded his head sagely. 'Yes . . . that would have been the time Blair Clayton was killed. What a waste of a brilliant man. I'm so sorry. He did a lot for this country during the war.' She looked at him with some interest now; at least he understood that much about Blair. She decided that if he ever telephoned, she would accept an invitation. Life without Alex had to be lived, somehow.

Rachel had accepted an invitation to the christening, but didn't attend. Dena's sister, Ellen, was there; Mark reckoned it was two years since he had seen her. Edward and Verity had sent regrets, and a modest present. Chris had come to the reception, between the Saturday matinée and the evening

458

performance. Her appearance caused a little swell of interest among the guests. Livy reflected that the young man from Dunston, Firburn, whose name she had already forgotten, would have done better to get Chris's telephone number. But he might have had a long wait for a dinner engagement with her.

They went back through the balmy early June evening, walking along the Embankment to Lambeth Bridge, and cutting through to Vincent Square. Livy planned to take Mark out to dinner at an Italian restaurant he liked, after they had packed his bags. He was to leave the next day for Washington.

She poured them both a sherry, and they opened up his bags. 'Next time I pack them,' he said grimly, 'it'll be for Eton.' They were made of old, stout leather. 'My father used them,' he said. 'I suppose my grandfather did, too. They probably know their own way to Eton.'

The telephone rang. Dena's voice, strangely hesitant. 'Was the christening lovely? I imagine Caro looked beautiful. I'm dying to see the baby. Our first grandchild. Mark's ready to fly tomorrow . . .?' There was a long pause. Livy sensed her unease.

'There's something wrong, isn't there? What do you want me to do?'

'Livy, could you arrange it with the bank to give you a little time off. Even a few weeks would be a help.'

'What's happened?'

'It's Nancy. Her mother says she's had a nervous breakdown. She's been put in some sort of sanitorium or nursing home in Maryland. Mrs Winterton says it's all the strain of Alex, trying to help him get well.' For a moment Dena's voice hardened. 'If the truth be known, I don't think Nancy can bear to look at Alex any more. A visit from you might help, Livy.'

'I'll see what they say at the bank. When they know where I'm going . . .'

She gave the news to Mark, tipped out the sherry, and poured herself a whisky. Then she sat and looked at the empty bags to be packed. 'Well, I always meant to give up that job. I need an economics degree. So what if they fire me? It doesn't look good on one's record, but I can always say it was part-time, which is what it's turned out to be.'

The phone rang again. Andrew McClintock came straight to the point. 'That stupid girl is having a permanent case of hysterics. You're needed here, Livy.'

'But what can I do?'

'More things than you know. You can chuck that job with my blessing. You can start a degree course at Georgetown University. I'll handle the immigration part of it. You'll be a student. Mark's flying tomorrow, right? Well, I've changed his booking to first class so he can be with you. What's that? Of course I've got two tickets. They'll have them for you at the airport. All you have to do is pack. Be on the plane with Mark. Did you give my new godchild my greetings? Trust Caroline to produce a son and heir with admirable promptness. I wish my granddaughter-in-law had done the same thing. It might have helped her keep her balance and given Alex something to live for. Well . . . perhaps it's just as well. Unstable stock. I knew it all along. It can't be helped now. I should have stopped it in the beginning. She never was right for him . . .' He allowed himself no further reflections. 'The flight is direct to Washington, with the usual stop at Gander. You'll be met on arrival.' He hung up.

Livy looked at Mark. Most of Andrew McClintock's shouted message over the rather crackling line had been clearly audible. 'Well what choice do I have? If I don't go he'll see that I'm fired from the bank. I'm supposed to be ready to go with you tomorrow. I'm supposed to enrol at Georgetown University. I'm supposed to help in ways I don't understand. I expect I'll be given a rather more generous allowance from the trust fund, and I'll live either with your mother and father, or with Aunt Ginny, or wherever I'm put. I'm supposed to lock up this flat tomorrow and walk away from here . . .'

'Do it! It's far better than that sticky job at the bank. You might be able to help. Probably you'll turn into everybody's dogsbody. But there are worse things than that. At least someone needs you.' Then he gave her his peculiar, enchanting, urchin's grin. 'At least I'll have you with me all summer.'

'I won't be your dogsbody, you wretch.'

'Nor will you. I'll be your slave and Alex's too. I'll be so nice to the Ambassador that maybe he'll decide I should go to school in Washington, just to be on hand so to speak. All kinds of possibilities.'

'Scheming little devil, aren't you? It will take hell and high water to get you out of Eton. The Ambassador knows what that signifies for the future.'

Mark's face darkened. 'It does mean, of course, that I won't be able to come to you for the holidays. It will be Caro or Chris, and neither of them really wants me.'

'There's Thea and Herbert. At a pinch, you're quite capable of looking after yourself in my cottage.'

He brightened. 'Yes, of course. Come on, let's go out to dinner, and then we can pack.'

'Don't you think we should make a sandwich and pack, and . . .'

'No! I don't mean to be cheated out of my dinner. There's plenty of time.'

He sat across the table from her, and, in the candle-light and the new, grown-up suit of clothes, the waiter seemed perfectly happy to serve him wine. He talked about what they would do that summer, as if it would be like all other summers. Did he forget Blair would not be there, Livy wondered? Did he forget that Alex could not be his companion on the tennis court and on horseback as he had been? Did he even realize that Ginny would be sad and lonely, that Prescott Hill would never again be the place he remembered? No. Why should he? He was going there to do what he could to help. She was already laying bets that he would face Alex's disfigurement with a complete lack of embarrassment. There was enough of the child left in him to be able to do that. He was the one who would not turn away.

The telephone began to ring as Livy unlocked the door. It was Alex. 'I've been trying to get you for hours. Livy, don't do it,' he begged. 'Don't get dragged into this thing. Don't you see, the Old Man's getting you at last, and he's using the worst of all weapons, pity. I don't need pity, Livy.

461

I don't *want* it! You can't help Nancy. You can't do anything for me. Don't play into the Old Man's hands . . .'

'Perhaps it's what *I* want! Perhaps I'm not doing it for you or anyone else. Mind your own business, Alex!' She hung up.

Mark was exultant. 'That's the way to talk! That's the way to make him think you don't give a damn! You can't pity him, or be soft with him. Don't ever let him think you're sorry for him. In a way, Chris is right. It might have been him and not Uncle Blair who died.' He began loading his bags with clothes, throwing them in haphazardly. 'Hurry up,' he ordered. 'We have to be out of here tomorrow morning.'

But in the midst of the rush and her own uncertainty, Mark showed an admirable practicality. 'I don't suppose you'll want to give up this place? Might need it if it doesn't work out in Washington. Well, I'd better get hold of Chris, or Rachel, and explain. Or even Caro. Yes, Caro might be better. She'd understand. You see, you can't leave Herbert's pictures here, or Thea's sculpture. Once the other tenants know you're not here . . . Yes, I'll get hold of Caro. I'll tell her she can have them on a "long borrow". Tell her they'd look nice in her hall. We can drop off a set of keys at her house in the morning . . .'

He planned and talked all the time they packed. He was up early and had breakfast made for her before she was awake. She didn't have a moment to ponder her decision. He didn't give her a chance. They dropped the keys of her flat through Caroline's letter flap early the next morning, as he had arranged. He talked as they waited in the first-class lounge. He bought her two novels from the bookstall. 'Cheap and nasty, no doubt, but a nice change from your old classics. It's a new life, Livy.'

He didn't stop talking until the doors had closed on the Constellation. He accepted champagne for them both from the hostess as soon as they were airborne. Then he slumped back in his seat. 'I thought I might not get you here. I thought you might reconsider.' He looked around him. 'Well, I hope they feed us well for all the money Mr McClintock is paying for this. I suppose I am the most awful snob, and totally different from Rachel, but when I get rich I intend to do everything first class.'

'How will you get rich?'

'I don't know yet. But when I do, I intend to have the most first-class restaurant in London. I won't just be the owner. I'll be the *maitre chef de cuisine* as well. That way, I'll be the king!'

Later when their berths had been made up, and Mark lay asleep across the aisle from Livy, his face wiped clear of all the spurious sophistication, Livy parted the curtains to gaze down on the endless reaches of the Atlantic. Mark sought a kingdom; she, unsure, bewildered, did not know what there might be for her. 'Alex . . .' she whispered. The hostess offered her another pillow and a blanket. But she did not sleep.

Dena and Ginny met them. 'Thank you for coming,' Ginny said. 'It could make a difference.'

'I don't know how, but I'm here.'

'I'm hoping that it will be you who manages to get him out of the house. He still goes to the hospital every day, but that's a protected environment. No one pays any attention to someone who's twisted and scarred there. There's usually so much worse to see. The elevator's been installed, and after all that trouble he insists on climbing the stairs most of the time, except when he's terribly tired. It was really that, moving in with me that triggered Nancy's breakdown. Once he was out of Mr McClintock's house, there was no reason on earth why she couldn't have moved in with us . . .' Ginny's voice faltered. 'With me,' she corrected herself. 'God knows, there's plenty of room. But she refused. She had a row with Alex, and she became hysterical. I called a doctor, who sedated her. When she woke up, her mother had arrived to take her off to a nursing home. They say she needs complete rest and quiet. That means she is not to see Alex. And I do mean see him. She can't quite hide her distaste, almost disgust. Alex isn't a freak, but that's the way she treats him.'

'Are we going to see him right away?' Mark asked. 'It would be better, wouldn't it?'

'No,' Dena said. 'You'll come home to me, as you'd

normally do. Have a bath, some sleep. Tomorrow you'll go over and have lunch with Ginny and Alex. Again, as you'd normally do. The Ambassador will be there. He sees Alex every day. Everything must seem perfectly normal. Livy, you're just accompanying Mark, taking the summer off, and you're excited about enrolling at Georgetown University for a course in economics. That's the only way forward in banking. The secretarial work would have been just a dead-end.'

'There's only one thing wrong with all this reasoning.' Livy told them of the telephone call from Alex. 'He knows it's all arranged. And he knows why. I denied it. I said I had my own selfish reasons for wanting to make the change. I don't think he believed me. But I was tough with him. No pity . . . no "I'm coming to help you" bit. In fact, I hung up on him.'

'Good,' Ginny said. 'That will have done a world of good. Everyone's been tiptoeing around Alex ever since the accident, so afraid of hurting him, never giving him an argument, letting him have things all his own way. If he has to be dragged back into the world, someone must do it. In fact, I feel more than a little sympathy for Nancy. She's simply not tough enough for that job.'

They met in the drawing-room of Ginny's house before lunch the next day. Alex was not with Ginny as she stood in the hall, and she nodded towards the drawing-room. 'He's in there. This is the first time anyone who's not seen him since the accident has come here.'

Livy did not approach timidly. She wore a simple green-patterned cotton dress which she knew flattered her. She let her running steps sound loudly on the marble floor. There must be no quiet, invalidish approach to Alex. She flung open the door, making more than the usual amount of noise.

'Well, don't you owe me an apology? No letter all this time. I'm tired of writing to an ungrateful friend.'

He was standing with his back to her, against the light from the windows, supported by crutches. The always slender frame now seemed stick-like. He turned clumsily on his crutches. 'Livy. Good to see you.'

464

'Is that all I get?' She ran towards him, reached up and kissed him fully on the lips. He could not fend her off. She held his head, and turned it to the light. 'Not bad! Not bad at all! Did you thank them for the wonderful job they've done! I swear to you, last time I kissed you, when you were all swathed in bandages, I wondered if there was ever going to be a time when we'd kiss again.' The scarred side of his face was a livid red, the skin shiny and smooth from the grafts. That side of his mouth was slightly drawn up, the eye socket was hidden by a quilted black patch. 'You look rather dashing, you know, Alex, the pirate! That's what they're going to say when you get loose in the banking world and Wall Street again. Watch out! Alex McClintock the pirate! Your grandfather's reputation won't stand a chance once you get loose. You'll be twice the man he is.'

She stood back from him. 'Don't I even get a hug? Here, let go of that crutch and let me feel your arm around me. You don't need it all the time on your right side. It functions perfectly well, as I've been told. *Alex! It's me, Livy!* You're not going to push me off and treat me like a stranger. Don't you remember, we've loved each other since we were kids! The prince in his castle and the scullery maid, if you want it that way. But we've loved each other. Oh, Alex, for God's sake, kiss me, hug me! Make me feel welcome at least!'

The crutch on his right side fell away. She felt his arm around her. The kiss he gave her was at first tentative, and then warmer. As he felt the response of her lips, and the strong embrace of her arms, it was near passion.

'Oh, Livy, I've longed for the sight of you.'

'Then there was no need to be so bloody rude on the phone. There's no plot, you know. I knew I was leaving Clayton's. I realized pretty quickly I needed a degree in economics. I was homesick for you all. This isn't the first summer I've spent in Washington . . . I enjoy it here.'

'Mind if I shake hands,' Mark said. 'Last time I saw you, you couldn't even raise that good hand, much less the bad one.' Livy was almost pitifully grateful to Mark that he didn't shrink from using such words, referring so openly to Alex's disabilities. 'I was looking at you through two lots of glass

465

windows, and thought maybe I'd never shake hands with you again. Well, you gave us all a big scare. Not fair. You're not supposed to worry a boy when he's taking his final exams at prep school. You might have ruined my career for ever! I might not have followed in the footsteps of my distinguished father and grandfather. In fact, I did a bit better than anyone expected. I captained the First Eleven, and I made the rugger team, and every time I was in the scrum and did a bit of dirty work, strictly against the rules, I thought "Here's one for Alex".'

'Thanks,' Alex said. He looked down at the crutch which had fallen, waiting.

'You don't expect me to pick it up, do you? Mark said. 'I'm your best friend, Alex, not your dogsbody.'

Alex was silent as he lowered himself on to the nearest chair, and used one crutch to draw the other towards him. He got both under his arms and rose. 'Neat!' Mark observed. 'Very neat. But you'll soon be able to do with just a cane, and then probably nothing. Unless you want to keep it for a status symbol, like that eye patch. Well, let's go. They're having sherry in the library, and if we hang about they'll probably ruin a very good lunch.'

Livy was appalled as she walked beside Alex to the hall, and then to the library. It took a long time. Mark covered the time with chatter, mostly about the christening. 'I was nifty as a godfather, but no one outdid the invisible but potent presence of Andrew McClintock, former Ambassador to the Court of St James's.'

It was as if one side of Alex's young body had been stricken by a stroke. He had learned to use the crutches with dexterity, but a sideways glance at his face showed her that the movements were a painful effort.

They had reached the library at last. Livy felt it had been one of the longest journeys of her life. Alex greeted Dena and Ginny with a little nod, seated himself and took a glass of sherry. Dena was a daily presence in his life. She moved swiftly to give him a light kiss on the cheek; Livy saw that she chose to kiss him on the skin graft. They waited for Andrew McClintock.

466

Alex's voice wasn't quite steady when he spoke, but he kept his words light-hearted. He was wearing cotton pants and an open-necked shirt, with rolled-up sleeves. Livy noted how powerful the muscles of the right arm had become, probably in an effort to compensate for what the left arm could not do. 'I hope you both realize what an honour I've done you by staying home for lunch. Usually at this time I'm labouring along under the whip of an Amazon physiotherapist.'

'Well, maybe you'll let me come along a few times as an observer,' Mark said. 'I'd like to see how muscles are built up – scientifically, that is. At school it's all brawn, but not much brain. If I'm ever going to make a go of Eton I'll have to . . .'

They were aware from the sounds outside that Andrew McClintock had arrived. He paused in the doorway. To Livy he seemed much stronger than when she had last seen him. Now he was secure in the knowledge that Alex would live; no one could yet tell him how Alex would choose to live what life he had.

'Good afternoon, Ginny. Dena.' He looked at Livy and Mark, who had risen to greet him. 'Well, it's wonderful to be young, isn't it? You two look very fresh after that journey.' Alex had come towards him on his crutches. A visible, though swiftly suppressed flicker of emotion crossed Andrew McClintock's face. 'You seem in fine fettle, Alex.'

'I'm starved,' Mark said. 'Aunt Ginny, can we go in to lunch?'

'Manners!' Alex said, with mock severity. 'But I'm starved too. I'm sure they're bored waiting for us. Let's go, Mark.'

Ginny and Dena waited. Andrew McClintock said to Livy, 'I don't know when I've ever seen you look prettier. Let me have the honour of your arm.'

They went to Prescott Hill, away from the humid heat of Washington. On the surface, most things seemed the same, but everything was different. Here, Livy found that she missed Blair the most. At the Washington house he had been a fleeting presence, a host taking care of his guests, the discreet banker forever being called to long, private talks on his telephone in his study. At Prescott Hill he had been more visible, swimming, riding, playing tennis. There was a silence over the place Livy was not accustomed to. There were no guests.

'People don't like to come unannounced, as they used to,' Ginny explained to Livy. 'But if I suggest a little lunch party or a barbecue to Alex, he panics. I think Mark understands how to treat him almost better than any of us. He's giving him no more sympathy than a boy at school recovering from chickenpox.'

A gym had been fitted up in one of the rooms, and Mark and Alex worked out daily together. One day, in a leotard Chris had sent, Livy went in to try out the various machines that had been installed. Mark let out an appreciative whistle. The male physiotherapist who came every day from Washington looked apprehensive. 'Oh for goodness sake,' Livy said haughtily, 'you've seen women before, dressed and undressed. I'm stiff and out of shape. Since everyone else is hell bent on getting fit, I might as well join in.'

This way she was able to see Alex in his gym clothes, to realize the extent of his injuries. Both his left leg and arm were twisted and somewhat wasted, the knee, hip and elbow were stiff. Once Alex had got over her unannounced entry into the gym, once he had tried but could not force her to go, the barriers of pride began to slip. He came to the pool to swim, knowing that there was nothing about his body she did not know. Mostly he ducked and floated about the pool, not able to muster the strength or dexterity to make the swift, beautifully executed crawl she remembered; the shortened and twisted muscles would not permit him that freedom. But after a few days Livy began to see that he enjoyed the simple pleasure of being in the pool, of the cooling water, of the childish splashing and horseplay Mark indulged in.

There came the day that he permitted himself to be hoisted on to the quietest old mare the stable possessed. His left hand wasn't strong enough to take the reins alone, but he held them with both hands, and tried to grip with both knees.

He, Mark, Livy and Dena went at a sedate walk to the nearest creek, about a mile from the house. Alex had to hold his back upright, though he did wear a light brace for support. The horses splashed about in the shallows of the creek; Alex lifted his left hand to brush away flies. For the first time he spoke to Livy of what he felt.

'I thought I'd never see this place again, unless someone drove me here in a jeep. You can't imagine how good it feels. I know I've never understood freedom before . . . not being tied. I don't have to live my life in a wheelchair.'

'You have to eat more,' Livy said. 'You're working it all off, you know. You have to be ready for the next operation.'

By this time she knew that the plastic surgeons would make another attempt on his face, taking skin from the unscarred right buttock. It would be in a few weeks' time, when he was judged strong enough. He had been doing exercises lying on his belly, knowing that would be his position after the operation, until the new skin grew. Livy and Mark exercised along with him. 'Ouch!' Livy said. 'I never knew tummy muscles could get so sore. I'd never do as a ballet dancer.'

Alex looked at her coolly in her leotard. 'You're rather too well-endowed for ballet, Livy. But don't let it break your heart.'

The summer went on. They became tanned and well-muscled; Alex started to cut down on sleeping pills and pain-killers. Each day they went a little farther on the horses. He tried, with success, to use only a cane to walk for short periods.

'Mother,' he said, 'why don't we invite some people over. Maybe a barbecue at the pool, no, not that, a dinner would be better so that people won't notice that I'm not quite ready to show up in swimming gear yet. Or is it too soon?'

'What do you mean too soon?'

He sighed. 'Oh, I thought maybe ladies still wanted to observe the official year's mourning. Proper Southern ladies, that is.'

'Have you seen me wearing widow's weeds? It's not what Blair would have wanted.'

'All right then, let's give a little party. Call it my coming-out. Let's have a bit of a bash before I have to go back into hospital. It'll be my going-in party too.'

They came, about forty people, those Ginny had carefully selected whom she could trust not to exclaim over Alex's face, or fuss over him, or try to help him except when he needed help. He had grown more used to asking for help, but they all noticed that he turned more often to Mark than to anyone else.

Ginny had telephoned Mrs Winterton, asking if Nancy could be present. 'Absolutely not!' was the reply. 'Her nerves are just starting to mend. Do you want to send her back to that nursing home? In any case, it's improper that that Miles girl should be living there in the house with Alex. It doesn't look right. I hear she does everything with him.'

'Olivia Miles has been an honoured guest in my house since she was a little girl. She grew up with Alex. Her mother saved my daughter's life, and gave her own. Livy is both daughter and friend to me. One day of her company is worth a lifetime of Nancy's.'

'Outrageous!' Mrs Winterton shrieked over the telephone. 'And I once thought you were a lady!'

'I have no such illusions. I will do anything in heaven or earth to make my son's life worth living. Mothers do that, Mrs Winterton. Ladies be damned!'

Dena, who had been listening to the conversation, doubled over with laughter. 'Ginny, you are wonderful! You are so sweet and gentle and good. And when you're angry, you have a marvellous Biblical wrath. Ladies be damned, indeed! That will go the rounds of Washington.'

The preparations for the party went ahead. Staff were brought from Washington to help, a small band was hired so that those who liked to dance could do so. Lights hung in the trees, the swimming-pool was lighted, and swimsuits were ready in the changing rooms.

Livy went into Alex's room when he had dressed. With patience he now managed that task for himself. 'It's like throwing away the damn crutches,' he had said, the first day he had managed it.

'If you don't agree, say so,' she began. 'If you want to take a bit of shine off that side of your face, you can do what women have been doing for centuries . . .'

He drew back from her. 'Make-up? No! Let them see me the way I am.'

She shrugged. 'Whatever you want. But don't throw out the idea altogether. Let me just show you . . . No one else will know. Just remember, after you've had the next operation, you'll have skin on this side of your face like a baby's bottom, or rather you'll have skin that closely resembles Alex McClintock's beautiful backside. Women were meant to love men this way, Alex, to look after them.'

'Rubbish! You inherited it all from your own gorgeous mother. All this looking after men, the way she looked after your father. You're not very modern, Livy. You're not up to the times.'

'I don't give a damn about the times,' Livy said. She stroked a little light foundation over the left side of his face, and added a trace of powder. 'And don't tell me men have never powdered before. It's just temporary. And you've just paid me the greatest compliment of my life, saying that I am like my mother.'

'I'm not the first one. My grandfather would have liked to snatch up your mother. And given the chance, he'd snatch you up. But, of course, he recognizes the age difference would be rather extreme.'

'There,' she said, giving him the hand mirror. 'You're beautiful, and I love it when you pay me absurd compliments.'

He studied his reflection for some seconds, then he reached for tissues and wiped off what she had applied. 'Good try, Livy. Quite effective, if I were in Chris's profession. But it won't do. People will just have to accept what they see.'

She fell back a little, recognizing her mistake, hearing the coldness in his tone.

'Well, shall we go down?' he said. 'By the sound of things, people have already arrived.' They walked along the corridor together; she had now become used to his slow pace. She pressed the button for the elevator Ginny had installed, but

471

he went straight past it, to the head of the stairs. She stifled her protest, thinking of how many eyes would be on him as he made his slow, painful way down.

'Don't lag behind, Livy.' His tone was sharp. 'Are you afraid to be seen with me?' He paused and adjusted his eye patch. 'A pirate, you called me. With this, and what's just about a replica of my grandfather's cane, I intend to strike fear into the heart of every corporation head down there who owes money to McClintock-Clayton, or is even thinking of trying to borrow it. If they think my grandfather's tough, just let them try to tangle with me . . .'

His right hand was on the banister, the left, resting on the cane, showed the knuckles white as he made a supreme effort to manage smoothly the progress down the stairs. Livy stayed one step behind him, not daring to offer assistance, conscious that already many people had noticed them, and a little pause fell on the talk and the greetings. Alex had reached the third step from the bottom when someone called 'Attaboy, Alex! Never thought we'd see you do that . . .'

It broke Alex's concentration. His hand trembled violently on the stick, the knee wavered. He slipped, rather than fell down the last steps, and sprawled at the feet of his mother's guests.

Only one man – possibly the one who had called to him, rushed forward to help him to his feet. 'Get your hands off me!'

People turned away, tried to take up their conversations again. The band decided to start a new selection. Slowly Alex slid himself back to the stairs, dragging his stick with him. He had sometimes allowed Livy to help him before when something like this had occurred, but now she did not dare offer. Very slowly he pulled himself to his feet, using the newel post as an aid. He drew his back erect, and balanced himself on the cane. He whispered to Livy, 'What was that someone once said about pride going before a fall?' Then in a much louder tone. 'Now, if you will do me the honour of giving me your arm, Livy, we'll say hello to our guests.'

She was conscious of the false jollity of some of the

greetings, from others a genuine expression of pleasure and concern. In the eyes of one woman, Livy saw tears well, but her grip on Alex's hand was firm, and she placed a light kiss on his face. 'You'll make it, baby,' she said, as if urging on a favourite racehorse.

Surprisingly, Alex returned her kiss. 'You bet I will.' He nodded towards Livy. 'I'm sure you've met our friend – the family's favourite girl, Miss Olivia Miles. Ah, and here's my grandfather. A bit sprightlier on his feet than I am, but I can still give him a run for his money.'

'Did I hear you offer me a challenge?' Andrew McClintock said. 'You'd better be very sure of yourself.'

'Oh, I am, grandfather.'

'Then you won't mind my borrowing Livy, she can show me to a seat and bring me a drink and a footstool, and all the other little comforts that my age demands. You do well enough on your own, young Alex.'

3

Alex delayed the next set of skin grafts until it was time for Mark to return to school. 'I'd rather the kid had a last sight of me looking reasonably healthy, than lying on my belly drinking from a bent straw.' So they stayed on at Prescott Hill until 1st September. Ginny grew visibly less strained as Alex's strength increased. Livy went through the procedure of enrolling at Georgetown University. 'I don't think economics is going to make much of an impression on me,' she said lightly to Alex, 'but I think I'd better do it just so I can have a glimmering of what you and your grandfather talk about. And if they throw me out after the first year, I suppose I might beg the favour of a job as a secretary at McClintock-Clayton.'

'If I had my way, you wouldn't be doing either. I'd send you back to St Just to dream and write . . . oh, poetry . . . or whatever came into your head.'

'That is just a dream,' she said. She kissed him lightly as they sat together on the front steps of Prescott Hill. There

473

was now an easy affection demonstrated between them, unselfconsciously. Livy longed for it to grow to passion, but she had learned the lesson of not trying to push Alex in any direction. She had seen the message in his eyes, his expression. A flicker of desire, and then a withdrawal. She knew all about his body, its strengths and deficiencies; she knew everything except whether he would ever again make love to her as he had done only once before.

Harry had decided to go back to England with Mark. 'I think I should introduce myself to his housemaster, make the acquaintance of my grandson, and see if I can coax a smile out of Rachel. I'll put my nose into the Private Office, too. Can't do any harm to remind them I'm around. The trouble is, if they see me, they might remember that the ambassadorship to Afghanistan is about to become vacant. Or Outer Mongolia . . .' He joked about his position as minister in Washington, when, at this stage of his career, he should have received an ambassadorship. But he did not hanker for some obscure posting, which was how the ladder was climbed. And he was aware that his knowledge of American affairs, including his relationship with the McClintock-Clayton empire was regarded as being of great value. He had become an American specialist, with a knowledgeable and watchful eye on America-Soviet relations, often asked unofficially by the State Department, for his opinions. He had no wish to uproot Dena from her present home, where she was happier than she had been in any of his postings.

Alex and Livy went with Dena and Ginny to the airport to see Harry and Mark off. The night before there had been a dinner party given for Mark at Andrew McClintock's house, for which Mark had been allowed to choose the menu. Alex now was beginning to get used to small gatherings. He had steeled himself to the curious glances, had strengthened himself so that now there was little danger of his falling. Just the day before he had gone with Mark to help to choose some new tennis racquets, the first time he had ventured out into a store, the first time away from the protected environment of Ginny's house or the hospital. 'Good to see you around again, Mr McClintock,' one of the older assistants had said. He had supplied Alex with sporting goods all his life, but he didn't venture any jokes about doing so now; he just concentrated on Mark's needs. The racquets were a gift from Andrew McClintock.

The surprise of the dinner party on that last night had been the arrival of Chris in Washington. She had not been back since her father's funeral. She had not seen Alex since the last look through the double glass door, when no one had been certain that he could hold on for another night. She had been in New York for a week, in rehearsal for the opening of *Tempo*, the play in which she had scored such an unexpected success in London. But this time she was playing the leading female role. An older, more brilliant Chris entered Andrew McClintock's house, lovely in the way her mother was, but brittle and wary. She walked straight to Alex. 'I should have come months ago and faced you! You'll have to forgive me for thinking that it was bad luck on daddy that he died, and hating you a little because you lived. Well, I've got over that.' Then she threw her arms around him, and held him with a force that rocked him, and nearly upset his still precarious balance. 'God damn it, but I do love you, Alex. I forgive you for living. I'm grateful that you did. May you live to be a hundred.'

'If you knew the aches and pains that go with growing old, Christine,' Andrew McClintock said, 'you wouldn't wish a hundred years on anyone.'

She went to him swiftly. 'I'm glad to see you, Ambassador. And your years sit lightly on you.' She took the martini she had ordered from the butler and downed half of it in one gulp. 'I hope you're around for at least a hundred years to keep pulling chestnuts out of the fire, at least in my life. I've a feeling little ole Chris is going to be putting an awful lot of chestnuts in the fire. I want to be a great actress. I want to be a producer. I want to be a director. As I look around me in the theatre, it all spells trouble.' She glanced around the family, who had assembled before the guests arrived. 'I hope all of you are good at pulling chestnuts out of the fire. Better start practising.' She nodded at the butler for another martini. 'That was wonderful. They have never learned to make them in England. No one ever has enough ice, or the sense to chill the glass . . .'

Ten other guests arrived for dinner. Chris by then had drunk another martini. 'God, what a family we are! Even with my father and Caro and Rachel missing, we still add up to a hell of a lot! Thank God for that. We'll still be needing each other.'

Alex returned to the hospital. The first of the operations would begin the next morning. He refused to let anyone accompany him. 'They know me quite well here. See you when I come around, and let's hope these guys know what they're doing. I don't fancy my ass being sliced off just to get another funny-looking, if different face . . .' They all knew, though, that this time the plastic surgeons could work with a patient who was not still suffering from the after-effects of burns and severe injuries. Patient hours could be taken working in minute detail; they would be able to straighten out the lopsided mouth, they could do work on the ragged ear. 'I don't expect miracles,' Alex had said to Livy. 'Maybe just a bit of an improvement.'

Chris stayed in Washington for a week after Alex's first operation; she visited the hospital daily until the angry calls from the producer forced her back to New York. 'The terms of your contract state that you can always be replaced for failure to carry out your part of the agreement.'

She said goodbye to Alex, who was still in considerable pain. 'I can take Sundays off to come and see you. I'm sorry I haven't been of any help in the past. Perhaps . . .'

He had trouble speaking because of the surgery to his lip. 'Sundays are for resting,' he whispered. 'I've got Livy to hold my hand.'

'Make sure you don't let go of it this time.'

Harry returned from London. 'I'm to hang on here,' he said. 'There were hints, but no promises, that the ambassadorship would be mine when Sir George goes in eighteen months' time. They're sorry about the delay, but they can't turn a good man out, and there's no other ambassadorship vacant at the moment that they know I'd want. I settled Mark at Eton, as much as he'll ever be settled. But he's being pretty philosophical about it. Caro's blooming, and so is our grandson. Toby Osborne's so smug it's hard to believe. Our Caroline and son are turning out to be all the things that his very careful, rather impersonal judgement hoped for. Motherhood has made her more beautiful than ever. She's a popular, clever hostess, already creating a little "salon" which will push along Toby's career. Damned if I don't think he's got his sights on Permanent Under Secretary some day. Caro seems to run her house like pouring cream. There don't seem to be any servant crises.'

'And Rachel?' Ginny pressed. She had come over to dinner at their house on the evening of Harry's return. Only Livy was with them.

'Rachel?' Harry sighed. 'I wish I knew what was ahead for her. She's working like a dog at the TUC, and everyone seems to know about her and Frazer Campbell. They're everywhere together. She mentioned that she might switch jobs to working directly for the Labour Party, which means she and Campbell would be thrown together even more. She refuses to talk about him. Told me mind my own business, which is her right. I wish I could see some future in it. But it's unlikely that Campbell will get a divorce. It doesn't look good in politics. She and Caro are barely on speaking terms. Rachel seems to be the one fly in the ointment of Caro's smooth life. Something she'd rather forget about.'

'Does Rachel seem . . . happy?'

Harry shrugged. 'How can I tell? She's not the sort of person one can ask that question of. I haven't a doubt that the Labour Party will run her as a candidate for some seat she can't possibly win when she's a bit older. Just to get her blooded, and see how she shapes up. One day she'll be in the House of Commons, no matter how long it takes. She may have to ditch Frazer Campbell to do that. Politics is her life, and for the moment that and Campbell are enough for her. There's not a thing we can do, Dena. She's been out of the nest for a long time now.'

They went up to New York for Christine's opening in

477

Tempo. The critics gave the play rave notices and, with some reluctance, Livy thought, praised Christine's performance. 'It must have hurt them to have to say nice things about the poor little rich girl,' Chris said. 'But if they're openly unfair, then all Broadway knows it. So I supposed they would be prepared to be even-handed, and this time around I won. But it's never going to be easy.'

She had given an 'after-the-show' party to wait for the papers at the apartment she was renting. 'I just couldn't bear Sardi's if the reviews had been bad.' It was a shock to Ginny to realize that the leading man, an English actor, was living here with Chris, and that he had a wife and two children back in London. She couldn't help liking the man, Hugh Meredith, who seemed to her extraordinarily humble for a man whose theatrical career had been spectacularly success- ful in the past five years, who had been highly praised as a stage actor, and had two very successful films to his name. He talked with Ginny quietly. 'I love Chris. I'd marry her if she'd have me. She says she's not ready for marriage.'

'Your wife?'

'My wife is fed up with the theatrical life. She would prefer something safer, duller perhaps. I have lovely kids, whom I don't want to give up. But they'll go of their own accord one day, so . . .' He looked appealingly at Ginny. 'Chris is lovely, and brilliant, and – may I say it? – unstable. And I love her. What am I to do?'

'That, Mr Meredith, will be your problem and Chris's. I'm not unsympathetic. I want happiness for my daughter, but it will never be a conventional happiness for her. She's still so young, when one thinks about it. Worldly wise, and yet . . . not wise. She'll always act instinctively. You'll just have to watch that instinct. I wouldn't begin to predict it, myself.'

As they flew back to Washington the next day, Ginny said to Dena, 'Well, our "twins" have certainly taken different paths. Both unusual and unconventional. I hope they find happiness in their own fashion, whatever that may be. Only twenty-four. Chris something of a star, and Rachel bound for a politician's career. And both involved with men who already have wives and children. Well . . . we can't work it all out for them, can we?'

'It's just as well,' Dena said, 'that the Ambassador didn't come up. I don't think he would have cared for last night's party, even if it was to celebrate a triumph for Chris. Less would he have liked Hugh Meredith.'

'I haven't the faintest doubt that Mr McClintock knows all about Hugh Meredith, and Chris's relationship with him. He has always made it his business to know about these things. And he can do nothing. She has her own money. She intends to live her own life, as distanced from the McClintock-Clayton tradition as possible.'

'Well, at least she hasn't made Alex's mistake of making an expected, predictable marriage, which didn't turn out at all as predicted.'

'Just like Chris, Alex was free to do what he wanted. He chose the conventional way, and it went wrong. Who's to blame Chris for trying it her way? They've both been hurt. The only person we can try to stop being hurt is Livy.'

'And we're as helpless in that as in anything else. Only Livy and Alex will decide what they will do.' Ginny looked bleakly from the window of the plane, and then back to the shining mass of Livy's red hair which rose above the cushion of the seat ahead. 'I miss Blair so much. At times everything seems whirling out of control, and he isn't here to steady me any more. I should be able to help my two children, but I feel totally helpless myself.'

After six weeks Alex was willing to leave hospital. He could have left earlier, going to his mother's house in the charge of nurses and attended by doctors. But he had chosen to remain. 'They have everything here to look after me. It saves a lot of trouble.' By that time the skin, though still tender and painful, had grown back on his buttock and the undamaged thigh. He had undergone another operation to strengthen his hip and knee; his left hand was straighter, though still not completely flexible. The upward slant of the left side of his mouth had been improved, though there wasn't much mobility to the lips. 'The doctors have told me

479

to practise smiling,' he said to Livy. The smile he gave to her was crooked, but had its own particular charm. 'So I spend half-an-hour every morning practising my smile for that impossible gorgon of a nurse who consents to bring in my breakfast . . . and then after lunch I practise smiling, waiting for you to come. And when you come, it isn't any effort to smile at all. The rest of the time I'm exercising or walking the corridors. How incredibly busy life is. I'm glad to go to sleep at night.'

Livy had been a month at Georgetown University; she was still shakily trying to find her way in a way of life so very different from Oxford, conscious that her voice and her mannerisms made her conspicuous. She was living with Dena and Harry, studying and doing some secretarial work for Ginny. 'When are you coming out of here?' she said to Alex. 'You'll have to come out sometime. You're so much better . . . you look so much better. In a year the scars will be hardly noticeable.' She tilted her head. 'You look rather interesting . . . Black patch, crooked smile. That slightly frozen look should give you a great advantage as a banker . . . You should be out at Prescott Hill, enjoying the fall weather. It's too nice a time to spend in hospital. This Indian summer . . . What lovely words they are . . . when they go with weather like this.'

'Not Prescott Hill, or Massachusetts Avenue. They're my mother's houses. Not the Georgetown house. That's Nancy's, and I never intend to return there again. I've found a little place to rent, just out beyond Alexandria. I've had the agents looking for something, and I think this would suit. It's not large, but it overlooks the river, and it's big enough for the time being. Furnished, not too badly, though a little too quaintly colonial for my taste. I've had myself driven out there. There's a cook and manservant who go with the package. They want a year's lease. If you'll come with me, I'll sign. What do you say?'

'Nancy?' It was what she had longed for all her life, and yet at this moment she spoke only another woman's name.

'Nancy can be taken care of. We will never live together again, that's obvious. I hate to admit that the Old Man was

480

right, but I made a stupid mistake. It should have been you from the beginning. Will you come and live with me, Livy? Live with me. Love me.'

'I've always loved you.'

'Is living with me when we're not married too much to ask? Eventually we will marry. Why wait? I've already lost so much time with you.'

'You're playing into Nancy's hands by going to live with me alone.'

'You surely don't expect me to play a game of living with you at Prescott Hill as if my mother were there as chaperone? Give me credit for more guts than that. I want the world to know that you're my woman, and that you will be my wife. No hiding behind my mother's skirts, or my grandfather's coat-tails. Are you hesitating, Livy? Would you rather have the protection, that shred of respectability until it's possible for us to be married? If that's what your choice is, then so be it. I'll wait, but I think it's a stupid waste of time.'

She was seated on the side of the bed. She leaned over and kissed him. 'Then let's waste no more time. We won't bother anyone else with our plans. We'll just do it . . .'

He slumped back against the pillows. 'Thank God! Let's run . . . I could run down the corridor now.'

'Easy, boy! Easy! You've got a tricky knee . . .'

'And a mangled hand, and a half-frozen face. And I'm glad I managed to live through that damned crash just to hear you say those words. We've years to make up for . . .'

The next day Alex informed his mother that he was leaving hospital with his doctors' permission, and was going to live for a while in a house he had rented down the river from Alexandria, and Livy would be going with him. Livy told Dena and Harry at breakfast that a car would be coming for her, and she would pick up Alex at the hospital. 'I haven't seen the house yet, and I don't care what it's like. You understand that I have to go with Alex, don't you?'

Harry sipped his coffee. 'Dear child, you don't make life easy for yourself. Nancy can do all kinds of things to Alex because of this. His living openly with you will give her

481

a very commanding position. She could hold out for an outrageous divorce settlement. At the very least, it will cause a tremendous scandal.'

'We just don't intend to wait while Nancy has another breakdown, or invents some other excuse for not facing up to the fact that the marriage is over. It was she who rejected Alex, but that's beside the point. We've waited long enough, and we're prepared to say be damned to the consequences. I'm sorry if this will hurt you with the diplomatic corps, but I really think they're all too sophisticated to bother about it too much. But the word would get around: we'd be at Prescott Hill or with Aunt Ginny at Massachusetts Avenue, and there would be all sort of snide stories and innuendos in the press. At least this way we're making an open declaration. It's the cleanest and simplest. At least we don't drag in you and Lady Camborne and Aunt Ginny. You're not turning a convenient blind eye.'

Dena gave a faint, nervous laugh. 'That just about says it. There's Rachel having an affair that everyone gossips about, and Chris living with her lover in New York. It seems Caro is the only one destined to do things the ordinary way. Good luck, Livy.' Unexpectedly she rose, and came around the table to kiss her on the cheek. 'You were never destined for an ordinary life. Even when it's possible to marry Alex, it will not be an ordinary or easy life. He's a very demanding man, and being married to the head of McClintock-Clayton won't be an easy position. I hope for your sake Andrew McClintock lives for many years yet. Of course, he'll expect the earth from you, as he's always expected it from Ginny. I'm sure you've thought of all this. Life won't always be an idyll of living in a nice little house with Alex, and the world leaving you alone.'

'I've thought about it. I don't like what I'm going into. I don't at all like the idea of McClintock-Clayton ruling our lives. But if that is what I must do to have Alex, then that's what I'll do. I'm not even planning to drop out of university. I'll drive into Georgetown every day. By the end of the year Alex might be fit enough to go back to his office. Our little house by the river will be only a very temporary thing. We'll enjoy it while we can.'

'Does the Ambassador know yet?'

Livy smiled. 'I think it's the one thing we've managed to keep from the Ambassador, though no doubt he's been expecting something like this to happen. Of course we'll telephone him the minute we reach the house. His reaction should be interesting. He'll either say, "What took you so long?", or maybe, "I told you so".'

He did both. He arrived that evening at the house on the river, and the chauffeur carried in the food he had brought from his own house. 'I thought the larder might be empty. The cellar as well.' He had brought a case of Romanée Conti. 'And if you don't think it hurts me to give that up . . . Well, you've done it. You've done everything that you, Alex, as a lawyer, know is playing into the hands of that girl, Nancy. But I have to respect you for not trying it any other way. It'll cost you a packet, and Livy will be worth it.' He inspected the house thoroughly. 'A bit pokey, isn't it?'

'For God's sake, grandfather, there's only the two of us. We won't be doing any entertaining. I need a few months before I can get back to the desk and do a full day's work. Livy's going to keep on at Georgetown . . .'

Andrew McClintock nodded, and ate some of the *pâté* he had brought with him. 'I'll be interested in seeing how things will be a year from now. Of course you'll be back at your desk, Alex. With Blair gone, we need you more than ever. These are difficult years. Blair perfectly filled the gap between you and me, but I'm seventy-seven years old. Still capable of doing a job, but not of running all over the world minding the shop. Too many decisions have been put off since Blair died. My fault . . . weakness. Fear for you, I suppose. But I have to keep looking over my shoulder all the time, watching out for who might be trying to have a go at the old man while he's unprotected by the heir-apparent. Thank God Ginny's such a steady woman. Her shares and mine will always block any sort of revolt from below, but you may be tempted to go out for more capital. To go public. That could be the crack in the dyke, that way, someday, someone could throw you out of McClintock-Clayton. Never be tempted to sell your shares to any other director, no matter how much you think you may trust him. There's real estate and pictures, and God knows what that can go before you sell any part of McClintock-Clayton, even to an insider. Let them think you're bankrupt if you have to, living like church-mice. But don't sell . . .' He looked as much at Livy as Alex. 'If things continue as they are going, you could be one of the most powerful men in the world. Just don't let greed for power tempt you into waters that are too deep. This accident has put white hairs in your head, Alex, as well as inflicting a lot of pain, emotional and physical. But it's made a man of you, and today you've made a man's choice. I'll drink to that.'

Alex's request, through his lawyers, for a divorce from Nancy was refused. He attempted to sue then for a divorce on the grounds that she had deserted him, and the reply which came from the lawyers was a long list of the doctors who had treated her, the evidence of her long stay in a nursing home because she was unfit to live outside of it. They cited Alex's refusal to return to the marital home in Georgetown, although from the evidence of the house he was presently residing in, it was evident that he was physically capable of living in the Georgetown house. The wrangle went on for almost two months, Nancy perfectly acting the part of the wife sinned against. The fact that Alex openly lived with Olivia Miles was her trump card, as they had always known it would be. 'Why doesn't she just name her price?' Alex demanded in exasperation. Instead of naming her price, she countered with an offer of a reconciliation. Alex would return to the Georgetown house, and they would take up their married life again.

'Bitch!' was Alex's response. 'She couldn't bear the sight of me, and now she says she's willing to live with me as my wife. It makes her look very good.'

Washington thoroughly enjoyed the sensation. Livy found she had to give up her course at Georgetown because the constant stories in the newspapers, the appearance of the press on the campus questioning, demanding replies, made attendance impossible. She retreated to the house on the river, reading with Alex, exercising with him, loving him. They walked daily along a river path; one day he actually broke into a stumbling, shambling run. That night they celebrated the run with Romanée Conti, and they made love as if they had never done so before. 'My love . . . my life,' Alex said to her softly. The next day the first snow fell, reminding them of the first storm of last winter when the plane crashed. 'It was my impatience,' Alex said. 'I wanted to get back to Washington that night. Blair was willing to wait until the morning . . . God knows I'd no pressing reason to get back except for meetings the next morning which could have waited. If I'd been wiser . . .'

'You were younger,' Livy said.

'I've had more than a year to regret it, and the rest of my life has to be devoted to trying to make up in any way I can to my mother for losing Blair. I know I can never do it, never compensate. Bringing you into my life is part of it. She was as doubtful of my marriage to Nancy as the Old Man, but she was too tactful to say so.'

Ginny came frequently to see them, as did Dena and Harry and Andrew McClintock. They went to dinner at the three houses and nowhere else, although invitations were beginning to come as people accepted the situation. Washington society was split over them: those who thought Nancy Winterton badly used, and saw Livy as a marriage wrecker, and those who would side with the McClintocks and the Claytons no matter what happened. Chris came early one Sunday morning, bringing Hugh Meredith with her, and stayed with them overnight. 'Nice,' she said as she walked along the river path. 'How nice. So peaceful.'

Alex laughed. 'And you couldn't stick it for more than two days.'

They all went to Prescott Hill for Christmas. Mark had flown over, even though the holiday period was short. Harry found that now he no longer had the expense of Caroline and Rachel, extras were possible for Mark. He cheerfully travelled economy class, even though his height was beginning to make such cramped conditions uncomfortable. Poor chap! 'There isn't any room with Rachel, and in any case I'd just get in the way. Caro and family are spending Christmas with the in-laws. Thea wrote to invite me, but when father came through with the fare, this is where I wanted to be.' He had stopped for a night with Chris in New York and seen the play. 'They all say she's very good . . . I wish she seemed happier. Perhaps that's asking too much. Hugh's nice . . .'

Chris came down to Prescott Hill for the few nights the show would be closed during the week before Christmas. She was disconsolate. She confided to Livy. 'Hugh dashed back to London because he just had to be there for Christmas Day with his children. His wife refuses to talk about a divorce. Someday she will, but the children are what holds Hugh. He adores them. Perhaps I should have a child of my own, so I'd have an equal card . . .'

Livy and Alex waited until all the presents, small and large, had been opened on Christmas morning. 'We have given a present to ourselves. We're going to have a baby.'

A short silence followed that announcement. Then there came the exclamations of pleasure, the kisses, the congratulations. But Andrew McClintock remained seated, and oddly silent. At last they all looked towards him. His face was set in a tight mask, as if he dared show neither pleasure nor pain. They waited for him to speak.

'Very good news,' he said carefully, though his tone did not express that sentiment. 'Now we will have to hurry. Nancy must be made to give you a divorce. We cannot have this child born illegitimate. Who else knows about this?'

'No one,' Livy said. 'Except, of course, my doctor . . .' She looked bewildered. 'I thought you'd be pleased.'

'I am pleased. It's what I always wanted. The nurse will know . . .'

'We only knew for sure the other day.'

'They always know. They always look at patients' records, especially when the patient is very much in the news. It would have been wiser to see someone who didn't know you, under an assumed name. What's the doctor's telephone number?'

486

'Oh, for God's sake, grandfather . . . it's Christmas Day! You can't disturb him.'

'I can disturb whom I please, if it's urgent enough. If we're not careful this will be the juiciest item in the New Year gossip columns.' He went to the library, and seemed to spend half the morning on the telephone. Through contacts, he found unlisted telephone numbers, he disturbed people at their Christmas dinners; at the end of the day he was only reasonably certain that he had stopped any possible leak of the news.

'We will have to be very careful,' he said. 'It is the most natural thing in the world to happen, that Livy should become pregnant. And I'm thankful for it. But any undue haste will alert Nancy's lawyers . . .'

'Poor little baby,' Mark said, as he and Ginny and Alex walked towards the frozen stream to which Alex had only been able to ride during the summer. 'It's hardly alive yet, and all this fuss already.'

'Don't worry,' Alex said. 'It will all be sorted out before it's born. It'll be the happiest baby you ever saw, Mark. You shall be godfather . . .'

In the New Year negotiations began in earnest. Nancy's lawyers seemed to sense the new urgency. The discussions were stretched out to interminable lengths. Briefs were written, submitted, dismissed. Counter briefs were written. The weeks dragged on. Andrew McClintock became visibly more agitated. He visited the little house on the river almost daily, inquiring intimately about Livy's health. Ginny laughed when she heard this. 'He did just the same with me. He wanted me both to exercise as much as possible, and still stay in bed all day and rest. Bear with him, Livy. This child is very precious to him. Very important.'

At last Alex had the news. 'She'll settle for five million dollars,' he told Livy.

She gasped. 'My God, no! It's not right. We can't agree.'

He shrugged. 'If I don't pay up, my grandfather will. When the papers are signed, and the lawyers see the money in escrow, she will depart for Reno or Las Vegas. Six weeks later I'll have a divorce, and the money will be hers.'

During that six weeks he went back to work at McClintock-Clayton. It signalled his return to the world, and Livy felt the pain of her first separation. It seemed long hours before he returned to the house at night. She began to worry about him when the roads were slippery with ice. For the first few weeks he had a driver, but then he rebelled against the restriction. 'I'm not an old man yet!' His grandfather insisted on a massively-built Rolls-Royce, which came from his own garage. 'Those damned icy roads, you could skid into anything. I don't want you flattened by some other maniac.' The car was fitted with automatic transmission, which Alex at first despised, and then admitted to Livy, 'It certainly does help my leg and hand, though I won't admit it to the Old Man. He's ordering another Rolls. Six months' delivery, even for him. It will be built like a tank, and I know he intends it for me. He's finally given in and ordered another company aircraft. This one will have four engines, and every navigational device anyone's invented, and a pilot will only be hired if he signs a statement to say that he will accept no orders from the passenger, no matter who it is, which go counter to his own safety instincts. That means if there's even a cloud in the sky, we don't take off.'

The day came in early April when Nancy returned from Las Vegas, and a cashiers' cheque for five million dollars was given to her. There would be no alimony, no further payments. 'That,' Alex said, 'is that! Now let's get married.'

But someone in the firm of lawyers which represented Nancy Winterton, jubilant at the size of the settlement and by now aware of Livy's pregnancy, leaked details to the press. The stories were hurtful. '*The five million dollar baby . . . The prince and the pauper.*' They carried stories of Livy which pictured her both as a scullery maid at Tresillian and the daughter of an admired poet. She was the offspring of fisherfolk, who had taken a first-class degree at Oxford. She was pictured as both a primitive and an academic. She was seen as the woman who had brought Alex back to life; other papers saw her as the penniless waif who had succeeded in snatching one of the richest marriage prizes in America from a wife whose agony over her husband had led to a nervous breakdown.

'Why look at those rags?' Alex demanded angrily. 'Next week they'll be pillorying someone else. And next week we'll be married. A year from now we'll be an old married couple with a baby to bring up, and they'll have forgotten all the fuss.'

The marriage took place in Ginny's house on Massachusetts Avenue. Only the two families were present, and they had believed the arrangements secret. But the story was front-page news in the next day's newspapers. Livy wore a dress which could not disguise her swelling shape. The baby would be born in July.

Andrew McClintock had already had discussions with Ginny, and they were both in agreement. 'I want you to have this house,' she told Livy and Alex. 'It's always been known as the McClintock mansion, even though Blair bought it from the Ambassador. I've been wanting to leave it ever since Blair died. I'm rattling around here. When you have the baby and there'll probably be others, you'll need more space. And you'll have to start entertaining, Livy, as soon as you're able. That dear little house on the river just won't do. In any case, it's too far from Washington. In time you'll learn, Livy, that McClintock-Clayton will absorb more of Alex than you want to give. You would begrudge the time it took him to drive in and out every day.'

'You can't give this up. I don't think I could live here. It's . . . it's too much.'

'That is part of the price of marrying Alex McClintock. There are other things you'll find out about. You can't ever own him completely, Livy. Most of him belongs to McClintock-Clayton. You've had your honeymoon, and it was much longer than I had. Now you must take whatever scrag ends of his time he has to give you. You have to admit,' Ginny added, 'that this house is all ready to move into – elevator and all.'

'But where will you go?'

'Don't worry. I have the nicest house you ever saw all

picked out. Less than half the size of this. Five blocks from the White House. Just a nice size for entertaining, but not for running a corporate giant from. Don't worry. I'm afraid I'll be on your doorstep every day. And Dena will be around the corner, or else, with luck, she'll be in residence at the British Embassy. And there's always Prescott Hill. Plenty of places for us to be together. It will be so good to have a grandchild, Livy.'

'I think,' Livy said, 'perhaps it's time to let the flat in Vincent Square go. And I should ask Caro to have Thea's piece and Herbert's paintings sent over.' She indicated the vastness of the house. 'They won't take up much space here.'

Just for a moment she was touched with homesickness, a longing for St Just. How good it would be to go to the cottage to wait for the baby, to experience the simplicity of the life her mother and father had known, without its hardships. She knew that was where she would have liked the child to grow up. But she had married Alex, and all that had become impossible. They would return to Tresillian and St Just from time to time, but it would be a holiday place for her child, not a home. She vowed they would go as often as possible. But first she must bear this child, and later explain to him his double heritage.

Even though she had few thoughts and no preference about the sex of the child, Andrew McClintock's unshakeable assurance that it would be a boy had its effect. 'I want another Alex,' he said. 'This family has had too few boys.'

It was May, and she was seven months pregnant when they left the small house on the river and moved into the McClintock mansion on Massachusetts Avenue.

Chapter 12

1

Harry strolled alone from the McClintock mansion where he
had had dinner with Livy and Alex, Livy struggling to adjust
to her new role as mistress of that vast place. Harry smiled
a little to himself as he recalled the history of those two,
whom he sometimes still saw as young children at Tresillian.
He could remember the lovely child who was drawn partly
from simple fisherfolk, but was no less the child of a poet.

The late May night was warm; he had told his driver not
to return for him after dinner, and had dismissed him for the
weekend. The short walk home would do him good. Home,
he called it, as diplomatic people must. It was a house, and
he'd had news that day that he would soon be moving on.
He could not yet release the news at the embassy, but he
knew it would be safe with Livy and Alex. Andrew McClintock had been present. He had continued his habit of just
turning up at the McClintock mansion whenever it pleased
him, just as he had always done when Ginny had been its
châtelaine. Now that Ginny had her own, smaller house, the
Ambassador used it in the same way. It was just another
place to go when the loneliness of his own house weighed
too much upon him. But tonight neither Ginny nor Dena
had been present. They had been in New York for four days.
Chris's play was soon to close, and she would be returning
to London, she said. There was another play to consider.
Ginny and Dena had decided on a shopping trip and were
staying at the apartment he still maintained on Park Avenue,
one seldom used, and with only one resident manservant to
take care of it. It was as though, having put down his roots
in Washington, Andrew McClintock preferred to stay there,
maintaining his contact with the Wall Street offices by tele-

phone. Blair had always been the one to make the trips to New York. The apartment had been used only once since Blair's death, when Dena and Ginny and Livy had gone to the opening of Chris's play. But it remained there, like Seymour House, like the house on the Zurich See, waiting for them.

Harry had wanted to telephone the news to Dena, and then, lest their telephone conversation be overheard, had decided to wait until her return the next morning. He wasn't entirely sure whether his telephone was not tapped, whether for the benefit of his own embassy or some other or for the CIA. He didn't hazard a guess.

They had sat quietly over brandy and coffee. In the dimness of the library, which was still Livy's favourite room in the house she had inherited, Alex had looked almost normal, Harry thought. The left side of his face was still somewhat inflexible: when he talked, it tended to stay still, while the other side was animated. Consequently his speech was a little affected, occasionally he tripped over a word in his impatience, but there was never any doubt about what he meant. He was still a young man in a hurry. Along the way since the accident he had learned a certain kind of patience; he had learned to tolerate his own defects. The livid skin had turned a better colour, though of a different texture from the rest of his face. The tiny marks of the stitches were fading. He walked reasonably well with his cane; he had become skilful with a knife and fork. He worked out in his own gym daily; the injured and permanently damaged muscles would not be allowed to grow weak again. For a young man who had been an athlete, and now was able only to walk with a cane, who permanently wore a back brace, Harry thought he looked extraordinarily content. Why should he not be content?

'I had news today,' Harry said when the butler had withdrawn. 'In about six months, Howells, who's ambassador in Paris, is retiring. Prematurely. He's developed some sort of heart condition, poor chap. Anyway, the post is mine.'

Alex levered himself up from the sofa, came to shake his hand. 'Congratulations!' He turned to his grandfather.

'There, sir! Soon we'll be asking "Which ambassador?" in this family.'

'Very glad to hear it, Harry. It's a bit overdue.'

Harry nodded. 'Yes, it is. But I've been riding behind some very good people, some very high flyers, all my career in the Foreign Service. Taking time out for the Army didn't help. I was almost tempted to say I'd rather stay on here in the hope that they'd give me this embassy when Sir George goes, but there's always the risk I'd be passed over. Next to Washington and Moscow, Paris is the most important posting. They didn't condemn me to Ghana or the Gold Coast, or even Outer Mongolia. The thing that troubles me is separating Dena and Ginny.'

Andrew McClintock waved his hand. 'Ginny has plenty of time and money, to visit Paris whenever she wants. There's always the excuse of going to buy new clothes. Don't worry, those two will be visiting back and forth for ever. When we get these new jet airplanes, crossing the Atlantic will be nothing.'

That long-ago prediction of Andrew McClintock's when he had arrived at Seymour House on Christmas morning after a long, cold and fatiguing flight, that the public would demand swifter and more comfortable long-distance flights had come true. The casual mention to Blair that they must look into the matter had resulted in McClintock-Clayton first lending money to Boeing, out in Seattle, and then acquiring a sizeable amount of stock. The prototypes were promising. A swift passage of the Atlantic would soon be possible. It was that magic touch that McClintocks and Claytons seemed to be endowed with, Harry thought, with only the faintest touch of envy. He himself had never had any money to invest in anything except his family's living needs. He was enjoying a good life now, and soon there would be the splendours of the Paris embassy. Dena would make a wonderful ambassador's wife. He knew that Ginny would insist that Dena borrowed tiara and jewels for the state occasions. And he didn't think Andrew McClintock would be able to resist adding gifts like the sable coat for Russia. And this time Harry wouldn't object. It would be something to be able to invite the former ambassador to the Court of St James's to be a guest at Her Britannic Majesty's Paris embassy.

These not unpleasant thoughts filled his head as he walked back to his house when he sensed that someone had fallen into step beside him. He knew that he really was not supposed to go anywhere unless he was driven, but it was a rule he often broke. It was dark under the trees that lined the side street off Massachusetts Avenue.

'Good evening, minister.'

Harry stopped and turned. He could not clearly make out the features of the man, but he was certain he had never seen him before. 'Who the devil are you?'

'You know very well that who I am doesn't matter, minister. I just have a simple message to deliver from our masters.' Once again those hateful, sinister words. 'They are not satisfied. Not enough reaches them through you. And some of it has been erroneous, if not deliberately misleading. They may have lost some valuable people through opinions of situations which you have written which turned out to be incorrect. And sometimes what you have conveyed has appeared in next week's newspapers, hardly a revelation. You are being watched, you must understand, through your own embassy. We have others in place.'

'Then use them! I send what comes that may be of value. A minister doesn't see everything, you know. I'm not in the confidence of MI6. I don't have great pals in the CIA. I only see what crosses my desk, and most of that is boring diplomatic routine.'

'You don't try hard enough, minister. You don't put yourself out to make those extra contacts. Your great friendship with McClintock-Clayton, for instance. They are heavily into research and development. In chemicals, in armaments, in aircraft. They have defence department contracts. Much of what they are doing would be of interest to our masters.'

'Then do it yourself, whoever you are!'

'Minister?' The tone was gently reproving. 'Have you forgotten Sonya Dimitriyevna, and your daughter, Irina? Whenever what you give our masters proves of value, they flourish. When it is useless, or at worst harmful, they suffer.

And your other women, minister. Your wife, your two daughters. Even this young woman, Olivia Miles, who was your protégée. We can reach all of them, you know. Mishaps, accidents. Things we can arrange which would not be pleasant. Our masters will expect better in the future.'

'What the hell more can I give you? I've never been trained in intelligence gathering. There are better placed people than I, you bastard.'

'Every small piece helps, minister. Your contribution has just been too small.' He held out an envelope to Harry. 'A small reminder of your past, minister. Study it well. Her life and wellbeing rest with you.' The man thrust an envelope into Harry's hand, and then turned away, walking rapidly into the darkness of the overhanging trees.

Harry started to follow him, and then checked his step. He looked about him carefully. They always found him in these places. No use to run after this man. Next time it would be someone different, and the next time. He walked the last few hundred yards to his house. The porch and hall lights were burning. The light in the apartment over the garage suggested that Thomas had retired early, as Harry had told him he might. He let himself in, wondering why they bothered to risk accosting him in the street, even in the darkness of the night. They might just as well have been waiting for him in his study. By this time he had come to believe that nothing was impossible for them.

He went to the drinks tray, where a bucket of ice was waiting. He poured himself a scotch, added some water. He sat down, looking at the envelope, fearing to open it. He relived the nightmare of that first encounter in Paris, and of the years since then. The information passed, the information doctored, the misleading information. He remembered the nights he had toiled over papers which indicated, with slight twists, the directions he believed the minds of his political masters were taking, all documents dictated to him by shadowy people he knew had nothing to do with the Foreign Office. Sometimes he was allowed to write the truth, because it suited whoever directed him that the truth be known in Moscow. He could never, and they knew it, send such things as photographs of research projects of such entities as McClintock-Clayton. But he was present at a great many meetings where policy was formulated and discussed. Even the indication of a research project being contemplated was enough – but not always. Sometimes he had been instructed to feed in the direct opposite, and that, he well knew, was extremely dangerous. He could only protest innocence, and ignorance, and continue with this deadly burden of dealing with two sides. He remembered over the years the galleries he had visited as indicated rendezvous points, the many times he had gone to share a sandwhich lunch with birds in the various parks, and always at an indicated bench. It had never been easy to escape his staff at the embassy. He had become ingenious because he had to. It was not in his nature to be skilful in facing both ways, but both sides had demanded it. Although there were people in London who knew of it, he was certain that his ambassadors in Paris and London had been kept ignorant. They could not have dealt so open-handedly with him if they had known of the double game. And all he had struggled to do was to keep alive whatever this envelope contained.

But always before it had been these two hostages they had threatened. Never before had Dena been mentioned, or Rachel or Caroline, and now Livy. He saw how her marriage to Alex McClintock had changed her situation. She had now married into the empire that was one of the goals of their thrust. How in God's name was he supposed to get the inner secrets of McClintock-Clayton research? Where was he supposed to look? He could reveal nothing he was not directed to reveal. And who were those within his own embassy who spied on him? Or was that yet another of their devilish inventions, to throw him off his guard? He reminded himself that nothing was impossible. It had been from within this very embassy that Burgess and Maclean and the ultimate spy, Philby, had betrayed their secrets to these same masters. He took a long swallow of his drink, and reluctantly opened the envelope.

This time no photograph of Sonya. Was she still alive? The face that stared into the camera, sharp and well-defined, was the grown, altered version of the other photos he possessed, particularly the last one. She was alone. The photograph was in colour, so that now he could see that her eyes were blue, not grey. There was still a vague resemblance to the Sonya he remembered, but not to the haggard woman of the last photo. This face was already more knowing, even more adult than the Sonya of the war-time years. It was sharper, longer, the jaw-line more pronounced; the hair, long and golden and pulled back, revealed a high forehead. She had a look of intelligence and terrifying wisdom. He saw Sonya's high, Slavic cheekbones. She was only Mark's age, hard to believe. He looked at the photo of his daughter with anguish. He didn't know whether her mother was alive or dead, but this girl remained, the tangible evidence of his brief love for her mother. Why the hell, he wondered, was he not able to tear it up? Tell them to do their damnedest. But as he continued to stare at the photo of the girl, the faces of Dena and Rachel and Caroline swam before him. And now Livy. Would there never be an end to it?'

The telephone rang. He snapped into alert attention. A call at this hour of the night usually meant something from the embassy. He wondered where the Ambassador was this weekend.

But the voice on the indistinct trans-Atlantic line was Herbert Gardiner's. 'That you, Harry? We've been ringing.'

'What's the trouble, Herbert?' He would not telephone except for an emergency. His thoughts instantly went back to the warning. 'Rachel?' he demanded. 'Caroline?'

'No, Harry. It's Mark. He's here with us.'

'Why?'

'Well, Harry, it's . . . well, the plain fact is that he left school. He packed up and left before they could formally expel him. No doubt the headmaster has been trying to get in touch with you also. He'll want his version of the case heard.'

'What in God's name has happened?'

'Mark, I think, in the terms of a proper public school, has done the unforgivable. He has knocked down a master, and broken his nose!'

497

'What? What made him do that?'

'The master, apparently, with all the vicious tyranny these little tin gods exert, insulted Rachel. Referred openly to her "dirty relationship with a Communist". In fact, Harry, he called her a whore. It seems he's one of these ultra right-wing fellows, and he just couldn't refrain from getting in that crack in front of an audience of Mark's classmates. With all the immunity from redress that his position gives him. He never bargained for Mark's return. Of course, no matter how right Mark was to defend his sister, he still has struck a master. I don't think you could get him to go back, even if they'd take him. He just packed his things and came here to us. The last person he could go to was Rachel. And Caro won't want to know him after this. I'll let you talk to him, Harry, but I have to warn you that my feelings towards him are wholly sympathetic. It seems from what he told us that this master has some personal grudge against Frazer Campbell.'

'Would you put Mark on, please, Herbert.'

Mark's voice sounded childishly troubled. 'I'm sorry, father. I just couldn't help it. He said it in front of the whole form. It wasn't anything that I could just sit there and swallow. They say he once had a try for the Foreign Office and got turned down. Perhaps it was as much against you as against Rachel and Frazer Campbell. Whatever . . . I couldn't let him say those things just because he's a master. He deserved everything he got, and more. But the other chaps dragged me off him before I did worse damage. I didn't mean to break his nose. I just . . . I just saw red . . .'

'In more ways than one,' Harry said. 'Well, old son, I'm sorry it's happened, but I can't say I'm sorry you didn't sit still under that filthy remark about Rachel. You would have gravely disappointed me if you had.'

There was a silence at the other end of the line. Harry thought he heard Mark sniff, but he made no comment. It wouldn't be surprising if there had been tears at the end of an episode like this. Mark was a boy, after all, who had taken it upon himself to respond like a man. What Harry feared, but did not talk about, was that the master might just decide to go for his full pound of flesh, and prefer charges of assault against Mark. He would look a fool if he did, but the consequences could be extremely serious. Somehow, Harry would have to persuade the headmaster that such a course of action would not be wise.

'Thanks, father. I was scared stiff when I realized what I'd done. But I wasn't going to apologize. And I knew they would expel me, in any case. The thing is, I've let you down. I've been expelled – and I don't suppose any other school will take me. I've even thought – well, if he wants to get nasty, I could be sent to Borstal.'

'Oh,' Harry said, in a tone of sanguinity he didn't feel. 'I wouldn't worry too much about that. I doubt he'd want to take it to court. He'd look such a bloody ass. And as for school . . . there are other places. Places that actually encourage rebels – especially when they rebel against the Establishment.' He said the words with false cheerfulness. The schools that would welcome a boy who had been expelled from Eton were few and far between, and of a type Harry mistrusted. He struggled to regain his perspective. 'Listen, Mark. You haven't done anything disgraceful. You haven't lied, or stolen or cheated. You haven't bullied anyone. You have nothing to be ashamed of.' They talked for a while longer. Mark asked to speak to his mother, and Harry told him she was in New York, expected back the next morning. 'Tell her I'm sorry, father.'

'I'll do that, but she won't be angry with you. She's more likely to be angry with Rachel. Well, try to enjoy yourself with Thea and Herbert. I'll have your mother telephone you tomorrow. It's almost the end of term, anyway, so you won't miss much. By September we'll have you fixed up at some other place . . . Good night, my son.'

Some other place – but where? He grew angry. Mark had done nothing dishonourable. It seemed so unfair that a boy's whole future should be shattered in one instant of protest. If only it had not been a master. Against a master there was no appeal. He was about to go to the desk to find the telephone number of the headmaster of Eton when he realized he was still holding the photo of his daughter, Irina.

Now, as he studied it again, the young face seemed to have a kind of severe bleakness about it. It was not young at all. What had that bastard out in the street said? That their conditions either flourished . . . or they suffered. Mark would never know anything of the kind of life this girl must lead, in fear, always in fear. He thought of them as half brother and sister, and then remembered that there was no actual blood link between them, since Mark was not his son. Whatever happened in his life, Mark could never know half the pain and fear this child had lived through. He probably could not even imagine it.

Harry got the old envelope again, the one in the locked drawer, with his signature and wax across the seal. He looked again at the two photos there, Sonya with the very young Irina, the one first given to him in Paris and Sonya with the older girl. In the single photo he now held, Sonya's absence made him grow cold. *They flourish . . . they suffer*. The child looked at him, faintly accusingly, with those old and knowing eyes, a solitary child. What had they done, Sonya and he? Only to love. To produce this child. It might have gone easier with Sonya if there had been no child. Her father's position might have saved her from the worst of their fury. But perhaps her father also had been caught up in the terror of the purges, one of the intellectuals condemned as Stalin had reigned. Perhaps the father too had disowned and abandoned Sonya. As he, Harry, had done. There might have been just the faintest possibility that he could have taken her out with him when he left. But not after he had spoken to his Ambassador. She had vanished then. Even in his time with her there had been the almost certain knowledge that they would never let her go. She had been a brilliant woman, daughter of a brilliant man. She may have possessed knowledge of some of the inner workings of the Soviet that they could never have permitted to be exported. And then there was the doubt he had at the time, the faintest doubt, the worry that she had been planted on him.

He looked again at the photo of the child. But she had done nothing, knew nothing. She was a mistake. But why should she be punished for it?

Harry took a fresh envelope, placed the three photos inside, sealed it as before. He locked it again in the desk. He knew it was foolish to keep them; they could always be discovered, and in any case their purpose was to torment him. But what else could he do, tear them up, burn them, rent a safety deposit box? He would keep them with him.

Then Harry remembered the threats of the man on the street. He had not mentioned Mark. Only Dena and the girls. Did they even know that Mark was not his son? Had they expected him to feel that Mark was expendable?

Dena came back next morning about eleven o'clock. Harry knew there was no need to meet her, or to send a car, because one was always available to Ginny. He greeted her on the doorstep, waved to Ginny in the departing car, and folded her in his arms. 'What's wrong, my dearest? You look tired.'

She kissed him, but shrugged off the enquiry. 'Oh, you know how New York is. Chris's set is so frenetic. All theatre and no real life. Of course, as soon as anyone knows Ginny is in town, the invitations come flooding in. We were always on the go.'

'You didn't ring me,' Harry said.

'Believe me, I did mean to. As soon as I thought you'd be away from the embassy. But by that time, we had a cocktail party in full swing, or we were on our way to dinner. Harry, it was only four days . . .'

'Yes, I understand. It's . . . It's just been lonely without you.'

She pulled a slight face at him. 'Don't tell me you missed me? I thought a few days to yourself would be a short relief. What did you do?'

'Nothing. Two routine receptions – I almost forget which embassies they were at. Last night I went to dinner with Livy and Alex. It seems to me that Ginny must be a little grateful that Livy has come to share the burden of looking after the Ambassador whenever he decides to show up.'

'I think she is.' Thomas had come into Harry's study with coffee, although Dena did not remember either of them

501

having asked for it. She added cream and sugar, and took her time before asking the question.

'And what's wrong with you, Harry? You don't look that fresh, either. Could it be that time is catching up on us both?'

'It just could be. Or perhaps the Foreign Office has decided that time is catching up on me, and decided to move me on.'

Her face grew more drawn. He saw lines in the downward planes of her cheeks he had never noticed before. 'What . . .? Where are we posted?'

'A very civilized posting, dearest. No hardship. I will be next ambassador to France. Howells is not well, poor chap. He'll resign soon, and in about nine months we'll be in Paris.'

Her face did not show any of the things he had expected. Not pleasure, not gratification. As a loyal and hardworking diplomatic wife she had the right to feel some gratification in the role she had played to make this elevation come about. He couldn't at all decipher the mixture of emotions which crossed her features. She moved swiftly to hide her face behind the coffee cup. 'What? Paris in one leap? I thought at the very least we'd have to go via Egypt or Pakistan. Or even Outer Mongolia –' always their joke. 'Paris. How glamorous!'

'Aren't you pleased, Dena?'

She put down the coffee cup and moved towards him, put her arms closely about him. 'Of course I'm pleased. How you've worked for it. The only other posting that would have pleased me more would have been right here, but we already have a very able ambassador. We'll just have to wait our turn. Paris, that's very grand, Harry. The French expect one to do things so well.'

'Which you will, my darling. You've always known how to do things well. And on a shoestring. Well, it won't have to be a shoestring, this time. Next to the Elysée Palace, you'll have the grandest residence in Paris, and a staff to go with it. Cars and secretaries. And I feel that on that salary I can even squeeze out the money for the clothes you'll need. Just think, my lovely wife, for once I'll be able to give you everything. You'll be one of France's grandest ladies.'

'I . . . I . . .' She went back to her chair, and took up the

502

coffee cup. Then he was amazed to see her put it down again and fumble in her handbag for a tissue to wipe tears from her eyes. 'Oh, don't pay any attention to me. But after waiting for so many years for it, always certain you'd make ambassador, I don't feel quite ready for it.'

'Nonsense, Dena. You've always been ready for it. From the day you married me you would have followed me to ambassadorship in Paris, or Outer Mongolia, or wherever fortune led us.'

She sighed. 'Ah, yes. But I was younger then. I could have sailed through any job the Foreign Office had assigned you. The blissful ignorance of youth. One grows diffident with age and experience.'

'Dena! You're in your prime. Just the right age to excite everyone with your beauty and social talents. You're not an old woman, or a young girl, inexperienced and bewildered. You've seen a lot of the diplomatic world . . .'

'And I've seen what's expected of one. Well . . .' She took up the cup and drank. 'It needs a little getting used to. I must go up and unpack. I expect I'll have to be going back to New York . . .' Her voice wavered. 'Well, I'll be going back to buy some more clothes. They aren't half as expensive here as the French couturiers. Clothes . . . yes, I'll have to be getting some more clothes.' To Harry her tone sounded nothing like the excitement of a woman bound for the Paris embassy or for a shopping spree.

'Dena, before you go upstairs, there's a telephone call you should make. It's about Mark . . .'

Now her face became a chalky white. She sprang to her feet. 'Mark! What's wrong with Mark? Is he all right? Is he ill?'

He drew her over to sit beside him on the sofa, and told her all the circumstances, all the details he could remember. He told her what he had said to Mark. 'I said he had done the only honourable thing. He didn't lie or cheat or steal, Dena. He did what any decent man would have done. I said so to the headmaster when I spoke to him. They will take no further action in the matter. It would make Adams look so bad. But they don't want Mark back at Eton.'

'Poor boy,' she said. 'Poor little boy. I'm so sorry for you, Harry. He should have been a son to follow you. Instead of that, he'll go off on his own tack, a renegade, always rebelling. And it's my fault . . .'

'What do you mean! Your fault?'

'I could never give Mark the love and attention he deserved. He isn't your son, and I could never feel anything but shame when I thought of him. I know what sort of mother I've been – I've done so little to help and support him. We were always being separated from him, and when we were together, it was always in the middle of a crowd. He hasn't any idea what a real mother would have been like. I've been too critical of him . . . wanting him to be perfection because he was the son you should have had. And in a peculiar way he's always known it. He's always sensed he was the outsider. I've done nothing to help him. I've always been so riddled with guilt—'

'Dena, stop this! I've never heard such a parcel of rubbish in my life. Mark is my son, as you are my wife. I love you both. For ever. Now I want you just to make one short telephone call to Mark. It's afternoon there now, and he'll have been on tenterhooks all day, waiting to hear from you. I told him you'd be back this morning, and you'd telephone. Say the right things to him, Dena. Let him know you love him. Just let him know it doesn't make any difference.'

'Of course it makes a difference, and we both know it. Where will he go to school now when he's been thrown out of Eton? What will become of him?' She began to weep.

He got up and placed the call to St Just, not knowing how long it would take to get through. While they waited he went and poured a brandy for Dena and brought it to her. 'Here, dearest. Drink, and try to get the tears out of your voice. Just say nice things to him. He's shown a courage few boys of his age would have done. Nothing to be ashamed of. Rather to be proud of . . .'

Her reaction to both pieces of news puzzled him. The fact that she was to be the wife of the Ambassador to France seemed to frighten her rather than elate her. The reaction he had expected would have been one of jubilation, not this shrinking away from a task, a job he would have been sure, until now, she would have joyfully accepted. He had told her that first, so that some of the pleasure he had been certain it would bring would carry in her voice when she made the call to Mark which she must make. But what he saw was guilt and shame and, yes, fear. He had never known Dena like this. He almost did not recognize the woman who sat on the sofa next to him. She had always been so bright and bold, ready for anything, ready for whatever came, good and bad. She huddled like an old woman, sipping the brandy. And when the call finally came through, that was how she talked to Mark. Obediently she repeated the words Harry had told her to say. She praised him, told him he had done the right thing, but her voice carried no conviction. He would have hoped to hear her laugh and joke with Mark, to tell him that he missed nothing by missing Eton. That there were other worlds. He could hear Mark's voice asking a question. 'What?' she said, as if the idea were foreign to her. 'Come here now? Well . . . well, darling, couldn't you just stay on for a few days with Thea and Herbert? Just a few days. It's a bit chaotic here . . . Yes, we'll arrange it. Soon, Mark . . . soon.' She hung up without asking to speak to Thea or Herbert.

Harry was appalled as she put down the brandy glass, and drifted out of the study in a kind of trance. Never in his life had he seen her look as she did. Withdrawn, closing him and Mark and the world out. She'd had two shocks – the posting to Paris and Mark's expulsion. Two things he might have expected Dena to take in her stride, with a joke or two thrown in. She must have known she was supremely fitted for her role in Paris; she should have known that alternatives could be found for Mark, that he had abilities that would find their outlet in some way, however unconventional. She had made it sound, through all the false words he had put into her mouth, that his future was dead.

She came down to lunch wearing slacks and a shirt. She seemed so much more relaxed when he made her a gin and tonic. 'I shouldn't. I've had Thomas bring me up one while I unpacked.' But she didn't refuse it, and asked for another.

She brushed aside questions about New York. 'Rachel!' she said angrily. 'It's Rachel I can't forgive. She's made a mess of Mark's life because she's made a mess of her own. *She's* the one we should telephone.'

'Dena, don't make it worse. Rachel has chosen her way. No doubt she never imagined it could bring hardship to anyone but herself. She must love this Campbell man or she . . .'

'Is blinded by him, Dena rejoined, with bitterness in her tone. 'Oh, God, why can't my children do anything right?'

'*Our* children, Dena.'

She hadn't seemed to hear him. She left the table, her lunch almost untouched, and poured herself another gin and tonic. 'One of them so smug in doing exactly what one might hope her to do that she's almost a parody. Our Caro . . . lovely . . . just about perfect. And totally lacking in a sense of humour. Perfectly suited to that dummy she's married.' She turned back from the sideboard to face him. 'And Rachel, now she might be full of humour, but it's a decidedly black humour. She's ashamed of her family. She wants nothing to do with us. And Mark . . . ah, Mark, the misbegotten.'

Harry's chair slid across the polished floor as he stood up. 'Dena! I forbid you ever to use that word. Mark is a wonderful and talented boy.'

'Talented? What talents does he have? If I did choose to bear a child who was not yours, Harry, I might have had the sense to choose a father who would give him some . . . some . . . ah, I don't know what. It's my fault, Harry. I've given you children who do not match up to you. *I* don't match up.'

His nerves seemed to disintegrate. All night long he had lain awake, waiting for it to be time to telephone Eton. And all night long he had stared into the darkness, seeing images of the girl in the photo, the young-old girl who was Mark's age, and the image of Mark himself before his eyes. Poor kids, was all he could think. And his guilt had been as great as Dena's now seemed to be. But last night she had not known about Mark. He had to give her time to adjust to that, and to the thought that their pleasant, cosy existence here in Washington, with Ginny as her *alter ego*, would soon end.

'Nothing to match up to at this moment, my dear. I'll just let you get over your nerves, and next time you speak to Mark, I hope to hear something kinder. I want you to welcome him here to Washington as soon as he can come. Our children are *ours*, Dena. We take them, warts and all.'

'Warts and all? Oh, go to hell, Harry! You know you've always wanted, expected, everyone to be perfect. Beautiful, talented, clever. It must be quite a dog's dinner to try to swallow both Rachel and Mark . . .'

The words ended as he reached to take her shoulder, as if to shake her, to stop the violent thrust of her emotions. 'You're becoming drunk and hysterical. I suggest that you go to bed and try to sleep. Then it will all seem different. Why on earth has the world suddenly collapsed?'

She didn't answer him; she leaned over the sideboard, her face averted from him. He closed the door as quietly as his mood would allow, feeling angry and dismayed. The stern face of the blonde child was before him. Dena didn't know the half of it.

Later that afternoon he was puzzled to hear the car Dena drove herself start up, and he watched from a window as Dena backed it out of the driveway. He went to Thomas. 'Where has Lady Camborne gone?'

Thomas permitted a little surprise to appear in his face. 'Why, Lord Camborne, I thought you knew. She's gone to join Mrs Clayton at Prescott Hill. She said Mrs Clayton went straight there after she dropped her off here this morning. I suppose Lady Camborne was hoping you could join them, sir. But with your work, and all . . .'

Harry knew that their quarrel, the tones of it, if not the actual words, would have been heard in the kitchen. Dena's departure was seen as the normal flight from a domestic upset.

'Yes, my work . . . lots of it, Thomas. It spoils a lot of good times.'

507

'Yes, sir. I know, sir. Work spoils things for just about everybody. 'Cept them that like it . . . Will you be alone for dinner, Lord Camborne?'

'Yes, just me, Thomas. Anything will do.'

'Cook would be offended if she heard you say that, sir. Simple but not "just anything".' The black man permitted himself a chuckle. 'Come to think of it, sir, Master Mark wouldn't like it, either. I seen that boy make a sandwich, and it was like a creation. I hope we're going to be seeing Master Mark this summer, sir. Sure does liven up the place.'

'Oh, you'll be seeing him, Thomas. Don't doubt it.'

Harry went and stared at the papers on his desk for the rest of the afternoon. He locked them up, habit making this imperative. Then he went upstairs to their bedroom. He was shocked by its appearance. The closet doors were thrown wide, hangers and some of Dena's clothes lay on the floor, as if she had plucked at random. Drawers containing her lingerie were left open. He tried to tidy up, not wanting the maid to see the disarray. He was amazed at the evidence of the storm that had shaken Dena, who was always so meticulous in the treatment of her clothes. She had taken only one small suitcase; he carried the other one she had used for the New York trip up to the box-room. Perhaps she had been right to go to Ginny at Prescott Hill; they would talk, as women and close friends do; they would walk for miles. She would breathe fresh air, and perhaps return on Monday with her perspectives changed, her fear and anger and shame gone, talked away with Ginny.

He had settled with a drink and the *New York Times* waiting for Thomas to call him to dinner, when the telephone rang. He picked it up, hoping it would be Dena. Ginny's voice. 'Hello, Harry. How are you? All well? That's good. I've just looked in on Alex and Livy. Glad to hear you were there last night. New York was . . .'

He felt himself grow cold. 'You've just looked in on Livy and Alex? Where are you, Ginny?'

'Why, I'm here at home, in Washington. I just thought I'd talk with Dena for a few minutes.'

'Ginny – Dena told Thomas that she was going to Prescott

Hill, and you would be there, expecting her. That you had gone straight there from the airport. She left hours ago!'

'Oh!' Ginny seemed to take a long time to gather her thoughts. 'Well, it's just some misunderstanding. I did say I thought I'd go there next weekend. But don't worry, Harry. There's always Landers and a cook at Prescott Hill, as you know. They won't be expecting her, but they're always very glad to see her . . .'

'Ginny, don't waffle with me! Dena came back here looking and acting as if the sky had fallen in on her. I had two pieces of news – one good, and one not so good, but not catastrophic. Her reaction to neither of them was what I would expect from Dena. Do you know something? Did something happen in New York? You have to tell me, Ginny.'

'I won't waste time. I think we'd both better go to Prescott Hill at once.'

'You'll have to drive. Dena's taken her car, and I told my driver I wouldn't need him this weekend.'

'I'll pick you up in a few minutes.' She hung up.

She was at his house in less than ten minutes. She gave the wheel of the car to him. She waited until they were beyond the hustle of the Washington Saturday night traffic, set on the road to Prescott Hill before she spoke.

'Drive carefully, Harry, and listen. I'll answer your questions when I've said my piece.'

'Go ahead.'

'The visit to New York was not for clothes. We barely saw Chris. Just told her we had full-time engagements. Dena was in hospital for those few days.'

'Hospital!' For a few seconds he seemed to let the car leave his control, then righted it. 'Why? What was she—'

'You said you'd hear me out. It's something that women dread, Harry. Some of us just can't face it. She told me only last week. A lump in her right breast. She's known it was there for some time, and she didn't do anything about it. And recently she discovered it had increased in size. Then she told me about it. She was in a near-panic and she didn't want you to know because she was certain it was benign. She didn't want you to have the worry of it, even for a few days. I suggested a surgeon I knew in New York. You might have noticed that we seemed to take off for that trip in rather a hurry.'

'Is she all right?'

'Harry, please. Let me tell it my own way. He examined her and said he must have a look at it immediately. I was there with her, Harry. She wasn't alone. She went into hospital that same afternoon. They took X-rays. She would sign only for an excision biopsy . . .'

'What the hell's that?'

'It means they take only a small section of the lump. It's frozen, and it goes at once to the pathologist. Mostly they hold the patient under anaesthetic until they hear the report, and if it's . . . malignant, they go ahead and perform a mastectomy.'

'A mast . . .?'

'They remove the breast and some surrounding tissue, lymph glands to find out if it's penetrated the lymph system. But Dena wouldn't agree to that. She would allow only the excision. That meant she was awake and fully conscious when he, the surgeon, came to tell her that they hadn't really needed the pathologist. It was evident to them all that it was malignant.'

He slammed on the brakes. They were on a dark and lonely stretch of the road. He edged the car over to the shoulder slowly, and stopped. 'What happened then?'

'Nothing. I was with her all the time. She refused to let me leave when the doctor came to tell her. He advised that a mastectomy should be performed immediately. He thought from what he'd seen that it could have progressed rather far, but that there was a lot they could do. She told him that as soon as he could remove that little drain they had put in her she would leave and come back here and think it over. I thought he'd explode! She got the usual lecture about not reporting the lump as soon as she noticed it. About letting vanity and fear put her life in danger. I finally succeeded in getting him out of the room. It was a stand-off between them. He wanted to operate the next morning, and she kept saying she had to get back to Washington to "think about it". He told her there was nothing to think about. She had to have the mastectomy, or she would die. She asked about having just the lump removed, and radium therapy. He said he'd never known it to work. They were shouting at each other, Harry . . .'

'Why wasn't I told? I would have insisted.'

'It wasn't something she could tell you over the phone. A few days wouldn't make a difference. I tried to get the surgeon to understand that she just needed time to get used to the idea. He took me into his office and told me that no matter how soon the operation, he didn't give her a very good chance. The lump was very deep-seated, and in what he called "an unfavourable position". It's bad, Harry, we've got to go on. We can't sit here discussing it. Dena shouldn't be alone.'

He obeyed her mechanically, but he drove very fast. The dusk was closing in rapidly. There were fifteen more miles to Prescott Hill.

'I could have made her,' he said. 'Why didn't someone tell me? Dena's life! Why did she even hesitate?'

'Harry . . . I think most men find it hard to understand what this operation means to a woman. At the very least, it's a mutilation. At worst, it may be more than that. It may mean that in Dena's mind she could see herself as only half a woman, or no woman at all. She's at a very vulnerable age, Harry. The age when a woman starts to feel that youth and all that goes with it have gone. And with this operation one of the things that made her a woman is taken away, leaving not just a void but a real ugliness. For a woman as beautiful, as feminine as Dena, that's a nightmare most men would find impossible to understand.'

'But doesn't she know that I love her? Whatever she looked like, I'd love and cherish her. All I want is her life.'

'Part of her knows that. And part of her also knows that if this treatment failed, if she were to die, the sacrifice would have been useless. She would have died ugly and mutilated in her own mind. She was trying to battle it out with herself. Trying to decide what to do.'

'You should have told me, Ginny.'

'I would have. If I found out she hadn't told you by tomorrow I would have broken my promise to her to say nothing. In fact, I have already broken my promise. But when I heard that she'd gone away to Prescott Hill by herself, I knew I had to tell you.'

'Then let's pray she did go to Prescott Hill. That was what she told Thomas. She could have gone anywhere – be holed up in some motel somewhere. Dear God, this is terrible. If I'd only known . . . and to think of the news I hit her with when she came home.'

'What news?'

He told her about the appointment to the Paris embassy, and then Mark's expulsion from Eton. 'I see now why she wasn't pleased about the prospect of being ambassador's wife in France, not with what she faced. She would be expected to be on her toes all the time. No depressions, no black moods. And if the . . . the operation and radium treatment didn't work, she would be dying in a very public position. No, I can't let myself believe it won't work. It will work. My poor love, my poor girl.'

'And then she blamed herself for what Mark did, I know it sounds irrational, but now I know she was, is, for the time being, irrational. My poor darling Dena. What on earth must she think of me that she couldn't tell me?'

'Harry, try not to blame yourself. It goes with the situation. No one wants to admit that it's happened to them. Close your eyes, and it might go away. She was even talking about another doctor, another pathologist, in case this one might have made a mistake. That's perfectly natural. It's what *I* would feel, Harry. I'd want to be sure. Give her time. Be gentle. Make her understand that it must be done. We can't just let Dena's life go down the drain without making every effort. We have both to push and support her.'

'And there's Mark,' Harry said. 'She taking the blame for something she could't possibly be responsible for. She accused herself of being a bad mother to him. Said all kinds of foolish things about neglecting him, and being hard on him because he's not . . . Well, that's another story.'

'You don't think I don't know that story, Harry? I was

there with Dena all the months of her pregnancy. I was there when Mark was born. I was the only one . . .'

'The only one besides me. No wonder she ran away. I wish to God she'd run directly to you. I wish she hadn't gone off alone. We had a row over lunch. Can you imagine it? Can you imagine that we should have quarrelled at this time, when I should have been the most loving, the most protective, the most reassuring?'

'You can be all of those things, Harry, now that you know. If necessary, if that's what seems best for Dena, you can give up the Paris embassy. The prospect of coping with it may be just too much for her. Convince her that it doesn't matter. Bring Mark over here when she has the operation, and try to help him understand how hard it is for a woman. Knowing Mark, I know that he will love and help her. It could be the thing that brings them closer than they've ever been.'

'She didn't want him to come. The last thing she said to him was that he should stay in St Just for a while.'

'It's your job to make her understand that he will need to be near her. That we will all be here. She has to have the operation, Harry. It won't go away. The surgeon didn't put her chances very high. They have to do further pathology on the lymph glands, but he's almost certain it's spread. He tried not to let her know this, but somehow it comes through in their manner. But the operation and radium treatment could save her. It has to be tried.'

'It will be tried. Everything will be tried. I'll tell the Foreign Office I'll just stay where I am. And if they don't agree, I'll resign. I've resigned before. I'll keep her and Mark together, and you, Ginny. We'll need you every minute of the time. Whatever time there may be left.'

'Wherever you are, I'll be. God knows, I have nothing left in my life now except what I may be able to give to you and Dena and Mark. I've always loved him so much. He was almost born into my arms. I so wished for a son myself. I would care for him . . . always. As I care for Dena . . .' He heard her voice waver.

'We're not going to lose her, Ginny. I don't think I could

513

live if we lost her. We won't. We'll fight this. We'll make her fight.'

They had come to the open wrought-iron gates of Prescott Hill. The car bumped over the cattle grid, and swept past the gate house where the head groom lived. As they carried on along the long drive towards the house, lights came on, and Harry caught sight, in the rear-view mirror, of a flash-lamp shining, as if someone had rushed out of the lodge and tried to read the licence plate. They would probably recognize Ginny's car, but in any case they would have telephoned through to the house before they reached it.

The butler, Landers, was on the steps. It was now fully dark, and every light on the wide porches surrounding the house was lighted.

'So glad to see you, Mrs Clayton. Lady Camborne said you might come tomorrow, but she wasn't sure. And Lord Camborne. Is Lady Camborne not well? She looked . . . well, she looked a little strange. Not her usual self.'

'What do you mean looked? Where is she?'

'We're not sure, my lord. We didn't think a thing about it until it began to grow dark. She had asked for drinks in the library, and said she just wanted to be alone. She said she'd come on ahead of you, Mrs Clayton, because you were detained in Washington. So I brought in the drinks tray, and left her. She said she didn't want any tea, and that just a sandwich or anything else light would do for supper. Not to take any trouble. As if it has ever been any trouble to do anything for Lady Camborne. Cook was . . .'

'Where is she!'

'Well, sir, that's what we don't know. We heard her out at the practice range with the guns. What she so often does that we didn't pay any particular attention. It got to be dusk, and we were busy preparing a meal to tempt her to eat something, as she didn't look very . . . very robust. And then suddenly I realized that it was almost dark. I went to look for her. So far as we know she isn't in the house. I've called Mac and Peter –' Harry was now aware of the head groom and one of the stable lads standing within the circle of light. 'We were just setting out to look when Mrs Mac

514

called from the lodge that Mrs Clayton's car had gone by. We just didn't know, Lord Camborne, that she hadn't come back.'

'The practice range, you said. How many shots did you hear!'

'Oh, the usual number. You stop hearing them after a while. That's why everything seemed quite normal, until we found that Lady Camborne hadn't come back. I'm sure it's quite normal. She's just taking her time walking back.'

For an instant Ginny leaned against the car. She was remembering the day her young husband had ridden away and not returned, and where he had been found. She was afraid to make the journey to the practice range.

They found her there, beneath the trees, curled up as if she were sleeping. The revolver seemed to have slipped from her hand. Harry fell to his knees and looked at the ugly sight of the bullet wound in her temple, and the other side of her head blown out. He bent and kissed that strange, cold face.

'Forgive me, my darling.'

The night seemed endless. First they had called the state troopers, who had come and looked at Dena's body, looked at the gun. Harry had immediately covered her head with his jacket, but he was required formally to identify her in their presence. The revolver was taken away, also the two rifles she had brought with her. 'Used to using them, was she, Mr . . .?' The trooper stumbled over Harry's title, and decided he didn't need to use it.

'Yes, since she was a child. Almost every time she came here to Prescott Hill she came out to target practice.'

'But the hand gun, sir.'

'It belonged to the late Mr Clayton. My wife used it whenever she wanted to, with his permission.'

'But she didn't have a licence for a hand gun, sir? You mean she just took it and practised with it whenever she wanted to? And Mr Clayton permitted it?'

'My wife is . . . is a very good shot. Mr Clayton trusted

her. It probably was illegal . . . but it was only ever used on the estate, never anywhere else.'

There was a noticeable care in the way the police dealt with the situation. First of all, it had happened at Prescott Hill, and that in itself would have made them wary and quiet in their ways, spare with their words. Then there was the added complication that Dena was the wife of one of the ministers at the British embassy. Diplomatic immunity was uppermost in their minds, if not diplomatic protocol. For them, it was a troublesome combination. The address of the dead woman, and of her husband, was the District of Columbia, not the state of Virginia. An ambulance came to take Dena's body to the morgue at Knottsville, the county seat. The guns, the revolver and two rifles, were taken away, wrapped in plastic. Police cars ringed the scene with the headlights blazing. Harry started to go in the ambulance with Dena's body. A state trooper restrained him. 'It isn't any use, sir. You can't help her now. The body, that is, your wife, will be released to you immediately after the autopsy.'

'Autopsy? My God, any fool can see how she died!'

'It's the law, sir. Routine. Sometimes these things are done to disguise something else.'

By now a captain of state troopers was with them. Landers, the butler, who had come with them to the practice range, had stayed at the scene. The captain asked only a few questions. 'Lady . . . er . . . Camborne, she was out there on the practice range for some time? Did you hear many shots?'

'Quite a number. As I told Lord Camborne, after a while you stop listening. Yes, quite a number . . .' The troopers, by flashlight, were searching the immediate area, picking up spent cartridges.

'So it seemed a normal thing to you. You were used to . . . to Lady Camborne coming out here and practising for quite a while.'

'It was completely normal. She used to say she worked off some nervous energy this way. We didn't think a thing about it, except that it would do her good to get some fresh air. She said she'd been in New York all week and I remarked to Cook that she looked a bit peaky . . .'

'Just the facts now. We'll hear your opinions later.'

Only two shots were fired from the six-cylinder revolver. Harry wondered, in agony, if she'd had the coolness to fire one shot first at the target to make sure the gun was in working order, before putting it to her head to fire the second shot. He shivered violently in the warm night air.

'We'll go back to the house,' Ginny said. 'No purpose, now, to stay here.' The ambulance had driven off, moving slowly across the grass until it reached the gravel road that led from the guest cottages to the house.

By now, the word had gone through the hierarchy at Knottsville. When they arrived at the house, a detective inspector was waiting. He knew Ginny by sight. 'Evening, Mrs Clayton. You are . . .' He glanced briefly at his note pad. 'Lord Camborne? Husband of Lady Camborne?'

He refused the offer of a drink. Ginny had poured a brandy for herself and Harry. Landers had already brought in a tray of small sandwiches and coffee. He and Cook were anticipating a long night. But the inspector was very brief in his questioning. 'Are you aware, sir, of any reason why your wife would want to take her own life?'

'May I answer, Inspector?' Ginny said.

'Certainly ma'am. If . . . if Lord Camborne is agreeable.'

'I have just spent the last week in New York with Lady Camborne. We returned this morning . . .' Ginny went on steadily, sparing Harry the agony of having to speak. She told him all that had happened in New York, the situation which Dena had confronted. 'It's understandable that Lady Camborne was terribly upset. She hadn't even told her husband about it when she decided to come out here . . . If I hadn't called Lord Camborne he wouldn't have known that I wasn't with her.'

Harry drained the brandy. 'I had better add, and you will certainly be able to verify this from my butler and cook in Washington, that my wife and I quarrelled at lunch. Over personal matters. Two pieces of news which seemed to upset her very much, and I didn't know why they upset her so much. She didn't tell me . . . she didn't tell me anything

517

about her own trouble, And I was dense enough not to be able to see that something terrible was eating at her.'

The inspector nodded. 'Understandable, sir. No one could be expected to guess . . .'

He asked a few more questions. He was treading very warily. What he was handling involved the McClintocks, since everything that happened at Prescott Hill involved them, the Claytons, and now this pair from the British embassy. 'One last question, sir.'

'Yes?'

'Did your wife leave any message, a note?'

'I thought of that,' Ginny said. 'I've asked Landers to go all through the house. There is nothing in any obvious place, but then she didn't expect us to come here.'

'Well, I'll be in touch with the DC Metropolitan Police. In fact, we've already been in touch with them. They are probably at your house now, sir. We will try to keep the press out of it as long as we can, sir. But naturally, they're going to want a statement. We'll stall as long as we can. Until you can let your family know . . .' He had begun to piece together the people involved. Alex's front-page divorce. The five-million dollar baby. Any news connected with Prescott Hill was big news in the county, in fact, it was news in Virginia and the whole country. He couldn't afford to make blunders. If it was too late for the Sunday newspapers, Monday would see the headlines.

'I'm sorry, Mrs Clayton . . . sir. We'll do our best with the press.'

He was gone, and Harry had to begin the task of telephoning. There was only one line from Prescott Hill, and so Ginny could not share the burden. He began with the Washington house. Thomas answered, and Harry knew he was weeping. 'Can't imagine why Lady Camborne would do so such a thing, sir. Must have been an accident. Always accidents with those pesky guns. The police been here. They just asked a few questions – like when Lady Camborne got back this morning, when she left this afternoon, when Mrs Clayton picked you up. Sir . . . I can't believe it.'

'I'll try to explain when I see you, Thomas. I probably

518

won't be back until early morning. I don't feel like driving right now. Now Mrs Clayton . . .' He couldn't bring himself to say that to return to Washington would seem to be leaving Dena behind, cold and lonely, in a little county morgue. It was still impossible for him to realize that he would never again hold her, that his words and his arms would never wake her. No warmth from him now would bring that cold flesh back to life. His chance to help her had come and gone, and he hadn't even recognized it. He felt as if he were forever damned.

'Let me do the rest of the telephoning, Harry.' But Ginny, now that the inspector had gone, and the last of the patrol cars seemed to be leaving, had begun to weep. 'I should never have left her, not for a single instant. I should have come right into the house this morning with her and insisted she told you. I should never have let her out of my sight until I knew she had told you. But I never guessed . . . about the Paris posting, and about Mark. Things that would distract you, and make whatever way she was acting seem understandable. I thought you would read it in her face. One just doesn't think of these other things.' She put her face in her hands for a few moments. 'I thought it was a matter of a few days until we had persuaded her to change her mind about the operation, or at least helped her to make up her mind that it should be done. Had to be done. I just couldn't imagine she would take it this way. It had to have been a deadly impulse. She came out with the guns to practise, and take her minds off things . . . and then she used the revolver on herself . . . A terrible impulse. That's why I should never have left her side. Oh dear God, Harry. I failed you both.'

'I failed her. That I will live with for the rest of my life. There can be no blame but mine, Ginny.' He wiped his brow with the back of his hand. 'Give me another brandy, Ginny. I've got a lot of telephoning to do.' He took it from her, staring across the room, seeing nothing in particular. 'Oh, my darling love. Why didn't I see, why did I let you feel so abandoned?'

Once the telephoning started, he wished he were back in

Washington. It could have been done more easily, not going through this rural exchange. He telephoned Alex. 'I hope Livy has gone to bed. Don't wake her if she's asleep. Let it keep until morning. Bad news is quick enough coming.'

Alex was shocked, but still the businessman in him came through, the practical training, and, as Harry well knew, the love and concern.

'Look, why don't you let me take all this off your back? I can do the telephoning. Mark, Caro, Rachel . . . anyone else you want. It's too hard on you, Harry.' It was probably rhe first time he had used Harry's first name. 'Let me do it.'

'Thanks, old man. But I'd never forgive myself if I didn't speak to each of them. I'm their father.'

'Yes. I respect that. I understand. Livy went to bed early. I'll let her rest. I'll call Chris, and my grandfather.'

But before Harry could place another call, Andrew McClintock was on the line. 'Your butler called me. Someone from the press had already tried to get in. This is very terrible news. I don't understand . . .'

'It's nothing I wish to talk about on the telephone, Mr McClintock,' Harry said wearily, now realizing the difficulty of explaining what had happened to people who were far away, and with the almost certain knowledge that his conversations were being listened to on the local exchange.

'If that's the case, then you'd better come back to Washington. Come to my house. I'll send a car immediately.'

As always, he had taken over and, as nearly always, his instincts were right. He had already begun to think of the reaction of the press, he would certainly have thought of the local exchange, he would think of unguarded words or actions. Far better to have Harry and Ginny, in their distraught state, under his control.

Harry sighed helplessly. 'I'm giving up, Ginny. I have to leave my darling here among strangers, but then I can't go with her where she's gone, in any sense. I'll let Mr McClintock do what is wisest. His secretary can place the calls, and then I can talk with the children. The embassy must be informed, if they don't already know . . . We'll wait for the car . . .' He stood up, and groped desperately for her. He wept in her arms. 'Why did I let it happen? I should have known . . .'

The telephone rang. Swiftly he jerked himself out of Ginny's arms. 'Yes?'

'Minister? It's been an unpleasant evening. We warned you. This is just to let you know that we mean it.'

'Who's this?'

'You know very well whom we represent minister. We watch very carefully, but you don't seem to take our warnings carefully. Your wife is dead. There are others. All your women, minister. We expect better of you in the future. We need say no more on the telephone.'

'You bastard! This has nothing to do with you. You know it!'

'How did we know that your wife was dead, minister? Think about it.' The connection was cut.

Ginny went to him. 'Who was that? What were you talking about?'

He had collapsed back into the cushions of the sofa. He breathed deeply, letting almost a minute go before he attempted an answer. 'A crank call, Ginny. A particularly horrible one. I think we had better not answer the phone again, or let Landers take it. If it's urgent enough, he can tell us . . .'

'But who . . .?'

'Some damn nut. Hell, it could even have been one of the police who was here. Or someone he talked to. Or someone on the telephone exchange.' He gestured savagely. 'Oh, God, Ginny. It doesn't matter. Nothing seems to matter now.'

2

The smooth mechanism of McClintock-Clayton, the embassy and the State moved into action. Harry stayed with Andrew McClintock, and Ginny returned to her own house. Harry had visits from Livy and Alex. He talked with Mark and Rachel and Caroline. He heard tears, and often wept himself.

521

He had little sleep, and what he did have was haunted, as were his waking hours, by the memory of that slight figure, curled up, with the gun just beyond reach of her hand.

The autopsy was performed, and confirmed that death had occurred as the result of a single shot through the right temple. It noted no other lacerations on the body, except the very recent evidence of an excision on the right breast. The pathologist's report confirmed that a malignant tumour was present, and that cancer had spread to the lymph system. The body was released for burial.

They had decided that the burial would be at Prescott Hill. 'It's as much a home to her as she's ever had. I can't go through with the farce of bringing her back to lie with her parents,' Harry said. 'Here, at least for a while, people will remember her. They will remember that Blair is buried here and maybe they'll spare a thought for her.'

Only Livy had objected. 'It should be St Just. There she would be remembered for ever. She would never be lonely . . .'

Harry looked at her bleakly. 'Dear love, perhaps you're right. But I haven't the strength to go through with it. I just wish her buried, and at peace, as soon as possible. Enough strange hands have touched her. She has suffered enough indignity.'

Livy wept, and Andrew McClintock, alarmed, sent her home. 'Rest, girl, rest. You have the living to think about. A healthy child . . . Don't give it away to the dead.'

The others had arrived. Livy had insisted, against every objection, on going to the airport to meet Mark. She saw his white, stern, and terribly grown-up face. He said only one thing. 'Did she do it because of me? Was she so ashamed?'

He almost fell into Livy's arms. 'Of course not. There was something else. Something she couldn't face.' She got back into the car, holding Mark. Ginny was with her, and on the way back to the McClintock mansion she tried to explain what had happened to Dena, her fears, the possibility that she would have died no matter what was done for her.

'She just took a quicker way, Mark. But it's a way that

requires more courage than to die slowly. This was her decision.'

'I don't believe it!' he stormed. 'She wouldn't have gone without a goodbye to anyone. Not even to my father. It must have been an accident. She would never leave us all this way.'

It was also what Livy thought, though logic appeared to rule out any possibility of an accident. She held the boy close to her, not caring that he pressed against her swollen body, that he felt the kicks of the child within her.

'None of us understands, Mark. I suppose that was why she couldn't leave a note. It was impossible to put what she felt into words. It was a sudden decision, just there, with the gun in her hand . . .' That was what most people thought.

'But she has hurt my father so much. She would never have done that to him.'

'Perhaps,' Ginny said quietly, 'she wanted to spare him the worse hurt of watching her die slowly.' She was murmuring in her despair at trying to make a boy of his age understand something she was very far from understanding herself. All she knew for certain was the desolation of a woman in Dena's position. She had tried often to put herself in that place, and understanding grew. But there was no way to tell to a young boy what she, as a mature woman, had only in the past few days begun to contemplate and comprehend.

Rachel arrived, stern and mostly silent. 'We failed her. She didn't trust any of us enough to help her through this. I blame myself. I blame my father. He was the one who could have made the difference.'

'If she had told him,' Ginny reminded her curtly. 'You had no small part in adding to her anguish. You do realize that Mark was expelled as a direct result of taking exception to that insult to you and your lover, Frazer Campbell?'

'Why on earth don't people mind their own business! I didn't need Mark to spring to the defence of my reputation. My life is my own.'

'And that, apparently, is what Dena thought about her life. Let it rest, Rachel. Leave her in peace, whatever her motives. Don't blame your father, or Mark, or yourself. Never blame your mother.'

Caroline arrived along with Toby. They had arranged to stay with friends in Washington, as if to distance themselves as much as possible from this disgraceful affair. 'How could she do it?' Caroline said. 'I would have expected mother to be more thoughtful of the family.'

'How dare you!' Livy shouted at her. They had come to see her at the McClintock mansion. 'Give a thought to what she must have been feeling! You expect her to die a graceful death, though a very painful and harrowing one, just so there should be no taint on you. She did what she decided to do. Perhaps any one of us would have done it in her situation.'

Andrew McClintock called at Massachusetts Avenue early in the morning to try to persuade Livy not to attend the burial that day at Prescott Hill. He was surprisingly gentle, not making demands, only giving a suggestion. 'I wish you wouldn't go, Livy. It can only distress you. Think of the baby. Only about six more weeks to go.'

'That's all you think about. How do you think I'd feel if I didn't go? Not say goodbye to her? In a sense she gave me life. None of us was permitted to see her, not after the autopsy. Except Lord Camborne. It must have been terrible. The very least I can do is be there when she is buried.'

Chris had come, and was gently touching Andrew McClintock's shoulder. She had arrived the night before, had paid a brief visit to Livy and Alex and Mark, and then had gone to stay with Ginny. 'Let her come, grandfather. She will feel worse if she's left alone. There's nothing worse than staying alone . . . and just imagining.'

He appeared to recognize the logic of this. 'Very well. But, Livy, spare yourself as much as you can. Stay in the car until the last moment. We won't forget you are there . . .'

The little church near Prescott Hill was packed with friends, the curious and the press. Andrew McClintock had made very special efforts to see that the press was excluded, but he had no grounds in law for keeping them out. The case had caused more than a mild sensation in Washington and beyond. It involved not only the McClintock and Clayton families, but the revelations of the autopsy had forcefully brought out the spectre of breast cancer, the tangled fears and nightmares such a thought raised in women. There had been pictures of Dena in the press, Dena at the height of her beauty, wearing a tiara borrowed from Ginny, attending a state function in Paris. Dena pictured with Ambassador McClintock. Even one taken from the British press of Dena on Coronation Day, with ermine-trimmed robes and coronet. There were pictures of her children: Mark recently expelled from Eton; Rachel, who was prominently linked with the left-wing politician, Frazer Campbell. There was a picture of Viscount and Viscountess Osborne arriving at Washington airport. One paper had even resurrected a picture of Alex and Nancy Winterton on their wedding day. And there was a single shot of Livy on the campus of Georgetown University. There were as many pictures of Christine Clayton as anyone wanted to choose from. It was something that not even Andrew McClintock could keep under control. Unlike Blair's burial, too much time had elapsed to be able to keep this event partially secret.

It turned out to be a stiflingly hot day, a foretaste of the worst of the Virginia summer to come. As soon as she entered the little church on Alex's arm, Livy began once again to long for the wind-swept graveyard on the hill at St Just. She endured the service, hardly knowing what was going on, the minister's words washing over her without meaning. What did he know of the woman they had all loved? Who could remember the war years when she had gone shooting for rabbit and hare to provide their meals? Only they in St Just would have remembered that and have understood the choice of a gun to end her life. If that was what had happened. In her grief, Livy had begun to see it as a piece of deliberate carelessness on Dena's part, the accident she had been hoping would happen. Part of Livy had begun to understand . . . it had been such an accident as she might have hoped for in Dena's place. Finally she knew why she had insisted on coming.

Mark kept close to her and Alex, wanting to cling to her,

525

and knowing her body would bear no more weight. Then there was Harry, his face grey, almost expressionless, lines carved deeply in its elegant thinness. He seemed to have aged uncountable years, in uncountable ways. His one close look at Livy, which seemed to blaze with yearning and love and a kind of compassion which could only spring from shared suffering, gave her the reason why she was there against all the dictates of good sense. She watched his face, as the coffin was lowered into the ground. As soon as it was decent, he plunged through the crowd towards the cars. Rachel followed him. Caroline waited, being careful that she did not ride in the same car as her father. Mark stayed with Livy and Alex. The crowd parted for them, a small gesture of sympathy towards her advanced pregnancy which they had not afforded to her before. She felt a wetness. 'Quickly, Alex, we have to get to Prescott Hill.'

On Andrew McClintock's insistence her physician had come to Prescott Hill. He advised against moving her to Washington. 'This funeral has already created a traffic jam of a sort. Even the ambulance would have trouble getting through to pick her up, never mind getting her back to Washington.' Livy did not know it, but she went into labour more than six weeks prematurely in the bed Alex had been conceived in.

In the heat, attended by her doctor and a midwife and an extra nurse who tried to invent duties for herself, Livy laboured for more than a day. Sometimes she heard herself cry out in pain, sometimes she was lost in a mist of drugs. She knew that Alex was there, coming and going through a haze. The doctor had summoned an ambulance ready to take the infant in an incubator to the county hospital. He would have liked to move Livy herself because the labour had gone on too long, but the birth was now imminent. The child was born as the sky darkened on the day after Dena had been buried in the little graveyard at the edge of the estate. They bore it in the incubator to the county hospital, a four-and-a-half-pound boy. Alex went with his son. Livy slept an exhausted, drug-induced sleep.

Downstairs Andrew McClintock raged. 'It would never

have happened if she hadn't insisted on coming. The heat, the crowd . . . She should have stayed in Washington, and at least she could have been in hospital . . .' Against his own inclination, Harry had stayed on also. Prescott Hill now had ghosts for him. He had stayed because he had believed and hoped that his occasional presence might give comfort to Livy. For him, there was no comfort.

Livy wakened and asked about the baby. He was well, the nurse said. He was holding his own. His weight was quite good: he hadn't been that many weeks premature. Alex came back to see her. The sight of him gave Livy little comfort. All the agony and tension of the time when he had struggled back to health after the accident had appeared to return. His movements were slow and uncertain. 'He's all right, Livy. Now try to sleep.'

'Will you sleep, then?'

'Yes.'

But they waited until the end of the second day to tell her that the baby had developed a respiratory infection, common in premature infants. Those were the words they used. She imagined the tiny infant struggling for breath in its little oxygen-fed cubicle. Even if she had been able to be there, she could not have placed her hands on him.

Andrew McClintock visited her briefly. 'Everything is being done. Two doctors from Washington. A more sophisticated incubator has been brought. Try not to worry, Livy. It will be all right.'

She was surprised that he had no words of blame or accusation for her. She had disobeyed his wishes, she had endangered the life of a much-wanted child. All he did was to say what he hadn't said downstairs, that it would probably have gone that way whatever she had done. 'I remember Ginny, all the care, the protection, the rest. Dena always with her, and still she lost her child. It's a mysterious thing, Livy. No one understands it, least of all men.'

And in the morning Alex came to tell her that during the night the baby had given up the struggle. It's little, underdeveloped lungs had given up.

Livy was not able to attend the swift burial in the little

graveyard in a plot beside the child's grandfather, Alex's father, near to where Blair and Dena lay. The press learned only after it was over. This time Andrew McClintock had used all his power to see that the death certificate and the burial came within hours of each other. The fact became known later, and the newspapers had their fill of the double tragedy which had befallen these families. The five-million dollar baby was no more. He was buried before Livy had seen his face. His birth and death and burial were registered under the name of Alexander McClintock III.

They took her back to Washington in an ambulance, so that she was spared the cameras of the press. When she was in bed, bathed and beginning to fall asleep from the drugs, Andrew McClintock came to see her. 'We don't seem to be a very lucky family, Livy. I rely on you to be here to share all our joys as well as our sorrows. Mourn your little one, but look forward to the next child. He will be conceived in peace. He will be born in peace. This has been . . . an accident. Like Dena's death. We will try to see that the next child knows no shadows . . .' He had spoken as if he had the power to assure that such a thing was within his compass. 'Rest now, Livy. We have need of you.'

Strangely the words did more to comfort her than anything Alex had yet said, but it was Alex's hand she felt in hers, his body she craved. She was amazed that only three days after giving birth to a child, she should want Alex's body beside her, within her. Even if no new life was created, she wanted him.

'I love you, Alex.' She fell asleep, and Alex limped wearily downstairs to face the wrath and storms of his grandfather, who seemed to take it as a personal insult that his first great-grandson had lived briefly and died. He was not the gentle man who had sat by Livy's bed.

'But she's strong,' he kept on insisting over and over. 'There'll be other children. If Dena hadn't died . . . if it hadn't been in that way . . . If Dena had kept the thing to herself until after the baby was born . . .' His wrath momentarily had turned on Dena, the trauma she had brought upon them all. 'Well, it will be different next time. There will be no disruption. There'll be none of the campus nonsense and the press. Perhaps she was right, perhaps Livy was right. If Dena had been buried in St Just, none of this would have happened. Livy would have had some sense of peace.'

Alex bowed his head into his hands. 'Grandfather, go home! Leave us in peace. Go home, and go to sleep.'

Andrew McClintock took up his cane. 'Damn you, don't you know that I never sleep?'

'Then let someone else have some sleep. Just for once, stop being a selfish old monster. Leave us alone!'

The inquest into the death of Lady Camborne was swift and came to its expected conclusion. The pathologist who had performed the autopsy stated the reason for death; he also gave information about the recent breast excision, and the biopsy he himself had performed on the breast and lymph glands. Harry was called, waiving diplomatic immunity, and told the coroner of the news he had given Dena when she returned from New York. He had feared the cloak of diplomatic immunity. It might for ever leave a ghost, a shadow of uncertainty. It was better that Mark and Rachel suffer for a time than for them to guess at what other explanation might lie behind Den's death. The forensic experts talked about the prints on the revolver. The prints on the two rifles Dena had used were clear; those on the revolver were smudged, though the only ones they could positively identify were hers. Harry had been instructed by his Ambassador and the Foreign Office to reveal that he had been offered the ambassadorship of France. It was easier to understand why a woman in Dena's situation might have panicked at the thought, might have concluded that she would be near death before that appointment took place. The court was infinitely sympathetic to Harry.

The inquest concluded swiftly: Lady Camborne had died by her own hand while the balance of her mind was disturbed.

No one, no one on or near the Prescott Hill estate had come forward to report the presence of strangers, or even one stranger, on that night. Not even the telephone operator had reported a strange and possibly unintelligible call. Harry sometimes wondered if he had imagined it, but Ginny had been a witness to that call, without knowing what was said on the other end. But they had never spoken about that. There had been no further contact from whoever had made that call. Harry was left to wonder, sometimes until he thought he would go insane, whether her death had been suicide, or murder.

Harry immediately talked with his Ambassador, and asked for leave, which was granted. 'I can't say how sorry we are, Harry. Dena was such a lovely woman. It's very difficult for us to understand, isn't it, how women take these things. I suppose, to use one's imagination, there are things that we, as men, we would find difficult, if not impossible, to face. We shall all miss her very much. Will you be coming back, Harry?'

'To this posting, sir? I rather hope not, although I shall be extremely sorry to leave you and Lady Halliwell. You've been wonderful, to both of us. No one could have asked for a better boss. But I think it's better that I go. I need some time to think. Perhaps it will end up with my resigning from the Foreign Service.'

'That's a very drastic step to take, Harry. You're more than due for an ambassadorship.'

Harry shrugged. And then he managed a faint smile. 'My career seems to have been dogged by too many good men ahead of me.'

'But Paris, you've been offered Paris. You won't take it now?'

'The offer may not stand. My heart isn't in it, without Dena. Now if they offered me Outer Mongolia, I might take that as some sort of challenge. Do we have any desert islands in the Pacific left which need an ambassador, I wonder . . .'

Sir George shook him by the hand. 'You need some rest, Harry. And a change from Washington won't do any harm. But I will miss my ablest minister. And that's what I'll write in my report.'

'Thank you, sir, for that and for everything else. Yes, I think a time away from Washington wouldn't do any harm.'

Neither of them said so, but in their minds were the sly

innuendos in the press about the fact that he and Ginny had driven together to Prescott Hill, while Dena had gone there alone. It had been so easy to twist the testimony at the inquest to suggest that they had intended her to be alone, and that Dena's death had been caused not only by her terror of death by cancer, but also of the feeling of abandonment and betrayal by her husband and closest friend. No one who had not been there would have known the difference if they had merely read the newspaper reports. Harry knew it was imperative that he leave Washington at once.

He told Andrew McClintock. 'What will you do?' the other asked.

'Take some leave. Try to recover. Keep Mark close by me. I expect I need him quite as much as he needs me. I have a lot to make up to Mark.'

'Where will you be? London?'

'No. I'd be meeting someone from the Foreign Office around every corner. I'll take Mark to Tresillian. We'll have the summer there. That's where he seems to thrive the most. See Thea and Herbert. Mess about a bit. Take picnics . . . fish . . . If at the end of the summer the Foreign Office still wants me, I suppose I'll go and do whatever job they have for me. But I'll have to see Mark settled first. A school to find and I have to be in some posting that's not too far away from him.'

'I would,' Andrew McClintock said, 'like you to take Livy and Alex with you, that is, if you're going to Tresillian. That's what the girl needs to set her up again. Alex needs it too.'

'Alex – all summer? Can you spare him so long?'

'I have to spare him. Haven't you noticed how much he's regressed since Dena and the baby died? He's in almost as bad shape as when he came out of hospital the second time. He drags his leg, and he can hardly lift his arm. There'll be precious little work coming from his desk for the next few months that'll be worth anything. To be back at Tresillian would set Livy up again, and I don't think Alex should be separated from her. It would be good for you and Mark to have them with you.'

'Yes, it would be very good.'

'Right, then do it the old-fashioned way. We'll arrange for you all to go by ship. That should put colour in Livy's cheeks. She might get Alex walking round the deck a few times a day. It would do you all good.'

They went by sea, and Andrew McClintock had been right. Time and distance was placed between them and the happenings at Prescott Hill in a natural way. Some of the greyness left Harry's face, though he still looked very remote and withdrawn. Early in the mornings, Livy and Alex walked the deck, early enough so that there were few to observe them. Mark was usually with them, but he was always ready to walk with his father when Harry seemed inclined. Early or late at night was their time for using the swimming-pool. The captain had assigned a sailor who was also a lifeguard to be on duty at whatever time they should appear. They always ate alone in the sitting-room which connected their staterooms. None of them had any desire to face the stares and murmurings of the dining-room, or to make polite conversation with strangers at the Captain's table. Livy was glad she didn't have to attempt to dress; the weight she had gained during pregnancy had still to come off. She was grateful that few eyes could see her as she slipped into the swimming-pool. They read, and slept and ate, drank good wines, and talked little. There was nothing yet they could say to one another. But their silence was companionable and close. The fresh wind seemed to sweep away some of the sticky, dull heat of Virginia. They all thought of the new graves at Prescott Hill, but they didn't talk about them.

They spent only two nights at Seymour House. Harry reported to the Permanent Under Secretary at the Foreign Office, and the Principal Private Secretary. 'Take as long as you like, dear boy. All this has been very shocking, very tragic. I'm glad Alex McClintock and his wife are with you. And, of course, your son. Too bad about Eton, but in his place I'd probably have done the same thing. That Campbell man has a lot to answer for . . .'.

Harry's closed expression did not invite further comment. The most important things he had to report had been said

532

earlier, to different people, those who supposedly had no connection with the Foreign Office. This was just an official send-off meant to ease Harry's mind. 'Let us know when you're ready again. We'll try to find something that won't be too burdensome.'

'I may just decide I never want to leave Cornwall again. Of course, there's the small matter of what I'd live on . . .'

'We wouldn't want to lose you, Harry. But I don't doubt there are many industries who would be glad to find a place for you. Starting with McClintock-Clayton.'

'I think not, sir. I'm very fond of all that family, but . . .'

'Of course . . . of course. Well, Harry, come and talk to us when you're ready.'

The next day they went down to Tresillian, and all of them slipped into a sort of mindless abandonment to the atmosphere, the sea, the fresh winds that blew from the Atlantic, the days when the wind was gale force and brought rain. The thunder of the sea on the Tresillian Rocks seemed to blank out other thoughts. Her Tregenna cousins and aunts crowded about Livy, vying with each other in little spoiling kindnesses. She exclaimed over new babies, the progress of toddlers, and her heart broke with longing for any one of them to be her own. Mark did as much cooking as he wanted to, always their breakfast: eggs, bacon, kedgeree, kippers, whatever they happened to fancy. He also prepared some dinners, and became bossy with the Tregenna women in the kitchen, who took it all with good humour and didn't always obey instructions. Thea and Herbert were often with them in the evenings. They took picnics to the familiar and loved places. Sometimes they pretended more pleasure than they felt. There were missing presences and voices: Dena and Ginny, Blair, Rachel and Chris, Caroline. Where had they all gone? They seemed a very small group now, who had all the time in the world to spend, when before it had always rushed away from them.

But the place slowly worked its magic on them. Livy recovered her spirits and her strength. 'And your shape,' Alex commented. But so had he recovered in subtle ways. He had sent to London for exercise equipment, and worked out daily,

Livy at his side. They walked each day, no matter the weather, down to St Just. They almost liked it better when it rained because there were fewer day-trippers on the streets of the little town. They were often in Thea's studio and her garden. Herbert had almost given up painting. 'I've become too old to feel enthusiastic about it, never mind that the old arthritis doesn't take kindly to the brush.' But that summer he did what he had rarely attempted before, a vague impressionistic portrait of Livy and Alex. It flattered neither of them, nor did it try to play down Alex's disfigurements. He was posed straight on to the viewer, the black patch and the grey streak in his hair prominently there. It was Livy he posed in profile, the sweep of red hair almost hiding her face. There was a sense of great intimacy in the portrait. 'What will you call it,' Thea asked when she viewed the finished picture. '"The Lovers?" It says it in every line, Herbert.'

'They've come through a lot, those two. That, I think is what it says.'

Harry had spent considerable time that summer hunting around for a school for Mark. They visited all those which seemed likely, and some that did not. Each time Harry had contact with a headmaster who sounded as if he ran the sort of school Mark could accept, they all visited it together, sometimes staying overnight in the local town to test the atmosphere. At last they tried one in Somerset Harry had thought least of all about, judging by its prospectus. It was noted for its lack of structured discipline; it was housed in a huge, rambling, somewhat tumbledown Victorian mansion, the gardens were rather unkempt, but the sporting facilities excellent. There was a swimming-pool, cricket pitches, playing fields. The atmosphere of the dining-hall and assembly hall, the classrooms and individual rooms was informal, and possessed an odd sort of charm. It had something to do with flowers being about, Livy thought, odd bits of pottery that might have come from St Just.

'The boys do more or less as they want. Within limits. The scholars study, and the athletes play, and if we're lucky, some of each rubs off on them all. We have an unusually high number who get into Oxford and Cambridge, but not because we claim to be expert crammers,' the headmaster said. It was a school which had been established just before the war, and was favoured for the sons of the recognized intelligentsia. For that reason it was regarded with some suspicion by the old public schools. 'We don't believe in corporal punishment here, Lord Camborne. If that shocks you, then you must look elsewhere.'

'I have never been more glad to hear anything. I don't think, in his present frame of mind, Mark would stand for it. He's already got himself thrown out of one school for hitting a master. What's happened to him in these past months has hardly put him in the frame of mind to accept much discipline. If he can work off his feelings playing rugger and cricket, I would be grateful.'

'Is there anything else he likes to do? Any special interests?'

'Yes. Something that won't get him very far. He likes cooking.'

'Good. The school catering could stand some attention – though I don't know how he'd react to having to cater for a hundred and fifty odd. If he can hit it off with the cook, he might be permitted an afternoon or two in the kitchen.'

'Cooks and butlers are the people he's never failed to hit it off with. They eat out of his hand.'

They decided on Wrisley, as it was called. They hadn't, by then, much choice. The new school year was just about to start. The September colour had come to the waters about Tresillian. The summer people were leaving St Just. What tipped the balance in favour of Wrisley, in Mark's eyes, was not just its easy-going air but the fact that it was only an hour's train journey from Penzance. 'I could go to Thea and Herbert at half-term, and any of the holidays . . .' Unspoken between them was the knowledge that Harry had seemed in no hurry to make up his mind about a return to the Foreign Office. He didn't even talk of it. If he did go back, no one had any idea of where he would be posted, since he had refused the Paris job. He was determined that he would not go where he would be half a world away from Mark.

'I think that's expecting rather a lot of Thea and Herbert,

son,' Harry said. 'They're not young. Having an active youngster about the house can be quite wearing . . .'

'But that's just it. I wouldn't be around the house, or underfoot. I was born in St Just. I have all the Tregenna boys to be with, plenty of fishing. I could live in Livy's house and just visit Thea and Herbert. Anything so I had somewhere to tell them at Wrisley that I was going. A home . . .'

Livy wanted to weep. He had no home. He could never stay at Tresillian by himself. His life had been pulled in a dozen different directions, and it had no centre. His mother had left him in what seemed a cruel way, though Livy still wanted to believe it had been an accident Dena had wished to happen, wished upon herself because she could not bear to let others, particularly Harry and Mark, watch her die slowly and in pain. Livy had never yet been able to face the fact that the gun had been fired by Dena in a way which could only have killed her.

'You can have my cottage whenever you like. And if there's a boy who can't get home for half-term, bring him. All the cousins and the aunts will look after you.'

'I don't need looking after. I can cook rings round most of them.'

'Well, I didn't mean exactly that. Just mundane things like bed-linen and clean socks.' Some humour was beginning to come back into their talk. 'And little things like not tearing the place apart. I'm going to need it when Alex and I are old and poor . . .' Now they could actually laugh.

'Don't be too sure of how things work out,' Alex cautioned, but still he laughed. 'I just might make one wild deal some time, when the Old Man's not there to give me the nod, which could bring the whole edifice tumbling. We could very well need Livy's cottage. You just keep it in good order.'

Harry was curiously silent through all this. He had not yet said whether he intended to resign from the Foreign Office; neither had he said anything about going back there.

They saw Mark settled at Wrisley; he had made a leisurely inspection of the kitchens and was in engrossed conversation with the cook, a fat, smiling man, when they left. They drove back to London, to Seymour House. In two days Livy and Alex would return to New York by ship, and would spend some months there. Andrew McClintock had decided that the Wall Street office could stand some attention. Livy guessed it was his way of easing them back into life in America; they would not be faced immediately with Washington and the painful memories it contained. Livy decided, though, that they must shortly pay a weekend visit to Washington. She missed Ginny. She could hardly bring herself to admit that in ways she also missed Andrew McClintock. Arrogant and authoritarian he might be, but he had been a rock in the shifting sands of her existence.

At Seymour House they were greeted excitedly by Knox. 'The Foreign Office has telephoned several times, sir. They would like you to ring at once – the office of the Permanent Under Secretary.'

Harry was stiff and tired after the long drive. 'They've waited all summer. Tomorrow will do.' But the old instinct had returned. He had been made curious by the seeming urgency. He telephoned, and made an appointment for an interview the next day.

'Sad news, Harry,' the PUS, the tag by which the Permanent Under Secretary was always known, said, 'Glendower has been in a Swiss clinic for three weeks. Cancer of the larynx. They think they've got it in time, but he'll never speak in more than a whisper again. So he resigned immediately. Wants to make way for the new chap. He'll be having radium therapy for some time, and feels he isn't up to even the routine work. Would the ambassadorship to Switzerland suit you, Harry?'

Harry hesitated fractionally. The summer had been no, serene, giving him the taste of how life without an implied or real threat could feel. There had been no contact from what they had kept referring to as 'our masters'. There had been no pressure to return to the Foreign Office by MI6; they were leaving it up to him. He was jolted into an answer by the thought of the three photographs which he kept with him, the bleak, staring, almost accusing eyes of the child.

He could turn down this offer, and abandon her for ever. He thought of Dena lying crumpled on the ground at Prescott Hill, and the price he might have forced her to pay. He had to go on.

'A nice, safe, neutral country. Nothing of very great importance will cross my desk. Thank you, sir. It seems the ideal posting.'

'Glad you agree. It should fit in very well. The McClintock-Clayton influence there is quite strong. That's an ambassador's job these days: keeping the trade links nice and firm. After all, we're hardly likely to be going to war with Switzerland. I expect you know Berne. A very pleasant city . . .'

Caroline and Toby came to dinner that evening. It seemed that the Permanent Under Secretary had decided to tell Toby about Harry's appointment, and Caroline had telephoned her congratulations. 'Come to dinner,' Harry said. 'We haven't seen you all summer.'

They came eagerly. Harry's position had changed in Caroline's eyes with the new appointment. At last her father had the position of Ambassador. It had been a long time coming, but it had come. She had been bitterly disappointed when he had turned down Paris, but after a safe year or so in Berne he might have a more important posting. Perhaps the plum of them all, Washington. So she and Toby were in good spirits, and happy to announce that Caroline was again pregnant. Even as she raised her glass to toast the news, Livy was pierced with a fierce envy. But she also recognized that something had vanished for ever between her and Caroline. Never again would they share quarters; never again discuss where clothes could be bought inexpensively. They were virtually polite strangers. It was almost the same with Rachel, though Rachel never bothered to keep up a façade of politeness. She had spent three days with them at Tresillian during the summer, rather uneasy days. None of them had mentioned Frazer Campbell, nor did Rachel talk about her hopes for the future. 'I know, in one way or another, I'll be working for the Labour Party all my life, either in the House of Commons or out of it. I will be an MP someday, you

538

know, if it takes twenty years.' But she said nothing of marriage. And no one dared, or indeed wanted, to ask.

Livy reflected sadly that they had both slipped away from her. Only Chris was on the same terms, easy, friendly, but that was Chris's whole life. She was friendly with almost everyone who crossed her path, and was often used by them. She was careless with her money and her friendship. She was now in Hollywood making a low-budget film of the play, *Tempo*, in which she had starred on Broadway. Hugh Meredith had either not been offered the role he had played on Broadway, or had turned it down. He was now starring in a successful West End production.

They dined together with curious formality. Harry was moving the next day to an hotel: he would not stay on at Seymour House, which belonged to Ginny, if Alex and Livy were not present.

Caroline seemed affronted when Livy asked if she would see to the shipping of Thea's sculpture and Herbert's pictures to the Massachusetts Avenue house. 'I have a place for them now, and I'd so much like to have them with me.'

'Very well,' Caroline said. 'Though I rather thought that with that house stuffed with art, you wouldn't miss these pieces. We've grown rather attached to them.'

Livy doubted that it was so. But Caroline would enjoy having a Thea Sedgemore in her hall when she was aware that her works were being increasingly sought by many galleries throughout the world. 'They were presents to me, Caro. I can't give them away. They'll always be very precious to me. Thank you for looking after them.'

Alex and Livy had decided to repeat the experience of travelling by sea to New York. Harry went down to Southampton to see them off. He went aboard the Cunarder, carrying flowers he had insisted on bringing from London. They toasted one another in champagne. He could even bring himself to recall aloud the time he and Dena had made their first visit to Ginny and Blair in Washington, and found that their suite had been the one always booked and ready for Andrew McClintock, should he want it. 'And not even a wine bill at the end of the voyage, I recall. We felt we were living way above our heads, and it was wonderful.'

He would be working every day from now on at the
Foreign Office, being briefed for his new posting. 'I wouldn't
have accepted anything except a job in Europe. I must have
Mark near enough so that he can come for holidays or I can
take a few days off at half-term and be with him. For all
those brave statements about being able to manage on his
own, he's due more of my time than I've been giving
him.'

Livy thought it all seemed to have worked for them, the
summer at Tresillian. Harry would go back to work, not as
gladly as he would have done if Dena had been with him, but
he would work, and in that there would be some distraction.
Mark had seemed happier at the prospect of Wrisley than
he had been about any other school. That night she and Alex
would dine at the Captain's table, both of them looking
well, their faces tanned, Alex walking more easily, his body
straighter, his hand once more flexible enough to manage
his food with seeming ease. And she would wear one of the
dresses she had dashed about to buy in London, for the first
time in her life suddenly aware that she need no longer look
at the price tag, and that any alterations she wanted would
be done in hours. That summer she had shed the weight
gained during pregnancy, her body was trim and taut. She
walked proudly beside Alex to their place in the dining-room;
this voyage there would be no meals in their suite except for
what she longed for again, the leisurely, intimate breakfast
that always seemed so much better after they had woken to
make love.

Andrew McClintock and Ginny had travelled up from Washington to meet them. The gratification on the old man's face
was evident when he saw them, but all he said was, 'Seems
to have done you both good.' But Livy noticed that he
followed Alex's every movement with his eyes. His talk of
the market was sharp and direct. 'Sorry, I'm a bit out of
touch with the market, grandfather. We decided we could
live without the *Financial Times* at Tresillian.'

Andrew McClintock grunted. 'Well, those days are over.

There'll be a pile of work on your desk both in Wall Street and in Washington.'

Livy was touched by the fact that Ginny had come; her presence softened the absence of Dena. Ginny said little, but Livy noticed there was often a sort of half-smile on her face as she listened to the talk, and watched Alex's movements. They were all staying at the Fifth Avenue apartment. Livy had the impression that although she might be expected to appear as its châtelaine, in fact it would still be the stopping-off place for any of the family who wanted it. There were, she thought wryly, more than enough rooms. Ginny wandered over its two floors speculatively. 'It really needs redecorating. Nothing's been changed here since before the war. All the colours are too dark. Why don't you start to brighten it up, Livy?'

'I don't think I know how,' she answered truthfully.

'There are such people as interior decorators who will do the running around for you. But don't let them push anything over on you that you don't feel comfortable with yourself. And look at the bills carefully. With a McClintock as a client, you may find hefty amounts of padding.' Then she laughed. 'I forgot. You once worked in a bank.'

'Clayton's Merchant Bank Ltd, hardly ever seemed to deal in ordinary money, not spending money,' Livy said, as if remembering an eon ago. 'I still haven't got used to spending money . . . not even buying clothes.'

'You will. It's a habit that comes all too easily . . .'

Andrew McClintock was quietly pleased about Harry's appointment. 'More than time. But I'm glad it's Switzerland. He'll be busy enough, without being overworked. It's nice that we have one of our own to look in on McClintock-Clayton in Zurich once in a while.'

Livy realized that he was speaking as if Harry's ambassadorship had been arranged for his personal satisfaction, and that the words 'one of our own' implied that he regarded Harry as being still solidly part of the family. And Ginny, Ginny, so long as Andrew McClintock lived, would never be released from the fact that long ago she had been married to his only child.

Ginny had been planning to return to Washington after a stay of only two days, but Livy asked her, as a favour, to stay on a little longer. 'I don't want to get under your feet,' Ginny said.

The doctor looked mildly annoyed as he finished the examination. 'Of course we must wait on the results of the tests, but I'm almost certain, even at this early stage. You really should not have allowed this to happen for at least a year after the birth of the last baby. It drains too much from you. But since it's happened, we must take good care of you. You must take care of yourself. I will hurry through the test . . .'

Ginny waited until the news ·was positive. They had a small and very quiet celebration that evening when Andrew McClintock and Alex returned from Wall Street. 'As I expected, things down there need attention,' the old man growled as he entered the apartment. 'Since Blair went, they've taken too much into their own hands, and I can't be everywhere . . . What's this . . . what's this . . .' He tried to wave aside the glass of champagne Ginny handed him. 'I'll have my usual whisky.'

'Just a sip, to celebrate the fact that Livy's going to have a baby.'

He shook his head. 'Too soon . . . too soon . . . but who am I to say?' Despite the words of disapproval, his eyes seemed to glow with renewed youth. 'You're right about those damned Rocks. They do seem to have a power of their own.'

He ordered then that only the minimum of redecorating in the apartment should be done. 'Make Livy's room pretty and light. But she shouldn't have workmen around her all day. The smell of paint . . . some new curtains, carpet, recover the furniture, but nothing that will disturb her. It all can wait. This time . . . this time . . .'

He couldn't help it, Livy supposed. He just couldn't help taking command. But she could imagine there would be many visits from him during the months of her pregnancy, just to make sure she was taking the proper precautions. And that was how it proved to be. Never with more than a few hours warning, if even that. She thought he hoped to catch her walking around museums, or on long, tiring, shopping sprees. Almost without her consent he engaged a housekeeper to complement the butler, and Livy suspected she was there mainly to make reports on her. It was an uncomfortable feeling, but the woman was pleasant and kindly, the sort of nurse one would like, Livy thought, if one could have chosen. Although her name was Mrs Hope, Livy secretly called her Mrs Timmins because she had exactly that fat, sleek air of Bess Bromley's cat.

Ginny came frequently, and Livy was always delighted to see her. She was a refreshing, welcome change from Mrs Hope's company on the morning walks and at the afternoon concerts. They went to the Russian Tea Room beside Carnegie Hall after the concerts, and the age gap between them seemed to shrink until it was barely there. Ginny had many New York acquaintances, who came for cocktails before going on to dinner elsewhere. There was a good deal of curiosity about Livy, the daughter of a fisherwoman who had upset the socially perfect union of Nancy Winterton and Alex McClintock, and apparently all with Andrew McClintock's connivance and approval, if Nancy's mother was to be believed. One man, who fancied himself as an art-lover, christened her the 'Pre-Raphaelite Girl', and the name stuck, even with those who didn't know what he was talking about. Livy came to enjoy, with rather malicious satisfaction, the surprise of those who expected to meet, in Alex's wild love, some sort of beautiful peasant. She went shopping with Ginny not only for baby clothes, but for increasingly sophisticated and expensive maternity clothes. It was, she thought, a long way from the quiet evenings in the house by the river in Alexandria, when it had hardly seemed to matter what she wore.

Andrew McClintock approved the changes; to a more or less degree, he approved Livy's social activities. He brought her small pieces of jewellery to prove it. The large pieces, he said, he would leave to Alex. The engagement ring they had never got around to choosing in the hectic days when they seemed besieged before their marriage, appeared. Ginny had insisted that the large diamond which had been her own

543

engagement ring from Alex's father was reset, and Livy now wore it. 'I'm ashamed,' Alex said. 'I never thought of it.'

'Do you think that in the midst of all that I cared?' She cherished it because Ginny had given it to her.

So long as he didn't smell paint, Andrew McClintock even approved the new, paler colours which were appearing through the apartment, the sheen of pale green and grey carpet, the watered silk wallpapers. They set off the collection of Chinese ceramics which Andrew McClintock vaguely remembered his father telling him he had acquired in settlement for a trifling debt a hundred years ago. These Livy and Ginny brought experts in to identify, and found they were K'ang-hsi *famille verte* baluster vases and Buddhistic lions. There were two T'ang horses and a collection of celedon that made the curators and dealers sigh. They were now displayed in lighted cases along the broad hallways. 'The Metropolitan hasn't anything as good as these, I'd say,' one guest murmured appreciatively. Somehow Andrew McClintock had hardly noticed the Chinese collection before. 'Probably because I didn't have to work for it,' he said.

Chapter 13

1

Harry found he liked Berne more than he expected. It was such a pleasant town, barely a city, even though it was the capital. He liked the food, the views, the almost village-like quality of its centre, its low skyline which never allowed its public buildings to be too dominant. It became his amusement to stroll through its fourteenth-century arcades, staring into shop windows, browsing in book-shops, buying a piece of bread and sausage and drinking it with good beer. It gave him a chance to brush up on his German. He spent weekends in the Bernese Oberland, trying to ski, but never venturing on to the difficult slopes, conscious of his age, and the need to maintain the dignity of his position. He felt it almost sinful to work to such an equable schedule for such a rate of pay. Something in him that needed order and rest appreciated the sense of quiet industry among the town dwellers, their carefulness, their punctuality, their tidiness. He did not miss the bustle and social frenzy of Washington. Almost daily he went to visit the bears, the city's mascots, in their pits. At first he felt sorry for them, pitying them their captivity. It became known that the British Ambassador always carried a bunch of carrots in his official car and that, whenever there was time, he stopped to toss a bunch into the pits and see the bears roll over with pleasure.

And yet, it struck him what a lonely thing it was for a busy man, an ambassador, to do. He kept thinking that Dena would have enjoyed it. He often found himself half-turning to her, to share a small pleasure, and the pain of her absence was acute. When Berne was garlanded in Christmas decorations and covered with real snow, Mark arrived from school. The first thing Harry did was to take him to see the bears.

They spent Christmas Day with the American Ambassador and his family, two children of about Mark's age, who seemed pleasantly surprised to find that Mark did not wear an Eton collar and a top hat. Harry had carefully bought and wrapped presents for Mark to give them. The day passed off well enough, he judged. It was the first Christmas Dena had not been with him; he was determined that if Mark could bear it with good grace, so could he.

The next day he took Mark to St Moritz, which gave him his choice of many ski slopes and a taste of grand hotel life. They stayed until New Year, and Harry allowed Mark to stay up to see it in, toasting it in wine. He looked almost completely adult among the crowd of revellers, and Harry was careful to stay near him, not trying to spoil his conversation with the pretty young girls, but still afraid to let him out of his sight. Dena would have managed much better, he thought.

They went back to Berne two days later. Mark had skiied every hour of daylight, and slept through the nights as if he would never wake. But he was bright and fresh every morning, saying complimentary things about the Swiss coffee and the Swiss cuisine in general. Once, in the lobby, the manager spoke to Harry. 'Ambassador, may I have a word? Your son has been in the kitchen. It is not a usual practice to allow guests in there. However the *chef de cuisine* did not complain. It was I who found him there. In fact, the chef seemed quite pleased with his company. He seems to know a good deal about . . .'

'Yes,' Harry said hastily. 'He does know. I'm terribly sorry.'

'No trouble, Ambassador. It is a pleasure to have you both with us.'

'But really, father, it was terribly interesting,' Mark said when Harry mildly reproached him. 'They have a lot of stainless steel. And a huge hanging and cooling room for the meat. Not exactly a refrigerator, just to age the meat, so it's tender. All the cheese, the fruit are beautifully stored. It was all so clean . . .'

'But you're not supposed to go in there without an invitation.'

'They didn't mind. All I have to do is say a few words in French, kitchen French, and they don't know I know.'

Harry had rather disturbing visions of Mark in every hotel and catering establishment they entered, asking if he could see the kitchen. In many places they would not be so pleasant to him as in this clean, polite and expensive hotel in St Moritz. Before he finished investigating kitchens, Mark might have some unpleasant shocks.

The rest of his holiday Mark spent roaming around Berne by himself, and shared his father's fascination with its ancient arcades. And every time he left the Residence he carried carrots for the bears.

Harry went with him to Zurich to see him off. 'Thank you, father. It's been a great holiday. I know how hard you tried to make it that.' It was an oblique reference to his mother, her absence, the thought of her that shadowed both their lives. He shook hands. For once he didn't seem to mind going back to school.

Late in March Harry's secretary asked if he would take a personal call from Mrs Blair Clayton. Alarmed, Harry asked for her to be put through immediately. But Ginny's voice was calm, and it sounded as if she were very near.

'In fact, right here at the Bellevue Palace. I have rooms with a wonderful view of the Alps.'

'To hell with the Alps! I want to see you. I'm coming to collect you this minute.'

She was waiting in the foyer of the hotel, with its fabulous glass dome. She walked towards him, holding out her arms. She was dressed in a white fur coat and matching cap, a miracle of elegance and smooth, groomed beauty. 'My god, Ginny, how good to see you!' They embraced without embarrassment, old friends meeting. It was the time of day when the ladies of Berne liked to patronize the Palace for tea and little cakes. In this small city many were familiar with the British Ambassador; some were amused and some a little shocked by this undiplomatic behaviour. Then the name of the lady was whispered. Many people knew of McClintock-Clayton's ownership of one of the world's biggest pharmaceutical companys and their majority holding in I. B. Amman. They knew of the villa on the lake in Zurich which was always kept ready, but seldom used, especially since the death of Blair Clayton. The Swiss usually knew these things, but they also knew how to mind their own business. Harry walked out to his waiting car arm in arm with Ginny.

'So sad for them both,' one lady said to her friends. 'Her husband killed, and the son maimed. The Ambassador's wife . . .' She did not finish the sentence. They did not like to speculate too much on the death of the wife of the Ambassador who had become so popular in such a short time.

Harry ended work for the day, took Ginny into the Residence, settled her before a fire in the drawing-room, enquired whether she would like tea or a drink. 'Of course you're staying to dinner. Thank heaven it isn't one of the nights I'm supposed to go out. I would have had to cancel, and everyone in Berne would have known the reason . . .' He laughed as he said it. 'All those dear ladies having tea at the Palace . . .' He gave her the light whisky she requested. 'Oh, Ginny, you just don't know how good it is to see you! This job has been a salvation, but I've never been so alone in my life. I've missed Dena so . . . and you . . . and the girls. Life has never been like this before. There are days when I actually have time on my hands.'

For the first time they were able to express, and share, pain and grief, in words, in memories uttered, in times recalled. The release for them both was like a torrent. 'I've never believed in the stiff upper lip bit,' Ginny said, 'and yet somehow it seems expected of one. You don't let down because it may upset other people. And yet one should be allowed to grieve. One should be allowed to speak the name. At times I find myself saying "when Blair and I —" and I stop. But at least his was a clear and straightforward death. When Dena died it was clouded and murky, sensational, even somewhat scandalous, some people thought. Though I know there was a lot of sympathy for her, and for you, Harry. Why couldn't I have come and talked to you then as I'm doing now?'

'I wasn't hearing then, Ginny. I felt deaf and blind and paralysed. I was afraid to feel in case I went totally to pieces. There was Mark to think of. Poor little devil, he did blame himself. He thought getting expelled contributed to her state of mind, the depression . . .'

They talked on and on. Dinner was announced, and served. They talked of unimportant things while the butler was present. When they were served coffee and liqueurs later, in private, they talked again. 'How long are you staying? I haven't even asked why you came.'

'What other reason would there be except to see you, Harry? I'm not needed in Washington or New York. Livy has a dear housemother, watching her every action. That is when Alex isn't hovering, or Mr McClintock asking embarrassing questions. She is very well. She has quite enough of a social life. I've done all I can. We will just wait for a perfectly healthy child carried to full term. It can get a little boring . . . unless, of course, it's one's own child. So I said I was going to Europe. The merry widow bit. It rather alarmed Mr McClintock. I looked in on Seymour House, to see if everything was well there. I gave a few parties, just to keep up the contacts. And then I decided I'd come and visit you.'

'I'm privileged. And so thankful . . .'

'We've talked half the night away, Harry. It's time I left.'

He had dismissed his chauffeur, so he drove himself, very carefully, down the icy roads to the centre of the city. He said goodnight to her on the doorstep of the Palace. 'I shall expect to see you every day, for as long as you can stay.'

For the next three weeks the diplomatic corps and the hostesses of Berne grew accustomed to Mrs Clayton accompanying the British Ambassador to receptions. When he was expected to dinner, a polite call from his secretary would enquire if the Ambassador might bring Mrs Clayton. Every hostess agreed, many fussing and fuming at having to rearrange the table, and finding the elusive single man to balance it. But there could be no question of not acceding to the Ambassador's request, most especially when his guest was Mrs Blair Clayton.

A magical spring broke early across Switzerland. All but the last patches of snow on the north-facing slopes of the valleys thawed, except for the places they could raise their eyes to and see where the snow was perpetual. They drove into the country and walked the meadows starred with spring flowers. 'It almost makes me feel young again,' Ginny said. 'I become very sentimental about Switzerland when it behaves like this but its a lot less sentimental when one sits around the table at a board meeting.'

'Do you often do that?'

'Not often. I never had to when Blair was here. Now I put in a token appearance, wondering how much of my ignorance shows. I've even had Livy and Alex coaching me on how to read the reports properly. I'm going to attend an I. B. Amman board meeting in Zurich next week.'

'And then?'

'Home, I suppose. I should be there when the baby's born in late May. I'll stay in the Zurich house for a few days. Doesn't hurt to put in an appearance.'

'May I come for a weekend?'

Until now their behaviour had been almost sterilely correct. They had said goodnight each evening under the eyes of the concierge at the Palace. Ginny had never accepted an invitation to return to the Residence when one of the dinner parties was over. Harry had never been up to her suite, though flowers arrived there for her daily. Sometimes, they were seen wandering the arcades of Berne, buying a little thing here and there, a book, a new design of clock, a silk scarf. They often visited the bears with carrots. That was all Berne had to say of them; it was disappointingly dull.

Harry drove himself to Zurich, simply leaving a telephone number where he could be contacted. If his butler guessed his destination, he said nothing to the rest of the staff. The Ambassador often took weekends in the mountains, or elsewhere. But this was the only time he had left only a telephone number, not an address or the name of a hotel.

Harry was received with great discretion at the villa. 'I almost feel as if I'm opening a secret account,' he said, trying to lighten his unease. The staff at the villa functioned as if they were accustomed to Ginny's presence every day of the year. The house was fresh and bright, great and lovely bowls of flowers were in every room and in the corridors, and fires burned in all the hearths. The first of the tourist ferries had begun to ply on the lake, glassed against the chill breeze. They walked the Bahnhofstrasse, the favourite pastime of tourists, took tea at the Baur au Lac, where Ginny was well known. She nodded to acquaintances in the foyer, but did not allow herself to be trapped into a conversation. 'We'll get asked to dinner,' she murmured to Harry, hurrying him on.

They dined alone, Ginny dressed in a simple green dress, wearing no jewellery except her wedding band. The dinner seemed unbearably long and formal, although the food was superb. A butler and a footman waited on them. The first of the spring asparagus had arrived, so they ate that, and at Ginny's request drank Fendant, the wine that is young and never leaves Switzerland. 'It does feel like spring,' Harry said. 'I'm beginning to feel renewed. Not like a staid old Ambassador, which is what I must remember I am.'

'Not to me,' Ginny answered. The butler had been dismissed for the night. They sat late before the fire in the library, saying little, mostly just watching the wood being consumed by the flames.

Clocks chimed eleven all over the house. The Mozart that had been playing on the radio ended. Harry rose.

'Will you permit me to come to bed with you, Ginny?' he asked softly.

'I thought you'd never ask. You've been the correct Ambassador for so long, I was beginning to think that the Foreign Office had finally turned you into a stuffed shirt . . .'

'Diplomacy,' he said, as they mounted the stairs together, 'is so often a matter of waiting, and trying to judge the right moment. If I had been mistaken, I would have lost you as a friend. I couldn't bear that.'

'You have me for a friend, always.'

At first they were tentative with each other. 'I feel almost shy,' Harry said. 'You know I've always loved you, but in a

551

different way. Every sexual thought and feeling was for Dena. You were the beloved friend . . .'

Their three weeks together, when they had felt able to talk of Dena and Blair in whatever way they wished, at any time, had yielded the fruit of knowledge and understanding. There was no sense of betrayal. When they did make love, no ghosts hovered beside them, there were no fears, no guilt. 'Your body feels as if I've known you for ever,' Harry said. 'Or as if I'd met you half an hour ago, and fallen madly in love.'

'Are you madly in love, Ambassador?'

'Yes, madly, overwhelmingly. If you had refused me this I would have been in despair. It's been so good, Ginny. So much shared, as well as this bed. May I share it again?'

'Yes,' she said. 'Please.'

She wakened him in the morning by pulling back the curtains to brilliant spring sunshine. The lake glistened and shimmered. She bent and kissed him. 'Good morning, Ambassador. The maid will be here in half an hour with breakfast. Perhaps it would be best if you weren't here. Not that they won't know. Servants always know . . .'

He sat bolt upright. She handed him a towelling bathrobe. 'Lord,' he said. 'I was so deeply asleep. I haven't slept like that since . . . since, oh, heaven knows when. Kiss me again, Ginny. It felt like being wakened by an angel. What a lovely face you have in the morning, Ginny. Kind and soft . . . and loving.'

He picked up the clothes he had discarded the night before. When he was at the door she stopped him.

'Harry?'

'Yes?'

'Will you marry me? That's the question I came to Switzerland to ask you. I thought of us both alone, both needing each other. Or at least I flattered myself that you needed me as I needed you . . .'

'Need you!' He flew back to her, dropping the clothes as he put his arms about her and kissed her. 'I love you. I wouldn't have dared ask. At least, I don't think I would.'

'That's what I guessed . . . I didn't see how I could bring

you around to it. After three weeks of waiting . . . you didn't even hold my hand. And yet you are the most perfect lover. Can I be so lucky again? It hardly seems possible.'

'When can it be?' he demanded. 'How soon?'

'Soon . . . I'd better go back to New York and get this baby born, and then . . .'

'That's too long. Will you mind coming to live in Berne? The diplomatic round can be terribly tedious, Ginny.'

'Not with you.' He was back sitting on the bed. He pulled her down beside him. 'Isn't there a "Do Not Disturb" sign to put on the door?'

'We'll have to go to a hotel for that. Or Tresillian, where no one would ever disturb us. There's time, Harry. We have all the time in the world.'

'No, we don't. Time begins now. I'm counting down the seconds. Tomorrow's Monday. We'll go and buy a ring in one of those fancy Bahnhofstrasse places. I'm sure I can get some sort of diplomatic licence to be married right away. Why wait? Why waste time . . . I'm getting older . . . and, strangely, younger, every minute.'

She hustled him to the door. 'We will have a quiet Sunday discussing our plans. Sundays in Switzerland can be very quiet.'

'I know something exciting to do. Right here.'

He went back to his own room. The immaculately tidy bed, sheets neatly folded down from the night before, amused him. He put on his pyjamas, opened the curtains, flung himself on the bed, and pulled its linen sheets awry. It wouldn't deceive anyone, he thought. And it didn't matter. He laughed aloud at this thought, was still laughing when the butler arrived with his breakfast, and the Swiss and English newspapers.

'Something is funny, sir?' The radio was not on. The Ambassador could have heard no one tell a joke.

'Yes funny! No, not funny. Delightful.'

'Well, that is very good, Ambassador. It is a fine spring day. Just as well to be cheerful.' The professional Swiss servant, correct, friendly, but not overstepping the mark.

Harry sat by the window eating his breakfast, watching

the few early sailboats already on the lake, enjoying the little cheeses and pieces of sausage, as he always did. He poured his second cup of coffee. He couldn't be bothered with the papers. They would only give him gloomy news, and he didn't want to spoil this hour. It was the first hour of complete happiness he had known since the moment they had, he and Ginny together, found Dena lying on the grass. He put out of his head the threat that had come that night, the voice of the stranger telling him that Dena's death was their responsibility. It could never have happened. If he allowed that through, he would have to reject Ginny, lest he bring the same fate on her. No, he was going to keep her. He was going to keep this chance of happiness.

He filled his coffee cup again, and went along the corridor to Ginny's room. He knocked, and went in. The maid was in the bathroom, running the water for Ginny's bath. Ginny raised her eyebrows at this entrance in pyjamas and robe.

'Oh, to hell with it,' he said. 'In a few days everyone will know. I thought what a waste it was to be sitting drinking coffee by myself when I could be with you.'

'Good morning, Ambassador.' The maid scuttled out, her eyes lowered, but her mouth twitching with a smile.

'Of course they'll all know,' Ginny said. 'We'll go for a long drive in the country, find a little inn, drink Fendant, and hold hands, like any young lovers. Why should the young have all the good things? Since it's Sunday, and the servants are off, we'll have a cold buffet in front of the fire in the library and we'll talk . . . or not talk . . .'

'And we'll make love. And we'll be happy.' He kissed her softly. 'We'll be happy . . . if not for ever, then for whatever time we're given. I'll never leave you, Ginny. Promise me you'll be with me for every hour there is.'

'What a strange promise. But yes . . . we both expected to spend out years and days and hours with someone else. So we'll use the hours. Every one of them.'

As they sat over a lunch of *bundnerfleisch* and raclettes, washed down with Fendant, Ginny said, 'There'll be a lot of talk, Harry. The nasty kind of talk that went around after Dena . . . died.'

'Let them talk. It wasn't true. That's all that matters to you and me, Ginny. The sort of talk that might bother me is that I'm marrying a very rich woman. That I won't like.'

'And equally they'll probably say that having all the money I can use, I've now gathered in a title, and the position of the wife of an Ambassador. By the way, will they let you marry someone who isn't British? I hadn't thought of that.'

'We'll need permission, but that's a formality. The Foreign Service, being what it is, is riddled with wives who were married when men were stationed in some far-off place. The FO isn't totally inhuman, you know. They do, though only in a vaguely embarrassed way, recognize that people fall in love, and it isn't always with suitable British ladies. Something else bothers me. The FO will be all too jolly pleased with this marriage. They always encouraged the friendship between you and Dena, and were pleased that our children all seemed to be one family. The power of big business is very persuasive, Ginny. I wish you were humble, and unknown . . . and poor. Then you would be sure I love you.'

'I am sure.'

The next day they went shopping for a ring from one of the jewellers in the Bahnhofstrasse. 'No,' Harry said, 'we're not going to your regular jewellers. Of course we'll call there, and we may end up there. But I want the fun of going into them all. I want to see everything. I want you to see everything.'

Ginny pulled a face. 'Alas, most of them know me. It's more customary for them to come to the house. No fun in that, I can tell you. The rich are very dull, Harry. Since they have most things, jewellery is about the only thing left. It requires little imagination, except on the part of the jeweller. What takes the lady's fancy? A tiger with ruby eyes, burning bright in the forests of the night? An elephant holding up an emerald log in its tusk? A horrible snake bracelet? Just ask. They have them all.'

He insisted that they tour the Bahnhofstrasse, and the little side streets where Ginny knew the good jewellers were. She was horrified at what Harry demanded to see, insisted she try on. She dragged him out on to the street after one session at which she had rejected everything. 'Harry, you can't afford those prices! It's monstrous! I won't let you! Why, one of those stones would put a new roof on Tresillian.'

'Damn Tresillian! I'll probably only be able to give you one gift of jewellery in my life. Let it be a good one. Something I can be proud to see you wear. I was on a very low salary when Dena and I were married. I wanted to give her something magnificent, and wasn't able. Don't spoil the fun this time around.'

Ginny, protesting, settled for a Columbian gemstone emerald, of fine quality, weighing almost six carats, surrounded by small diamonds, mounted in platinum. She felt guilty over what it cost, and tried to stifle the thought. The news had spread through the small and tight circle of the exclusive jewellers of Zurich that Mrs Clayton and a man swiftly identified as the British Ambassador to Switzerland were shopping for a ring which Mrs Clayton would wear on the fourth finger of her left hand. The ring she chose was adapted to that size within half an hour, while the jeweller chatted with them over coffee. Many of his colleagues knew by sight and repute the size and quality of the Kashmir sapphire Blair Clayton had given her. They had never seen the fabulous diamond that Alex's father had given her. That had been put away when she had married Blair, and only now appeared on Livy's hand.

Ginny said later, when they were having tea at the Baur au Lac, she displaying the new emerald as if she had never possessed a jewel in her life, 'Did you remember that you are going to be my third husband? They're soon going to start referring to me as "the much-married Ginny . . ." whatever my name will be.'

'Let them. Third or fifth or tenth. Just so long as you marry me.'

2

Ginny returned to New York two weeks before Livy's baby was due. 'Thank God you've come,' Livy said. 'I was running

556

out of things to say to Mr McClintock, who's here every chance he has. And I really don't know how I'm going to stand all this cossetting for two more weeks.'

'Just try to remember how precious this child is to him, and be patient a little longer. He's old, Livy. He can't possibly see the baby grow up. You must remember that in his life a generation is missing. When Alex's father died, he lost that generation. He relies on Alex, and now on this baby. Bear with him. It was bad enough when Alex was on the way, but now that he's so much older, he will fuss that much more.'

The child came on time, Livy's labour was only six hours, the child was a healthy eight-pound boy. 'Almost a nonevent,' Livy said to Ginny, when Ginny came to see her grandson. 'All routine. No drama.' Then she retracted. 'No . . . no . . . forget I said that. I never want drama again. And this is an event.'

'Yes, it is, in the McClintock dynasty. It has hung on such a slender thread. If Alex had not survived that crash, there would have been no more. I know what the baby means to you, Livy. Just imagine what it means to an old man who had seen his family almost extinguished.'

'I wonder,' Livy speculated, walking slowly around the room to exercise, as the doctor had instructed, 'why he never married again? He could have had a dozen children. Wives aren't hard to come by when you're as rich as Mr McClintock.'

'I think he has a taste for the exotic. The Russian princess. And who knows who else? He can't have lived entirely as a monk. But he never married any of them. The only woman he's ever talked about with admiration, I suppose a degree of fascination, was your mother. I suppose she's the only woman he ever encountered to whom jewels and furs and money, in quantities more than enough to get by on, meant nothing. She didn't have any real idea who Mr McClintock was or what he represented, apart from being Alex's grandfather. She might have been the only totally innocent woman he ever met. I suppose that's why he wanted you, Livy, for Alex. He didn't want more money, he wanted the strain, the blood line.'

Livy looked at the child in Ginny's arms, who had a tangle of thick, quite long red hair. 'He's got the strain, all right.'

Andrew McClintock had been several times to see his great-grandson, and had commented on the red hair. 'I always heard that gipsies had red hair.'

'And so do Celts, Mr McClintock. Being sprung of that stock yourself, you ought to recognize it. Highlanders. Gaels. Big, tough, strong brawny men. Pale skin and blue eyes and sandy hair. Walk twenty-odd miles a day shepherding their sheep, and not think a thing about it. Alex researched the McClintock family while he was at Oxford. The branch he believes you're sprung from are Highland crofters. Gaels.'

'Well, I won't live to see this one walk twenty-odd miles, but at least, I hope, a few steps . . .'

'You'll see that, and more. Perhaps another one or two beside him. In a sense, he disappoints me.'

Andrew McClintock was outraged. 'What's wrong with him?'

'He doesn't look like Alex. Now that I have a healthy, living baby, I'm disappointed he doesn't look like Alex.'

'Don't ask for the moon, girl. The next one may or may not resemble Alex. I don't, myself, give a damn. I have now what I wanted.'

A trust fund of how many million dollars Livy didn't at the time fully realize was set up in the name of Andrew Alexander James McClintock. He was christened at the Episcopalian Church of St Thomas on Fifth Avenue. There were eight godparents, and Ginny held the child for the ceremony. He was only a month old, and he bawled lustily. When they went back to the apartment on Fifth Avenue for the reception – to which every leading family and firm on Wall Street had sent a representative, the Claytons from England, the Swiss partners from I. B. Amman – the baby was docile but alert, revelling in the attention he received. 'What will he be called?' someone asked.

'Well,' Alex said, 'his great-grandfather and I have taken up his first two names. There's only James left. Jamie, I suppose.' He smiled proudly at Livy. He sat beside her on a sofa, holding the baby, not relinquishing him to anyone else. He held that bundle, clad in a long lace gown over a hundred years old which belonged to Ginny's family, and he looked defiantly at the crowd about them. Slender, almost frail, with his hair half-silvered, and his black eye patch, his cane by his side, he seemed to declare to Ginny, who watched the scene carefully, and to all the others present, 'We beat the odds. I survived, and we beat the odds.'

'Well,' Ginny said, when the guests had departed, the baby had been asleep for hours, the glasses and the other débris of the party had been cleared away, 'I suppose I've been patient long enough. I have waited for weeks, for Jamie to be born, to grow up enough to be christened, and now it's my turn. I'm getting married very soon.'

Alex went to her and kissed her. 'Mother, did you think it was a secret? Not after that parade you and Lord Camborne made up and down the Bahnhofstrasse? Not after our good, grey Swiss partners had heard the news.' He took her hand which only today had displayed Harry's emerald, though Blair's sapphire had not been worn since she had returned from Europe, and kissed it. 'You deserve all the happiness in the world. We all wondered when on earth you'd get around to announcing it.'

'At my age,' she ignored the laughter from Alex and Livy, 'one knows how to be patient. The baby was the first thing. Now we oldsters can think about what we will do.'

'Do it as soon as possible,' Alex said. 'I want to make it a gala occasion. I want everyone to come and drink to your happiness.'

Ginny shook her head. 'We wanted something very quiet. Just the family. It's such a short time since Dena . . . and Blair, died.'

Andrew McClintock thumped his stick on the floor. 'All the more reason to make an occasion of it. Anyone who can find happiness is entitled to it. I won't countenance any hole-in-the-corner stuff. I won't let anyone think we don't wholly approve of this marriage.' By this, Ginny knew that he meant he approved of it, and that was all that mattered.

'Let's see . . . I think it should be in Washington. Harry has lots of friends there. Almost as many as in London. It should be at the McClintock mansion. Alex should give away the bride. For once, let them splash it all over the newspapers. Harry is a loyal, decent man, a member of the House of Lords, Her Britannic Majesty's Ambassador. Why shouldn't it be a splash! This family has had enough tragedy in these last years. Now, a reason for a celebration. A baby. A marriage. Let the whole world in on it!'

The sacred boundaries of privacy Andrew McClintock had cherished, his suspicion and mistrust of the press, seemed all swept away. 'Let's show them how we welcome this marriage.'

'I don't think Harry . . .'

He didn't even hear her. 'It should be arranged as soon as possible. If we press, the printers can have the invitations ready in a few days. Just give the foreign people three weeks to make their arrangements to be there. The catering people will do the rest. But I think it would be wise if my great-grandson were at my house, or Ginny's house, or even Prescott Hill on the great day. Too many people will want to slobber over him. Too many germs flying around. Anyone can see he's strong as an ox, but still, he's only a few weeks old . . .'

He was still doing it, Ginny thought. Five weeks later, as she walked through the assembled guests in the McClintock mansion on Alex's arm (he had given up his stick for this short walk) she thought that Andrew McClintock was still doing it, organizing their lives, ordering things to suit himself. The whole world seemed to be there, but she was fully conscious that her strength lay in the man who waited for her at the end of that short walk. Harry placed on her finger a simple, thin band of rare Welsh gold, which Livy had suggested, and vowed to love, honour and cherish her. It marked the end of her grieving. She was approaching fifty, and she had a new life.

The family had come. Ginny wasn't sure if the invitations hadn't been reinforced by letters from Andrew McClintock, but they were all there: Chris, Rachel and Caroline. Mark had gone to Berne, and had travelled over with Harry. He was full of joy and excitement at this happening. 'It's wonderful,' he said to Ginny when he first saw her. He held her very tightly. 'He's happy. I know that. He's been trying so hard since mother died to seem all right. Getting over it, getting on with life. Now there really is a life for him. After mother, you're the only person in the world I would have wanted . . .' It was a school-boyish, slightly awkward way to phrase it, but she knew there was nothing contrived or calculated about what he said.

Caroline and Toby came. Ginny didn't think their presence had needed any personal urging from Andrew McClintock. In their eyes, this marriage, so lavishly celebrated, probably took away any of the lingering stigma and questions surrounding Dena's death. Caroline's father, now of ambassadorial rank, was making one of the best marriages possible. Suddenly the doubt and suspicion about any former relationship was resolved. The two couples had been the closest of friends through many years, hadn't they? What was more natural than that the two survivors of a tragic period of their lives should come together in this way? That was how Caroline talked through the reception. That was what she and Toby said to anyone who would listen.

Rachel came, more mellow and more in a wedding mood than anyone had expected. 'I'm so glad for father,' she said to Livy when they were alone. 'The two of them have had a rotten deal. They need each other. There's no one else either one of them would ever understand half as well. It's a marriage of friends. They don't have to get used to each other. No unpleasant surprises.' Rachel had come a few days before the wedding, which surprised most of them. She demanded immediately to see Jamie, and Livy took her to the nursery. Rachel, rather hesitantly, asked if she could hold him. The nanny, brought from England before Jamie's birth, gave over her charge with some misgivings. Miss Penrose, in her opinion, didn't look as if she knew how to hold a child. Rachel sat down in a nursing chair, holding the infant carefully and quite expertly. He was lightly clad for the Washington summer: he squealed and kicked vigorously,

561

and laughed when she touched him under the chin, let his fingers grasp hers. His hair was thicker, and, if possible, even more firy red than at his birth. 'A real little Celt, isn't he?' Rachel said. 'Fighting already. What a triumph, after all you and Alex have been through.' To Livy's amazement, Rachel bent and kissed him lightly on the forehead. 'Go on, fight, little man. It's only the fighters who make it. If you weren't so disgustingly rich, I'd say you were my favourite baby. But then, I don't know many babies, or they don't know me. So you'd better be designated my favourite baby. And mind you live up to it, now.' Nanny had drawn away, apparently satisfied that this young woman meant no harm to her charge. Rachel murmured, so softly that even Livy, close by her, hardly heard the word so they were not meant to be answered. 'I wonder if I shall ever have anything like you, little Mister Fisticuffs?'

As they went downstairs Livy asked about Caroline's children. 'I never see them,' Rachel replied. 'You must surely know that my name is anathema in that household. I'm the Red. The Communist. I might contaminate their little darlings. They certainly wouldn't want to introduce me to their friends. And yet . . .'

'What?' It was so seldom Rachel volunteered a confidence, that Livy didn't want it to falter.

'There's a bit of talk about him, Toby. He's always been a bit of a man about town, though what anyone could see in a cold fish like that is beyond me. But still . . . Now, as a respectable married man, father of two, he doesn't exactly have girls on his arm. But there are an amazing number of "secretaries" and "research assistants" with him at cocktail parties. Because, he says, dear Caro got involved with the children at the last moment. Of course, at formal dinners she is always there. He'd never be so indiscreet. But I feel our dear Caro is doing a slow burn, and her mantle of matronly bliss might soon slip. Toby always was a calculating type, and Caro won't be satisfied with playing the dutiful wife for ever. I don't for a moment think there'll be a divorce. Perhaps just some friendly arrangement. They're capable of it . . . the two of them.'

They sat now together in the library sipping iced tea. 'And isn't that what you're involved in,' Livy asked, made bold by Rachel's unusual forthrightness. 'An arrangement?'

Rachel shrugged. 'Yes, of course it's an arrangement. Frazer couldn't possibly be divorced. Not in these times. But perhaps later. One day we may marry. Or we may break it off completely. While the Labour Party's in Opposition, he'll never have a national role to play. But when Labour tosses the Conservatives out, he will be in the Cabinet, in some capacity. It could create problems. At the moment, I'm content to let it run its course. After all, I have the pleasure of his company, freely given. He's nice to me. Still courting. She has all the wifely chores. All the appearances to make, all the bloody silly dinner parties. She's welcome to them.'

It was a view of marriage Livy had not considered before, but she realized that it was possible that Rachel was talking to her this way because her relationship with Alex before their marriage had been so widely known and written about. She had, in fact, stepped further over the line than Rachel had done; she had lived openly with Alex, been pregnant with his child before they were married.

'Oh, yes, just one other piece of news, and that completes my domestic news. I've graduated to a flat with two bedrooms in Dolphin Square. Such luxury. I actually have a study. More places to put books.' With a wave of her hand she cut short whatever Livy might have said. 'No, Frazer isn't paying for it. Has never paid for anything I own or rent except for some books. I've just moved up in the job league a little, that's all. I'll be independent for ever, if I have to starve. You know that, Livy.'

Andrew McClintock roared with delight when he heard Rachel's nickname for the baby. 'Mr Fisticuffs! That's good. I wish I could live long enough to see Mr Fisticuffs begin to tear them apart on Wall Street.'

They had given up meeting each plane Chris said she was coming on. Her non-arrival in Washington was always followed by a telephone call of apology. 'I'll be on the next one. I will certainly be there on the day.' She was going through the throes of enjoying what had unexpectedly come.

The low-budget film of the Broadway play, *Tempo*, had turned into a 'sleeper'. The reviews were so good that it had been booked into major movie house chains across the country, and was attracting very big and appreciative audiences. Box-office good news spreads quickly. It was appearing in places which would not have considered it on its cast and director. In the past month Chris had turned into what was most unlikely in film history, a near-star who had made only one film. The promotion people and the press were never slow to combine magic; this was the reverse story of the little girl who had struggled from a very ordinary background, or one of poverty and little education. Here they could indulge in the novelty of the girl who had been born with it all and the automatic bars which go up in show business against such a person. On film, she photographed with all Ginny's subtle beauty, the long neck, the very defined jaw and cheek bones, the long sweep of dark blonde hair. Her skills as an actress were commended, as if the critics were surprised that anything as good as Christine Clayton could possibly come from the ranks of the rich. In writing stories about her, the press searched around for every detail they could find: the McClintocks and the Claytons were prominent, but they liked better the story of the developing child who had spent the war years at Tresillian, the child who had roughed it with the Cornish fisherfolk, but had a tutor. Those who had shared those years were also highlighted. There was hardly need to explain them. The focus was on the reunion of those four girls who had grown up at Tresillian, the one little boy among them, and the two women who had mothered them all. The marriage of Ginny Clayton and Ambassador Lord Camborne was all grist to the publicity mill of the rising star, Christine Clayton.

The press had not neglected to point out that the man who had co-starred with her on Broadway in *Tempo*, Hugh Meredith, had not been offered the same part in the movie. Their close friendship, as it was called, had broken apart then. He was now starring in a revival of a Shaw play in London. That fact seemed to condemn him to the oblivion of the English stage.

Ginny did not much care for the man Chris had brought to Washington with her. As a gesture to her family, Chris had decided that she would stay the required two nights with Livy and Alex; her lover, Jeff Rigghouse, was famous, an actor with many successful pictures behind him, and three failed marriages. Circumspectly, he stayed at the Hay-Adams, but he was there with Chris at the marriage and reception, and the press found the combination fascinating. He came from a background that Washington society would never recognize, if it were not that he was famous, and that Christine Clayton had brought him.

So the marriage was celebrated in the presence of all those who were closest to Harry and Ginny, and even some who had not been expected. Edward and Verity, Dena's brother and sister-in-law, Lord and Lady Milroy, had come, to everyone's surprise. Ginny's brother, Robbie, was there with his family, keeping rather in the background. He seldom attended social functions. Her father, Senator Jackson, was there, looking frail and infirm by comparison to the older Andrew McClintock. Ginny's sister, Lucy, had curtly refused an invitation; she continued to live in Los Angeles with her husband, a permanent invalid after the war and never saw her family. Sir George and Lady Halliwell were there, smiling and affable, and many of Harry's old colleagues from the British Embassy staff. Many of Harry's State Department contacts had come, and even, at the last minute, the Secretary of State himself. Andrew McClintock had been right in his judgement of how this marriage should be staged. No quiet ceremony, as they had first suggested, but one which drew the best of Washington society, the most important names in government and finance, with the nice little icing of British titles. It was thought within the family that the presence of Lord and Lady Milroy had been entirely Andrew McClintock's doing: Harry was sure their first-class fares had been paid for, and they would incur no expenses. One of their daughters had come with them; the day before the wedding the Milroys were joined as Andrew McClintock's guests by Dena's sister, Ellen, and her husband. Julia had sent her regrets, and a water-colour of the Scottish castle, by one of her daughters as a wedding-gift. The presence of Dena's family put the last touch of respectability that Andrew McClintock had sought on this marriage.

Mark stayed the rest of the summer with Livy, spending most of the time at Prescott Hill. Alex came at weekends. Andrew McClintock was there almost constantly. His house in Washington was being torn apart to put in central air-conditioning. 'Can't stand those box-things sticking out of the windows. At my time of life I need a bit of comfort.'

'Southern Comfort, sir? On the rocks, with branch water on the side?' Mark said, with mock deference.

'Don't be cheeky, young man. And yes, I'd like a mint julep.'

Mark rushed to the kitchen, delighted to have an order to execute. 'The Ambassador asked me to make it myself,' he said to Landers. The kitchen staff didn't mind. He was only a kid. Let him fix the drink, if that was what pleased Mr McClintock. Let him fiddle about with his ragoûts and soufflés, so long as he cleans up the mess himself. They could be vastly tolerant of kids playing around, but this one took the job very seriously, and he always cleaned up after himself.

Chapter 14

1

At Tresillian the weather was mostly kind, and Harry and Ginny lazed away the days in the sun. Most afternoons they went down to St Just to have tea with Thea and Herbert, or Thea and Herbert came up to have dinner with them. The Gardiners had not felt like making the journey to Washington for the wedding; Herbert did not say so, but from his slow walk and sometimes laboured breathing, Ginny realized he was far from well. He had painted nothing for months. 'I suppose it's all just gone out of me. The last picture I really wanted to paint was the portrait of Livy and Alex.'

Ginny and Harry made the round of their favourite picnic places, the small, almost secret coves, the ruins half-hidden in the earth and debris of the centuries. They revelled in each other's company, not talking very much, occasionally wordlessly reaching out a hand which swiftly found a response. They lay with the windows open at night, listening to the surf on the Tresillian Rocks, and the almost eerie quiet which prevailed when the tide was far out, and the sands uncovered in the moonlight. They made love in a leisurely fashion, with no haste, secure that there was world enough, and time.

'There's a sort of magic here,' Ginny said. 'Even in the hard times of the war, I loved it. Even when we were being pushed around by the evacuees, and Dena was out shooting rabbits . . .' They could speak her name as naturally as they spoke Blair's. Their grieving had come together, and had seemed to strengthen the love they both had for the ones who were lost, and still strengthened it further for each other.

'This should be the place we come back to when you retire, Harry.'

'What's the hurry to retire me? I'm only fifty-six.'

'I thought retirement as an ambassador for the FO was mandatory at sixty.'

'Well, so it is,' he admitted grudgingly. 'Sometimes they keep you on a bit longer if there's no one quite ready to step into your shoes.'

'Well,' Ginny said, 'I don't fancy keeping the Washington house. There's no purpose to it. We can always stay with Livy and Alex when we go there. There's Prescott Hill and Seymour House. There's even the house in Zurich, though I've never thought of that as a home, but just a sort of convenience. What I'd really love to do . . .' She had been lying stretched out on a rug in the meadow where they had picnicked, feeling sleepy from the bottle of Devon cider they had shared. Now she sat up. 'What I'd really *love* to do is rehabilitate Tresillian. Do it from head to foot. Kitchen, bathroom, plumbing, central heating, never mind a new roof and replacing all the timber that's got dry rot in it.'

Harry himself sat up. He looked alarmed. 'That would mean tearing the place apart. It would cost an absolute fortune! You've no idea what these rehabilitation jobs cost, Ginny, because you don't know what problems you'll run into. Can you imagine what it would cost to put new wiring and plumbing into those old walls? In some places they must be four feet thick.'

'And I'd like,' Ginny continued serenely, as if he had not spoken, 'to rehabilitate the Tower. Oh, not put it all back in place, I like that pile of stones around the base, but just to make it safe. One lovely, great, stupendous folly. We could fence off the cliff top, discreetly, so that our grandchildren could play safely. Such a lovely lot of things to do.'

'You're mad, Ginny. Look, you don't even know what it costs to make the most necessary repairs to the place, just to keep the rain from running down the walls.'

'I have an idea,' she said drily. 'I've always examined my own bills carefully. I know what it costs to keep up the McClintock mansion, and Prescott Hill.'

'But those places are modern by comparison with Tresillian. This is a bloody great castle, Ginny, built before they even thought of plumbing.'

'Oh well,' she said airily, 'if you're so dead against it . . . we could just do something boringly ordinary like renovating a palazzo in Venice, and live with our feet in water, and water running up the walls.' She turned to look at him. 'This is your place, Harry. We don't have to buy it. There are centuries of your family's history here.'

'And what about when I'm gone, when I'm history? The place will have to go to Mark, who won't be able to afford it. Unless there's some way around the entail. All your work and money will go for someone else.'

'I didn't know you were planning to die so soon, Harry. Only a minute ago you were grumbling because I was thinking about what we would do when you were retired. You have years, Harry. Years and years. Wouldn't you like to spend some of them here?'

'Yes,' he admitted. 'Yes, I would like that. I hate to see it just fall down. How you ever stuck it all through the winters during the war I'll never know. It's always been a place for a summer idyll for me. Something I never expected to have, and didn't know what to do with when I got it. Oh, you are mad, Ginny. It's really not to be thought of!'

'Well, just let me do the thinking. You have your job to attend to. This needn't bother you. Just think how splendid those rooms could look. Just think about a bathroom with every bedroom, and loads of hot water. And a stainless-steel kitchen for Mark to mess about in. Just think how snug and cosy we could be when the winter gales roared outside. Oh, Harry, that great old pile has withstood those gales for so long. It would be a damned shame to abandon it to them.'

'Mad!' he repeated testily, beginning to pack up the picnic basket. 'There just would be no end in sight to the money you'd have to spend on it. Oh, a few modest improvements I wouldn't say no to, but this . . . this is a gigantic undertaking.'

She sighed. 'Oh, well, I guess it will just have to be some old palazzo in Venice . . .'

They didn't talk about it at all as they drove back, but when the car bumped up the rutted drive and rounded the

569

last clump of rhododendrons, and the house came into sight, Ginny just nodded silently. Harry took the picnic basket to the kitchen, and from the way he banged the doors, Ginny knew his mood.

But when he came back to the sitting-room they always used because it was the smallest, and therefore the easiest to heat, he was laughing. 'And wouldn't you just know it? This is the day the iron on the range has finally burned through. Jacques was doing something with a leg of lamb, and the damn thing just fell through to the bottom of the range. They're still trying to salvage it. And the refrigerator has gone on the blink. It won't make us even a little cube of ice for a drink. I'm not very popular in the kitchen right at this moment. I've told them to dry their tears, and make do on some *pâté de foie gras*, or a cheese sandwich. We'll take Thea and Herbert out to dinner somewhere. And I've promised them a new stove and a new refrigerator first thing tomorrow, or I'm afraid they'll be packing their bags and heading back to Seymour House. Knox thinks I've let the side down. And let you down.'

Ginny seemed unperturbed. 'I'll just ring Thea. It's time we had a night out somewhere. She'll know some place to go.'

The next morning, while workmen were struggling to rip out the old iron range and install a large electric cooker, and another lot were putting into place a new refrigerator, the largest the shop in Truro could supply, an architect arrived. 'Mr Penleigh,' Ginny said to Harry, 'has kindly come from Truro to give the place a quick look-over. I've told him there are only cheese sandwiches available for lunch, but we've some quite nice wine . . .'

Mr Penleigh was mostly silent as Ginny led him through the house, the grand staircase, and the little back staircases, the broad corridors, and the small twisting passages. Harry trailed along disconsolately. 'It's useless, Ginny,' he protested at one stage. 'I'd forgotten how much of the bloody place there was. I think there are rooms here I've never even seen before.'

'That was how we lost so many evacuee children during

570

the war,' she said gaily. 'Sometimes they didn't go to school, and we didn't know it, because we could never find them. They just drifted in and out of the kitchen and ate anything that came to hand. We never could keep track of when the sheets should be changed because we really didn't know where half of them were sleeping. It all added to the fun . . . though it didn't seem like fun then, but a big headache.'

Jacques, cheered by the sight of the new stove and refrigerator, had decided to forgive them. He gave them a splendid lunch of smoked salmon, cold meats and potato salad, a huge mixed salad, and fruit salad in Kirsch. Knox had taken it on himself to choose the wine, a Meursault.

Mr Penleigh sighed in satisfaction. He was a man in his thirties, and all through lunch he had carefully avoided the subject of the house. With coffee and brandy which he had at first refused, but which Ginny persuaded him to take, he said, 'It would be the biggest challenge of my professional life and it would cost an absolute fortune. At this stage, I couldn't even begin to give you an estimate . . . I would require help from experts. I mean, the sort of people who know every different period during which this house was built. It has to be properly done, or not even started. In fact, my best advice to you is just to replace the worst of the rotten timbers, put on a new roof, and leave well enough alone.'

'Exactly what I think,' Harry put in.

'But, Mr Penleigh, that wasn't what I asked for. You're a Cornishman, aren't you? Wouldn't you like to see this place restored to what it should be? With all its oddities. Its medieval bits, its Elizabethan bits, its Georgian bits. This is a house that's grown out of Cornish history, Mr Penleigh. Supposing I said "be damned to the cost". Could it be done? Could we restore it, I mean with all the things we're used to? I'd want a bathroom with every bedroom, or almost that. Turn the little rooms into dressing-rooms, store rooms. Look behind the panelling and make sure there isn't rot there.'

'It would mean, Lady Camborne, really creating a modern house inside the shell of an ancient house. Could you . . . would you be prepared for the cost of that?' He looked

571

around him wildly, as if he didn't want to see either of their faces. 'It could be one of the splendours of Cornwall, as it was in its greatest days.'

Harry groaned. Ginny said quietly, 'Then let's do it. Call in any experts you think you need, Mr Penleigh. I assure you the bills will be paid, promptly. Let's do this. Let's say it's a sort of a thanksgiving for the life of my son. It's a gesture to the lovely woman who was born down there in St Just who is his wife. It is a wartime memory for me, when I lived here with beloved friends. We all have our reasons. I know I must be mad to embark on this, but let's say, over my husband's wishes, I intend to be mad. But I want it soon, Mr Penleigh. I can't wait ten years. Life has taught me to seize the day, if not the hour.'

2

Harry and Ginny returned to Berne, and Ginny settled down to the not very exacting duties of the wife of the British Ambassador, in a small and sedate community. There was the usual social round, parties given and parties attended, protocol strictly observed. By comparison to one of the major embassies, it was a quiet life, and many weekends they went to the chalet they had rented in the mountains, or to the house on the Zurich See. Ginny wrote to Andrew McClintock of her plans for Tresillian, not seeking his approval, but simply to inform him of what she was doing. He wrote back that he thought she was wasting her money, but that it wasn't a bad idea, all together. She didn't know what the 'all together' signified, but she let it go. He treated it as if it were some expensive hobby she had taken up, but from which there would be no reward except some personal pleasure. *'Since you can afford it'*, Andrew McClintock wrote, *'there's no one to say you can't do it.'*

Once Harry had been convinced that she was serious in her intentions he had started the lengthy procedure of breaking the entail, and splitting Tresillian and its immediate grounds from the rest of the estate, so that on his death, it would be solely Ginny's property. Mark would inherit the title, there was no way he could escape that, but Tresillian Castle and the death duties that would go with it would not be his. Mark's letter in response to this news was one long sigh of relief.

Ginny put her Washington house on the market, and suggested to Andrew McClintock that the house in Zurich was something of an extravagance, since it was seldom used.

An answer came back promptly.

The house in Zurich is the property of McClintock-Clayton, and, in my opinion, it should be kept. We have extensive holdings in Switzerland, as you know, and Alex will need to make many trips there in the future. It should be regarded in the light of the Fifth Avenue apartment. It is for company use, when it is needed.

Ginny was glad, when she read that, that Seymour House had been bought solely by Blair, and now belonged to her. That fact would not stop Andrew McClintock or any other member of the family using it whenever they wanted it, but it could not be sold at the whim of McClintock-Clayton.

Letters from Livy came regularly from Washington. They sounded, Ginny thought, a little too sedate and settled for a young woman of only twenty-five. But, as Livy had noted, who wanted anything else but a smooth existence, when the alternative could be so terrible? Ginny was twice Livy's age; it was all right for her to enjoy a settled existence with Harry. Livy would find something other than her charitable committees and the inevitable dinner parties.

For Ginny there was the mostly hidden excitement of Tresillian. She made a few journeys to London, only staying overnight at Seymour House, to meet Mr Penleigh and some associates he had brought in on the project. They had completed the almost impossible task of making a plan of Tresillian. 'We have to have this, Lady Camborne, but some of it doesn't make sense. There are some walls too thick to be only walls, one suspects secret rooms, or priest holes. I really don't know what to expect when we start to tear it apart.

'I thought I'd leave these plans with you for your approval: the placing of the bathrooms and dressing-rooms that sort of thing. The small rooms on the upper floors must have been used for servants. I wondered if you intended us just to put them in good repair and leave them or would you like us to throw some of them together to make larger rooms, and keep others as bathrooms? There may be a problem of which are bearing walls, and how much we dare take out. That we'll more or less have to decide as we go along. Of course, the reception rooms, one should almost call them the state rooms, will remain as they are, with repair, of course. The library will be one of the most beautiful rooms in the whole of Britain.' They conferred with Jacques over the kitchen. When he sensed that no expense was being spared, he described the kitchen of his dreams, almost the sort of kitchen he would have liked to see in some of the hotels where he had trained. He wanted a massive dish-washing system, such as a restaurant would have, a walk-in refrigerator, a hanging-room for meat and poultry, a range of stoves, chopping tables, a chef's room . . . Mr Penleigh raised his eyebrows over some of the suggestions. 'Aren't they rather excessive?'

'No, Lady Camborne will do much entertaining, as she does here, when she is in residence. Here, the kitchen is not up to these standards, we are cramped for space, and everything must go by the little lift to the dining-room. At Tresillian, it is all on the same level, with plenty of space. Make the best while you are doing it, is my advice, m'lady. Make it the easiest. People don't want to be servants anymore, not since the war. Not the young. Here in London they will do it for the money, and because there is some place to spend the money in their time off. Down there, who is there? The Tregenna ladies: good-hearted, but not very well trained.' He pointed to the plans, not understanding half of what was on them. 'Make a nice cosy little room for the Ambassador and Lady Camborne to eat in when they are alone. Make it close to the kitchen. Some day Lady Camborne may have to do the cooking herself . . .'

Ginny laughed. 'It wouldn't be the first time, at Tresillian.

But it's a good idea, Jacques. It should be here, Mr Penleigh.' She touched the plan. 'That used to be the room the girls used as a school room. It looks out on to the orchard. And this still-room area, Mr Penleigh. That could be made into a very attractive staff-room. A place to eat, and relax. It has the same view . . .' Jacques beamed at her.

She talked to people who would do the restoration of the panelling, those who would catalogue the library, and repair the books which needed repair. She saw decorators' schemes for the colours in each room, and asked Christie's and Sotheby's to inform her when suitable furniture of the appropriate period came on to the market. There were many magnificent pieces at Tresillian, but mostly heavy items of the Elizabethan and Jacobean periods. She guessed that smaller, more elegant pieces might have been sold. Lighter chairs and small tables and commodes would be needed for the drawing-room. She was having her own Chippendale dining-table with sixteen chairs shipped from Washington. 'I know we will have to be rather grand in the reception rooms,' she told the decorators, 'but remember it's a country house. We ought to have a few homey touches of chintz in some of the bedrooms and the little sitting-room.'

She made a point of seeing Rachel and Caroline whenever she went to London, though never together. She thought Caroline seemed rather reluctant to see her, though she and Toby appeared dutifully at Seymour House. Ginny went to visit the children, bringing them toys, so she could report back to Harry. They were two good-looking little boys, with just enough spirit of naughtiness to make them normal. 'You must be so pleased with them,' she said over tea to Caroline.

'They're all right,' Caroline said, with something of a shrug. 'It's a relief to know one's done what was expected of one.' She seemed distant, and strangely defensive, as if she expected criticism.

Ginny mentioned this to Rachel. 'I don't think the perfect marriage is all that perfect, as I said before,' Rachel answered. 'But now Caroline has started out on her own. She's often at functions without Toby. No man in particular,

I think, but Caro doesn't sit at home and wait for Toby any more.'

Ginny kept that information, as well as many other things, from Harry. She didn't involve him in the plans for Tresillian; she was afraid he would object too strongly to what was being spent. Rather carefully, he didn't ask. He didn't know that she had set a team of workmen to clear up the grounds of the Castle – trim back the shrubs, clear the deadwood from the trees. A separate firm of restorers had begun the delicate work on the Tower; it would still appear to be what it was, a ruin, but one that was safe to walk into. 'Ginny's Folly' she knew well they would call it. The last thing she did was select the room that would be hers and Harry's bedroom, with its adjoining bath and dressing-room. She made a deliberate choice to have it at the front of the house, the side which looked down to the town and bay of St Just, rather than facing the Tresillian Rocks and the force of the Atlantic gales. The Rocks had their own fascination, but she did not want to hear the pounding of the seas against them, she did not want to think, each time she looked from her window, of Chris down there, helpless, and Isa running for her life.

The short trips to London were only a small departure from the routine of Berne. She noticed that Harry seemed abstracted at times, but he had never talked about his work, so there was nothing unusual about his behaviour. She quietly planned for the retirement that would not now be long in coming. 'Do you think you might be moved,' she hated to use the word, because Harry didn't appear to like it, 'before your retirement?'

'If I am moved, I hope it's to some other quiet and peaceful place. But Ambassadors are supposed to pick their way through minefields for their governments, though these days we're being bypassed. The age of the telephone. The Foreign Secretary talks directly to foreign ministers, and sometimes the ambassador doesn't even know what's going on. Eden's cooking up something right now. I can smell it. God help him if he goes ahead without Eisenhower's approval. And he won't get that this side of the election in November, if at all.'

576

A week before the American election Britain and France moved in to take over the Suez Canal, under the pretext of defending lives and property after Israel had attacked Egypt. A furious Eisenhower instructed the US Treasury to sell sterling, a move which shook the British Cabinet. In a week it was all over; Israel, Britain and France were out of Egypt, the Canal was blocked by sunk shipping, and the powers concerned were denying that there had ever been any collusion. Eden collapsed as a man and as a force after a rumoured threat from Eisenhower of oil sanctions. Under cover of the fuss, and with scant attention paid to it by the world's press, the Soviets invaded Hungary.

Harry was in despair. 'We've lost everything. We can't hold our heads up. No one seems to have noticed that Israel inflicted a stunning defeat in one week on Egypt, which has the latest weapons from Russia. Then they're ordered to pull out. Why in hell didn't Eden wait until after the election? He might have had a chance with Eisenhower. Well, Ginny, this is the end of it. We haven't been a real world power since the end of the war, no matter what we've pretended. This stupid, ill-conceived little episode only makes it more abundantly clear.' He said this bitterly as they both dressed to attend a reception to mark the National Day of one of Britain's former colonies. Harry had a drink while he dressed, something he seldom did. 'Put on your best smile, Ginny. We're going to have to face a mob who must be politely rubbing their hands at our humiliation. The British Ambassador is going to eat humble pie tonight. God, what stupidity . . . They say Eden's ill. I think he must be mad as well.' Just as they were about to go down to the car, he placed a kiss on her cheek. 'Maybe the idea of putting Tresillian in order wasn't such a bad one. I think I'll take a little trip to London when the dust settles and see what my pension position is. I really haven't got much stomach for this job now, Ginny.'

She wore more jewels than she would ordinarily have done, and the smile Harry had asked of her. She parried snide little remarks, expressions of sympathy which she knew were expressions of triumph. The diplomatic corps were politely indicating that the British had better give themselves no more airs. They were the vassals of the United States.

Ginny caught just a snatch of conversation she was not, she was sure, meant to hear, as the speaker was someone she regarded as a friend among the diplomatic community. 'Poor old Harry. Hard to take this. It's lucky for him he's married to an American, a rather powerful American lady. Or at least, the former daughter-in-law of an extremely powerful American who likes to keep his finger on all his family, no matter how remote . . .'

Ginny kept her smile, and moved on through the crush, rage in her heart against Eden and Eisenhower and everyone else involved in the mess that made Harry feel humiliated, made him feel that he wanted to retire from the scene. In all the plans for Tresillian, she had never envisaged it as a bolt-hole for an embittered man.

Then two weeks later Harry was summoned to London to the Foreign Office. 'Can't think what they want . . . I haven't had any indication that they're dissatisfied with what I've been doing here. Any rate, it'll be a chance to see the grandchildren, and maybe Mark can come up to London for the weekend. I'll telephone the headmaster . . .'

Ginny made her own telephone calls to Mr Penleigh, to the decorators, made notes to view some furniture coming up for auction. She was pleased that Harry would be with her; she had no fears that the summons to the Foreign Office indicated trouble, that it was other than routine.

They arrived in London on a wet morning late in November. Mark was travelling up to London by train that day, a lenient headmaster being quite agreeable; Wrisley encouraged all and any contact between parents and pupils. Ginny spent part of the day closeted with Mr Penleigh, and with her principal decorator. Harry had gone at once to the Foreign Office; the appointment had been with the Permanent Under Secretary, but there had been a hint that the Foreign Secretary himself might want to see him.

He returned late, after seven. Mark had arrived, and was upstairs having a bath. Ginny had briefly let him examine the plans for Tresillian. His face glowed with pleasure. 'It'll be just wonderful! How wonderful that you and Father will be spending so much time here. I thought . . . well, I thought you'd naturally want to go back to Washington.'

'We'll do that, but only for visits. I think your father would be happier at Tresillian. And for myself, I've taken a fancy to being a country lady, arranging flowers, having walks with golden labradors . . .'

'You'll do it beautifully!' Mark looked amazingly grown up, she thought. He seemed happier. He did not complain about school. But he confessed a worry about Herbert. 'When I went there at half-term he seemed hardly able to breathe. Something called emphysema, Thea says . . . Nothing they can do to help him.' Ginny wondered if she should stay on after Harry had gone back to Berne to go and visit them. She could make the work at Tresillian the excuse; there was no point in conveying to Herbert her sense of alarm and impending loss.

Harry's return put the thought out of her head. He looked quite haggard when he came in. He kissed her absently, and went and poured himself a whisky. He nodded towards her own glass, but she shook her head.

'What's the matter?'

He slumped back into his chair. 'Washington. That's what's the matter. George Halliwell was due to retire in October. Of course, when Suez blew up, it was no time to replace him. And now Eisenhower is so furious with the Prime Minister and the Foreign Secretary, Selwyn Lloyd, that he refused to have Peter Simmons, who was to replace George Halliwell. It seems he's tainted by the "collusion" theory. At any rate, Dulles is against him, so that's that. They put forward my name to Dulles, and it seems I'm acceptable, barely. If there has to be a British Ambassador, then it might as well be someone who was safely away from London and Paris when the plotting about Suez was supposed to be going on. And someone who's married to an American puts more than a little jam on the pill.'

'Harry!'

'Well, they didn't exactly say that, but it was implied. We

have one huge job of fence-mending to do in Washington. If George Halliwell hadn't been on the verge of retirement, I haven't any doubt Dulles would have asked for his withdrawal. Things are that bad.'

'Don't you want to go?'

He swirled the liquid in his glass. 'You have to know that the embassy in Washington is one of the dreams of a career diplomat. But now it's come, no, I don't think I do want it. I've grown used to a quieter life. I don't fancy being summoned to the State Department to be rapped over the knuckles for every little thing that goes wrong. I don't want to be eternally apologizing. I've grown selfish in my happiness with you, Ginny. This is both a demand of duty, and an honour. And I don't feel much like living up to either of them.'

'But you'll do it.'

'I've asked for the weekend to think it over. I hate to admit it, but since I am married to you, they are thinking I can afford to resign, and not take up any job at all. It isn't a thought I relish.'

'So you'll do it. I know you will. You have a few years left that you owe them. You might as well spend them at the top of the tree. You'll have earned Tresillian, and anything else you fancy by then.'

'What do you think about it? Do you fancy Washington?'

'I married the Foreign Office, didn't I? Whither thou goest etc. At least I don't have to learn another language. Livy and Alex will be just down the road, and of course Mr McClintock will be a frequent caller.'

'Ginny, do you realize that the more spiteful will say that you, that McClintock-Clayton, bought the ambassadorship, that Ginny Clayton rather fancied being the ambassador's wife in Washington, not just nice, quiet little Berne? You're the one who'll be top of the tree. White House parties will have to try hard to keep up with the British Embassy. Don't you see, Ginny, that for the Foreign Office you're the ace in the pack? It doesn't hurt that although Andrew McClintock is a well-known Democrat, he has contributed evenly to the campaign funds of both parties. He knew Eisenhower would win.'

'Harry! Harry! Stop it! Either you swallow your pride and take what comes with being married to me, or don't say another word about it. If you decide to return to Berne, or resign, then do it. But I know you'll take Washington. You say: "They'll say this and they'll say that." And I say: "Let them say." Will I have to watch you sulking at Tresillian for years, thinking that you should have made this one last effort? You know you want to give the job your damnedest to the end. Then you can retire with grace and pride. You'll do it, Harry.'

He raised his glass to her. 'You're a very persuasive woman, Ginny, and a very perceptive one. Even in this so-called enlightened age, it's sometimes hard for a man to accept that what he achieves might, in part, be due to his wife.'

'What a man achieves has always partly, if not mostly, been due to his wife. If he loves her, he may work harder for her sake. If he loathes her, he may work to get away from her. Marriage is such a funny situation, Harry. I sometimes wonder how any of us put up with it.'

'Well then, that's it. I'll work my hardest, and for the rest, I'll rely on you.'

'The way I see it is that they are taking a very seasoned diplomat and giving him the top job. I really wonder that they didn't offer it to you in the first place, rather that Peter Simmons.'

'Never question the will of our political masters, Ginny. Perhaps they thought they'd just let me rest content in my cosy little niche, with my lovely wife. That is, after all, what I asked for. Not for this.'

Mark came downstairs. Harry got up to shake hands, and then could not resist the embrace. 'You look wonderful, old son. This Wrisley place seems to suit you.' Harry told him the news. 'I'm afraid it means you're going to be flying the Atlantic again, back on the same old route.'

'You'll do a splendid job, Father.' They talked on, and Ginny realized that Mark was far more aware, politically, of the task of fence-mending Harry would have to undertake than she had expected. They talked about Suez, the mistakes, the bungling. Harry was careful not to apportion blame to Eden or Selwyn Lloyd. He could never say things like that to Mark, only to his wife. She listened to them, watched them. Could Harry have loved a child more if he had been his own? She and Harry were now the only people in the world who knew that Mark was not Harry's son. With the possible exception of Mike Goodrick. But Mike Goodrick had kept his word, and faded out of Mark's life. Mark was Harry's son, and always would be.

3

By March Harry and Ginny were installed in the British Embassy. Harry was greeted, after the formalities, by one of the Ministers with whom he had previously worked. 'Welcome back, Harry. If George hadn't been such a great chap you'd have been here sooner.' The splendid rooms of the embassy, built by Sir Edward Lutyens to look as much as possible like a grand English country house, familiar to Harry and Ginny, took on a new meaning, because they were now their home. Ginny couldn't remember the number of times she had ascended the great staircase with its flying bridge leading to the reception rooms; and how many summer parties had she attended held in the great portico with its thin grey slate, set on edge, parties which had spilled over, into the famous gardens? She remembered the embassy cat. For her it was a return to a place she had known almost all her life, but in quite a different fashion. She had been mistress of a great Washington mansion, but not one over which she presided but did not own, of which she was the temporary occupant, but where she was expected to set a standard and run, after the fashion of a country which was not hers as a native. She, used to all the splendour Washington could offer, felt strangely diffident and shy. She was grateful that the McClintock mansion was just down the Avenue, and Livy's cosy sitting-room, which she herself had once furnished, was there for her to retreat to, Jamie's nursery was to be visited whenever formality grew too much.

Harry went to the White House to present his credentials, and was received with rather more warmth that he had expected. He knew he was the new man, sent to paper over the cracks of the Suez misadventure, but that did not seem to be held against him personally. He was regarded as an old Washington hand, someone who knew the ropes, knew the diplomatic corps, perhaps most importantly, knew the press corps. And he had married a lady who combined the McClintock-Clayton money with some of Virginia's most honoured names. The last fact was a matter of much comment in the social pages. The British Embassy had always been a place of glamour and fascination in social Washington; now it seemed to have found its most perfect mistress, one of their own daughters. There was speculation about what sort of parties Lady Camborne might give; Ginny could have told them that they would be very little different from the parties given before. The Lutyens house imposed its own rules and procedures.

There were the usual receptions given all through diplomatic Washington to welcome Harry as ambassador; that was expected, and each night was occupied. But the first party they gave at the embassy was private, and one for which they paid, as they had to. It was to honour Andrew McClintock on his eightieth birthday.

Everyone who could get an invitation was there; it was spring, and the gardens had come to life, the doors of the great portico were open. Later, when the reception was over, there would be a private dinner just for the family, and the most intimate McClintock-Clayton associates. As she surveyed the list Ginny reflected that 'intimate' seemed to encompass a lot of people. Some were coming from Europe for the occasion. Even her brother, Robbie, had been enticed, but her father was not well enough to attend. Lucy had sent the usual refusal. Caroline and Toby were coming. It was too good a social occasion to miss. To her surprise, Ginny received an acceptance from Rachel. The formal note of reply came, and then a personal letter. *'I don't like the things for which the old bastard stands, but he's a fascinating man, and I've had some glorious rows with him. I'd rather*

583

like to be there to drink his health,' Ginny decided that, despite the coolness, the near hostility that existed between them, she would accommodate both Rachel and the Osbornes in the embassy. They were both Harry's daughters. She had written a pleading letter to the headmaster of Wrisley, asking for Mark to be allowed time off to come. It was granted readily; Harry's status was now one which not even Wrisley could be nonchalant about.

Chris was coming from Los Angeles with the husband she had married in Las Vegas a month ago, the film star, Jeff Rigghouse. Ginny and Harry had received a call from her only after the ceremony, just before the press had time to print the news. Ginny felt shut out, excluded, by the fact that her only daughter would choose to marry first, and tell her later. Not that she had ever expected Chris to marry in a formal manner, especially not to someone who had been married three times before, but Chris's phone call had only just preceded the first call from the press to the British Embassy. A secretary had been instructed to give a formal reply, the very least they could give. 'We are very pleased. We hope she will be very happy.' Ginny couldn't help thinking back to Hugh Meredith whom she had found so warm, so endearing. She 'hoped for Chris's happiness; she feared it was something that would elude her.

The embassy was thronged on the evening of the reception, the upstairs reception rooms, the portico, the gardens. Ginny had set dinner for a very late hour, knowing that it would be difficult to get rid of some of their guests. Slowly they trailed off, as if reluctant to leave the scented gardens, the sense of a dynastic family, of American origin, ensconced in the British Embassy.

There were more than fifty around the dinner table. Andrew McClintock had stood for most of the hours of the reception, receiving congratulations. That day's Washington and New York newspapers, and many abroad, had carried profiles on him, all of which recognized the autocrat in him, his passion for requiring to know the details of his vast empire, his unwillingness to delegate, seen by them as a weakness. One paper had observed:

> There seldom can have been a businessman of the acumen of Andrew McClintock's father, followed by a son of such talent in the very diversified businesses he undertook, a talent, which in the eyes of some, amounts to near-genius. His hope of a son to follow him was cruelly thwarted by the very early death of that son. He was more than fortunate in the talents of his partner, Blair Clayton, who married his son's widow. This support he was deprived of by the death of Blair Clayton in an airplane crash in 1953. Now the international business community looks with interest at the developing abilities of his grandson, Alexander McClintock. It will need a master to follow this grandmaster of the game.

'Got me in my grave, already,' Andrew McClintock had commented sourly to Alex, and tossed the paper aside.

'Well, I've got a birthday present for you that I think you'll like better than all the newspaper articles, flattering or otherwise; and all the cashmere robes and gold desk sets. Livy's going to have another baby. She's two months pregnant, and healthy as a horse.'

Which news possibly explained why Andrew McClintock had seemed in an unusually jovial humour that evening; he had beamed on everyone alike. He even found some polite words to say to Chris's new husband, a man he was believed to detest, although he had only seen him twice. 'You should have come and let us give you a proper family wedding.' Livy, who was standing near by, knew perfectly well that there was nothing Andrew McClintock would have liked less. If the wedding had been in Washington, he probably wouldn't have attended.

Chris seemed buoyed up by excitement, and possibly she'd had rather too much champagne. 'Ambassador, it's so exciting. I'm becoming a woman of business. I mean real business. Jeff and I have just bought *The Way West* – you must have heard of it – the novel that's been an enormous best-seller.'

She knew perfectly well that Andrew McClintock never read novels. 'You know – the pioneering saga – three generations conquering the West. Jeff and I are going to co-produce it, and we're going to be in the cast. Apart from Jeff, we're getting some big names. Real money-in-the-bank names.'

'Are you going to be the bank?'

She looked a little startled. 'Why, yes, that's what we planned. That way we own it, lock, stock and barrel. Every penny's ours . . .'

'Profit, you mean? I've heard of films that don't make any profit. Then every penny of loss will be yours, too. Well, good luck. I hope you don't lose your shirt, forgive me, your husband's shirt.'

'Miserable old bastard,' Chris remarked later to Rachel. 'Age certainly doesn't mellow him. He just can't bear to think that someone besides Alex or himself might have a bent for making any money. And come to that, we don't have any proof that Alex has any particular talent for making money. He has so much expert back-up . . .'

'Time will tell that, too, won't it?' Rachel replied vaguely. She wandered off. Chris stared after her. Not many people wandered off from her these days. She had wanted to tell Rachel about a 'little' film she would start working on in the next week, called *Arriving*, not obvious box-office, but of which she would be the star. In the midst of all the grand plans for *The Way West*, she was conscious of needing more experience. She remembered, as she hadn't done for a long time, the days when everything had been shared so naturally with Rachel. She shrugged. It wasn't her fault that Rachel had become so anti-social, so aggressively against the sort of life she, Chris, lived. But who was Rachel to pass judgement? At least she, Chris, was married to Jeff.

Andrew McClintock had been very gracious to Rachel when she offered him birthday greetings. He even leaned towards her, indicating that she might kiss him on the cheek. 'Very nice of you to take the trouble to come. And at least you had the good sense and manners not to wish me many happy returns.'

She laughed. 'That's just it. You probably will have many,

many happy returns of the day, and confound all of us who think bloated capitalists are doomed to early graves. I'd really miss you, Mr McClintock. We've had some pretty good rows. I look forward to many more.'

'That's a date, Rachel. We won't have one now, because that would spoil Ginny's evening. I'd like you to come and have lunch with me, if you have the time before you go back. I'd like to hear what the Young Turks are thinking these days.'

'I'd like that too, Ambassador. Tomorrow?'

'Tomorrow,' he agreed.

There were toasts to him at the long table, and short speeches. He rose to reply. 'I thank you all. I thank you for coming, especially those who have come long distances to be here. Some of the things you have said have been flattering, and some false. Some have been flattering, and perhaps true. I can't attempt to summarize eighty years in a few sentences, and I have a horror of turning into a windy old bore. I am grateful for you, as a family. I am grateful for friends who are real friends. I am grateful for such a wonderful woman as Ginny, who put up with me for so many years. But eighty is eighty, and has to count as old. So I give you a toast to youth, and the continuance of the McClintock family. I give you a toast to life and the new baby that Livy and Alex will have.'

And so the news came out in an unexpectedly public way.

The three women she had grown up with came to congratulate Livy afterwards. Livy sensed, of what was said to her, that only Rachel's words were genuine, if a little wistful. 'How lovely . . . I'm so glad.' Caroline was perfunctory. It was, she indicated, nothing to make a fuss about, having another baby.

Alex offered to take Chris and Jeff back to the Hay-Adams, where they were staying. 'Thank you, we have a car waiting.' Chris's manner indicated plainly that film stars did not have to accept lifts. In the car she said to Jeff, 'Well, just like him to make such a to-do about a baby, the old fool. You'd think it was something unusual.'

Jeff leaned back and pulled on his cigarette. 'Want a baby,

Chris? We could make a baby any day you like.' He had already fathered five children, and he said it with a casual arrogance.

'What? With my new film ready to go – and *The Way West* to handle? You must be mad.'

'Well, the news about Livy seems to have upset you.'

'Oh, she's getting so damn smug. I could have six children, and it wouldn't make any difference to the Old Man. My name isn't McClintock.'

4

Time seemed to move very slowly for Livy in the weeks following Andrew McClintock's eightieth birthday. She was less excited about this pregnancy than the other two. Now the new pregnancy seemed dully routine. She was shocked to find that she was bored. She would hardly admit it even to herself, but that was the truth. She was bored and annoyed by Andrew McClintock's daily calls, his fussing about her health, the visits to the nursery to see Jamie. She tried to make allowances for his age, his anxiety to see another great-grandchild safely born, to think that there was a good chance that there would be others. She was horrified to find that she even grew bored and indeed irritated by Alex's solicitude. What was the matter with her? In having Alex, hadn't she everything she had ever dreamed of in life? And good sense told her that in expecting Alex to fill every moment of her being, she was asking too much. But good sense didn't seem to help. She was irritable, and often snapped at him. They entertained less frequently, but that didn't mean that she had more of his company; the affairs of McClintock-Clayton seemed to absorb all his free time. Sometimes she wondered if the late evenings at the office, the arrival back at Massachusetts Avenue just before dinner didn't indicate that he was seeing some other woman, that he too was bored with the details of domestic life, and having a family. Sometimes he told her that he would be stopping in at the Cosmos Club for a drink with a business associate.

She snappishly asked him why the associate couldn't come to their house.

'Because my business associates bore you, Livy. Anyhow, it is business. It isn't social. There are things that have to be said privately. If it pleases you, I'll invite these people here, and have them into the library. But you won't be able to join us, because they won't discuss their affairs in front of anyone else. The club is a good place. Sometimes one can get just that little bit of extra information . . . Besides, if I ask them here, we really should have them to dinner. And I know that bores you, as well as tires you.'

Of course it made sense, but she didn't like it. She was fretful and irritable, and she knew she didn't present an attractive spectacle in these moods. She often walked up the Avenue to the British Embassy to visit Ginny, and found that Ginny was usually fully occupied with her social secretary. The wife of the British Ambassador had a crowded life. Harry was very dependent on her. But Ginny always sent the secretary away when Livy appeared. They talked, drank coffee, Livy confessed some of her feelings. 'God knows how Alex keeps his temper with me. I must be such a drag . . . But he's so engrossed in his work or at least, I hope that's what he's engrossed in.'

'He is engrossed in his work. He's trying to do all that Blair did, as well as relieve Mr McClintock of some of the load. He's taking on far too much, trying to prove to the Old Man that he can do it.' Ginny spread her hands. 'Of course, the whole thing's become far too big. Alex is finding it as hard to delegate as ever his grandfather did. And the Old Man still tends to see things in the terms he did when I was first married to his son. It was so much smaller then. Times were simpler. And yes, Livy, feeling bored is often part of being pregnant. Being bored is often part of being a rich woman without a job. If you had to take care of Jamie all by yourself, you wouldn't have time to be bored.'

'I wish I were allowed to take care of Jamie. I wish life were simpler. I hate being treated as an invalid. Even these charity committees I'm on bore me. Everything centres around gala events. I never get my hands dirty raising money the hard way.'

'I raise money right here at the embassy handing out tea and little sandwiches. That's all I've ever been able to do, so I do it.'

Livy would walk back to the McClintock mansion, walk with her car crawling at the kerb behind her, listening to the honking of the cars which had to go around it. She was perversely pleased to be causing trouble, and at the same time, ashamed of herself. Then sometimes she would have herself driven to one of the galleries, where she could walk without causing a disturbance, sit down when she felt tired, eat a tuna sandwich at the cafeteria, and have the luxury of the car waiting to take her home. Once she went to one of the women's clubs of which she had membership – every club in Washington invited her to join once she and Alex were married. She sipped orange juice, and leafed through magazines, and came home just before dinner.

Alex was home, and frantic. 'Where on earth have you been? If I hadn't known you had the car, and Malcolm . . . well, anything could have happened. He could have had a breakdown . . . you might have been in an accident. You should have telephoned.'

'Oh, I stopped in at the club for a drink,' she said maliciously, because that was often what he said to her. 'I didn't think you'd be here, or even notice.'

'Oh, damn you! Don't tell me you're turning into a bitch. Whatever happened to the Livy who only wanted life with me, and nothing else?'

'I don't have much life with you. There's nothing to it except waiting for you to come home, and then watching you disappear into the library and dive into the briefcase the moment dinner's over. If I were knitting little booties on the other side of the fire from you, I might find it bearable. But, unfortunately, it's too ludicrous for a McClintock child to have knitted booties when it can have every pair in every shop in Washington.'

'Well, why don't you try knitting them for the poor, and stop feeling sorry for yourself?'

They ate dinner in almost total silence, only striking up a completely artificial conversation when the butler came to serve them. That was part of the trouble, Livy thought. If she could just cook dinner for Alex, serve it to him, do something.

She went to bed early, feeling tired and sore in her heart, knowing she was being unfair, but not knowing how to say so. It took her a long time to fall asleep, but when she did it was a heavy sleep. She woke late, and realized that Alex had not shared their bed that night. She got up and went into the dressing-room, where there was a single bed. He had used that, and he had already left. She felt the weight in her heart like some huge lump; her throat tightened. She sat on the edge of the bed he had used for the first time since they had moved into this house, and wept. At ten o'clock, the butler dared to ring on the house phone.

'I wondered if you were ready for your breakfast yet, Madam?' It was two hours past her usual breakfast time. They knew too well the rules of the diet of a pregnant woman. Breakfast must be served, whether she called for it or not. It came, and she drank only the orange juice, and nibbled at the corner of a piece of dry toast. She felt sick, and it wasn't the sickness of pregnancy.

She had herself driven to the embassy, and when she asked to see Lady Camborne, she realized she was interrupting a meeting Ginny was in with members of the Red Cross committee. Ginny came out at once, and Livy felt racked with guilt. 'Just give me ten minutes, and I'll wind this up. Then I'll be right out.'

Ginny had ordered coffee in her sitting-room. She poured it slowly. 'What's happened?'

Livy told her, feeling ashamed. It all sounded so trivial, and yet there was something serious at the core. 'You've both had a pretty rough time since the plane crash, one way and another. Sometimes a kind of – fatigue, sets in – years after the events themselves. If I didn't have Harry, I think I might be quietly going out of my mind. Alex has fought such a battle to get back to a normal life. Remember, Livy, this

591

is your third pregnancy in three years. That's too much, even though I know how much each baby was wanted.'

She got up and took her coffee cup with her, staring for a few minutes down over the embassy gardens. 'Let me just think . . . Mark finishes school this week, and he's going to visit Thea and Herbert for two weeks before coming here. I think we should go and meet him in St Just. By ship . . . Take no notice of what Alex says, or Mr McClintock. I'll do the arguing for you. We'll get the next sailing, and we'll go to Tresillian for a while – at least a month. Or rather, we'll go to your house in St Just, because Tresillian isn't habitable.'

Livy took a deep breath, and already felt better. It was almost as if she could smell the sea, the salt air, hear the waves, feel the peace and friendliness seeping into her body.

'Oh I would love that. Will you be able . . .?'

'Well, I have to have a look at Tresillian, don't I? Let the men say what they like . . .' In fact, the thought of being separated from Harry for a whole month dismayed Ginny, but then so did the expression Livy wore. She didn't know whether it would be the worst mistake she ever made to separate Livy and Alex right now, but if things drifted, there would be disaster.

Over everyone's objections they were on the next sailing of a Cunarder. Mr McClintock had been furious at the idea of Livy travelling when she was pregnant, and of Jamie going with her. Of course Nanny was accompanying them. Alex had said almost nothing, neither indicating approval or disapproval. He was tight-lipped as he said goodbye to Livy and his son. 'I hope,' Livy said to Ginny, 'that I'm not throwing him straight into the arms of someone else.'

'He won't be in your arms if you go on snarling at each other.'

When they were settled on board in the usual string of staterooms and sitting-rooms, Mrs Hope, nominally still in charge of the apartment on Fifth Avenue, presented herself. 'You'll have to forgive me, Mrs McClintock. It wasn't something I would do myself without consulting you. But Mr McClintock – the old gentleman – insisted. My instructions are just to help out when I can, and otherwise stay out of your way. I'm to find a room in one of the hotels in this . . . this St Just place, and come over and spell your nanny when she has time off. Just generally make myself useful.' The woman looked pleadingly at both Livy and Ginny. 'I'm sorry I'm pushing in where I'm probably not wanted. But Mr McClintock said you were having a vacation and a rest. You weren't to have any extra chores, just enjoy yourself. It was more than my job's worth to go against him. I hope I can help.'

Livy said politely, 'It was very thoughtful of Mr McClintock. I'm sure there'll be many ways in which you can help.' She saw the look of relief flood the woman's face, and hated herself for resenting her presence. A job was a job, and Andrew McClintock had sent her to do one. She should be grateful to be relieved of the day-to-day chores which Mrs Hope would take on, chores her Tregenna cousins and aunts would gladly have done. She could see that she would have to fight for possession of her son, even for a few hours a day. She closed her eyes for a moment, wondering if there was nothing Andrew McClintock would not involve himself in. 'I hope you have a pleasant voyage, Mrs Hope. You can work it out with Nanny about taking care of Jamie . . .' Three women struggling over the possession of one small baby.

Mark had made his way by train to Southampton to meet them. His face was joyful as he tried to embrace all three, Ginny, Livy and Jamie at the same time. 'How marvellous! I hadn't dreamed of such good luck. Thea and Herbert are dying to see you all. You can't believe what's happening to Tresillian! It's going to be wonderful if they ever get it finished.'

The inevitable cars were there from McClintock-Clayton. For once, Livy was grateful for their ease. She put Nanny and Mrs Hope firmly in the second car, and established her right to have Jamie to herself for the hours of the journey.

Thea and Herbert were waiting at Livy's house in St Just, the rooms decked with flowers from their combined gardens, and dinner of cold salmon ready, and Nell and another cousin smiling from the kitchen. There was the unavoidable time while everyone exclaimed over Jamie, who, having slept all the way down in the car, was extremely lively. It shocked and amazed Livy to realize how grateful she was to hand him over to Nanny. Mrs Hope was taken to her small hotel, and because the Tregenna women had made the arrangements, and the proprietor was married to a cousin, Mrs Hope got what she didn't realize was a special luxury in small English sea-side towns, her own bathroom. 'I'm going to enjoy this,' she said, staring out at the bay of St Just in the flush of the summer twilight. There was hardly a more beautiful sight in the world, Livy fondly thought.

The only thing that dismayed her about their return was the sight of Herbert. When they arrived, he had difficulty in pulling himself up from his chair. His speech was punctuated with long pauses as he struggled for breath. 'Forgive me, my dears,' he said. 'An old man, paying for a misspent youth.' He would be, Livy guessed, in his middle sixties, and he looked older than Andrew McClintock.

The next morning they all drove up to Tresillian. One of the McClintock-Clayton cars had been left at their disposal. They drove, when they would have preferred to walk, because Herbert was unable to climb the hill, or even walk for more than a few yards without stopping for breath. He stayed in the car with Nanny and Jamie.

As far as the builders and the scaffolding would allow them, they roamed over the house, Mr Penleigh in anxious attendance. The roof, the first priority, had been completed months ago. All the work now was being done in shelter from the weather. Livy pointed to a small ditch filled with coarse gravel which surrounded the whole building. 'What's that?'

'Drainage, Mrs McClintock. The house, fortunately, is pitched on a slope. Water will always take the easiest course, so we're giving it one, away from the walls, and down the hill. We've lined this back gulley with lead and tar. I hope now that the central heating won't be trying to suck up the damp that would normally lie here after a heavy rain. We're dealing with old walls, Mrs McClintock. We are trying to find a way to divert the water around the house, and not into it.' Livy nodded, remembering the days when she and her

594

mother had come up here, and huddled around the kitchen stove at lunch time, watching the rain streaming down the windows.

'Yes, I should think it could benefit from it.'

They climbed as far as they could to see what was happening. Most of it was hidden in scaffolding and huge dust sheets. 'It's a constant war between us and the decorators, Lady Camborne. They want to come in, but the place isn't ready. But it will be soon, and then we can let them loose. It will be a triumph, Lady Camborne. A real showplace!'

'Well . . . that wasn't exactly what I intended, but so be it. A very nice job, Mr Penleigh.' They saw where the panelling was being taken off, the walls behind cured and insulated, with the panelling rubbed and restored. A lot of books had gone from the library. 'To London for restoration,' Mr Penleigh said. 'It's a very good library. We even found some of the logs belonging to the very ships the Admiral sailed in. There's some wonderful Cornish history printed on little local presses.' The sketches were there of how the Georgian rooms would look. 'The ceilings were still in quite good repair. Some lovely mouldings. And the fireplaces are Adam, we're assured. Of course we wouldn't touch the hall, except to get at bits of dry rot. I would imagine it's the finest of its kind in Cornwall.'

Ginny went away smiling, satisfied. 'Do try to get it done quickly, Mr Penleigh. I can hardly wait to come and live here.'

The days passed quietly, gracefully in St Just. They were with Thea and Herbert a part of each day, but not staying so long as to overtire Herbert. Ginny and Livy and Jamie went to their usual, rather hidden places, and found to their delight that no one else, even in the summer season, was using them. Livy felt herself revive in the sweet, fresh air. Tentatively, she started to write letters to Alex, trying to tell him how she felt, trying to explain. None of them satisfied her. Once she lifted the telephone to call him, and then decided against it. What would she say? 'Forgive me . . . I love you.' Hard things to say when silence had grown between them.

She was able to say it when Alex banged the door knocker late one afternoon, the car he had rented at London Airport in the narrow street outside. She stepped into his arms.

'It was wrong of me to leave you. How I've missed you . . .'

'No more than I've missed you and Jamie. It's been so lonely, Livy. Even just a few weeks. I've founded my life now on you. I have to keep you.'

Ginny moved over to Thea and Herbert's house to make room for Alex. She had been quietly happy at her son's appearance. She left them to picnic alone, to walk the beaches together. A tension that had been with Alex ever since the plane crash seemed to lift, as it had done on their last visit to Tresillian. They played together with Jamie, took him, without Nanny, on some of their picnics. Alex scrambled, with difficulty, through the maze of scaffolding at Tresillian. 'It's better than a workout at the gym.' He was covered with dust and plaster when he was finished, but exultant. 'I know what Mother is doing – she's building a rest-cure place for us all.' He was even able to negotiate the cliff path to the Tresillian Rocks at low tide. He gazed at them for a long time, from the safety of the bottom of the path; they didn't venture out more than a few yards from the cliff. There would be no possibility of them running from the tide when it turned. 'They're like some magnetic pole: they pull this family,' he said. 'Destructive and restorative.' They made their way slowly, and Livy knew, for Alex with some pain, up the cliff path. It was a way of pilgrimage for them now, Isa and Chris in their minds, always. They circled the Tower, its restoration almost complete. Three skilled master masons worked on it. 'A grand job, sir.'

'No one would imagine anyone had laid a hand on it,' Alex said. 'I used to come here when I was young. We were always forbidden to go near it, in case it collapsed.'

'That I know, sir. My father used to come here from time to time. He remembers you as a young lad. A bit of repairing, whatever was necessary in the house. Lord Camborne could never have started on the Tower itself, it's taken us nearly a year as it is. But it's a landmark in Cornwall, sir. You can

596

see it from far out at sea. It gives the people a deal of pleasure that it's not going to fall down.'

They walked back to St Just. Alex always refused to use the car for short distances. 'It's very satisfying. It's like keeping Prescott Hill as a symbol of what Virginia used to be. My mother has a great instinct for these things. But then, so does Harry. So did Dena. It's a complex relationship, Livy. Mixed up lives.'

'Let's not get ours mixed up again, Alex. I nearly . . . I could have lost you.' That night she showed him the letters she had attempted to write to him. He read them thoughtfully. They had shared a bottle of good Nuits St Georges over dinner. Their son slept peacefully upstairs. Footsteps outside reminded them they were in a tiny town, where people walked in a public street only feet away. 'But these aren't letters, Livy. They're all beginnings of some story. Something you're trying to say . . . Sometimes addressed to me, sometimes to Jamie, sometimes to the baby.' He referred to the unborn child.

'It was all I could do. Tales of the sea. Old Cornish legends. Things I've learned from my family . . . How else could I tell you, and our children, why I wanted so much to come back here? And somehow Ginny knew I needed to come back. You are right, Alex. It is magnetic. When I stand on the cliffs up there, I seem to go back in time.'

'Livy, Livy, don't leave me again. Don't go back so far in time that I can't follow you . . .'

They travelled back by ship, Alex never once saying that he should have gone by air, and been back at his desk. The restorative effect of St Just remained with him. He walked the deck in the early mornings with Livy, swam when the pool was deserted, and was gracious about appearing with his wife and mother each night at the captain's table, when he would have preferred to eat in their stateroom. 'After all,' he conceded, 'why should I begrudge a sight of you two beauties to all the others who want to see you?'

But he clung to Livy's company, almost as he clung to his cane. Livy remembered Ginny's words about the effect, the fatigue of great stress perhaps biting much later. All that she and Alex would accomplish would be a mutual effort; they had lived through their times of trial, and now understood what the aftershocks could be.

As the ship berthed in New York, Andrew McClintock was with the first immigration officers aboard. He was led directly to their stateroom, when they were finishing breakfast. He allowed the steward to pour coffee for him, then nodded his dismissal.

'I'm very sorry to bring you this news. Thea sent the cable to me because she didn't want to spoil your voyage. I had to come and deliver it personally. Herbert Gardiner died the night after you left. He is buried and, I trust, at peace.'

Mark looked at him in anguish. Then he rose and left the stateroom. Andrew McClintock spoke awkwardly. 'Livy, he was your adoptive father. In a sense he was a father to all of you children when you were growing up.'

Alex limped to the porthole, apparently surveying the scene of unloading beneath him. 'I'm privileged to have shared his last days.' He came back and took Livy in his arms. 'He will always be with you, my love . . . like your people.'

Livy and Alex's second child was born in November, a small, perfectly-formed boy, with very pale skin, dark hair, and Alex's dark grey eyes. There seemed to be no creases or redness, the features already seemed defined. He was much smaller than Jamie had been; he didn't thrust out and punch at the air. He seemed to Livy, even in those first hours, to conserve his movements.

She mentioned this to her doctor, who nodded, and didn't laugh at her. 'Some babies are like that. But don't worry. That little heart is pounding very normally. He isn't delicate or puny. He just may be one of those fellas that nature has already taught how to make the most of everything.'

Andrew McClintock came after Alex had left. He spent a long time gazing at the child in his cot beside Livy's bed, when she had just finished feeding him. 'I'll say something. He looks a lot like Alex. Even at this early stage anyone can see that. But something even more. He looks the image of my son, even hours after he was born. Alex, the Alex Ginny married. The Russian's child, if we want to recall that. You've given us back a generation, Livy. You've given us back my son.' He said the words very slowly, as if weighing each one of them. Livy thought he must have gazed wordlessly then at the child for almost ten minutes; after the feeding, the baby's eyelids drooped, and he slept. 'Well, I won't poke him, or breathe any more germs over him, Livy.' He got up and straightened himself. His body was beginning to shrink with age, but standing erect, he could still look formidable. 'It's a kind of miracle for me to see my son again. Thank you, Livy.'

A present of jewellery followed this visit, jewellery such as Livy had never had before, even from Alex. Sapphires – a necklace, earrings and bracelet. She was awed by them, and asked Alex to take them immediately to be put in the safe. She had come into hospital wearing only her wedding-band. Now she asked for the opal. 'It's something I love. I miss it.' And when she held the new baby, she moved the dark-coloured stones across his field of vision, his unfocused gaze only seeing the myriad-coloured light refracted back. It delighted her when the small hand reached tentatively towards it. 'That's right, my darling. There it is, your home, the sea.'

Ginny had seen him when he was only a few hours old. When she returned the next day, she studied him as carefully as Andrew McClintock had. 'He's almost right, the Old Man. Of course I didn't see Alex, his son, Alex, when he was a baby, but all the marks of the two of them are here. Alex and his father. What a gift for the Old Man at this time in his life. He really does think his son has been born again. You'll have a struggle, Livy. He'll want to possess this one even more than dear old Fisticuffs.'

Two months after he was born he was christened Alexander Andrew Oliver Herbert. At the last minute Livy had insisted on tacking on the name Tristan. That had caused some raised eyebrows, but she had her way. 'Oh, well, what does it matter? It's a name no one will ever use. It's just a sort of memory of my mother.'

The christening party, held in the aftermath of a January snowstorm, had brought the same people who had attended Jamie's christening. People from Clayton's Merchant Bank had come, representatives from Switzerland, most of Washington society, except those who still clung to the Wintertons. There were some strange mix-ups when ambassadors from countries who did not know the family history assumed that it was Harry's grandson they had come to toast, and yet there were puzzled frowns because most of them knew of, even if they had never met, the legendary Andrew McClintock, who was the child's great-grandfather. But what did it matter? It was a gathering of social and diplomatic Washington, with the nice touch of two Supreme Court Justices. It was the sort of occasion for which the McClintock mansion had been built. Clearly the baby was important, that was what mattered to the puzzled ambassadors. The baby became even more important when there was a sudden invasion of the large hall and reception rooms by what were obviously security men. The butler's voice was heard over the sudden hush.

'Ladies and gentlemen. The President of the United States.'

They all rose. The President stayed five minutes, patted the baby's head, took a sip of champagne, a morsel of the christening cake, and then escorted the First Lady out.

He had not made the gesture of coming to the British Embassy; that would have been going too far. But who could make anything political of his attendance at the christening party of an infant who was no blood relation to the British Ambassador, but the great-grandson of one of the most influential men in the land?

His father and great-grandfather already had his first two names, so the baby began to be known as Oliver. Secretly, though, Livy, when she nursed him, or laid him in his cot to sleep would whisper 'Tristan' to him. Sometimes he opened his eyes and looked at her as if he understood their shared secret.

5

That Easter they saw pictures of the marchers from Alder-
maston to London to demand nuclear disarmament headed
by the aged Bertrand Russell. 'Silly old fool. At his age he
ought to know better,' Andrew McClintock said. Beside him
was the very vigorous figure of Frazer Campbell. Caroline
sent her father and Ginny a large, front-page photo from one
of the tabloids which plainly showed Rachel's face behind
Campbell's. Caroline wrote.

It's quite disgraceful, I hate to admit she's my sister.
Did you know they locked her up for a few hours, until
Frazer Campbell, or one of her other commie friends
came and bailed her out? She'll probably be fined for
disturbing the peace, and if she decides not to pay, she'll
go to gaol for contempt of court.

Rachel did refuse to pay the small fine, and forbade anyone
else to do it; she was sentenced to four weeks in gaol. The
popular press didn't know whether to make more of the fact
that she was the daughter of the British Ambassador to
Washington, or her relationship with Frazer Campbell. The
latter could only be implied, and the laws of libel were strict,
so they played up the Washington connection.
Daily Harry expected a summons from the Foreign Office
and a demand for his resignation. Rachel wrote after three
weeks in Holloway, that she had been given a week's remission for good behaviour.

I'm sorry if I've hurt you, but my conscience tells me
this is the only way to go. I can't believe they'll be so
unfair as to punish you for what the Establishment sees
as my mistaken point of view.

'I think she's right about that,' Livy said, when Ginny
discussed this with her. 'It would appear to be such obvious
victimization, that the Foreign Office would look like preju-
diced fools. He's made such a great success of the job, and
then there's you.'
'Yes,' Ginny agreed. 'Harry did point out to me before
we married that I would be regarded as something of an ace

in the pack. I didn't think it very flattering at the time, but I suppose he was right.'

Mark wrote from Wrisley.

Half the school's for nuclear disarmament, and half against, so either Rachel's a heroine or a traitor, whichever way you look at it. Are you coming to Tresillian this summer? Father must surely be due a few week's leave. Thea would be awfully glad to see you all. She must be so lonely at times. She says Tresillian's finished, give or take a few details.

Ginny did plan some weeks at Tresillian, and Harry had promised he would come with her. At Andrew McClintock's urging, Alex, Livy and the two children would join them. 'I might even come and take a look at the place myself.' He had recognized, as Alex had, the need Livy had to return to her birthplace. The world of high finance and commerce, of power plays and take-over bids, would always be alien to her, but she had begun to play her part in it very well, or at least she made it seem that it interested her. She gave, and attended the parties required of her, she wore the gowns and the jewels that seemed fitting. She had regained strength very quickly after Oliver's birth, and she seemed to glow with a beauty that was more mature, and even more sensual than before. She stuck closely by Alex's side, and their silences were not taken for strain. She had had a second desk placed in the library, and when he went there at night with his papers, she sat and either read or wrote. 'What are you writing?' Alex had once enquired, wondering if he dared ask.

'I'm not sure. Fairy stories, I think. Things for children and a little for you. Sort of a continuation of what I tried to write to you last summer. Never ask to see them, they're not good . . .'

He did not press her. He lived with the hope that at some time she would offer to show these fragments, if that was what they were, to him. But he knew that they were part of the private, almost secret world Livy inhabited, the world that had nothing at all to do with his own world of power and money. Sometimes he fiercely envied her the escape, as he sometimes wondered why he continued to toil in the affairs of McClintock-Clayton as he did. On his twenty-fifth birthday he had become totally independent of his grandfather. He could have walked away from the endless work, the papers, the meetings. But he saw about him an empire in change, and he knew he had to forge that change, to shape it in the way he believed it should go. He had dragged from his grandfather grudging consent to some radical reforms of structure, giving a desperately needed semi-autonomy to the various divisions of the company. He and his grandfather still stood at the head of them all, but the structure began to resemble more and more a pyramid on a solid base, instead of a giant needle. He often brought his mother into discussion of the company's affairs, in broad outline, because her voting shares were always needed. A good deal of the power Blair Clayton had had now rested with her. More and more he discussed these things with Livy also.

'I don't want to bore you, but the McClintock line is still perilously thin. You've given it two young men who will probably want to make their contribution, but if I suddenly disappeared in another air crash,' he saw Livy wince, but he went on, 'I'd want you to know what's what. You'd be looking after their interests for some time. You and Mother between you.' Then he smiled at her, hoping to wipe away the look of terrible anxiety which had come to her face at the mention of another disaster in their lives. 'But then, you never know what those two young hellions are going to decide to be. It wouldn't at all surprise me if one of them turned out to be a poet and the other a painter. Or maybe a sailor, or something equally impractical.'

'Would you accept that? If that's what happened?'

'Livy, I'm not my grandfather. I don't demand that they give their lives to McClintock-Clayton unless they want to. By the time they're ready for it, it may have bypassed them. It may have grown into such a giant that they could only look after some small part of it. It might have gone bust . . . these things happen. Someone smarter than either of them might have taken it away from them. While my grandfather's alive, I have to keep going. But it's a different world they'll inherit. They might not like it. In the meantime, you write your stories for them, and I'll try to be the breadwinner.'

She teased him. 'You forget, don't you, that Mr McClintock is still busy making me into a modestly well-off lady? Oh, not rich, but rich enough to live in St Just. You know, don't you, that every three months we have our formal lunch together, and we go over what he calls "my portfolio". He still keeps it up to date himself. And it isn't all in McClintock-Clayton shares, either. There are too few of them around, and he'd like to keep them all for himself. He's tried to set me up so that I am independent of the crash of McClintock-Clayton – if the unthinkable ever happened. It would be the crash of what I see the financial papers are starting to call one of the corporate giants of the world, and are starting to warn that it's almost sinful that it still is held by so few people.'

Alex laughed delightedly. 'Good for him – canny old Scot! Well, one day, my love, perhaps you'll be supporting me in St Just.'

Livy shrugged. 'And, of course, we'll only have a few Renoirs and Degas and a small truckful of jewels to use for eating money.'

He was more serious. 'I think you'd prefer it that way – in St Just, with the boys and me, if I were lucky enough to be let in.'

'You have the key of the door, don't you?'

Ginny had written to Rachel and Caroline, outlining plans for the summer, inviting them to come and stay at Tresillian.

I need family to help break it in. If the plumbing doesn't work properly, I'll need sympathy. There seem to be as many bathrooms as bedrooms, so the plumbing had better work, or we're in trouble. The only way to test it all is to use it, so if any of your friends fee like being adventurous, do invite them.

To Rachel she wrote a special postscript.

Isn't it time we met Frazer Campbell? If you care to bring him to Tresillian? If that seems too much, then perhaps just a dinner at Seymour House?

Rachel wrote back at once.

You are the most forgiving woman, or is it that your abundant good grace and sense tells you that I'll never be different, but that you and Father will just put up with me? I hope that will always be so. Maybe Seymour House, rather than Tresillian. That would be less public. Frazer will probably make or break himself on this nuclear issue. He might become leader of the Labour Party, or be shoved to the farthest reaches of the back benches. Or the lunatic fringe. He's planning to go to Russia when Parliament recesses. It's just possible that I may go with him. That could be a very public declaration of many things. If he wants me to go with him, I'll go. And the fat will be in the fire. I doubt that even the fierce loyalty of his constituents would survive such a thing. But times, they are a-changing . . . People in public life dare now to think of divorce, and still survive. I don't know if Frazer dares go that far yet, but if he asks, I'm with him. It will be either glory or oblivion.

Ginny did not think that they would see Rachel at Tresillian that summer.

Ginny's letter reached Chris in California, outlining the plans, the hopes.

I wish we might all be together for just a little time. You girls were old enough to remember what it was like during the war. I'm not expecting to relive those days. They're gone, as are Dena and your father. But I would like us to be together, even briefly. I'm tired of these great social occasions when we only peck each other on the cheek, and utter platitudes. Come, and bring Jeff. It's time we got to know him. I've invited Rachel, and even Frazer Campbell. Time we got to know him, too.

Chris read the letter once again – about the fourth time –

by the light of a candle shielded in a hurricane glass set on the table on the deck of her beach house at Malibu. She had fled there for a few days of solitude; there was a much grander house in Beverly Hills which she hated, but which Jeff's status as a star demanded. It was never mentioned that her money had bought it, and maintained it. A great deal of Jeff's money went in alimony to his three former wives; they had had large settlements at the time of the divorces, but there was still alimony to pay until they remarried, which none of them had done. There would be the maintenance of his five children until they reached majority. Perhaps that was why he played the tables so recklessly at Las Vegas. Chris had come to dread his periodic visits there. Sometimes he won, and that made things worse, because it encouraged him to think that he was on a winning streak.

The 'little' film, *Arriving*, she had made last year had been recently released, and it had had an unexpected critical success. It had not been big box-office, but had done very well in the 'art' houses. Her acting had been praised. It wasn't enough. It hadn't made her into a star of the magnitude that *The Way West* demanded. She rose, and slipped Ginny's letter under the hurricane lamp, and went down the steps to the beach. She thought it must have been very late. Few of the beach houses still had lights on. The surf glistened under the pale crescent of the new moon. Bare-footed, she walked just at the tide's edge.

The Way West was beginning to assume the proportions of a nightmare. Two writers had had a try at the screenplay, two very expensive writers, and neither of them had captured the novel's momentum. A third, Rod Gibbins, had been hired, was living and working in a bungalow of the Beverly Hill's Hotel, at the company's expense. He kept telling Chris that she could see nothing until the script was complete, and she was getting reports of the many hours a day he spent in the Polo Lounge, or at the swimming-pool, where he ostentatiously scribbled on paper on a clip board, ordered drinks and lunch, and invited others to join him. It didn't sound like work to Chris. 'Relax, will you,' he had snapped at her when she had put this to him. 'Listen, I stay up half the night getting the stuff I make notes on during the day into the typewriter . . . You'll see it when it's ready, and it'll be worth the wait.'

Too often Jeff joined him at those sessions in the Polo Bar or by the swimming-pool. 'Just checking,' he would tell Chris. 'That's what a producer's supposed to do, isn't it?'

She saw the problems looming ahead, and they made her shiver. She had too little experience, and Jeff had never worked out a budget in his life. It had been in the heady days just after their marriage when he had persuaded her to buy *The Way West*. With him as the star, and the first money-in-the-bank name, the rest would follow. Those had been the days before his last film had been released. It had been a very high-budget film, and it had been a well-publicized, resounding flop. The Hollywood law that you're only as good as your last picture went rapidly into force. Suddenly, Jeff was bad box-office news. The stars they had hoped to sign were not available, or would not commit themselves until they saw a script. She was a relative new-comer to Hollywood, with only two films to her credit and Jeff, she now realized, was on the point of becoming a has-been. He had even begun to live the life of a has-been. Gradually, the lean, taut look, which had won him his millions of fans, seemed to blur: there was more than a perceptible sign of a double-chin, and he struggled to hold in his stomach. He insisted on holding the 'has-been' label at bay by giving lavish parties at the Beverly Hills house. 'You've got to be seen around this town, or you're dead.' Suddenly his superb confidence, that trace of arrogance his fans had found appealing, had degenerated into a kind of puffy bravado.

Something of her father's good sense, his business sense, told Chris that it would be wiser if she wound up the whole project right now. Paid off the writer, paid off the secretary who staffed the office Jeff had insisted was necessary for the image of Clayhouse Productions. She should get out while she could. It was one thing to have a fortune whose income she couldn't spend. It was something different, as their accountant pointed out, to have to finance a film whose budget, by the very nature of its subject, would have to eat up that fortune before it showed a profit. She wished it were possible to back out, to cut her losses. But for Jeff that would be the end. There was no other film in sight for him. None were offered. His future depended on *The Way West*. If she pulled out, it would destroy him.

And what about her? What in her was being destroyed? Useless to blame Jeff for what was no longer there. They had been in love, but she was beginning to recognize that what they had both loved most was success. With *Tempo* she had been the success story of the Hollywood year, the London-Broadway actress who had starred in a 'sleeper' which had caught the critics' attention, and, amazingly, the public's also. He had been the famous name, the star of many glittering box-office successes. He had just been through his third divorce; she had just lost irretrievably, Hugh Meredith. Together they had been a pair who had been the focus of every press camera within range. When the afterglow of the flash bulbs had gone, they had found little else.

She watched the sea in the faint moonlight, and wished it could be possible to go back to Tresillian, not for the few weeks her mother suggested, but simply go back and start over. The sea always had its particular terror and lure for her, it had so nearly taken her and Isa's life at the Tresillian Rocks. Isa had saved her, but for what? She thought of the three who had shared those years, and those hours after Isa's death.

She ground her heel into the sand. On the surface the four girls who had lived out those war years at Tresillian were all right. It was in the next years the cracks would show. She turned and headed back towards the house.

She looked for her mother's letter. She must not have placed it very securely under the lamp. It must have blown away. Perhaps it now rode on the waves out there, growing damp and heavy, and finally sinking. It didn't matter. She would say she was too busy to come to Tresillian. She and Jeff were too busy. Her mother was mistaken to think they could recreate those times when they had all been innocent and facing a life hardly even begun. She doubted that she would ever go back to Tresillian.

Then she brought a bottle of brandy and a glass out on to the deck. She was still there when the pre-dawn light outlined the mountains behind her. She felt alone and afraid, terrified of what seemed to be happening to her.

Chapter 15

1

Ginny thought afterwards that she had been naive in her fond thoughts of a reunion that summer at Tresillian. At first the idea had been wonderful. Then she had approached the house with some doubts. Would the mess of dust and plaster really have become an ordered house, furnished and livable? She had placed a great deal of faith in Mr Penleigh and the experts he had summoned; she had relied on the decorators not to overstep the line. She had received regular reports in Washington on what was being done, but reality might appear very different from the sketches and the photographs. But she had paid the bills and hoped.

There, two years after she had conceived the idea, two years after she and Harry had been married, the project was completed. The cars that carried them all, she and Harry, Alex and Livy, the two children and Nanny, from London had wound their way up a smooth paved drive, where the rhododendrons had been pruned, but not too severely. They did not look quite tidy, which was what she had ordered. Nor did the house itself, at first sight, look much different, except that the flower beds and the lawns surrounding it were neat. The Tower stood, as it always had in her memory, pieces missing, the gulls wheeling about its height, its roof still open to the sky.

Inside it was different, and yet very much the same. The great hall and staircase were as they had always been, the same massive pieces of furniture stood about. The rather indifferent portraits of Camborne ancestors, carefully uncleaned, were in the darkest places. But new crimson damask curtains hung at the windows, one golden velvet wing chair showed off the aged sheen of the carved Jacobean chair

and long stretcher table. Flowers were massed in the great
fireplace. Somewhere in the house a decorator, or perhaps
Mr Penleigh, had found some heraldic banners; they hung,
splendidly faded, from the gallery. From room to room they
went, like eager children. Here the differences showed. The
drawing-room was a cool silver green, colours which matched
the old, but still splendid carpet which had always been
there. A few fine pieces of furniture belonged with the
Adams fireplace. Harry walked slowly, silently, into the
library. It looked untouched, but it was fresh. The ominous
stains on the ceiling were gone, new curtains hung at the
windows, there were comfortable sofas and chairs, and a
magnificent desk he had never seen before. Best were the
books, the beloved books, which had not been rebound, but
restored. 'My God, Ginny, you've had every book restorer
in London busy these past two years.'

'More likely in the whole of England. They're hard to find
these days.'

He touched the faded leathers lovingly. 'I never imagined . . .'

'No, it wasn't your job to imagine. I asked you to trust
me, and not to worry. And I had to trust Mr Penleigh, and
an army of other people.'

'I'm afraid to ask what it cost.'

'Then don't ask. It's none of your business.'

The four of them went all through the house. Ginny's
beautiful Chippendale dining-table and chairs sent from
Washington looked as if they had always been there. The
dining-room had taken its colour from the blue Wedgwood
medallions the craftsmen had found when they had cleaned
the grime from the mouldings of the ceilings. The seats of
the chairs had been recovered in tapestry made by the ladies
of the London School of Needlework in a slightly darker
blue; the silver candlebra reflected the soft blue of the walls
and curtains. The best of Guy Denham's beloved landscapes,
inherited by Dena, hung here, quite compatible with their
setting. Harry just stared at it, voiceless. 'Why Ginny . . .'
He could say no more, and she was moved to see that his
eyes grew bright with tears.

611

'A triumph, Mother,' Alex said. 'Was this the room where we all made such messes? I can remember adding to the scratches on the marvellously beaten-up old table. I hope that hasn't gone into the bonfire. I was fond of that.'

'There's a sort of play-room upstairs near the nurseries. I think we'll find it there.'

Knox, who had risen at dawn to get there before them, opened a door leading from the dining-room. There was a short corridor from which the butler's pantry opened, and which led on to the kitchen. 'We thought you would enjoy this, Lady Camborne. Do you remember Jacques saying something about a small room for you and Lord Camborne to eat in when you were alone?' Ginny smiled. It had been there on the plans which Harry had always seemed too busy to look at carefully, or had not wanted to look at because he dreaded the cost of what he saw. Livy gasped as she saw the room that had been the school room during the war-years, where Rachel had guarded the books from the evacuee children. It was heavily carpeted for warmth; double-lined chintz curtains hung at the windows which looked into the orchard. There was an old, gate-legged table, with six windsor chairs whose seat pads matched the curtains. Before the old wooden fireplace one of the decorators had found somewhere, were a sofa and easy chairs. Pewter candlesticks and plates lined the mantle. For contrast, on the shelves of an old Welsh dresser were some fine pieces of pottery by Bernard Leach.

'Yes, this is the room for Harry and me when there's no help in the house, and we're fending for ourselves.'

Livy looked around her, and then at Alex. 'I wish we had it.'

'You haven't reached that stage of life, yet,' Harry said, pleasure and pride in his voice, as if the idea had been his. 'This is for when you've earned it. Ginny and I shall have many happy years in this room.'

They examined the pantry, locked cupboards for the silver, racks of glasses, and then Knox opened the door to the kitchen.

Mark burst upon them. 'There! I'll bet you thought we'd

612

deserted you, or forgotten the day you were supposed to come!' He threw himself into Ginny's arms, or rather, he seemed to lift her from her feet in his embrace. He had gone directly from Wrisley to stay with Thea, waiting their coming. Ginny had been more than a little disappointed that Mark and Thea had not stood on the doorstep to meet them. Thea now rose from the seat by the large kitchen table where she sat.

'Welcome home. I just wish Herbert were here to see this day.'

Mark skipped around impatiently while they all exchanged greetings. 'I just have to show you . . . look . . . look . . .' The two huge refrigerators had to be inspected, the dish-washing equipment, the cool-room for meat and bacon and game. He touched the stainless-steel counters lovingly, pointed out the features of the two cookers. 'It's wonderful, isn't it? Can you even remember the old range . . .?'

'I can,' Livy said. 'I seem to have grown up beside it.'

'And I can remember how I cursed it, and wondered how Dena coaxed such wonders from it.'

Jacques was there, crisp in his white jacket and tall hat. 'A marvel, Lady Camborne. I could not believe my eyes. Perhaps at Seymour House these same kitchen people . . .'

'I guessed that might be the next on the list,' Harry observed, pretending gloom.

'The food had better be bloody marvellous to match,' Mark said, and Ginny wanted to reprove him until she realized that it was a joke that Jacques fully understood and shared.

'You remember the old scullery and still-room, where we had natural refrigeration as the draughts were so bad?' Mark showed them the room proudly, as if he had achieved it himself. It had become an attractive staff dining and sitting room, as Ginny had requested. There was even a small, glassed-off cubicle for Jacques alone, for him to do his accounts and write up his menus. 'I didn't remember there was so much space here.'

Upstairs some of the large bedrooms with the four posters seemed unchanged, except that they had been repaired and

613

cleaned, and hung with fresh curtains, made more human with sofas and chairs. Bathrooms had been squeezed in wherever Mr Penleigh could find space, sometimes sacrificing one room to make two bathrooms. There were radiators in large numbers. Thick carpet covered the old wooden floors. 'I just had to make grandeur give way to comfort,' Ginny said, faintly apologetic. Livy felt a serenity and charm in these rooms, a softness that had always been noticeably lacking at Tresillian. It was no longer a spartan house, to be loved, but also endured. It was the ideal of a beautiful country house, furnished with a happy mingling of grace and cheerfulness, down to the last Wedgwood ashtray.

The little cramped rooms on the next floor had given way to space and light. Nanny gasped with relief and pleasure when she saw the nurseries. There was even a small kitchen to prepare nursery teas. 'I don't believe it,' Livy said. She tried to find the room she and Caroline had shared when the evacuees had crowded in, and became confused. 'Well, it must be this room, but it's bigger, and it's got the bathroom. Yes, that's the view . . . from this window . . .'

'Yes, that's the window,' Harry said. 'When Bully died, I was here with you both . . . and I opened the window so his spirit could go.'

'Yes,' Livy said softly. 'You did that. I shall never forget.'

They dined that evening in a splendour none of them except Ginny had ever thought to experience at Tresillian. Jacques had put himself out to prove what the new kitchen could produce. The wine seemed better than anything Livy had ever tasted. And yet there was a little after taste of nostalgia. She kept thinking of her mother, and of Herbert, who should have been with them. Afterwards she went upstairs to the nursery where her two children lay sleeping, just to reassure herself that the losses of the past were being replaced, as best they could. then she went to the empty room where Bully had died, and just for a few minutes stood at the open window, listening to the pounding of the sea against the Rocks.

Harry had said he couldn't be away from Washington for more than three weeks, so Caroline and Toby and their children came during the first week. They brought their own nanny, and the nurseries were almost filled. At Ginny's suggestion, Caroline had invited another couple and their young child, the husband of a colleague of Toby's at the Foreign Office, for the weekend. 'We might as well stretch the house a bit, and see if everything holds up,' Ginny said.

Caroline examined every room in thorough detail, had been out to look at the central-heating plant, the water pumps, even looked at the cisterns in the attics. She looked at the lovingly restored stables, most of which had become discreet garages. 'It's amazing,' she said. 'I was expecting some changes, a bit more comfort, but not this.' She looked closely at Ginny. 'It must have cost a fortune.'

Ginny was not to be drawn into figures. 'It cost enough.'

'Father tells me the entail has been broken, so this will not belong to Mark.'

'It belongs now to Harry and to me, and when we're gone, it will belong to whomever we think should have it. Mark was consulted, and was relieved that he wouldn't have to try to support the place.'

'Mark's a child, and doesn't . . .' Caroline bit off her words. But afterwards Ginny was uncomfortably aware that each time Caroline's eyes roamed about a room, she seemed to be costing everything. 'My great-grandfather's paintings were left to my mother, weren't they?' she said pointedly one evening during dinner.

'Yes,' Harry answered, 'and left to me in Dena's will. Your turn will come, Caroline. Just try to be patient.'

It was while Caroline and Toby were there that the news broke about Rachel. They watched the nine o'clock news on television in the library, and suddenly there flashed on to the screen a picture of Frazer Campbell being greeted at Moscow airport by both a representative of the Soviet Foreign Minister and a member of the British embassy staff, a courtesy which would have been extended to any visiting Member of Parliament. Among those who followed him down the steps from the plane was Rachel. Frazer Campbell's wife was not in the party.

'That's done it!' Caroline said. 'Why can't she keep her nasty little affair private? She makes it impossible for Frazer Campbell's wife to ignore this.'

'Perhaps that's what was intended,' Harry commented. 'She obviously is there because he wants her there. In a sense, one has to admire him. He could be risking his political life on this one. It will be interesting to see what his constituents make of it.'

'What they'll make of it!' Caroline snapped. 'They'll probably say "good luck to him". He represents some nasty little slum where the people adore him. It's hard to believe he went to Rugby and Oxford. Those lovely dishevelled working-class clothes. That nicely cultivated rumpled look.'

'He is a brilliant politician,' Toby observed.

Caroline rounded on him. 'Don't tell me you're defending his politics.'

'I didn't say that, dear girl. I merely remarked that he is supremely skilful in manipulating his own party, and provoking the members of the other party into near apoplexy. And he can almost wring tears from any crowd he addresses about the plight of the working classes, even if they are now enjoying a welfare state such as they never imagined. He could go very far, perhaps to Prime Minister if Labour gets back in. Or he could over reach himself, and be ruined. It will be interesting to watch.'

'And my sister will go with him.'

'We'll see. She might never be a Prime Minister's wife, though Eden was divorced and that didn't stop him being Prime Minister. But she could go to ruin with him.'

'And you don't care!'

'No, my dear, I don't. It is purely a matter of academic interest to me.' He spoke, Livy thought, with the sureness of a civil servant, and a civil servant who was independently rich as well, whose job on the permanent staff of the Foreign Office was secure, no matter which government came or went. His tone was cold and calm. Toby would never, ever, Livy thought, take the risk Frazer Campbell was taking. But in that quick glimpse they had had of her, Rachel had looked slightly defensive, as if she were even more aware of the risk than they were.

Three weeks they stayed at Tresillian. Friends visited, friends from London, from New York, from Washington. Colleagues from the Foreign Office came. Mr Penleigh came anxiously several times, tapping gauges, testing valves. All that had gone into Tresillian seemed adequate to the strains placed upon it. He and Ginny heaved a sigh of relief, and shared a glass of champagne with Harry in the small sitting-room with the view of the orchard. 'We've already had requests from *Country Life* to come and photograph it, and write it up,' Mr Penleigh said.

'I think that's the recognition due to you,' Ginny said, 'but when we've gone, Mr Penleigh. Just give us these few weeks in peace.'

Then they all departed except Livy, Jamie and Oliver, and Nanny. Ginny went with Harry up to Seymour House so that he could have a week in London, conferring at the Foreign Office, entertaining colleagues, 'catching up' as he called it. Alex had to return to Washington.

'I can't leave the Old Man too long,' he said. 'But you stay, my love. Write your pieces, whatever it is you're writing. Let the boys get to know their cousins. Take them for picnics when it's fine. Tell them stories when it's not, and listen to the rain. If Thea will permit it, take them to her studio.'

Livy moved into her own cottage in St Just. There was room for them, if Mark stayed with Thea. Ginny wanted them to stay on at Tresillian.

'No,' Livy said, 'you need Knox and Jacques in London. All the girls, my cousins, will look in on me, and see that we don't need anything. It's time Jamie began to see, even if he can't understand it yet, that there's a different sort of life.'

She spent the rest of the summer there. She wrote, putting together a vague plan the sketches were beginning to trace for themselves. *'It's like following a snail's track,'* she wrote to Alex. Every night she and Thea and Mark had dinner together. And every night there was a different cousin, or an aunt, preparing food in the kitchen, infinitely tolerant, even amazed at Mark's interference. Food, traditionally, was not the concern of men. And yet Mark was still accepted on any of the fishing boats in the harbour, stood his round of pints in the pubs, while keeping within the law himself by drinking sickly orange drinks, which he loathed.

They drove to the little coves, the high headlands for the usual picnics. They lay among heather, or on the firm sands, listening to the songs of birds, the plaintive cry of the seagulls. Mark took Jamie by the hand and led him away from the picnic basket. He showed him how the seagulls would come at the offer of food. Jamie watched in wonder as Mark tossed the scraps high into the air, and the gulls fought one another to be there first. At first Jamie was frightened of them, their size, the power of their dive. Then he began to laugh, to clap his hands.

In late August Ginny telephoned from Washington. 'Mr McClintock,' she announced, 'has decided to go and visit the bank in London. I think he just wants to show them that he's still very much alive. He may call into Zurich before that. I'm just warning you that he intends to come down to St Just. Livy, I hate to ask it of you, but would you open up Tresillian for me. Knox and Jacques will come down to take care of you all – and I hope your family will help out. Mr McClintock has to stay at Tresillian, Livy. There's no other place. He'll have his own valet with him. He'll have his own car and chauffeur. But he can't be at Tresillian alone. It wouldn't be right. Will you be there in my place?'

'Of course.'

So they moved back to Tresillian. Nanny was delighted to be back in the spacious nurseries. Jamie thought it quite natural that they should have two homes, but he didn't like it when he discovered that the young playmates he had had among the widely spread Tregenna family were no longer so conveniently close. Livy promised that she would take him down to see them every day, and they would come up and play with him on the now fenced-in cliff-top. Mark moved to Tresillian with Livy. 'I'll need a man around. Even though I get on very well with him, Mr McClintock can be . . .'

'Yes, I know. Don't worry. I'll be there every second with him. At least until it's time to go back to school.'

They waited for several days after what Ginny estimated would be the date of his arrival. Knox and Jacques had arrived, the Tregenna women were waiting for a summons, though several of them came daily to Tresillian to clean, whether or not anyone was living there. Then came the telephone call from the Ritz. He would drive down the next day; expect him by evening.

Livy had imagined, after the long journey, that Mr McClintock would be too tired to tour the whole house, but he insisted on it. He spent the most time in the library. Livy unlocked a brass-screened bookcase which held the papers and the log books of the Admiral. Andrew McClintock grunted in satisfaction. 'Good stuff.' He made a few derisory remarks about the portraits of the ancestors hanging in the great hall. 'Just as well to keep them in dark corners where no one will pay much attention to them. And just as well to leave them uncleaned. They don't bear close inspection. Ginny should find a few decent pictures for the drawing-room . . . Maybe I'll lend her some . . .' He went to see his sleeping great-grandchildren in their nursery. 'Fisticuffs seems to have grown about a foot since I last saw him.' But he lingered for some minutes silently over Oliver's cot. The baby lay sideways, so his face was in profile; his fingers lay lightly on a small stuffed white rabbit Andrew McClintock had given him at his christening. No one ever mentioned the trust fund which had been set up at the same time. 'I hope that isn't a plant, just to please me.'

'Oh, no, Mr McClintock!' Nanny breathed. 'It's his favourite. He always goes to bed with it. If I try to give him something else, he just howls.'

Andrew McClintock grunted again. Of course he would remember which toy he had given to each child, even though he had given them dozens. 'He looks well, but he almost needs a haircut.'

He moved on to an inspection of the other rooms on

619

that floor, even Knox's and Jacques's rooms, although Livy regarded this as an intrusion. 'Nonsense! I just want to see how English architects treat servants these days. Not badly . . . not badly, at all. They must be learning something.' They descended by the narrow back stairs to the kitchen. Mark was there, but he managed to keep silent, and let Jacques show Mr McClintock what had been achieved. He looked at everything, examined the equipment, touched the gleaming stainless-steel counters, deliberately, Livy thought, just so that he could put finger marks on them.

'Well, it may be efficient, but I liked it better the way it was.' He pointed his cane towards the big new central table, and the butcher's chopping block. 'I had some of the finest breakfasts of my life right there. In the company of a beautiful and charming woman. I don't suppose that'll ever happen again.' Then he went out to the drawing-room where Thea now waited, and accepted a scotch from Knox.

'Well . . . well, I suppose Ginny's thrown a pot of money into this place. And I suppose there are worse things to do with it.' He looked directly at Mark. 'D'you mind, young man, that it won't go to you automatically when Harry dies?'

Mark answered him as directly. 'You know very well, sir, I couldn't have afforded to keep it. I would have had to try to sell it, or to walk away from it and let it fall down. What's happened is much the best thing. Father and Aunt Ginny will have a comfortable house, and I won't have a load on my back.'

'Just as well you know it,' Andrew McClintock said, ungraciously.

They went into dinner, and Livy realized that Mark was hanging anxiously on every mouthful of food the old man took. His face became radiant when Mr McClintock requested a small second helping of the lobster *bisque*. He couldn't help blurting out, 'I made that, sir.'

Andrew McClintock laid his spoon down, as if the soup no longer interested him. 'It's time you took up other pastimes. How's your cricket? How's your schoolwork?'

'My cricket's fine, sir. I expect to be captain of the First

Eleven next term. The schoolwork's . . .' he shrugged. 'It's all right. Not brilliant. But then I know I can never come up to Father, so nothing's ever good enough.'

'Well, if you were clever enough to get yourself kicked out of Eton, everything else should be simple for you.'

Mark's face darkened. 'I try, sir. I've done better at Wrisley than anywhere else. And they let me into the kitchen there,' he added, giving a twist to his words. 'We don't get things quite like this . . .' he indicated the food on his plate, 'but it isn't bad. Sometimes, on half day, I go into Bath and buy some ingredients, and I cook them up, and the cook and I have a bit of a feast. I buy the best wine I can afford. Wrisley doesn't mind one doing things like that, so long as it doesn't interfere with what other people are doing. They call it "creative" work. Some chaps just lie on the grass and look at the sky. A few of them paint pictures, or try to. There's one chap there who offered me five pounds if I'd get Thea to autograph a postcard of one of her pieces he'd bought at the Tate.'

'And did you do it?'

'Yes. Thea . . .' He nodded to her across the table, 'was very decent. She didn't mind at all.'

'And did you take the five pounds?'

'No, sir.'

'More fool you! That would have been your first step to being rich.'

'I'll never be rich, sir. I know that. And I'll never make any money out of Thea.'

Andrew McClintock raised his eyes to the ceiling, seeming to survey the delicate moulding, the Wedgwood medallions. 'There must be something in the air of this place. No one ever seems to care about money.' He looked at Livy. 'Your mother didn't. She didn't expect anything from me.' Next he looked at Thea. 'You'd go on working if people paid you a song for your pieces, instead of a fortune, as they're now doing. And your husband, that last picture of Alex and Livy that Ginny's put in the drawing-room, in my opinion it was the finest thing he ever did, but he just handed it to them. *I* would have paid him handsomely for it. And Livy would

621

be just as happy to live in her cottage as the McClintock mansion.'

Thea gave a hoarse chuckle, and signalled to Knox that she would have more wine. 'Just so long as you know it, Mr McClintock. Just so long as you know there are some things money can't buy.'

He sipped his own wine slowly. 'That, my dear, is the beginning of knowing how to make money. Knowing what it can't buy. In a sense, young Mark has learned his first lesson. If he'd taken that five pounds, I would have marked him down as a greedy fool. Being able to wait is more than half the game.'

'The game . . .?' Livy said.

'The game of power, of money . . . of artistry.' In an elaborate gesture he raised his glass to Thea. 'Of genius. All must learn how to wait, and when to move.' He leaned towards Mark. 'I hope at that fancy "creative" school, you've learned to play chess.'

While Andrew McClintock was there, Rachel telephoned. 'Please give my regards to him, Livy, and I mean that. But I don't think I could bear to talk to that cynical old man just now. You're going to read stories in tomorrow's newspapers. I thought I should warn you. I hope those lovely children are well and flourishing. Give my love to Mark.' She hung up.

Livy went down early to St Just to buy all the newspapers, though *The Times* was delivered at Tresillian. She spread them on Thea's kitchen table, and they drank coffee while they read what Rachel had warned them of. The popular press made a field day of it, freed from the law of libel, because it was now public knowledge. Frazer Campbell's wife was suing for a legal separation from her husband, citing his continuing relationship with the Hon Rachel Penrose. She had done the unexpected, and publicly named 'the other woman'. She would not be suing for a divorce; she was a Roman Catholic.

'Well,' Thea said, 'that's that. If the woman won't agree to be divorced, Rachel will never be able to marry him. And

I'd bet anything Mrs Frazer Campbell is as beyond reproach as Caesar's wife, so there'll be no grounds on which he can divorce her. Some day there could be a change in the divorce laws, but for the moment she holds all the cards. The wronged woman. She doesn't want him any more, but she won't free him. And the world being what it is, Rachel will take the blame.'

There was nothing about it in *The Times*, which didn't print such items, but Livy could not hold back the popular press from Andrew McClintock. He would have been told about it, or one of his colleagues or his employees would have sent the cuttings, if not, it would have come from the press-cutting agency he employed. Anything that was written about the Penrose family was of equal interest to him as what was said about the McClintocks and the Claytons.

He read them all. 'Yes, it's an old weapon of revenge. I used it on my own wife, the Russian. I never did agree to a divorce, but then it hardly mattered as none of her many lovers seemed to want to marry her.' He spoke so dispassionately that he might have been referring to someone who had never existed. 'I hope Rachel and Frazer Campbell have enough going between them to compensate for what they will lose.' That seemed to be his final comment on the matter.

The first of the autumn gales hit the Cornish coast. The sea boiled white around the Tresillian Rocks, and the tide reached its highest mark on the cliff path. The St Just fishing-fleet stayed in harbour. When the rain let up, Livy walked with Andrew McClintock and Jamie to the edge of the cliff top, to witness the spectacle of the waves and spray shooting high into the air. Jamie shouted with excitement. Andrew McClintock clutched his cane and his hat, and said, 'Something seems to indicate it's time we all went home.'

Mark was already back at school. They had a final grand dinner with Thea, Livy handed over the keys Tresillian to her cousin, Nell, and they travelled up to London in the wake of Knox and Jacques. They had two nights at Seymour House. Caroline and Toby came to dinner. Caroline didn't mention Rachel until she and Livy were in the downstairs cloakroom.

'Well,' she observed, as she applied powder and fresh lipstick, 'she's made a real mess of it. Just imagine allowing yourself to be so publicly associated with Frazer Campbell knowing that the wretched wife would probably never let him go. She should have thought of that years ago. It could ruin him, and it'll probably ruin any hopes she has of getting into Parliament herself. It's a lot to give up for a man like Frazer Campbell.'

'That obviously isn't how she sees it, or him.' Livy didn't say that Rachel had been around to see her that afternoon, to have tea in the nursery with the children, to give them soft, carefully-chosen toys.

'Unless I defy every convention I'll probably never have children,' Rachel had said. 'It's one of the choices one has to make. I don't think I'd want to try to bring up a child who was illegitimate. It's too tough on the child. Frazer and I don't exactly "co-habit" as that quaint expression has it. We've kept our separate flats. It's awkward, it's inconvenient. But that's what we've decided.'

'You must love him very much.'

'If being willing to give up so much for a man means loving him, then I suppose I do. But there never, that I can remember, has been any "grand passion". Just, for me, a clear and overwhelming feeling that there's no one else I could care about in that way. To live a day without talking to him is an agony. I have to know what he's thinking and feeling. I suppose that has to count as love.'

'I would say it does,' Livy replied softly. She had been acutely aware of the way Rachel had fondled the two little boys, a look almost of hunger in her eyes, the sharp planes of her handsome face breaking into a smile as she listened to Fisticuffs's almost indecipherable chatter; she was patient and loving with him. Of all four of them, Rachel might have made the best mother, Livy thought.

The journey back with Andrew McClintock was novel, and exciting. The first transatlantic jet air service had just been inaugurated. The first-class compartment no longer converted into sleeping berths; there were just large, reclining seats and leg rests for those who wanted to sleep for part of the non-stop journey to New York. The aircraft rose with unnatural speed on take-off, and levelled out at about thirty-three thousand feet. They were far above the cloud layer in brilliant sunshine. the motion of the plane was less than riding in a car on a smooth road. 'They really paved it up here, didn't they?' Andrew McClintock remarked as the hostess served cocktails and hors d'oeuvres. He had backed swift air-travel for the public since the war, had watched the disasters of the British Comets, and placed his faith and his money in what the engineers of Boeing had shown him. He was soberly triumphant when, even with headwinds against them, they landed in New York seven hours after take-off from London. 'Well, this is the beginning. It will get better and faster. The public in a few years will be going on an almighty travelling spree. And poor Alex and Harry will be back and forth across the Atlantic more times than they can count. Passenger liners will be a luxury, and there'll be very few of them.'

2

It was almost two months since Livy had seen Alex, and the sight of him waiting for them at Washington airport frightened her. There was something heart-wrenching in the way he tried to hurry towards her, leaning heavily on his cane, his foot dragging, his face twisted in a lopsided smile. He looked frail and tired, but there was nothing frail about his embrace and his kiss, nor the way he managed to lift Jamie to kiss him, or how he insisted on taking Oliver from Nanny's arms and carrying him to the car. Oliver wasn't quite sure who this man was. He didn't mind being carried by this stranger who made pleasant noises at him, but his curiosity was aroused. He tried to take away Alex's eye patch. 'Here, you little monkey! Stop it!' He reached with his left hand and put the patch back in place, but to the child it was a game, and he kept it up all the way across the concourse to the waiting car.

Alex dumped him unceremoniously into Nanny's lap. 'There, you little devil. Plague someone else! He's grown like a weed, Livy. What are you feeding him on there?'

'Oh, fresh air and fish scraps,' she answered lightly. 'The usual diet for St Just.' They had a wave from Andrew McClintock's cane as his own car bore him away. They talked innocuously during the drive back to Massachusetts Avenue, because of Nanny's presence; but Alex managed to keep Jamie perched on his lap, and to hold Livy's hand. The gentle pressure he applied from time to time racked her with guilt; she had had all summer long to do as she wished, and he had endured the enervating heat of a Washington summer, and the endless grind of McClintock, Clayton. 'You look as if you could stand some fresh air yourself. I noticed in your letters that you always managed to avoid telling me whether you went to Prescott Hill at the weekends.'

He sighed. 'Mother managed to drag me out there a few times, but honestly, I preferred to stay and work at home. Now that the air-conditioning's complete, it was less effort. Mother's so busy entertaining. It never stops. Being an ambassador's wife is damned hard work. If I felt the need for company, I took myself down to the Cosmos . . . a rather dreary bachelor's existence.'

With quick glances she studied his face; the left side with the eye patch was next to her. He looked worn, almost old. He was only thirty-one. A terrible fear engulfed her; suppose he had used up half his life's force in that fierce struggle to survive? Suppose he could not look forward to a normal life span. She looked at her two children and realized again how precious they were, the part of Alex that would endure. Then she shook the gloomy thoughts away. She returned the pressure of his hand. He would survive; she would have him at least another thirty years, and more.

The car drew up at the McClintock mansion. The butler hurried down the steps to open the doors. 'Welcome back, Mrs McClintock. Lady Camborne is on the telephone . . .' Livy hurried inside.

'My dear, just to say "hello". We have to attend a reception tonight at the Brazilian Embassy – a trade delegation is visiting. But we're free for dinner. Could you and Alex slip over here? Just the four of us. And tomorrow morning, if it's convenient, I have a couple of hours free, and I'd love to see my grandsons.'

'Yes, to both,' Livy said. 'We'd be happy to come.'

The children and the luggage were being taken upstairs. Livy realized that a woman, a handsome woman of indefinite age, dressed in a plain white blouse and neat dark skirt, stood at the door of the library as if waiting to meet her. Alex motioned her forward. 'Livy, this is Mrs Tennant. I know she is ludicrously young to be retiring from McClintock-Clayton, but that's what she's doing. I thought perhaps you could use a little help – with the committee work, and so on. Just part time.'

The woman smiled tentatively. 'How do you do, Mrs McClintock? I couldn't bear not to take up Mr McClintock's offer. If I don't suit you, of course, this is only a trial period. But Mr McClintock seemed to think you could use some help. Judging from the pile of mail on your desk, I'd guess he is right.'

Momentarily, Livy felt a flush of anger that Alex had done this without consulting her. Then, as swiftly she realized he was probably right. She thought of the telephone being answered, the routine mail being taken care of. It seemed such luxury, but such good sense. And yet part of her was still in revolt. She was only twenty-seven. But she was a matron with two children, and social responsibilities to take care of. She saw the anxiety in Alex's face. This step had been taken out of concern for her. Perhaps he had decided that it would give her some extra hours for whatever was in that manuscript she played around with. He was making her a gift of time. And yet she saw Mrs Tennant as a symbol of what was expected of her, of the relentless pressure of social Washington. After the freedom of St Just, gilded gates seemed to swing shut again. She forced herself to smile, and she held out her hand. 'I'm sure you'll be a great help, Mrs Tennant.' And every fibre of her ached for freedom again. But she saw Alex's expression relax into relief. She realized he had been worried about this moment. Her smile became full and real.

'How good of you to think of it, Alex.'

He put out his hand to her. 'Come on, let's go and help Nanny put the kids to bed . . .' From his tone he might just as well have said, 'Let's you and I go to bed.'

Andrew McClintock's prediction that the new jet services would mean more transatlantic crossings for both Alex and Harry became a reality. Harry and other ambassadors could now be more readily called to London for consultation; at times it was easier for Alex to go to London or Zurich to settle a problem, or call all the directors of McClintock-Clayton into conference, than to attempt to do the work by telephone or letter. But they were beginning to discover the peculiar tiredness which accompanied this form of travel, the inability to sleep when the clock of local time said it was time to sleep, and when sleep came the awakening at the time which was usual in Washington. 'I can't get used,' Alex said, on returning to Washington from a trip that had lasted only four days, 'to being faced with dinner when something tells me it's almost breakfast time back in London.'

But this new phenomenon did not stop them making plans to spend Christmas at Tresillian instead of Prescott Hill. At least, Ginny made the plans, and not willing to disappoint her, Livy and Alex fell in with them. 'I want to be at home in my new house,' she said. 'I'd love a beautiful tree in the great hall, lights, food, all the things we weren't able to have during the war. I want the carollers to come, and we'd feast them on mince pies and mulled wine.'

'I think Mother's been reading too much Dickens,' Alex said, 'but if she wants to see her house decked with holly, well . . .'

It had all been arranged with the agreement of Andrew McClintock. 'There's no question that I'd leave him here all through the holidays alone;' Ginny said. She wrote invitations to Caroline, Rachel and Chris. 'Still trying,' she said to Livy. 'I feel I must try to do what Dena would have done. And I haven't seen my own daughter since last January. Mark needn't come over . . .'

628

Caroline replied that she would come for Christmas and bring the children, but that she doubted that Toby could be with them. *'His mother isn't very well. He feels perhaps he should go home for a few days then.'*

Rachel's reply was evasive.

'Damn Christmas!' Chris almost screamed when she read her mother's letter. 'Doesn't she understand we haven't time for the holly and the ivy and all that nonsense? Doesn't she understand about the picture?'

'Heh! Steady on, Baby,' her husband advised her. 'Perhaps it isn't such a bad idea. We're not going to be able to do a thing over the Christmas-New Year period. You know that. You have to pay golden time to keep the crew working. Any rate, Dunbar's headed for Acapulco that week. It's in his contract.'

Chris sagged down in the chair. 'We could shoot around him.'

'What with? Half a crew?'

She dropped her head into her hands. 'I wish,' she said, her voice muffled, 'I'd never heard of *The Way West.*'

They had started in July with the script in an unsatisfactory state, but the writer, Rod Gibbins, promised he'd stay with them all through the shooting, just to fix things up if they were needed. His agent had negotiated an extra fee for that service. They had been compelled to start because the only big star they had been able to sign, Jackson Dunbar, was committed to another film in February. Chris had known if they lost him they might as well fold up the project. Pride wouldn't let her do it. As part of the price of getting Dunbar, they had had to agree to sign up his mistress. Chris had desperately longed to give the role to an older woman, a character actress she knew would be ideal for the role, and whose strength and experience the film desperately needed, but they had signed Dunbar's mistress, virtually unknown in the movie world, and they had to artificially age her. She hadn't liked that, and it showed in her acting. Of course Jeff believed that the Rigghouse name was just as good as Jackson Dunbar's, and there had been an intense rivalry between the men. It didn't help Jeff's attitude that he had been cast as

Dunbar's father in the movie. He hadn't seemed to realize when the script was taking shape that that was the role he would play.

No other big name had come forward for the cameo roles as she had envisaged. Either she couldn't pay enough, or they weren't interested. Or the word had got around that the whole project was in trouble. So they had picked up character actors who were 'resting'. 'All these people are very fine actors, Baby, with a hundred years experience. They don't have to prove anything. They'll just slip into their parts like silk gloves.'

That hadn't proved to be the case. Chris had relied on Jeff's knowledge of the movie industry in casting them. Almost all of them had decided it was a wonderful chance to show that they really were stars who had somehow been overlooked. On location, in the dusty, windy Arizona desert, where a flock of expensive air-conditioned trailers had been necessary to keep cast and crew sane, all of them had played their parts to the hilt, and in most cases, overplayed them. Chris had had to fire their first choice of director after four weeks because Jeff quarrelled with him almost daily. He wanted the big scenes focused on himself, and not on Jackson Dunbar. Cannily, the director had waited to be fired, rather than walking out, so that he could collect his full fee. There had been a hiatus while they found a second director, John Cullen, who hadn't worked for three years, and had to be dug out from Zihuatanejo, up the coast from Acapulco. He was a man of fine reputation, great sensitivity, and he was a drunk. He read through the script aloud with Chris and Jeff. 'In God's name, where did you get this crap? The script stinks, the casting stinks.

'I've looked at the rushes. They stink, too. There isn't another director around who'd touch it. Not the way it is now.'

He had gone on the wagon, worked a seventeen hour day with the screen writer, Rod Gibbins, and wrung out of him something that had promise. And the cast waited in their motel, and not a foot of film was shot. They began again, finally, but the break had disorientated them. The script was different, the director was different, and Christine Clayton, whose money propped up the whole venture, showed signs of extreme nerves. She seemed to count the seconds as they shot. She would open her mouth to protest when the director called for yet another take. She played her part woodenly, as if her mind were on what the scene was costing rather than what it was supposed to achieve. Every night she conferred with John Cullen, trying to urge speed on him, instead of the perfection he desired. It was, after all, his chance too. They reached an uneasy compromise, and the results satisfied nobody. But at last the location shots were finished, and they could move to the studio and the back-lot shooting. They were two months behind schedule, and already over budget. Jackson Dunbar's agent had written into his contract that he would have two weeks at Christmas and New Year off. And that his services would terminate on the last day of February, whether the film was finished or not. Of course he would take his mistress to Acapulco with him, and that virtually ended any hope of John Cullen shooting around them, even if Chris had been willing and able to pay golden time to the crew. In all these months Jeff had carefully distanced himself from the money problem, the script problem, and anything else that was outside his sphere of acting. On paper he was co-producer with Chris, but he shrugged at the problems during the day, and eased himself to sleep with drink at night.

As the money poured out with frightening speed, Chris thought more and more of her father. Without a good script Blair would never have gone ahead. She thought of the night in the summer when her mother's letter had come inviting them to Tresillian, when she had paced the beach and wondered whether she ought to abandon the whole project, and pride, and the knowledge of what it would do to Jeff had stopped her. Now pride was in the dust, and Jeff was no better than before. When the film was released, his reputation would probably suffer, even if John Cullen did manage to salvage something from a basically flawed script. When they had returned to Hollywood, faced with the February deadline, and knowing that she would have to pay overtime to both cast and crew, Chris had gone quietly to the bank and raised money on her McClintock-Clayton shares. The bank had given the loan readily. McClintock-Clayton was not a public company, so the shares had no market price on them, but the bank reckoned that if Christine Clayton defaulted on repayment of the loan, the bank would own what they believed had to be a highly rated investment, and they would have forced a wedge into what was almost an impregnable fortress. She hated to think that she had betrayed her father by making this move, but she still clung to the hope that *The Way West* would at least break even at the box office, the loan repaid and the shares safe. Even more frightening to her was the wrath of Andrew McClintock if the shares passed from her hands into the bank's. Why hadn't she gone to him for the money? she wondered, and the answer had been simple. He would have loaned her monly only on the condition that she pay off cast and crew, and abandon the whole project. She hadn't yet reached that stage of desperation.

'Well, come on, what do you say, Baby? What do you say we take a spell away ourselves? Go to this Cornish place of your mother's. You haven't seen your family in a long time, Baby. It wouldn't hurt to say hello to them . . . especially the Old Man.'

'If you think . . .' she began slowly. 'Yes, why not? It'd do us good to get away for a while. No more than ten days. We have to be ready to roll the second Jackson gets back from Acapulco.'

Early the next morning she telephoned John Cullen to give him the news. He didn't even try to disguise the relief in his voice. 'Say, that's great! A real English Christmas, eh? In a castle. I heard your mother'd got a wonderful old castle.'

'It isn't a castle, it's a country house. It's just called a castle, and it belongs to my stepfather, Lord Camborne.'

'Well, whatever. Have a great time, Chris. See you right after the New Year. We should all be fresh as daisies by then, and ready to roll.'

So she sent a cable to her mother, and two days before Christmas she and Jeff were on board one of the new jets crossing the Atlantic. Jeff had seen that their departure was much publicized in *The Hollywood Reporter*, and in *Variety*, much blown-up stories about a fairy-tale castle, and a gathering of the English upper classes, complete with the British Ambassador to Washington. Chris had cringed at the thought of using her own family for publicity, and Jeff had laughed at her. 'Baby, this is show biz. It's great publicity. It makes it all sound so solid, you and all the McClintock-Clayton clan together for Christmas. It all helps the picture, Baby.'

A chauffeur-driven car took them straight from London to Tresillian. The day before they left Jeff had shopped extravagantly for presents for the whole family. She had tried to restrain him. 'Jeff, English Christmases aren't like Hollywood. Simple things are best. You don't have to load all the children with six presents each.'

'What? And let them think I'm some sort of cheapskate? Aw, come on, Chris. Let yourself go, Baby. It's Christmas!' The presents were all brightly and expensively wrapped by the stores, and charged to her account. They filled an embarrassingly large suitcase, and she knew they would be out-of-place beneath the Christmas tree. But Jeff was supremely pleased about them. It was his idea of how a film star behaved.

It was Christmas Eve when they arrived, tired after the plane journeys from Los Angeles to New York, and then on to London. But Jeff seemed fresh and alert as they greeted everyone. Caroline had arrived the day before with her two boys. Jeff asked to be allowed to visit them for nursery tea; the four boys, presided over by two nannies and one of Livy's young cousins, were bewildered by this stranger who seemed intent on having something to say to each of them, helping them to eat their tea, making smacking sounds over it to encourage them. The women were round-eyed at the sight of the person they had only witnessed larger than life from the darkened cinema stalls. True, he wasn't quite as handsome as he had once appeared, but he made up for it in enthusiasm and charm. Then he was downstairs for tea in the drawing-room, fulsome in his praise of the children. Chris knew what an effort he was making not to ask for a drink before the proper time. Andrew McClintock was not present. He did not have English afternoon tea, and he was either resting or working in his room. Chris waited with some nervousness for his appearance.

During tea Livy was called to the telephone by Knox. 'It's Miss Rachel,' he said quietly, as she made her way to the private little booth Mr Penleigh had constructed in one of those mysterious spaces uncovered when Tresillian was being restored.

'Rachel?'

'Hello, Livy. We're here in St Just. Frazer and I.'

'Well, why on earth aren't you up here?'

Rachel answered. 'You know very well why not. I just had a feeling I'd like to be with you all on Christmas Day, but I'm not going to put Frazer through the hoop by asking him to stay up there. We only made up our minds last night to come down. St Just seems pretty booked up, but we managed to find a room at the George . . .'

'That won't do,' Livy said. The George was one of the local pubs, pleasant enough, but she hadn't realized before that they even had rooms to rent. It would be very much a bed and breakfast style, with little privacy. 'Look, go round to Nell's. She has the key to my cottage. She'll have you fixed up in no time. There's plenty of booze there – and she'll have something for you for breakfast in the morning. The rest of the meals you can have here. Aunt Ginny would be very hurt if you didn't come. As it is, she won't understand why you didn't come here in the first place.'

'Yes, she will. She'll understand very well, being Ginny. We'll be travelling back on Boxing Day.'

'Why not stay just a little longer – or as long as you like?' Livy urged. 'The cottage needs using.'

'Well, we'll see. Yes, I'll go around to Nell. Thanks for the cottage, Livy. The room we have you can't swing a cat in, and of course there are all sorts of snide looks at us because we're not Mr and Mrs. I'll look in to say hello to Thea.'

'Try to get here by seven. Dinner's at eight. Caroline's

here, and the boys. And Chris decided to show. Her husband is being so charming to everyone I'm about to be sick. You'll be a breath of fresh air. Ginny will be delighted.'

'I hope so,' Rachel said drily, and rang off.

There was electric tension in the air that evening. Rachel had arrived at seven with Frazer Campbell. Livy and Ginny had made sure to be waiting in the drawing-room by then, but Jeff Rigghouse was there before them, and Knox had already served him a drink. He couldn't understand why such a fuss was being made of Rachel bringing Frazer Campbell here. 'I understand he's a big shot politician, and all, but . . .'

'No, you don't really understand. There'll be sparks flying every minute Caro's with him, and that might go for Mr McClintock too – but he'll probably be more subtle about it.'

'Well, hell, Rachel is Lord Camborne's daughter . . .'

'That's precisely why I'm very happy she's come,' Ginny said. 'She hardly ever sees her father. Now everyone get your own drinks. Knox has quite enough to do.'

'Let me,' Jeff said eagerly. 'I'm a real mean bartender.' He refilled his own glass before anyone else's. Alex came down, and decided he wasn't going to fight with Chris's husband for the honour of watching to see that everyone had what they wanted to drink. So he sat back and only got to his feet when Rachel and Frazer Campbell arrived.

Livy thought Rachel looked surprisingly lovely. She wore a red dress, and it was one of the times when her beauty, so much like Dena's when she was feeling expansive, showed through. There was a rush to greet her. Mark was there first, his arms flung around her. 'Rachel, you look smashing. It's great that you've managed to make it.'

There was a little awkwardness while Rachel went through the routine of introducing Frazer Campbell to everyone. They all, except Jeff, had seen many photos of him, but in the flesh he came over as a man of surprising warmth, with a sense of power which was coiled, but always ready to be unleashed. He was good-looking, Livy thought, in a way that didn't quite come across in his photographs, but which she had once witnessed as she saw him in a television debate. He was very large, tall and broad, with massive dark eyebrows, a thatch of untidy dark hair. He had a bear-like appearance, but his eyes were very dark grey, not brown, and Livy thought that in debate or anger, his bear-like qualities could turn savage. His voice was full of dark colour, a voice for the crowds and the hustings, a man to love, if you agreed with him.

'Say,' Jeff murmured to Livy, 'he could have been in pictures. He could have made a fortune playing character roles. You know . . . on a horse, protecting his territory . . . that sort of thing.' Livy was the one Jeff found easiest to talk to. Ginny seemed, as the ambassador's wife, very much a figure of the Eastern Establishment, to be rather too much a *grande dame* for his taste, even though she had been so welcoming and gentle. Caroline had looked at him with such frank scorn that he had wondered what he had ever done to her. He was put off by Chris's half-brother, Alex, too. He and the Ambassador, Lord Camborne, seemed very much to be reserving judgement on him, glad that Chris has come, and were making an effort to include him in the family. It was, he realized, the first time he had ever been alone with them all before. Any other time it had been at a big gathering, and there had been plenty of other people around who had been only too happy to talk to Jeff Rigghouse. He was glad that this Frazer character had shown up to take some of the heat off him. Already he was beginning to wonder if it had been a good idea, after all, to have made this visit. And where was the Old Man? It was a quarter to eight, already.

Andrew McClintock appeared a few minutes later; without thinking everyone in the room stood up, including the women. He greeted Chris gravely, gave a bleak smile to Jeff, a much warmer one to Rachel. 'I was very pleased to hear you had come. You'll be very comfortable in Livy's cottage, though I'm sure Ginny could have put you up here . . .' Rachel murmured something about not wanting to be any trouble. Then Andrew McClintock turned to Frazer Campbell. 'Well, sir, I'm very interested to meet you.'

'I sense, Ambassador, that that is said very much in the spirit of "won't you come into my parlour said the spider to the fly".'

To everyone's surprise, Andrew McClintock laughed. 'You look like a man who could fight his way out of any spider's web. Here, man, come and sit down and have a whisky with me. There's much I'd like to discuss with you. I know the Russian Ambassador in Washington pretty well, in fact, we've had a few commercial dealings. There's a lot of McClintock-Clayton technology he'd like to buy, but I imagine your experience of the Russians on their home ground is quite extensive.'

'Ambassador, I am a Socialist, not a Communist. So long as that is understood, I'll be happy to talk to you about any subject you like . . .'

They retreated to a sofa at the end of the room, and Ginny delayed dinner by fifteen minutes so that Andrew McClintock could sip his whisky slowly and talk with Frazer Campbell. The atmosphere in the room had eased considerably. They might argue, these two men, but it began to seem, of all unlikely things, that they would get along together.

Andrew McClintock was seated as always at Ginny's right at dinner, Frazer Campbell on her left. Jeff experienced a surge of anger as he saw the seating arrangement. He expected to be at Ginny's side. Didn't anyone here understand that he was famous. And who had ever heard of this two-bit politician?

Except on formal embassy occasions Ginny did not observe the tradition of withdrawing to leave the men alone with the port. They all went together to the drawing-room for coffee. But within half an hour Andrew McClintock, Frazer Campbell and Harry were in the library, seated around the fire, and Knox had left a bottle of brandy with them. Jeff, feeling shut out, tried all his charm on the women, and witnessed them thaw a little, even that bitch, Lady Osborne, who still had not given him permission to call her Caroline. She would, he thought, she would. But God, even with her high-and-mighty attitude, she was a dish, a real dish. He would have loved to have taken her to bed just to see how her icicles melted. But he was aware that he must not attempt anything of the sort. Too much depended on Chris now, and perhaps, in turn, on that old bastard, McClintock. It was, he thought, going to be a pretty boring week. But the whisky was very good, and there was plenty of it.

It was already Christmas morning when Rachel and Frazer walked down the hill to Livy's cottage. The fire Nell had made was just beginning to die down. But the house was warm, and Nell had laid holly along the mantlepiece. Rachel put on another log. 'Drink?' she said.

Frazer shook his head. He slumped into the big sofa. Andrew McClintock, aware that sleep was now always slow in coming to him, had not hesitated to keep Frazer with him long after all but Harry had gone upstairs. Rachel had joined them as a silent listener in the library. 'Funny,' Frazer said, 'what a good friend one sometimes thinks one can make of a man whom one knows, by all counts, to be an enemy.'

Jeff watched the next morning in amazement at the ceremony of opening the presents under the huge tree which decorated the great hall. He had been impressed by the great hall; it was better than any movie set he had ever seen, and he was pleased that the presents he had brought, in their spectacular wrappings, made such a terrific splash under the tree. Better, and far more numerous than anyone else's. Because of the children, and their impatience, the opening had to be before breakfast, although they had all received little stockings with small gifts in them in the nurseries. 'Santa came to you first,' Livy explained. The children sat, in pyjamas and dressing-gowns, happily around the tree, as Ginny handed out boxes and oddly shaped little packages to everyone, each labelled with little tags. 'I'm sorry, we didn't have much notice you were coming,' she said to Jeff. 'Your presents are probably waiting in Beverly Hills for you . . . Just a token . . .'

A token it was. A tie that Jeff wouldn't be seen dead in, probably bought in a hurry in that crummy little place down the hill. There was one miserable scarf for Chris. Where, he wondered, were the jewels and the gold these people were supposed to give one another? They were rich, for God's sake, but they seemed to have taken more trouble over presents for their servants than for their family. The kids got toys, but nothing out of the way. No box contained a fur coat, though Andrew McClintock seemed to have collected a pile of cashmere socks. The kids were tooting little cheap trumpets, and none of them had yet figured out what to do with the expensive train set he had given the Old Man's first great-grandson, the red-headed fury they called Fisticuffs. He sat, thumb in his mouth, listening while Alex, seated awkwardly beside him on the floor, read the first page of a story book to him. Jeff suddenly realized that there were more books than anything else coming out of the packagers. Some of them just cheap colouring books for the kids, others expensively bound volumes for the adults, containing God knew what. Biographies, histories . . . where was the glamour? It would have been thought a poor show in Beverly Hills. Jeff watched Alex and his son for a while. Hell, that guy took some getting used to. How could that gorgeous piece, Livy, ripe and beautiful, stand the sight of him, twisted, and one-eyed, two fingers missing, and half his head white? Well, money could buy lots of things, Jeff concluded. Then he saw that Chris was gazing at him with an 'I told you so', look on her face. Caroline had barely been able to finger the beaded cashmere sweater he had bought for her – Italian design, the very best label. 'How kind of you,' she said coldly, dropping the sweater back into the box without even folding it. 'But it's rather personal, isn't it? I mean, I hardly know you.'

Bitch! He was sick to death of this English Christmas which was supposed to be so jolly. It hadn't damned well even snowed! In fact, rain was splattering the windows, which wasn't the same thing at all. He began to wonder when the pubs in that little place down the hill opened – if they opened at all on Christmas Day. He'd have to persuade Chris to take a walk with him, or he'd slip something to the butler, and take a bottle of Lady Camborne's expensive whisky up to their room. It was the one thing, in the orgy of buying Christmas presents which weren't appreciated, he had forgotten. Before leaving London he hadn't stocked up with his own supply of whisky.

Jeff endured the tedium of Christmas Day, the formal dinner in the middle of the afternoon, after the Queen's speech, which had seemed a bore to him. 'The servants,' Chris explained, 'have to have their time off, too. So we'll be having cold buffet for supper.' Jeff had tried to give Knox a ten pound note when he asked for and had been given a bottle of seventeen-year-old scotch. 'Oh, no, sir. Anything in the house is yours. Lady Camborne wouldn't be at all pleased if I didn't see that you had everything you wanted.'

Damned snobs, he thought. They all looked down their noses at him, even the damn servants. As if he were trash, who had, by a horrible mistake, got enmeshed with the only daughter. And yet that Livy woman, the one they all seemed to fall over for, was a cousin to every second fishwife in the little place below. If this was an English Christmas, he'd had it. What he couldn't stand, most of all, when they arrived on Christmas Day, was the expression of well-being on the faces of Frazer Campbell and Rachel. They had produced only simple toys for the children, explaining that Santa had left them at Livy's cottage by mistake. For the adults, there was nothing, and no one seemed to expect anything.

On what they called Boxing Day – Chris explained to Jeff that it was the day when, at one time, the servants of the family had traditionally received their Christmas 'Boxes' – they drove to attend the meet of a local hunt. It was all a bore, Jeff thought. Just a lot of haughty-looking women in severe black coats, their hair in nets, and the men, some of them in scarlet coats, which everyone called 'pink'. They must be colour-blind. There were local farmers, with some good-looking horses. And all the damn yapping dogs, each of which had a name, but which, for the life of him, Jeff couldn't have told apart. There was a stirrup cup passed around – not nearly enough of it. Then there were hours of following a string of cars with the faint hope of a distant sight of the chase. Jeff felt like cheering when he heard that the fox got clean away.

Caroline left the next day. 'I really have to take the children to Toby's parents. It's expected.' The decision seemed to have been made after a telephone call which she said was from Toby. Her hurried goodbyes did not include Rachel and Frazer Campbell, or Thea. She left early in the morning. 'It's a long drive to Northamptonshire,' she said. Jeff Rigghouse had not yet appeared. She barely remembered to wish Chris good luck with the film. 'Do say goodbye to your husband for me, won't you?' Her tone clearly implied that she would be glad if she never saw him again.

Her departure was followed the next day by Chris's and Jeff's. 'Baby, I've had it. Let's get up to London and have some fun. This place just gets on my nerves.' She knew it was useless to protest, and in any case she did not want to stay on any longer herself. Jeff's charm was beginning to wear very thin; Andrew McClintock seemed barely to notice his presence. In fact, he preferred to spend time talking after dinner to Frazer Campbell. Each day Rachel and Frazer said they would be leaving; each day they postponed their departure.

Chris and Jeff went to her mews house in London, which she had arranged to have opened and cleaned. He inspected it in a cursory fashion. 'Nice, cute, but it's a bit pokey, isn't it? I mean for someone like you. But still . . . listen, Baby, why don't you call some of your friends and organize a whing-ding? I have a few buddies living over here. We have a few more days before we have to go back. Let's start to have some of the old Christmas spirit . . .'

Chris gave the party, organized hurriedly, and was surprised to find how many people from her theatre days in London, were available and dying to fill in part of the dead week between Christmas and New Year. They were joined by a few acquaintances Jeff had made through the years who now lived in London. Through one of these he got a temporary membership of the most fashionable gaming club in London. He played for two nights, and then Chris had to sign a large cheque for his debts. 'Not to worry, Baby,' he said, and kissed her tenderly. 'It'll all come rolling back in when the movie's released.'

They spent New Year's Eve on a jet flight to New York. Chris wished they had never left Beverly Hills. She did not feel rested or refreshed; she felt no new surge of hope. She could only look at the man sleeping in the reclining seat beside her, and wonder if she could manage to stay with him until the picture was finished. She thought of London, and the people who had come to the party, most of them the usual hangers-on, who would have come to anyone's party. And she thought of the few who had been genuinely pleased to see her. Although she had not contacted him, the thought of Hugh Meredith was often with her. One afternoon, when Jeff had been lunching with one of his friends, and planning an afternoon at the gaming club, she had attended the matinée performance of a play in which Hugh Meredith had the lead. She had sat in the stalls, engrossed, realizing again what a very fine actor he was. The sound of his voice was with her still during the sleepless journey across the Atlantic.

Rachel and Frazer Campbell stayed almost the whole week in St Just, and most nights they were at Tresillian for dinner, where Thea was always a guest. To Rachel it was a small slice of time that seemed nearly perfect. There was nothing to disturb them, no one knew where they were, except Frazer's secretary, and with the House in recess, there was no urgent business he had to attend to. He had brought the usual briefcase full of papers to be studied, but they lay there almost unread. They slept late, and woke to pale winter sun. It was warm enough to picnic most days. She took him to the usual places the families had discovered over the years. He munched his sandwiches happily, shared a bottle of wine with her. She had never known this side of him, at peace, gazing across the rugged coast line, watching the birds swoop and wheel. 'I could stay for ever,' he said.

'No, you couldn't. The first little row in the Commons, and you'd be charging back there, like an old war horse sniffing battle. I just wish you could take these breaks more often with me.'

'I'll try, my Rachel. I'll try.'

It was Thea who brought over a copy of the *Express*. 'I don't know why I read it, but sometimes there's something amusing. This particular piece didn't amuse me much. I wonder if they get the *Express* up at Tresillian?'

'They get a whole raft of papers.' Rachel read the small item in William Hickey's column.

Lady Osborne flew off to Monaco yesterday to join the yachting party of Sir Bruce Abbott, whose New Year Party is reckoned to be the highlight of the Christmas week. Sir Bruce and Lady Abbott, formerly the model, Jean Furgus, have recently divorced.

'So where did she put the children?'

'Probably exactly where she said, with Toby's parents.'

Ginny, nodded when Rachel mentioned it. 'I guessed there was some problem . . . She didn't seem at all certain how long she'd stay . . . taking the children to their grandparents wasn't even mentioned when she came down here. There was just that one telephone call, and she was gone. Would it have been from Bruce Abbott?'

'I imagine so,' Rachel said. 'She's been seeing a lot of him. Caro is rather less the perfect Foreign Office wife than she used to be.'

'Bruce Abbott . . .' Andrew McClintock mused. He had read the item. He seemed never to miss anything that was in the papers. 'The entrepreneur extraordinary. He collects businesses like other men collect neckties. When it comes to money, Toby Osborne isn't in the same league, no, not at all. I've met him a few times. Handsome fellow, attractive in a sort of rough way, and as deadly as a shark. He's come to Clayton's a few times for extra financing for some project he wants to get into. He really isn't Clayton's sort of customer. But he always gets his money somewhere.'

'And Caro?' Harry said bleakly. 'Is she really involved with him?'

'It seems so. He's a great ladies' man, they say,' Rachel offered. 'Impossible to say with him whether it's a serious thing, or he's just playing about.'

'But Caro's taking a terrible risk with her marriage,' Harry objected. 'Why doesn't someone *tell* me these things?'

'What could you do?' Ginny answered. 'Caro lives her own life, and everyone in the Foreign Office has known for a long time that Toby played around a bit. Perhaps she's just giving him a bit of his own back. Or perhaps . . . perhaps she's intending to get Bruce Abbott. The way he lives would be a lot more exciting than the Foreign Office round.'

'Poor Father,' Rachel said. 'Your two daughters are turning in a rather poor showing in the matrimonial stakes.' she tried to laugh, but it came hollowly.

In February Caroline wrote to Ginny and Harry.

I hope this reaches you before kind friends send the newspaper cuttings. Toby and I are separating immediately. Toby is going to take a flat, and I'll stay on here in the house until Toby and I are divorced. He's agreed to a divorce, with as little wrangling as possible. We've agreed over the children. He'll have access at all times, and they will go to stay with him at specified times. Don't weep for him. I think he'll be pretty quickly consoled. It was really a question of which one of us made the first move. Of course I couldn't be sure until Bruce asked me to marry him. If he hadn't I'd have had to hold on to Toby as long as possible. I'm sorry if it upsets you . . . but you must have known that things haven't been right between Toby and me for quite some time now. At least, Father, it can't hurt you at the FO, as you'll certainly be ambassador to Washington until you retire.

Ginny called Livy and Alex over to share the news privately with them. 'I worry about the children . . . I think she should have stuck it out. Toby's too lazy to go through all the bother of a divorce if it weren't forced on him.'

'It was bound to happen,' Alex said. 'If not Bruce Abbott, then someone else. Caro married Toby because she wanted money. Then a very much bigger piece of money came along, and she grabbed it, as well as a more exciting life. Just as well she's so much younger than Bruce Abbott. He's the sort whose fancy lightly turns . . .'

'For heaven's sake,' Ginny said, 'don't say things like that in front of Harry. He's pretending to shrug it off, but I know he's terribly upset. He wanted happiness for them both. We

644

know Rachel's position can never be happy, except for what Frazer can give to her personally, and I believe now that that is quite a lot. But for Caroline . . . Harry just feels that this is one more turn on the merry-go-round, and she could easily fall off this time, too . . .'

'Well, while we're about it,' Alex said, 'let's not forget our Chris. That marriage is finished right now. Probably was finished a few months after it began. They may just stay together long enough to see this wretched movie finished, and then that will be that.' Not caring about his mother's presence he reached out and grabbed Livy's hand. 'Now, for God's sake, don't take it into your head to fall for someone else. I won't be a bit obliging. I'll lock the doors and chain you up. I'll fight to keep you the way only my grandfather knows how to fight. There'll be no question of giving way gracefully. You understand, now?' He leaned over and kissed her.

'I'd better start growing my hair, so my lovers can climb up to visit in my tower. Or start saving sheets, to escape. But it really wouldn't work. I'd come running back. We seem to be stuck with each other.'

'And you can thank God for that,' Ginny said drily.

Chapter 16

1

Chris telephoned Livy from Beverly Hills. 'I'd like to stay a night with you, if it's convenient. I could go to a hotel, but I'd rather be with someone whose shoulder I can cry on a bit, and naturally I'd rather that the press didn't know I was in town. I can't go to Mother and Harry because the embassy's so public, and it wouldn't be fair on her.'

'Of course you can stay here,' Livy said. 'But what's the matter? Why the tears?'

'I'll tell you when I see you. Just don't tell anyone I'm coming. Not Mother. Especially not Alex.'

Chris was in Washington the next day. She had flown all night, but stayed away from the McClintock mansion until she could be reasonably certain that Alex had left. 'I didn't want Alex to know,' she told Livy. 'I'll just have a shower, and change. I'm seeing Mr McClintock at eleven o'clock. Perhaps it wasn't fair of me to come here, because it might seem to the Old Man that Alex is backing me up. But I couldn't face being alone just now.'

'The film?' Livy asked.

'The film might be terrible, or it might just scrape through. That will pretty much depend on what John Cullen can do in the cutting room on the editing. We have to wrap it up by the end of this month or at least we have to be finished with our star, and I'm not talking about Jeff Rigghouse. The mighty box-office draw, Jackson Dunbar, leaves our happy little company then. We'll probably have a week or two more of shooting. Interiors mostly. And back-lot stuff. But I'm paying double time now to the whole crew for extra hours on the lot to get it finished. They're all delighted except the ones who have something else to go to, and I'm holding

646

them up. Or they're just taking their pay and leaving. If we can just keep our principal cameraman; he and John Cullen work very well together, and we need that particular magic desperately. It's about the only thing in the whole damn movie that actually works.'

'It can't be a total washout,' Livy said. 'You've got two big stars, even if you don't think of Jeff that way anymore. And John Cullen has won an Oscar, hasn't he?'

'Twelve years ago. If there's an ounce of justice in the world, he deserves a success. What he won't get, I'm afraid, is a triumph. A triumph wasn't written into the script.'

'So you're here . . .?'

Chris laughed harshly. 'Give me a drink will you, Livy? I'm here to see the Old Man. I'm here to go down on my knees and beg Andrew McClintock for a few million dollars. I need it. We're well over budget, and over time. The studios have to be paid, the crew has to be paid. The last instalment of our fee to the great star comes due the day he leaves, and he'll put a lien on everything we have if he doesn't get it. I'm broke, Livy, and I owe a couple of million dollars. My husband's gambling debts are petty cash by comparison.'

'But can't you borrow from a bank? It'll be hell to go to Andrew McClintock.'

'Don't I know it. I've been to a bank. They're already holding all my McClintock-Clayton stock as collateral, and they're just dying for me not to be able to repay so that they can keep the stock, and edge their way into McClintock-Clayton. You know, Livy, you don't finance movies on the income from stocks. It needs millions. I had a few loose millions that weren't in McClintock-Clayton stock. I've used those up. So I suppose everyone assumed that McClintock-Clayton money was behind it all along. No one but a fool would risk their personal fortune on a movie. They shouldn't, but a lot do. You see, I wanted to show just how good I could be at making money. I wanted to own the whole thing, lock, stock and barrel. It was supposed to be the big movie. But I guess I'm just too inexperienced. All I can see is a lot of jumbled rushes, and a cast who think the whole thing is down the drain. They'll take their money and run, and they'll never boast that they appeared in *The Way West*. But if the film's to be finished at all, I have to have the money.'

'Alex?'

'I couldn't ask Alex. He'd probably give me the money just for the sake of Mother. And I'd feel I'd stolen it from him. No. If I'm to get it, it'll be the hard way. From the Old Man himself. And I haven't any misconceptions. If he gives it to me, just so the movie can be finished, everything will belong to Mr Ambassador Andrew McClintock. Livy, give me another drink will you? I shouldn't have it, but I can't face him without some Dutch courage.'

'Your mother? She'd help.'

Chris shook her head. 'I don't think you know, or possibly you don't remember the details of my father's will. My mother has a large income, a very large one. But the shares that provide it are in trust during her lifetime until they go to Alex. You see, Livy, my father left me my shares outright, after a certain age. And he included shares in other companies which I used to get the film on its way. After all, I am Blair Clayton's only child. He could afford to be generous with me. But to give Ginny a handsome income, but still safeguard McClintock-Clayton, her shares are in an unbreakable trust. They can't be sold by her. You have to remember that my father was *Blair Clayton*. It was a name and a reputation he was proud of. He, like the Old Man, wanted the company closely held.

'My share of my father's estate was small by comparison to hers. So when I was twenty-five, I got control of it. And look what I did with it! No, I can't go to Mother. Can I ask her to sell a few paintings, my father's greatest joy? Will I ask her to flog her jewellery? If you do that in a hurry, it doesn't raise much cash because everyone knows you need the cash. After restoring Tresillian, she's going to have to be a little careful with her money. I couldn't ask her, Livy. I just couldn't ask her!' Mutely she held out her glass to be refilled. 'It's important that Alex doesn't know I'm going to the Old Man. I want your sacred promise, Livy, that when I go upstairs to shower, and gargle away the smell of the booze, you won't rush to the telephone, to Alex. I have to do it my way, Livy. I've told you all this because I had to talk to someone, to get it straight in my head. But the responsibility begins and ends with me. I walked into it. I want to come out with my head up, not bailed out by Alex or my mother. A scrap of pride is about all I've got left.'

Chris came back after two o'clock. Livy had taken only a sandwich lunch, too nervous to try to eat more. She was at the desk in the library with Mrs Tennant, trying to clear up some routine letters, when Chris came in. Mrs Tennant rose at once. 'I'll just start to type these up, Mrs McClintock. Just ring through when you want me again.'

Chris slumped down in the chair Mrs Tennant had just vacated. The light from the big windows behind Livy was directly on her face, which was pale, and drawn in tight lines. She had asked the butler to bring her a drink as she had come in. It was brought, and she took a swift gulp of it. Livy thought she fought against tears.

'Well, I have it. I have the money to finish. The bank is being paid off immediately, and all my McClintock-Clayton shares will belong to the Old Man. He also owns the film, the whole thing. He will absorb the losses and he'll get the profits, if there are any. Or let's say he'll get the gross receipts, because it isn't necessary, really, to show any profits. Jeff was only a nominal partner, more for his pride than anything else. The attorneys who drew up the contract made sure he really didn't get anything but his fee, and the credit as co-producer. They weren't so dumb.'

'Mr McClintock has everything? Your shares and the film?'

'Yes. I gambled with my shares, and I've lost. The movie's probably a dead duck, there might be some returns, since there won't be any outstanding creditors now that I have the money to finish. But that's the end of it for me in the film business, at least as a producer. I just hope there are a few jobs offered to me as an actress.'

Livy said slowly, unable to quite comprehend what she heard, 'You have nothing? No shares, no returns from the film?'

'Nothing, or almost nothing. The Old Man was being magnanimous. He's allowing a small income from a number of the McClintock-Clayton shares to be paid to me quarterly. For my mother's sake, he said, and Blair's. I won't starve or go barefoot. But he's making damn sure I'll never again have the money to get grandiose ideas about being a producer. And I'll never again have enough money to make any man want to marry me for it. I broke all the rules. I gambled with McClintock-Clayton shares. That's not permitted. The only sensible thing I did was finally to go to the Old Man and give him time to buy them back. The unforgivable sin would have been to let them go out of the family.' She took another large gulp of her drink. 'So it's all signed and sealed. There's enough money to finish the picture, and buy time for John Cullen to do a decent job on the editing. And that's it. *Finis*. I'm an out of work actress looking for a job. Of course the Beverly Hills house and the Malibu house are part of the deal. But I've already mortgaged them for as much as I could get. Perhaps the Old Man forgot about the mews in London. Or perhaps he'd prefer that I went back there, and got out from under everyone's feet.'

Livy lifted the telephone to the kitchen, ordered sandwiches and another drink for Chris. What did it matter now? 'Sweet of you, Livy. I don't think I could eat a crumb. The Old Man had some sent to the desk while we hammered all this out, and the first mouthful nearly choked me. But I could use the drink.'

'Chris . . . I don't know what to say.'

'Nothing to say, Livy. I made two terrible blunders. The first was to marry Jeff Rigghouse, and the second followed on that. So as soon as we've finished shooting on the film I'll be taking up quiet residence in Nevada for six weeks, and wait it out for a divorce. I'd go tomorrow, but if I did, what's left of morale on the set would totally fall apart. I'll talk to John Cullen quietly, assure him that he has the backing to do a good job on the editing and then I'll move my things out of the two houses, and advise Jeff he'd better do the same, because when the Old Man pays off the mortgages the two places will belong to McClintock-Clayton. They're good real-estate buys. There shouldn't be any problem disposing of them.' She got up to where she knew the bar was concealed behind false bookshelves. She poured for herself this time, a large drink, neat, without water.

'You'll probably have to pour me on to the plane tomorrow, but at least I can go back with a precious piece of paper I can wave. Money!'

It was only a little after four o'clock when Alex returned home. He came into the library, his face thunderous. The sandwiches lay untouched on a table beside Chris, and she was more than a little drunk.

He dropped gracelessly into a chair opposite her, his expression tense and angry. 'Why on earth didn't you tell me, Chris? I could have helped out with a loan myself. The very least I could have done was hammer out a better deal for you. Damn it! The old scoundrel showed me what you signed. He's skinned you alive! You signed without even having another attorney look at it. Surely you know that contracts that McClintock-Clayton draw up are always in favour of McClintock-Clayton.'

'Hadn't got the time, dear brother. Kind of you, though. Didn't see why I should involve you in my folly. It was none of your making. You would have advised me against it long ago if I hadn't been too damn proud to ask. No, the Old Man won legitimately, if not quite ethically. You see, time wasn't on my side. There wasn't time for attorneys to argue it out. I had to have the money now, or the film would fold. When people finally take their goods to a pawnbroker, they're desperate. I wonder if the Old Man's ever been called a pawnbroker before?'

'You had an hour when you could have talked to me! You could have demanded that I be called to the Old Man's office while those papers were being prepared. There was a little time. I could have done something, Chris.'

Chris sighed, and sipped her drink. Her voice wavered. 'Dear brother – decent of you. Very decent. But I made my own bed. Why shouldn't I get into it? I have a little pride about that, too. And don't you dare blame Livy for not telling you, or I'll never speak to you again. I made her promise. Livy knows a thing or two about pride. She wouldn't strip me of the last I've got left.' She waved her glass towards him. 'You saw, I'm sure, among all those papers I signed, and those he signed, that the old monster has made me an allowance. Fairly generous in the circumstances. It won't keep me in style, but it'll keep me. If little 'ole Chris wants jam on her bread and butter, she'll just have to get out and earn it. You never know, it just might turn me into one hell of a good actress.' Then, slowly, the tears started to slide down her face.

Alex rose, and went to her chair. Awkwardly, he went down on his knees, and took her head and placed it on his shoulder. 'Sorry, Chris. I wish you'd told me. It needn't have been this way . . .'

She raised her head. 'Thanks, Alex. I won't keep anything from you in the future. When I have a future to talk about. Don't tell Mother. Not yet. Don't tell her I've been in Washington. It would hurt her terribly. Try never to let her know the deal the Old Man and I made. Little Chris got to be a woman, and made a woman's decision. Pity it turned out to be such a rotten one.'

Chris returned to the set; she talked at length with John Cullen, and the final scenes were finished. Cullen was worried about a few of the interiors, which he would have liked to reshoot. But the sets had been struck, and the end of February was upon them, and the star departed. Scenes were reshot on the back lot; a feeling had spread through the cast and crew that money was available, and they visibly relaxed. Finally, John Cullen said of the last scene he decided to shoot, 'That's it! Print!'

They had the usual 'wrap' party. Chris and Jeff were showered with congratulations and good wishes. The last thing, privately, Chris said to John Cullen was, 'Take your time with the editing. Make it good! And here is the number of the person you call when you're through.' She gave him the number of Andrew McClintock's private office. 'It all belongs to them, John. They'll have people ready to do whatever has to be done, exhibitors, promotion, everything. They're nothing if not efficient. Good luck.'

He surprised her by giving her the first genuine kiss she had had from any member of the cast or crew. 'You're a sweetheart, Chris. You may have saved my life.'

She said to Jeff in the parking lot, 'I'll be at Malibu for a few days. I'd like you to be gone from Beverly Hills by then. I have some packing to do. Anything that's left behind may end up belonging to Andrew McClintock. Goodbye, Jeff.'

'So long, Baby. Pity. I think you're making a mistake.' He shrugged. She remembered he had been through this scene at least three times with the women he had married, and possibly many more with the women he hadn't married. He had known, without her needing to tell him, that they would part.

'I'll be in Nevada, probably Reno,' she said. 'My attorneys will be in touch. There isn't any such thing as a property settlement, you know. I don't have any property, except some clothes, and I don't suppose you're interested in them.'

'You know, I think you did it deliberately. You handed it all to McClintock so that I'd have to deal with him, not you. He's got a hundred lawyers on retainer, and I can't even get near him.'

'We finished the picture, didn't we, Jeff? At least you'll have a chance to see yourself up there on the screen again. It won't all be filed away in cans.'

'I think you're making a mistake, Baby. It'll be a good movie.'

'I hope so. Goodbye.'

She drove to Malibu, stopping at a shopping centre to pick up some food, and a supply of whisky. For the next three days she lived on sandwiches, topped off with scotch. She locked her car in the garage, so that none of her neighbours would know she was there. She didn't answer the telephone. She walked on the beach only at night when the surrounding darkness told her that everyone should be asleep. The Malibu house was the one thing she minded parting with. She had been tempted to plead with Andrew McClintock to exempt it from the bargain, but pride had not permitted her. It had been all or nothing.

After about a week she called her attorney, went to him to hand over the deeds of both houses to be consigned to McClintock-Clayton, and went for the last time to the Beverly Hills house. Here there were no regrets; she had never liked nor wanted this place. It had all been for Jeff. His closets were empty, and she noticed that some fairly valuable items were missing. Some pieces of jade, two pre-Columbian figures she had been fond of, and a magnificent Persian rug. She shrugged. No inventory had ever been taken, so McClintock-Clayton would not miss them. If Jeff could flog them for some money, good luck to him. It was the last money he would be able to get from her.

She bought a lot of books, mainly classics, and drove to Reno. She found a small, inexpensive motel on the outskirts of the town; it was barren and unlovely. The place had a swimming-pool that seemed hardly larger than the marble bathtub Jeff had had installed in Beverly Hills. There was a little coffee shop next door, and an Italian restaurant next to that. It would be her home for the next six weeks. She followed her attorney's instructions about contacting another attorney he had recommended. After signing some papers, she went back to the motel, and began the six weeks wait until she would be free. She had registered under the name of Mrs Miles Oliver, with a prayer for forgiveness to Livy. She spent her days reading and sleeping. She read the almost forgotten poetry of her youth. She read, more than once, the two small volumes of poetry of Oliver Miles, which she had taken from the Malibu house. She thought often of Tresillian, and the time when these poems had been new to her. She remembered Bess Bromley, and what that bright, energetic mind had tried to impart to four young girls who hadn't then appreciated what they were getting.

She looked at the flame-red Mercedes parked before the door of her motel room. In her mind she began to trace the itinerary of the journey she would make East. She knew she was trying to turn back the clock of her life, and it could never be done completely, but this would have a semblance of a journey to find again some of the innocence and the spirit of the young Chris. She would drive back slowly. She would stop and see places she had only heard of before. She would see the Grand Tetons, the Great Salt Lake, she would stand and listen to the thunder of the Niagara Falls. She would drive down the fishing villages of the East Coast. She would drive far up in the mountains of New York State so that she would not even be within striking distance of Manhattan. By back and slow country roads she would gradually make her way down to Virginia. It would be the American odyssey she had never made before.

From Prescott Hill she would call her mother and Livy and ask if they could come and spend some time with her there. She wanted nothing of Washington. She would exercise, and lap the pool, and give up the booze. She would play with Livy's children. And when she felt she was ready, she would sell the Mercedes, and take a plane for London. In London she would try again.

Then one afternoon, very close to the time when her decree would be granted, she was approached as she sat reading on the porch which ran along the length of the motel. The man was well-dressed in a dark suit, wore dark glasses, and spoke softly. 'Mrs Rigghouse.' It wasn't a question.

'Yes,' she said. He didn't look as if he was from the press, but if he were, what did it matter? Everyone would know in a few days.

'We know you haven't seen your husband for some weeks, but we wondered if he had been in touch with you?'

'What business is that of yours?'

'Do you mind if I sit down?' He gestured to a chair nearby. She nodded curtly. He went on. 'It is more than a little of our business. Your husband has been in Vegas for the last six weeks. He's been gambling quite heavily. Nothing wrong with that, except he's been losing heavily, too. Of course, in the past, the casinos have been happy to extend him credit, because he's been a good customer, and he's always paid up, eventually. They've been continuing to extend credit on the strength of the film you both own that'll shortly be released. We hear it won't be any blockbuster, but his share should redeem his debts, which have grown rather large. Now, we hear from sources other than Mr Rigghouse, that in fact he doesn't own any of the film. That he's had his last payment. We would like to know if that's true.'

'Who are you?'

'It doesn't really matter, Miss Clayton.' The change in her name jarred her. 'I just represent a number of casinos in Vegas who would like their debts settled.'

She shook her head. 'It's useless coming to me, and I won't bother asking how you found me. The film doesn't belong either to Jeff or to me. All the rights in it were sold to keep it in production, and get it finished.'

'Well, then, other assets. The two houses.'

'They've gone to the same source who loaned the money. Neither of them were in Jeff's name. I once owned them. I don't any longer.'

'And that source? We've been to the bank who supplied the first capital. They assure us all debts have been repaid.'

'Then guess,' she said shortly. She was angry, and was beginning to be afraid. There was almost positive identification between organized crime and most of the casinos in Nevada. She was uneasily aware of the dark good looks of this well-dressed stranger, whose eyes she couldn't see. His tone was detached, but in that very detachment there was a kind of menace. He was not the sort of mobster who carried a gun. He was one of their smooth-spoken attorneys.

'Well, I would make my first guess McClintock-Clayton.'

'Right first time. How clever.'

'Then you really do still own the movie, the houses . . .'

'You obviously don't know Andrew McClintock. I own nothing. I'm living in this place by courtesy of Mr McClintock who has generously given me an allowance you would call peanuts, so that I don't embarrass the family by being picked up as destitute. If you take time to look up the real estate records in LA, you'll see what's been transferred to McClintock-Clayton. Copies of the papers I signed in Washington are on file with my attorney in LA. I'll call him if you like, and tell him that you may see them. That is, if I'm permitted to know your name.'

He rose. 'I really don't think that will be necessary. I believe you, Miss Clayton. We made a few enquiries before I came here. What you say seems to corroberate the information we have. Just checking to make sure. Your husband's debts amount to quite a sum. It's a bad example to other gamblers if one of them is seen to walk away from debts like that.'

'In two days he won't be my husband. I don't care what he told you, he knew from the beginning there was no money.'

'Gamblers are a strange breed, Miss Clayton. They always come back. My clients should have done a bit more investigating before they let him start. But the magic of the McClintock name goes far. The casinos can absorb the loss. It is only a theoretical loss. The mistake was in letting him go so far that other people knew the scale of his losses.'

'Please don't lecture me on the psychology of gamblers. I've already had too much experience of that. And as for the mistakes the casinos made. Their mistakes, not mine. I made mine a long time ago.'

'Thank you for your time, Miss Clayton. You've been very helpful. And candid. If you had had any other story to tell . . . well, you didn't. Do you mind?' He reached down and picked up the book she had been reading, looking at its spine.

'Ah, yes . . . Walt Whitman. I'm quite a fan of him myself. Good day, Mrs Oliver.'

She wondered how many other smooth, well-educated lawyers the mobs hired. Many, she thought. Maybe her own lawyer hadn't minded disclosing what should have been confidential information. Perhaps he had been frightened, too. Well, they knew they could get nothing from her, and they couldn't even get near Andrew McClintock. No pleas for Jeff Rigghouse would get a hearing from him. They would just have to hope that *The Way West* would be a success, and that Jeff would get more offers of parts. But he'd be barred from every casino in Nevada, and he'd be in hock for the rest of his life.

She had come out of the whole mess just a little better. At least she had the money to eat.

Two evenings later she routinely picked up a copy of the *Los Angeles Times* as she went into the Italian restaurant. As soon as her regular waitress saw her she brought her her usual scotch, but this time Chris realized that it had to be a double. 'I'm real sorry, Miss Clayton. Real sorry. It's been a privilege to know you.'

Chris thought she was referring to the divorce, which had been granted that morning. 'Oh, you know . . .'

'Oh, sure I knew. I saw that first movie you made. Saw it about four times. You looked a lot like a sister of mine – same sort of story, too. Born loser, she was. I cried . . . But I guess this is a real bad day for you. Fact is, I didn't expect to see you here tonight. I thought they'd want you down in Vegas . . .'

'What for?'

The woman's expression changed abruptly. 'Thought you'd have known by now. The LA paper comes late. The Reno daily's got it splashed all over the front page . . . 'scuse me. Got a customer waiting . . .'

Chris gulped at the drink, grateful for its size, and briefly scanned the front page of the *Los Angeles Times*. It was a small item at the bottom of the page. The *Times* did not go in for sensationalism.

The body of the film actor, Jeff Rigghouse, was discovered this morning on a dirt road leading out of Las Vegas. He had a single bullet wound to the temple. No weapon was found, and no vehicle was near the scene. The police are treating it as homicide.

She had drunk the whisky in the Italian restaurant, staring at her own reflection in a window; she had paid and left, without ordering any food. She took her car, which she'd hardly used in these six weeks, and headed south on Route 395 towards Tahoe. She had circled the lake twice before she realized it. She was back at the strip of casinos just over the state line from California. Before she left this blazing patch of light, she noticed that the car was almost out of gasoline. While the attendant filled the tank, she walked across the road to a liquor store and bought a fifth of scotch. Then, as she rounded the lake again she suddenly swung off on to Route 98 into the Tahoe National Forest. Up there was Mount Lola, more than nine thousand feet high. She found a place to pull off the highway, and switched off the engine. The air was thin, the night cool and clear; she shivered a little, and slumped down in the seat so that she could see the stars. They seemed huge and pulsing in the clear night sky. She reached for the scotch, unscrewed the top, and drank straight from the bottle.

She wondered if it had been night when they had murdered Jeff, if the stars in the cold desert had been the last things he saw. Or had it been sunrise? Had he been terribly afraid, or hadn't he believed it was actually going to happen? Had he thought they had taken him on that ride just to frighten him, and would abandon him far out in the desert and tell him to keep on walking? He might have believed it until the last minutes. Gambler's luck. He had always been lucky.

She drank from the bottle again. Could she have done anything? She had told that quietly-spoken man that she was broke, and that all her assets belonged to Andrew McClintock. Going to Andrew McClintock to pay off Jeff Rigghouse's gambling debts they knew was useless. But she hadn't done anything to help him, hadn't even asked how much he owed. She hadn't believed they could do anything more terrible than rough him up, at the worst, and ban him from every casino in the state. But the man had threatened no reprisal, had mentioned no punishment. If he had done that, she could have telephoned Alex. Alex would have helped in some way. Even though he despised Jeff, he would have warded off a sentence so terrible. The guilt for what she had not done seemed to crush against her heart like a weight. She could at least have lifted a telephone; she could have asked more questions. She could have pleaded for time . . . for anything they would give. The mysterious 'they'. The hit men who would have no known connections with the casino owners. They had chosen Jeff because he was famous; the news of the ultimate punishment would spread like wildfire through the gambling fraternity. Vegas did not like those who played, lost, and could not pay.

She drank again and wept and drank. It was cold, and she had never felt so alone. Some rational part of her said it would have happened, one way or another. Only this one time she might have been able to help. But there would have been another time, and another. But rational thought and guilt were warring partners in her heart, and for tonight guilt was much stronger. She drank until the bottle was two-thirds empty, watching the cold stars, thinking of the man she had once believed she loved. In the early hours of the morning, exhaustion and the drink overcame her. She slumped across the seat and fell asleep.

The sun woke her, but she was still cold. Her body felt stiff and painful; for a second she wondered where she was, and why – stretched out on the seat of a car in this wilderness. She slowly crawled out of the car, walked around to stretch her numbed limbs. The brightness of the sun smote her eyes; her head throbbed unbearably. She got back into the car, started up the engine, uncertainly eased her way back on to the highway, her eyes screwed up into slits to try to ease the pain. She thought of the motel room, and darkness, longingly. She had to get there quickly. In her hurry she shot straight across Highway 80 which led back to Reno. The blast of the horn of another car on Highway 80 told her that she had crossed without stopping. She backed and turned around, and this time stopped dead before entering the main road. It was still early; there were few vehicles. The thought of a shower and bed. She would leave the telephone off the hook. She tried to think about how she would talk to the police about the man who had come the day before yesterday. Yes, that's what she'd do – when she had slept, when she felt better. She was approaching Reno. She would soon be there. Darkness, oblivion, how she longed for them. Unwittingly she pressed her foot more firmly on the accelerator. The houses were now close together. Automobiles were parked along the street. The turning to the motel was three blocks down, or was it four? She tried to read the numbers, but she couldn't see properly. She certainly didn't see the child on the tricycle until she was almost on top of him. He shot out of a driveway between two parked cars, peddling vigorously. Even in her fogged state she knew it was too late for the brakes; with all the strength of the reflexes she still possessed, she jerked at the wheel, away from the child. She missed him, side-swiped a parked car on the other side of the road, bounced off it, and ricochetted across the road again and hit a telephone pole. There was searing pain, a burst of flame; and then the blackness, the oblivion for which she had longed.

2

A pall hung on them all after Chris's death. Ginny seemed wrapped in silent grief which could find no outlet. She did only the most necessary entertaining at the embassy, and no one expected more of her. For almost three months she did not attend any reception outside the embassy, but asked Livy to accompany Harry when she thought one of the family should be with him. Quite unexpectedly, Rachel had come to Washington to attend Chris's burial at Prescott Hill. She had come unannounced; simply turned up in a taxi at the McClintock mansion. 'I had to come,' she said to Livy. 'I have such a terrible sense of guilt. We all let her grow away from us . . .'

'Don't say that to Ginny or Alex. They feel too much that way already. Alex seems to think he's solely responsible. He thinks he should have been able to do something . . . once he found out what she'd turned over to Mr McClintock to save that wretched film.'

'No one could have saved Jeff Rigghouse from himself. If Chris's death . . . Oh, God, we'll never know what was in her mind . . .'

No one ever knew about the child on the tricycle. He had screamed in terror when the car had crashed into another across the road, then hit the telephone pole. He had turned and cycled back into his yard, calling to his mother. She and his father were only two of the many who rushed out from the neighbouring houses to try to help; the child had stayed behind, whimpering softly.

The autopsy on Christine Clayton had shown the level of alcohol in her blood, and the fact that she hadn't eaten for many hours. The waitress at the Italian restaurant had gone to the police and told them what she knew, of her last sight of the woman who had called herself Mrs Oliver, but who she had known was Christine Clayton. Because of the double tragedy of the deaths of Christine Clayton and Jeff Rigghouse, the newspapers had carried the story prominently. The gas station attendant had studied the photograph in the paper, and told the police he had gassed up her car that night, and that the lady had gone into the liquor store. The liquor store clerk remembered her because of a trace of a British accent. The driver of the car she had nearly collided with at the intersection of Route 80 had not had a chance to get the licence number, but he remembered the colour and make of the car. He gave evidence at the inquest. 'Didn't see her face, but I knew it was a woman. Tore across the highway like a bat out of hell. I damn nearly ploughed right into her. It wouldn't have been my fault if we'd both been killed. I was so goddamn mad I would have gone after her, and reported her, but I had an appointment in town . . .'

When the news of the deaths of both Chris Clayton, whom he had admired, and of Jeff Rigghouse, whom he thought of as a man with potential whose character had been pulled awry by too early and easy success, reached John Cullen in his retreat in Mexico, he had poured himself a whisky. It hadn't tasted good. He tossed it down the sink, and went out and watched the sunset. She'd given him a chance, and he'd given her his all.

Mark arrived in Washington at the start of the summer holidays. Even in the bustle of the embassy, a small core of silence and sadness seemed to entrap the Ambassador and his wife. As often as Harry could manage he went to Prescott Hill with Ginny, but the relentless pressure of the work kept up. 'I'm a glorified salesman,' was how he put it, but it was truly his job and his staff's to ease the way of any businessman who was trying to sell in America. The commercial attaché was the member of the staff most often in his office. Harry wrote introductions, he made speeches, he entertained delegations, and he did it that year with a sore heart. There was something in the tragedy of Chris's death that had not been present in Blair's, the sense that it was a death that could have been averted; it could have been stopped if there had been someone to reach out to her.

The summer heat descended on Washington. They spent languid weekends at Prescott Hill, and sometimes Ginny did not return to the embassy during the week. She never spoke of going to Tresillian; she seemed to have no plans except to keep functioning, with little interest or enthusiasm in anything. 'Poor Mark,' she said to Livy. 'It must be so boring for him. And he's so good about it. He rides by himself, and laps the pool endlessly, and always seems cheerful, makes an effort to cheer me up. I wish I could do something for him.'

'He knows you love him. That's all he ever wants.'

Andrew McClintock seemed to have retreated into his own world. He seldom visited Livy and Alex, never attended functions at the embassy, to which, however, he was always invited; rarely, and only on Ginny's insistence, did he come to Prescott Hill. Ginny's initial rage at his treatment of Chris had simmered down to resentment. 'I don't know why I should have expected any different. He's always been that way. Capriciously generous, but in business, always fighting for a bargain. I suppose I should think him generous even to have given her an allowance. He could have left her without a cent. He's an old man . . . I've coped with him all my adult life. It isn't fair to abandon him now.'

But her forgiveness wasn't complete, and sensing something in Ginny which had never been there before, Andrew McClintock stayed away.

It was that summer that Ginny's father's life finally came to a close. More and more, as strength failed him, he had retreated into a secluded life at Pointerstown, sustained by his son Robbie, and his wife, visits from Robbie's children and from Ginny. He had spent his last afternoon rocking gently on the tall shaded porch of Pointerstown with Ginny and Mark, and had quietly slipped away during the night. 'He gave up too easily,' Andrew McClintock said to Alex, and Alex knew his grandfather was remembering that he was one year older than Senator Jackson.

3

Alex had intensified his long struggle with his grandfather to go public with McClintock-Clayton. 'He just can't seem to accept that even he hasn't enough money to go on expanding, to go on with research, and the new products we need, without more borrowing, and that means inviting the public in. It would be a share issue that Clayton's in London could handle. We could sell many millions worth of shares, and still keep a comfortable control of the company. But he can't bear the thought that anyone but he and the family, and a few of the directors, should have any stock. That was what he couldn't forgive Chris. She risked some of it going to that bank. Now, for example, there's a beautiful, rather small electronics company in Texas which we could use very well. It could be bought. But we'd have to borrow again. I keep watching. There are companies here and there, ones that would mesh very well into our group. They need capital, they're ripe for take-over, and we need their particular expertise. And we're strapped for cash.'

'I never thought I'd hear that said of McClintock-Clayton.'

Alex sighed in frustration. 'The well isn't bottomless. I agree with the Old Man in certain respects. I know how far we can borrow and still be safe. But if we went public, we'd have money to do the things we must do if we're not to wither, and die of conservatism. In the new technology, we'd better be with it, or we're dead. It's all changing so quickly. Livy. In defence contracts we're not getting the orders we should because we're not coming up with the right ideas. In pharmaceuticals we're holding our own, but just barely. Steel is dying, and we should cut back there, but the Old Man has a sentimental attachment to what first started his father, and on which he built. We've moved our textiles to the South, to save money, but we're watching the Far East, because they can do it much cheaper there. If only he'd go public. Do I have to wait until he's dead before I can see that day? By then it might be too late. We might have missed the boat. We have the chance to remain one of the great diversified companies of the world. But if we don't move, in a few years we might be moribund.'

Livy smiled quietly. 'Then that would give me the chance to support you! I have the cottage in St Just. And Mr McClintock has carefully diversified my stocks, so if the mighty McClintock-Clayton shrunk to a dwarf, we could still eat.'

He reached over and touched her cheek. 'My lovely Livy. What a lot of good you do me. You bring me down to earth. I sometimes think that that may have been how your father regarded your mother. A lifeline, an anchor. You see, he must have been physically frail, as I've become. Since I passed thirty, dragging this body around with me, I've thought a lot about your father. How he must have relied on Isa, loved her in many different ways, for many different reasons. Livy, I've been thinking . . .'

'Yes?'

'Why don't we take that honeymoon we never had? You're a woman of wide education, and yet you've never walked some of the great galleries of the world. You know the Paris Embassy, and therefore the Paris galleries. But you've never been to Vienna or Venice. Between looking after me, and having babies, we've kept you chained. Let's take off for a few weeks, for a month. There's too much sorrow and mourning here.'

'The babies?'

'Forget the babies for once. There are plenty of people to take care of them. My mother would be delighted to have them at Prescott Hill. Looking after them, amusing them, might take her mind off Chris for a time. Mark would be delighted to help her. Let's go and look at what's been reconstructed since the war. We're almost into the sixties . . . It's time you and I saw what's happening.'

She knew it was an expression of his frustration with his grandfather, but she welcomed this return to a youthfulness he seemed to have left behind him forever. There was no mention of Tresillian or Seymour House or any of the traditional things they had both known. And yes, he was right. There never had been a honeymoon.

Chapter 17

1

They did as he suggested. They went first to Vienna. It was still trying to repair itself after the battering of the war, as was almost every other great city they saw. The galleries and opera houses and palaces, the cathedrals of Milan, Munich, Cologne, were being restored. Florence and Venice were the easiest to enjoy, because so much of their beauty could be seen by just standing in a piazza, or riding in a gondola. Livy soon realized that more than a few rooms of a great gallery were beyond Alex's strength. In cathedrals he would take a seat at the back and let her wander. It brought the fact crushingly home to her that there was so much he would never see, except from catalogues, or from small salerooms. He was not blind, but he was lame: palaces and galleries were alike to him. He could not drag himself beyond the first few rooms. He would sternly send her on. 'You have to be my eyes, Livy. I'll buy the catalogues, and you'll have to report to me where they went wrong with the colour, and how the thing really looked.' He absolutely refused the use of a wheelchair.

When she saw that he could do no more, they retreated to an island off Venice, Torcello, where a very small hotel, owned by a great and famous one in the city itself, had only four rooms for guests. For lunch hundreds came there, by water taxi and vaporetto. But at night, the whole island was deserted except for the few people who worked for the hotel, and the fishermen who hung on to its small coast-line. Livy and Alex occupied the suite of rooms where, the proprietor told them, Hemingway had come to avoid the distractions of the city across the lagoon, and finish a book. 'Alas,' he said, 'not a very good book.'

They had silence and sun, and at dusk, mosquitoes. They ate out under an arbour of ripening grapes, and the quiet was something almost palpable; in the early morning they would walk to the small church near the hotel. Strangely, for this tiny congregation, there was always a priest celebrating mass. The ninth-century cathedral next to it had a great Madonna in golden mosaic in need of restoration. 'Now, I'd like to have the money to do something about that,' Alex said. 'But my grandfather would never hear of it. It wouldn't belong to him.'

In the face of the August heat they retreated finally to St Just. They stayed at Livy's cottage, went up the hill to Tresillian, picnicked in the orchard near Bully's gravestone. They inspected the house, but did not stay there. Livy's cottage was small and homely, and with the help of her family, it ran smoothly. She was more than ever grateful for what Bess Bromley had done to renovate and extend it. Alex did not have to pull himself up the difficult and steep stairs. They spent their days peacefully, visiting Livy's cousins and their abounding children, driving through the country, coming to rest at the end of lonely, unsurfaced roads which only served the local farmers; evenings were spent with Thea. As they gazed out on the dangerously wild, beautiful panorama of the Cornish coast, Alex said, 'I expect you'll always keep coming, won't you, Livy? You so much belong here that it shows in your face. Your eyes reflect the sea. Your voice changes when you talk to your family.'

'If Chris . . .' she began slowly. 'If only Chris had had some place like this that was truly her own, where people accepted her, no matter what, she might have been saved. The rich seldom have places like that.'

'Prescott Hill . . .' he ventured, but only half-heartedly.

She shook her head, and her hand closed on his. 'Prescott Hill is McClintock territory. She had her house in London, and that was all. It wasn't enough.'

They stayed a few days at Seymour House before returning to Washington, and Alex again took up the reins of the McClintock-Clayton business. There were many cables from Andrew McClintock to be read, and answered, the usual matters that had become his life to go into, investigate, discuss, decide. He found a mood of near rebellion among the board of Clayton's Bank, and even in the Swiss directors who had come to attend meetings. The need for McClintock-Clayton to expand, to acquire more capital for research and development was evident, but Andrew McClintock still blocked it. Alex promised, once more, to try to change the Old Man's mind. He looked around the boardroom. 'I'll do it, even if I have to threaten to resign.' He added, 'I don't doubt some of you might welcome that.'

Livy gave dinner parties for the directors of Clayton's, and other business people it was useful for Alex to see. She suddenly was aware how much the weeks they had taken away from Washington had helped him. He did not now appear to be the man who could explore only a few rooms of a gallery. He was tanned and invigorated. As she listened to him in conversation with those he was either in partnership with, or was about to do battle with, she saw no signs, except the ones obvious to everyone, of frailty. 'He looks as much a buccaneer as ever his grandfather was,' Rachel observed, the night she and Frazer Campbell came to dinner. 'Black eye patch and all.'

Livy was surprised at the interested, if not wholly warm, reception Frazer Campbell received among the banking fraternity. Rachel waved her hand in dismissal when Livy commented on this. 'It's all one world. If there were a revolution tomorrow, if the Labour Party were in power, and Frazer were Chancellor, all these people would want to know him. They'd want to remember some things he said. They'd want to claim some knowledge about him . . . In politics, and in business, you never turn down an opportunity to learn to know your enemy.'

'They're really enemies? Frazer still feels so strongly?'

Rachel paused for a moment and let her eyes rove around the vast and beautiful hall of Seymour House, which they were crossing on their way to the drawing-room. The spiral staircase swept upwards in all its simple beauty, the Adam fireplace, lovingly restored after the war, gleamed as if the master craftsmen had just put down their tools; Blair's great collection of Impressionist paintings still hung there, and in the drawing-room, splendidly lighted.

'No, he wouldn't tear down all this. It would just simply belong to the people. It would be the museum it really is. People would be free to come and see it, not just enter its portals by invitation . . .' Her voice was slightly dreamy, as if she could envisage the future. Livy was strongly reminded of the great golden Madonna of Torcello, the beauty which still belonged to anyone who cared to walk into the basilica. It could never be owned by an Andrew McClintock or a Blair Clayton.

The next evening they had Caroline and Sir Bruce Abbott to dinner, with a guest list that reflected more than Clayton's Bank; it still amazed Livy how readily an invitation to Seymour House was accepted, even at short notice. Caroline looked beautiful in a carefully-tended, expensive way. She checked her appearance in the long mirror in the cloak-room, looking at Livy behind her. 'Livy, dear, I hope you don't get blowsy when you're thirty-five.'

Livy looked into the famous icy-hot eyes that Harry had bequeathed to his younger daughter, looked at her trim, exercised body, the immaculate hair, lips, nails. 'I hope not, too,' she answered.

On her last day in London she went to see her father's publishers, Venables. The elder Venables was now dead, the one Dena had dealt with. His son had come back from the war in hardly better shape than Alex, except that he had both eyes. He came down to the reception room to meet her, and, far less agilely than Alex, climbed the stairs after her to his office. They sat at a desk that Livy realized must have survived the bombing of their original premises. It was scarred and battered, and no one had tried to restore it, as if it were a frayed and honoured battle flag.

He tapped the manuscript on the desk. Livy had sent it, without Alex's knowledge, before they began their trip. 'I hardly know what to say, Mrs McClintock. It's a fairy story, a child's story, and yet it's every bit as much an adult story. A fantasy, an allegory. Your *Kingdom of the Sea* could belong in any time, in any place. Its loves and hates, the wars, triumphs and defeats belong as much in our time as they did in the time that never was, where you've placed them. There's beauty and wisdom in it, Mrs McClintock. I think your father would have been proud of you. But I don't think we should publish it.'

She experienced the disappointment she had always expected would come. 'It isn't good enough. I wrote it for my children . . .' She tried to shrug it off. 'Well, it's only a first attempt. Perhaps I'll move on to something that is publishable.'

He held up his hand to silence her. 'I didn't mean that. What I meant was that I don't think it's for Venables. We could do it. We could find an excellent illustrator. It will make a beautiful book. Brought to the attention of the right people, it could get wonderful reviews. But we're so small, you see. It would be regarded by the trade as a specialized literary work, with a small potential market. It would be praised and it would sell a few thousand copies. It deserves more than that, I think.'

'That is what Lady Camborne told me your father said to her about *This England*. Look what he did with it, in the end.'

'With help, Mrs McClintock. With the help and backing of Andrew McClintock.'

'No!' Livy said sharply. 'I won't have that. No one knows this book exists. One day I'll read it to my children, but I won't have it published because Andrew McClintock thinks it should be published. It's my own . . .' she said defensively.

He sighed. 'Well . . . there's such a thing as co-publishing. We could actually handle it editorially, arrange for the printing, the illustrator, all that sort of thing. It would have to be a very beautiful book visually. And if we can interest one of the big boys, the one with the promotion department, the big sales-force, the one who knows how to generate the excitement and interest in the media.'

'All I want is for it to be published.'

'It deserves more than that. Will you trust me with it? I'll pass it on to one or two people whose judgement I respect, but who are highly commercial. If they don't see it the way

I do, then Venables will gladly publish it, in our own rather quiet fashion, and just hope that some critics will notice it, and praise it highly enough to generate some excitement. But I'd rather take the other course. I want to make the public notice it. After all, Mrs McClintock, we owe your father's memory a great deal. *This England* gave us a best-seller such as we've never had before. Publishing in small firms is always a struggle. *This England* kept us going at a difficult time. Will you leave it with me for a while?'

She went away only half-satisfied, and a little afraid. She hadn't minded sending her book, a fairy tale spun in the swirling mists of ancient Celtic times, the story of a kingdom of land and sea which had no physical counterpart, except that it was peopled by two warring races of Celts; it was all the Cornish legends she had ever heard, mixed with the legend of Arthur and his knights, of Tristan and Iseult; there was love and jealousy and death. She had meant it for Jamie and Oliver, but as she had written it, she had not been certain that they should hear or read it until they were grown up.

So she left it with Mr Venables, and returned to Washington, prepared to let the book find its own way, glad it was finished and out of her hands.

They found Ginny in better spirits. Jamie and Oliver had absorbed so much of her time that there had been little left for brooding over Chris. Her pleasure in seeing them was evident. 'It's done Alex a world of good, Livy. You must try to do it each year. He can't give his whole life to McClintock-Clayton.'

She asked them for a family dinner at the embassy the evening after their return. 'It's time I took up my chores again. Everyone has been very indulgent, but an ambassador's wife is expected to work.' For the first time since Chris's death, Andrew McClintock accepted an invitation to dinner with Ginny and Harry. He had remained in semi-seclusion all summer, working quietly at his office or at home. He seemed to Livy somewhat thinner, and more stooped, his old face sere and lined.

'Well, you've been gallivanting around as a young couple should. I'm pleased to see that it seems to suit you.'

'Does that mean that you now think Alex is fit enough so that you can start to work him to death again?'

'Alex is free to go tomorrow if he wants to. He's rich enough. If he chooses to stay . . .'

Livy nodded her head. 'I know. He's a McClintock. It's in the blood. What would he do if he left? He'd be bored silly.'

'I know exactly what I'd do,' Alex answered. 'I'd grow roses, I'd buy a vineyard, and cultivate the vines. I'd help restore the Madonna of Torcello.'

After dinner they had coffee in Ginny's private sitting-room. Harry poured port for Mr McClintock, brandy for the rest of them. He had been very quiet through dinner, just listening to what Alex and Livy had to tell. Livy still hugged to herself the secret of *The Kingdom of the Sea*. She would tell them when, and if, something came of it.

Andrew McClintock began in what was, for him, almost a diffident manner. 'There are some things I think I should now tell you about Christine's film, *The Way West*. It has been edited and cut. It has been musically scored. I have seen it myself, but having little judgement of these things, I invited the heads of some studios and some big distributors to view it also. I sensed the thing was right, and they agree. I have a contract with a major distribution chain. They tell me, and they should know, that the direction is first rate. Almost inspired, given that the script was not promising. And John Cullen found a young man to do the musical score. He's written a theme that the professionals say sweeps the whole film on. Not a song, a theme. And . . .' He could not help his face puckering with the same distaste he had always shown towards the man. 'They tell me Jeff Rigghouse has turned in an excellent performance. He almost outshines the star. They say he's certain to get a nomination for best supporting actor.'

The news fell into the silence like a stone. No one said anything. It was left to Andrew McClintock to continue.

'I am advised that all-out promotion is the thing for this film. I have engaged the right people to do it. It could be, they tell me, what is the word they use? Big box-office? It

673

seems this Cullen man has rescued it. With luck, and the right promotion, it might even be nominated for an Academy Award.'

'These professionals,' Alex said. 'Are they saying this because you are paying them to promote it? Are they suckering you in?'

The old man's face twisted in a bleak smile. 'I'm too long in the game, Alex, to be "suckered in". These are the distributors. It is *their* money, their movie houses. If the film is a flop, they stand to lose money. If it is the success they expect it to be, we all make money.'

'Out of Chris's film. Poor little Chris. You cheated her out of the lot, didn't you?' Alex said. 'You took her shares away from her, and you took her film. You may have taken her life.'

Andrew McClintock heaved himself to his feet, and stood leaning on his cane. 'I gave her the money to finish her film. What happened after that was none of my doing. If she had lived she would have enjoyed a triumph, and that dissolute creature, Jeff Rigghouse, would have paid off his debts to the mob. Only to contract more debts.' He looked around the room. 'I am no one's keeper. You all make your own decisions. If I am involved, I try to see that they are the right decisions. Good evening. Don't trouble to see me out, Harry. I know the way.'

Ginny sat on the sofa, Harry's arm about her, and wept quietly. 'My poor Chris . . . my poor Chris,' she murmured. 'We didn't help her. We didn't even try.'

'We didn't even know,' Alex said.

'That makes it worse. We should have known . . . we should have asked . . .'

The summer seemed over and finished. The gloom of the bright spring day when Chris had died was back with them. Livy thought this was not the time to tell them, as she had not yet even told Alex, that she was now certain that she was expecting a baby.

In November *The Way West* was released, and it received a generally favourable, if not ecstatic press. But in the cutting room John Cullen had spliced together scenes that were memorable, in the shooting he had extracted from Jeff Rigghouse a performance no one believed he had left in him. Even Christine Clayton had moments when she came to life and showed the talent which made her two earlier films a success with the critics. And it was true what Andrew McClintock had reported of the score. The young, virtually unknown composer, Daniel Seeburg, had produced a theme of brooding power and beauty, something audiences remembered after they had left the cinemas. It, and its variations, knit together the skein of the film. It was as if he and the director had thought with one mind, and their union was perfect.

In every major city the advertising for the movie was extravagant and nearly omnipresent. It became a movie to go and see. The violent deaths of two of its principals that had made such shocking news reading, the fading star and the rising star, added a kind of prurient interest. Audiences looked at their doomed faces, and the lesson that neither money nor fame and power had saved them. It was a potent mix of sensationalism and tragedy, and *The Way West* played to packed houses, and was held over for many weeks longer than even the most optimistic distributors had hoped.

'I hear on the grapevine,' Alex told Livy, 'that the film could even get a nomination for an Academy Award. Not much of a chance of winning, but its popularity will probably put it there. And, of course, there's the sympathy vote. A kind of last tribute to Jeff Rigghouse, and to Chris who had the courage to go ahead and make it, and stick with it, even when she knew she'd got in over her head. Well, we'll see. And the Old Man thinks he did it.'

By then Livy was past the difficult months of pregnancy; she felt well, and excited by the prospect of the child. 'Let's hope it's a girl,' Alex said. 'It would do our two little bully-boys good to have a sister.'

Livy just smiled. The dynastic requirements had been fulfilled in Jamie and Oliver. She didn't care what the coming child would be, so long as it was healthy. She had never been so happy in a pregnancy before. The child, she believed, had

675

been conceived in the peace and stillness of Torcello, had been growing as a tiny creature within her during those brief idyllic days in Cornwall. In its blood would be the pearly mists of the Venice lagoon, and the tearing of the sea against the Tresillian Rocks.

There was something else to make her happy. She had received word from George Venables that the first publisher, Harold Harding, to whom he had shown *The Kingdom of the Sea*, had been very pleased and intrigued with it. 'Perhaps,' George Venables had reported him saying, 'this is something we need for our late spring list. Something totally different. It could be a flop, but there's a chance of a great success.' With extra money in hand, Venables had hired an illustrator who was regarded as a minor genius in his field.'

Livy's joy faded when, through a chance remark the co-publisher, Harold Harding, made to a fellow dinner guest, a director of Clayton's Bank, the news about the work of Olivia Miles was passed on to Andrew McClintock. Andrew McClintock asked his grandson about it, and when he learned that Alex knew nothing about publication plans, he had himself driven at once to visit Livy. He was quite gentle, as if he feared upsetting a pregnant woman or perhaps, Livy thought, he may have learned something from the way he had dealt with Chris.

'My dear,' he said, 'this is very good news. But I know nothing about it. Nor does Alex, except that he knew you were doing a bit of writing. But now it's being published. You've told none of us about it.'

She waved her hand impatiently. 'It's a bit of nonsense. A fairy story. Full of hobgoblins and unicorns and witches, and warriors and damsels in distress. I wrote it for the children.'

'From what I hear, Harding doesn't publish fairy stories. I'd like to read it.'

'I didn't know you read fairy stories, Mr McClintock.'

Within a short time he had gathered all the information about publication plans, and even had received a copy of the manuscript, and the preliminary sketches for the illustrations. He made the almost unprecedented move of going to see Alex in his own office. 'I haven't read it yet, but Harding is very enthusiastic. And the illustrator is top of the ladder in his field. But they've made no plans for American publication. They say they're waiting for a finished book so that the whole package can be shown together. Well, that seems to me to be wasting time. If it's going to be a best-seller, it will do better, be bigger news, if it's a best-seller on both sides of the Atlantic. And we haven't much time unless we buy sheets from Harding's . . . And that won't do. That's what they do with high-priced art books of which they only sell a few thousand copies between them. Livy's book has to do much better than that.'

'Have you read it?' Alex asked.

'No. But what does that matter? Professionals have. Hard-headed professionals. We must arrange a publisher here at once.'

'I don't think Livy would like you to arrange anything. I think you would be wise, Grandfather, to leave this strictly alone.'

'I didn't leave *This England* alone.'

'This is different. This is Livy's own, very personal thing. Let it take its chances. She knows enough about the business to know what they are. For God's sake, for once . . .' Alex rose to his feet, as if he wanted to terminate the discussion. 'For once, I beg you, don't arrange things. Let them just happen! Now, if you'll excuse me, I have a meeting. They're waiting . . .'

Andrew McClintock had not been dismissed from someone's presence since he had been a child. His face twisted with anger.

'You know very well, Alex. Things do not happen. If they do, they are nearly always a mess. They are better arranged.'

'Just for once in your life, can't you let something just happen? Let it happen to Livy. It's her work, her imagination. Let her have the joy of something happening because she's Olivia Miles, not Alex McClintock's wife! Don't interfere in something so precious. You're risking too much!'

Alex never told Livy of the interview with his grandfather, but he did read a copy of the manuscript sent to him from

677

Andrew McClintock's office. He read it and wondered and yet understood. He understood both Livy's reluctance to have any interference from McClintock-Clayton; he also began to understand his grandfather's attitude. The book had a certain strange, fantastical magic about it. It was the sort of thing that might go entirely unnoticed and unread; but it could also generate a cult following. It made no claim to the conventions of adult fiction. In this way, it was a truly original piece of work and might just succeed as such.

He told Livy he had read the manuscript, and how he had come by it. 'If you'd offered it to me, I would have been more prepared for the Old Man's reaction. I could have been two jumps ahead of him.'

'But I wanted something just of my own, something that would owe nothing to the McClintock name, or anyone else's.'

'Then, my darling, you should have submitted it under another name than Olivia Miles. You should have taken that heart-breaking journey through dozens of publishers who could have turned it down without reading it. It might never have been published . . .'

'But Venables . . . they're not that sort of firm.'

'Any publisher worth the name should know what is good, and when it is written by someone called Olivia Miles, he would be mad not to exploit it. There is no sentiment in business, Livy. You should know that by now. Not even in small, old, gentlemanly firms like Venables. They have to make their bread and butter to stay alive . . .'

'You're on his side. You'll take it away from me.'

'No, my darling. It's already been taken away from you. You can't stop the process now – not unless you cancel the whole thing, and make up the money so far spent on it. You can't do that, Livy. You can't just kill it. It's your work, yours alone. Far more than the child you're carrying. I had something to do with that . . .'

Within two weeks an American publisher offered a contract, a very generous contract, with a large promotion budget. Alex read it over, and nodded his approval. Livy wasn't sure that it hadn't all been arranged by him and

Andrew McClintock. He read her suspicions immediately. 'No, Livy, I didn't have a hand in it. And if the Old Man's been at work, then it's only in a very peripheral way. Believe George Venables when he says it was submitted in the usual way. After all, no real publisher believes in vanity publishing. They won't put their imprint on it. Good God, Livy, you got a first in English. You know this isn't rubbish. Venables, Harding and Wingate –' he named the American publisher '– don't play games like that because they know they could end up being the laughing stock of the trade. Just let it take its course.'

'Yes, just as *The Way West* is taking its course, with an almighty assist from Andrew McClintock.'

'I don't think you'd have preferred Chris's picture to be allowed to die unnoticed. No, I don't think you would.'

She let it go, telling herself that in the end, all writers had to let their work go. And she didn't want it unread. She was torn between a rage against Andrew McClintock, a sense that, once again, in his authoritarian fashion, he had totally invaded her privacy, and the hope that somehow the book would make it on merit. After all, he couldn't bribe all the reviewers, all the newspapers. But she was also aware of the power of massive promotion, how huge advertising can quietly corrupt even those who thought they were incorruptible. Alex was right. If she had wanted *The Kingdom of the Sea* to make it on its own, she should never have gone to Venables, and she should never have used the name Olivia Miles. It would serve her right, her and the lot of them, Andrew McClintock, Alex, George Venables, Harding's and Wingate's, if it proved to be a well-publicized flop. She knew enough about publishing to know that they could push a hundred thousand copies into the bookshops, and have ninety thousand returned. She looked forward to its publication next year with foreboding. Perhaps this was the moment when the public would reject a product of this McClintock, Clayton machine.

Then something happened which made *The Way West* and *The Kingdom of the Sea* unimportant. Ginny telephoned

Livy one morning from Walter Reed Hospital, and told her she'd like to come for a cup of coffee. 'I just can't face the embassy staff, and their kind enquiries right now.'

Livy had coffee waiting when Ginny arrived. Not even when the news of Chris had come, had Livy seen Ginny so shaken. 'Those last times, Blair and Chris, it was all finished and done. And there was Alex to worry about, to hope about. But this . . .' She set her cup down, and it clattered against the saucer. 'Harry went into Walter Reed for a check-up. He's always refused anything but the routine thing in the doctor's office before. But this time it was different. You don't see him every day. You couldn't have noticed how tired he sometimes looks. A little shortness of breath. But I've woken up a few times in the last couple of months, and he's been in the bathroom drying himself off, getting fresh pyjamas . . . His pillow has been soaked with sweat. His legs and arms are covered in bruises. I forced him to tell the doctor this, in fact, I telephoned him and told him myself, and arranged for his check-up before it was scheduled. So his doctor handed over to the Walter Reed. They did all the tests, did a complete work-up. A bone marrow biopsy. Livy, it's leukaemia. That's what they say. Tomorrow they're giving him a blood tranfusion. I don't understand it completely. It's all about multiplying white cells, out of control. They say . . . they say there can be remission for many years. He can go into remission, Livy. But it can't be cured. He could die of old age, but he can't be cured. Oh, God, Livy, I'm so frightened. I can't lose him. I couldn't bear to lose him.'

Livy telephoned Alex. He came at once, sat by his mother, listened to her talk, and then went into the library. From there he telephoned the various doctors who were taking care of Harry. He learned some things, and forced other information from them. Then he telephoned the Minister at the British Embassy. A smooth curtain of secrecy was drawn about the Ambassador and his mother. He did not telephone his grandfather.

Harry came out of hospital after ten days. 'A little bit of

a repair job,' he said cheerfully. His staff and the press assumed he was referring to a prostate condition. He went about his job with what seemed to his staff his usual vigour. The day he returned from hospital he hosted a reception for a delegation from Hawker Siddeley, who had designs they were hoping to sell to the American aircraft industry.

Andrew McClintock attended, and mingled with the guests. As part of the industry himself, he had every right to be there. Harry stood and talked and introduced people during the more than two hours the reception lasted. But when it was over, and the family went to dinner alone, Andrew McClintock was aware that Harry looked exhausted. He barely touched the food placed before him. His clothes, always tailored in Savile Row and perfectly fitting, seemed too big for him, his shirt collar was loose on his throat. Ginny did not urge a second coffee on anyone. 'I feel rather tired,' she said.

The next morning Andrew McClintock came to Alex's office. His visit was so unprecedented that it startled Alex. Alex immediately lifted the telephone and asked that no calls be put through. 'It's about Harry,' Andrew McClintock said. 'There's something wrong. And something I'm not being told.'

So Alex told him. He stressed the possibility of remission for a long period, but he also told him what he had learned about the speed with which the white blood cells could multiply. 'It's totally uncertain. No doctor in the world will give a prognosis. They can treat it with blood transfusions, and drugs, but they have no cure.'

Andrew McClintock bowed his chin on to the cane resting between his hands. 'Is there nowhere else we can try? No other doctor?'

'They called a leading cancer specialist down from New York. He agreed with the finding, and he could offer no other treatment. At my suggestion he called some colleagues, here and overseas. London, Zurich, Frankfurt. They could offer nothing different. These people keep in touch, in any case. They publish and share their research. The only thing they could offer was slight variations of the drugs, but nothing

681

more. Nothing that isn't known and tried here.'

'This will go very hard with Ginny,' Andrew McClintock said. 'She's had too much. Blair, Chris . . . and even all that time ago, my own son, Alex. Your father. Does Harry know?'

'Of course he knows. He knew it wasn't just a routine check-up. You don't have a bone marrow biopsy and a transfusion if you're all right. He demanded to know the truth. He guessed there was something pretty seriously wrong. They couldn't just tell him that it was all right. That it would go away. He's going to be having treatment from now on. Naturally a man like Harry would want to know what for.'

'His plans? Will he be able to carry on?'

'It depends on how he responds to the treatment. He could go on functioning very well for years. At the moment he's tired, but the transfusion seems to have helped. And the drugs should start to have an effect . . . It's impossible to say. If the job gets too much for him, he'll have to resign. He's due to retire when he's sixty. That's next year.'

Very slowly Andrew McClintock rose to his feet. He left Alex without another word. He telephoned Ginny and arranged to meet her at Livy's house. A visit to the embassy might appear too public. He was waiting when she arrived. He took her hand. 'I have nothing to offer. No help. Little comfort. I just wanted you to know that there's nothing in the world I wouldn't do to spare you this. But there is nothing.'

She nodded. She had learned to retain a façade of calmness; if she sometimes seemed remote, and a little distracted, her staff remembered the shock and horror of her daughter's and Jeff Rigghouse's deaths. 'It may be many years,' she said. I have to keep hoping for that. Just one day at a time, that's how Harry and I live.'

She straightened her shoulders. 'Now, let's not waste an opportunity to see the children. They're growing out of sight.'

They went up to the nurseries and found seven children and three nannies there. 'Play school, it's called,' Ginny said.

'And Fisticuffs settles all the arguments. Do you realize he'll be going to a proper school next year? He'll be five in May . . .' They watched the activity for a few minutes, the building of block houses, the scrawling of crayon on paper, the occasional scream of protest as one child took another's toy.

'We'll have to make a very good Christmas at Prescott Hill this year,' Ginny said, and Andrew McClintock knew she would not be making it just for the children.

In February *The Way West* was nominated for Academy Awards in several categories. Andrew McClintock had heavily loaded the newspapers, particularly the Los Angeles papers, with advertising. Most members of the Academy acknowledged that the film would receive a sympathy vote, but was unlikely to win any Oscars. There was an element in the story of Christine Clayton and Jeff Rigghouse which struck a cord with most of the members of the Academy. The struggle to get the film made at all, and to get it finished was something most of them had experienced, and Christine's courage was applauded. The resurrection of John Cullen from his drunken obscurity was a story in itself. The whole industry knew that Cullen had found a major talent in the young composer, Daniel Seeburg.

No one of the family was there to represent Christine or her husband. They watched together in the library of the McClintock mansion; they often gathered these evenings for dinner, either at the embassy, or with Livy and Alex, and occasionally at Andrew McClintock's house. Livy's baby was due in May. She did not entertain; she read, excused herself from the meetings of her various charities, and Mrs Tennant complained that she was taking her salary for nothing. Whatever free time Ginny had, she spent at the McClintock mansion, mostly in the nursery. She planned a summer at Tresillian. Harry seemed to hold his own. He continued his treatment; it was difficult in the hotbed of rumour and gossip that was Washington to stop speculation about his health. 'Mildly anaemic,' was all the press secretary would say, and any further discussion of the Ambassador's health was discouraged. He appeared well, and almost outrageously cheerful. Now they all sat and waited to hear what would become of·The Way West.

It was John Cullen whom they had selected to receive any awards the film might gather for those who were not present. But it was Daniel Seeburg who rose the first time to take his award for the best original musical score. It was a highly popular award. When John Cullen was called to take his own award for best director his voice broke when he made his acceptance speech. 'You all know what has happened to me. You all know this is a come-back that no one expected. This award is owed to a very gallant and courageous lady, and a brilliant actress, Christine Clayton.'

Then he rose once more to accept the award for best supporting actor for Jeff Rigghouse. 'Jeff mightn't have liked the fact that he was a *supporting* actor,' John Cullen said, 'but the truth is that he gave the most honest performance of his life, and I thank the Academy for recognizing it.'

The Way West did not win the Best Film Award. But a myth was gathering about it. It would endure to be shown again and again on television. The acting of Jeff Rigghouse and Christine Clayton would be studied as the mature performance of a man on the edge of decay and desperation, and of a young woman of infinite promise. It was seen as a new lease of life of the talents of John Cullen.

Ginny wept openly there in front of the television; she wept for the loss of Chris, for the loss of her youth and beauty, her talent. Those around her would forgive her for weeping. What she could not say was how frail Harry's arm about her shoulder felt, how she knew it was she who must support him. Tears were permissible now because they would be seen as springing from another source. She must never be seen to weep for Harry.

Early the next morning there was a telephone call from Rachel. 'If only she could have been there . . .'

And then there was Caroline. 'Isn't it exciting! You must be thrilled!'

There was even a telephone call from Mark. 'Damned wonderful,' he said to Ginny and Harry. 'If only Chris could have got up and taken the award for Jeff herself. What a thing to happen after she's dead.' He did not try to disguise that he was weeping. The headmaster had given him the privacy of his study to make the call. 'We'll always remember her as she was, won't we? When I was a kid she was so good with me. But they were all brilliant, in their way. What sisters I've had . . .' There was no distinction in Mark's mind between any of them.

Livy's baby was born in May; she was a sweetly perfect child, weighing seven pounds, but looking more delicate because her features seemed so clearly defined. She looked like Alex, and she looked like her brother, Oliver, with dark hair and dark grey eyes. Ginny sat by her cot in the hospital room for a long time, just gazing. 'She's so perfect. I'm grateful she's a girl, Livy. In some strange way she makes up a little for Chris.'

'Shall we call her Chris?'

Ginny shook her head. 'No. Not as a first name. I don't think I would want that. I would like it if there were no one in the family ever again called Christine. It should stay as a name that was special to her. What about calling her after Dena? Why not call her Geraldine?'

Andrew McClintock came to see his first great-grand-daughter. 'She has the look of the Russian. Like Alex, like his father. Same eyes, same long fingers. She'll probably be a raving beauty. But I don't think we should give her the Russian's name. Irina Tatiana. Did I ever tell you that was the Russian's name? Call her Iseult. That's a name I'd like remembered in this family.'

The christening was the usual grand McClintock-Clayton affair, though this time there was no one of the Clayton name present. Once again the President attended briefly; this was seen as a signal honour. It was the last year of Eisenhower's second term; he would not run again. He needed nothing from the Democrats, Andrew and Alex McClintock. 'I just came to see the baby's beautiful mother,' he said to Andrew McClintock.

'Just a "thank-you" gesture,' someone remarked sourly. 'I wonder how much Old Man McClintock has slipped into

685

the campaign fund, in return for defence contracts, of course.'

'And here's one of the new hopefuls coming up,' his companion replied, as Senator John Kennedy and his glamorous young wife approached the baby. 'Not that he has a hope being Catholic. But I wonder how much he's hoping for from the McClintocks?'

'Don't worry. Andrew McClintock will spread it around, and say nothing. And all in good time he'll collect the due bills – from whomever becomes President.' The same experienced observer of the Washington scene gazed around the crowd present. 'I must say, Harry Camborne looks more than a bit the worse for wear. This is his last year at the embassy, isn't it? Won't stand up to the rest of it from the way he looks now.'

'They say it's acute anaemia. It seems to me he needs more than a good plate of liver . . . Yes, thanks,' he said as a waiter paused with the laden champagne tray. 'Well, what do we drink to . . . little what's her name? You could say, I guess, she's been born with more than a silver spoon in her mouth. I hear that everyone of these McClintock, Clayton, Camborne kids got a gold christening mug from the Old Man. A rather exclusive club.'

The baby was indeed called by a string of names – Geraldine, Christine, Iseult, Olivia. She was automatically called Isa. 'She isn't a Gerry, never will be,' Alex had observed. 'And Dena's name belongs solely to her, as Chris's does. So Isa it is . . .'

When she was only six weeks old they sailed for England. The reason was partly given as the launch of Livy's book, and Caroline's marriage to Sir Bruce Abbott. Harry said goodbye to his staff exactly as if he were going on holiday. 'They'll be kicking me out as soon as I'm sixty,' he told the senior members of his staff at the small party he gave for them and their wives the night before they left. 'When I get back I may be able to tell you who my replacement will be.'

They paused briefly in London. Harry had a series of appointments with doctors, and with the Foreign Office. For Livy it was the time to see the first finished copies of *The Kingdom of the Sea*. They had put off publication when they learned that Livy was coming to England after the baby's birth. Venables had made a beautiful volume of it, and Livy was breathless with pride, but alarmed when she learned that there was to be a big launching party at the Savoy; Venables had written vaguely of a party, but not one of this size. 'I'm afraid, Mrs McClintock,' George Venables said, 'it's all part of the promotion campaign. Harding's won't be pushing you all around the country – that would be too much to expect of the mother of such a young baby. But they would like you to record just a few interviews for radio and then there will be some journalists coming to visit you in Cornwall. I know it would be more easily done here in London, but they all want to see you in the setting of *The Kingdom of the Sea*. You must, I'm afraid, expect some Fleet Street plain curiosity as much about you as the book. They'll want to see where you were born and grew up and of course they'd like a glimpse of Lord Camborne's castle. The idea has caught on. A very romanticized idea, I'm afraid, but better than no attention at all.'

After three days in London Harry returned from an interview with the Permanent Under Secretary at the Foreign Office. They gathered for tea at Seymour House on the afternoon before the reception for Livy at the Savoy. Rachel had come to join them. He looked around them all. 'Well,' he said, 'it's all settled. I have resigned, and they have a free hand to appoint whom they like in my place. I was invited to give my own recommendations, but they don't have to act on them. It would have been more proper if I'd announced it before I left Washington, but I just couldn't take the round of farewell parties. Let them think I'm coming back for a while. At any rate, I'd be retired before the end of the year. I just don't like the idea of having to drag myself back there. I took the precaution of clearing out my desk before I left, and only my private secretary knows it. Ginny did the same. We couldn't move too much that was personal. It would have given the game away.'

Ginny sat beside him and held his hand as he spoke. 'As you all know, there can be periods of remission in this illness. I could have many happy years at Trésillian with Ginny. That's what we plan for ourselves. That's what we hope for. I've had enough parties to last three life times. I didn't need any more. Ginny perfectly understands and agrees. She and my secretary have made lists of all the things that are our property at the embassy. In due course they will be packed up and stored, or sent to Tresillian. This was the best way we could manage it. A lot of people know in Washington that I'm ill, but have been too tactful to talk about it to my face. At least we'll be spared tearful farewells, and presents we don't need.'

Livy stared at them, and her hand went to Alex's. She twisted it with an intensity which she didn't realize caused him pain. 'You're . . . I can hardly believe it. You're taking it so . . . so . . .'

'Philosophically? What other way, dear Livy? We may only get months together, Ginny and I. We may get years. It could be weeks. We were determined to spend them in as much peace as we could find. I know you, Alex, can't stay on long, but we'd be grateful to have Livy for as long as you can spare her, until Fisticuffs has to go to school. There'll be the baby and Oliver to play with. Mark will be there . . . a lot to look forward to.' He turned to his older daughter. 'I hope, Rachel, you can spare us a little time now and then. Bring Frazer with you, if he'll come. I enjoy his company. I don't expect to see much of Caro because she's going to be very busy just being married to Bruce Abbott. But she knows. I've made sure she knows. I don't want unnecessary burdens laid on Ginny. She's had enough. She has been all my strength in these last months. I hope you all in your turn will try to give her even a little part of what she's given me.'

He continued to hold Ginny's hand. 'I'm saying this while I'm still able to say it rationally and clearly. They know all the reasons at the Foreign Office. There will be no fuss.

There's no reason why there should be. I'm looking for the years, not the months. Now, I think it's time we all went and got ready for Livy's party.'

Tears were rolling down Livy's cheeks. 'How can I go? I can't appear just now. I couldn't face it.'

'My dear, you must. You've known for a long time what's wrong with me. Nothing has changed, except that the Foreign Office, who also knew what was wrong, have accepted my resignation. But don't worry. There will be no announcement from them until we're well and truly settled at Tresillian, and by all but the few that are in the know, it will just be taking my retirement a few months early. Come on, Livy. this is your night! I know you'll hate it, but it's due to you. I hope you have a lovely dress all ready, and I want you to wear your most beautiful jewellery. You owe it to these people to dress up to the part of the princess of *The Kingdom of the Sea*, which you truly are.'

She squeezed herself into a dress she was not quite ready to wear so soon after Isa's birth. She had had her hair done that day, and the hairdresser, knowing about the party at the Savoy, had persuaded her to wear it in an apparently simple but contrived fashion. Because she had become a friend over the years she had brought him a copy of *The Kingdom of the Sea*. He had poured over the illustrations. 'You met the illustrator, Mrs McClintock, didn't you?'

'Yes, he came to Washington to consult about the preliminary sketches. Why?'

'He's put you into some of these. The princess . . . I love the way he's managed the hair. I'd like to try to copy it. With your permission, of course. I hope your dress is a lovely blue-green, like your opal.'

So her hair was twisted to one side, and hung in a single shining rope over her left shoulder. She dressed and began to take out the sapphires Andrew McClintock had given her when Oliver was born. Alex came into the dressing-room. 'Ever since I read *The Kingdom of the Sea* I've been trying to get these ready for you. They've taken some hunting down. I'm sorry they come at this late date but maybe it's just at the right moment.'

She saw in the velvet-lined boxes a collection of black opals that made her gasp: a necklace, earrings, bracelet, set in diamonds which refracted their myriad colours. 'I gave our usual jeweller the commission to find them,' Alex said. 'They had to be fit for a sea princess. He sent one of his men, who knows about opals, to Australia, in fact, all the way to Lightning Ridge. Matching them up was a problem. They don't quite match, but opals never do. That's part of their magic. So, my darling, wear them with my grandfather's ring. He must have known something about you years ago when he gave you that ring. You look very beautiful, my Livy. I wish I were a fit knight for the sea princess.'

She kissed him. 'I wish we all had Harry and Ginny's courage. Like him, we'll plan for years, not months.'

She endured the reception at the Savoy. It was a test of stamina and control. Every time she glimpsed Harry through the crowd, seeing him in animated conversation with someone, no doubt someone who could help *The Kingdom of the Sea*, she firmly set her lips against their tendency to quiver. Rachel and Alex stayed closely by her. She knew after the first hour he must have longed to sit down, as Harry must, but they stayed on their feet. Ginny was always close to Harry; she wore a simple dress, of grey silk, with pearls, and only her wedding ring and Harry's emerald. It was not in Ginny's nature to distract attention from Livy on this evening. Some of the women journalists commented on the opals. Livy explained very simply. An Australian journalist who had come on a routine assignment, seized on them. She telegraphed the story to her newspaper that same evening, and it was given the front page, not the women's page. *'Millionaire husband sought gift of rare black opals to celebrate publication of wife's book.'*

Two days later they were present at Caroline's marriage to Sir Bruce Abbott at the St Marylebone registrar's office. No advance plans of the marriage had been given to the press, but still there was a small crowd of photographers waiting for them as they left the building. Bruce Abbott's love of making a splash might not have been satisfied with the quietness of the ceremony, but he was pleased with the reception which awaited them at Seymour House. Almost a hundred and fifty people were there to drink their health, and wish them well. How, Livy wondered, could it possibly have been the quiet, almost secret wedding Caroline had spoken of when so many people had been invited? Rachel arrived, and held back from the wedding group until the bride and groom were momentarily alone. 'I couldn't not come to wish you luck, Caro, and happiness.'

'Perhaps it'll be your turn soon,' Caroline answered, and knew there was little chance of that. She was full of a nervous kind of gaiety, but there was almost an air of relief about her that Livy sensed had only come when the marriage had finally become a fact. Bruce Abbott had been known to be volatile in his attachments before. But he had married her, and she was satisfied. She had exchanged the comfortable, but to her, somewhat dull circle of the landed gentry and the formality of the Foreign Office. She would now move in a wider, much more exciting world of Bruce Abbott's entrepreneurial style, a world of large parties and international celebrity, a world where the display of wealth was not held to be vulgar.

Livy went upstairs with Caroline when she went to change. She caught the expression on Livy's face reflected in the mirror. 'Oh, for God's sake, don't look like that! That's the way the world is. It isn't filled with fairies and princesses and knights in shining armour. I'm taking what I can get while it's on offer. I mean to enjoy life – and I don't ever intend to be poor again.'

Chapter 18

1

They went down to Tresillian, and in the wake of the boom-
ing sales of *The Kingdom of the Sea*, the press followed.
There were photographs of Livy walking in the streets of St
Just, pictures of her in the garden of the cottage which had
belonged to her poet father, Oliver Miles, with Jamie
and Oliver by her side, the baby Isa in her arms. There
were pictures of her with her famous adoptive mother,
Thea Sedgemore, who in the most recent Queen's
Birthday Honours, had become a Dame of the British
Empire. By request of the famous photographer the *Sunday
Times* had sent, there was a picture of Livy standing at the
base of the Tower, the wind blowing her hair, the Tresillian Rocks a misty background. The editors of a powerful
glossy magazine begged, but could not get, a photograph
of her with Alex and Mark, Ginny and the just-retired
Ambassador. They had to make do with a photograph
of her on the stairs of Tresillian's great hall, where, they
didn't mind pointing out, Livy's mother had once polished
the floors.

They could not, however, get her Tregenna cousins to talk
about her. Only once did someone slip, and mention the
dog, Bully, and how Thea Sedgemore had made a headstone
for him. There was a photograph of the beautiful stone which
marked his grave. Again and again the photographs of Livy
at the Savoy reception were reprinted. Almost always, aware
of the McClintock-Clayton background, the news editors
captioned the photo with the term Harry had first used of
her 'The Princess of the Kingdom of the Sea'. The opals
became famous. Someone had found out about Andrew
McClintock's gift, on her twenty-first birthday, of the opal

she always wore on her right hand. It was regarded as further evidence of the astute old man's ability to sense talent, even a touch of genius. They harked back to his promotion of the great war-time success of *This England*. They cited his sponsorship of *The Way West*, which was still attracting crowds to the cinema. The golden McClintock touch, they called it. Wingate, Livy's American publisher, avidly seized on all this, demanded further interviews from representatives of the American press bureaux in London. America knew Livy as a young Washington hostess, unconventional, rather shy and distant in her manner, but nevertheless, Alex McClintock's wife. Here the other side of her was revealed, a magically romantic side. She was the girl who had grown up with Christine Clayton, the young woman touched with the golden but sometimes tragic hand of the McClintock, the Clayton and the Camborne families. They couldn't get enough of it, and from Wingate's reports, they couldn't get enough copies of *The Kingdom of the Sea*.

'I only wrote it for my children,' was about as much as Livy would say of the book, and didn't comment on the different meanings people read into the fable, or morality play, as some of the more romantically minded journalists called it.

'I've had enough!' she said to George Venables on the phone after ten days at Tresillian. 'My family's had enough. I've done what you asked. Now let us have some peace.'

Andrew McClintock was on the phone from Washington. 'Just one television interview, Livy. An exclusive for NBC. You'll get the book into millions of homes that never hear about this sort of book.'

'No!' she said. 'No!'

He seemed to rethink the situation rather quickly. 'Perhaps you're right. Perhaps it's better to leave a little mystery about . . . The book is mysterious, after all.'

She lay and sobbed in Alex's arms. 'He's taken it all. Just the way he took *The Way West* from Chris. We came here for peace. For Harry to feel well and rested, and it's turned into a circus. I feel as if my father's and mother's graves have been dug up, and even poor old Bully's. All this . . . this hysteria has made me feel that I'll never write another word in my life.'

'It may take years before you are able to forget *The Kingdom of the Sea*,' Alex said, rocking her gently. 'But one day you'll write, and it will be all your own. My grandfather will not take you or anyone else over, ever again, if I can help it.'

After two weeks Alex had to leave. He had been away a month, and he knew the amount of work which was piling up for him. But he was reassured, as they all were, that Harry was looking better, appeared to have more energy. 'Perhaps just the fact of having laid down the burden of that job has helped him,' Alex said. 'I sometimes wonder how old I have to be before I can do it and maybe Fisticuffs and Oliver won't even want to take over.'

'There's always Isa. The brains don't always go to the boys.'

'You're right. By that time, perhaps McClintock-Clayton will be ready for her.'

She went up to London with him. He urged her not to come. 'That long journey there and back . . .'

'It's worth it.' She didn't tell Venables or Harding that she was going to be in London; *The Kingdom of the Sea* could look after itself now, so far as she was concerned. She was hostess at a dinner party just for the Clayton Bank directors; she sensed an atmosphere of unusual excitement carefully kept under control. Alex smiled as he closed the door after bidding the last of their guests goodnight. They could hear Knox making the rounds, locking doors and windows as they went upstairs.

'Derek Arnold's just back from Washington and New York,' Alex said, 'as you probably gathered. The gossip, very private as yet, is that the Old Man's beginning to climb down. He can see we have to have more capital. He can't continue for ever to borrow from one company we already own to buy another we need to own. He has given just the faintest hint that he might be ready to agree to a stock issue. Of course, it would all be contingent on him and Ginny and

694

me holding the majority of voting shares. No question of who would be in charge. But the public would go for it, I think. In quite a big way.'

'Would you be richer, Alex?' She hated the thought.

'Depends. It will be very tricky to set a price per share. There's many months of work in preparing for a thing like this. We might issue at a certain price. The public might buy or not. If the share price shot up, all the quick-money boys would dump for a profit, and we could find the stock dropping, and ourselves a few million poorer. The stock-market is always a gamble, as you well know. But to stay as we are isn't even a gamble. We'll just stagnate, and there could be nothing for Fisticuffs or Oliver or Isa, to take over.'

'What about the vineyard you were going to buy to cultivate your vines?'

'Oh, we'll keep a lookout for the right vineyard . . . maybe some day it'll be just what I need. Somewhere it's warm, and we can lie and listen to the grapes ripen . . . Well, I can dream, can't I? I'm so glad that, at last, Harry has his place. How wise Mother was, almost prescient. She couldn't possibly have known how badly they'd need Tresillian, in peace and order and quiet. It's Harry's best hope. I believe.'

She saw him off next day, and returned by night sleeper to Penzance. There were four more weeks left before she had to return to Washington so that Jamie could start at school. She was greeted by him and Oliver as if she had been gone for months. She took Isa into her arms, and said to Nanny, 'I think she's grown about two inches since I left her. And she seems pounds heavier.'

Mrs Hope, still nominally in charge of the New York apartment, now always accompanied them when the children travelled. 'Two small, very energetic boys and a young baby is too much for one woman to cope with,' Andrew McClintock had decreed.

Mrs Hope now beamed down upon Livy and Isa. 'She's going to be a beauty, Mrs McClintock. You can see it, even now. She'll be even better-looking than her brother, Oliver, and he's as handsome as a young prince.'

'I think we've heard and read enough about princes and

695

princesses in the last few weeks, Mrs Hope. I just want them to be happy children. And what about my poor Fisticuffs? Doesn't he stand a chance with these two?'

'Well . . .' Mrs Hope said what she wouldn't have said if the two boys had been present. 'He's got a lot of your looks, Mrs McClintock, but the strange thing is that you hardly notice what he looks like, because he's always making a scene about something. Ordering someone around, arranging something else, arguing, shoving, getting himself dirty and not caring. Whoever called him Fisticuffs got it right. He's for all the world like Mr Andrew McClintock. But, you know, he isn't a bully. I've been watching for that. He looks out for Oliver, and I've seen him just stand and look at Isa in her cradle. That's when his thumb goes back in his mouth. He might take everything by storm, Mrs McClintock, but his brother and sister are going right along with him.'

The night after Livy's return from London, Mark's headmaster, Matthew Fletcher, and his wife, Anne, came to dinner, and to stay overnight at Tresillian. To honour them, everyone dressed for dinner. Livy thought how handsome and how well Harry looked, or was she merely deceived by the suntan he had acquired during these warm summer days? The house was cool and beautiful, and decked with flowers. Anne Fletcher was alone in the drawing-room when Livy came down; she rose to meet her. 'I came down early, with the hope that you'd be here too. You must be tired of hearing it in these past weeks, about *The Kingdom of the Sea*, but I'm Cornish. I recognize some of the legends, and I so much admire the way they've been put together. Mark is beside himself with delight over the book and the way it's selling. He's still at the age when he wants the people he loves to succeed in whatever they aspire to. He loves you very much. He wants the world for you. And from what I've learned about Mr Andrew McClintock, it isn't easy to retain the world of Cornish legends in his company.'

'I love Mark too, Mrs Fletcher. I think he exaggerates a little.'

Anne Fletcher smiled, and nodded. 'Perhaps. There's just one thing I'd like to know isn't an exaggeration. I'm disappointed you're not wearing the opals. I had hoped to see them. Mark hasn't seen them, either. I imagine they epitomize this place.'

Livy stared at her in amazement, but knew at once that this finely tuned lady possessed no idle curiosity. She had seen Tresillian, and knew its spirit. She wanted more of it. 'I'll go and put them on at once, Mrs Fletcher. For you and Mark.'

After dinner, they sat in the drawing-room with the last long flush of sunset fading on the Atlantic and the Rocks. Finally they discussed what Matthew Fletcher had come for. Mark was eighteen. He had refused, so far, to sit for the entrance exams for Oxford or Cambridge. And no one, in these last months of anxiety over Harry's health, had had the energy to press him.

'You could always go to a crammer's,' Harry said, introducing the subject gently. 'Your work at Wrisley has been pretty good in the past few years – am I right, Mr Fletcher?'

'Good enough. With a bit of extra work, he could make it, I think.'

'But what for?' Mark said. 'What would I do with a degree? You know I'm not for the Foreign Service, Father. Even if I could make the grade, it isn't for me. It just isn't for me.'

'Then what?' Harry spoke mildly. 'Any ideas? Perhaps you need a few years at university before you make up your mind.'

'I'm going into the army, Father. I could defer it by going to university but it's a bit late for that now. I have to do two years National Service, no matter what. I'm going to have my medical in a few days, and I expect I'll be inducted pretty soon.'

Harry frowned. 'I'm sorry, Mark. I've been a bit preoccupied. Hadn't really thought of it coming up on you like that. You've only just finished school. But still, I could get in touch with some friends . . .'

'Father . . . no! I'm not going to try to get into a guards regiment. I'm not going to be a cadet officer. In fact, if I can wangle it, I'm going to get myself into the army catering corps. As a private.'

Harry drew in his breath. 'Catering . . .? You mean you want to peel potatoes?'

'Well, I suppose I'd get a bit further than that. But the experience wouldn't hurt, since I have to go into one of the services. Where I would like your help is when I come out.' He looked from his father to Ginny. 'I would want an introduction to some famous restaurant or hotel, to start in the kitchen. I'd have to go to chef's school, as well, but someone would have to take me in as an apprentice.'

'My God,' Harry paused for a moment. 'But that's a kind of slavery, Mark. Could you take it? The rotten hours, being ordered around and shouted at, and paid damn-all?'

'Father, in a more genteel way, was it much different for you when you started at the Foreign Office? Worse, I'd expect, because your father was Permanent Under Secretary. They must have tried to trip you up whenever they had the chance. Weren't you ordered around, and shouted at, in the politest possible way, of course? And could you say you were handsomely paid? One day, of course, I'd hope to be a *chef de cuisine*. To be my own boss. I'd hope to run a kitchen, and be reponsible for it, as you have had to be for your embassies. Of course, all chefs have to show a tangible profit. It has to be there on the books. You don't actually have to show that in the Foreign Service. You don't have to prove that such-and-such a reception brought in such-and-such an order, or made the Russians any friendlier. You don't know what tilts the scales whether you're selling armaments or socks. A chef has to sell food, and if it's no good, he's out, or the restaurant is broke. It's a high-risk business, Father. There are no little nooks or crannies of privilege where you can hide, and be safe. If you're in charge, you have to make the place pay.'

'I thought you were rather more concerned about the romance of the cuisine, cooking as an art.'

'Cooking is an art, but it isn't one you can practise by yourself out in the desert. You need instant customers, consumers. A great chef is an artist, and probably a slave-driver, and a tyrant. And a book-keeper. Have you ever heard shouts coming from the kitchen of a great restaurant, Father?'

698

'Yes . . .'

'I'm sorry that you have, but it's bound to happen, now and then. If the fish isn't ready the moment the sauce is, the fish chef gets hell from the *saucier*. If the vegetables are ready too soon, they'll go limp being kept warm. It's a kind of orchestration, Father. The maestro has to be in charge of everything, has to conduct the lot. And it has to be beautifully presented, quietly, but with some flair, to the customer. They don't want to hear the rows that are going on in the orchestra. They just want the music of great food.'

'You're beginning to make me hungry,' Ginny said. 'But I'm certain we all had dinner . . .'

Harry looked around them all, to Ginny, as if for guidance, to Matthew Fletcher, who carefully kept quiet, as if he wanted to hold his arguments in reserve, to Livy, who had always known that some day it could come to this.

'Well, I couldn't be more surprised if you'd announced you intended to be a . . . a . . . well, I don't know what. I always thought this was an amusing, if very practical hobby of yours. I never saw it as a career.'

'What did you imagine, Father? A lawyer? A parson? Tinker, tailor, soldier . . . diplomat? You've known for a long time I'd never make a diplomat. There's just one thing I think I can make a real success of. I don't have a talent for anything else.'

Harry spread his hands in a gesture of submission. 'Well, dear fellow, if you're willing for the drudgery and the slow climb to the top, if you have the inspiration, in fact, I think I mean the genius needed for it, what can I say? It's full of risk. But then, what isn't? I wouldn't like to think of you shoved all around the world as third secretary in hardship postings because the FO didn't suit you. If you're going to be a high-flyer, Mark, you'd better get cracking, the sooner the better. Ginny and I will just put our heads together and think of people we know who can steer you into the right places. If you drop the baked Alaska just as you're about to pass it to the head waiter, we can't protect you from that. But then, I couldn't protect you from writing damn foolish dispatches for the Foreign Office. Better get this army thing over with, too. You may have other thoughts by then.'

Harry looked at Matthew Fletcher. 'Mr Fletcher, you haven't said a word.'

'I am only here to say a word if you had totally disagreed with what Mark's thinking. Two years in the army may indeed change his mind. He might long for some other form of slavery by then. My life at Wrisley is dedicated to trying to find the natural talents and bents of the pupils. That's why we're not a conventional school. I see you're wise enough to let the stream take its natural course. In my opinion, Mark is doing, for the moment, the right thing. Any other job, if you're going to do it well, requires no less slavery than what he's chosen.'

Ginny rose, and put her hand on Harry's arm, gently. 'I think we'll have a nightcap of champagne. But don't call Knox. Let Mark get it. Let him present it as it should be done, draw the cork without splattering the room, the right glasses . . .'

'How wise you are, my darling,' He touched her hand lightly. 'Yes, we'd better let this stream take its natural course.'

To Livy he looked terribly tired. Not disappointed, almost relieved. Mark had made his own decision. Harry had not had to push or guide or coach him. He would not be responsible for any of his failures. He might be modestly pleased with whatever success he had. She was suddenly aware that Harry had passed the point where he wanted to make any more decisions.

Every day Livy took Jamie and Oliver down to play with their Tregenna relations. There were plenty of about their age, second cousins, third cousins. They had long ago lost track of the exact relationships. The children gathered at Livy's cottage, which was well-stocked with toys. Unless it was raining, they played in the little garden. There was an amount of good-natured brawling, but there was also the stimulus young children give to each other. Often Mark came with her, to help keep order. Thea sometimes came over from her studio, and they gossiped, sitting in the sun. Several

700

of the Tregenna women would take ten minutes from their household chores to share a cup of coffee. At lunch time they came to collect their children. Livy gave Jamie and Oliver lunch at the cottage, and then they would slowly climb the hill to Tresillian. Nanny and Mrs Hope were there to settle them down for their nap.

On the surface, it was a serene, peaceful existence, but beneath the tension grew because they realized that Harry was not holding his own. He grew more gaunt, more frail. He spent most of his time lying out in the sun in the walled garden, and after lunch he went as readily to his bed as the children did. There wasn't even the suggestion of the picnics which used to be a part of their times at Tresillian. Mark stopped coming down to Livy's cottage in the mornings. He spent every moment possible at Harry's side.

'He's going through a bad patch,' he said to Livy. 'He'll pull out of it, won't he?' He had only been told what was wrong with Harry when they had come down to Tresillian that summer, and Harry's resignation had been announced.

'I don't know,' Livy said. 'A remission is just a sort of pause, however long it lasts. I don't know if one ever gets any better. I don't think anyone knows that much about it . . .'

'He's not getting any better!' Mark cried, panic seeming to rise in him suddenly. 'He's getting worse. Livy, sometimes I can't bear to look at him. I'm so frightened he won't last. I was so happy when I knew he and Aunt Ginny were coming back here to live. I thought finally they'd always be in the same place, and I could come whenever I wanted. I've never had a home that was permanent. He doesn't even ask about the army or about my wanting to be a chef. I suppose it's a great disappointment to him . . . but he never says anything to try to dissuade me.'

'He's too wise to say anything. He loves you too much to want to interfere. Perhaps he's seen too much of what Andrew McClintock has tried to do with the lives of those around him . . .'

Ginny had written to Andrew McClintock about Mark's decision. A troubled telephone call had followed. 'I can help him. There's plenty of things he can do at McClintock's. It doesn't have to be here in Washington, it can be any place. He can almost choose his own spot.'

'He has to get through the army first,' Ginny said. 'He may have changed his mind by then.'

'True.' He was thoughtful, rather than angry. 'If he's bound and determined to go through with this thing, we can get him into the best restaurant, anywhere he wants. He can start at the Ritz.'

'I think he'd prefer somewhere smaller, where he'd get a better variety of jobs.'

'If it's a bit of experience he wants, there are plenty of canteens at the McClintock plants. He can go over to Switzerland.'

'You just have to let him go, Mr McClintock,' Ginny said quietly. 'I know you're trying to help, but he has to do it on his own. Can you imagine how the rest of the staff would treat him if he took a job in a McClintock plant? He'd have a dog's life. It's hard enough for him to try to get out of Harry's shadow, and Eton, and all the rest of it . . . what people have expected him to do. He has to go down his own road, and it's just as tough as if he'd said he intended to be a painter or a musician.'

'But we could do so much for him. He could come here and work with the chef in our own kitchen. He'd get his experience very quickly that way.'

'That isn't enough. Just preparing a set lunch every day for middle-aged and elderly gentlemen who are all watching their diet. It's too quiet. He needs to be in the thick of things. I think he actually looks forward to having a saucepan hurled at his head, and listening to an argument going on in six languages . . . He's got no illusions. He expects to be kicked around, until he's sick and tired of it, or he's got to the top.'

'Well . . .' Andrew McClintock said, rather grudgingly, 'I suppose when he's come through it all, we might stake him to the price of setting up on his own. It'd be a small investment compared to what we lash out here every day.'

'That's years off,' Ginny answered. 'We'll wait and see.'

'Well, if you're all going to be there until the end of

September, I might just pay you a visit. Alex is giving me such a battering about going public, I'd like a break from it. I suppose I ought to talk to the London directors.'

'We're not just here until the end of September. It's our thought that we're here for good. Remember? Harry's retired. We won't be coming to Washington except for visits.'

'Yes, I keep forgetting. That's what they're all hinting here. I'm getting old. I want things to stay the same. I'll tell you, Ginny, I don't want this company to go public. But they're forcing it on me. Perhaps it's time, like Harry, I resigned . . . Well, maybe I'll see you soon.' He hung up.

The next day Ginny looked at Harry's face, noted the weakness of his movements, and telephoned the specialist in London who was taking care of him. They went up to London, and Harry was admitted to hospital. They took blood tests, and gave him a transfusion. Dr Bernon faced Ginny when the results of the tests were known. 'It doesn't look good, Lady Camborne. Your doctors in Washington tried the usual cytotoxic, anti-cancer, drugs. And variations of them. And I've carried on the treatment. But he's showing every sign of becoming immune to the drugs. The white cells have multiplied very rapidly since the last tests. This is a very rare disease, and we're only beginning to try to treat it. None of us pretend we have a cure. You see, he's becoming totally open to infection . . . We can't stop it. Sometimes it will hold itself in remission for years and then suddenly it gallops ahead.'

'Is that what's happening now?'

'I think it is. That's what the blood tests show.'

'How long?'

He shook his head. 'I can't answer that. We'll continue with the drug therapy. And hope. I'll see him again in a month. Or sooner, if his condition seems to warrant it. But we've almost shot our bolt on treatment. I have to warn you that there might be a total collapse in a few weeks. I've even seen some cases where it was only a few days. But we'll be with him all the time, I promise you. If taking him into hospital seems justified . . .'

'I'll have to talk to Harry.'

'You're not going to tell him? Let him have whatever time there is . . .'

'Harry knows he's very seriously ill, and he's going downhill. He may not want to end his life in hospital. You'll have to leave it to him to decide what he wants to do now. You'll have to trust me to tell him.'

'Shall I tell him?'

'No. I think he'd prefer to hear it from me. I don't want him to make any effort in thinking he's keeping the truth from me. He needs all his strength, and whatever I can contribute. He may not even want to stay on in London.'

'I'll come down to Cornwall, of course, at any time you want. I've already consulted with your man in the Truro hospital. He has a good reputation. I have to repeat, though, that it's a rare disease, and none of us have that much experience of it.'

Harry heard what Ginny had to say. 'Let's get down to Tresillian, Ginny. I'll carry on with the drugs, if that's all they can do. We can get nurses, can't we, if things get bad?' He held out a frail and bruised hand to her. 'I hate hospital, Ginny. Will it place too much of a burden on you if we go back to Tresillian? I'd like to breathe the air there . . .'

'We'll do whatever you want, Harry.'

They were driven back to Cornwall. Dr Bernon had suggested an ambulance as being less tiring, but Harry refused. 'I don't want to frighten Livy and Mark. Especially I don't want the children to see an ambulance.'

They made the journey back to Cornwall, and Ginny knew it would be the last time Harry would make it. She tried to see things through his eyes, and felt overwhelmed by the weight of it. It was a golden day in early September. The familiar pieces of the landscape came and went. The rivers, the bridges, the views of the moors, crossing the moors. Harry looked around him constantly, as if he could not get enough of the sights. Very many times during the journey he reached out and took her hand, fondled it, and then let it go, as if even that small gesture tired him. As they started up the drive to Tresillian, Harry once more took her hand. 'In case there isn't time to say it, thank you, my darling.

There may be no time left, but the little time I've had with you has been precious and rare.'

They reached the house, and Livy and Mark came out to welcome them. They asked no questions: Ginny had talked by telephone with Livy before she left London. They both knew the situation, but it did not prepare them for the sight of Harry, who seemed much frailer than when he had left. After Ginny had seen him to bed, Livy told her that Dr Bassett had telephoned from Truro. 'He'll come any time you want him. And he says he can get good nurses round the clock. They'd have to live here, of course. I told him there was plenty of room. I'll try to keep the children quiet . . .'

Ginny shook her head. 'No, everything must be as normal as possible . . . for as long as possible. That's why he wanted to come back. It might stop here, Livy. There might be months, even a year. Life has to go on. You must go back to Washington. As it is, Fisticuffs will be late starting at school . . . Mark has to go into the army at the end of October.'

'No, I have to stay with you. Alex will understand . . .'

'That's not what I want. How do you think it will seem to Harry? That you are waiting for him to die. I told you he might even have a year. Dr Bernon changed the drugs. They may work.'

'I can't bear to think of you being here all winter.'

'I shall be with Harry. That's enough. I have Dr Bassett, who can be here in an hour. And Dr Bernon, if he's needed. Harry is seeking peace, Livy. Not the flurry of a hospital where they'll make every last-ditch effort to give him an extra day, and ruin that day for him. This way there'll be dignity. That's what he wants most of all.'

Livy let it go, as she knew she must. She continued with the routine of taking the children down to St Just every morning, and they didn't notice that Harry grew weaker. She managed, by watching, to stop them hurling themselves on to him. Once, when the boys had done it at the same time, Harry had rocked under their assault and nearly fallen. And yet she knew it was what he wanted, what he had desired. These were not children of his blood, but of Ginny's; he needed them, their vitality, their innocence, the noise they made as they tried to explain everything that had happened that morning in what they thought of as the 'play' house. They thrust their toys and their drawings at him. He was ready, seated on the sofa, when they came back each day. They climbed up to sit one on each side of him, vying for his attention. He sat there, both enduring and loving the giggles and their squeezes, their hugs, until Nanny and Mrs Hope came down to take them off for their nap. Then he would rise wearily and go to his own bed.

It happened very quickly, as the doctors said it might. Two weeks after he returned from London came the day when Harry staggered back from the bathroom to his bed with Ginny, and she knew he probably didn't have the strength to get out of it again. Ginny telephoned Dr Bassett, and he came. By that evening the first of the nurses had been installed. The next day Dr Bernon arrived, but it was a gesture only. He had stopped at Truro to see the results of the tests of the blood samples Dr Bassett had taken the day before. They conferred over the drugs, altered them slightly, and Dr Bernon went on to see his patient. He knew enough not to offer false words of hope. 'We'll keep you as comfortable as possible.' He walked to the window and looked down on the bay of St Just. 'I understand why you wanted to come back. I met your grandchildren . . .' Like most strangers, he made no distinction between their being Harry's or Ginny's grandchildren. 'I've walked around the cliff face. This is the end of England or Cornwall, as you'd probably want me to say. There's nothing beyond it, just the sea. I looked at the Rocks. Yes, wonderful . . . formidable. Sometimes it's good for us doctors to be taken out of our clinical environment. People turn back into people . . . instead of being patients.' He did not say that that afternoon two more nurses had been installed in rooms on the third floor.

He stayed the night, and from the window of his room he could both see and hear the sea against the Rocks. Dinner was in the large dining-room. Dr Bassett had only been able

706

to stay for a sherry before dinner. In the candlelight the room was very beautiful. The food and wine seemed exceptional. It was as if Knox and Jacques had known that this might be their last chance to serve a meal to a guest in an atmosphere of tranquillity before an onslaught began. The nurses ate in the sitting dining-room Mr Penleigh had provided for the times when Harry and Ginny would be alone. It had never been used by them.

Dr Bernon drew them out. He talked about the Rocks, the Tower, the pretty town nestling under its hill. They told him of when Tresillian had not been like this. Ginny talked of the war years, the evacuee children, how Dena had gone shooting to fill the pot on the old stove, how there had always been fish of some sort to eke out the rations, and much of it rejected by the evacuees. They even told him the story of Isa and Chris, and the race before the tide swirling about the Rocks. They didn't even bother to try to explain the tangled relationships. 'I was born down there,' Mark said, jerking his head in the direction of the town. 'Aunt Ginny got Mother there just in time.'

Bernon looked around the three of them, the two women, the shadow of grief already on their faces, the boy who was struggling towards manhood, and trying to choke back his tears. Despite what he had said to Harry upstairs, it was a mistake ever to come too near the families of patients. And yet it was necessary, he reminded himself, to remain human. Some day his own time would come. He fell asleep listening to the sea on the Rocks. He knew why Harry Camborne had wanted to come home.

2

So there came, finally, the afternoon when Livy walked up the hill from St Just, with Jamie ahead of her, impatiently calling to her when she paused to look at the house, as she always did, more lingeringly now because a sense of sorrow already lay upon it. The walk was still too long for Oliver, and she pushed him before her in the pushchair. He was

707

sleepy after his lunch; he crooned unintelligible words to himself, and sucked his thumb. The flowers in her hand, which she had brought from her mother's garden and would arrange for Harry's room, momentarily brushed Oliver's head, and he looked up, startled. Then he smiled at her, and his hand reached for the biggest, reddest of the chrysanthemums. Jamie had gone on ahead, and had now reached the front door, and was struggling with the big brass knob. It was then she glanced up to the windows of the room where the Ambassador lay. She saw the curtains being drawn, a gentle motion, as if there were no hurry. Harry slept little these days, and they saved the strongest drugs for the night. He liked the daylight in the room for as long as it lasted. She recognized the gesture then, and what it meant. The flowers dropped from her hand, and she pushed Oliver before her, running. She flung open the door to the great hall. Ginny was half-way down the stairs. She paused momentarily when she saw them. Then she continued her way down. Her eyes were very bright, as she struggled to hold back tears. Livy knew she did not want the children to see her weep. When she spoke, it was barely more than a whisper.

'He's gone,' she said. 'He's gone . . .' Then she bent and took Jamie's hand.

'We'll go up to Nanny now.'

'Gramp! We'll go and see Gramp.'

'No, darling. Not just now.' She said to Livy, 'I'll take Oliver up. I was just going to find Mark. I think he's in the orchard . . . he's about somewhere. He was here a little while ago. Would you . . .?'

Livy found him in the orchard, seated beneath the tree closest to Bully's headstone, his knees drawn up to his chin. He saw her coming, and got slowly to his feet. She opened her lips to speak, and no words came. But he knew what she struggled to say. What she finally did say was: 'He loved you . . .'

'He loved us all.' They shed their first tears there by Bully's headstone, away from everyone's gaze, and the wind from the sea blew softly around Tresillian's ancient walls.

They came quickly. Rachel was first. 'I wish I had given him more happiness. I know he worried about me.' Her arms still around Ginny, she added, 'How thankful I am he had you in these last years. For him you made them worth living.'

Caroline arrived alone. 'Bruce will be down for the funeral, of course. Oh, poor Father. He didn't have time to enjoy it.' She looked at Ginny and tears rolled down her cheeks. 'It's not fair that he didn't have more time with you, in peace.' Livy felt herself soften towards Caroline; this was the Caro she had grown up with. The woman who had married Bruce Abbott had melted back into the child who had grown up here.

Alex and Andrew McClintock came at the same time. No one had expected that the Old Man would come at such short notice. He looked weary and haggard after the journey. Uncharacteristically, he brushed Ginny's cheek with his lips.

'I never expected this. I never thought I'd come to see Harry buried.'

Alex embraced his mother, and then went with Livy to visit their three children in the nursery. It was late – just before dinner – and they were sleeping. He stood for a long time in silence, looking at the faces of his two sons, bending to lower the cover a little so that he could look at Isa. Long dark hair already flowed over the pillow.

He put his arm around Livy. 'Thank Heaven we have them. I never expected such riches from life.' In their own room he lingered beside the window, looking past the walled garden to the Rocks. 'I know I'll always have to share you with this place. I'll take what you'll give me.'

'Alex, I've always loved you. From that first day when you came into the kitchen . . .'

'Before you ever saw me you belonged to this place. I understand now that I can only have part of you. I'm grateful, Livy. You'll come here, year after year, and I won't begrudge you that. I'll miss you, but I'll never again try to stifle whatever it is this place gives you. I'll gladly take what's left.'

They changed clothes and went down to dinner. Two of the Clayton directors had arrived. Unexpectedly, the

Permanent Under Secretary of the Foreign Office had come, with only a few hours, telephoned notice. And the Foreign Secretary had sent his Principal Private Secretary. The Tregenna women had come in force to prepare rooms, make up beds, distribute towels and soap, and fresh flowers. Jacques was almost overwhelmed by the amount of food they had brought with them, hams and cheeses and fish. All of the new arrivals were gathered in the drawing-room, Knox dispensing drinks.

'Where is Mark?' one of the Clayton directors asked.

'Yes,' the Permanent Under Secretary said, 'I should like to meet Lord Camborne.'

The use of the title shocked Livy. Harry was dead, and Mark was Lord Camborne. He appeared eventually, wearing chef's checked trousers, the buttoned white jacket, and white neckerchief knotted about his throat.

'I had to help Jacques,' was all he said.

There was a flood of telegrams and letters from the Foreign Secretary, the Prime Minister, even from the Queen. There were many telegrams and letters from strangers for Livy, people who had read *The Kingdom of the Sea*, and now read of the death of this man who had been so important in her life. The obituary in *The Times* was very long, and mostly praised Harry's work, but laid emphasis on the charm and goodhumour which had characterized it. A surprising number of people came from London for the funeral, although there would be a memorial service in London later. Colleagues came, friends . . . Harry's retiring brother, a Fellow of All Souls, appeared, the first time any of them had seen him for years. Frazer Campbell came. Tresillian was filled; people stayed overnight in St Just and Penzance. Mark spent all his time in the kitchen with Jacques; he needed the work Jacques assigned to him for distraction, and it was a way for him to avoid talking with people who had come such a long way, those who would insist on calling him Lord Camborne.

The burial was over, the people had gone. A quiet descended on Tresillian, and there was time and space to realize that

Harry was dead. For just a day Ginny gave way to her grief, and did not appear among them. Jamie and Oliver, who had been bewildered by the sudden influx of people, were beginning to notice Harry's absence. Livy and Alex took them for a walk along the cliff-top, and tried to explain what had happened. Disbelief showed on Jamie's face. 'I won't see Gramp again? Never again?'

'He's still with us, in a way,' Alex said, fumbling for words that Jamie might comprehend. 'He loved you very much, and the love is still here, with you, sort of looking out for you.'

'I don't see him,' Jamie said stubbornly. 'I don't believe you.' He pointed out to sea, and swung around and looked at the Tower. 'He isn't here. If he was here, I could see him. Nanny said he's in Heaven. But he was taken away to the churchyard, and they wouldn't let me go with him.' He started to cry, a sound that was like a bellow of rage. He shook his fist at the sea and the Rocks below. 'I don't see him. How can he be looking out for me?'

His tears in turn started tears of fright in Oliver. He didn't know what he was crying about. He'd only vaguely heard of Heaven, and he didn't know where it was. He had a feeling that all the people who had come were the cause of his beloved grandfather being taken away. He screamed and reached for his father. Alex caught him up in his right arm, struggling desperately to keep his balance. It had never been easy for him to lift his children, and Oliver's weight was almost beyond him now. Livy knelt and took Jamie in her arms. 'Hush, my darling – Daddy and I will try to make it up to you. Gramp is always going to be with you because he loved you.'

These were the moments in which she truly knew that Harry was gone. They sat on the grass, all four of them, and Livy's thoughts were of Harry – his generosity with whatever he had had to give, his friendship and approval being the highest prize she sought. She thought of Blair, who had been his friend, and Dena and Ginny. All the war years seemed to flash before her mind in little frames, like still photos, the years when Alex had been missing, the years when the four

711

girls had become one family. She looked at the two children beside her. They were the tangible reminder of momentous years.

3

Harry's solicitor had stayed on at Tresillian until Ginny felt able to come to listen to the formality of the reading of the will. It was very simple. He had placed the house and the acres which made up its garden in Ginny's name once she had begun the restoration. The entail had been broken. The rest, the small income he had shared with his brother from his father's estate, together with the few farms left in the Camborne name, rented to tenant farmers, the uneconomic tin mines, were to be equally shared between Mark, Rachel and Caroline. He left some personal mementoes to Livy, one of Guy Denham's paintings, a pair of cuff-links, the leather blotting-paper pad he had used all his life in the Foreign Service. The bulk of the death duties would fall on Ginny, because she had so much increased the value of the house.

'There won't be much for you to pay,' the solicitor said, looking at the three children. 'The value of the farms isn't that great. But still, there will be an assessment . . .' He hardly glanced at Ginny as he said this. There would be no difficulty for her in paying whatever was levied on the house and surrounding acres of Tresillian. He had known that the restoration had been undertaken with the thought that it would be the place they would live in Harry's retirement. It seemed cruel to underline the fact that the retirement had been only the brief time it had taken for the illness to overtake him.

He packed up his papers and prepared to leave. If they wished, he informed them, he would continue to represent them, to obtain probate, to engage accountants. But he knew that in the case of Ginny, batteries of McClintock-Clayton lawyers and accountants would come before him. 'It was a privilege to serve Lord Camborne,' he said to Ginny as he shook her hand. He had a taxi waiting to take him to the train at Penzance. Caroline had a chauffeured car waiting to take her to London, but she did not offer to share it with him.

After the solicitor had left, Caroline looked at Rachel and Mark. 'Well, I think I'll leave all the details to you. He shouldn't have included me, really, since I'm so much better off. I mean Bruce has got more than he knows what to do with. I can't be thrown out, penniless. And I'm fulfilling his greatest wish, so I'll be decked in diamonds for quite some time. I'm having a baby.'

They made little sounds of pleasure and congratulations, but they were hollow. Caroline herself did not seem pleased, except that her pregnancy made her marriage more secure. She went off, and as she settled back in the car, they could see her features relax. Death and mourning was behind her.

'I wonder,' Ginny said, 'if she'll ever come to Tresillian again?'

It seemed as if, with Harry's burial, the last of the summer weather went with him. That night, with Caroline gone, the solicitor gone, they were only a small number around the dining-table. Mark had been banished from the kitchen by Jacques, who said it was time he stayed with his family. The weather forecast gave a warning of gales and rain, and as they settled round the table, they could hear the thrust of the wind against the house, the sharp pattering sound of the rain penetrated even the muffling of the heavy curtains. They were mostly silent during dinner; the talk of the last days when so many had gathered about them, had exhausted any desire for conversation. The sadness of Harry's absence, now that they knew it would be for ever, was beginning to hit deeply.

'Will you stay on here now?' Andrew McClintock asked when they were settled in the library where Ginny had asked Knox to serve coffee and liqueurs.

'I don't know. I don't know what I'll do. Tresillian was only left to me because Harry knew, even if he left the whole estate to Mark, that he couldn't possibly afford to maintain it, and he couldn't pay the death duties on it. He'd be forced to sell it. He broke the entail because he thought it was unjust that I was restoring Tresillian at such expense, only to have it belong to Mark. Of course, it's now up to me whether I sell it or not. I didn't plan to live here alone. This is Harry's house, and I meant it for him. I meant to make some arrangement so that Mark should eventually have it. Harry hated to be the Camborne who finally let Tresillian go from the family.'

'I'm glad he did what he did,' Mark said. 'It would have been no gift to me. What would I do with a house like this? He was right to see me free of it.'

Ginny looked around them, as if gathering this attention totally to her. 'There is something I have to tell you. There is something Harry left for us, for all of us. A task, a trust, if we can carry it out.'

She rose, and went to the tray where the liqueurs and glasses were set out. Mark sprang to his feet. 'Let me, please.' Andrew McClintock and Rachel both shook their heads. 'I think you'd better,' Ginny said. 'It may help.' She waited until Mark had poured and handed around brandy to each of them.

'Harry finally told me, the day his resignation was accepted by the Foreign Office.' She had taken a key from her handbag, and went to the drawer of the big library desk where Harry had kept papers. 'I've taken this from the safe upstairs. These are not things to be left lying around. Harry kept them in a safe-deposit box in London, but after the last stay in hospital, he knew he was never going back to London. He brought them down with him.'

'Mother, what is it?' Alex said quietly. 'Don't torture yourself trying to explain too much. Tell us what you want us to know.'

She nodded. She gestured to Mark. 'Give those to Mr McClintock, please. And then pass them around.' She waited as Andrew McClintock studied four photographs. There was a hush among them as they were passed from hand to hand. Mark was the last to gaze at them. He laid them back on the desk beside Ginny.

'Those photographs are of Sonya, who was Harry's mistress when he was in Moscow, and Irina, Sonya's daughter by Harry, whose existence he wasn't aware of until the first photo came to him in Paris. Only four,' she added. 'That was all he ever had. The first of Sonya and Irina when the child was very young, another some years later, also when he was in Paris. And then, while he was in Washington as minister, the one of the girl alone. The last one, which seems to be very recent, came to him in London just after his resignation as ambassador. With it came confirmation of what he had guessed, from her absence from the photos, that Sonya was dead. She died in a labour camp.'

She tapped a sheaf of papers she held in her hand. 'He wrote it all down here in the weeks after he resigned. He guessed he would have very little time, and he wanted the details clear. You remember how long he was away in Moscow? War and absence does strange things to people. Dena once said to me while we were here at Tresillian that she didn't expect to see Harry again. She thought he would die there in Russia. Absence placed a great strain on both of them. She even suspected that he could have a Russian mistress. But when he arrived back in London that time, coming out with Beaverbrook, Sonya had already disappeared. God knows, enough people disappeared in Russia in those days, but she had been in a favoured and protected position. Her father was a leading intellectual and a physicist. Harry told me he loved Sonya, not the way he loved Dena, but the sort of love that grows when you feel you are trapped, and will possibly die soon. The love of desperation. Sonya was fluent in several languages, and was assigned to various jobs connected with the diplomatic corps. That in itself would make her suspect. Harry, at times, thought she might have been a "plant", someone put there to seduce a senior member of a diplomatic mission, never mind the fact that they were allies, to let slip to her little things. Any sort of thing that she could report back to her masters. But he said, he told me, that he was certain, whatever her mission, that she did love him.'

She looked down at Harry's emerald, twisted it slightly on

715

her finger. 'He told all this to Dena when he got back to London. He had told his ambassador, who seemed to regard it as a minor peccadillo, and didn't include it in his report back to London on Harry. Everything was quiet for so many years. Sonya had disappeared. He even wondered if she had been used again on some other diplomat posted to Moscow after the war, but he didn't think so, because someone, any one of the dozens who had been there during the war, would almost surely have seen and recognized her. He had hoped that she was working obscurely in some safe place away from Moscow, or she had got her reward in a nice apartment and a dacha, but with no contact with the diplomatic circles. Then he got the photograph in Paris. Sonya, and his daughter, Irina. She was in a labour camp, they implied. When the second photograph came, they said the daughter was being brought up in internal exile. The lives of both of them depended on Harry's co-operation.'

'Co-operation?' Andrew McClintock said. 'What sort of co-operation?'

'It was very cruel,' Ginny said. 'He had told his ambassador in Moscow about his affair with Sonya. The ambassador did nothing. Harry knew that he had not talked about sensitive things with her, that he had been very guarded. But once he spoke to his ambassador, Sonya disappeared. She was, quite simply, no longer there. It either meant that she had been a plant, and was now no longer useful, or that they had decided to remove her because she had been guilty of falling in love with a foreigner. He never discovered how the Russians found out he'd told the Ambassador. It was a time when terrible things were happening in Russia.

'All the war years went by. There was no word from her. There was no way he could reach her. After the war, when the Russians had managed to grab so much territory and the Cold War was on in earnest, he knew that any communication from him, even a simple enquiry, could put her in terrible danger. The first contact came in Paris . . .' She pointed to the photos on the desk. 'The first photo of Sonya and his daughter. Then came the demands. They wanted whatever information he had which might prove useful –

716

anything. Details of NATO strength, details of contracts Britain made with other countries. Anything that remotely dealt with defence. Each and every piece of information that could be of the slightest use. He was to report attitudes in and outside the embassy, the opinions people held, the way the wind was blowing. Anything, they said, and everything. The price was the life of Sonya and his daughter.'

Alex broke in. 'But he didn't . . .'

Ginny's raised hand silenced him. 'He did everything he should have done. First of all he told his Ambassador in Paris. Then the Foreign Office sent for him to come to London. It was not their affair, and they could have washed their hands of him, demanded his resignation. But there were devious circumstances most of us hardly begin to guess at. His political masters saw an opportunity. They conferred with both MI5 and MI6. There was a chance, just a chance, that the Russians might accept from Harry some ideas they wanted planted. They were even willing to give away some information they believed the Russians already had, or which would be of only minor importance, to make the misinformation they wanted sent look more realistic. They had a chance of a double agent in a high position. Not too high, not too important, and with a genuine reason for wanting to be co-operative. It was difficult even to get the two services, MI5 and MI6, to talk to each other, to agree on what it was safe to let Harry divulge. But they used him. They used all the power of the photographs of those two women to force him to go through with the whole charade. He lived all those years with the fact that he was being used in some dirty and brutal game, and never knowing the outcome of it. They sent him to Washington. The McClintock-Clayton connection could prove extremely useful, the fact that Dena and I had been such close friends for so long could not be faked. It was a fact. It was well known. And small details of the McClintock-Clayton involvement in armaments could prove useful. Even the pharmaceutical side. The electronics. There were many areas of technology where the Russians knew they were behind. They didn't expect plans – nothing as dramatic as that. Plans don't pass over embassy desks to be photographed. But he was a man in a sensitive position whom they could manipulate . . . through these two Russian women.'

'I find it hard to believe. Father wouldn't . . .'

'He didn't,' Ginny answered sharply. 'He told the Foreign Office everything. He went to anonymous places and talked with anonymous men, received instructions from them. He thought it would be the end of his career, and possibly the end of the lives of Sonya and his daughter. But Harry could never have spied for a foreign power. And the Foreign Office knew that. So he became the tool of the security services, both of them. Mostly counter-intelligence, but to a degree espionage itself.'

She pointed to one of the photographs on the desk. 'This one, the first one of the girl alone, came at the cruellest time of all. The night, the night before Dena died. She and I were still in New York, and Harry was approached as he walked back from dinner with Livy and Alex, and you, Mr McClintock. The night he told you about being appointed ambassador to Paris. They said they were not satisfied. They were not getting enough. Some of the information did not fit what they already knew. They threatened him again. The lives of Sonya and his daughter. Possibly something worse . . .'

Outside the wind shrieked about the chimneys of Tresillian. Now the rain was slashing against the windows. The fire blazed, a powerful upward draft caused the flames to leap high above the logs.

'You all know that when Dena got back from New York that morning he had greeted her with the news that he would be ambassador to Paris. No doubt the secret service had told the Foreign Office that this would be the next most favourable place Harry could be put. His rise to a very important post would convince the Russians that he still was trusted. Something of the information Harry passed on, on instructions of the security services, seemed to have been worthwhile, or that was their information. In Paris it would be natural for Harry to hear a good deal about NATO. So he was to be raised to the rank of ambassador in one of the most important embassies.

718

'He told Dena this when she came back from New York. She didn't tell him what she had learned about her cancer in New York. She kept that to herself.'

'Why,' Rachel said, 'are we talking about this when what you've just told us is that my father was being used as a counter-intelligence agent? My mother's suicide had nothing to do with that.'

Ginny looked upwards at the ceiling, as if gathering her thoughts, remembering things she would rather have put behind her. 'You know we drove together that night to Prescott Hill. We found Dena's body. The police took over from there. There was something which came out at the inquest which they weren't quite satisfied about, but there was never any explanation of. There's no doubt Dena went alone to the practice range. She took several guns with her, including Blair's hand gun. There were no prints on the gun, except hers, but they were a little blurred. But the police inferred, though they didn't exactly say it, that they found the angle at which she was holding it not quite natural. But then, Harry or I, or both of us, might have touched her, disarranged things, without either of us meaning to. As I remember it, the gun appeared just to have slipped from her hand.'

Andrew McClintock spoke. 'I want to be quite clear about what you're leading up to, Ginny.'

'And I want you all to be quite sure of what I'm telling you. Everyone had gone. The ambulance, the police. Everyone had been very polite. Very understanding. Harry began telephoning . . .'

Alex nodded. 'Yes, he telephoned me. And I told him I'd do the rest of the telephoning.'

'Then I telephoned him,' Andrew McClintock said. 'I told him I was sending a car to bring you both back to Washington. I knew from Harry's butler . . . the press were already on to it.'

'But then there was the strange call,' Ginny said. Her voice was slow, and now weary. 'There was the call which came . . . a call from no one who would identify himself. Harry called it a crank call. A ghoul call. He said it was

719

because everything had to go through the local exchange, and that the whole world could know that Dena was dead, and how she had died. I only heard his side of the conversation. It was very brief. And Harry was in deep shock. He didn't tell me what the other person had said.'

'But you know now?' Rachel asked.

'When he resigned, when Harry told me the whole story of Sonya and Irina, and what he'd been doing in those years, he told me the other side of the telephone conversation which I'd listened to at Prescott Hill. It was them, the Russians, whomever. They implied that they had killed her. Said they'd followed her . . .'

'The Russians aren't allowed beyond certain points in the Washington area,' Alex said.

'There are plenty they could pay who are. American citizens can go anywhere they want, and some will do anything if the money is right. The Russians are perfectly aware of this. They do employ other people for jobs they want done, surveillance, and heavens knows what else. They said . . .' Ginny's voice wavered. 'They said Harry must take her death as a warning. There were his daughters . . . they actually said, all of them. The young Mrs McClintock. All your women – that's what they said. All your women. The threat was no longer just to Sonya and Irina. It was a most monstrous cruelty. They said it was they who had killed Dena.

'You know what happened after that. Harry gave up. He retreated to Tresillian. He first told the Foreign Office everything that had happened. The threat to his whole family. He said he'd had enough. He wanted to resign. They told him to take some time off. And then they offered him the embassy in Berne. They promised that they wouldn't ask him to have further dealings with agents of the Russians. There was little sensitive information coming from Berne. It was a backwater, except when they needed a neutral country.'

She slumped in her seat. 'And I inadvertently threw him back into the mess by practically asking him to marry me. By then he'd been left in peace for so long he had begun to

720

think it would be permanent. All he ever wanted was to be left in Berne until his retirement. Instead, and probably because of me, and all that goes with the McClintock-Clayton connection, they offered him Washington. They persuaded him that it was his duty to take the post. That he would be uniquely placed to deal with the Russians on many levels. No documents need change hands. Just a hint now and then from Harry on the way the wind was blowing. And then, the security services really gave him his instructions. They had been desperately worried about the Washington embassy ever since the Burgess and Maclean affair. They suspected there still was a real spy in place there. Harry was to wait for some contact from within the embassy. He pointed out that none had been made all the time that he had been there as minister. But they wanted him there. He was the only one who had ever come to them voluntarily and told them he was being blackmailed. They felt he was the only one they could really trust. They wanted him back in place.'

'So they never believed that Dena had been murdered by the Russians? They didn't take his fears for the rest of us seriously?'

Ginny shook her head. 'Dena would not have been the first woman to act as she did in that circumstance. But there were two things that haunted Harry. That she had left no note, made no gesture to tell him that she needed help, or to help him over the shock of that act. Nothing to help him understand why she had done such a thing. Nothing to absolve him from blame. That telephone call had come appallingly soon after her death. Yes, people did know, the police, the local telephone exchange. But the Russians knew so soon! He never resolved it in his own mind. He was never sure she had taken her own life. He never knew that if she had not gone out to target practice she would have lived. Would they have dared murder her when everyone would know it was murder? Had she just been followed on the off-chance that some opportunity would come so they could hurt her, and put more pressure on Harry? Was the fact that she had a hand gun with her just a stroke of convenient luck? Did one of the hirelings go too far? Harry never knew.

'He only told me these things when he knew he was dying. He was of no further use to the Foreign Office, security services, or the Russians. He had reached a point beyond blackmail. Or perhaps not quite. It was at that time, in London, before he came down to Tresillian, through another contact, that they let him know finally that Sonya had died in a labour camp. That's when they also sent him the last photo.' She placed her finger on it. 'His daughter, Irina. Growing up. Just a little older than Mark . . . He took this final cruelty with him to his death.'

Andrew McClintock broke the frozen silence which settled on the room. He gestured to the photographs on the desk. 'I'll look at them again.' Mark brought them to him. They all remained silent while he gazed at them again, comparing one to the other. 'Harry would have recognized Sonya, of course. The child he never saw. Photographs have been faked before, of course. There may never have been a child, but this one, as indefinite as she looks in the early ones, bears a vague resemblance to Harry, but she's more like her mother. Then there is the rather long period before the third, the photograph of the girl alone. She has changed, but children do change. The child's face is gone, and the adolescent's face is there. The same shaped eyes, the same brows, but more defined. The jaw-line is stronger. This recent one, a lovely, if rather frightened-looking young girl, who might become a beautiful woman, as is evident her mother once was.'

'What,' Alex said, 'are we expected to do? Nothing? Something?' He looked at his mother. 'You've told us all this for a reason, and I suspect we already know it.'

Ginny sighed. 'I expect you do. Harry wanted her out. He always wanted her out, Sonya too, if that were ever possible. But he hardly believed that could happen. That last picture of Irina, this one obsessed him. Ever since he had known of her existence, he'd begged the Foreign Office to try to do something about getting her out. He was willing to acknowledge her as his child, if that was necessary. He was willing to give up his whole career if the truth came out. After all, Dena had been aware of his affair with Sonya. He believed

722

that she would accept the girl once she knew that there was a chance she might get out to the West. It would not be the first time an illegitimate child has appeared in someone's family. Or Irina could have come under another identity. He pleaded with the Foreign Office to try, and they swore they did, very quietly, in Moscow. It had to be made to appear as if it was being done by one of Harry's friends in the Foreign Office as a favour, a very secret favour. The Russians must not know that Harry had told the Foreign Office everything, otherwise the credibility of what he passed on to them would be destroyed. He suspected, in fact, that they did nothing at all. Harry knew he had assumed the same bargaining weight as Irina. The Russians wouldn't give her up as long as they could use her in any way, to bring even the smallest pressure on Harry. She had no importance except where she was. She was no one the British or anyone else wanted; only Harry wanted her. She couldn't be "exchanged" for someone convicted of spying here or in the US. She just wasn't important enough. Harry once threatened to go to the press here and make it all public. The Foreign Office simply pointed out what Harry already knew, that the move would be counter-productive. It would be assumed to be the ravings of a madman, or if the Russians went to the length of denying all knowledge of the girl publicly, then she was as good as dead. If you don't exist in Russia, you just don't exist.'

Ginny folded her hands in her lap, deep folds of grief and weariness in her face. 'Harry died still wanting her out. He hadn't any idea how she'd been treated. He didn't know if she knew about him. He didn't know, God help him, whether she would even want to come to the West. His ignorance about her was total. Internal exile means people are unreachable. She might never have been near any of the cities Westerners are allowed to visit. She might have been brought up in a labour camp or by foster parents who were peasants. He had hoped, all through the years that he played his double game, that when the time came for him to retire, the Foreign Office might help. He hoped he might make his own private bargain with the Russians though he would have nothing to bargain with. He planned to go to Russia himself when he was retired, and try to find her. God knows, it was a forlorn hope. What would he have done if they'd closed the books on him and on Irina? They could just deport him, and that would be the end.

'The real end was that Harry just wasn't strong enough or well enough to do anything. His only hope was the Foreign Office, and they refused to get involved officially. They laid the whole situation at the door of the secret intelligence service, and MI5. And they had closed the door. Harry was of no further use to them, nor was the girl. She was simply the result of an indiscretion on Harry's part all those years ago in Moscow. Harry was beaten every way he turned. He gave up, and he came back here to die.'

Her voice grew bitter. 'I wondered how they dared show themselves at his funeral, coming here and offering me condolences. But I'm not even sure that the ones who came here ever knew about the situation. All that side of it was handled by people who seemed to have no real identities. Harry kept reminding me that the Foreign Service was not the secret service. He just happened to get caught in the middle.'

'Do you want this girl out?' Andrew McClintock said to Ginny.

'Would I have told you this if I didn't? He told no one but me. I could have kept quiet. Regarded it as a lost cause. I thought you . . .' She looked from the old man to her son. 'I thought between you, you might be able to do something. Find some way. It is a debt I feel I owe to Harry, though he never ever asked me to try. I think he knew I would. In the end I could always do as Harry had threatened. I could go to the press – tell the story. It would make very big and scandalous news.'

'And the girl, Irina, would most certanly die,' Alex said. 'Just as Harry knew.'

Ginny's body sagged. 'Well, am I beaten, then?'

Andrew McClintock, as if to deny what she had just said, straightened himself, leaning forward on his cane. 'No, not beaten. There may be ways. There may be ways which will have to be quietly and carefully explored. I have a few friends in high places . . . Let me think You are sure you want to go through with this? If it could be managed, we –' now he included them all '– would be landed with a stranger. Perhaps an unwilling stranger . . .'

'Not a stranger,' Ginny said. 'She is Harry's daughter.'

He got slowly to his feet. 'Very well. We will try. Now I think I'll go to bed. Not that I'll sleep, but there'll be many new thoughts to occupy the waking hours. I'll be leaving early in the morning, Ginny. And Alex will be coming with me. There's much to attend to in Washington. Do you want to drive with us to London, Rachel? I know you have a job to hold down.'

'Thank you,' she said quietly. 'I'd be grateful.'

'That leaves you, Livy,' Andrew McClintock said. 'Stay as long as Ginny needs you – but not too long. Alex needs you also. I wish you, Ginny, would come back to Washington for a while – but that's for you to decide. Jamie is already late starting school. We'll be using Seymour House for the next few days, Ginny. I cannot place certain telephone calls through a hotel switchboard. If you hear nothing, don't think we've abandoned the idea. It may take a very long time.'

Mark held open the door. As Andrew McClintock passed, he murmured, 'Thank you, sir.'

'What the devil are you thanking me for?'

'For trying. If I could, I'd go in there and get her out myself.'

'You, boy, are a romantic. There will be no knight on a white horse dashing in to rescue her. It will be cold, and painstaking and slow.'

'Yes, sir.' Mark closed the door behind him.

'You know, of course,' Livy said, when she was certain that Andrew McClintock was well beyond earshot, 'why he is willing to make this effort?' She looked at Ginny. 'He's trying, in some odd fashion, to give you back a life for Chris's life.'

'Livy!' Alex sounded outraged that she should make the comparison.

'But it's true,' Ginny said. 'If there's no other way, if he ever gets an opportunity, he'll try to buy her out.'

4

After ten days Mark left them to be inducted into the army at Catterick, in Yorkshire. This was to be his three months basic training. 'Don't worry about me,' he said. 'I'll do just fine. I'll learn to shine my shoes properly, make my bed, hate the drill sergeant, and with luck, after that, I'll learn to do a bit more than peel potatoes.' He went off with a determinedly cheerful expression.

'I wonder how he will do,' Ginny said, when he was gone. 'God help him if any of the rest of them learn he's Lord Camborne. He would have been Mark Penrose on his draft papers. I hope it can stay that way.'

'I think he's become very tough, or he will be,' Livy said, 'when it's all over. The day he broke that teacher's nose at Eton he made a break for himself. He knows that the world his father went into doesn't exist anymore. He's fully prepared to create his own. But I wish he could have had his father just a bit longer.'

'He still has me,' Ginny said. 'I think he knows it.'

After another week Ginny announced to Livy that the children had to be taken back to Washington. 'I've been very selfish, keeping you here. Jamie is already many weeks late starting school. You've seen so little of Alex this summer. It's no way to run a marriage.'

'What about you?'

Ginny shrugged. 'What about me? It isn't the life I planned. Harry was to have been here with me. We were supposed to be cosily ensconced here, with Knox and Jacques, and Seymour House for when we wanted a break. I always looked forward to us having a lot of time together. Now there's far too much time for me alone. And I'll be alone, no matter where I go. I might as well stay here.'

'Not here alone,' Livy urged her. 'Not here just yet. Come back to Washington with us. You know there's loads of room at Massachusetts Avenue. There's Prescott Hill. You might decide to have a house in Washington again . . .'

'I should do something about organizing a memorial service for Harry,' Ginny murmured. 'But I don't feel up to it yet. But I should really stay in Europe. I have to wait for her.'

'You mean Irina. How do you know that she'll come to England? If they can manage to get her out, I would suppose that they'll arrange an American entry visa for her. It would be . . . well, I'm not sure. If Mr McClintock has any influence in the matter, she'll come to the States. She'll come to Washington.'

With some reluctance Ginny agreed to come with her. 'Suddenly I feel old and unsure of myself. I feel as if I'm finally leaving Harry behind. Leaving his house closed and shut up. No life in it.'

'He wanted you to have it. Being very practical, you're the only one who can afford it.'

On the last day they took their usual cliff-top walk. Jamie and Oliver, when they reached the base of the Tower, began to scramble among the huge fallen stones. 'I can't bear to sell it,' Ginny said. She turned and looked back at the house. 'I have a little dream, Livy . . . just the beginning of a dream, and you're the only one I can tell it to. You will have to promise me it will stay with you.' For the first time since Harry died, Livy saw some glimmer of enthusiam in Ginny's face.

'Suppose I keep on this place . . . suppose I just come here in the summer, and keep open the house for anyone else who wants to come. Suppose I keep it on for as many years as it takes Mark to finish his training. Until he has the confidence and experience to run a kitchen himself.'

'You're surely not thinking . . .'

'It would make a beautiful, small, rather grand hotel. Or simply a restaurant. Where is there to go around here? Not a lot of places. People are starting to travel more. They want something different. I think you'll see a number of these sorts of hotels starting up, and their guests will probably mostly be American, looking for something different. This already has several advantages for that sort of carriage trade. All the bathrooms. It's got a magnificent wine cellar already laid down. That would cost any restaurateur just starting up a fortune.'

'Mark running a hotel? He's only eighteen.'

'One day he'll be twenty-eight. He'll be capable . . . Well, I hope he'll be capable of running it. You remember, Livy . . . Harry left it to me because he knew there was no way Mark alone could keep it. It would have to be sold. So I feel it's been left to me in trust. What can I do but hope that one day it might pay for itself? The rent from the lands could never do it. There has to be some way for it to make money. I can't just hand it over to Mark with a huge amount of money to keep it running as a private house. He'd never accept it, and if he did, idleness, having no need to make a living, would ruin him. If I could make him see it as a business deal, lease it to him. See if he can make a go of it. It's a nice, smallish, comfortable stately home. It has great historic associations. And can't you just imagine a Thea Sedgemore gallery in the stable block? Tresillian would come to life, Livy. It wouldn't be inhabited just in the summer by an old woman and her grandchildren. Of course, we could always visit . . . as paying guests.'

'Mr McClintock would say you're incurably romantic.'

'Perhaps I am. I would feel, if this worked out, that I was keeping faith with Harry and Dena. And Mark. He was the only one born here. If ever there was a natural godmother, I'm it. Well . . . I can dream, can't I? At least I see some future for Tresillian. Just a glimmer, if Mark proves up to it. But we must never speak to him about it. Not for a long time. Don't let him expect anything. And above all, let's not put a burden of expectation on him. He'll have to find his own way. When he's older, I'll tell him, so he'll work harder to earn it. I suppose he'd even have to think about taking a hotel-management course.' She sighed. 'Perhaps it's all nonsense. But at least I have something to think about for it . . .'

Jamie and Oliver came dashing out of the Tower, shrieking with laughter at a game of 'wreckers' they had played among the stones. They had assimilated many of the games their young relations played and 'wreckers' along the Cornish coast was an old and favourite one. False lights set to lure ships and people to their deaths, to plunder cargo. Livy supposed it was no more bloodthirsty than cowboys and Indians, but it still made her shudder.

'Time for tea,' she said to them, holding out her hands. 'Aunt Thea is coming, to say goodbye for a little time. Up early tomorrow. A big journey. In two days we'll be seeing Daddy. And school for Jamie . . . and next summer we'll be back.' She was determined that the leave-taking would not be sad. Above all, she did not want Ginny to feel sad, or alone. The children raced on ahead of them towards the house.

'One thing Mark will have to have besides experience and the capability of running a small, smart hotel,' Livy volunteered.

'What?'

'He'll have to be lucky enough to find a wife who won't mind her house being invaded by strangers. Who'll be tactful and loyal and welcoming. She'll have to be a paragon, in fact. Perhaps you shouldn't leave it too long to tell him what you hope for him and Tresillian. It wouldn't do for him to marry a Caroline, or even a Rachel. And a Chris couldn't be buried in Cornwall all her life.'

'Well, there's always the hope that he'll find a Livy.'

That night Ginny half dozed away the hours, lying in the single bed she had had put in Harry's dressing-room when he had needed a nurse with him all through the night. She thought of what she had talked to Livy about, the small, secret hope that had begun to grow in her that there might be a way to keep Tresillian for Mark, even after her death. She smiled a little wryly as she remembered Livy's warning of the kind of wife Mark would need. Someone charming, but hard-headed, a worker. Someone who would perhaps, one day, name this suite of rooms the ambassador's suite. Would there be an admiral's suite? She hoped they wouldn't name the rooms rose and blue and green. Perhaps there could be an Olivia room, a Rachel room, a Caroline room, even, even, a Christine room. Then she turned her head into the pillow and wept as she did only at nights, when no one could see or hear her. She wept for Harry, and their lost future. She wept for Blair, and for her beloved young husband, her first love, Alex. She wept for Dena, and the lonely way she had died. She wept for Chris, and the blazing horror of her death. And as she wept, she grew more determined that this house would survive, and Mark would be its master. She was conscious that she was now the only person alive who was certain that he was not Harry's son. Mike Goodrick might suspect that that was so, but he would never know, not for certain.

And in the middle of her tears, she thought, as she had thought many times in the months she had known of her existence, of the girl, Irina. The part of Harry that still lived. The part she was determined she would one day share.

Eased with this thought, at last she slept.

Chapter 19

1

Autumn merged into early Washington winter. Ginny stayed at Prescott Hill, making infrequent journeys into Washington to stay overnight with Livy and Alex. She went nowhere, socially, and social Washington respected that desire. Some people who were asked to quiet dinner parties at Massachusetts Avenue when Ginny visited, expressed open regret that she was not still mistress of the British Embassy, and then were quickly silent as an expression of disapproval registered on Ginny's face. As the widow of a former British Ambassador, she still observed the protocol of never criticizing her successor or predecessor.

Accompanied by Livy and Alex, she had been obliged to attend a packed memorial service for Harry in St Margaret's, Westminster. She had not wanted what she saw as a show of hypocrisy arranged by the Foreign Office, which she had believed had used Harry, and then discarded him. She wondered which of the many of his colleagues who had attended had known the double life they had forced him to live. Every face now seemed to her to be tinged with duplicity.

There were frequent letters from Mark. They were deliberately lighthearted; through them he clung to Ginny and to Livy as he could not to Rachel and Caroline. When he had a few days leave he spent it on the long journey to Cornwall to visit Thea. He wrote,

I'll survive this army, if it doesn't kill me first. Eton would have been a better preparation for it than Wrisley. Here I know they're totally uninterested in me as an individual. If I bust the sergeant-major's nose, they'll shove me in the can for the rest of my two years. I can't say the army's very interested in *sole bonne femme*.

He was moved to Aldershot.

Things are looking up. I've landed a job in the kitchen of the officers' mess of the Grenadier Guards. Usually, all I'm allowed to do is chop the vegetables and give an occasional stir to the soup. In about three months they'll assign me to waiting at table, or carrying drinks. I'd rather stay in the kitchen. Some of the chaps out there, the subalterns, were at Eton in my house for the little time I lasted. I'm afraid they might recognize me. That could make things a bit awkward in the barracks. I lay myself out flat for the chef, so he'll think I'm his right hand, and won't let me be assigned to Outer Mongolia. That was always Father's favourite expression of extreme disapproval from the Foreign Office.

As if she hadn't heard that expression dozens of times from both Harry and Dena, Ginny thought. He always ended his letters the same way. *'I wonder about news of the girl. Is there any news?'* He never mentioned her name, but Ginny and Livy always knew that he referred to Irina.

There was no news to give him of Irina. 'It's being worked on,' was all Alex would tell Livy. 'The less you know about it, the better. If we can get her out, it would be better if you just knew her with whatever identity's been given to her.'

Andrew McClintock would tell them no more than Alex. He was invited to dinner, and came, each time Ginny visited from Prescott Hill. 'Don't ask,' he said, whenever Ginny ventured to raise the subject. 'Better not to know. It isn't accomplished yet. It may never be.' Each time he visited, he went to see his sleeping great-grandchildren in their nurseries. Mrs Hope was now a permanent member of the household. Like Mrs Tennant, she had just slipped in. There was never any doubt of her affection for the children, and she got along with Nanny, which was vital. Livy knew that it was useless now to try to escape from the regimen of the rich. There were people there to serve her and Alex and their children, and she must accept it. She wrote some poems, and tore up most of them. *The Kingdom of the Sea* was still hanging on in the lower half of the best-seller lists.

She had become a minor Washington celebrity in her own right, not just the girl who was said to have broken up Alex's first marriage, and managed to hold on to him for herself. For her, Harry's death had so overshadowed the success of *The Kingdom of the Sea* that it seemed it had taken place in another life, that it had little to do with her. She still resented Andrew McClintock's interference in its promotion, but in her calm moments she realized she ought to be grateful. Without him, it might have gathered dust on booksellers' shelves, and already be on its way to being remaindered. She still cherished the dream that it might have made it on its own, and half the time was willing to acknowledge that it was only that, a dream. Sometimes she even found herself believing Andrew McClintock's maxim that things seldom happened, they were made to happen.

They went for Christmas to Prescott Hill. Ginny made it festive, with a huge tree dominating the hall, because the children were still young enough to enjoy it. Someone at his school, an older boy, had told Jamie there was no Father Christmas, and being a McClintock, he was half-inclined to believe it. But he watched his father solemnly lay out wine and cake in the hall, and make sure that no fire was lighted, so that the way was clear down the chimney. So he was convinced again, and Livy knew that for another year, Jamie would not try to disillusion Oliver.

Among the Christmas cards there was a letter from Mark.

I've met a smashing girl. Her name's Gill. She's working as a sort of secretary-companion to an old lady in Aldershot – in fact the widow of General West. She doesn't get much time off, and it isn't always the times I'm free. But she's great to be with, when we can meet.

Had a rather awkward experience a few weeks ago. I'd been temporarily assigned to duty in the bar of the officers' mess. The regular chap was sick. Not mixing

733

drinks, just serving them. Well, I was waiting on the table of a group of the brass, and the guest of honour was General Goodrick. As I've noticed in a lot of Americans, he tends to look at the faces of the people who serve him. Then someone called me Penrose. The General just about managed to clamp his mouth down on saying something to me. He knows that doesn't go in the army. But I had a note from him two days later, inviting me to dinner at a London club, which he's an honorary member of, for whenever I had a night off duty. I didn't want to go, because it might come out, and my life would be hell at Aldershot and generals aren't supposed to consort with other ranks. But then I thought of how decent he'd been to me when we met at Prescott Hill, and it seemed rude to say no. So I went, in civvies, of course, and he signed me into the book as Penrose. Then one of those bloody club servants with a memory longer than an elephant's trunk, remembered Father as Penrose, and he remembered a photograph of me in the papers when Father died. Well, General Goodrick bribed him to shut up, and I wasn't called Lord Camborne. No one was any wiser at Aldershot. I enjoyed his company, once I'd got over the scare. He asked me to give his regards to all of you. He talked about Mother and Father, and you, Aunt Ginny, and how much he still missed Blair. He said when I was out of the army we should get together, and he gave me a permanent address at the Pentagon where they'd always forward post. He's just on the verge of retirement, and doesn't have much idea of what he'll do with his life, or where he'll live. He's been moved around a lot. Being a bachelor, of course, they've been inclined to post him wherever he could be useful at short notice. But having been in the army a while now, I just have to say I was scared as hell having dinner with a four-star general. But he's a nice man, and he didn't treat me like a kid. If I hadn't been so overwhelmed by rank, and afraid someone might recognize me, I'd have thoroughly enjoyed myself. He isn't at all 'military', and he didn't find it shocking that I was working in the catering corps. He asked me what I was going to do when I came out, and he didn't laugh when I told him. 'Tough life, soldier,' he said. 'You've chosen a tough life.' I expect I have, but it's still what I want.

The letter ended, as always, *'I wonder if there's any news of the girl? I think about her so often.'*

At last Andrew McClintock gave them a crumb of information, too slight to be passed on to Mark. 'The British Foreign Office want nothing to do with it. So far as they're concerned, she doesn't exist, or if she does, it's no business of theirs. Without their help, we can't get near MI6. Harry is dead, and the whole matter is ended. But I have my contacts at the State Department, a few people who owe me favours. I have succeeded in seeing the President, for a few minutes. This is information which is strictly secret. Kennedy cannot be seen to be involved in any fashion. But he can give the nod to State. No one can expect Kennedy to pick up the telephone and talk to Khruschev, or even write him, about an unimportant girl. These people deal only in far bigger chips. But he owes me a little something. I presented my due bill. Then, we are always negotiating business deals with Russia. McClintock-Clayton men are frequently in Moscow. I have flown to Cleveland to see Cyrus Eaton about it. He is interested, and said he'd try to help. He could speak to almost anyone in Russia, and they'd listen. He's the one capitalist of whom the Russians appear to entirely approve. He has talked me into a project of supplying really huge harvesting machinery to Russia. Would they let go of a girl in order to get their hands on a few hundred more giant harvesters? We'll have to wait and see . . .'

Andrew McClintock and Alex had other preoccupations that winter and spring. On 1st June, McClintock-Clayton would be offered on the New York stock exchange. The work of preparation was intense. 'We have to be very careful about the number of shares we offer, that's the Old Man's price for agreeing to it at all,' Alex said. 'And there's the tricky business of the price at which they're offered. The public won't buy if it's too high. If it's too low, we've devalued our own stock, and given part of McClintock-Clayton away. We'll have to work like mad between the offer of shares, and the final parcelling out of them. We don't dare let too many shares go to too few people, or we'll end up with a take-over battle on our hands. That's why we've got to reserve so many shares for ourselves, and it doesn't leave a lot to go public with. The Old Man insists that fifty-one per cent isn't enough for us to keep. If any one of the directors of Clayton, in particular, decided to sell even the small number of shares each has been given over the years, or worse, if a couple of them got together to sell because they decided they hadn't been given enough, we'd have lost the balance. It's all very fine tuning, and it's got to be done if McClintock-Clayton is to stay alive.'

The first of June arrived, and the shares of McClintock-Clayton were heavily oversubscribed. The financial press had been in a paroxysm of speculation over the rights issue for weeks. Andrew McClintock and Ginny met with Alex and Livy that night at the McClintock mansion. The Old Man looked grim, despite the fact that the day had established a great victory, proof of how Wall Street and the public regarded the worth and solidity of McClintock-Clayton. 'My father,' he said, 'would have hated this day. I myself don't see it in a very different light. But it's time Alex's generation took over. I won't be around much longer. Probably the first action of the new board of directors will be to vote me chairman for life, and ask me to retire to a non-executive position and let them get on with the business of the second half of the twentieth century. Well, so be it.' Livy offered champagne, which Andrew McClintock took grudgingly. 'Well, Alex, have you calculated yet how many millions you're worth today? From now on you'll be able to look it up in the *Wall Street Journal* every morning, and see how many you're up or down on the day before.' He nodded to Livy. 'I bought a few shares for your portfolio, and of course the children's trusts bought too. Have to keep it in the family.'

Then his tone changed. 'I have some news that might be

more in keeping with champagne. The ⸏⸏⸏ ⸏⸏ ⸏
Austria. Very soon she will be on her way t⸏ ⸏⸏
few months there, she will be permitted to enter ⸏⸏
States as an immigrant. We had to find a very obscure pe⸏⸏
who is also very discreet, to be her sponsor. It wouldn't do
to have her directly connected with our names.'

Ginny's hand went to her throat in a fluttery, nervous
movement. 'The poor child. Is she to go to a complete
stranger?'

'What are we except complete strangers?' Andrew
McClintock answered. 'As a formality she will see the person
who has sponsored her. Then she can take up a position as
a secretary with Livy. I've persuaded Mrs Tennant that it's
finally time she fully retired.'

'But . . .' Livy protested. 'Supposing she . . .'

'Doesn't like us? Doesn't want to be that close? That will
all be revealed in time. If it's Harry's daughter you want,
Ginny, then she must be placed somewhere within the family.
If she doesn't like the situation, then she'll get out on her
own. That's her choice. Once she has her green card, she's
free to seek employment anywhere in the United States. If
she should happen to marry an American, she will be free
to become a United States citizen in three years. If she
doesn't marry, she will wait five years. In the meantime, she
will carry an Israeli passport. It was the least obvious way
we could arrange it. They let a certain number of Jews out
of Russia each year, a very few. So for the time being, she's
Jewish. She understands all this.'

'How do you know?'

'People have talked with her. Have very easily talked with
her. This is no child who'd been brought up by peasant foster
parents, nor in a labour camp. Her English is excellent. So
is her French. She speaks fairly good German. In preparation
for travelling on an Israeli passport, she had managed to
learn some Hebrew. I'm told she has some little talent on
the cello.'

'The languages sound like Harry's daughter.'

Andrew McClintock gave a light shrug. 'Yes and no. She's
obviously very intelligent. But the report on her personally

. . . she seems rather . . . rather characterless. Not like Harry at all. In appearance she resembles him, though not startlingly, as you saw from the photos. She's very attractive, but beyond answering questions like a polite child, she seems to be a nobody.'

'Isn't that exactly what she is?' Ginny said. 'A nobody. For nineteen years she hasn't had much identity, or, at least, the only identity she had was one she'd rather, probably, be without. And now she's being pushed into another situation she doesn't know anything about. It's a wonder she isn't speechless with fright.'

'That could be. Perhaps the capitalist West has no attractions for her. Well, she's being landed right into the nest of capitalism. If she leaves, we'll understand why.'

'But why is she coming to me?' Livy asked. Once again she was resentful of arrangements being made without consulting her. Once again Andrew McClintock had done exactly what he thought should be done. 'Why not to Ginny?'

'With Ginny she would be too obvious. She is too young to fit in as a companion-secretary. However excellent her English is, it will take a year or two before she will seem a normal part of any scene here. And there's another reason. I was thinking of the girl's chances of some happiness. She is more likely to find that in the midst of a family with small children, with the normal comings and goings of a family, than with, forgive me, Ginny, but you know what I'm saying is true, than with a rich woman who spends most of her time alone. If Ginny were to come back to Washington, then you could share her. Between two households she would very quickly get used to American life. Your tastes, Livy, in Washington are considered rather odd. You're different. It will be far less noticeable if you decide to employ a young foreigner than if Ginny did. Fewer questions asked. Fewer comparisons to Harry, if she happens to resemble him in some mannerisms.'

'Yes I see. You're probably right. When do we expect her?'

'That hasn't been decided. Leave her a little while to absorb some Israeli colouration. She will be, of course,

Russian. But she should also have just a few touches of Jewishness. That would be expected. So we will all go about our normal lives, and wait.'

Livy had brought out some bottles of her precious stock of Romanée Conti for the occasion. At dinner, they did not talk of the girl. When the wine was poured, Alex rose. 'There's only one possible toast tonight. To the man who created McClintock-Clayton.'

Andrew McClintock did not respond. He had turned eighty-four that spring. He must soon give up what he had created.

2

The girl came at the end of the summer. Ginny and Livy had gone to Tresillian in July with the children, Nanny and Mrs Hope. Andrew McClintock had developed a chest ailment, and the doctors advised him to leave Washington's humid heat for some weeks. 'They might as well have said months,' he had declared sourly, 'for all the use I am now to the company.' He had, as he predicted, immediately assumed an non-executive chairmanship; he still retained his office at McClintock-Clayton. He still attended board meetings. But he no longer had the deciding vote. That belonged to Alex. So instead of the journey by air, they travelled by sea with Andrew McClintock with the thought that the voyage might restore him. But he was pale and thin, and seemed shrunken. He sat for long hours in a deckchair, wrapped in rugs. He held a book in his hand, but did not read. He watched Jamie and Oliver play with the few other young children in first class. 'Would do them more good if they were down with the kids in steerage. A bit of rough and tumble just for practice . . .'

The baby Isa was beginning to walk unsteadily. Nanny hovered over her, but Isa more often put her hand trustingly in Andrew McClintock's when he took his one stroll around the deck, leaning heavily on his cane. 'What a sight,' one Wall-Street broker, on honeymoon with his third bride, remarked when he saw them from his seat in the bar. 'The great Andrew McClintock, a merciless old cutthroat who's pretty well up there with the robber barons, and his sweet, innocent little great-granddaughter, who'll probably inherit the earth.'

They settled in at Tresillian: Alex would come later in the summer. The rhythm of their lives was resumed. Jamie's play-house was opened up, and the young Tregenna and Trevithick relations gathered every morning. Thea came to Tresillian most nights to dinner. She observed the children playing in the garden of the cottage as she slowly drank her coffee in the mornings. 'I feel age creeping into my bones, Livy. At times I'm too tired to work. And yet I have to go on. There's so much to finish . . . I almost feel I have to work to make up for what the others didn't have time to do. Harry went too young. Dena. And your own father. Chris . . . One doesn't make such friends again. The circle is closing.'

Livy dared not intimate that it might be widened to include one other. That would be the one sadness if the girl, Irina, should come to them, and stay with them. They might in time treat her as one of the family, but they could never acknowledge her as such. Harry would never see her, never know . . .

Towards the end of August there was a small flurry of activity; Andrew McClintock was on the telephone to London a number of times a day. He placed only one call to Alex in Washington, and asked him to come at once. Alex would fly the next night. In less than two days he would be at Tresillian.

He arrived, driven directly down from Heathrow. As always, the long journey tired him, but he went enthusiastically to the nursery. Isa was asleep, but Jamie and Oliver were having their supper. They greeted him joyfully. Jamie's words tumbled over themselves in his excitement. There was a pony coming. They could all have it to ride in what remained of the holiday at Tresillian, and then the Tregenna and Trevithick children would have him for the winter. 'But we'll have to get another one. He'd be awfully lonely up here all by himself and anyway, there are just too many of us to share one small poor pony.'

'Jamie, you're breaking my heart,' Alex said, as he hugged him. 'How do you know you can afford two more ponies? You have one at Prescott Hill.'

Jamie rocked a little on his heels; his father never talked about money. 'Well . . . maybe we can work it out. Maybe it could come out of my allowance. Maybe Oliver could chip in . . .' In true McClintock fashion, Oliver was silent about committing his small allowance. 'All the Tregennas and the Trevithicks would like the ponies, Dad,' Jamie went on. 'And they'd come every day to groom and feed them. They wouldn't be lonely. There's plenty of stable room here.' A young Andrew McClintock was trying to figure out the logistics of it. 'Well, maybe one pony, then. John Trevithick says his pa has a shed at the back of the house where they could put the pony in the winter . . . but of course it would be better to have two ponies up here so all the kids could ride in the orchard. They'd take great care of them, Dad, and they'd be waiting for us next year. Dad, how much does it cost to keep a pony?'

'I suspect even more than your and Oliver's allowance. But we'll go into that tomorrow, very carefully. We'll see what can be managed. Now kiss your tired old father good-night.'

'You tired, Dad?' Jamie's face clouded. 'You're not going to get all tired to death, like Gramp?'

'No, Jamie, not that way. Don't worry. Nothing that a bath and a meal, and a night's sleep won't put right. We'll sort out the pony tomorrow. I promise.' He went into the night nursery and kissed Isa softly, stroked the long, dark hair. Then he put his arm around Livy as he went tiredly, and carefully, down the stairs, to the room they always had at Tresillian. 'I sometimes think I'd go mad if I didn't have you and them. Let's try to get some ponies and gladden not just their hearts, but all the Tregenna and the Trevithick and the Trencom kids. It wouldn't hurt to stable a few ponies up here, give the kids something to think about during the winter, and our kids something to look forward to. That's

741

one of the reasons I think this place is so special and so precious. So long as our kids keep coming here, they'll never forget what they're descended from. They have strong sea-going blood in them. They should be able to come back, and feel at home. I'll do my damnedest to see that no stupid snobbery ever separates them from their friends and relatives here. Ginny's instinct was right about this place, as yours always has been. We must never let it go.'

Andrew McClintock was waiting for them, with Ginny, in the library. 'She is due to arrive in London tonight. She will be met . . .' He held up his hand. 'No, not in the usual McClintock-Clayton style. A very ordinary young man, in a very beaten-up car. They'll stay at a hotel near the airport tonight. He'll drive her down tomorrow. Her visa permits her to stay in Britain for six months – but not to be employed. She is a student on her way to the States. And a boyfriend to meet, and a romantic holiday in Cornwall. They will stay in St Just, like any other holiday couple. They will stroll up the hill. They'll look at the Tower, and the Rocks, unaware that they're trespassing. And she will just come in . . . the young man will wait in the orchard.'

'Just like that?' Alex said.

'Just like that. Over the next few weeks she and Livy will become friends. Livy will offer her a job. She will travel on to the States, but not with us. She will turn up to Massachusetts Avenue, and the job will be there – if she wants it.'

Andrew McClintock went to the table and poured himself another malt whisky. 'Sometimes I have a real need of this stuff. I have to say that you mustn't think I'm not as nervous as you all are.' He looked around at them, as if he were annoyed by something. 'I haven't been nervous for as long as I can remember. We might be doing totally the wrong thing. And I'll have wasted a hell of a lot of money, and what's worse a lot of time, to accomplish precisely nothing. At my age, time is what you can't afford. Damn, don't know when I last poured my own drink, either. If young Mark was here . . . Well, I hope I've arranged that. I had one of my friends at Clayton's who's an ex-Grenadier himself telephone the CO at Aldershot and tell him that Old Man McClintock was at his last gasp. Could Mark Penrose, Lord Camborne, be granted compassionate leave for a few days? I think he can manage it. And I've telephoned Rachel. She's coming down tonight. I left Caroline out of it. She wouldn't keep her heart, or her tongue still.'

'It's all arranged, then,' Ginny said.

He glared at her. 'If I don't arrange things, who will? That's one thing you'll all miss about me when I'm finally gone. I can just hear you saying it . . . "He was a mean old bastard, but he did get things done".'

It was the last day of August, a day calm, clear, the afternoon warm and golden, the sort of day in Cornwall when the sea most resembled Livy's opals. Rachel had arrived, Mark had come by a roundabout route by train; Livy and Alex drove to pick him up. They had a late tea, and then sat about in the library, starting up fragments of conversation which petered out into nervous silence. Mark kept getting up and going to the window from which he could see the orchard. The tide was out. The Tresillian Rocks showed all their powerful, cruel beauty.

Knox had arrived to ask if anyone would like drinks poured. Andrew McClintock waved him away. 'We have an excellent bartender here,' gesturing to Mark. Knox had brought water and ice with him. He put it down, and departed. Quietly Mark poured and served drinks for all of them.

'She should be here,' Rachel said. 'Did something go wrong?'

Then she was there. While Mark had been busy with the drinks she had approached from the orchard to the door and the back passage which led to the great hall. She knew exactly where to go. She knew where they would be waiting. The plan of the house had been shown to her, and she had memorized it.

She was wearing a simple cotton dress, blue, which looked slightly faded from washing; she wore a darker blue scarf tied at the back of her head from which long, golden hair fell on her shoulders and back; she was bare-legged and wore

743

rope-soled sandals. Her face and arms and legs were tanned, as if she had absorbed a lot of sun in Israel. She was above average height, with a slender, graceful body. She had finely-drawn features, a mouth with a slightly sensuous curve at the corners, very straight eyebrows darker than her hair, and blue eyes.

She closed the door gently behind her, and stood and faced them. 'Irina,' she said in a soft, almost accentless voice. Alex got to his feet; Mark stood by the window just staring at her.

But it was to Andrew McClintock she went first. 'Mr McClintock? Good evening. You sent for me?'

He struggled to his feet. He held out his hand. 'Yes, I sent for you. The goods went by a rather indirect route, but they have arrived, and seem to be in good condition. I'm glad to see you here.'

She moved next to Ginny. 'Lady Camborne. I understand it was at your most express wish that this has been . . . been arranged. How very kind.'

She did not for a moment hesitate between Livy and Rachel. She went to Livy. 'You are Mrs McClintock – Olivia Miles, the poet's daughter. The daughter of Isa, who was very beautiful, and very kind. I have read your father's poems, and they say much about war which I did not understand before. I have read *The Kingdom of the Sea*, and looking at your Tresillian Rocks, perhaps I understand just a little.' She moved on to Rachel. 'And you are Lord Camborne's eldest daughter, the brilliant Rachel, who believes in socialism, and one day will be a member of your Parliament. I have looked forward to meeting you.' To Alex she said simply, 'Thank you. I know you did much to aid your grandfather's efforts on my behalf.'

Finally she went to Mark, who was still standing by the window, his mouth slightly open, as if he could not believe what he was seeing. 'And you are Lord Camborne.'

'Mark,' he said. 'Mark Penrose. Oh . . . you'll get used to the difference in time.' He added, quite gratuitously, and with no trace of shyness, as if she, the girl, were an object, rather than a person, 'You're very beautiful.'

744

For a second, the unnatural calm which had seemed wrapped about her was shaken. She flushed. She had been, it seemed, prepared for everything else, but not this. She had moved among them as if in a rehearsed part, knowing her lines perfectly, knowing exactly where to place herself on this stage which she had never seen before, knowing exactly who were the *dramatis personae* of this play, but Mark had fed her the wrong line.

'Oh, do you think I look like him?' She turned back to the others in the room. 'Do you think so?'

It was again Mark who spoke the lines then which perhaps had never been written into the script. 'Not really. You have blue eyes, but not his blue eyes. They were very distinctive. You don't really have his features. I expect you look more like your mother. We only saw two photos of her. When she was older than you. But she looked ill.'

'She was ill. She didn't live for long after that second photograph was taken. I was in the camp with her for a while, and then they sent me away, to live with some people in Gorky, rather privileged people. Intellectuals. Later they told me she died.'

'Shall I pour you a drink?' Mark said. 'What would you like? Vodka?'

She shook her head emphatically. 'No, not vodka. May I have a scotch whisky, please?'

He brought it to her. 'I made it with ice and water. I should have asked . . .'

She nodded. 'How kind.' She raised the glass, and then looked around all of them again. Hastily Alex took up his own glass. 'Welcome,' he said.

'Thank you,' she answered, as the rest also took up their glasses. '*L'chayim*. To life.' After one small sip, she set it down. 'I have never tasted scotch whisky before. A strange taste.'

'You'll have to get used to many strange tastes,' Livy said. 'Many things are very different from what you have known. It will be difficult at first. But you did want to come, didn't you? You weren't forced? We wanted to welcome you into the family, but if you don't want to stay, we wouldn't want

745

to make you stay. That was agreed, wasn't it, Mr McClintock? That is what you said. Once here, she, Irina, is free to stay or to make her own way.' She looked directly at the girl. 'Freedom may seem a strange concept to you. Here, on this side of the world, you rarely have to do what you don't want to do. If you don't like life with us, you are free to walk out any time you want to. If you decide to stay, then you will be bound by the natural rule any family relationship imposes on its members. We give and we take. I hope we don't take too much.'

'That is how the peasant lives in Russia, the ones far out in the country. The officials are not forever on their backs. They raise vegetables for sale, beyond what they have to give to the collective. They barter, sometimes they help one another. Outside of that, there is no "give and take". We are told what we must give. We don't give any more than is required. We give less, if we can get away with it.'

'But you haven't been a peasant,' Alex said. 'You haven't lived as a peasant. You're educated . . .'

'Ah, yes, but I suspect that was part of the "give" that was required of the people who took care of me. They gave me education. They started me in languages. They liked music, poetry. They liked their books . . . and their vodka, and their good boots, and the other, not small things, they were able to buy, where others were not. They went to the special shops. They were warm and well-fed. Had good clothes. And I had learning crammed into me as if I were one of those Strasbourg geese, having its liver stuffed.'

'How long did you stay in Gorky?' Ginny asked.

'Until four years ago. Then I was sent to Leningrad. It was very exciting. A big city. Many things to see. Concerts. The ballet. The Hermitage. A new set of foster-parents, who had two children of their own. About my age. We did not discuss where I had come from – where I had been. We did not discuss who I was. I was there to learn. Languages were very important. Especially English.'

'And what else?' Ginny asked.

'What else?' The girl hesitated. 'What else?' She walked to the deep mullioned window where Mark still stood. She

746

looked out, gazed at the orchard wall, beyond that to where she knew the Rocks were. She turned and faced them again. 'At the end of last summer, at the beginning of the autumn, I was sent to Moscow. I was sent to Moscow to learn how to be Harry's daughter.'

She walked back into the middle of the room. She stood in the centre of the circle of sofas and chairs they occupied. It was a theatrical gesture, but now there was no sense of it being rehearsed or practised.

'I learned about you. About Harry's family.' She looked at the great height of the room, the second floor gallery, the tooled leather ceiling. 'I learned about this house, about Seymour House, about Prescott Hill, about Massa . . .' she tripped a little on the pronunciation of the word . . . 'about Massachusetts Avenue. A mansion, they called it. As fine as the mansions of Petrograd, Leningrad. Harry's world. They told me about the woman Harry had loved in Moscow. The ambassador's woman, they called her. They told me about McClintock-Clayton. They told me it was possible that I might go and live in these places. They told me it was possible that I might be part of this family. They had given me this education all these years . . . to achieve this.'

Andrew McClintock leaned forward on his cane. 'Was there any reason why you shouldn't be a member of this family?'

'Yes. It is very simple. I am *not* Harry's daughter.'

She hurried back to the window, turning her back on them, staring out. It seemed to be a flight, and yet she was confined. She glanced quickly at Mark, as if she thought he might aid in an escape, up on the sill, out, away to the freedom of the orchard, the Rocks, and whatever lay beyond. But she went no further than that single glance. She turned and faced them again.

'Because Harry's daughter is dead. She died long ago. Before her mother died. We were briefly together. In the same camp. I hardly remember them. We were not friends. Who has friends in places like that where it is everyone for oneself? No give and take there. My own mother died, and they took me to some other place, hardly better. And then one day they came and took me to somewhere warmer, and more comfortable. I had a bath, and they took a lot of trouble with my hair, to make it nice. They brought in a woman I hardly recognized. We were photographed together. I never saw her again.

'Things became easier. Much better food, warm clothes. And then the move to Gorky. It seemed like heaven to me. I was expected to work very hard at my lessons, lessons in everything. It didn't seem hard to me. I did everything I was told to do. I didn't ask questions. If I asked, I might have been sent back. Even when I was sent to Leningrad, and there were two children in the family, I didn't ask questions. That would have been foolish. They resented me a little, those two. As if I might have been someone special. I didn't mind being someone special, so long as they didn't send me back . . . back to the camps. I kept quiet, and I studied hard, and I made no noise. Then they sent me to this special place in Moscow. There I had teachers all to myself. I didn't see anyone my own age. They started to tell me about my father. My father – Lord Camborne. They told me he had loved my mother in Moscow, and that she had committed a crime against the State in loving him. But I didn't believe them. I could remember that woman. I could just remember her daughter. I wasn't her daughter. Therefore I wasn't Harry's daughter. After a while they knew it. Then they began to tell me a little of what I was supposed to do once I had been sent to be with you. It was a great pity, they said, that I wasn't a boy. Whoever had sent that first photograph of Sonya and the real Irina had made a great mistake.'

'Why was it a mistake?'

'Because if I had been a boy there would have been a greater chance of my being taken into McClintock-Clayton. I might have been like the young ones.' For a moment she fumbled for their names. 'Like Jamie and Oliver. Yes . . . like them, but older. Perhaps given a place of trust with you. There are many things they would like to know about McClintock-Clayton – and through the connections they have. But even I, as a girl, might be useful. I might have been taken into McClintock-Clayton. The very least would be that I would know what you discussed in private. The best they could do was to send me out as well taught as they . . . and I suppose I . . . could manage. Languages. American and British history, which they said was corrupt. It is corrupt. So is our Russian history corrupt. We don't talk about it.'

'Then why are you talking to us now?' Alex asked. 'Why are you telling us this? Aren't you sending yourself right back to where you came from? Worse than that. Right back to the beginning. To the labour camps?'

'Because I am *not* Harry's daughter. I couldn't keep playing their game for ever. I didn't want to play it in the beginning, but no one asked me. I was sent for a purpose. I can't fill that purpose. I didn't think I would tell you. I thought I would go on with the lie, and have a nice, comfortable existence. But I came into this room and I knew I could never be Harry's daughter. Better to tell you right away. You might have guessed or you might not have. But none of you are fools. And I am not a fool.

'I can ask you for some favours. A little time, a little time with you. So that they will think I am trying to do what they sent me to do. If I leave you, then it will just look as if it didn't work. As if you really didn't believe me, take to me. Once I'm in America I can get a job. I speak languages. That is a skill I can use. They even began me on shorthand and typing, in English. That was to be the first entry into McClintock-Clayton. I could use that. I need not bother you. I ask for a little time. When I'm used to America I could just go . . . go . . . maybe to California. Maybe anywhere. It doesn't matter. I am not Harry's daughter, and I know it. I can't live this lie for ever. If she had died just a little younger, Harry's daughter, they might have been able to convince me that I was his daughter. But I was just old enough to remember her. I remember their camps. I remember so many things. I don't want to go back . . . I'm frightened of them. Just give me a little time . . . to deceive them for a while.'

She sat down. She had chosen a seat as far away from them as she could find, almost hidden behind the globe on the long library table. Her eyes once more sought the window, and encountered Mark's gaze. She looked away. She looked down; her hands were clasped together, the attitude of someone awaiting judgement.

Mark went around the silent group, taking their glasses, refilling them. He came at last to the girl, Irina. Was her name really Irina? She shook her head. Her glass was far away, on the table by the sofa where Ginny sat. The silence continued. The warm golden sun of a long summer's evening flooded the westward facing room. It was possible to tell, in the stillness, that the tide had turned. They could hear it begin its hiss and rush about the base of the Rocks.

Andrew McClintock spoke. His tones quavered; was it emotion, or simply the voice of an old man? 'I've been taken!' His cane crashed down on the floor. 'By God, I've been taken! I can remember no other time in my life when I've been so completely and utterly hoodwinked. I've gambled before, and very occasionally I've lost. But I've always known that the game was a gamble. But this time they've worked the sting. Their gamble has been the hope that Harry, or I, would make some move to get this . . . this girl, whose real name we don't even know, out. For years they've been preparing their plant, with just this hope. And it nearly worked. I might have come to trust her. I paid a very high price, and I got defective goods. I should send her back. Tell them the goods were not what we ordered. I've been beaten . . . God damn it! *At my age, I've been beaten!*'

Andrew McClintock got slowly to his feet. Then he picked up his glass. He nodded to Mark to bring the girl's glass to her. He walked slowly to where she sat. As he approached, she rose. 'I'll take your toast. "To life!" They haven't really beaten the old man yet. Here, girl . . . drink!'

She raised her glass to her lips. They were all shocked to hear Andrew McClintock's sudden, rather wild laughter. 'By God, they've had me! But the game isn't finished yet. I'll find a way . . .'

In the hall, Knox sounded the gong for dinner.

Andrew McClintock nodded his head to the girl. 'You may go.'

Ginny's voice cut in, quietly, but decisively. 'We have dinner early here in the country, Irina. You'll get used to our customs, our little habits. Alex, will you take Irina into dinner, please . . .'

'You can't!' Andrew McClintock almost shouted.

'But I can.' Ginny answered coolly. 'I find the goods satisfactory. I have no intention of using them for any purpose but my own.'

Alex came forward. He offered his right arm to the girl. 'I expect we'll go on calling you Irina. It's a pretty name.'

She struggled against tears. 'It's the only one I know.' They walked slowly through the hall, following Ginny. Andrew McClintock was the last to move. For a time it seemed doubtful that he would move at all.

Knox was waiting in the dining-room. He said not a word when he saw the girl, but hurried to the sideboard, and swiftly brought another place mat, and napkin. Before he could turn back, Mark was laying knives and forks. He brought up an extra chair.

Ginny indicated to Irina that she should take her place at her right hand. 'No!' Andrew McClintock's voice from the doorway halted them all. 'So long as I am in Ginny's house, I occupy the place at her right hand. You,' he said to the girl, 'may sit opposite.' Mark drew out the chair for her.

Knox came forward to serve the soup. He hesitated just fractionally, then went first to the girl, instead of Ginny. Someone he had never seen before, had not expected to be at the table, was the guest. She would be served first. But Andrew McClintock's upraised hand caused him to halt.

'We will say grace.'

Those around the table had never heard Andrew McClintock utter a prayer in all their lives. It was possible that he prayed, but never audibly. He, and whatever god he thought might exist besides himself, had talked together, had settled things between them, privately.

He said: 'Now, God be thanked Who has matched us with His hour . . .'

Livy took up the poem of Rupert Brooke, strangely twisted for this occasion: '. . . And caught our youth . . .'

751

Another voice, Irina's, softly continued the poem: '. . . and wakened us from sleeping . . .'

The tide was coming in very fast. They heard the familiar crash against the Rocks.